HAROLD
COYLE

TRIAL
BY
FIRE

A NOVEL

SIMON & SCHUSTER
New York   London   Toronto   Sydney   Tokyo   Singapore

SIMON & SCHUSTER
Simon & Schuster Building
Rockefeller Center
1230 Avenue of the Americas
New York, New York 10020

Designed by Irving Perkins Associates
Manufactured in the United States of America

1   3   5   7   9   10   8   6   4   2

Library of Congress Cataloging-in-Publication Data

Coyle, H. W. (Harold W.), date.
Trial by fire : a novel / by Harold Coyle.
p.   cm.
I. Title.
PS3553.0948T7   1992
813'.54—dc20   91–47865
ISBN 0-671-73255-2   CIP

ACKNOWLEDGMENTS

There are many people who have made this book possible. Their comments and encouragement have been critical, for without them, none of this would be possible. In particular, I would like to thank Jan Ciganick and Chet Burgess for their reviews and comments.

Paul McCarthy, from Pocket Books and on detached duty to Simon & Schuster for this project, has been instrumental, both as an editor and as a cheerleader, in getting *Trial by Fire* together. Books simply do not happen without support from people like Paul and the editorial staff of Simon & Schuster. Many thanks to everyone in New York City involved in this effort.

Professionally, I owe a great deal to the people with whom I served during the last two years. Colonel Richard M. Swain III, Director of the Combat Studies Institute and Historian for the 3rd Army during Operation Desert Storm, is a mentor of the first class. He provided me an insight into many areas of military history and thought that I had not considered before, and encouraged me to explore them. Lieutenant General John J. Yeosock, Commander, 3rd Army, during Operation Desert Storm, and his deputy, Brigadier General (Promotable) Robert Frix, provided me more than an opportunity to apply my professional skills during Desert Storm. They, along with Colonel Karl Ernst and Colonel Flynn of the 3rd Army TAC CP, showed me what it meant to be a professional soldier. Like Colonel Swain, they provided me with an insight into the American way of war and serve to remind me that wars are fought and won by men, not machines. To all of you, and everyone I have had the pleasure of serving with at Leavenworth and during my Saudi duty, I thank you and wish you all the best of luck in everything you do.

Finally, I wish to thank Pat, my partner. Her encouragement, her support, her love, and her understanding in everything I do make all of this possible and worthwhile. She is, in word and deed, the wind beneath my wings.

This book is dedicated to the memory of the soldiers, sailors, airmen, and marines, male and female, who lost their lives during Operations Desert Shield and Desert Storm, August 1990–March 1991.

The nation that forgets its defenders will itself be forgotten.

—Calvin Coolidge

TRIAL
BY
FIRE

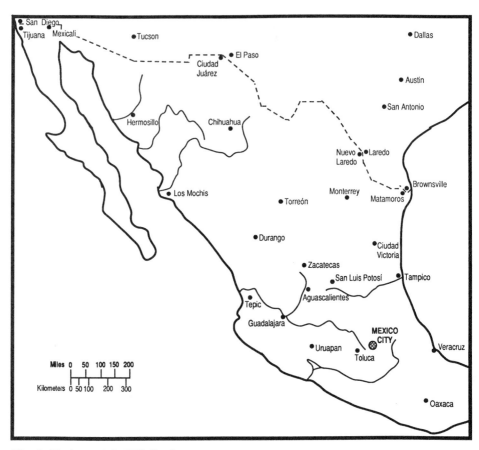

Map 1: Mexico and the U.S. Border

Prologue

In the gathering darkness, the predators of the night began to stir. From burrows, holes and crevices, the creatures of the desert crawled, slithered, or scurried from their habitats into the cool of the late afternoon. For the next several hours they would seek, strike, and consume those things that would allow them to survive another day in their harsh environment. It was a cruel existence that demanded something die so that something live. There was no grand plan or reason for such things. Nor was there compassion, feeling, or regrets. Only survival.

From one of thousands of holes dotting the barren desert floor, a scorpion sallied forth. Like a missile being released from its launch tube, the scorpion moved forward mechanically, purposefully, unstoppably. As it cleared the narrow confines of its hole, the scorpion prepared to kill. Once it was free to do so, even before its head was in the open and able to see, the scorpion swung its massive right claw out, and then the left. There was no pause, no hesitation as the scorpion continued to move forward, finally clearing its tail. Like the fin of a missile, the tail automatically deployed into a fully erect position. Unlike the fin of a missile, the tail was more than a mere accessory; it was the scorpion's main weapon. The stinger at the end of the tail was, for now, curled under, but ready.

As if the scorpion had known where it was going before it left the dark hole, it continued straight ahead into the gathering darkness. As it did so, for a brief moment, the long shadow of an eagle flashed across the scorpion. There was, however, no danger to the scorpion. The eagle was not seeking so small a creature. Instead, the large powerful bird had its senses tuned to seek what it needed to survive. Flying high above the desert floor, the eagle scanned the barren terrain for other prey. The small, seemingly insignificant scorpion, moving about in the long shadow of the eagle's powerful wings, never caught the bird's eye.

If the crossing of their paths was an accident, their purpose was the same. Each sought that which would allow it to survive, to continue. That those two particular creatures of the desert would ever meet, let alone come into conflict, or even cross paths again, was improbable at best. But in a harsh and cruel world where killing meant survival and survival was all that mattered, everything that could do so pursued that goal unhesitatingly. So anything was possible.

And if something is possible, then it will be, if only in a dream, or a nightmare.

1

The Service isn't what it used to be—and never was.

—Service saying

Manning Mountain, Fort Hood, Texas
0645 Hours, 28 June

Perched upon a flat rock, Captain Stan Wittworth lazily ate his breakfast of cold ham and chicken loaf while he watched to the south. A cedar tree, its growth stunted by the Texas heat and lack of water, gave some protection from the sun, but did little to protect Wittworth from the heat. The heat of a new Texas day, less than an hour old, was already oppressive, soaking Wittworth's BDUs with sweat. Within two hours the heat would be unbearable.

From his Humvee parked in a concealed position behind Wittworth, the blaring of a radio speaker announced the beginning of a report. Identifying the radio call sign as that of the platoon leader of his 2nd Platoon, Wittworth stopped eating and listened. The report announced that they had cleared checkpoint one-four without any contact and were proceeding north. Looking down at a map of Fort Hood's maneuver area laid out at his feet, Wittworth looked for the blue symbol that identified checkpoint one-four. He found it at the point where Old Georgetown Road crossed the Cowhouse Creek. Popularly known as Jackson's Crossing, it was indeed a critical point to any force attacking north or south. Reaching the Cowhouse and crossing it unopposed would give the 2nd Platoon a decided advantage in the upcoming engagement.

Leaning the brown aluminum-foil package that contained his ham and chicken loaf against a rock so that the contents wouldn't spill, Wittworth lifted his binoculars to his eyes and looked for the vehicles of the 2nd

Platoon. Though he couldn't see them, the dust clouds thrown into the still morning air by the tracks of its vehicles marked their progress. Unless the tank company undergoing evaluation reached the point where Wittworth was sitting in the next ten minutes, his 2nd Platoon, playing the role of the opposing force, or enemy, would be here instead. The tank company, instead of holding superior firing positions such as the one Wittworth's Humvee was in, or fighting the 2nd Platoon in the open ground between Manning Mountain and the Cowhouse, would have to fight in the cedar forest on top of Manning Mountain. In a fight on the mountain, in the woods, the 2nd Platoon would be able to use its infantry against the tanks in close terrain. That was what Wittworth was hoping for. In a fight in the open terrain of the Manning Mountain Corridor below, the 2nd Platoon's four M-2 Bradleys, with its infantry, would be eaten alive by the fourteen tanks rolling down from the north.

Wittworth watched Old Georgetown Road intently for the first of the 2nd Platoon's Bradleys to roll into the open. In the distance, he could hear the Bradleys' high-pitched whine. Suddenly, however, the sound changed, almost dying out. Searching the tree line on either side of the road where the 2nd Platoon should have been emerging, Wittworth saw nothing. Even the large dust cloud was dissipating. That could mean only one thing; Lieutenant Shippler was stopping to regroup and deploy before crossing the open area at the base of Manning Mountain. Slowly dropping his binoculars from his eyes, Wittworth unconsciously began to shake his head, mumbling and calling Shippler every foul name he could think of. Instead of being bold and rushing for the high ground, Shippler was exercising great textbook caution. Unless the tank company commander, moving south along Old Georgetown Road from Royalty Ridge, had a severe case of the slows, he would reach the southern edge of Manning Mountain and gain superior positions from which he could engage the 2nd Platoon as they moved north across the open area below.

As if drawn by Wittworth's dismal thoughts, the cracking of dry cedar branches being crushed under the treads of M-1 tanks and the squeak of steel drive sprockets announced the arrival of the tank company. Turning, Wittworth caught glimpses of the green, brown, and black camouflage paint of an M-1 tank as it slowly picked its way through the cedar trees toward the edge of Manning Mountain. The tank's commander, standing waist-high in his cupola, was leaning forward, watching the right front fender as he directed his driver forward through the trees. The tank's loader was also riding high out of his hatch, located on the turret's left side. Like his commander, he was leaning forward, watching that the left front fender cleared the trees. It was obvious that the tank commander had been there before, for he neither referred to a map nor stopped and dismounted his loader to move forward to recon a spot for the tank. It didn't take officers and NCOs of the armor and mech units stationed at Fort Hood long to figure out that there were only so many ways to skin the cat when maneuvering on Manning Mountain.

Ignoring Wittworth and his Humvee, the tank commander pulled into a position to the left of where Wittworth sat. When the tank was where he wanted it, the tank commander ordered his driver to stop. As the driver throttled back and locked the brakes, the commander dropped down in his cupola, snatching up a pair of binoculars that had been tied to the cradle of his .50-caliber machine gun, and began to scan the far horizon. The turret also began to move slowly, from left to right, as the gunner began his search for targets. Even the loader watched for telltale signs of the enemy. The movement of one of Shippler's Bradleys simplified their task.

Like a hunting dog who has spotted game, the tank's main gun suddenly jerked to one side, then froze once it had its prey in sight. Even before the gun stopped moving, the tank commander, no doubt alerted by the gunner's acquisition report, had already disappeared into the tank where he could use the commander's extension of the tank's primary sight to control the engagement. Wittworth stood up, watching the tank prepare for action. Then he turned to the south, scanning the tree line where Shippler's platoon had disappeared. In the distance, Wittworth could see a Bradley move out from the tree line and begin to angle to the left toward Old Georgetown Road.

That maneuver presented the M-1 tank next to Wittworth with a good quartering shot. But the tank commander was in no great hurry. He knew Bradleys rarely traveled alone. To kill the first one would only have served to warn the others that they were in danger. So he and the other tank commanders in the tank company, who had moved into fighting positions along the lip of the ridge after him, watched and waited. Just as the first Bradley reached Old Georgetown Road, their patience and discipline were rewarded as a second Bradley broke out of the tree line and began to follow.

Watching, Wittworth hoped that the tanks would fire soon. It was obvious that Shippler was using one section of two Bradleys, still in the tree line, to overwatch the movement of the two Bradleys now moving toward the road. While the two Bradleys in motion would have little chance of surviving the initial volley of fourteen tanks, at least the stationary Bradleys in overwatch would be able to return fire and take out one or two of the offending tanks. But even this hope was soon dashed as

Wittworth and the tanks now lining the southern edge of Manning Mountain watched the last two Bradleys of Shippler's platoon come trundling out of cover and into the open. As if they had all the time in the world, the last two Bradleys began to move toward the road to join the others already there.

Still, the tanks held their fire. Every second they waited drew the Bradleys away from cover and closer to the tanks. With the MILES laser engagement system, the ideal killing range for the tanks was 1,000 to 1,500 meters. A well-trained crew with their MILES device well bore-sighted and zeroed and with fresh batteries could score a kill out beyond 2,000. But this tank company commander wasn't taking any chances. He didn't need to, for Shippler's platoon, now formed in a wedge on either side of Old Georgetown Road, was gradually closing the range.

To Wittworth, it was like watching a bad movie, or a play that showed the actors casually walking into a trap that the audience knew of but couldn't do anything about. Unable to watch his own platoon any longer, Wittworth looked over at the tank to his left. The tank commander was hunched down in his cupola with only his head and shoulders showing. As he watched the oncoming Bradleys without the use of binoculars—for there really was no need for them anymore—the tank commander spoke into his intercom microphone. There was no way for Wittworth to tell if he was giving last-minute instructions to his gunner or simply engaging in idle chitchat in an effort to pass the last few nervous seconds before they fired.

From the corner of his eye, the tank commander caught Wittworth staring at him. Ending his conversation with the unseen crewman, the tank commander turned to Wittworth. With the broadest, toothiest grin he could manage, the tank commander looked at Wittworth and gave him a thumbs-down, meaning that the Bradleys were about to die. This gesture pissed Wittworth off, and the tank commander, knowing who Wittworth was, meant it to piss him off. Wittworth could feel the blood rushing to his head and the hair rising on his neck as he shot a glare that could have burned through the tank's armor plate.

Wittworth's rage was still building when the tank commander's grin disappeared. Leaning forward, the commander's right hand went up to his helmet. For a second, he stood there like that, listening to something coming in over his earphones. It had been a radio call, for Wittworth saw his right thumb push the transmit lever forward into the position for transmitting over the radio. The tank commander shouted something into the mike, stopped, pushed the transmit lever to the rear, or intercom position, and shouted something to his crew. Turning from watching the tank commander, back to Shippler's platoon, Wittworth realized that the tank commander had, in all probability, just received the order to fire. Shippler's platoon was about to be engaged.

From hidden positions along the southern edge of Manning Mountain, half a dozen loud booms announced the beginning of the engagement. Below, Shippler's platoon continued forward for a few more seconds. Then the MILES receivers on the Bradleys began to register hits and near misses. Even before they knew for sure whether or not they were "dead," two of Shippler's Bradley commanders cut on their on-board smoke generators and began a sharp 180-degree turn in an effort to hide in their own smoke. The other Bradley commanders, seeing the two turn away, also cut on their smoke generators and turned.

From where he stood, Wittworth listened to the radio in his Humvee tuned to Shippler's command net for the initial report. There was none. Nor was there any kind of order from Shippler. Any actions taken within Shippler's platoon were the result of decisions being made by each Bradley commander, not by Shippler. Not that there was much that he could have done. The first volley of tank fire had "destroyed" two of the Bradleys. As soon as the commanders of those two vehicles realized that the orange kill light was continuously flashing, they stopped, cut off their smoke generator, put their gun tube over the rear deck, and waited. The other two Bradley commanders maneuvered wildly in an effort to hide in their own smoke while seeking cover. The tanks, able to determine who was left, turned their attention to the two fleeing Bradleys.

The chase lasted less than a minute. In the next volley, the Bradley on the left was hit, its kill light flashing without pause. The last Bradley survived several near misses, indicated by three quick flashes on the kill light. In the end, however, despite the wild gyrations, sharp turns, and the efforts of the Bradley's puny smoke generator, it too was overwhelmed as every tank on the mountain that could tracked it and fired.

Disgusted, Wittworth turned his back on the massacre of Shippler's platoon and walked back to his Humvee. As he did so, he pondered what he would say to Shippler when he saw him next. After all, Shippler's maneuver had been, according to the manual, correct. After crossing the Cowhouse Creek, he had regrouped, switched to bounding overwatch when they had reached the open area, and then moved into traveling overwatch with his whole platoon when there appeared to be no danger. Wittworth had hoped that Shippler would make a high-speed mad dash for Manning Mountain. But that would have been unorthodox, a gamble based on knowledge gained from fighting over the same ground time and time again and not the application of sound tactics. And there was no guarantee that that gamble would have paid off. After all, the tanks had come on rather fast. For the gamble to succeed, Shippler would have had to depend on the tank company commander to make an error or be slow. Basing one's plans on hope or depending on the enemy to make mistakes is a bad habit. Still . . .

When he reached his Humvee, Wittworth swung the door open and prepared to climb in. His driver twisted to the right in his seat, switched the two radios off to prevent the electrical surge of the ignition from damaging the radios, started the engine, and then turned the radios back on. Instead of getting in the Humvee, Wittworth stopped, told his driver to wait, and went back to the rock where he had been sitting to retrieve his breakfast. Approaching the rock, he noticed something moving on and around the brown aluminum foil package. Stopping, he looked down and watched as a horde of ants assaulted the remains of his ham and chicken loaf. With a sigh and a muffled curse, Wittworth kicked the foil package with all his might before he turned away and headed back to his Humvee.

As much as the slaughter of Shippler's platoon and the loss of his breakfast pissed him off, they were nothing to compare to what Wittworth knew awaited him back in the rear. Today was "The Day," the day when Second Lieutenant Nancy Kozak, the first female to be commissioned as an infantry officer, was to report to Wittworth's company. The mere thought of females assigned to combat arms, let alone one assigned to his company, still was enough to send Wittworth on an emotional roller coaster that took him from blind anger to almost total despondency.

As he and his driver rode back to the rear in silence, Wittworth wrestled with his own feelings and beliefs. Though he had known that this great experiment in equal opportunity had been coming for over six months, he had done little to mentally prepare himself. The briefings by the Test and Evaluation Command officials and data collectors, Wittworth's chain of command, and the Equal Opportunity reps from the Department of Defense had explained how the twelve-month evaluation would work. They had even tried to provide a system for everyone involved to overcome their prejudices through a series of rap sessions, educational seminars, and "encounter" groups. These efforts, however, had failed for the most part. Instead of eliminating prejudices, they had only served to harden them in some of the men in Wittworth's company, Wittworth included.

As hard as he might try, he could not separate out emotions from the problem. Why in the hell, he thought, is it necessary to allow women in combat arms branches? As it was, a number of good infantry officers were being forced to turn in the coveted crossed-rifle brass in order to fill vacancies in combat support and combat service support branches, branches where women already served without problem. Why the people in Washington couldn't leave well enough alone, and let things continue as they had been since the United States Army had been created, baffled Wittworth. It was as if someone in the Department of Defense wanted to see just how much shit they could pile onto combat arms officers before their jobs became impossible to carry out.

Breaking out from the rough and rutted trails, Wittworth's driver crossed the main tank trail and turned the Humvee south onto West Range Road. Wittworth didn't notice. His mind was still wrestling with how he would greet Kozak, an event now only a few hours away. That, coupled with the poor performance of Shippler's platoon, the loss of his breakfast to ants, and the oppressive heat, conspired to crush any tact Wittworth might have begun the day with. And tact was one commodity that people who knew him would never accuse Wittworth of having an overabundance of.

MAIN POST, FORT HOOD, TEXAS
0745 HOURS, 28 JUNE

Turning her light blue Chevy Suburban from Hood Road onto Headquarters Street, Second Lieutenant Nancy Kozak slowed and prepared to turn into the parking lot across the street from Building 108. To say that she was nervous would not do justice to Lieutenant Kozak's state of mind at that moment. After years of physical and mental preparation, The Day had arrived, the day she was reporting into her first unit. All the theoretical exercises in leadership, "what if?" drills, and "how to" training sessions that had permeated the military instruction at West Point and during her officer's basic course were over. From here on in, everything was for real. No role-playing, no hypothetical situations, no neat, clean classroom solutions. Her decisions and actions would affect real people and be judged by professional soldiers, those entrusted to her care, those who were her appointed superiors, and those who considered themselves her peers.

As if the simple act of reporting to her first unit wasn't difficult enough, Nancy Kozak would also have to deal with the trauma of being the first female to be commissioned in the U.S. Army as a combat arms officer. For the next year, she and the unit she was reporting into would be the subject of an evaluation that would attempt to answer the question of whether it was possible for American women to serve effectively as frontline soldiers.

The evaluation plan was quite simple in concept. Three units—one tank battalion, one mechanized infantry battalion, and one field artillery battalion—would receive a number of female officers and enlisted personnel. Within these units, some companies would remain all male. These were the "baseline" companies. Other companies, referred to as "mixed units," would consist of both male and female soldiers. Special teams from the Army's Test and Evaluation Command would study the performance of both the baseline companies and the mixed companies while those companies conducted their normal training and duties. The final test, though no one referred to it as such, would be a rotation to the National Training Center at Fort Irwin, California, at the end of the one-year evaluation. Based upon the performance of the units throughout the year and at the National Training Center, and the observations of the evaluation teams, a decision, or so it was hoped, would be made concerning the future of women in combat arms.

To start the evaluation, a number of female officers, one assigned to each of the mixed companies, were to report in first. It was felt that the female officers would be better able to handle the initial shock and "difficulties" that were anticipated when females were introduced into the combat units. The female officers had three months to adjust to the unit, and allow the unit to adjust to them, before the enlisted female soldiers began to arrive. In this way, the female officers would have an opportunity to achieve a level of competence and acceptance, making it easier for the enlisted females.

Unstated in either the evaluation plans or the briefings was the belief that a buffer would be needed between the male officers and noncommissioned officers and the enlisted females. The female officers would serve as this buffer, ensuring that training, discipline, and duty assignments were handled in a fair and even-handed manner. Otherwise, there was always the possibility that the all-male leadership would sabotage the evaluation by harassing the females or pushing them beyond accepted limits. While there was concern over the fact that the female officers were junior to everyone, it was generally accepted that this was preferable to introducing female officers of higher rank, lacking combat arms experience and baseline training, into the evaluation. Besides, as the briefers in the Pentagon pointed out, you can't get any closer to combat than at platoon level, so that was where the focus of the evaluation had to be.

*   *   *

So Second Lieutenant Kozak was exercising extreme care in everything she did. From reading everything she could to prepare herself technically and tactically, to obeying every traffic law on post. Even the manner in which she dressed was taken into account. After sliding into a parking slot and turning off the engine of her conservative and nondescript car, Kozak paused before getting out. Turning the rearview mirror toward her, she gave herself the once-over one more time before leaving the safety of her car.

Her auburn hair, normally worn long, was pulled back and pinned to the back of her head. The length of her hair had been a matter of concern and great debate, not only for herself, but for her fellow female classmates at West Point. Many had opted to get it cut short rather than mess with it when in uniform or in the field. Others had it cut so that, wet or dry, it fell just above the bottom of the uniform collar, which was the extreme limit that regulations permitted. A few, like Kozak, couldn't part with all of their hair. "After all," she had once told a friend, "everyone knows you're a woman, so why try to hide it." So they tolerated the inconvenience of washing it, tangling with it, and putting it up when in uniform so that they could maintain their pride and joy. Through trial and error, and with a lot of help from other female officers, Kozak had learned how to deal with her long hair in and out of the field. She of course had no way of knowing what her company commander would say about it. Technically, so long as she wore it above the bottom of her uniform collar, he could say nothing. Just in case, however, she had prepared herself mentally to get a butch cut if it became an issue.

The makeup she wore was light and hardly noticeable. Like her hair, this too had been a subject of great concern. For the last two weeks, she had debated with herself as to whether it would be wise to wear makeup when she reported. Just as she convinced herself of the wisdom of not wearing any, she found herself rejecting her own decision. In the end, she opted for a compromise of sorts. The foundation she wore was the sheerest she could find and applied with a light touch. A single coat of mascara, also applied with a light hand on uncurled lashes, was her only eye makeup. There was no blush and only a hint of lipstick to add a little color to her otherwise pale face. In addition, in order to keep from drawing any more attention to herself than she needed to, Kozak had avoided the use of any type of cologne, perfume, or anything that gave off a strong feminine scent. What she didn't appreciate, as she prepared herself, was that many of her products, from shampoo to face cream, gave off a decidedly feminine fragrance that lingered with her. Continuous use had made her so accustomed to them that she didn't notice it. Unfortunately, in the all-male world of a mechanized infantry company where the faint scent of diesel mixed with the musky smell of male sweat and gun oil permeated everything, Kozak would stand out no matter what she did.

Satisfied and yet not satisfied with the job she had done on her face, she checked the brass of her uniform one more time. The two gold bars of a second lieutenant sat mounted five-eighths of an inch in from the outside of the shoulder loops. Set exactly midway between the seam of the sleeve and the button that held the shoulder loop in place was a green felt tab one and five-eighths of an inch wide, a leadership tab that designated her as a leader of a combat unit. The leadership tab was topped off with the unit crest of the 13th Infantry Regiment. On each lapel of her green class A uniform blouse, exactly five-eighths of an inch above the cut of the lapel, were the brass letters u.s. Five-eighths of an inch below the cut of the lapel was the symbol of the infantry, a brass representation of two model 1842 muskets, commonly referred to as the crossed rifles.

Were it not for these two highly polished pieces of brass, each weighing less than an ounce, Nancy Kozak's appearance at Fort Hood that morning would have been routine. She would have been just another female officer, representing fourteen percent of the Army's total, reporting for duty. But, by her own hand and drive, she was different. She was, and always would be, the first. In no small measure, the future of women in the Army depended on what she, and five other females commissioned in the combat arms, did in the next year.

Overwhelmed by this sense of history, Kozak opened the door and got out. Standing upright, she slung her regulation black purse over her shoulder, smoothed her skirt, pulled the blouse of her uniform down, and set out for Building 108 to sign in.

BUILDING 108, FORT HOOD, TEXAS
0755 HOURS, 28 JUNE

Casually sprawled on a chair in the first row of the room where he had been directed, Captain Harold Cerro waited for the admin clerks to settle down and begin their arduous task of inprocessing a new batch of officers. As the clerks shuffled reams of papers and huge computer printouts, Cerro sipped coffee from a Styrofoam cup and read *USA Today*. Based on the headlines, Cerro decided, the day before had been a complete bore. The top news story was about a series of four murders in New York City.

Cynical as ever, Cerro wondered why these particular murders, in a city where an average of six people a day were murdered, were different from any others. Besides, in Cerro's mind, four dead people were almost negligible. After all, there had been days when Cerro would account for the loss of four men killed in a firefight simply by reporting, "Casualties light, continuing mission." How odd civilians were, he thought.

It was not that Cerro was an intrinsically cruel person. On the contrary, most of the people he allowed to know him thought Hal Cerro was a nice guy. But that nice guy happened to be both a soldier and a realist. People, Cerro knew, die. It was a part of life. As a veteran, he had not only seen death up close and personal, he had participated in the process. In doing so, Cerro, like any soldier in combat, had faced the possibility of his own death. Death, therefore, held no mysteries for him. It was to him, instead, simply another fact of life. People eat, they breathe, and they die. In Cerro's trained mind, it was that simple. Clear, simple, and cold. Besides, it was the only way he could rationalize what he did in order to maintain his sanity.

From the doorway, the clicking of heels on the tile floor announced that a woman had entered the room. Glancing up from his paper, Cerro's eyes tracked the female second lieutenant who had just entered the room as they would track a target. His mind, conditioned through years of training, began to assess the target.

He immediately established, based on the rank, the manner in which she carried herself, and her appearance, that the lieutenant was newly commissioned, putting her at twenty-two—at the most, twenty-three—years old. As she walked over to the desk where the clerks sat, Cerro judged her height to be five-eight, tops five-ten, even when the two-inch heels were taken into account. The lieutenant's auburn hair was drawn up in a simple bun which was pinned tightly to the back of her head. Her face was set in a deadpan stare fixed on the clerk she was approaching, confirming Cerro's belief that the lieutenant was reporting to her first unit. Despite the lack of expression, and dearth of makeup, the lieutenant's face had potential. The lack of clearly visible cheekbones was more than offset by a well-molded nose, a soft chin, full lips, and big brown eyes.

At the desk, the lieutenant cleared her throat and informed the clerk that she was there to sign in. The clerk stopped what she was doing, looked up at the lieutenant, and cocked her head to the side. "We started at oh-eight hundred, ma'am. If you would please take a seat, we will be with you shortly." Without waiting for an acknowledgment, the clerk went back to shuffling the papers on her desk. While this exchange transpired, Cerro utilized the time, and the fact that no one else was watching, to conduct a detailed terrain analysis. He decided that the lieutenant was five foot eight, weighed 150 pounds, probably wore a B cup, maybe a C, had a waist measuring no more than 28 inches, and had a nice tush.

Cerro was still considering this last item when the lieutenant turned on her heel and walked over to the row of chairs where Cerro was seated. With measured ease, Cerro looked back at his paper, taking a long sip on his coffee while he continued to track the lieutenant out of the corner of his eye. Once she was seated, Cerro turned his attention back to his paper. All thoughts of the female lieutenant were quickly relegated to a file in the back of his mind labeled "Lieutenant, Female." That he had regarded the lieutenant in the same way he would a woman on the prowl at a singles bar never crossed his mind as he turned to the weather page. As an old first sergeant had once told him, "Regardless how you package them, they're still women."

Promptly at 0800 hours, one of the clerks at the front of the room called out Cerro's name and rank. Looking up from his paper, Cerro turned to the clerk. For a moment, he simply stared at her. "We're open now, sir."

Feigning surprise and excitement, Cerro carefully folded his paper, packing it away in his briefcase for later, then slowly rose and casually strolled over to the clerk. When he arrived at her desk, she announced she needed two copies of his orders and all amendments. Once she had them, the clerk referred to a computer printout. Finding Cerro's name, she ran a finger across the appropriate line while she copied the information on a blank form.

Finished, she took the form, turned it so that Cerro could see it, and began to explain what he was to do next. "This confirms your assignment to Headquarters and Headquarters Company, 2nd Brigade, 16th Armored Division. You'll start your inprocessing with finance in room . . ."

Cerro wasn't paying attention to the clerk. He had tripped into a mental lock when the clerk had announced that he was assigned to a brigade's headquarters and headquarters company. Simply put, that meant that he would be on the brigade staff. For the first time in his military career, Cerro would not be in a real troop unit. Instead of working with real soldiers and tromping about in the boonies, he would be living in a world ruled by a lieutenant colonel executive officer in search of his eagles, populated by high-speed, low-drag majors out to make their mark on the Army, and run by sergeants who were either too old to be in line units or had been thrown out of them. Such an assignment, to Cerro, was akin to being sentenced to a salt mine in Siberia. The old question, "Father, why have you forsaken me?" kept running through his mind as the clerk continued to give him instructions he ignored.

With his mind cluttered with visions of doom and damnation, Cerro didn't notice the appearance of the female second lieutenant when she was called forward by the clerk seated next to the one mumbling instructions to him. The lieutenant was up out of her seat and at the front of the room in a flash when her name was called. As Cerro's clerk had done, the clerk attending to the lieutenant asked for two copies of her orders and all amendments, then leafed through the great computer printout until he found the lieutenant's name and automatically began to fill in an inprocessing form for her.

The clerk's hand stopped, however, when he reached the column on the printout that listed the lieutenant's unit of assignment. Running his finger back across the line, he first checked to make sure he hadn't inadvertently dropped down a line while writing. Once he was sure the line on the printout was correct, he looked at the orders the lieutenant had handed him, checking that the name and social security number on the orders agreed with those on the printout. Only after he was satisfied that he had the correct entry did he look up at the lieutenant. "I'm sorry, ma'am. There must be a mistake here. According to the printout, you're being assigned to A Company, 2nd Battalion, 13th Infantry."

The lieutenant spoke for the first time. "Oh, there's no mistake. I'm an infantry officer and that's the unit I've been assigned to."

The clerk looked at Kozak for a second before he responded. "Oh, so you're one of them."

As in the old E. F. Hutton commercial, everyone in the room momentarily stopped whatever he or she was doing, turned, and looked at the five-foot-eight female second lieutenant. Even Cerro, shaken from his thoughts of gloom and despair, turned and looked at the lieutenant next to him. For the first time, he carefully studied her profile. Every hair was in place, neatly combed back and secured in the tight little bun at the back of her head. Small gold ball earrings sat nestled in her soft white earlobe. Her face, set in a firm, dispassionate stare, was flawless, if somewhat colorless. Cerro paused for a second, as if he was afraid of what he would see, before he allowed his eyes to drop down to confirm what the lieutenant had already announced. When he did, a sudden shudder ran through his body as his eyes locked onto the shiny brass symbol of the infantry secured to the lieutenant's collar. It was her! The day had finally come. They had arrived.

The sudden and unwanted attention had caught Nancy Kozak by surprise. She had hoped that all the advance publicity and media coverage would have softened the shock and allowed her to quietly slip through the initial processing without a scene. That hope, however, was shattered before she even got out of the starting blocks. The introduction of females into combat arms units was simply too emotional an issue to quietly slip by. "Well," she thought, "so much the better." Regaining her poise, Kozak bent forward slightly toward the clerk. "Yes, the orders and the printout are correct. I am Nancy L. Kozak, Second Lieutenant, Infantry, and, according to my sponsor and orders, I am to report to A Company, 2nd of the 13th Infantry." And, as an afterthought, Kozak added, "That's right, soldier. I'm one of them."

It took a few more seconds for Kozak's confident, almost defiant retort to register with the clerk. Blinking his eyes, the clerk apologized, blushing from embarrassment as he did so, then mumbled that he was just confirming that the printout was correct. For an awkward second, there was silence before he went back to filling out the form. Satisfied with herself, Kozak straightened up, then turned to face the captain standing next to her, who was staring at her. When their eyes met, she tilted her head to one side and arched her eyebrows slightly, giving a quizzical look.

The captain, an infantry officer with master parachutist wings and a collection of ribbons that was quite impressive, looked into her eyes for a moment, then down at the infantry brass on her collar, then back to her eyes. Though he said nothing, his actions and expressions spoke legions.

Only the intervention of the clerk filling out Cerro's inprocessing form broke the stare-off between Kozak and Cerro. "Sir, if you take this, you start your processing at finance." Without taking his eyes off Kozak, Cerro took the form from the clerk with his left hand while picking up his briefcase with his right. Even when he responded to the clerk with a barely audible and perfunctory "Thank you," he was still staring at Kozak. Then, with an abruptness that almost startled her, he turned and fled out of the room.

When he was gone from sight, Kozak turned back to the clerk filling out her form. He too was staring at her again. Rather than feeling uncomfortable, Kozak found herself becoming angry. "Is there something else wrong, soldier, with my paperwork?"

The sharp question caused the soldier to blink. "No, ma'am."

"Well then, let's get on with it, soldier."

With that little incident, Second Lieutenant Kozak passed from reaction to assertion.

THE PARKING LOT ACROSS FROM BUILDING 108, FORT HOOD, TEXAS
1035 HOURS, 28 JUNE

It was more than the heat and his assignment to the division staff that was bothering Cerro as he approached his car. It was the female infantry lieutenant. As much as he wanted to ignore the fact that she was there, he could not. All morning, as he had inprocessed, she had always been right behind him as she inprocessed. It wasn't the fact that they were now commissioning women in the combat arms that surprised Cerro. On the contrary, he, and most of the Army, had been following the debates, decisions, and processes involved in making all of that happen. The pros and cons of the issue, and what impact the final decision would have, had been the subject of many discussions wherever Cerro had gone. Though he had reconciled his mind to the fact that whatever happened was beyond him and he had no choice but to live with decisions made by the Department of the Army, it was still unsettling to see his first female infantry officer.

He was just beginning to convince himself that it was foolish to get so worked up over an issue that he had no control over when, suddenly, as if all of his dark thoughts had made his worst nightmare a reality, there she was, standing next to his car. Cerro stopped in midstride and paused, wondering what she was doing there and why she was following him.

Taking her black handbag from her shoulder, she began to rummage about in it, looking for something. Pulling out a set of keys, she turned to the car next to Cerro's and began to open the door. She wasn't following him, after all.

Feeling like a fool, Cerro continued to walk over to his car. As his was backed in and the lieutenant had pulled hers in forward, the driver's doors of both cars opened out together. As he approached from behind, Cerro watched the lieutenant bend over and unlock her door. She was beginning to open it when she saw him approaching. Turning to face him, the lieutenant came to attention, her right hand coming up like a crisp karate chop to salute Cerro.

Though he shouldn't have been, Cerro was surprised by this. Taking another step before stopping, he casually returned the salute. As he did, he heard the sound of a small piece of metal hitting the pavement between them. Looking down, he saw a small clip roll on the ground. Automatically, Cerro assumed that one of the clips holding his brass, badges, and ribbons had fallen off. Breaking off the salute, he began to feel about his uniform under his lapels and jacket to confirm that it was his clip that had been lost.

Kozak had also heard the clip hit the ground. Seeing that Cerro had dropped his salute and was checking his uniform, she did likewise. For several seconds the two infantry officers stood there, facing each other without a word as they checked their uniforms. To a casual observer who had never served, their actions would have seemed strange, giving the appearance that they were checking themselves for bugs. To a soldier, it was part of life.

Though Cerro had started first, Kozak, with far fewer badges and ribbons, finished first. She held on to the post of the unit crest underneath the right shoulder loop of her green blouse, and a look of delight lit up her face as if she had found the prize. "Oh, I think it's mine, sir."

Cerro stopped searching his uniform and immediately turned his attention to the ground. Locating the offending clip between his feet, he squatted down and policed it up, holding it between two fingers like a dead bug. "Here you go, Lieutenant. One stray clip."

Reaching out, Kozak took the clip from Cerro, thanked him, and began to fumble about in an effort to fasten it to the post of her unit crest. The unit crest, set in the center of her green leader's tabs on the shoulder loop of her uniform, was located midway between her shoulder and the collar of her uniform. This made it difficult to work on while wearing the uniform. Cocking her head back and to the right in order to see what she was doing, Kozak tried holding the crest on the loop with her right hand as she attempted to fasten the clip using her left hand. Cerro watched without saying a word, a fact that made Kozak nervous and the task more difficult. After two attempts, the clip slipped out from between her fingers and fell to the ground again. Sheepishly, Kozak looked at Cerro, shrugged her shoulders and began to bend down to retrieve it.

Cerro, however, was quicker. Scooping up the clip for the second time, he stood and stepped forward. "Here, let me help. Otherwise you'll be here all day."

Kozak straightened up and looked forward over Cerro's shoulder as he held the unit crest in one hand and attached the clip. Since they were about the same size, this was not difficult. Finished, he stepped back. Not knowing what else to say, Cerro blurted, "There! Now, you're back together."

"Thank you, Captain. I'm just a little nervous and all. This is my first assignment."

Her smile, her statement that was nothing short of a brilliant flash of the obvious, and her manner were disarming, sincere, and, more important, very human. Cerro was at a loss for a response. Suddenly the personification of every infantryman's worst nightmare had turned into a real person he had to deal with. Without thinking, he reacted instinctively, treating Kozak as he would any brand-new infantry lieutenant. "Yes, I know. And we certainly can't have you reporting to your CO with your uniform looking like shit, can we?"

As if a great weight had been lifted from her shoulders, Kozak relaxed, a slight smile returning to her face. "No, sir. That wouldn't do. I appreciate your concern and help." And she did. For the first time all day—in fact, for the first time in weeks—someone had been kind, had shown genuine concern for her, and had treated her as an officer. But even more important was the fact that it had been another infantry officer, a captain who was a combat veteran to boot.

Nodding, Cerro turned to unlock his car. "Well, if you'll excuse me, I have to report to division headquarters."

Saluting one more time, Kozak wished him luck in his new assignment.

Chuckling as he returned her salute, Cerro shook his head and began to climb in his car. "I'm afraid all my luck has been used up. I'm going to 2nd Brigade to become a staff wienie."

Though she didn't understand Cerro's obvious displeasure at being assigned to such an important position, Kozak nodded and watched as he started his car and pulled away. Perhaps, she thought, things weren't going to be as hard as she had imagined.

It doesn't take a majority to make a rebellion; it only takes a few determined men and a sound cause.

—H. L. Mencken

CIUDAD VICTORIA, TAMAULIPAS, MEXICO
1545 HOURS, 28 JUNE

The small delegation that awaited the arrival of the president of the Republic of Mexico was exhausted from days of dealing with a crisis that seemed to come from nowhere. The problem had no apparent beginning or goals, only chaos, disruption of the daily routine of the state, and now, violence. For seven days oil field workers had disrupted, then stopped work in most of the oil fields throughout the state of Tamaulipas. At first it was thought that the troubles were nothing more than an extension of the labor unrest that had been bubbling up throughout the industrial cities of the republic. On several occasions the oil field workers had more than made it known that their sympathies were with their brothers and sisters who worked in the cities. It came, therefore, as no great surprise, to those who chose to pay attention at least, that the rash of strikes should spread to the oil fields.

While his assistants and advisors sat and waited or held hushed conversations, the governor of Tamaulipas paced the length of the small VIP lounge as he awaited the arrival of the president and his party. Every now and then he would glance out the window to the spot where several Air Force personnel waited in the late afternoon heat for the president's plane. It had been decided, at the recommendation of military zone commander Colonel Alfredo Guajardo, that the meeting between the president and governor be kept short and secret. Guajardo, who was now seated against the far wall of the room, had explained to the governor that a simple meeting at the airport would make security easy and would not put the governor in political jeopardy. "After all," Guajardo told the governor, "how would it look to the people of Tamaulipas if the president had to be called every time you had a minor problem with the workers. Besides, *el presidente* is growing tired of his vacation and family. He will be glad to use an excuse to fly here and then return to Mexico City and his mistress."

Although the governor did not consider the problem minor, he had agreed. After all, the president, and whomever he designated to succeed him, would have to be lived with for a long time. It would not be in the governor's best interest to be too much in the young president's debt publicly, or to have the president's role in solving the problem inflated at the governor's expense. By keeping the meeting secret, the governor could deny that it had ever happened, even though it had and everyone knew it. With his mind wrapped up in such concerns, the governor had never thought to ask Guajardo how he knew about the president's mistress or what the president might or might not want to do. Not that it mattered, for the governor also favored spending a single night with his mistress over an entire week with his own family.

When the door of the room opened, all movement stopped as every face turned to see who was entering. The young Air Force lieutenant who had opened the door froze in midstride when he saw the roomful of solemn faces staring at him. Unsure what to do, the lieutenant looked to Guajardo. For a moment, he stared into Guajardo's eyes, eyes that were as cold and expressionless as his face. Guajardo said nothing, jerking his head to indicate that he wanted the lieutenant to come over to him.

Moving around the room, and keeping as far as possible from where the governor had resumed his pacing, the lieutenant came up next to Guajardo, bent over, and whispered into his ear. There was no change in Guajardo's expression, not even a nod. Instead, when the lieutenant had finished and straightened up, Guajardo stood, straightening the blouse of his uniform as he did so. Turning to face the lieutenant, Guajardo issued several orders to him in a low voice. The governor neared that end of the room in time to hear Guajardo emphasize that the lieutenant was to personally see that the president's plane was taken care of, as arranged. The lieutenant's response was a simple, almost curt, and solemn, "It will be done." With that, the lieutenant left the room.

Turning to the governor, Guajardo quietly announced that the president's plane would be on the ground in five minutes. The governor paused. For a moment, there was a pained expression on his face. Only after it cleared did he acknowledge the news of the president's arrival with an absentminded nod. He resumed pacing, stopping only when the Mexican Air Force Boeing 727 finally came into sight. With a sigh, the governor nervously tugged at his tie in a failed effort to straighten it. Ready, he headed for the door. Behind him his aides and advisors, save Guajardo, scurried to follow.

The governor emerged from the terminal just as the 727 rolled to a stop. From nowhere a throng of security men, some in uniform, others in short-sleeved white shirts, flooded onto the field and formed up around the aircraft. Behind them a truck-mounted stairway was moved into place while a fuel tanker lumbered up on the far side of the plane. When the president emerged from the 727, he paused briefly at the top of the stairs while his eyes adjusted to the bright afternoon sun. When he was able to see, the president looked about for the governor, beaming a broad smile to him when their eyes locked, a smile that belied the deep concerns he had.

Carlos Montalvo's pace as he bounced down the stairs wasn't quite as spry as it had been when he had been campaigning for the office of president six months ago. In those days, anything and everything had been possible. He had, or so he thought, plans and programs that, when in place, would see Mexico and its people through the social and economic problems they faced. Repayment of a staggering debt, reversal of a population explosion, halting of inflation that set new records almost daily, and, most importantly, resurrection of the people's faith in the ruling political party, all had appeared to be within his grasp. His party, the Partido Revolucionario Institucional, or PRI, had been losing ground for years to both the left, represented by the Partido Socialista Unificado de México, or PSUM, and to the right in the form of the Partido de Acción Nacional, or PAN. The last election, won by the narrowest of margins, had been won only through sheer determination, willpower, and the loss of many ballot boxes in districts where the power of the PRI was questionable. As he walked down the stairs, Montalvo doubted that he had the strength, political or physical, to defeat a challenge from either the PSUM or the PAN again.

The problems faced by the republic were difficult but manageable. Or so the young president had thought when he took office in December of the previous year. The reality of the social and economic collapse that threatened Mexico had been a rude shock even to someone with as much political savvy as Montalvo. "Truth," he had found, changed dramatically when he was handed the red, white, and green sash that represented the office and responsibility of the president of Mexico.

So too did the political landscape. Seemingly overnight the scattered and quarreling parties on the political left had found new unity and popularity. While the PRI still held a majority of the Chamber of Deputies, four hundred seats, more than ever before, had been lost to non-PRI candidates, mostly to the PAN who cried for a return to the "true Revolution." The once orderly and safe processes of legislation were disrupted and endangered. The non-PRI deputies, taking advantage of the disenchantment with the PRI that had so nearly defeated Montalvo in his race for president, were unwilling to rubber-stamp legislation proposed by him—legislation that was necessary to make his dreams a reality. The debates that raged on every issue, both on the floor of the chamber and in the news, stalled all effective action and brought to the surface again and again the corruption, fraud, and indifference to the suffering of the Mexican people that had become the grim legacy of the PRI's rule.

In these troubled times, the parties of both the left and right found new popularity and support from all facets of the population that traditional PRI methods could not discourage or beat back into line using the "usual" methods. The left and the right seemingly took turns twisting Montalvo's programs into inflammatory issues that divided, rather than united, the people. The church, through an unnatural coalition with the socialist PSUM, saw Montalvo's programs aimed at population control as a threat to its dogma. Students were finally convinced that the continuation of PRI dominance would favor the well connected, not the best and the brightest. And the workers were shown that they, not the elite, would pay the bill for retiring the massive debt accumulated in the days of brighter hopes and foolish investments. Instead of being able to lead the country down the road to a brighter future, President Montalvo found himself struggling to maintain control as barriers to prevent his programs from going into effect were erected, both in and out of the government.

It did not take long for the specter of a socialist, or even worse, a communist revolt, to appear. Though no hint of preparations for insurgency or threat of violent overthrow of the government by the PSUM could be uncovered by the Mexican intelligence community or special security forces controlled by the PRI, the Army insisted that those threats were real. Caches of weapons, presumably smuggled across the border from Texas into Tamaulipas, had been seized by Colonel Guajardo's soldiers in surprise sweeps along the border. Together with the rhetoric of the PSUM, which reeked of the classic communist manipulation of the people and the situation, the regional Army commanders began to increase their vigilance and the state of readiness of their troops. As a result, security was tightened as intelligence and security forces redoubled their efforts to discover the threat that the Army claimed was everywhere and was responsible for the growing unrest that was beginning to sweep the country.

The Army, long excluded from the inner circles of policy-making and decisions, remained silent and aloof from the growing political unrest and debates, turning their attention instead to preparations designed to deal with the dangers that only they saw so clearly. The only comment senior staff officers would volunteer in public were pledges to "uphold the traditions of the Revolution and the honor of Mexico" and defend the people and the Revolution from all threats, both internal and foreign. Had any of the president's advisors paused and carefully analyzed what the colonels were actually saying, the true danger would have been appreciated.

So the president and the governor greeted each other with minds clouded with many concerns and problems. Though Montalvo wore the stress better than the governor did, each man knew that the other was desperately searching for solutions to his own problems. The president's concern over the problems that threatened their way of life and the political system that had ruled Mexico since 1928 was no less real than the governor's concern over political survival. Their greetings, and the introduction to each other's staff, were, therefore, perfunctory. As President Montalvo and the governor walked into the terminal, questions immediately turned to the matter at hand. Had there been any new outbreaks of violence? Were the police able to contain the oil workers? Had there been any acts of sabotage?

From the lounge, Colonel Guajardo watched with detached interest as the presidential party and the attending cluster of lackeys and functionaries moved to the terminal door behind a screen of security men. He was not really interested in the president's party. Instead, he watched the crew of the fuel truck go about their task under the scrutiny of the security personnel. The Air Force lieutenant who had informed him that the president's plane was inbound was nowhere to be seen. The colonel, however, had no doubt that everything was in hand. With nothing more to do, he turned away from the window and left the lounge for the conference room to listen to the discussions that would last well into the night.

*   *   *

The flight back to Mexico City was quiet. President Montalvo had started
to work on a speech he was scheduled to give to the Chamber of Deputies
in two days, but he was unable to concentrate. The secretary of finance,
the secretary of national defense, the secretary of programming and budget, and the comptroller general, all of whom had accompanied the president on this trip for the express purpose of working on the speech, were
already asleep, as was almost everyone else. Even the ever-watchful chief
of his security detachment, seated in the aisle seat of the last row of the
cabin, was nodding between consciousness and sleep. It seemed that
President Montalvo alone, though tired, could not sleep. His mind was a
tumble of thoughts and feelings, most of them negative.

His most recurring thought was that he might fail to solve Mexico's
problems. The discussions with the governor of Tamaulipas had only
served to further befuddle his grasp of the scope and nature of problems
facing his administration. Because of this inability to achieve a clear and
precise focus, instead of being the savior of his nation, the Revolution,
and its people, he now was being portrayed as a Quemando, someone too
naïve to be trusted. In six months Montalvo had been unable to hack
through the bureaucracy that fed on corruption at every level and protected itself from within.

Seeing no changes, the people heeded the call for civil disobedience
and strikes, actions that Montalvo saw as a direct challenge to his authority. Though he instinctively knew it was wrong, Montalvo had, at the
urging of his advisors, resorted to harsh repression and the selected suspension of civil liberties. The left seemed to be employing anything and
everything to alienate him and his party from the people. Unless something could be done to stop the current trend, he would have no choice but
to employ those means of restoring stability to the government and the
nation that could also bring about its eventual downfall.

Though his eyes demanded he close them, President Montalvo cleared
his head as he shuffled through the papers on his worktable. Forcing
himself to concentrate, he carefully underlined selected passages of the
speech he would use in an interview with an American journalist that had
been arranged for later that morning. The curtailment of his vacation and
early return to Mexico City was, in his opinion, an opportunity. By
leaking some of the more important items of his new program through the
American media in advance of its official presentation, he and his advisors could gauge how it would be received by both the Chamber of
Deputies and the public. Everything for the next few weeks would be

critical. Nothing could be left to chance. If the opposition's reaction to the information he would leak during the interview was deemed adverse, he could always blame it on misquotes or poor understanding on the part of the American journalist. If the reaction was favorable, he would leave the speech and program intact.

For a moment, President Montalvo paused and allowed himself to think about the interview, now only six hours off. Even though it would be crucial, and he would have to exercise great care in what he said and how he presented himself, he was looking forward to it. The thought of being interviewed by an American woman of Jan Fields's stature and beauty aroused him. By reputation, he knew that she was as bold as she was beautiful, beguiling, and manipulative, and captivating to the point of being an enchantress. A sudden twitch and pain in his groin broke President Montalvo's train of thought. He shifted in his seat so as to allow his reaction the additional room it demanded. As he did so, President Montalvo sheepishly looked about the cabin to see if anyone was watching. Had someone noticed, how could he possibly account for getting an erection while reading one of his own speeches?

President Montalvo was pondering this rather unpresidential question when the first engine lost power and died. The cockpit crew, lulled into inattentiveness by the late hour and monotony, stared at the red warning light for a moment, refusing to believe they had a problem. The copilot looked out the window to see if there was a fire in the engine, but saw nothing. The pilot began to struggle with the aircraft, compensating for the loss of the engine while attempting to restart it. The flight engineer hit the FASTEN SEAT BELT sign and paged the flight attendant, to warn her, and in turn the president, of the problem.

In the passenger cabin the first sign of a problem was a change in the pitch of the engine followed by a series of jerky maneuvers. President Montalvo looked up toward the front of the aircraft, waiting for someone to tell him what was wrong. His aide, who had been asleep, woke with a start and looked about for a moment before getting up to go forward and investigate the nature of the problem. Immediately behind him was the chief of security. Both men were halfway to the crew cabin when the door swung open and the flight attendant, in a near panic, came running out, headed for the president. She was about to explain the problem to the president's aide when the second engine cut out, sending the aircraft into a steep dive and throwing everyone in the aisle sprawling.

President Montalvo grabbed the armrests of his seat and pushed himself back. He watched as those who were not strapped into their seats were hurled forward into the seat backs before them or into the aisles. The plane jerked from side to side as the pilot struggled to gain some degree of control. He failed, however. Without power there was nothing he could do to lessen the angle or speed of descent. In a matter of seconds the plane was almost on its nose and slowly spinning to the right.

Everything not secured, including people, the president's speech, pillows, blankets, and suit jackets went crashing past President Montalvo into a great tumbled heap at the rear of the cabin. The screams of fear and panic mixed with the cries and moans of the injured. President Montalvo braced himself with his feet on the seat back to his front in order to keep from being wrenched from his seat and into the heap at the rear of the cabin.

The descent seemed to take an eternity. Without having to be told, President Montalvo understood his fate. He knew he was going to die. In his mind, there was no panic, no desire to know why the plane was going down. There was only regret, regret that he would die a failure. The image of him riding into Mexico City on a great white horse to save it and its people would go up in a great ball of fire, just like the aircraft.

The only witnesses to the crash of the aircraft into the side of a mountain in the Sierra Madre Oriental were two F-5 fighters that had been trailing the president's plane at a discreet distance. The pilots of the F-5s watched the president's aircraft collapse upon itself, its wings pitching forward as the sudden impact ripped them from the fuselage and spread fuel over the entire area. The fuel and its fumes ignited and exploded, enveloping the aircraft in a ball of fire. President Montalvo, key members of the cabinet, his personal staff, and the air crew were dead. The contaminated fuel that had caused their death incinerated their bodies beyond recognition and wiped away all traces of sabotage.

3

Many wearing rapiers are afraid of goose-quills.

—Shakespeare, *Hamlet*, ii, 2

PALACIO NACIONAL, MEXICO CITY, MEXICO
1045 HOURS, 29 JUNE

Despite the hour of the day, there was little traffic along the Avenue República de Brasil, which pleased Corporal José Fares, Guajardo's driver. The events of the morning, the wild rumors, and the somber, almost dark mood of the colonel made Fares uncomfortable. Guajardo, slouched in the backseat of the sedan, had said nothing since getting into the sedan. In his rearview mirror Fares watched the colonel sit motionless, as if in a trance, staring vacantly out the window at the near-deserted streets. Though no one told him as much, Fares understood that the tall colonel in the backseat was one of the members of the coup that had swept Carlos Montalvo and the PRI away in a matter of hours and was now, no doubt, seizing control of Mexico. The very thought of being so close to a person with such power was somewhat frightening. Without realizing it, Fares drove the car with great care, acting as if he were carrying a bomb, rather than a colonel.

Guajardo did not notice the empty streets or the manner in which the corporal drove the sedan. Even when they reached the *zócalo,* or main square of the city, he paid scant attention to the gray stone and marble façade of the Catedral Metropolitana or any of the massive buildings that ringed the *zócalo.* Even in the best of times, Mexico City had little that excited Guajardo. The events of the last twenty-four hours, weighing heavy on his tired mind, did nothing to change how Colonel Guajardo felt about the capital. A native of Chihuahua, Guajardo viewed Mexico City and the government that ruled the country from it with suspicion. Like his forefathers, he had been raised to be self-reliant and an individual, traits that were as necessary for survival in the political world of modern Mexico as they were in the harsh and remote northern state.

Mechanically, when the car stopped, Guajardo opened the door and was out of the sedan before Corporal Fares had a chance to get out and open it for him. Without a word, Guajardo walked away from Fares, passed two guards at the South Gate of the Palacio Nacional, and headed for the offices of the president. Like Corporal Fares, the guards knew instinctively who, and what, Guajardo was. Stepping back, they saluted with a crispness seldom seen in Mexico, and allowed him to pass.

As with Corporal Fares, Guajardo did not acknowledge their presence. He walked out of the sun into the dark shadows of the Palacio Nacional, lost in his own thoughts, fears, and concerns. For now he was moving into the unfamiliar halls from which political power emanated, a world that he was not trained to deal with. Behind his every thought, self-doubt hovered like a buzzard, leaving him to wonder if the skills his grandfather and father had passed on to him would see him through the revolution he and his co-conspirators had embarked upon.

Through the corridors, courtyards, and halls of the palace, Guajardo trudged, past colorful murals and paintings that recorded Mexico's history. Only briefly, as he passed a mural depicting the heroes of the last Mexican Revolution, did Guajardo pause. For a second, his eyes glanced from the face of one hero of the Revolution to another, looking into their eyes in the hope that they could give him the answers and inspiration that he himself could not find.

But they could not. The colorful images, larger than life but lifeless, betrayed no secrets or answers. They only looked down on Guajardo, a mere mortal, returning his stare. There was no strength or knowledge to be drawn from the images on the wall. Disappointed, Guajardo let out a slight sigh as he wondered if the real men who had inspired the images on the mural had felt the self-doubt, exhaustion, and fear that he was feeling then. They all had been, he told himself, humans themselves. It was their actions that mattered. Standing there, Guajardo wondered if that was their message. Perhaps what the mural really said was, "Look at us! We were mere mortals. We are here because we overcame the limits of our bodies and the fears in our minds to do what was necessary." Drawing in a deep breath, Guajardo scanned the mural once more, nodding his head as he did so. Yes, they were only men, he thought, no better than he. With the dark cloud of self-doubt tempered by that thought, Guajardo turned and proceeded down the corridor with a determined stride.

*   *   *

Entering the outer office of the president's suite, Guajardo casually glanced about as he continued on, without breaking stride, to the closed doors of the president's office. The outer office was crammed with military officers, senior police officials, and government civilians. Some were engaged in heated discussions, others in hushed conversations. A few sat alone, lost in thought. It was easy to tell, by the expressions they wore, who believed they were on the "inside" and who didn't know and were waiting to find out. On this day, the first day of the New Revolution, the faces of the outsiders betrayed their feelings. By far, concern, fear, panic, and gloom were dominant.

Guajardo, along with twelve other Army and Air Force colonels, were the only true insiders. Those filling the outer office who did not know this by prior knowledge soon understood by the manner in which Guajardo crossed the room. Guajardo wore a cold expression on his face as he moved through the crowd. His gait, his posture, his carriage were not those of an arrogant or pompous man. Instead, Guajardo emitted an air of confidence and power that could only be described as a commanding presence, a presence that was as much psychic as it was physical. Everyone responded to his presence without a word being spoken or a cue given. Like a bow wave, the crowd parted to allow him to pass.

Though Guajardo knew who each person was, he didn't acknowledge their presence, for none of them were part of the Council of 13. On the other hand, the officers and civilian officials filling the room paused in midsentence or momentarily emerged from their lonely dark thoughts when Guajardo passed by them. Most acknowledged him with a slight bow of the head. Two officers made motions, which he ignored, in an effort to catch Guajardo's attention. One civilian, alone in the corner, shaken from his thoughts by Guajardo's passing shadow, looked up at Guajardo and grimaced as if he had just seen his own hangman. Regardless, all kept their eyes on him as they stepped aside, allowing Guajardo to glide by.

It was only when he reached the door of the president's office and began to turn the brass knob that a voice from the center of the room called out. "Colonel Guajardo, Colonel Molina is in conference with Colonel Zavala. I do not believe they want to be disturbed."

Guajardo paused but did not remove his hand from the doorknob. He merely turned to where the voice had come from, knowing all too well that it belonged to Major Ricardo Puerto, Molina's adjutant. Sensing a confrontation, the crowd in the room parted, clearing the line of vision from where Guajardo stood and Puerto sat. In an instant, only a large desk, strewn with haphazard stacks of papers and files, separated the two men. Puerto made no attempt to stand. If anything, he eased back in his chair as he eyed Guajardo.

As Molina's adjutant, Puerto had served as the recording secretary whenever members of the Council of 13 had met to plan the Revolution or as a special courier when Molina needed to pass information discreetly to other members of the council. It was therefore quite natural that Puerto began to regard himself as a part of the Revolution's inner circle and assume an air of importance that was as unbecoming as it was inappropriate. Guajardo, and most of the other colonels who belonged to the council, never missed a chance to put the pretentious junior officer in his place. Guajardo's eyes met Puerto's for a moment as the room again fell silent and everyone waited to see who really held the upper hand.

Why, Guajardo thought, did young officers always feel the need to exaggerate their own importance at the expense of someone else? There was no reason, other than self-gratification, for Puerto to challenge Guajardo. Puerto was a young fool playing a fool's game. This, Guajardo thought, was no time to play such silly games. Besides, to respond to, or even acknowledge, Puerto's challenge in any manner would only diminish Guajardo's character in the eyes of the people filling the outer office. Such ignorant behavior, Guajardo thought, deserved to be ignored. Still looking at Puerto, Guajardo turned the doorknob and flung the door open in an exaggerated manner. Without further ado, Guajardo snapped his head forward and stepped smartly into the president's office, leaving Puerto to hold down the anger he felt at the rebuff as best he could.

From behind the desk, Colonel Hernando Molina looked up as Guajardo entered the room. Behind Molina stood Colonel Salvado Zavala, the member of the council responsible for domestic affairs. With one hand on Molina's chair and the other on the desk, Zavala was leaning forward over Molina's right shoulder, reading a document Molina was reviewing. Looking across the room at his fellow conspirators, Guajardo suddenly felt self-conscious about the state of his uniform. Having stopped only to wash his hands and shave, he wore the same uniform that he had worn for the last twenty-four hours. Besides being dusty with a sprinkling of dirt, mud, and grass stains, it had a peculiar smell that was a mixture of aviation hydraulic fluid, sweat, and the pungent odor of burnt flesh.

Any reservations Guajardo had about his appearance were soon brushed aside by the greeting given him by Colonel Hernando Molina, chairman of the Council of 13, president of the provisional government, and god-father to Guajardo's oldest son. As soon as Molina saw Guajardo, a smile lit his face as he practically jumped up out of his seat. "Alfredo! My friend! How glad I am to see you."

Guajardo's unexpected appearance and Molina's sudden and exuberant reaction to him caught Zavala off-guard. He was practically knocked down as Molina moved around the desk in a rush and grasped Guajardo's right hand with both of his and began to pump it vigorously. "We have done it, my friend. We have stepped forward and done that which should have been done years ago."

"It has only started."

Without acknowledging Guajardo's laconic response or expressionless face, Molina led Guajardo to a large, overstuffed leather chair. "Yes, yes, we have much to do, but at least we are finally doing something. Come, sit and give me your report."

Before he turned to sit, Guajardo's eyes fell upon the red, white, and green sash that had been the president's badge of office. The sash was haphazardly draped across the back of the chair where Molina had taken him. For a moment, Guajardo wondered if Molina's choice of seating was an intentional insult to the office that the sash represented, or if he was simply overwhelmed by the enthusiasm of the moment and the over-powering feeling of relief one experiences when action allows the release of nervous tension and stress. If there was a hidden meaning in this action, it was far too subtle for Guajardo's practical, and tired, mind. Turning his back to the sash, he sat down and eased himself into a comfortable position.

Moving to a chair similar to the one Guajardo was seated in, Molina sat. His actions, his expressions, and his manner were those of an excited man, a man with much to do and little time. Molina's excitement was not based on panic, fear, or confusion. Guajardo and those members of the council who considered him a friend knew better. Molina, a colonel of infantry, had the reputation throughout the Army as a man who feared no one and nothing. Even in the greatest of adversity, he kept his head and functioned with a cold machinelike precision, efficiency, and ruthless-ness, earning him the nickname "the Shark." Guajardo surmised that it was the sudden rush of events of the past twelve hours that animated Molina, for he had felt the same. No doubt, all the members of the council, after secretly planning and plotting for months while suppressing the fear of betrayal or failure, felt great exhilaration at finally being able to release their stress through action.

"So, tell me, my friend, is everything in order?"

Guajardo closed his eyes and nodded slowly. He then opened his eyes and recounted his actions since leaving Victoria in a low, steady voice. "The president with his party, including the secretaries of finance, national defense, programming and budget, and the comptroller general boarded the presidential plane. The two F-5 interceptors that were to track the presidential jet were airborne and in a holding pattern north of Victoria when the presidential jet departed. According to the Air Force, based on transmissions from the president's plane and the manner in which it flew, no one on it detected the interceptors during the flight.

"As soon as possible, I left Victoria and followed the president's plane in my helicopter. En route, the interceptors reported when the president's plane went in and its location. They remained on station over the wreckage until I arrived. Before departing, the flight leader reported that, as best they could tell, no one arrived at the site before I did. The team with me confirmed this once we were on the ground." Finished, Guajardo leaned back further into the chair.

There was a momentary silence as Molina waited for Guajardo to continue. When he didn't, Molina, in a quiet and almost faltering voice, asked the question that bothered him the most. "Did you, could you confirm that the president was dead?"

Under ordinary circumstances, Guajardo would have lost his patience and not have answered such a stupid question. But these were not normal times. Molina, like Guajardo, was operating under a great deal of stress and pressure as they carried out an intricate and fast-paced plan to decapitate the government of Mexico and replace it with the Council of 13. In such an operation, it was wrong to assume and sometimes the obvious must be confirmed.

Before answering, Guajardo looked up at the ceiling. He continued to stare at the ceiling as he spoke. "When the aircraft impacted, it was almost completely vertical and nose-down, causing it to collapse upon itself. Imagine, if you can, a full-size 727 compacted into a heap less than a fifth its original length." Guajardo paused to let this image sink in. "Fire broke out almost immediately and covered not only the wreckage but the area immediately around it. When I arrived, it was still burning. The molten aluminum and twisted wreckage fused into a single great smoldering lump. Even if I had been able to get close, there was no way to sort out what charred remains belonged to the president." Turning his hard gaze toward Molina, he added, "I doubt even our best pathologist could."

With that, both men lapsed again into silence, averting their eyes to the floor. Without looking up, Molina spoke first. "I am sorry for being so boorish, my friend. I simply had to hear you say it. You understand. The vision of the failed Soviet coup several years ago still haunts me.''

Without looking at him, Guajardo shook his head before he responded. ''The Russians were fools. They didn't have the stomach to do what was necessary.'' Then, Guajardo chuckled and looked up at Molina. ''You know, it's almost ironic. The very people who made the saying 'You can't make an omelet without cracking a few eggs' a cliché didn't have the nerve to eliminate Yeltsin and Gorbachev. Who would have thought that we would live to see the day when the head of the KGB would hesitate to pull the trigger?''

Molina sighed, smiling as he spoke. ''Yes, who would have thought? At least, my friend, we were able to learn from their errors. It seems none of our brothers suffer from a weak stomach.''

Then Guajardo, his face reverting to an expressionless mask, asked point-blank how much longer he and the other members of the Council of 13 were going to have pretend that the president's death was an accident and not the first stroke of the New Revolution.

Molina, glad that Guajardo had changed the subject, smiled. ''Soon, my friend, soon. In fact, at noon, I will make a public announcement. In the meantime, we say nothing. Our deception has worked. All the key officials, as well as the leadership of the opposition parties, rushed to their offices when they were informed that Montalvo's plane was missing. It seems that everyone was anxious to see how they could further their own position as a result of the president's death. Without exception, none of them were prepared for the reception they found.''

Yes, Guajardo thought. What they found must have come as a shock to many of them. He could almost envision the scene, repeated a hundred times in the last few hours across Mexico. Informed that the president was missing, Montalvo's advisors and assistants, as well as the leaders of the PSUM and PAN parties, would immediately rush to their offices. Instead of finding their own trusted staffs ready to take advantage of such a crisis, each of the president's men and opposition leaders found a young Army or Air Force officer, hand-picked by members of the Council of 13. Accompanied by two or three armed soldiers, the officer executed his instruction to the letter, either placing the surprised official under arrest or, as the American CIA liked to put it, ''terminating the target with extreme prejudice'' on the spot. Few would live long enough to realize that the officer and the soldiers with him were the same people who had been responsible for agitating the workers across Mexico to strike, pre-cipitating the crisis that had set the stage for the New Revolution. In retrospect, Guajardo had to agree that it had been better to do things this way, rather than send bands of armed soldiers careening about the country like a bunch of American cowboys hunting their targets.

From where he had been left standing, Colonel Zavala broke the trance that both Molina and Guajardo had lapsed into. "Colonel Molina, should I come back later to confirm the names on this list?"

Suddenly remembering that Zavala was in the room, Molina pivoted in his seat toward him. "No, there is no need for me to confirm the list so long as it has not changed from last week. Simply take it over to Colonel Obregón at the Supreme Court. With everyone on the first list accounted for, it is time to begin collecting the next level." Zavala, realizing that he was being dismissed, picked the list of names off of Molina's desk and briskly left the room. The list Zavala carried contained the names of those members of the old government, officials, and private citizens that the council referred to as level-two threats. These were people who had to be dealt with as soon as all level-one threats, such as the president and the governor of Tamaulipas, had been "removed." Some of the people waiting outside Molina's door were on the second list.

With Zavala gone, Molina turned back to Guajardo. To Molina's surprise, Guajardo was standing, his peaked cap tucked under his left arm. "Since it is time to move on to level two, I must be on my way. We must not keep Señor Alamán waiting."

Motioning to Guajardo to resume his seat, Molina surprised him by announcing that Alamán could wait. Other matters, according to Molina, required Guajardo's immediate attention.

Thrown off guard, Guajardo, with his cap still under his arm, sat down on the edge of the chair. What, he thought, could be more important than crushing Alamán and his private empire built on drugs and corruption? As it was, Guajardo thought it had been a mistake to not to classify Alamán as a level-one threat. At every opportunity, Guajardo had pointed that out. Any delays would most certainly play into Alamán's hands, especially since his private army was superior to the Mexican Army in every way when it came to weapons and secrecy. "What could possibly be more important than eliminating Alamán?"

Leaning back in his chair, Molina let Guajardo hang for a moment before he answered. "The Americans, my friend. The Americans, and what they think, are very important to us right now."

Impatient, Guajardo blurted, "Yes, yes, we knew that going into this. But dealing with the Americans is Barreda's task. As the acting minister of foreign affairs, he is better prepared to deal with that. I feel it would be a mistake to have me, charged with defense and national security, becoming involved in diplomacy and foreign affairs."

Molina patiently waited while Guajardo stated his objections. When he was sure that Guajardo was finished, Molina responded with smooth, controlled tones. "Yes, that is the way it should be and will be, except for one interview. This morning, we found out that our former president had an interview scheduled with an American film crew from Austin, Texas. The correspondent conducting the interview is a very famous, well-connected international correspondent, a female by the name of Jan Fields. At first, we were going to cancel the interview. But Barreda thought that we could use her, and the scheduled interview, as a means of presenting to the American public the goals and objectives of our actions. Therefore, on his own initiative, he contacted Miss Fields this morning and offered her an opportunity to interview one of the leading members of the Council of 13. She, of course, accepted."

Listening to Molina, Guajardo nodded in agreement. Yes, he thought, this made perfect sense. But what did that have to do with him?

Seeing the quizzical look on Guajardo's face, Molina continued. "After the decision to keep the interview had been made, the next question was who would be the best person for the task. As you have pointed out, Barreda, who is responsible for foreign affairs, should do it. Unfortunately, Barreda does not speak English and physically, he does not present the kind of image we want the Americans to have of us."

The last part of Molina's statement was surprisingly blunt, but true. Barreda's ancestry was heavily Indian, giving him dark skin and features that could best be described as chiseled. To say that Barreda was not photogenic would have been an understatement.

"Besides, Barreda is unknown to the Americans. You, on the other hand, my friend, speak English like a yanqui, attended their staff and war colleges, and you are almost pure Spanish."

Guajardo did not like how or where the conversation was going. "None of those things should make a difference. We had a plan of action and methods of dealing with such things. I see nothing that indicates that we need to . . ."

Putting up his right hand, Molina cut Guajardo off. "You, of all people, know that in any operation, plans seldom survive initial contact with the enemy. We must continuously assess the situation and alter the plan to take advantage of opportunities that were unseen when the plan was created. This revolution, our revolution, is no different."

Resting his elbows on the arms of the overstuffed chair, Molina settled back a little deeper into its cushions and put his hands together, with his fingers interlocked and held just below his chin. "This interview, and your presence in Mexico City, is one such opportunity. By having you do the interview, the American public will see a member of the council who looks like them, talks like them, and uses terms that they are used to. Your experience with the Americans and knowledge of their culture will be invaluable in a free-flowing interview. In addition, the American intelligence community will be able to access your files with their military and quickly see that you are both intelligent and reasonable. As you were trained in their staff and war colleges, they may believe that there is the possibility of influencing the council and its decisions through your training and association with Americans. While all this is merely a hope, we must do everything that we can to keep the American government and public neutral while we consolidate power and institute our reforms.''

As Molina spoke, Guajardo watched his friend's face and expression. By the time Molina had finished, Guajardo knew there was no point in arguing or protesting his new assignment. It was not so much the words and logic Molina had used, although both were convincing in their own right. Rather, it was Molina's expression and the manner in which he presented himself. In his mind, there was no other solution. He had seen a problem, considered it from all angles, and evolved a remedy. Besides, Guajardo thought, when you're in his home waters, it's pointless to argue with a shark. Shrugging, Guajardo indicated his acceptance of the task. ''So, my leader, when and where do I meet my fate?''

Relieved that Guajardo was agreeing without further protest, Molina smiled and leaned forward, patting his friend's right arm. ''It's not so bad. It will definitely be more enjoyable than sticking a pointed stick in your eye.''

Caught up in Molina's lighthearted mood, Guajardo chuckled. ''Obviously, my friend, you have never worked with American women. I have a chance of controlling a sharp stick.''

''Don't worry, Alfredo. Jan Fields is a beautiful and spirited woman. Treat her like a thoroughbred.'' Molina, holding his hands as if he held the reins of a horse's bridle, moved his body ever so smoothly as if he were riding. ''You must make sure you are in control, using a gentle hand and soothing voice to control your mount.''

Shaking his head and smiling, Guajardo stood. ''You could sell the devil ice in July. But unfortunately, my fearless leader, you know nothing about American women. If I try to handle her like a horse, she will bite my arm off up to here, or worse.''

Molina laughed. ''In that case, keep your hands in your pocket and your legs crossed.''

4

Truth can never be told so as to be understood, and not be believed.

—William Blake

Throughout her years as a correspondent, Jan Fields had been asked many times, "What is the secret of your success? How did you make it in such a demanding business?"

Jan enjoyed playing down her considerable success, answering that question using the same charming and graceful style that she used to disarm people she interviewed. With a slight, almost imperceptible flick of her head, she would toss her long brown hair to one side. For a moment she would pause while she looked from the corner of her eye at the person talking to her. Turning her head slowly back toward the other person, a simple, almost mischievous smile would cross her face. For a moment, she would avert her eyes, looking down at her hands as if to ponder the question before answering. When she did respond, her tone was soft, almost shy. "Well, I've just been lucky, I guess, *very* lucky." Then, quickly glancing up, she would look at the questioner, her big brown eyes wide open now, a broad smile lighting up her face. Throwing her hands out to the side, palms up, she would repeat her response: "Luck, nothing but dumb luck."

Those who worked with her, however, knew better. If there was any luck involved in Jan Fields's success, it was because she made it. Her current assignment was a good case in point. Sent to Mexico City to do a story on the impact of American investments and American-controlled business in Mexico, Jan had worked sixteen hours a day for three days

48

scheduling interviews. By wrangling invitations to several cocktail parties and affairs, including a formal state dinner, Jan was able to meet people who consented to being interviewed by the charming señorita with the dancing brown eyes.

In arranging for interviews, and while doing them, Jan worked like an artist selecting the proper brush and color, employing a variety of skills and talents to get what she wanted. When talking to one official, she would be all business. With another, all smiles and charm. And with yet another, shy, almost timid. Jan was not to be taken lightly, however. When hacking through the layers of bureaucracy, she could be as determined and tough as she needed to be when someone stood between her and a story.

As to the technical side of her profession, not only was Jan dedicated and a perfectionist, she demanded no less from those who worked with her. Yet she could be professional without being impersonal, in control without being overbearing, by using the same charm and graceful manner on her camera crew that she used to put her subjects at ease. She understood that the process of putting a story together was a cooperative effort and acted accordingly. By making everyone a member of one team, Jan was able to extract the best from those who worked with her and for her.

When she was preparing for an interview, no detail was too small and no angle was left unconsidered. As part of her advance study of the interviewee, Jan made it a point to study how the person dressed. If the person was a man, she would examine photos of his wife, noting the style and even the color of her clothing in an attempt to find out preferences. Anything and everything was used to put the subject at ease.

There was an aspect of Jan Fields's work, however, that most people in her profession would frown upon. Jan, for all her technical skills, was, first and foremost, an artist. She did not simply cover a story, she created. Everything—the lighting, angle of the shot, her attire, the background—was considered against an overall concept, an image, an idea that she wanted to communicate. Of all her skills, her ability to take abstract thoughts and images and translate them into images that could be captured by the camera was the most difficult to define, yet the most important.

Still, there was no denying that luck did play a part. June 29 was to be the last day of shooting. After an interview with the president in the morning, Jan and her Austin-based camera crew had been scheduled to leave for Texas. The death of the president, however, changed all that.

The morning started when her "fixer," a Mexican hired to make arrangements for hotels and transportation, as well as to deal with government bureaucrats, called her at 6:30 and told her that the president was dead. With rumors of a coup, he warned her that it was important to leave the city immediately. Naturally, Jan would hear nothing of that. Instead, she insisted that the fixer, an elderly man named Juan, arrange for an interview with a spokesman from the new government. Juan, not wanting to leave his home, let alone become involved with the new government, tried to talk her out of it. Jan, however, hung tough and demanded he try or lose his commission. Reluctantly, Juan agreed.

No sooner had she hung up the phone and turned to begin dressing, than it rang again. Without waiting for Jan to respond, a male voice, in impeccable English, identified himself as a captain in the Mexican Army calling on behalf of a Mexican Army colonel Jan had never heard of. In a very crisp yet polite voice, he informed Jan that in reviewing the president's daily schedule, his colonel had discovered that Jan was listed for an interview at the Palacio Nacional later that morning with the president. Jan, a little leery about where this conversation was going, paused before answering. Caution, however, was not one of her strong points. "Yes," she responded, "that's right. I am, I mean, I was scheduled for thirty minutes." Then, as an afterthought, she decided to push her luck and see what she could get the captain to confirm. After all, he didn't know how much she knew. "Is there something wrong with the time or the length of the interview, Captain? I have a very flexible schedule and can easily change it in order to accommodate the president."

Now the hesitation was on the other end of the line, while the captain thought before responding to Jan's probing questions. Finally, in a hushed voice, he informed Jan that President Carlos Montalvo's plane was missing and that an assassination attempt was suspected. He then went on, stating that, in order to ensure public safety and internal security, as of five o'clock that morning the Mexican Army had declared a state of emergency and imposed martial law.

Jan was becoming excited. She had confirmation, from an official source, of Montalvo's death. Furthermore, she knew that an Army captain, representing a colonel, wouldn't be calling her at a time like this if there weren't something that they wanted. Deciding to push a little further, she asked, in a soft voice preceded with a slightly audible sigh, "Oh, how tragic. I don't know what to say." Then, before the captain could respond, Jan added, "I guess that means there is no point in my coming to the Palacio Nacional."

Jan's ploy worked. When the captain responded, he spoke quickly in order to soothe her fears. "Oh no, Miss Fields. On the contrary. My colonel has instructed me to advise you that it would be his pleasure to meet with you at noon, if that time is suitable for you. He will provide you with a summary of the past twelve hours and actions being taken by the Mexican Army to deal with the current crisis."

Pausing for dramatic effect before responding, Jan informed the captain that it would be a pleasure to meet with his colonel at noon. After a few pleasantries, they both hung up. Jan, excited by the manner in which the morning was developing, smiled and leaned over, pumping her right arm up and down and shouting, "Yes, yes." Fame and fortune, she knew, belonged to the lucky.

Once she was off the phone, Jan roused her crew, informing them of the news and getting them ready to go out into the street to shoot whatever they came across. There was no sense, she thought, of wasting the valuable time before her interview with the colonel. Next she called World News Network, her employer. When she informed them that she was still in Mexico City and had been contacted by people who claimed to be in charge, they were all ears. Though WNN already had two camera crews and a full production team, with direct feed capabilities, preparing to fly in from Dallas, Jan knew it would be hours before they were there and longer before they were ready to start covering the story. With some deft negotiating, she managed to get them to agree that she would be their chief correspondent in Mexico for the duration of the current crisis, with the right to edit her own material before beaming it back to Washington.

With that settled, Jan called back to Juan to check on his progress. His news, presented in a rather unconvincing manner, was discouraging. According to him, he was unable to contact anyone who knew what was going on. "Everything is in chaos, Señorita Fields. Everyone is very uncooperative. No one knows who's in charge."

Without hesitation, Jan fired back. "Then I guess we need to go down to the government offices and find someone who is in charge."

"*No! No!* We can't do that, Señorita Fields. This is a coup, a revolution. There may be trouble. That is no place for a woman to be."

Juan's last comment tripped a harsh response. "Listen, mister, that's what I'm paying you for. Either you take me down there and do your job, or kiss your commission, *and* your reputation, good-bye."

There was a moment's pause while Juan pondered his choices. Jan wondered which threat was more damaging, the loss of money or the loss of prestige. Not that it mattered much to her. All that mattered right then was getting a story, any story, shot and on the air.

Finally, Juan answered, "Sí, yes. I will take you. But we must discuss my salary. Things have changed. This is now a very dangerous time, señorita. You understand."

Softening her tone, Jan responded. "Yes, Juan, I understand. What would be fair pay for a man of your talents in the current crisis?"

Feeling that he had regained a measure of control, Juan pondered the question out loud. "Well, things could become dangerous. They say government troops are all over and that other government police officials across the country are being arrested. There could be fighting."

Jan listened, responding with, "I see," and "Ah-huh," as Juan built a case for a higher salary. When he was finished, Jan repeated her question.

With the confidence of a man who knew she would never agree to such an outrageous sum, Juan demanded double his current fees. What he had not realized was that Jan was prepared to pay four times the current fee. Without hesitation, she agreed to double his fee, told him to meet her in the lobby of her hotel in thirty minutes, and hung up before he had the chance to say another word.

Prepared for scenes of chaos and open fighting, Jan was somewhat disappointed as they drove through the deserted streets of the city with her tiny crew consisting of Juan, a cameraman, and a sound technician. After taping ten minutes of empty streetcorners and closed shops, they drove to the main plaza where the Palacio Nacional was located. Again, except for an occasional jeep filled with soldiers, there was nothing. Leaving the van, Jan, followed by the camera crew, began to walk toward the Palacio Nacional in an effort to attract attention or provoke a response from the Army patrols. Again, however, she was quite disappointed as the mounted patrols and guards posted at the doorways of government buildings ignored Jan and the camera.

When they passed the Palacio Nacional, Jan decided to take advantage of her invitation to interview one of the colonels who was supposed to be in charge. She stopped and looked at a knot of soldiers standing about the main entrance. "We had an interview scheduled with the president of Mexico this morning. Now, we have one with his replacement." Then, with a smile on her face, she turned to her sound man, Joe Bob. "So, my loyal friends and crew, that must mean we are welcomed and sanctioned. Let's take advantage of that welcome and do some serious reporting."

Joe Bob took his cue and pulled the van up to a good place to park. Without asking or waiting for the opinion of the others with her, Jan turned away and moved with purpose toward the Palacio Nacional. From what she had seen, if there had been a military coup, it had been efficient, quick, and controlled. If those assumptions were true, there was an organization in charge and operating. And if there was a system, it could be manipulated. Since the news wasn't going to come to them, it was time to dig for it, and what better place to start than at the top?

Juan, however, was shaken by the events of the morning, the presence of so many soldiers, and the brazen attitude of Jan Fields. Never missing a chance, he tried to persuade Jan to return to the hotel until things settled down. Jan would not be put off. Angered by Juan's timidity, Jan turned to him, throwing her arms out and shouting as she did so. "Settled? If things get any more settled, they'll roll up the sidewalk!"

Neither Juan nor Jan took into account that while they were looking at the same situation, each was dealing with it based on an entirely different perspective. For Juan, the sight of vacant streets in Mexico City populated only by armed soldiers was a new and disturbing sight. The Federales and their fat officers, after all, could not be trusted. Jan, on the other hand, who had seen firsthand bloody street fighting and cities choked with tanks and troops, began to wonder if the military was, after all, in charge, let alone behind the coup and the unrest that Juan kept worrying about.

After spinning about and looking at the deserted streets, she turned back to Juan. "Settled? If this place becomes any more settled we'll die from boredom." Dropping her arms, Jan stood there for a moment and thought. Slowly, a wicked smile lit her face. "What we need to do is stir something up." Without waiting for a response, she turned and walked right into the middle of the soldiers.

HOUSE OFFICE BUILDING, WASHINGTON, D.C.
1000 HOURS, 29 JUNE

Like clockwork, everyone in Congressman Ed Lewis's outer office dropped what they were doing and turned to the television monitor whenever WNN reviewed the top news stories of the hour. Even the congressman, like a figure on a German cuckoo clock, came out of his own office every half hour to watch the news. Ever since Lewis, a Democratic representative from Tennessee, had been appointed a member of the House Intelligence Committee, both he and his staff took a keen interest in any news that involved foreign crisis or conflicts. An avid reader of just about anything in print and a news junkie, Lewis was capable of absorbing and retaining tremendous amounts of information and storing it away, ready for use. Only partially in jest did his fellow representatives refer to him as the next best thing to the Library of Congress.

Yet no one would think of describing Lewis as being bookish or an intellectual. At forty-two, he looked more like a college basketball coach than a U.S. congressman. His six-foot two-inch frame was lean without being skinny. His brown hair, streaked with stray strands of gray, was cut short, not styled. Though he often wore a warm and friendly smile, it was his eyes, more than any other feature, that expressed his moods and betrayed his thoughts. They could be warm and inviting to a new acquaintance, cold and cutting to an opponent, and friendly and mischievous to a friend. His eyes told everything and, like the college basketball coach, missed nothing. More than one witness who appeared before a panel on which Lewis sat commented on the manner in which Lewis used his eyes to unnerve them. An interdepartmental memo circulated within the CIA to members of that agency slated to appear before Lewis, advised that its members read or pretend to read notes and avoid eye contact with Lewis when answering questions.

As he stood in his doorway watching the news on the situation in Mexico, Lewis compared the story to the information he already had. That, unfortunately, was not only skimpy, but contradictory. Official statements and contacts he had cultivated at the CIA, the Defense Intelligence Agency, or DIA, and the National Security Agency, or NSA, provided only bits and pieces of the story, bits and pieces that didn't fit together.

What he had heard was not at all satisfactory. From the CIA, he got the impression that the coup in Mexico was a bolt out of the blue. Though he was given few details, the DIA described the coup as an efficient and comprehensive operation that had decapitated the Mexican government. The NSA, on the other hand, noted that the situation was confused and quite chaotic. Based on his experiences with intelligence people, Lewis knew that, in reality, the situation in Mexico contained all those elements. The material from the nation's intelligence agencies, after all, was no better than the sources they used and the opinions of the people doing the data analysis. Each agency depended on different sources and used different criteria when determining what was relevant and what could be ignored. While the information they provided was nice, it wasn't what he needed at a time like this. What he and the nation's decision-makers needed was a clear, concise, and comprehensive overview of the situation, a view that brought all the stray pieces together. Unfortunately, Lewis knew it would be days before anyone in the intelligence community would be able, or willing, to commit themselves to such a summary. So until then, all they would get was raw data and bits and pieces.

Still, Lewis was disturbed that no one had seen the coup coming. It was like the fall of Cuba in 1959, the invasion of Czechoslovakia in 1968 and of Afghanistan in 1979, the reunification of Germany in 1989, the invasion of Kuwait in 1990, the Soviet coup in 1991, and a score of other "bolts out of the blue": America's leaders were handed a crisis which they had not been prepared to deal with, leaving them no choice but to throw together a policy on the fly. What made this failure even more disturbing was the fact that the U.S. had massive resources deployed in Mexico and along the border as part of the drug-interdiction mission. Surely, Lewis thought, someone working with the Mexican military or government must have come across something. No one, he knew, could hide an undertaking massive enough to topple the Mexican government in a matter of hours without someone noticing.

As he watched the news, he considered his next move. He would give the chairman of the House Intelligence Committee until noon to begin asking questions before he did anything. If, by noon, no one else had, Lewis would throw a few turds in the punch bowl and start hounding people, not only for information but for answers. With the amount of money the Congress sank into the intelligence community, there was absolutely no excuse for the nation's depending on a twit like Jan Fields to provide them with their only source of information on world events.

As if by magic, the image of Jan Fields flashed onto the screen across the office. With the Palacio Nacional as a background, the bright-eyed journalist stood reporting from the heart of Mexico City. Flanked by well-armed and grinning soldiers, she casually recapped what she had seen, mentioning that she had arranged an interview with a member of the Council of 13, the organization she described as comprised of Army and Air Force officers who had assumed control of the government.

Lewis could feel his anger building up. Mumbling, he turned away. "Christ, in a few hours she knows more about what's going on than the CIA. What a farce! What a bloody farce!"

PALACIO NACIONAL, MEXICO CITY, MEXICO
1235 HOURS, 29 JUNE

Sitting across from the Mexican colonel, Jan couldn't be more pleased with herself. In a matter of a few hours, she had shot a piece, made contact with the ruling council, arranged for an interview with a member of that council, and even got the Mexican military to help her transmit her first story to WNN headquarters in Washington, D.C.

Seated across from her was, from what she had been told, one of the architects of the coup that had brought to an end "the corrupt and self-serving government of the few,'' as an official spokesman had called President Montalvo's administration. Although the Mexican colonel's uniform was slightly wrinkled, and specked with dirt and dust, his presence and carriage were commanding. That, coupled with his extraordinary command of English and his position on the Council of 13, provided Jan with an opportunity to create a piece that would be head-and-shoulders above anything the other news agencies could possibly hope to put together for days. Now all she needed was to get this colonel to give her a few interesting comments that she could add to the framework of the official comments she had in hand.

"So, Colonel Guajardo, what finally convinced you and the other members of the council that the duly elected government of Mexico no longer represented the people?''

Though the question by the American correspondent bothered Guajardo, he didn't show it. Looking straight into Jan Fields's eyes, he framed his response, translating his thoughts from Spanish to English in his mind. When he was ready, Guajardo leaned forward, toward Jan. "There is no simple answer to that question, I am afraid. In the past few weeks, I have often pondered that same thought.'' Guajardo paused, allowing himself to settle back in his seat before continuing. When he began to speak, he waved his right hand about, sometimes throwing it out to the side with the palm up and open, other times pointing his index finger at Jan to emphasize a point. "Is such a violent response, I asked myself many times, really necessary? Isn't there a better way? Not a day passed that I didn't say to myself, you are not giving the system a chance. Perhaps, just perhaps, things will get better.'' Pausing, Guajardo let out a sigh, letting his right hand come to rest on his right thigh while he let his head drop down as if to study his resting hand. "But, alas, nothing changed. The politicians, they came and went. Programs to solve our debt, create jobs, and remedy our social problems were launched with great fanfare and wonderful speeches. For a while, whatever problem the program was aimed at solving would improve.''

In a flash, Guajardo changed. Jan was startled by the sudden transformation. When their eyes met, she was greeted by eyes that were cold and distant, set in a face contorted in anger. Though she didn't notice, Guajardo's right hand was now clenched into a fist, a fist that he was slowly using to pound his right thigh as he spoke with a harsh, cutting voice. "But then, when no one was looking, the politicians went back to their big houses and the programs were forgotten. The only thing that did not change was the faces of the people. In their eyes, you could see the flame of hope slowly dying, drowned by the harsh reality of survival in modern Mexico.''

Jan, momentarily caught off guard by Guajardo's response, paused. After thirty minutes of simple banter and short, crisp answers, she had finally gotten the colonel to react. Sensing it was time, she seized the mood and drove on. "So, you and your fellow colonels decided that you had to act. But I wonder, was it necessary to eliminate the entire government *and* the leadership of the PRI, as well as the other political parties? Surely there was no need to turn on the PAN and the PSUM. If anything, wouldn't they have been better as allies, not rivals, in your efforts to establish a new government?"

Again Guajardo paused before answering. He continued to look into Jan Fields's eyes while he thought. She was attempting to provoke him. It was as if she had driven a knife into him and was slowly twisting it. Well, he thought, if you want a reaction, you shall have one. But Guajardo, ever the professional soldier, sought to maintain control.

"The PRI has rooted itself throughout our nation like a great cancer. It is everywhere, it touches everything and everyone. And everyone it touches it infects. For decades, men like my father struggled to cure the cancer from within. He served the party well, doing what was asked in the belief that he was doing something important for Mexico. And all the while, he closed his eyes to the graft, the corruption, the fixed elections, the misappropriation of funds. I would hear him at night telling my mother that someday, when he had the power, he would do what was right. He would come forth, like the knight on the white horse, and change everything."

Pausing for a moment, Guajardo shifted in his seat, turning his head to look up at the great mural depicting the heroes of the first revolution. Without looking back at Jan, he continued. "I think, in his heart, he really believed he was doing what was right. Just like the politicians in the PAN and PSUM, I truly believe he was trying as hard as he could. But the cancer had seized him. Its roots slowly wrapped themselves about him, squeezing every trace of compassion out of him. By the time he died, he was like a man who had stared at the sun too long, he was blind to the reality of the world around him, a reality that threatens to destroy everything that the Revolution stands for."

"Is that how you see yourself, Colonel, a savior on a white horse, coming forward to correct all the ills of Mexico by execution and terror?"

Guajardo could feel the blood rush to his head. He snapped his entire body about and faced the American female. For a moment, he eyed Jan Fields, fighting hard to maintain his composure. What arrogance, he thought. How can she, sitting here, dressed in clothes and shoes that cost her more money than the average family in Mexico made in half a year, understand what we are trying to do? What does she know of poverty, of crushed dreams and stillborn hopes? How dare she come into my country and impose her morals on our people when she has no idea what it means to be a Mexican?

For the longest time, Jan watched as Guajardo glared at her. Perhaps, she thought, she had gone too far.

As if in response to Jan's thoughts, Guajardo stood up, coming to a ramrod straight position of attention in front of Jan. There was a moment of silence as everyone waited for Guajardo to announce that the interview was over. Instead, Guajardo summoned, with a slight motion of his hand, a captain who had been patiently waiting in the background.

As the captain came forward, Jan looked at her crew. Ted the cameraman, nicknamed Theodore because of the round wire-rimmed glasses he wore, not seeing any cues from Jan, had his eye glued to the camera as he continued to shoot. Joe Bob, her sound tech and the only native Texan in the crew, looked at Jan, shaking his head. Also at a loss, Jan shrugged her shoulders and threw her hands out, palms up. Only Juan, standing against the wall, was visibly upset. Like a barefooted man on a hot beach, he nervously moved and shuffled his feet about, his eyes jumping from the spot where Guajardo stood conferring with the captain to the door at the far end of the room. To Jan, it appeared as if Juan were mentally measuring the distance he would have to run if something happened. Did he know something, Jan thought, that we didn't? Or was he just overreacting? For the first time, Jan began to take the situation seriously, reminding herself that the man standing in front of her had something to do with a revolution that had begun by killing the same leaders he had, as a soldier, pledged fidelity to.

The clicking of the captain's heels as he turned and walked away caused Jan to turn back and face Guajardo. In a moment, he had changed. His face was transformed, his eyes, his whole attitude had changed. The calm, relaxed man in the overstuffed chair was now towering over her. From her chair, she looked up at him. In his brown uniform, he looked like a great grizzly bear. The soft brown eyes that had been so disarming were now dark, vacant, and piercing. Whether he intended to be intimidating didn't matter as far as Jan was concerned; she was duly intimidated, though she tried not to show it.

"Ms. Fields, a minute ago you asked me what finally drove me to turn against my government and the political system that kept it in power. Come, I will show you." Without waiting for an acknowledgment, Guajardo turned and left the room.

The colonel's announcement had been an order, plain and simple. Although she had no idea where he was going to take them, Jan knew she had hit a nerve and that whatever he was going to show them could only enhance the material they had collected during the interview. Without hesitation, she was up out of her seat and scurrying across the floor, leaving Ted and Joe Bob scrambling to grab cases and cables. Juan, seizing the confusion of the moment, deciding that he had greater need of his life and liberty than of double pay, quickly and quietly slipped away through the door he had been eyeing.

With Colonel Guajardo leading, Jan and her crew trotted through the corridors and down the grand staircases, in an effort to match the colonel's great strides. None of them noticed that Juan was not with them. Even when they walked into the great courtyard where a military sedan and the rental van Jan's small crew was using sat waiting with doors open and engines already running. Neither Jan nor Joe Bob, the driver, thought to ask how or by whom the van had been moved. Such details weren't important at that moment.

What was important was where they were going and what the colonel wanted them to see. Pausing at the open side door, Jan all but shoved Ted and Joe Bob in, shouting, "Go, go, go," as they passed her. As soon as Joe Bob was clear, Jan turned to follow, but was held back by a hand on her arm. Turning, she saw that the captain Guajardo had talked to was holding her. With a slight smile, he informed her that Colonel Guajardo would like her to come with him in the sedan. Caught off guard, Jan looked back to Joe Bob, noticing for the first time that there was a soldier in the van's driver's seat.

In an instant, Jan realized that she was no longer in control of the situation. Her first reaction was to turn on the captain and explain that she had to stay with the rest of the crew. That, however, quickly passed from her mind when she noticed for the first time that Juan was not with them. Instead of defiance, Jan decided to stall in an effort to gain some time to assess the situation.

"Juan, my fixer, is not here yet. We must wait."

The captain, still smiling and still holding her arm with a gentle but firm grip, simply shook his head. "I am sorry, Ms. Fields. Your man has already left. The colonel is quite busy and we must leave, now."

"I assume the man you have driving our van knows where we are going."

The captain nodded his head. "He is a very good man. The van will follow. Please, Ms. Fields, we must go. The colonel is waiting." With that, he gave a slight tug on Jan's arm, a tug she initially resisted.

Wanting the last word, if for no other reason than to show that she was going of her own free will, Jan called to Joe Bob and Ted. "I'll be with the colonel. Keep the camera ready and roll on anything that might be of interest.''

Looking at Jan, Joe Bob wondered if she meant that as a threat to the captain, reminding him that they were filming in case he had evil intent, or if she was just giving simple directions. Regardless of what she meant, Joe Bob began to regret leaving his .357 Magnum back home in Austin. There ain't nothin' more pathetic, he thought, than an unarmed cowboy surrounded by a bunch of pissed-off greasers. ''Okay, Miss Fields, we'll be right behind you.'' Not that we can do squat, he thought.

Guiding her around the van, the captain led Jan to the sedan where Colonel Guajardo waited in the backseat. Jan had hoped to sit up front, preferring to have some distance and a nice seat back between her and the colonel. But the captain took her to the rear door, which he closed behind her with a quick, crisp slam.

Guajardo, without a word, looked over to Jan while she settled herself. His cold, hard expression hadn't changed. Even when she smiled and told him she was ready, Guajardo said nothing to her, greeting her announcement with a slight nod. Turning to the driver, Guajardo rattled off instructions in Spanish.

To Jan's surprise, instead of a simple nod or *sí,* the driver suddenly stiffened. In the rearview mirror, she could see an expression of shock on his face. The order the colonel had given had certainly upset him, a fact that did nothing to calm the tightness Jan began to feel growing in the pit of her stomach. Moving only her eyes, Jan glanced back and forth between Guajardo and the driver.

When Corporal Fares, the driver, failed to respond to his order, Guajardo leaned forward and repeated it. Fares, his face now contorted with an expression that reminded Jan of the same frightened look Juan had had, whispered what sounded like a hesitant plea in response to Guajardo's second order.

In a flash, Guajardo raised his right hand, made a fist, and pounded his right thigh with it as he hissed his order for a third time. Choking out a ''Sí'' that was barely audible, Corporal Fares mechanically released the parking brake, shifted the sedan into gear, and began to drive. Satisfied, Guajardo eased back into his seat, not bothering to look at Jan, who was trying to sink into her corner as far as she could.

Once out of the courtyard and on the streets, Jan did her best to avoid attracting Guajardo's attention. Looking out the window, she tried to suppress the fear that was gnawing away at her. Though she had been in difficult spots before, she had never been the focus of attention as she was now. Before, she had always been the casual observer, able to keep herself apart from the event she was reporting or the person being interviewed. What was happening now was totally out of control. Knowing that she had put herself and her crew into such a situation so willingly and without weighing all the consequences didn't do anything to assist her efforts to calm down and collect her thoughts.

And the presence of Colonel Guajardo was also troubling. Even though she kept her face turned to her window, Jan could sense his presence. In the large room of the Palacio Nacional where they had conducted the interview, she had noticed mud on Guajardo's boots and traces of dirt and soot on his uniform. Now, in the confines of the car, Jan noted the unusual mixture of odors that permeated Guajardo's uniform.

Without looking at the colonel, Jan began trying to determine what he had been up to by analyzing the scents that emanated from him. The dominant odor was that of a man who had been very active and either not taken the time or hadn't had the opportunity to shower. Jan was familiar with the musky smell of masculine sweat. Her lover, Scott Dixon, who was a lieutenant colonel in the American Army, usually smelled like that when he came back from a field exercise. Guajardo had another smell to him that often permeated Scott's field gear, the odor of hydraulic fluids. As the operations officer of the 16th Armored Division, Scott often used a helicopter. So it was not uncommon for him to smell like one after a field problem. A third scent, fainter than the others, yet quite distinct, reminded Jan of burned flesh. The question of how Guajardo had managed to pick up that odor intrigued her while, at the same time, it brought her back to the realization that the man sitting next to her was no soapbox politician. The power he held was the result of direct and brutal action. For a brief second, Jan felt the urge to look at Guajardo's hands to see if there was still blood on them. She quickly dismissed that thought, however. After all, modern man had progressed a long way from the Old Testament, becoming quite adept at washing hands.

Jan began to concentrate on the scenes that flashed by her window. Without her noticing it, they had passed from the almost deserted streets of the center of the city to a residential and shopping district crowded with cars, trucks, people, shops, small stands and stalls. Outside, on the street, shoppers, workers, vendors, and beggars jostled each other as they went about their daily business as if nothing had changed in Mexico. Jan sat up when she realized this and began to look for the soldiers that had been so evident in the center city. She saw none. She didn't even see any police. For all practical purposes, whatever was happening with the government had, so far, had no effect on these people.

When the sedan reached an intersection and stopped for a light, a young man ran out from the curb and came up to Jan's window. He looked at her, smiled, and turned his head. Puzzled, Jan wondered if he was a beggar or peddler. Then, without warning, as he held a lighter inches from his face, he spit out a ball of flame from his mouth.

The sudden feat of the fire-breathing man startled Jan, causing her to jump backward, bumping Guajardo in the process. Guajardo, who had been lost deep in thought as he looked out his window, turned to see what had startled Jan. The fire-breather, finished with his act, had turned back to wait for his reward. Only then did he notice that Jan was seated next to a colonel of the Mexican Army. Slowly, the fire-breather's face turned from a broad smile to a quizzical frown. Still, the man stood there, not moving. He was still staring at Jan and Guajardo, as if in a daze, until the light turned and the sedan pulled away.

Suddenly realizing that she was leaning against the colonel, Jan sat up straight and moved back to her side of the seat, running her hand through her hair. As she began to regain her composure, she glanced over at Guajardo. He was looking at her.

Seeing that he was studying her, waiting for her next action, Jan faced Guajardo. "I'm so sorry, Colonel. I wasn't expecting that. He caught me off guard."

"They are called *tragafuegos,* our slang for fire-breathers."

"Why do they do that? I mean, isn't it dangerous?"

Guajardo looked at Jan and let out a cynical laugh. "To live, my dear Ms. Fields. They do what is necessary to live. On a good day, a *tragafuego* can make eight or nine thousand pesos."

Doing some quick mental math, Jan figured how much nine thousand pesos was in dollars. Guajardo watched as she did so, smirking when Jan's expression turned from a blank to a look of surprise. "But that's only a little more than three U.S. dollars."

With a self-satisfied look on his face, Guajardo nodded. "Yes, somewhat better than the average minimum wage."

"But it is dangerous. It must be easy to burn himself."

Realizing that he had her, Guajardo played with her. "Oh, if they are careful, and use diesel instead of gasoline or cooking oil, they do well." As he talked, Jan's face showed signs of surprise. In a rather nonchalant manner, Guajardo continued to drive his point home. "The problem is not the burns. They can heal. What does not heal is the damage the *tragafuegos* do to their health. The first thing they lose is their sense of taste. The petroleum products, regardless of what they use, are corrosive. They eat at the human tissue. Eventually, the *tragafuegos* lose all feeling in their mouth, followed by their teeth.'' Then, as an afterthought, he added, lightly, ''And of course, ulcers on the tongue are not at all unusual.''

Jan's expression was slowly turning to disgust. ''That, however, is only the beginning, Ms. Fields. The worst is the brain damage. The speech becomes slurred as they become brain dead, unable to fend for themselves. The process is slow, taking eight to ten years. Eventually, they will simply disappear, their places on the streetcorners taken by younger men who are still able to perform.''

Jan was becoming uncomfortable. In part Guajardo knew that it was because she was no longer in control. Like most Americans, Jan was used to having things her way. That she couldn't, bothered her. Even more disturbing, though, was the fact that she no longer had the option to pick those things that fit neatly with her preconceived ideas and images. She had not been ready, or willing, to face the reality of Mexico. That face, one easily ignored, was not pleasing to her. Guajardo could see this and was quite pleased. The trip was paying off. ''And what, Colonel, is the government doing? Aren't there social programs, or welfare, or something better than that? Doesn't he know what he is doing?''

Turning his face away from Jan, he looked out the window as he answered. ''Yes, Ms. Fields, he knows.'' Then, looking back to her, his eyes narrowed. ''But he is a man, a proud man. What you just saw was the result of failed or sham programs that the former government used to justify its existence. I have no doubt that somewhere along the line, a politician or social worker arranged a mediocre job for the *tragafuego* that we saw. And no doubt, the *tragafuego* worked at it until the funds ran out or the program closed down after the politician was re-elected. As for welfare, I shouldn't need to remind you that we are a proud people. Your North American ideas of welfare serve only to break the spirit. That man, the *tragafuego*, would rather die a slow and miserable death than lose his pride.''

No sooner had Guajardo said that than the sedan stopped. Jan turned to see where they were. She had been so absorbed in her conversation that she had not noticed they had driven into an area that was little better than a shantytown. The sudden transition, from the clean, broad boulevards of the city center to the squalor of this slum of Mexico City, was unsettling to Jan. She was not ready to deal with this. In her travels, she had been in such ghettos before. Still, she never grew used to them. She had a great deal of difficulty accepting that people had to live in such conditions, and that there was nothing she could do to change that. Whenever she knew she would need to go into a ghetto or into a place like this, it took her days to condition herself to deal with the despair, filth, and poverty she knew she would see. She had not been able to prepare herself for this trip, and it threw her mentally and emotionally off balance, a condition she was struggling to correct as Guajardo prepared to leave the safety of the sedan.

The driver opened his door, jumped out, and ran to open Guajardo's. When Jan looked back at the colonel, he smiled a sly smile, one that reminded Jan of a cat eyeing a bird. "At the Palacio Nacional you asked what motivated us to do what we did, Ms. Fields. Come with me, and I will show you." Without waiting, Guajardo turned away and exited the sedan.

The stench hit Jan before she even left the car. A dizzying combination of decaying garbage and human waste assaulted her nose, irritating its lining like pepper and causing her to gag. Pausing, Jan instinctively brought her hand up to her mouth and nose. Guajardo, waiting for her several feet from the sedan, watched in amusement. For a moment, he felt like calling out a snide comment, but decided to wait. There would be ample time to rub her nose into the reality of modern Mexico.

Regaining her composure, Jan swung her legs out of the sedan, planting her feet into the discolored goo of the unpaved and rutted street. Again, a momentary expression of disgust registered on her face, causing the smirk on Guajardo's face to broaden.

Jan, looking up at Guajardo, realized that she was not only making a spectacle of herself, but was reacting in a way that Guajardo, no doubt, had anticipated, perhaps even had counted on. This, and her own inability to control her reactions, suddenly angered her. Determined to show that she was made of sterner stuff, she sucked in a deep breath, distasteful as this was, and forced herself to stare back at Guajardo with a face that was as determined as it was defiant.

The change in Jan's demeanor wiped the grin off of Guajardo's face. Realizing that she had managed to rally to his first challenge, he decided it was time to press on. Time was valuable and he was already falling behind. In a tone that was, for the circumstances, artificially polite and sweet, Guajardo invited Jan and her crew to follow his driver, Corporal Fares.

As if on cue, Ted and Joe Bob came up, equipment at the ready, on either side of her. Placing a free hand on her left shoulder, Joe Bob leaned over and whispered in Jan's ear, "You okay, Miss Fields?"

Reaching across her chest with her right hand and lightly grasping the hand Joe Bob had on her shoulder, Jan nodded. "I'm fine. Now let's go see what the good colonel wants to show us." With that, she let go of Joe Bob's hand and stepped off.

The strange procession caused the people in the streets of the slum to stop what they were doing and watch as it went by. Corporal Fares, wearing a nervous look on his face, led the group. Every so often he looked to the side, nervously nodding his head at a neighbor who recognized him. Behind him came Guajardo, walking tall, erect, and seemingly unconcerned with the squalor of his surroundings. Several feet behind the colonel were Jan, Ted, and Joe Bob, all traveling in a tight little knot with Ted and Joe Bob holding their equipment at the ready. Only the soldier who had driven the van for the camera crew remained behind, occasionally shooing away dirty children dressed in rags when they came too close to the sedan and van.

The tumbledown shanties, shacks, and hovels that lined the filth-strewn dirt street were constructed of every imaginable material. Some were made with cinder blocks, either loosely piled up one upon the other or cemented together with uneven layers of mortar used by the amateur builders who laid the blocks. Scattered between the hovels made of cinder blocks were other homes built with irregular scraps of plywood or wooden boards. These, like the cinder-block homes, varied depending upon the skill of the builder. All were no more than six or seven feet high, had a single door, often without a frame, and few if any windows. Their roofs, flat and barely visible to Jan, were either boards covered with a thin layer of tarpaper or loosely connected strips of corrugated metal.

As they trudged along, Jan began to take note of the people. They parted as Corporal Fares and Colonel Guajardo approached, slipping away into their homes or into the dark, narrow spaces between them. Jan looked at them as she passed. In the spaces between the homes, amid heaps of rubbish and discarded building material, small children and women watched as she went by. In one alley, Jan was shocked to see a woman, her back to the street, squatting over an open hole, relieving herself. That, no doubt, Jan thought, accounted for part of the stench. For a moment, Jan wondered why she was doing that in the open. Then, looking back at the size of the houses, she realized that they were far too small and crude to hold a bathroom inside. For the next few feet, Jan looked between the homes, searching for any signs of an outhouse, but saw none. Satisfied, and disgusted at the same time, she stopped looking.

Other details began to jump out at her. Above the houses, a wild patchwork of electric wires and extension cords running from telephone poles crisscrossed, running into access holes in the houses. On the ground, running between the houses, garden hoses of every color and size snaked in and out of other holes chipped or cut through the walls. It took no great genius to figure that this was how those fortunate enough to afford the material provided their homes with water and electricity.

In their wanderings, Jan could not find any street markings or numbers on the houses. She began to wonder if there were any. While she was working on this problem, Corporal Fares stopped in front of a cinder-block house, no different than many of those they had already passed. Sheepishly, he looked up at Colonel Guajardo. The colonel, without changing expression, simply nodded, giving permission to, or ordering, Fares to enter.

Turning to Jan and her crew, Guajardo finally spoke. "Before, Ms. Fields, you asked me what made me decide to raise my hand against the government to which I had pledged undying loyalty. I tried to think of the words that could describe this to you." He paused, stretching out his arms, palms up, and rotating his torso as he looked away from Jan and at the crowded slum in which they stood. Dropping his arms, he turned back to Jan. "But I could not. How, I thought, could I describe this in words that a well-bred, cared-for, and educated yanqui woman such as yourself could understand. Better, I thought, that I allow you to see, for yourself, what it meant to be a Mexican under the callous rule of the PRI. So I have brought you to the home of my driver, Corporal Fares. Perhaps, when you have seen this, you can better understand what is causing not only me, but millions of others like me, to take desperate steps. You may, if you like, film this. Perhaps you can think of the words that have escaped me."

Suddenly, the confrontation with his driver, the nervous silence in the sedan, and Corporal Fares's uneasiness as they had walked down the street, made sense. The corporal, obviously ashamed of his home, was being forced to expose it to strangers. That, and the fact that Jan realized that the colonel was making a crude effort to use them for propaganda, angered her. Her dark expression, displaying the anger and contempt she felt for Guajardo, was returned by the colonel, who, for his part, felt hatred for a person who sought only the truth that fit her own clean perception of how the world should be.

Jan turned toward Joe Bob and barked out her instructions in a tone that betrayed her disgust with Guajardo. "All right, let's get on with this. Give me a hand mike."

Pulling out his earphones and sliding them over his head, Joe Bob turned on the recorder, listened for a moment, then reached into a side pocket and pulled out a mike for Jan. While he was doing so, Ted hoisted the camera onto his shoulder and waited for Jan's cue to start shooting.

Without any of the normal preliminaries, except for a quick check of her long reddish-brown hair, Jan gave the cue to start shooting. When she saw the red record light and Joe Bob give her a thumbs-up, indicating the mike was hot, Jan began without really knowing what she was going to say. "Jan Fields from Mexico City. About an hour ago, while interviewing Colonel Alfredo Guajardo, a member of the council of colonels responsible for today's dramatic coup here in Mexico, I asked the colonel why he decided to turn against the popularly elected government of Mexico. His response was to take me, and my camera crew, to this slum in the suburbs of Mexico City. The home we are standing in front of, barely better than a shack, supposedly belongs to his driver, a corporal in the Mexican Army. While it is not unusual for rebels to claim that they represent the will of the people or justify their actions by publicly displaying the plight of the people, I thought it would be appropriate to allow the colonel an opportunity to state his case. So here we are, at the home of Corporal Fares, Mexican Army."

Giving Ted the signal to keep rolling, Jan turned to enter the cinderblock house. For a moment, she felt good. The brief piece before the camera, her little introduction, had had a calming effect on her. For a second, she felt she was back in control, running the show. All she had to do now was maintain the edge and keep Guajardo from dominating the interview. Like a fighter entering the ring, she was ready.

The scene that greeted her, however, shook her. With the trained eye of an observer, in a single sweep of the one-room house, she took everything and everyone in, and was appalled. A single light bulb, precariously dangling from a cord in the center of the room, provided the only source of light. Guajardo, standing just inside the door to the right, was silently watching Corporal Fares as he hugged a girl of six or seven. She was thin, bordering on scrawny, with jet black hair pulled together in a braid. Her big eyes, wide with fright, were turned up to her father as she held his leg with a viselike grip.

Across from Fares, on the wall to the left of Jan, was a small portable two-burner stove, the only kitchen appliance in evidence. Next to it stood several wooden boxes, neatly stacked and attached by boards on either side, creating a shelving unit in which pots and pans occupied the lower section, or box, while other cooking utensils and boxes filled the top two. In the corner, next to the stove, was an old kitchen table with a broken leg, surrounded by four chairs, none of which matched. Against the far wall was a mattress sitting on the floor. Though Corporal Fares partially blocked Jan from seeing the entire mattress, she could see that someone was on it. Curious, and anxious to see what was so important about this particular home, Jan moved around the corporal.

As she made this move, Jan's head struck the bulb, causing it to swing haphazardly from its long wire. Distracted, she moved farther into the room, almost up to the edge of the mattress, before looking down to see who was on it. When she did, she gasped in horror.

The child lying there was little more than a skeleton. It was hard to judge her age because her face was distorted by bulging eyes sunk deep into their sockets and surrounded by black circles and hollow cheeks. Still, based on her length, the girl had to be ten, maybe eleven. Her arms and legs showed no sign of muscle; the joints, both kneecaps and elbows, were clearly visible. The only indication that she was alive was a shallow, raspy breathing that caused her chest to rise and fall ever so slightly.

Once she was over the initial shock, Jan began to notice that, for all the misery that wracked the girl, she appeared to be well cared-for. Her hair, long and black like her sister's, was neatly combed and arranged to either side of her head. Her nightgown, and the single sheet that covered the mattress, though frayed and threadbare in spots, were spotless.

"Her name is Angela. She is ten years old." Jan, startled by Guajardo's statement, turned away from the girl and looked at the colonel. To his right, in the doorway, stood the rest of her crew, Ted taping and Joe Bob listening to the quality of the sound recording and adjusting it as necessary.

Looking back at Angela, Jan asked what was wrong with her.

Guajardo grunted. "Mexico City, Ms. Fields, Mexico City and poverty."

Jan looked up again, first at Corporal Fares and his other daughter, both of whom were watching her intently, then at Guajardo. For the first time since entering the room, she noticed it was terribly hot and she was sweating. Except for the door, there was no other opening in the room. The sun, on the exposed tarpaper on the roof, was turning the room into an oven. Guajardo was using her.

Though she knew in her heart that what was happening had not been a setup, Jan felt anger. She didn't quite know why she was angry, let alone who she should be angry at. Was she angry because she was unable to handle the sights of poverty, sights that were part of the real world that was so much a part of her profession? Was she angry at the arrogant Mexican Army colonel for rubbing her nose in that poverty? Was she angry because she wasn't in control of the situation? Was she angry that she was being manipulated so skillfully by the colonel? She didn't know. At that moment, surrounded by the grim reality of real life in Mexico, all she knew was that she was angry and had no one to lash out at. Determined to regain her mental balance and establish some degree of moral ascendency over the colonel, her retort was sharp, almost bitter.

"Cities do not kill children. Nor do governments. This poor creature has an illness that, I am sure, can be cured if properly cared for."

Guajardo, in a very controlled and even voice, slowly responded, carefully picking his words for effect. "How naïve you are, Ms. Fields. Naïve and arrogant. You come south, into Mexico, from your rich middle-class world in the north where everyone has an education and there is always an answer, always a solution to the problems of the poor. Yet for all your sophistication and knowledge, you know so little. Or is it that you choose not to know the truth? Cities do kill people, Ms. Fields. Just look about you, out there in the street, if you care to call it that. It is an open sewer, a dung heap. People and animals who live here leave their waste out there, day in and day out. In the heat of the day, human waste, uncovered, dries and flakes. Tiny microscopic flakes of feces are picked up by the wind, mixed with exhaust fumes from hundreds of thousands of cars, trucks, and buses that run on leaded gas and poor exhaust systems, and are carried about the city. These people, living in these slums, breathe this mix in, every day of their lives. Some, like Angela, aren't strong enough to survive."

Guajardo paused, looking away from Jan and at the frail figure on the mattress. "Perhaps she is the lucky one. Her lungs, corrupted beyond repair, will kill her before she becomes a woman. Death will save her from living in a hole like this, scratching out a living and raising a family where the children have no hope, no fantasies, no dreams. Angela will not have to watch her son stand on a corner and breathe fire to make a few dollars a day, killing himself as he does it. Angela will not have to watch her daughters become old and haggard before their time, scrubbing floors or doing laundry in the homes of the rich. And Angela will not have to be told that her husband, or son, was gunned down in the streets by the thugs of a rival drug lord."

Turning, he began to walk away, but then stopped and looked back at Jan. As he spoke, Guajardo breathed in deeply, struggling to control his anger and tears. Between breaths, his choppy words hammered Jan like blows. "No, Ms. Fields, if you have tears to shed, shed them for Angela's sister. She is a girl with no future. A child who cannot go to school because she must care for Angela while her mother earns two dollars a day scrubbing floors and her father serves in the military. It is the sister, not Angela, that I can save. And if I fail, if the old system is allowed to return, she will be condemned to live and die in a hole like this."

Finished, Guajardo took another deep breath, held it for a moment as he looked back at Jan, then left the room, brushing aside Ted and Joe Bob as he did so. Seeing the colonel leave, Corporal Fares quickly bent down, told his daughter something, gave her quick hug, then followed Guajardo out the door.

For a moment, Jan stood at the foot of the mattress, at a loss. Her anger began to swell up in her again. Needing to do something to dissipate this anger, to give it a name and a target, Jan ran out the door after Guajardo, practically running him down.

"And what about you, Colonel? What makes you any different? You knew about that girl. You are a man who is obviously well off, who has the power to help that girl. Why have you done nothing to save Angela?"

To Jan's surprise, Guajardo's response was neither hurried nor angered. On the contrary, at first, he smiled and merely shook his head. When he spoke, his voice was soft. "I see. Your solution is to save one child. If I do that, I suppose, I can rest in peace, just like you yanquis do."

Jan, her anger still unchecked by Guajardo's calm demeanor, asked him why that was such a bad thing.

"I remember, Ms. Fields, when I attended a course in Kansas, I was taken to a restaurant in town that had a small container shaped like a loaf of bread next to the cash register. The sign behind that loaf of bread claimed that a fifty-cent donation could feed a hungry child in a poor country for two days. I looked at that sign and became quite angry at my host and his countrymen. I could not understand a people who could so easily dispose of the poor and hungry of the world and, for such a small amount, create the impression that they had done a good, meaningful deed. For just fifty cents, they could feel good for a whole week, maybe a month, and go back to their homes with their fat children who wanted for nothing and would never know the agony of hunger."

Stopping for a moment, Guajardo looked about him before he continued. Jan did likewise. "No, Ms. Fields, we are playing for much bigger stakes, as you would say up north. I will not rest until not only all of this is gone, but the system that created this is gone as well."

As he looked at Jan, Guajardo's face suddenly became cold, his eyes narrowing into mere slits. "Yes, you are right! I could save Angela. I could go back there, right now, and take that girl away from here and save her. But who would save the others like her? You, Ms. Fields, with a fifty-cent donation? No, because the screams of hunger or Angela's pain do not reach far enough north for you to hear. We are fighting for the very soul and existence of Mexico. We want nothing less than you want; freedom, security, and a life worth living. That, Ms. Fields, is well worth fighting for and, if necessary, dying for."

Finished, Guajardo walked past Jan toward the sedan, brushing her aside as he did so. The interview had finally ended. But the anger and confusion that Jan felt hadn't. For the longest time, she stood there, letting his words, mixed with the sights, sounds, and smells of the barrio, hammer away at her. By the time Joe Bob reached her, Jan was able to begin to think clearly. Guajardo was right. He knew it. And so did she. Now all that remained was for her to figure out what to do with that revelation.

5

He who risks nothing gets nothing.

—French proverb

NORTH OF MEXICO CITY, MEXICO
0335 HOURS, 30 JUNE

With nothing to do while they waited their turn to be inspected by their platoon leader, the men designated Group D, for "Distrito Federal," shuffled, yawned, and stretched as they stood in the ranks. From across the dilapidated hangar, Guajardo occasionally glanced up from the maps and diagrams laid out before him on a rickety table, watching the inspection with the same detached interest as the men undergoing it displayed. As of yet, only the captain who was serving as their platoon leader knew where they were going and what their objective was. Even the majority of the helicopter crewmen who would be moving Group D as well as three other groups, did not know where they would be going.

Looking back down at his charts, maps, and diagrams, Guajardo wondered if his intricate scheme of deceptions and precautions had been necessary or effective. At times, during the planning process, even he had experienced difficulty remembering what was deception and what was actual. The need for tight security was not imaginary, since the target was one of the most effective and cunning criminals in Mexico. Referred to as El Dueño, or "the Manager," Señor Hector Alamán had created an empire that spread across the entire Caribbean and included in its ranks politicians, police officials, judges, and officers in the armed forces of every country in the region, including the United States.

Alamán did not directly involve himself in the growing, transporting, or marketing of drugs. Instead, he provided services to those who did.

72

These services included planning, coordinating, and orchestrating all aspects of the business for his clients. With a vast data base that tracked the demand and flow of drugs like those of any commodities market, Alamán and his advisors could provide information to both growers and shippers as to what product would be most profitable and where the best price could be had. Additionally, for a little extra, Alamán's banking associates provided the growers and shippers with a wide variety of financial services for moving and investing profits and business expenses from their illegal marketplace into legitimate banks, institutions, and markets. He even provided insurance policies, either long-term, which were quite expensive, or for single events, such as a shipment. Alamán's insurance, which was nothing more than an elaborate system of bribes, allowed his clients to operate their business free of official interference.

The network of contacts and "employees" needed to ensure that operations and shipments were not interfered with was created through a variety of methods that ranged from simple bribery to terrorism. Using an intelligence network that provided timely and accurate information on threats and potential threats to the industry from any quarter, Alamán and the members of his "Action department" sought to neutralize them. When possible, the people who generated the threats were encouraged not only to change their minds, but were actively recruited by Alamán. When they could not be swayed, they were eliminated in a manner that would serve as a warning to anyone wishing to follow in their footsteps. Guajardo himself had experienced Alamán's power.

Alamán ran these operations from a villa located in the state of Tamaulipas, where Guajardo served as the military zone commander. Under Guajardo's very eyes, and those of the police and the government of the state, Alamán had built a fortress twenty-two kilometers southwest of Ciudad Victoria. The fortress, named Chinampas, was manned by a staff of experts and advisors in every imaginable field, most of whom had PhDs and years of practical experience in banking, trade, intelligence, transportation, law enforcement, and other disciplines needed to make the drug industry profitable, efficient, and safe. This staff, supported by a computer and communications system that put the one possessed by the Mexican Army to shame, lacked nothing, especially security. Protection was provided by a garrison of fifty well-trained mercenaries recruited from the best agencies, armed with the best weapons money could buy, and backed up by a security system similar to that used to protect Israel's nuclear-weapons depots. Chinampas, with walls that could resist a direct hit by a 105mm tank cannon, represented a formidable challenge to anyone who might consider testing its defenses.

Not that anyone ever thought that such an event would become a reality. Chinampas's best defenses came from the benevolent, well-paid, and well-tended judiciary at both state and national level. It would have been bad enough, in Guajardo's eyes, had government and state officials simply been unwilling to consider initiating an investigation of Alamán and his operations. Guajardo could have accepted the excuse that perhaps the government and police officials being bribed didn't fully understand what Alamán was about. The openness, however, with which Alamán associated with and entertained those officials made such a defense unsupportable. Even before Chinampas was finished, Guajardo had watched a parade of officials whisked away to Alamán's paradise for weekends and vacations. Tending to every need, legal and illegal, of local, state, and national government and police officials provided Alamán security that most men in the shadow world of the international drug trade could only dream of.

Only a man of Guajardo's temper and conviction could conceive of such a mission. The destruction of Chinampas, however, had become more than a task for the professional soldier; it had become a quest. When the existence of Chinampas came to Guajardo's attention, he had conducted an unauthorized reconnaissance of the site accompanied by one of his trusted captains. Though it had still been under construction during his first visit, Guajardo had understood its potential. He saw it as a tumor that had to be removed before it grew and killed the state which he was responsible for. Foolishly, Guajardo had gone to the governor of Tamaulipas with his findings and a recommendation that the growing fortress be destroyed immediately. The governor reacted with a controlled sincerity that Guajardo naïvely believed. Thanking him for his concern, the governor dismissed Guajardo, assuring him that appropriate steps would be taken.

For a month, Guajardo had heard nothing more on the subject. Then, one morning, he had discovered what those steps were. Opening the front door of his home to leave for work, he found the naked body of the captain who had accompanied him on the unauthorized recon of Chinampas nailed, upside down, to his front door. The severity of the corruption that permeated the government was hammered home when the head of the state's police force came into Guajardo's office the next day and personally advised the colonel to leave Chinampas alone. At first, Guajardo could not understand why the captain, and not he, the man who had led the recon and recommended action against Chinampas, had been murdered. The answer was provided by a friend at the funeral of the captain. Guajardo, a senior and well-respected member of the Army, was more valuable to Alamán if, through a simple demonstration of power, Guajardo could be won over to Alamán's side. Failing that, Alamán's action would serve to frighten Guajardo into inaction.

The shock of the incident and the reasoning behind it were slow to wear off. When it did, however, anger and hatred, not fear and complacency, replaced the shock. It was then, even before Guajardo knew of Molina's plans to conduct a coup, that Guajardo dedicated himself to purging his homeland of those who made it a prostitute to be exploited by the highest bidder. While the reasons he had given the American TV correspondent for joining the Council of 13 were real, they paled in comparison to his goal of crushing Chinampas, and all who lived there. The coup, even the murder of his president, were merely chores that needed to be tended to before Guajardo could pursue his quest of striking Alamán down, avenging his pride and freeing Mexico of men like him in the process.

Conviction and good intentions, however, would not reduce Chinampas. Only a well-planned and violent attack with overwhelming force could achieve that. Working on his own, Guajardo had learned everything he could about Alamán's operations, Chinampas, and the curtains of security that shielded it. He soon knew more about the capability of the defenses of Chinampas than Alamán himself.

Through frequent visits, often at night and always alone, Guajardo had learned everything he could about the terrain surrounding Chinampas and its defenses. Slowly, with the drive of a zealot, the eye of a professional soldier, and the patience of a native-born son of Chihuahua, Guajardo collected information and devised plans of action. When, at Molina's invitation, he joined the Council of 13, Guajardo found he had access to funds secretly diverted from the Mexican Army budget.

Using Alamán's own techniques, Guajardo used the funds to obtain information. This included the purchasing of the original plans for the construction of Chinampas from the American construction firm that had built the fortress. By pretending to be a Colombian businessman, he easily obtained schematics and technical data of the security system used at Chinampas from the Israeli firm that had installed the original. Through a friend, himself a mercenary, Guajardo not only managed to obtain detailed dossiers on every man who comprised Chinampas's garrison, but, through the Belgian firm that handled Alamán's weapons contracts, Guajardo purchased copies of every invoice for both weapons and ammunition used to arm that garrison.

Chinampas itself was built for no other purpose than to protect its

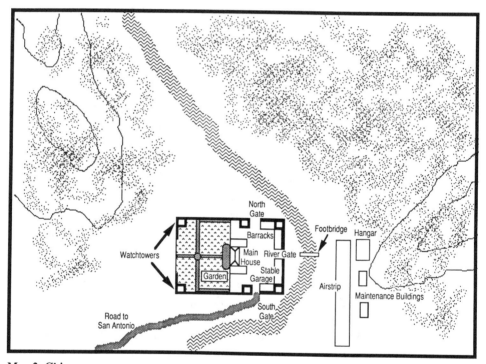

Map 2: Chinampas

occupants. Its twelve-foot-high walls, though not overly imposing, were high enough to prevent scaling without the aid of ladders or ropes. Even if these were used, smooth metal rollers that rotated out and away from the interior of the fortress, similar to those that had been used on the former Berlin wall, lined the top of the wall. Anyone trying to climb over the walls would start the rollers spinning, causing the climber to fall off the wall. The walls themselves were reinforced concrete measuring four feet thick at the base, tapering to two feet at the top. The angle of this tapering was all on the outer side of the wall. This reduced but did not eliminate the dead space, or blind spots, at the base of the wall. To cover any dead space that did exist, command-detonated anti-personnel mines were placed in recesses in the outer wall.

A tower standing twenty feet high was located at each corner, with two intermediate towers covering the long northern and southern walls and the north and south gates. These six towers, also built of reinforced concrete, provided the garrison with excellent observation and served as weapons platforms. From them, every inch of ground surrounding and within Chinampas could be covered by automatic-weapons fire. Provisions for the firing of antitank rockets and guided missiles, as well as surface-to-air missiles, stored at the base of each tower, were incorporated in the design.

Even the buildings themselves were built with an eye for defense. Although the façades of the main house, barracks, stable, and garage were stucco, the core of the walls, like the outer walls and towers, was all reinforced concrete. Apertures, cleverly designed to appear as ornate masonry, provided the occupants with firing ports. Even if the outer walls and towers failed to keep attackers out, each building could defend itself.

As formidable as these integrated defenses were, there were weaknesses. The six towers were built in such a manner that they could not cover the base of the outer wall. Once the command-detonated mines were expended, or neutralized, assault forces could freely move about in the lee of the outer walls. Each tower also depended on overlapping fire from another tower or building to cover its own base. While the loss of one or two towers or buildings would do nothing to break the integrity of Chinampas's defense, the rapid loss of several would.

The surrounding terrain dominated Chinampas. Though the fortress was well sited to take advantage of the natural beauty of the area, the cool breeze that came down the valley from the north, and abundant water for the garden, the high ground to the northwest and east looked down into Chinampas. Finally, and most significant, while Chinampas could withstand and repel a raid, it could not withstand a siege against a large and determined force. Alamán had no forces, other than those within Chinampas and the benevolent intervention by friendly government officials, that could be rushed in to lift a siege.

Satisfied that he had all the information that could be safely obtained, Guajardo had begun the methodical process of exploring all options of attack available to him. Once all realistic options had been developed, Guajardo would wargame them, looking for the strength and weakness of each, comparing the advantages and disadvantages of each option before making a decision. This process, which took place in almost total secrecy, spanned several months and, like all obsessions, was never far from Guajardo's mind.

Some options had fallen out almost immediately. A ground attack was impractical. Ideally, such an attack would be conducted at night with no warning. But the Mexican Army lacked night-vision devices and the training that would make such an operation easy and ensure success. The garrison of Chinampas, on the other hand, was lavishly equipped to deal with such a threat. Numerous limited-visibility vision devices, both manned and automated, backed up by several belts of unattended ground sensors and remote monitoring stations, made an undetected approach by more than a handful of men highly unlikely. Besides, all units trained to conduct such commando operations were heavily infiltrated by informers either directly or through those who controlled their deployment and operations.

Unable to use stealth, Guajardo next considered the other extreme: direct and overwhelming conventional attack by regular Army units. As a professional soldier, he could easily organize and conduct such an operation. Though its weapons were not the most sophisticated, the Mexican Army possessed sufficient firepower to wipe Chinampas, and all within its walls, off the face of the earth.

An operation of that nature, however, could not escape detection. As with Mexico's special operations forces, every unit within his military zone, down to company level, had informers either in Alamán's pay or in the pay of another drug lord. Guajardo knew that any movement of major forces would be known in Chinampas even before the troops left their barracks. And even if, by some chance, such advance warning from within the ranks could be prevented, it would be impossible to hide the movement of troops through San Antonia, then north over the only road leading to Chinampas. Either way, while the troops and weapons could be brought to bear, and Chinampas destroyed, Alamán would be long gone before the Mexican Army could fire its first round.

Discarding direct ground attack, Guajardo explored the possibility of reducing Chinampas with air attacks. Together with an Air Force colonel who was a member of the Council of 13, Guajardo worked out the mathematics of such an attack. After looking at every possible combination of aircraft and ordnance available to the Mexican Air Force, both officers agreed that such an attack, though possible, could not guarantee success.

Though Guajardo desired to use a simple, direct, and quick solution, all the options that fit that description failed the most critical test: they did not offer a better than even chance of catching, or killing, Alamán and his key personnel. In a fit of frustration, anger, and irrational rage, Guajardo threw all the data, maps, draft plans, and working papers into his safe, changed the combination, locked it, promptly forgot the combination, and walked away from it. There the matter rested for several months.

It was during a conference at Fort Benning, Georgia, that a viable solution to the Chinampas problem began to form in Guajardo's mind. In one of the sessions dealing with special operations and raids, the briefer presented a short lecture on the American raid on Son Tay. Executed on 21 November 1970, that raid had been meant to liberate sixty-five American POWs held there. Although the operation was expertly executed, it failed because the POWs that had been held there had been moved days before the raid. As Guajardo listened to the lecture and studied the colorful diagrams, he could not help but compare many of the problems that faced the Son Tay planners with those that faced him at Chinampas. Even before the lecture was over, he realized that he had been given the key to the solution. Though a detailed plan had to be developed, from that moment on, Guajardo knew that Chinampas, and all who worked within its walls, would fall to him. All that was needed now was someone to open the safe he had locked.

Realizing that it is a mistake to take the solution to one military problem and apply it blindly to another, Guajardo carefully created his own plan, selectively using tactics and techniques used at Son Tay. An example was the manner in which the Son Tay raiders used helicopters to neutralize the guard towers in 1970. There, a CH-53 with miniguns on both sides flew between two guard towers, hovered at the same level as the towers, and fired the miniguns directly into them. The wooden guard towers at Son Tay, pulverized by miniguns firing 6,000 7.62mm rounds per minute, were, in effect, sawed off their supports. This allowed the initial assault group to come in and land unhindered in an open space in the compound.

Though Guajardo did not have a helicopter as big as the CH-53, or miniguns for that matter, he could improvise. For aircraft, four Bell 206 helicopters, each with a crew of two and capable of carrying five passengers, would be used. Since the Mexican Army had few helicopters, only the towers in the west and the center would be attacked. These four helicopters and their passengers, code named Group Z because it was staging and launching from Zacatecas, would hit Chinampas first. Coming in from the west, each helicopter would fly directly to its designated target, one of the four towers. Flying nap-of-the-earth, Group Z would use the hills west of Chinampas to mask their approach. Once clear of the hills, the pilots would only have a few seconds to orient themselves and line up on the tower they were to hit, all the while making a final high-speed approach.

The challenge that faced each pilot in Group Z was covering the last few meters of open ground as quickly as possible, clearing the outer wall, then rapidly bringing their helicopter to a hover a few meters away from the tower. With a main blade diameter of 11.3 meters, the closest the Bell 206s could come to the tower, or any other obstacle for that matter, was six to eight meters. That, however, was close enough.

Once the pilot or the co-pilot had brought the helicopter to a hover, the other crewmen, armed with automatic rifles, would fire out of their open windows into the guard tower. Guajardo knew this fire would be wildly inaccurate, especially since the crews would not be permitted to practice before the operation in order to preserve secrecy. But it didn't need to be accurate. Guajardo was counting on the surprise assault from the air, coupled with the suppressive fire from the helicopter crew, to allow the passengers enough time to rappel out of the helicopter onto the ground at the base of the tower.

The passengers carried by the Bell 206s were four teams of combat engineers armed with automatic rifles and a variety of explosives. Each team, consisting of an officer, a sergeant, and three sappers, had been hand-picked by a colonel of the engineers who was a member of the Council of 13. During the assault on Chinampas, while the helicopter hovered and the crew fired on the occupants of the tower, the engineers would exit the helicopter using the speed-rappel technique pioneered by the U.S. Army's special operations helicopter group, Task Force 160. The nylon rope used was two inches thick and stiff. The engineers, wearing leather gloves, would slide down it like firemen dropping down a fire pole. Since the drop would only be twenty feet, even if someone let go, the chances of severe injury would be minimal. Once on the ground at the base of the towers, the engineers, using explosives, would force their way into the tower and clear it as rapidly as possible using gunfire and explosives.

Unlike the pilots, the engineers were allowed to practice exiting the helicopter and the techniques to be used in clearing the towers. To ensure security, each team in Group Z, along with the helicopter and crew that would transport it, was trained in isolation in a different part of Mexico. None were told what their actual target was. Instead, the men, even the officers in charge, were told that they were being trained to deal with prison riots. To make this cover story more convincing, the dummy towers and compounds they drilled on were patterned after actual prisons within the state where they were located. Even with this cover story, all rehearsals were classified top secret. Only on June 29, the day before the actual raid, would all members of Group Z be brought together at an abandoned airfield outside of Zacatecas. There, Guajardo himself would issue the actual order for their real target.

Since there was no way of knowing what helicopters and helicopter crews would be available on the day of the raid, Guajardo, who was not a pilot, decided to keep them out of the mission planning. To protect the security of the operation, Guajardo made it a habit to use different helicopter crews. An Air Force colonel on the council advised Guajardo to include the pilots in the rehearsals, but was rebuffed for his efforts. "This is," Guajardo told him, "a ground operation. All the helicopters are needed for is transportation. And for that, all the pilots need to be given is a course, speed, and destination." Unstated was Guajardo's dislike of aviators, a breed he considered to be overpaid and underworked. So the pilots, like many other participants, would learn of their role at the last minute.

With the two western and two center towers seized or under attack, the door to direct insertion of the main force into the compound itself was open. The open spaces needed to grow the beautiful gardens of Chinampas, which is the name given ancient Aztec floating gardens, provided ample space for helicopters to land within the walls of the fortress. Two assault groups, one coming in from the north and one from the south, would use these open spaces as landing zones.

The assault group coming down from the north, designated Group M for its staging area near Monterrey, was commanded by Major Antonio Caso, Guajardo's deputy commander for this operation. Consisting of two Bell 205 helicopters and twenty-four infantrymen, Group M would land in the northern half of the garden, seize the northern side of the main house, and engage the barracks with automatic rifle, machine gun, and recoilless rifle fire.

Converging on Chinampas from Distrito Federal in the south was Group D. It consisted of twenty-four men transported in two Bell 205A helicopters, nicknamed Hueys by the American military. Guajardo's com-

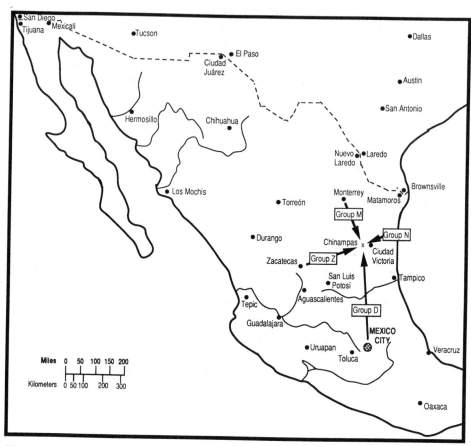

Map 3: The Converging of Forces on Chinampas

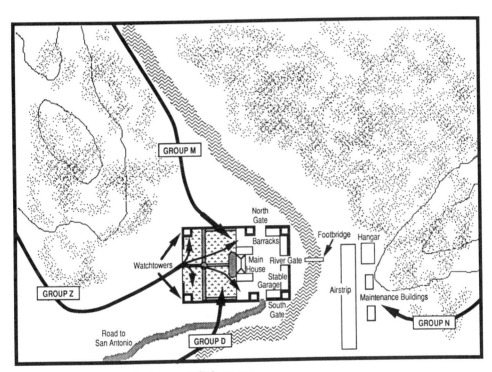

Map 4: Routes of Assault Groups at Chinampas

mand group, in a Bell 206 like those used by the engineers, would follow Group D into Chinampas. Consisting of himself, two radiomen, and two riflemen to be used as runners as needed, Guajardo would move along with Group D once on the ground. Landing in the southern half of the garden, this group would seize the southern half of the main house and, from there, engage any of Alamán's men holed up in the stable or garage. So as to prevent confusion, the east-west walk in the garden served as a boundary to separate the landing zones and areas of responsibility for groups M and D.

A fourth assault group, Group N, consisting of 24 infantrymen commanded by a lieutenant, would approach from the east. Staging out of Nuevo Dolores, hence its designation "N," this group would not enter Chinampas. Its mission, instead, was to seize the airfield east of Chinampas, clear all buildings there, and capture, or if that was not possible, disable all aircraft on the field. Once this was completed, Group N was to deploy itself on either side of the footbridge, establishing fields of fire so as to prevent anyone from escaping from Chinampas. Though there was concern over the use of so junior an officer to command one of the assault groups, Guajardo dismissed it. The lieutenant, a graduate of the Mexican Military Academy at Chapultepec, was highly recommended by Colonel Molina.

If all went well, and all groups secured their objectives, any occupants of Chinampas or its garrison surviving the initial assault would be disorganized, perhaps leaderless, and trapped in the buildings along the eastern wall within ten minutes, maybe less. After a brief pause to regroup and assess the situation, Guajardo intended to begin a slow, methodical clearing operation to eliminate any remaining resistance. Covered by suppressive fire provided by Group M from the main house and Group Z's teams in towers 2 and 5, Guajardo would lead Group D, reinforced by engineers from teams 1 and 6, against the garage.

By blowing a hole in the east side of tower 5 from the inside, Guajardo's force would gain access to the narrow gap that separated tower 5 and the garage. The engineers, covered by fire from every weapon that could be brought to bear, would cross that gap, blow a hole into the garage, and clear the way for Guajardo and Group D. Once inside the garage, Group D, assisted by the engineers when necessary, would be free to clear the garage, tower 4, and the stable room by room. With the stable cleared, if the garrison was still resisting from the barracks, Group D and the accompanying engineers would cross over from the stable into the barracks and tower 3 using the same techniques that had been used to gain access to the garage from tower 5.

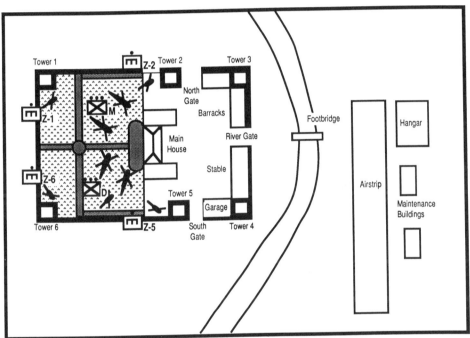

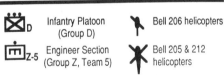

Map 5: Initial Landings of Groups D, M & Z at Chinampas

Few, however, including Guajardo, thought that it would go that far. Unable to escape, the garrison's occupants would be faced with the choice of surrendering or dying. As these men were either mercenaries or criminals motivated by money alone, once the hopelessness of their situation became obvious to them, Guajardo expected their will to stand and fight to collapse and resistance to cease. Guajardo hoped to forestall such an event for as long as possible. From the very beginning, his goal was nothing less than total eradication of Chinampas and all who lived and worked within its walls. Once he started, Guajardo had no intention of stopping.

Such thoughts, however, were clouded by apprehension as Guajardo watched the men of Group D complete their final preparation. Like an anxious groom, he felt second thoughts begin to creep into his tired mind. The nervous flipping through maps, orders, and diagrams scattered before him was pointless. He knew every word, every detail on every map. There was nothing more to do, nothing left to say. After two days of ceaseless activity that had begun the day before the coup and had taken him from one end of Mexico to another, not to mention months of planning, plotting, and preparation, Guajardo found himself with nothing to do but wait for lift-off. What he should have done was sleep. Yet he could not, despite the fact that he had less than four hours' sleep in the last forty-eight, all of it while being flown from one place to another, and never for more than an hour at a time.

Instead, Guajardo pushed himself away from the table, stood, and stretched, then began to pace. First he circled the small table where he had been seated. Tiring of that, he walked over to the door of the hangar and looked outside, checking his watch before he did so and after. After standing there for a few minutes, he walked back to the table and began to circle it again, absentmindedly.

In his head, thoughts rattled about, thoughts, apprehensions, and fears. It was only natural, as Clausewitz once wrote, for a commander to become uneasy with his plan when the moment of execution drew near. After all, the attack on Chinampas was no longer a theoretical drill. Men, weapons, and aircraft were, at that moment, in the final process of staging for the attack. The 124 soldiers and pilots participating in the operation were real human beings with all their frailties, vulnerabilities, and weaknesses. Each man, officer, NCO, and enlisted, understood what was expected of him. The question that kept cropping up was, Could they do it?

For all the planning, for all the security, there was much that was against them. As part of the security plan, the four groups had never worked together. In fact, until a few hours ago, the commanders of each of the groups not only had not known what their true objective was, they had not even known that the other groups participating in the attack existed. Throughout the entire preparatory phase, each group had drilled and rehearsed on its own, all, like the engineers, believing they were training for an entirely different mission. The first time the entire force, with the pilots added in, would be brought together was within the walls of Chinampas itself.

Few commanders ever created such a potentially deadly self-imposed handicap. Even Colonel Molina had not taken Guajardo's plan seriously when he first presented it to the Council of 13. His efforts to convince Molina and the others that his plan was the only solution often reminded Guajardo of his grandfather's story of a man trying to sell a blind, three-legged mule that had gone lame. Yet through sheer stubbornness and persistence, the other members of the council had finally allowed Guajardo to have his way.

Looking down at his watch for the second time in less than three minutes, Guajardo saw it wasn't even four o'clock. There was still better than half an hour to go before lift-off. The group he was traveling with, Group D, having the farthest to travel, would be the first airborne. They needed to be skids up at 0424 hours in order to cover the 483 kilometers and arrive at Chinampas at 0700 hours, H-Hour. Group Z, perhaps the most important of the four, with 362 kilometers to travel, was scheduled to leave at 0515, followed quickly by Group M, leaving Monterrey at 0536. Group N, nearest to Chinampas and with only 121 kilometers to cover, would not leave Nuevo Dolores until 0621, thirty-nine minutes before the engineers went in.

Even this thought gave Guajardo little comfort. Though he was the commander of the raid, he had no way of knowing if the other groups were ready or, when the time came, if they made it off on time. Another feature of the security plan imposed total radio listening silence on all groups until Group Z actually opened fire on the guard towers. The commanders of the other groups could not even contact Guajardo by phone if they needed to, for none of them, except Major Caso, knew where everyone was staging and launching from.

That thought triggered another, causing Guajardo to automatically begin to recite, in his mind, a litany of options and responses he had generated, in case one or more of the groups failed to arrive or reach their initial objective. This process, however, was cut short by the sound of helicopter blades beating their way through the still predawn darkness.

Also hearing the approaching helicopters, the platoon leader turned to his senior NCO and told him to have the men prepare for embarkation. With a series of short, crisp orders, the sergeant set the men in motion.

For Guajardo, and the men who would make his quest a reality, the waiting was over.

FORT HOOD, TEXAS
0615 HOURS, 30 JUNE

It was easy to tell it was Friday morning. The entire 16th Armored Division, by battalions and separate companies, was out doing their morning run in formation. For a two-mile stretch, from Cedar Creek Road in the west to Hood Avenue in the east, massed ranks of soldiers ran along Maintenance Row. In the lead, their unit commanders and regimental colors and guidons set the pace. On the flanks, sergeants counted cadence and made corrections as tired soldiers wavered and slowed, causing disruption and disorder of the ranks and files. In the rear of each formation, other sergeants ran, encouraging those who were lagging or had fallen out. The words used to encourage or threaten the offending soldiers varied, depending upon the soldier or the personality of the sergeant. Those shouts and threats mixed and mingled with the cadence and the commands of officers and NCOs as well as with the panting, moaning, and griping of soldiers reaching their limits, real or imagined. The whole disjointed chorus echoed and reverberated off the buildings along the entire two-mile stretch of road, then drifted across the rolling ground into the distance to remind all those who heard that this was a military base.

From a side street, Captain Harold Cerro paused before entering the endless stream of running soldiers. The spectacle of soldiers training, whether it was on the range or simply doing PT, never failed to excite him. Cerro loved being a soldier and loved being with them doing, as his wife often referred to it, soldier things. That he happened to be where he was, watching the massed formations go by, was no accident. Cerro had learned early in his career that you could tell a lot about a unit by watching it during PT. Two units, passing to his front as he watched, provided him with a good idea of what the 16th Armored Division would be like.

The first unit to run past Cerro was an artillery unit. It was in the process of passing a slower-moving unit. There was no mistaking their vocation. The artillerymen, wearing Army-issue running shorts and red shirts decorated with yellow crossed cannons that symbolized their branch, looked like a unit. And they moved like a unit. To a man, they were in step, creating a strange muffled slapping noise as hundreds of pairs of sneakers hit the pavement in unison. In the front, their battalion commander, closely followed by the battalion colors, moved out with a purpose. Behind him came the companies, in solid formations of four men abreast and led by their young company commanders and company guidons. Each company was in step, every soldier gliding forward almost effortlessly as they repeated the chants sung by their NCOs.

In stark contrast, the unit the artillerymen were passing showed little sign of either cohesion or pride. There was no guidon or flag to betray their branch of service or unit. No two soldiers were dressed alike. The shirts and running shorts they wore were a riot of colors and styles, ranging from the Army-issue brown T-shirt to shocking-orange designer sleeveless running shirts. From what Cerro could see, not only was no one in step, there appeared to be no effort on the part of the NCOs to get them in step. Nor was there anyone in the rear of the formation, a term Cerro loosely applied to the gaggle, to police up a line of stragglers that trailed behind. By ones and twos, the soldiers of the second unit were dropping out, unnoticed by their commander, who kept on running, oblivious to the disintegration of his unit. Rather than a unit, the second group was simply a collection of people moving in the same general direction.

Shaking his head in disgust, Cerro was about to move out when he saw an infantry battalion moving down the road. From the pace and the determined look of its commander's face, Cerro had no doubt they had but one goal in mind, to pass the artillery battalion that had just gone by. The soldiers of the infantry battalion, like the artillery unit, were outfitted in matching T-shirts and running shorts, their T-shirts embossed with their unit crest and motto. A history buff, Cerro recognized the regimental crest as that of the 13th Infantry, although he couldn't place the battalion based on the motto, "Forty Rounds, Sir."

Deciding it would be unwise to jump out in front of the infantry battalion, Cerro waited for it to pass. With a measured pace that now bordered on a dead run, row after row of infantrymen passed by. In step and leaning forward as their commander picked up the pace, the troops, on cue from their sergeant major, began to clap their hands every time their left foot hit the ground. Like a locomotive, the infantrymen bore down, closed the gap separating them from the artillerymen. In their rush, they never noticed the rabble that the artillery unit had passed.

For a moment, Cerro felt a pang in his heart, knowing that he would not be able to join a unit such as this one. His assignment to the brigade staff condemned him to a unit that, when it ran as a unit, would no doubt resemble the rabble that the artillerymen had passed. The only reason

Cerro had escaped the unit run that morning was because he was still inprocessing and new. This had saved him from that morning's run. Nothing, however, would save him next week.

As he was silently bemoaning his fate, Cerro looked up just in time to see a female, dressed in the same T-shirt and shorts as the infantry battalion, go by. It took him a few seconds to recognize her as the same woman he had run into the day before while inprocessing. Her long auburn hair, pulled back and held by a clip, swung from side to side as she ran. That, coupled with a physique that was unmistakably female, set her apart from the rest of the formation. Her appearance caused Cerro to reconsider his own plight. As much as he knew he would be like a fish out of water on the brigade staff, his predicament, he thought, was nothing compared to what the female lieutenant faced.

When the infantry unit finished passing him, Cerro shook himself out one more time before stepping off and joining the flow of running soldiers, adding the sound of his pounding feet to that of a division on the move.

The pace, even when the battalion commander picked it up to pass an artillery unit, was easy for Second Lieutenant Nancy Kozak. At West Point she had earned three letters in track and field, and at the Infantry Officers Basic Course at Fort Benning she had maxed the standard physical fitness test, the same one the male officers in her class had been required to pass. Physically, she was ready. Mentally, however, she wasn't sure. While she had gone over in her mind, again and again, what she would do and how she would handle herself, no mental drill could prepare her for her introduction to the unit, in particular the men in the platoon she was expected to lead.

From the company commander down to the lowest private, everyone in the unit treated her with the respect and deference that was appropriate for her rank and position. Her conversation with her platoon sergeant, the only NCO in her platoon she had had any time to talk to, had been short, functional, and punctuated with many "yes ma'ams" and "no ma'ams." Throughout that conversation, she had been unable to gauge how the sergeant—Sergeant First Class Leon Rivera—felt about her. His manner, like his conversation, was functional and correct. Nothing in his tone of voice, in his expressions, even in his eyes, betrayed his feelings. The only thing she noted was that Rivera, like everyone else in the company, had a tendency to stare at her, and that the term *ma'am* did not come easily to him. More than once, Rivera, used to operating in an almost exclusively male world, had responded with "Sir."

The staring, more than anything else, affected Kozak. As hard as she might want to, she could not blend in. Through a simple biological function, started at the moment of conception, Nancy Kozak had become a woman. While that was not a curse, it would definitely be a handicap in her efforts to become an effective combat leader. That thought, and a thousand others, tumbled through her head as she ran beside her platoon, her long auburn hair gently swaying from side to side.

6

Promptness contributes a great deal to success in marches and even more in battles.

—Frederick the Great

NUEVO DOLORES, MEXICO
0615 HOURS, 30 JUNE

From the edge of the runway's apron, Lieutenant Rafael Blasio watched the young infantry lieutenant supervise the loading of his men into Blasio's Bell 212 helicopter. With quick, nervous jerks, Blasio alternated between puffing the half-smoked cigarette in his left hand and drinking cold coffee from a paper cup in his right. The rest of his crew, a co-pilot and crew chief, were scurrying about the helicopter, performing whatever preflight checks on the aircraft they could in five minutes while simultaneously helping the infantrymen strap themselves in. Blasio was already on edge, and caffeine was the last thing he needed. Caffeine, however, was the only thing he had to keep him going.

The day before had started at four o'clock when his commander woke him with orders to report for duty immediately. At the airfield in Tampico he and his crew were informed that the military had assumed control of the government after an assassination attempt on the president of the republic and that a state of emergency existed. For Blasio and his crew, this meant they spent the entire day shuttling troops loyal to the new military council up and down the east coast of Mexico. It wasn't until he and his crew arrived back in Tampico at eight o'clock in the evening that they received the whole story concerning the coup. By then, however, he was too tired to care. The only thing that interested him at that point was food and a bed, and which came first didn't make any difference.

Checking in with the military dispatcher at flight operations, Blasio was handed a sealed envelope stamped SECRET instead of directions to the nearest mess. Inside the envelope was a one-page order that instructed him to fly to the airfield at Nuevo Dolores, arriving there not later than ten o'clock that evening. It was signed by a Colonel Alfredo Guajardo, who used the title Minister of Defense. Blasio handed the orders over to the flight operations officer and demanded that they be verified.

Expecting a long delay, Blasio prepared to leave flight operations in search of food. His escape was cut short by the military commander of the airfield. Storming out of his office, and followed by the flight operations officer, the airfield commander literally leaped in front of Blasio, waving the one-page order in his face. "Who in the hell do you think you are, Lieutenant?" demanded the commander. "Are you insane, or are you a traitor?"

The suddenness of the confrontation and its violence startled Blasio. Speechless, he stared at the airfield commander, trying to come up with an explanation. But before he could answer, the airfield commander continued, yelling louder. "Why are you trying to get out of this mission? Can't you see that it is signed by Colonel Guajardo?"

Like a fighter hit with a series of blows that could not be deflected, Blasio reeled under the airfield commander's attack. Finally, Blasio took a step back, came to attention, and yelled as loud as he could, "Sir, I do not wish to evade my duty. But I must explain, sir."

The ploy worked, causing the airfield commander to relent and allowing Blasio a few more seconds with which to frame his response. "All right, Lieutenant, explain."

Stating his defense in the strongest possible terms, Blasio recounted the activities of his crew throughout the day, ending his account by stating that his crew needed both food and rest while his aircraft was in desperate need of a thorough maintenance check. For several minutes, the airfield commander listened in silence. When he had heard enough, he raised his hand, signaling Blasio to stop speaking.

"We have all had a very difficult day. And tomorrow, no doubt, will be no different. That remains to be seen. What I do know is that your day is not yet over. You will, Lieutenant, refuel immediately and depart for Nuevo Dolores as soon as possible. Do you have any further questions?" From his tone, Blasio had no doubt that his explanations had been summarily dismissed and he was being ordered to move out quickly and without further protest.

Angry and tired, Blasio saluted, turned, and left flight operations.

*   *   *

Arriving at Nuevo Dolores at five minutes to ten, Blasio had been greeted by a young infantry lieutenant. The lieutenant had escorted Blasio to a maintenance shed at the far corner of the airfield while a ground crew prepared to tow Blasio's helicopter to the same building. In the building, serving as quarters for the lieutenant's platoon, Blasio met Major Caso, the pilot of a second Bell 212 helicopter, and the senior sergeant of the infantry platoon. Caso, who identified himself as Colonel Guajardo's deputy, was there to brief the pilots and infantrymen on an impending raid against a place called Chinampas.

Under ordinary circumstances, Blasio would have been all ears. But, as the airfield commander in Tampico had pointed out, these were not ordinary times. Worn out from the nervous strain of flying nonstop and of having no food all day, only the growling of his stomach kept Blasio awake during the briefing. Not that there was much that concerned him. Quickly he determined that, except for the fact that they were going to land in a confined area, and there might be some small-arms fire, this was just another troop-ferrying mission. All he had to do was take off at 0621 hours, fly southwest toward Ciudad Victoria at 115 knots for thirty-nine minutes, land in the garden of some drug lord's hideout, drop his load of troops off, leave the landing zone, and fly to a rally point three kilometers southwest of the landing zone where he and the other pilots would wait for further orders. As to the rest of the briefing, Blasio paid scant attention. While the name Alamán was vaguely familiar, sleep and food were what mattered the most at that moment.

When the briefing was finished and Major Caso departed for Monterrey, Blasio returned to his own aircraft, now parked in the hangar and guarded by two infantrymen. Both his co-pilot and crew chief were asleep on the floor of the aircraft when he reached it. For a moment, he considered waking them up to inform them of their mission, but decided against that. It was late, well past midnight, and there was no food to be had. There would be plenty of time when they were awakened at five o'clock by the infantry platoon. Instead, he pulled a blanket out of his flight bag, threw it on the floor next to his helicopter, and lay down. Despite the fact that the floor was concrete, Blasio dropped right off into a deep sleep. Only the persistent shaking of the infantry lieutenant woke him at 0610, eleven minutes before scheduled lift-off.

CHINAMPAS, MEXICO
0615 HOURS, 30 JUNE

Despite the beauty of the morning, Señor Alamán felt no joy. He descended the massive spiral staircase that dominated the main entrance of his home as if he were carrying a great weight. He stopped every few steps, pausing and looking about. He paid scant attention to the bodyguard seated next to the front door at the base of the stairs and, in turn, the bodyguard paid scant attention to Alamán. The other mercenary, a massive blond American, didn't concern himself with the comings and goings of Alamán or his staff. What they did was their affair. As a mercenary, he had no politics, no imaginary loyalties to principles or nations. All he had was a contract that obligated him to protect and defend Alamán and his staff. So long as Alamán fulfilled his portion of the contract—i.e., paid him on time—the American mercenary would fulfill his end. That Alamán paid no attention to them was all right by the American.

While the American mercenary suspected that Alamán's somber mood and increased security were due to the military coup that threatened to bring an end to his operation, he could not know that it was the safety and preservation of Chinampas that was foremost in Alamán's mind. The mere thought of losing the paradise he had built from nothing hit Alamán's heart like nothing ever had. In many ways, Chinampas had grown to become the personification of Alamán himself.

Born in Veracruz, Alamán had moved with his family to Mexico City while he was still a young boy. His parents, like millions of other unemployed Mexicans in search of a better life, had been drawn to the capital city. And, as with many before them, the life they found in the barrios of the city destroyed them. After several months of wandering the streets in search of work, Alamán's father went north to the United States. His mother, unable to wait for her husband to return, found work as a laundress. Alamán, left to fend for himself, began to create a life of his own.

Even as a boy, Alamán had been very unimposing. Of average height and build, he could easily have held his own against most of the other boys in the barrio. While he enjoyed being in the company of other boys, he was not interested in doing everything they did. This included fighting and conforming to the macho image that was the mark of a true Mexican male. Instead, beauty as expressed in the arts, fashions, and flowers—especially flowers—captured his imagination. As he grew, Alamán would seek to escape the barrio, and travel throughout the city in search of beautiful things to look at and hold. He spent hours walking through the art museum, watching painters work their oils along the boulevards, or doing petty jobs at the flower markets just to be near the beauty that so captivated him.

Such pursuits, however, left Alamán open to criticism and abuse by the other boys in his school and the barrio where he lived. Whenever possible, he avoided placing himself in positions that required fighting or exposed him to harm. When he could not, he made arrangements for others to do his fighting for him. Since he was poor and unable to pay cash for his own protection, Alamán arranged things for those who defended him. Aided by what he saw and contacts he made in his travels throughout Mexico City, he soon realized not only that he had a knack for "arranging" things for his friends, but that the process was challenging and potentially profitable. Without realizing it, he began creating a lucrative business out of what had begun as a simple quest for survival.

Over the years, as he grew and matured, so did his business. The discovery that people would pay for just about anything, coupled with his knowledge of the city and lack of moral or parental restraints, opened unlimited vistas to Alamán. While Mexico City had many who could arrange for a prostitute, drugs, or perversions of any color, Alamán had a personal charm and class that made dealing with him enjoyable both to locals and to foreign visitors. Seizing upon this advantage, Alamán developed his social graces, manner of dress, and knowledge of culture and the world. In the process, he not only improved his marketability, but his own enjoyment as well. For no one could ever claim that Señor Alamán didn't take care of his own needs, or find people willing to take care of them. One of his greatest thrills came from appearing in public with tall, thin, beautiful young women, some of whom, it was rumored, were actually female.

As he became more socially acceptable, Alamán gained access to men of greater power and wealth, for they too had vices that needed to be tended to. A better clientele meant higher fees. Higher fees resulted in greater wealth and access to art, culture, and social circles. Introduction into better social circles meant meeting new and more powerful people. More powerful people provided Alamán new and better information, clients, and access to others. The speed with which he had amassed power, influence, and access to information was matched only by Alamán's drive to possess the beautiful things that he had only been able to view from afar when he was poor. And once he began to taste the pleasures that money and power could provide him, Alamán had become more determined to do whatever was necessary to serve those who could provide him with the beauty that he so admired.

The coup of June 29 had come as a shock to Alamán. Suddenly, a world that he had carefully nurtured, with the same care and love that a gardener uses when he tends to a rose, was threatened. For the first time in many years, Alamán didn't know from where the dangers came, and felt powerless to protect himself. Many of the government officials that had provided him with business, information, and protection were, if the rumors were true, dead. Even more ominous than that, however, was the fact that he had had no warning of the coming coup. It puzzled him, and wounded his pride, that his system of informers and friends within the ranks of the Mexican military had so utterly failed him. Such a failure cast his skills and reliability in doubt.

His slow descent of the spiral staircase was, to him, symbolic of what might happen if he could not come to terms with the new military government. Reaching the base of the staircase, Alamán paused, looking out through the glass doors onto the garden patio where his staff and several business associates sat picking at breakfast and waiting for his arrival. Even from where he stood, he could see that they, like himself, were confused and worried. Their solemn expressions and dejected stares did nothing to inspire Alamán.

Turning to the blond American mercenary, Alamán asked if any military or police units had been shifted during the night into positions that might threaten Chinampas. The blond American, who went by the name of Randel Childress, stood up before responding. "Señor Delapos himself flew to Ciudad Victoria and San Antonia this morning and talked to our people there. Nothing out of the ordinary was reported there or anywhere else throughout the state, Señor Alamán."

Delapos, Alamán's chief of security, was both thorough and utterly reliable. Thanking Childress, Alamán studied the American for a moment. The American's smooth face, with soft, fine features and hardly a trace of beard, didn't match the massive body that made him an effective bodyguard. What a shame, Alamán thought. What a shame.

Pushing such thoughts from his mind, Alamán turned away, facing the glass doors that led out onto the patio where his associates, now refugees from the coup, awaited his appearance. Still, he hesitated. Perhaps, he thought, the new military council was waiting before striking Chinampas. After all, they had an old government to dispose of and a new one to create. Or maybe they were waiting for him to come out and offer a deal. After all, his contacts were international. There was much he could offer the new military government, a government that needed both time and money to establish itself and gain international recognition. Alamán's friends in the American Congress could be a great help to the fledgling military government. And, if what he had been told was true, one of the officers on the Council of 13 shared Alamán's preference in "women."

Sighing, Alamán pushed all thoughts out of his mind for a moment as he allowed himself to enjoy the beauty of the early morning. The fact that he was still in Chinampas and there was nothing threatening on the horizon were good signs. Given time, he was sure that he could come to some kind of accord with the military rulers of Mexico. They were, after all, men, men who had weaknesses and vices and ambitions. If there was anyone who understood this, Alamán did.

25 MILES SOUTH OF CHINAMPAS, MEXICO
0645 HOURS, 30 JUNE

The wild gyrations of the Bell 206 helicopter flying nap-of-the-earth, mixed with the sweet smell of warm hydraulic fluid, were intoxicating to Colonel Guajardo. Looking to the radioman to his left, Guajardo could tell from the pained expression on the young soldier's face that he did not share the pleasure Guajardo derived from flying at better than one hundred knots less than fifty feet off the ground. Ahead, the two Bell 205As carrying the infantry of Group D were, like Guajardo's, skimming just above the ground as they raced north to Chinampas.

Flying in such a manner was for more than the colonel's pleasure. Unsure if the air traffic controllers or the radar operators in Ciudad Victoria were in Alamán's pay, Guajardo had directed that all the helicopters participating in the raid on Chinampas make their final approach low and fast, using valleys and mountains to mask detection by any radars. No one outside the Council of 13 and the men actually participating knew of the raid. Guajardo, intending to come down on Chinampas like a thunderbolt, had taken every precaution imaginable to protect the plan.

Now, with only fifteen minutes to go, he could feel his heart begin to pump adrenaline into his system. Like a runner straining at the blocks, he could feel every muscle tense, preparing themselves for sudden and violent action. In his mind, Guajardo imagined he could see all eleven helicopters screaming along at one hundred knots as they skimmed the surface of the ground. Like great javelins, the assault force was converging on their target. "Nothing," Guajardo whispered, "nothing can save Chinampas. It is mine!"

25 MILES EAST OF CHINAMPAS, MEXICO
0645 HOURS, 30 JUNE

Absorbed in flying his helicopter, Blasio didn't notice the warning indicator until his co-pilot brought it to his attention. Even when he finally did acknowledge the co-pilot, the danger was slow to register in Blasio's tired mind. Turning to his left to the rows of warning indicators, Blasio focused on the orange flashing light, trying to read the small lettering on it between flashes. After several seconds, he decided it was the main gearbox chip collector light.

Instinctively, Blasio simultaneously pulled back on his cyclic with his right hand, eased his collective down with his left, and nudged his right pedal with his foot to reduce their speed, searching for a place to land as he did so. Noticing the change in pitch, the infantry platoon leader leaned over and asked the crew chief if they were approaching the landing zone. Having monitored the conversation between Blasio and the co-pilot, the crew chief told the lieutenant that there was a mechanical problem and they were preparing to land.

Without hesitation, the lieutenant pushed his way past the crew chief. Yelling so that Blasio could hear, even through his flight helmet, the infantry lieutenant demanded that they not stop, that they continue on. Turning control over to his co-pilot, Blasio twisted in his seat to face the lieutenant. "We must land. Particles, tiny bits of metal chipped off the main rotor's gears, have reached a dangerous level in the gear box. If we do not stop and clean off the chip collector, a little magnetic plug that gathers these stray chips out of the transmission oil, the metal chips will foul the gears of the main rotor and cause it to seize up. And if that happens, we will drop from the sky like a rock and, boom, no one goes anywhere anymore."

The infantry lieutenant was persistent. "No. We cannot stop. We must continue on to our objective. We must not fail."

Tired and angry, Blasio was in no mood to risk the lives of his crew, not to mention his own, executing what he considered to be a simple troop-ferrying mission. The young lieutenant, like the major last night, was fired up by the passions of the moment. And, like most infantry officers, he could not understand the harsh reality that aircraft, and their crews, cannot be pushed beyond a certain point without paying a price. Blasio, not really understanding the passions of the moment, and unwilling to pay the price he knew he would pay if he pushed his machine too far, was not going to relent from his decision. Besides, as Blasio recalled, even Major Caso himself had told them that their task, securing the airfield, was a supporting operation. "Look, Lieutenant, we can land, clean the chip collector off, and be airborne again in ten minutes. Flying at full throttle, we can make some of that time up, arriving in plenty of time to secure the airfield."

In response to his proposal, the lieutenant lifted the muzzle of his rifle to the level of Blasio's eyes. "We will continue on. We will not land."

Fury overcame Blasio's common sense. His face contorted in anger, Blasio screamed at the top of his lungs. *"Go ahead, shoot me, you stupid bastard!* Either way, we are going to land now."

Without a second thought, Blasio turned away from the lieutenant. Grabbing his cyclic, Blasio jerked it to the right and forward as he prepared to set the helicopter down. The second Bell 212, with the rest of the infantry of Group N, traveling astern and left of Blasio, watched his maneuvering. Slow to respond to the unexpected change in speed and course, the second helicopter flew past Blasio's before its pilot could bring it about. When the second aircraft returned to its station astern of the lead aircraft, its pilot conformed to every maneuver Blasio performed, landing fifty meters from where Blasio had landed.

SOUTH OF CHINAMPAS, MEXICO
0659 HOURS, 30 JUNE

When San Antonia was to their right, the three helicopters of Group D changed formation from single file to a V, with the two troop carriers abreast and Guajardo's behind them. Unable to restrain himself, Guajardo released his seat belt, grabbed the rear of the pilot's and co-pilot's seats, and pulled himself forward, straining to catch a glimpse of Chinampas as he did so. To his left, out of the corner of his eye, he saw the Bell 206s of Group Z as they swung around the southern tip of a hill mass and began their final run toward the towers. For a second, he watched them. They were on time, and like Group D, deployed and ready. Satisfied, he turned his head to the right, in the direction in which they were headed.

Before him, as if it had suddenly popped out of the ground, was Chinampas. In an instant, he took everything in. All was in order. All was as it should be. After months of detailed planning and study, the moment was here.

Intently Guajardo looked for telltale signs of flight or resistance. There were none. No tracers from machine guns, no puffs of smoke from surface-to-air missiles being launched, no hasty activity on the airfield. Surprise appeared to be complete.

Looking north, above Chinampas, he tried to find Group M. That he did not didn't concern him. They, no doubt, were coming on as fast as Group D and already descending. And, even if they weren't there, there was no waiting for them or stopping. Two groups were on time and committed. There was no more time for planning. No more decisions needed to be made. There was no recall. Now was the time for action. One way or the other, the problem of Señor Alamán was about to be resolved.

CHINAMPAS, MEXICO
0659 HOURS, 30 JUNE

Díaz Bella, long associated with every illegal sport in Mexico City from prostitution to cockfights, was animated as he barked at Alamán. Like most of the men sitting about the table, men who had built their fortunes by exploiting the corruption that was a way of life in Mexico, Bella felt himself lucky to have escaped from the grasp of the military coup, a feat few of their fellow associates had managed. The rolls of Bella's fat belly bumped the edge of the table, causing it to shake as he ranted and raved, throwing his arms about to accentuate his displeasure. "I am sorry if I do not share your confidence, my friend. But I do not trust these colonels in Mexico City. They are zealots. They actually believe in what they say. They have conviction, determination, and, for the moment, power and popular support, all of which is a very dangerous combination." Finished, Bella allowed himself to settle down, taking his two hands and smoothing back his hair as he leaned back in his chair and waited for Alamán's response. Like the half dozen other men seated at the table, he had come to Chinampas to seek refuge and advice, and to plan a common response to the new threat to their livelihood.

Alamán did not immediately respond. Instead, he took a sip of his coffee, looking around the lush green garden just beyond the patio. They were excited, he thought to himself. Shaken and excited. Now, if he could maintain his composure and forestall calamity from either the new government or from within the ranks of the drug cartel and Mexican underworld, he, El Dueño, would become the undisputed leader of every aspect of organized crime in all of Mexico.

Savoring that thought, Alamán set his coffee cup down and began to speak. "My friend, time is on our side. So long as we don't lose our heads and hang together, I have no doubt that we can reach some type of understanding with this new government." Pausing, he looked at each man. Each man, in turn, looked into Alamán's eyes in an effort to see if he really believed his own words. Though half were still skeptical, Alamán was satisfied he had their attention. As he prepared to continue, the heavy beating of helicopter blades drawing near caught his attention. Turning his head away from the group gathered around the table, Alamán looked across the garden toward the west wall.

For a moment, he saw nothing. Then, in a flash, two small Army helicopters came screaming across the top of the wall headed right for them. Never having seen a raid before, Alamán and most of the men at the table were mesmerized by the scene unfolding before them. Even as a second pair of helicopters came over the west wall, slowed to a hover, then began to fire on the towers while a stream of soldiers descended ropes from both sides of the helicopters, Alamán simply sat, as if he were rooted to his chair, watching in amazement as the engineer teams took out the towers. Only a loud explosion coming from the direction of the north wall, and the appearance of Childress, the American mercenary, shook Alamán from his immobility.

Grabbing Alamán's arm, Childress pulled him up out of his chair and back into the main house just as a swarm of troop-carrying helicopters popped up over the south wall and dropped down, like giant grasshoppers, right in front of the patio.

Only after his helicopter lurched up to clear the south wall did Guajardo see the two helicopters of Group M approaching from the north. Already excited, the appearance of Group M and the scene unfolding before him was both overwhelming and a relief. For never having been rehearsed, everything seemed to be coming together magnificently. Glancing to the right to see if Group N had arrived, Guajardo was caught off guard when a fireball suddenly erupted near tower 2.

Forgetting about Group N for the moment, he turned his attention toward the north wall, where tower 2 was located. Since his own helicopter had already dropped into the garden and the main house lay between him and the tower, he could not see the tower or what had caused the massive explosion. He could, however, see the fireball, now laced with black smoke, rising in the sky above the main house. In an instant, Guajardo knew that one of the helicopters had crashed or had been shot down. Judging from the angle, it had to be the Bell 206 carrying Engineer Team Z-2.

The thumping of the skids on the ground alerted Guajardo that they were in the garden. Pushing away from the pilot's and co-pilot's seats, he turned for the right door, drew his pistol, and, in a single bound, was clear of the aircraft and running for the main house.

Once he was on the ground, Guajardo began to look around in an effort to assess his own situation and the progress of the attack. At that moment, he could not tell if things were happening the way he had intended them to or not. Everything seemed unreal. Although they were running, the movement of the men of Group D to his front seemed painfully slow. Beyond them, from the main house, there were flashes of gunfire. And beyond that, billows of black smoke from the unseen fire at tower 2. All these images flowed together and merged into a great blur one instant, then like a snapshot, a single scene became crystal clear, almost frozen in his mind. Mixed with the unfolding spectacle was a cacophony of sounds. Muffled explosions reverberated from the walls as the engineers broke into the towers. The crack of rifle fire and the sputter of automatic weapons from his men, return fire from the house, and the zing of near misses punctured the air. Above the gunfire and explosions came the shouts of officers giving orders, sergeants driving their soldiers on, and the screams of wounded and dying men, bombarding Guajardo's ears as he tried to make sense out of the chaos in the garden.

Just short of the patio, a young private in front of Guajardo suddenly threw his arms out and went sprawling across the grass. He had been hit in midstride. His forward momentum carried him forward while his automatic rifle flew out of his hands. Without pausing, Guajardo continued past the dead soldier, grabbing the rifle and exposing himself to the same gunfire that had struck the soldier. That he was doing so did not occur to Guajardo. In fact, very few conscious thoughts crossed his mind in his mad rush for the main house. All that mattered was to reach the house and clear it as quickly as possible.

Only the quick action of Childress saved Alamán from going down in the first volley of fire that had taken out most of the associates he had been meeting with. The speed, violence, and overwhelming force of the attack made an organized defense of the house impossible. Childress realized this immediately and acted accordingly. Rather than stand and fire at the attacking Federales in what would be nothing more than a futile gesture, Childress grabbed Alamán in an effort to hustle him out of harm's way as best he could, leaving the others on the patio to fend for themselves.

The sudden and violent takedown, as well as the weight of Childress's body on his, knocked the air out of Alamán's lungs. Not realizing what had happened, he began to get up onto his hands and knees, shoving Childress aside as he did so. Back on his own feet, Childress rearranged his hold on the collar of Alamán's jacket and began to push Alamán off the patio, through the house, and out the front door.

As they reached the door, Alamán began to protest. "Maria! We must get Maria! She is upstairs!"

Childress, however, ignored his plea. Without a word, he shoved

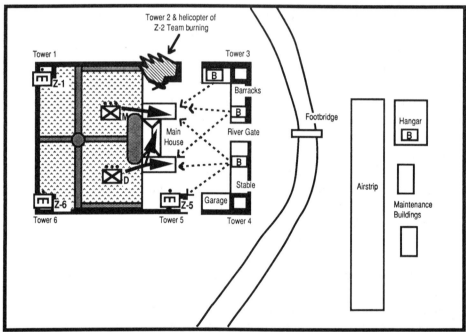

Map 6: Seizure of the Main House & the Firefight in the Compound

Infantry Platoon (Group D)

Engineer Section (Group Z, Team 5)

Groups of Alamán's men

Bell 206 helicopter

Alamán, assisted by a knee in the back, out the front door, glancing over his shoulder toward the patio as he did so. Alamán's organized, businesslike meeting of less than a minute ago was now a scene of bedlam and horror. Several of the men who had been with Alamán were already lying lifeless on the ground or draped across the table and chairs in awkward positions. One man, a fat dark Mexican whom Childress recognized as Díaz Bella, jumped up from behind the body of one of his fallen associates and began to lumber toward the door of the house. An unseen assailant from somewhere in the garden ended Bella's flight with a hail of gunfire. Hit from behind, Bella jerked straight up, arching his huge belly forward as if punched in the small of the back, before he fell forward, crashing through the glass doors that led from the house to the patio.

Once in the open courtyard, Alamán looked about as the American hustled him toward the barracks buildings. To his left, the entire tower next to the north gate and the twisted wreckage of a helicopter were engulfed in flames. The fire created a thick, choking smoke that lingered in the courtyard. To his front, figures with weapons at the ready rushed out of the smoke, passed them, and ran into the house. They were members of the garrison. Childress considered stopping them and telling them that the house couldn't be held, but decided not to, not in the middle of the open courtyard.

As if to underscore how bad things were, Childress and Alamán began to take fire from somewhere to the right. At first, Childress thought the guards in the tower next to the south gate were confused by the smoke. This time he did pause to yell at them to cease fire. Then he saw the tan uniforms and dark helmets of the federal soldiers popping up over the edge of the tower as they fired down into the courtyard below them. The tower had been lost. In a few more seconds, the house would be too. Unless they reached the barracks before that, they would be caught in a deadly cross fire.

With another great push, Childress shoved Alamán toward the barracks and kept him going.

Guajardo, flanked by two soldiers, rushed past bodies of the criminals who had been gathered on the patio and behind overturned furniture. Without pausing, he went through the open patio doors and into the house. As they reached the base of the spiral staircase, Guajardo and the two soldiers with him ran head-on into two of Alamán's mercenaries coming through the front door. Surprised to see the soldiers, and realizing the soldiers had the advantage, both of the mercenaries threw down their weapons and raised their hands in surrender.

Unfortunately for the occupants of the house, giving quarter to his enemy had never entered Guajardo's mind. With his blood up and seeking to strike out, Guajardo stopped, turned toward the nearest mercenary, leveled the rifle he had picked up, and squeezed the trigger.

The mercenary who was his first target took the full burst in the chest and was thrown against the wall. Even before the first mercenary had crumpled into a bloody heap on the floor, Guajardo turned on the second.

Seeing that the federal soldiers were in no mood to compromise, and determining that he had thrown his own weapon too far to grab it back, the second mercenary pivoted and ran back out the door.

Guajardo had no intention of letting him escape. Bringing his rifle up to his shoulder, he took careful aim this time before he squeezed off another burst. Panicked, the mercenary made no effort to bob or weave, providing Guajardo an easy mark. The first rounds struck in the lower back. The climb of the gun muzzle, lifted by firing on full automatic, raised the strike of the following rounds up the mercenary's spine to the back of his head.

Like a man who had just quenched a burning thirst, Guajardo stood motionless for a moment. With the rifle still tucked to his cheek, he looked down the barrel, through the open doorway, at the corpse of the mercenary lying in the courtyard. For a second he was oblivious to everything and everyone about him. The scurrying of the soldiers who had accompanied him into the house did not break his concentration. Nor did the popping of gunfire and roar of grenades upstairs and in rooms to either side bother him. Instead, he just stood there, savoring his success and enjoying the exhilaration of the kill. Months of stress and strain, fear and apprehension, self-doubt and second thoughts, were suddenly forgotten in the heat of action.

Only the sudden appearance of his deputy, Major Caso, snapped him back to the present. That, and the announcement that Group N was missing.

20 MILES EAST OF CHINAMPAS, MEXICO
0705 HOURS, 30 JUNE

In his haste to get the helicopter back into operation, Blasio's crew chief had stripped the threads of the chip collector, making it impossible to get it back into the main rotor gearbox. Carrying the small spark-plug-shaped chip collector over to where Blasio and the infantry lieutenant waited, the crew chief began to apologize, but was cut short by the infantry lieutenant.

With eyes wide from shock and disbelief, the infantry lieutenant pointed at the part in the crew chief's hand and yelled at Blasio, "You mean to tell me that that little thing will keep your helicopter from flying?"

Embarrassed, Blasio threw out his hands and shrugged his shoulders. "There is nothing we can do. Without the collector, there is a hole in the gearbox. We can't fly without it."

The infantry lieutenant, horrified by Blasio's announcement, was unable to speak. He had already lost valuable time waiting in the vain hope that both helicopters could still make it. Now, realizing he had made a bad choice, he spun about and began to run toward the one good helicopter. Jumping in, he didn't even bother strapping himself in. Instead, he wedged himself between the pilot and the co-pilot, and ordered them to take off immediately and fly to Chinampas. When the pilot told him to sit down and strap himself in, the infantry lieutenant grabbed the pilot by the collar, pulled the pilot's face to his, and yelled at him to fly his damned helicopter. The bulging eyes, red face, and spit that sprayed all over when the lieutenant spoke convinced the pilot that he had best comply immediately.

Without a second thought, as soon as the infantry lieutenant let his collar go, the pilot lifted his collective, depressed his left pedal, and eased the stick forward, lifting his aircraft off the ground and leaving Blasio with his crew and half of the infantry platoon behind.

CHINAMPAS, MEXICO
0707 HOURS, 30 JUNE

From either side of a second-story window in the north wing of the main house, Guajardo and Caso looked out into the courtyard below. Gray and black smoke from the burning helicopter wreckage and tower 2 drifted across the courtyard, obscuring their view of the barracks, the stable, and the river gate beyond, making it difficult to pinpoint where the gunfire was coming from. The mercenaries, no doubt, were also hamstrung by the same lack of visibility. Even so, they were maintaining an effective cross fire that covered every inch of the courtyard, making a direct assault impossible. Although Guajardo had anticipated this, the failure of Group N to appear and seize the airfield made his methodical clearing operations impracticable. Time, instead of being an ally, was now against him.

A quick search of the house by the assault teams revealed that Alamán was not among the bodies there. That meant either that his primary target, Alamán, was not at Chinampas, which Guajardo thought highly unlikely, or that he was now sitting safely somewhere in the barracks building obscured by the whiffs of smoke that drifted across the courtyard. Regardless, Guajardo knew his troops needed to end the fight quickly, or find some way of keeping Alamán's people from reaching the airfield. Otherwise, the success of the entire operation would be in jeopardy.

At the other side of the window, with his back against the wall, Caso carefully looked down into the courtyard while Guajardo searched for a solution. "As you can see, we are, as the Americans would say, at a Mexican stand-off, sir."

Guajardo didn't care for Caso's attempt at humor at a time like this. But he said nothing, for he knew Caso was right—and there were far more important matters to be dealt with. His mind was already busy seeking a solution for the problem they faced.

The defenders of Chinampas were in a very strong position and, without Group N at the airfield to the east, they had an escape route. With the helicopters already clear of Chinampas and en route to their rally point, Guajardo had only the men of the assault force available to do whatever needed to be done in order to find and kill Alamán. Direct assault was out. Such an effort would be too costly, and he didn't have enough men for a human-wave attack. The methodical approach was out. Too slow. Closing his eyes, Guajardo created an image of Chinampas and the area around it in his mind. Blocking out all other thoughts, he forced himself to concentrate on that image, seeking a solution.

A young engineer lieutenant, the commander of Group Z, came running into the room where Guajardo and Caso were. Seeing the colonel and the major at the window, he began to head straight for them. He paused, however, when he noticed his path was blocked by a body lying in the center of the floor. The flowing satin and lace of the young woman's nightgown was stained by blotches of blood that seeped from multiple gunshot wounds and soaked up by a vast pool of blood that surrounded the woman's torso. Though appalled by the sight, the engineer lieutenant stood there for a moment transfixed as he studied, with a macabre fascination, the body of the tall, thin woman with boyish features. Only after Caso, turning to see who had entered the room, warned the lieutenant to stay clear of the window, did the engineer lieutenant move. Pulling himself away from the heap of body, satin, lace, and blood in the center of the room, the lieutenant came up next to Caso, carefully avoiding the open window. "Sir, I am here to report to Colonel Guajardo on our situation."

"The colonel is busy right now. Give me your report."

Looking over at Guajardo, the lieutenant wondered what the colonel could possibly be doing with his eyes closed. It looked as if he were asleep. Since he was a senior officer, and the lieutenant still did not understand the ways of senior officers, he ignored the colonel and rendered his report to Caso.

"Towers one, five, and six are secured. We lost one sergeant dead as well as an officer and a sapper wounded in taking them. Team Z-2 was wiped out to a man when the helicopter crashed into tower two. I have myself, one other officer, two sergeants, and eight sappers left." The lieutenant's voice was slightly hoarse but controlled.

Caso nodded his approval, noticing that, as he spoke, the lieutenant could not help himself as he glanced back at the body in the center of the floor. "This is your first action, Lieutenant. You will soon grow used to such sights."

The lieutenant of engineers looked at the body, then back at Caso. Closing his eyes as he nodded, the lieutenant indicated that he was all right, wondering if he, or anyone, could really become accustomed to such sights. Opening his eyes, he probed the major's, trying to see if Caso himself believed what he said. Caso's stare, however, betrayed nothing. "Yes, sir. I, I've never really seen anything like that." He looked back one more time at the body in white behind them. "It seems a shame, such a beautiful woman should die like that."

Case restrained his laughter. "Wastage, yes, but unavoidable. Our task was to clear the building quickly and completely. 'She,' unfortunately, simply found herself in the line of fire. It could not be helped." He paused, looked from the body back to the engineer lieutenant, and then shot back: "Status of demolitions?"

"Excellent. We used only one satchel charge in each tower to gain access. All doors and gates in the towers were open. The guards had not had time to close them."

Suddenly Guajardo, without opening his eyes, called out. "Did you capture any machine guns in the towers?"

Turning from Caso to the colonel, the lieutenant responded that they had. There had been two American 7.62mm machine guns in each tower. All were still operational.

"Do you think your men could work them, Lieutenant?" Guajardo asked, his eyes still closed.

With the confidence of a young officer who believes in himself and his men, the engineer lieutenant responded to Guajardo's inquiry in a manner that bordered on being boastful. "Yes, we can. The sergeants took them right off and checked that out. They are really quite simple weapons to . . ."

Guajardo, his eyes flying open, turned to the lieutenant, firing orders to him as he did so. "Have the team from tower one drop down from that tower, with both M-60 machine guns, outside the wall and move toward the north gate. The team from tower six will also drop down outside the wall, take their machine guns, and move to the south gate."

Looking to Caso, Guajardo continued to issue orders. "Leave Captain Castro and half of his Group M in the house to keep the mercenaries busy. You, my friend, will take the rest of Group M, move through the garden, go over the north wall, join the engineers at the north gate, move to the base of tower three, and set up your machine guns to cover the footbridge and airfield from the north. The engineers, if they can, will blow a hole into tower three to gain access. Take the tower if you can." Guajardo paused, then emphasized his intent. "Regardless of what happens, set up the machine guns and keep anyone from escaping."

Caso thought for a minute. "What about the rollers on the walls?"

"They roll only one way, out. They were meant to keep people out, not in. Your landing may be hard, but you can do it. Any other questions?"

"I assume, Colonel, you will do the same in the south."

In his excitement, Guajardo had not told his men his complete plan. "Yes. That is correct. I will send half of Group D with their commander over the south wall to join the engineers from tower six and set up their machine guns at the base of tower four. That should trap Alamán's men. With the rest of Group D and the engineers in tower five, I shall begin the process of clearing the garage, stable, and barracks, as planned." Finished, Guajardo looked at Caso, then the lieutenant. "Do you have any questions?"

Both men shook their heads. "Good. Now hurry. Time is against us."

Exhausted from the sudden and unaccustomed exertion, Alamán sat in the corner of a barracks room, forgotten for the moment. Overwhelmed by shock and pain from his rough handling by Childress, El Dueño watched with detached interest the scene before him. It all seemed so unreal, like a nightmare. The sudden and brutal death of his associates before his eyes paled in comparison to the destruction of his beloved Chinampas. Everything that had ever mattered to him was being destroyed, piece by piece, as he sat there, and there was nothing that he could do, nothing.

Across from where Alamán sat, several of the mercenaries, who served

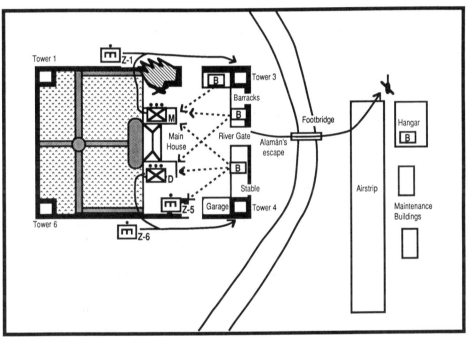

Map 7: Attack on Towers 3 & 4 and Alamán's Escape

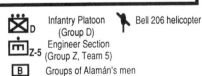

Infantry Platoon (Group D)

Bell 206 helicopter

Engineer Section (Group Z, Team 5)

Groups of Alamán's men

as the garrison, took turns firing out into the courtyard and in the direction of the house. The fumes from the firing of their weapons, mixed with the smoke from the burning tower and helicopter, filled the room with a stench that seared Alamán's lungs as he gasped to catch his breath. A few feet away from him, Delapos, his chief of security, and Childress were conferring in English. Though he could only understand half of what they said, with much of the rest drowned out by gunfire, Alamán gathered that they were in agreement that their situation was hopeless and that they needed to escape.

Though he wanted to protest, demanding that they fight for Chinampas, Alamán had neither the physical strength, nor the moral courage, to make such a demand on the armed mercenaries. Although he was confused and stunned, he still had enough common sense to realize that his paid garrison did not possess the same love for Chinampas that he did. Nothing he could say at that moment, not even the promise of more money, could motivate them to do anything to save the place. Survival, the desire to live and collect that which was due to them, was all that mattered to the mercenaries. As a businessman who had made his fortune dealing with such men, Alamán understood this. Still, the thought of losing Chinampas, and all that it stood for, brought him to the verge of tears.

While their boss struggled to control his emotions, Delapos and Childress quickly reviewed their options. Neither man could understand why the raiders, who appeared to be so well organized and led, had neglected to seize the airfield. Not that it mattered. What did matter was that this error provided them an avenue of escape. That it would soon be closed was without question. The only thing that needed to be decided was how to get Alamán, the man who paid them, and as many of the men as possible, out of the trap they were in before escape became impossible.

Despite the fact that Delapos was in charge, Childress's training as a Green Beret in the U.S. Army equaled and in some ways surpassed the skills and experience of his boss. At times Delapos treated Childress as an equal, even deferring to his judgment. So it was not surprising that, at that moment, Childress took the lead. After all, both men were professionals, and results, not formality, mattered. "Are the pilots still at the airfield?"

Delapos shook his head. "I do not know. Someone said they took off in that direction as soon as the firing started. I assume that they are still there. But even if they are not, we still need to go through there anyhow."

Childress nodded in agreement. "That's true. Now, who takes Señor Alamán and who covers the rear?"

Before answering, Delapos looked over at the men firing in the court-yard. At times like this, it was hard to predict how they would react. As much as he wanted to leave with Alamán, he knew he had to stay since he could best control the mercenary force he had built. Looking back at Childress, he ordered him to pick three men, get Alamán to the airfield, and get him away as best he could. He, Delapos, would give Childress two minutes, then follow with as many men as possible.

Stirred from his stupor when he heard that his men were going to abandon his beloved Chinampas, Alamán yelled from across the room, "And how, my friend, will you do that? There are not enough aircraft at the field to get everyone out."

Surprised by Alamán's sudden outburst, Delapos stood up, put his hands on his hips, and looked at his employer. "That is not your concern. If necessary, we will evade the Federales on foot and work our way north." Turning back, he looked into Childress's eyes, lowering his voice so that Alamán could not hear, as he continued to issue his orders. "Now, my gringo friend, get our fearless leader out of here. If he doesn't get out, none of us will get paid."

Childress laughed. "Ah, a true mercenary to the last." His face serious again, he asked Delapos where they planned to rally.

"Meet us at the old training grounds, the one with the airfield, in five days. If we are not there by then, enjoy your bonus. Now go."

Guajardo had no sooner sent Caso and the engineer lieutenant off than he regretted not giving himself a more active role in the plan to finish Alamán and his men. Though it made sense in that it nearly conformed to the orig-inal plan, Guajardo didn't feel comfortable delegating such important and dangerous tasks to his subordinates while he stayed safe, secure, and worse, unable to personally expedite their execution. With everyone gone, all he could do was wait and watch. After a few more seconds of thinking and looking around the room, now empty except for himself, one soldier firing from another window, and the body in the center of the floor, Gua-jardo decided to vent his nervous energy through action.

Leaving the main house through the back patio doors, Guajardo cir-cled around to tower 5. The part of Group D that had been ordered over the wall was preparing to move out when he reached the tower. The other men of Group D, who would go with him into the garage, were already waiting at the base of the tower. Telling the sergeant in charge of that group to stand by, Guajardo entered the tower in search of the engineers.

His climb up the stairs of the tower was hindered by the bodies of three dead mercenaries, left where they had been shot by the engineers who had seized the tower. For the first time, he realized that he had yet to come across a live mercenary or member of Alamán's staff. This should not have surprised him: the same rage that had driven him minutes before to kill two unarmed mercenaries had infected all of his soldiers. That morning, in the heat of intense and close combat, no one was taking any chances. Dead men, after all, were not a threat.

Just as he reached the firing platform of the tower, a burst of automatic fire from the barracks across the courtyard hit the protective wall and roof, showering chips of concrete all over Guajardo and the engineers in the tower. Lunging forward for the safety of the wall, Guajardo plowed into the back of the engineer sergeant in charge of the team in tower 5. The sergeant cursed, then apologized when he saw it was Guajardo.

Twisting themselves about so that their backs were against the wall facing the enemy fire, Guajardo assured the sergeant that it was all right, then asked him for a report. "They have increased their rates of fire. They're not hitting anything, just firing very fast and all over."

Concerned, Guajardo turned around, got to his knees, and began slowly to raise his head up to the edge of the protective wall in order to see what was going on. A volley of bullets, some smacking the other side of the wall while others streamed overhead, convinced Guajardo that this was neither the time nor the place to expose himself. Dropping back down, he thought for a moment. They were probably getting ready to break and run. The increased rate of fire by some of the mercenaries was to cover the escape of the rest. Time was running out.

"Have any helicopters landed at the airfield, Sergeant?"

"No, sir, not that we have seen or heard. Of course, they could have driven a train through the gate below us and we wouldn't have heard it, or seen it. Here, we are pinned and useless."

Guajardo looked around at the four engineers in the tower, all crouched and seeking cover as best they could. In their faces he could see what he took to be anger at being ordered to such a position, with their lives so endangered, and unable to do anything. The sergeant was right. They were useless there. Turning back to the sergeant, Guajardo issued his orders, ignoring the steady hammering of bullets on the other side of the wall that offered both of them protection. "Yes, there is nothing you can do here. Take your men, go to the base of the tower, and blow a hole big enough for a man to crawl through into the space between the tower and the garage. When you have done that, and before you blow a hole into the garage, open the south gate. Do you understand?"

"Yes, we will do that." Happy to be ordered away from the tower's firing platform, and to have something to do, the sergeant smiled, got the attention of his engineers, and ordered them down to the base of the tower. As soon as the last one was gone, Guajardo stuck his head up quickly, looked about, then ran down the stairs behind the sergeant.

Without looking back, Childress led the small party out through the river gate and ran for the footbridge. Two men on either side of Alamán, holding him up as well as dragging him along, followed Childress. A third man, taking up the rear, waited a few seconds, then ran after them, twisting about every few steps to check for danger from behind.

As he ran, Childress expected to be fired on at any moment. But nothing happened. Once they were clear of the gate, Childress noted that the smoke that obscured everything within the walls of Chinampas was absent. This both pleased him—for he could finally catch a deep breath without coughing—and worried him, for there was no smoke to cover their flight. Still, as he reached the bridge without taking any fire, Childress began to believe they would make it. He waited until he reached the other side before he stopped and looked behind.

The two men with Alamán were nearing the bridge and coming on fast. The rear guard, still twisting about as he ran, was about twenty yards behind.

Suddenly, the rear guard stopped, dropped to one knee, and began to fire. Looking at where his fire was directed, Childress saw a group of Mexican soldiers coming around the north corner of the wall just below tower 3. One of the men in tower 3, not realizing the Federales were at the base of the tower until he saw the rear guard firing, leaned over to see what was going on below. A Mexican soldier, prepared for such an occurrence, killed the man in the tower with a single burst, sending the dead man headlong out of the tower and into the middle of the soldiers setting up a machine gun below, surprising them and disrupting their efforts to bring their weapon to bear on Childress, Alamán, and his escort.

Yelling for the men with Alamán to hurry, Childress continued his own flight to the airfield, missing the death of the rear guard when the soldiers finally were able to open up with the machine gun. The rear guard's sacrifice, and the interruption caused by the dead mercenary's body falling on the machine-gun crew, however, allowed the others in the group hustling Alamán along to clear the bridge and reach the airfield.

There, Childress found the pilots of two helicopters in their aircraft preparing to depart while the guards at the airfield were gathering in the hangar. Running to the nearest helicopter, he ordered the pilot to wait for Alamán. At the next, he told the pilot to wait for him. The second pilot, clearly shaken, reluctantly agreed. Childress next made for the hangar. In his haste, he hadn't noticed the rucksacks stacked up and secured in the helicopters.

At the door of the hangar he saw Jean Lefleur, leader of the group charged with protecting the airfield. Lefleur, a veteran of the French Foreign Legion, did not like Childress and resented the relationship he had with Delapos. As Childress came up to him, Lefleur leaned against the doorframe.

Out of breath as much from excitement as from exertion, Childress came up to Lefleur and began to issue a string of orders. Lefleur listened in silence as Childress told him to send two reliable men with Alamán and his two men in the first helicopter, while Lefleur led the rest, on foot, north to escape and rally at their old training site, where he would meet Delapos and whatever men managed to escape from the firefight still in progress in Chinampas. Finished, Childress waited for Lefleur to act.

The sudden appearance of Childress, with Alamán in tow, put Lefleur in an awkward position. If he did as Childress instructed, then he and his men would not have the helicopters to escape in, as Lefleur had been preparing to do. Yet, if they did escape without Alamán, they wouldn't get paid. While he pondered his options, Lefleur stalled, looking down at his fingernails, casually asking if those were Delapos's instructions or Childress's.

Suppressing a desire to smash Lefleur's face with the butt of his rifle, Childress replied that they were Delapos's orders. Then, so that the other mercenaries gathered about Lefleur could hear, Childress warned Lefleur that unless they got Alamán out safely, not only would there be no pay, their chances of getting out of Mexico alive without Alamán's contacts would be nil.

For a second, Lefleur considered killing Childress where he stood. That thought, however, quickly passed. After Childress's comments about the need to save Alamán in order to get paid, Lefleur had no way of knowing how his men would react. Therefore, Lefleur opted to take the safest option. Still, he was determined to maintain the show that he was in charge. Looking about for a moment, Lefleur paused before he turned to his assembled men. "You two, into the helicopter with Señor Alamán. The rest of you, grab your rucksacks out of the aircraft and meet me over there, at the base of the hill. Bring only food and ammo, no personal items. Now, move.'' When the men had scattered, he looked at Childress, an arrogant smile lighting his face. ''Satisfied?''

Too angry to respond, Childress simply turned and ran to the helicopter he had told to wait for him. Before he got in, he watched his men and Lefleur's bundle Alamán into the other helicopter. Only after they were off did Childress climb in and order the surprised pilot to fly into the courtyard of Chinampas.

Impatiently, Guajardo watched the engineers he had found in tower 5 carry out his orders. After blowing a hole low to the ground at the base of the tower near the gate, the engineer sergeant and Guajardo noted that the smoke nearly obscured the garage wall, only a few meters across from them. Cautiously, the sergeant stuck his head out of the hole to see if his men could low-crawl out without being taken under fire from the barracks. Satisfied that it was possible, he yelled back for one of his men to follow, then went through the hole to the gate without pausing.

Though they worked quickly and efficiently, to Guajardo the efforts of the sergeant and his engineer to return to the safety of the tower before setting off the charge appeared slow and clumsy. From the base of the tower, Guajardo watched the engineers moving back and forth from one side of the hole to the other. Only after the sergeant and his engineer had returned and the cord to set off the demolitions to blow the south gate had been pulled, did Guajardo realize that some of the men he had sent outside the wall might be on the other side of the gate. As the fuse burned its way to the demolitions, Guajardo cursed his own stupidity while he prayed his haste wouldn't result in the death of any of his own men.

The roar of the explosion, followed a few seconds later by a shower of debris, announced that the south gate was gone. Even before the remains of the gate stopped falling, Guajardo was up and running for the opening.

Once he was in the clear, he looked about, relieved that there were no dead or wounded Mexican soldiers on the other side. This relief was short-lived, however, when he heard the sound of a helicopter leaving the airfield. Although he hoped that it was Group N finally arriving, in his heart he knew it was Alamán leaving. The flash of a red and white Bell 206 helicopter confirmed his fear.

Dejected, Guajardo stood there, watching the helicopter disappear. All of his efforts, all of the sacrifices of his men, everything, was for naught.

Chinampas might be gone, but what it stood for still lived. And so long as Alamán lived, he was dangerous.

As if to underscore his failure, Guajardo watched as a single Army helicopter coming in from the east landed at the abandoned airfield and disgorged Group N troops at exactly 0716.

Lost in his own dark thoughts, Guajardo missed the final act of the day's drama. Knowing that Delapos would never be able to make it across the bridge, Childress ordered the pilot to land in the courtyard. Both he and the pilot realized that they were in as much danger from friendly fire as they were from the Federales. Still, Childress was counting on the fact that the surprise of a helicopter landing in the courtyard would buy them enough time to get Delapos and a few men out.

What Childress couldn't know was that he had more than surprise on his side. Guajardo's order that sent most of the men outside the walls, coupled with the engineers abandoning tower 5, had left fewer than six Mexican soldiers in positions that could fire on the courtyard. Rather than a meat grinder, the courtyard was probably the safest place at that moment for the mercenaries.

The unexpected appearance of the red and white helicopter dropping into the center of the smoke-filled courtyard worked as Childress had expected. The Federales, unsure of whose helicopter it was, ceased fire. On the other side, in the barracks, Delapos knew immediately what Childress was up to. Without a second thought, Delapos turned to the men in the room and yelled for them to make for the helicopter.

As soon as the mercenaries came out of the barracks, the few soldiers left in the house began to fire on them, but not on the helicopter. While Childress fired out of an open window at the house, Delapos threw the rear door of the helicopter open and jumped in. After two other men piled in behind him, he yelled to the pilot to go.

For a moment, there was a panic as another mercenary jumped in and a second, missing the door, grabbed the skid of the helicopter. Others, midway between the barracks and the departing helicopter, stopped, watching the helicopter lift off. Seeing that they had been abandoned, the remaining mercenaries turned around to run back to the barracks.

The soldiers, fully recovered from their surprise, fired at the exposed mercenaries. None, however, fired on the helicopter, or the mercenary hanging onto its skid. As quickly as it had appeared, it was gone.

With all hope gone, those mercenaries still in the barracks, towers 3 and 4, and the stable decided they had had enough. So too had the soldiers. It was as if the final free-for-all in the courtyard had satisfied their lust for killing. This time, when the mercenaries appeared with their hands up, no one shot.

Chinampas was finished, but Señor Alamán, Guajardo's real target, was not.

7

Man shall be framed for war, and Woman for the entertainment of the Warrior. All else is folly.

—F. W. Nietzsche

HEADQUARTERS, 16TH ARMORED DIVISION, FORT HOOD, TEXAS
0915 HOURS, 3 JULY

From his office, Scott Dixon could look out his window onto the parade ground in front of division headquarters. He enjoyed his window, especially in the summer, when a large number of units conducted change-of-command ceremonies on the parade ground. During June and July, a week didn't go by without a ceremony, or rehearsals for it. Despite the fact that most Army parades lacked the precision and pomp of a VMI parade, they were still the best free show in town.

What Dixon enjoyed about the 16th Division's parades was the ceremonial horse platoon and the field artillery section. At the insistence of a former division commander, the 16th had formed a horse platoon to match the one used by the other armored division at Fort Hood. The next division commander, being an artilleryman, created a two-gun artillery section, patterned after the ceremonial half-section of artillery at Fort Sill, to go along with the horse platoon. The only difference between the guns used by the Fort Sill artillery section, which used World War I–era guns and uniforms, and those used by the 16th Division's, was that the 16th used two 12-pound smooth-bore Napoleons and matching caissons while their crews wore post–Civil War uniforms.

With the addition of the two ceremonial units, 16th Armored Division parades had a flair that few other units could match. During the ceremony, the horse platoon, outfitted with broad-brimmed Stetsons, dark blue shirts, and sky blue trousers seamed with broad yellow stripes, would form to the left of the battalion or brigade that made up the bulk of the parade. The artillery section, with similar uniforms but red stripes on the seams of their uniform, formed to the left of the horse platoon. When the two ceremonial units had been formed, there was lively debate by traditionalists over this, referred to as the great horse debate. According to tradition, the more senior service or branch held the position to the right, the position of honor. Artillery officers argued that the field artillery, the more senior branch, should be posted to the right of the horse platoon. Armor officers, who were in the majority within the division, argued that they deserved the post of honor. The infantry officers in the division, like the third child in a family, switched sides depending on their mood, just to piss the other side off. Before Dixon became the G3, or operations officer for the division, the placement of the guns of the artillery section and the horses of the horse platoon was often switched, based upon the leanings of the officer in charge of a particular ceremony.

Dixon had no sooner assumed his duties as the G3 than he was confronted by two of his high-speed, low-drag majors concerning the great horse debate. The majors, in an apparent effort to put the bum's rush on the new man, cornered Dixon and tried to convince him that the artillery should be on the right. Dixon, befuddled by the seriousness these men attached to what he considered such a trivial matter, made a snap decision, his first as the G3. Without allowing them to finish their argument, he put up his right hand in order to silence them. When they had stopped speaking, he announced that, so long as he was an armored officer and the 16th remained an armored division, the horses would go on the right, period. Thus, on his first day, he unilaterally ended the great horse debate and established himself as an officer who neither tolerated nor offered bullshit, in any way, shape, or form.

Now, over a year later, Dixon was pleased every time he saw the horse platoon and artillery section march by. Though he hadn't given the decision any serious thought, it had been the right one, for it looked right. The horse soldiers, led by their platoon leader and the guidon bearer, belonged in the lead, as the cavalry always had. Then came the guns, the heavies who did the real killing. And finally, the supply wagon, the ever-necessary tail of any unit, with its four-mule team, teamster, and mascot dog.

After passing the reviewing stand, while the battalion or brigade performing the ceremony and the division band moved off to one side, the horse platoon would wheel about and come back to form a skirmish line, pistols drawn and at the ready. The guns of the artillery section, galloping up from the rear, would pass around the flank of the horse platoon, unlimber, and prepare to fire. Each gun, under the command of the section leader, would fire two rounds. After the reverberation of the second volley drifted away, the horse platoon leader would raise his saber, signaling the bugler to sound the charge. Bringing his saber down while spurring his horse, the platoon leader would scream "Charge!" so that all could hear and lead his platoon past the guns, at a dead run, on line, across the length of the field while the division band played "Gary Owen." The artillery section, limbering their guns as soon as the horse platoon had passed, would follow at a gallop, the gunners waving their hats at the applauding crowd as they went by. And as a grand finale, the supply wagon would bring up the rear as fast as the four mules could take it.

Regardless of how many times he saw it, Dixon loved the show. Like most officers, he was conservative, finding security and comfort in the traditions, order, and regulations that governed military life. The horse platoon and artillery section were a link to the past, a salute to the simpler days when soldiers did soldier things and everyone understood what being a soldier was all about. How wonderful, Dixon thought, life in the Army would be if all we needed to worry about was being a good horseman, a decent shot, and a capable leader.

Leaning back in his chair with his feet propped up on the windowsill, Dixon was sipping coffee and watching a battalion of the 2nd Brigade prepare for a rehearsal when his sergeant major walked into his office. With a booming voice that could wake the dead and a cheerfulness that Dixon could never muster that early in the morning the sergeant major announced his presence. "Ain't it a great day to be in the Army, sir?"

Without moving from his position or turning toward the sergeant major, Dixon responded with a touch of sarcasm in his voice. "Sergeant Major Aiken, *every* day is a great day to be in this man's Army."

"This person's Army, sir. Remember, the Sweet 16th is on the cutting edge of social and cultural advancement."

Although Aiken couldn't see it, he knew Dixon had winced. Dixon winced every time someone referred to the 16th Armored Division as the Sweet 16th, a nickname applied to the division in private conversations ever since it had been selected to be the unit to conduct the Evaluation of Female Combat Officers, EFCO for short.

"Yeah, right, Sergeant Major. How foolish of me to forget." Not that Dixon could forget. It was easier to forget how to breathe than to be a member of the 16th Armored Division and forget that they were about to become the test-bed unit for the introduction of females into combat arms units. Everyone in the division, male and female, officer and enlisted, had an opinion. Even the wives had an opinion. For three months the division, in particular the three battalions that would be receiving the first female officers, had been preparing for the evaluation. It had not been easy.

Though most of the officers and men in the targeted units were prepared to accept the inevitable, there were a few holdouts. Some combat arms officers had voiced their objections, and a few had threatened their resignations, including the commander of one of the battalions selected to participate in the evaluation. All of that ended, however, when Major General Alvin M. Malin, the commander of the 16th Armored Division, was "adviced" of the situation. Nicknamed "Big Al" because he was so short, Malin was a man who neither tolerated dissent when an order had been given nor believed in half measures when action was called for. Within minutes of hearing of the battalion commander's threat, Big Al personally marched down to the commander's office, walking in unannounced. Taking a seat across from the surprised commander, Big Al, in a very friendly voice, told the lieutenant colonel that he was there to personally pick up his resignation and approve it on the spot. Flabbergasted, the battalion commander tried to explain, but Big Al cut him short, telling him to shut up and support the program or hand over his resignation.

The commander of the 2nd Battalion, 13th Infantry, backed down, apologizing for running off at the mouth and promising to support the program, one hundred ten percent.

Big Al's surprise attack had, for the most part, the desired effect. Unquestioning cooperation and team playing became the order of the day. Still, there were whispered comments and dissent in the ranks. Even in Dixon's own section, there were doubts about the wisdom of putting women in combat units. On the previous Friday, to Dixon's surprise, the captain in his section charged with coordination of the overall program for the division came in and asked Dixon to reassign him to other duties on the grounds that he could not support the program. While Dixon admired the man's honesty, he could not allow an officer who did not support Army policy and the Army equal-opportunity program to walk away without comment. After all, Dixon knew that officers could not be allowed to pick and choose what they did and did not want to support.

To Dixon, a graduate of the Virginia Military Institute with twenty-one years of active duty and two wars behind him, it was an all-or-nothing proposition for an officer. Within a matter of hours, the officer was reassigned and Dixon had prepared an adverse evaluation that, in a peacetime Army, would effectively be a show-stopper to the captain's career. The entire affair was made easier since the captain had waited until the very last minute, just as the female officers were coming on board, to make his opinion known. That he chose to do so on a Friday, putting the coup de grace on an already doomed weekend, allowed Dixon to actually enjoy writing cutting comments on the captain's evaluation report.

Two months before, Dixon had planned to take a long weekend in conjunction with the 4th of July and go down to South Padre Island with his two boys and Jan Fields, the woman he had been living with for the past three years. The military coup in Mexico, however, had caused Jan to drop out. The chance to be the World News Network senior correspondent in Mexico City was simply too tempting for Jan to pass up. Dixon, though put out, didn't complain. After all, she had given up a better position with WNN to become, as she referred to herself, a camp follower. The loss of the project officer for EFCO had finished the weekend. Instead of sitting on the beach on South Padre Island with his two sons, Dixon had sat in his office at Fort Hood with the division personnel officer looking for a suitable officer to become the new stuckee for EFCO. After looking at dozens of officers' records, they both agreed upon a new officer just coming into the division, a young captain by the name of Harold Cerro.

Waiting to go in and be interviewed by the division G3, Captain Harold Cerro sipped at the coffee he had been offered and watched the comings and goings of the people around him. He was already pissed off by the fact that his assignment to a brigade staff had been changed, removing him still farther from "real" soldiers. At least at brigade level, Cerro thought, he would have had an opportunity, every now and then, to smell the horseshit and gunpowder. On division staff, all he'd get to smell was the horseshit.

Already in what could be described as a deep funk due to his sudden reassignment, Cerro could find nothing impressive about the division staff that morning. Everyone, officer and enlisted, seemed to move at a half-speed, lackadaisical pace. In most of the line units he had been in, there had always been a high degree of crispness in everything they had done, including their conversations. Here, everyone just sort of moseyed about, lost in their own little world as they drank coffee, shuffled paper, and became annoyed anytime a telephone rudely interrupted their sedate pace and required them to answer it. This, Cerro thought to himself, was going to take some getting used to.

As he pondered his fate, a sergeant major came up to him, a smile on his face and his right hand stretched out. "Captain Cerro, I'm Sergeant Major Aiken. Welcome to the G3." -

Caught off guard, Cerro shifted his coffee cup from his right hand to his left, stood up as he did so, grasped the sergeant major's hand, and lied. "It's a pleasure to be here, Sergeant Major."

Aiken looked into the captain's eyes for a moment as they shook hands and smiled a shy, knowing smile. "I'm sure it is, sir. I'm sure it is."

The smile and comment did not escape Cerro's notice, and the look of concern on his face did not escape Aiken. "Sir, the G3 will see you now." Without waiting, Aiken turned and stepped off to lead Cerro to the G3's office. After quickly putting his half-empty cup down on the floor next to the seat where he had been sitting, Cerro turned and scurried after the sergeant major.

By the time Cerro caught up to the sergeant major, he was standing outside the G3's door. Without a word, Aiken motioned that Cerro was to enter. As Cerro passed him, Aiken mumbled, *"Vaya con Dios."* Although he didn't respond to the remark, Cerro wondered why in the hell the sergeant major had said that.

The G3's office was, relatively speaking, small. At one end was a simple and functional wooden desk facing the door. In front of the desk, a long wooden table with five chairs around it was set perpendicular to, and butted up against, the wooden desk. To Cerro's left was an overstuffed chair and an end table with an old unit history of the 16th Armored Division on it. Farther along the wall to his left was a wooden bookcase filled with a combination of field manuals, military history books, and loose-leaf binders of assorted colors and sizes. On the wall where the bookcase sat were two small-scale maps, one showing Germany and Eastern Europe and the second showing the Persian Gulf region. A third map, on the wall behind the desk, was a special overprinted map of Fort Hood that showed all the ranges and training areas on post. Behind the desk, seated in a large executive-style chair, with his feet propped on the windowsill, sipping coffee as he watched a parade rehearsal, was the G3.

Coming up to the edge of the long table, Cerro stopped, came to the position of attention, saluted, and reported. "Sir, Captain Harold Cerro reporting for duty."

Dixon had heard the captain enter his office. He had even heard the sergeant major's snide comment. The booming voice of the young captain, artificially dropped a couple of octaves so that he sounded huskier, more masculine, did not surprise Dixon. In fact, Dixon half expected the captain to end with the traditional, "Airborne."

Without facing the captain, Dixon took another sip of coffee before moving the cup from his right hand to his left and returning the captain's salute rather casually. "Take a seat, Captain Cerro."

For a moment, Cerro was taken aback by the casual, almost slovenly attitude of the G3. No wonder, Cerro thought, the G3 staff moves around half-stepping. They get it from the top. Heaving a sigh, Cerro dropped his salute, and took a seat at the head of the long table, waiting for the G3 to speak. The G3, however, didn't pay any further attention to Cerro. Instead, he continued to watch the parade rehearsal outside his window. With nothing better to do, Cerro turned in his seat and also watched.

Down on the parade ground, the marching unit was just completing its final turn before passing the reviewing stand. The battalion commander, followed by his four staff principals, was in front of the reviewing stand, saluting the reviewing officer. As this was only a rehearsal, a major from the G3 shop was acting as the reviewing officer, returning salutes and taking notes on deficiencies as elements of the marching unit went by. Following the battalion staff came the companies, led by their captains and guidons. Cerro watched as the commander of each company gave his orders. First came the exaggerated preparatory command, *"Eyes,"* which alerted the company to what command was about to be issued. At the same instant the commander gave the preparatory command, the guidon bearer hoisted the guidon as high as he could. This was an old tradition, done in the days when commanders used the guidon to signal their commands to subordinates who could not hear them over the sounds of battle. After a pause, the commander shouted a crisp, curt *"Right,"* the command of execution. In unison, the commander's head turned to the right as his right hand shot up to salute the reviewing officer. The guidon came down with an audible snap to signal the command of execution had been given. In the ranks of the company, the right-hand file continued to look straight ahead while every head in the two files to the left snapped to the right. The company held this position until its commander had passed the reviewing stand and reached a marker that told him the trail element of his unit had cleared the reviewing stand. At that point, he gave the order, "Ready," pause, "Front."

Company after company marched by, with the national and regimental colors between the second and third company. As they passed the reviewing stand, the regimental colors dipped to a forty-five-degree angle in salute to the reviewing officer, but the national colors remained aloft, dipping for no man. This was the only time the reviewing officer initiated the salute, honoring the national colors.

Cerro had seen all of this before and didn't really understand the G3's fascination with the parade—since, no doubt, the G3 had seen it far more often. Cerro was becoming quite uncharitable in his thoughts concerning his new superior until the horse platoon came by. Though the sequence was the same, there was more flair and drama, a flair and drama that Cerro found himself caught up in, as the horse platoon leader brought his drawn saber up before his face as he gave the preparatory order. Bellowing *"Eyes"* for all he was worth, the horse platoon leader snapped his saber down, catching a glint of sunlight on the polished blade as he did so. He held it there, with a stiff extended arm, as he issued the execution order, *"Right."* The horsemen and their mounts, passing two by two before the reviewing officer, did so with a precision and a casual ease that Cerro marveled at. No doubt, he thought, the horses, their heads held high, required as much drill as the troopers did. Following the horse platoon came the field guns. Each gun, pulled by four horses, had a crew of four, two men riding the trace horses, the ones on the right, and two men riding on the caisson.

While their passing in review in itself had been interesting, the maneuvering and mock battle, followed by a mounted charge afterward, was, for want of a better word, exhilarating. As Cerro watched in fascination, he could feel his pulse rate increase. This, he thought, this was a ceremony worthy of the United States Army.

As the horse platoon leader rallied his troopers, Dixon spun around in his chair and faced Cerro for the first time. "Ever see a cavalry charge before?"

Cerro, surprised by the G3, shook his head. "No, sir, not really."

Leaning back in his chair, Dixon spoke, studying the new captain as he did so. "Back when the Army did things like that for real, everything was simple, manageable, understood. The commander, riding a few paces in front of his troopers, would see and study the enemy, the land, and his objective. He could take it all in with a single glance. Using what he saw, along with his training, experience, and judgment, he'd issue a quick and simple order. He could do it on his own, since units were only as large as a commander's voice could carry. And the maneuvers were simple drills, something that a good troop had practiced many times. When he, the commander, felt all was ready, he would raise his saber and give the order to charge. In a matter of minutes, it would be success, or failure. Simple, clean, and quick. In the words of Major Joel Elliott at the Washita, 'Here goes for a brevet or a coffin!' "

Cerro, sitting at the far end of the table, waited for the G3 to continue, or to tie his little story in to some profound thought. As he waited, he couldn't help but get the feeling that he was being set up for something, especially since Dixon had used Major Elliott's quote. Elliott, an officer assigned to the 7th U.S. Cavalry Regiment in 1868, was last seen alive leading a group of eighteen troops in pursuit of a group of fleeing Cheyennes on the first day of the Battle of the Washita. His body, and those of all eighteen troopers, were found almost two weeks later. Elliott had gotten his coffin. Was that, Cerro thought, what the G3 was preparing him for, a bullet or a brevet? That suspicion was justified as the G3 continued.

"Have you ever heard of the program called Evaluation of Female Combat Officers?"

That was it. Without another word, Cerro knew what was coming. Still, he hesitated for a moment before answering. When he did, Cerro tried hard to maintain an even, calm voice. "Yes, sir, I am familiar with the program."

Dixon picked up a small square paperweight and began to play with it, looking at the paperweight instead of Cerro, causing Cerro to wonder if Army lieutenant colonels used paperweights in the same manner that Navy captains used ball bearings.

As Dixon spoke, Cerro could feel his shoulders, already dangerously close to the floor, slump down even further. "Well, by this time next week, you will be more than familiar with it. I have decided to assign you to the G3 training section as the individual training and gunnery officer for the division. One of your responsibilities will be monitoring and coordinating the EFCO program for the division. While you will have other duties, including being the division point of contact for the skills qualification testing, small arms and gunnery training, special schools, etc., none of them compare to the importance of EFCO. That is a very high-vis program that I expect you to remain on top of." Stopping his fiddling with the paperweight, Dixon looked up and into Cerro's eyes before continuing. "Understood?"

Although Cerro didn't have any idea what all his responsibilities and duties concerning EFCO would entail, he understood the sensitive nature of the program, the publicity it had received and would continue to receive, and the controversies that would be generated when the results were released, no matter what those results were. For a moment, Cerro pondered all of this, trying hard to come up with an appropriate response. Looking back at the G3, he suspected he was waiting for some comment that would offer him a clue as to how Cerro felt about his assignment. Remembering that a little humor, employed at moments like this, had more than once gotten him out of a tight spot, Cerro smiled. "Gee, sir, you had me going there for a while. I thought you were going to give me something really tough to deal with."

Caught off guard by Cerro's comment, Dixon looked at Cerro, then smiled. Well, he thought, if he wants to fuck with me, two can play at this. Leaning forward, putting his elbows on the desk and his hands together, Dixon looked Cerro in the eyes. "In that case, do you think you could also handle training ammunition?"

The first thing that popped into Cerro's head was "Oh, shit, I misjudged this guy." That thought must have turned his own smile into a worried look, for after a brief pause, Dixon winked and smiled. "Next time, trooper, look before you leap. Understand?"

Cerro shook his head. "Target, sir, cease fire."

Standing up, Dixon walked to the door. "Your period of grace is over. Time for you to go to work. Follow me and I'll introduce you to Major Nihart, the G3 training officer."

HEADQUARTERS, 2ND BATTALION, 13TH INFANTRY, FORT HOOD, TEXAS
0945 HOURS, 3 JULY

Turning off the road on which 2nd Brigade headquarters was located and into the parking lot behind the headquarters building for the battalion, the soldiers of 2nd of the 13th Infantry prepared to come to a halt. For Second Lieutenant Kozak, it had been a good start. Drill and ceremony, after four years at West Point, including one year as a cadet battalion commander, had at least prepared her for parades. Now, she thought, if the rest of the next year goes this easy, we've got it made.

That she considered her success as a matter of "we" and not "I" was a subconscious admission that her success or failure would affect more than herself. Her performance, and that of five other young female officers like her, would determine if female officers would be allowed into the mainstream of the Army. So long as females, both officer and enlisted, remained restricted to combat support and combat service support branches, there would be barriers to promotion and ascent to the highest levels. Only by becoming members of the combat arms branches could women achieve real and unrestricted equality. And for this to be achieved, Nancy Kozak knew she had to succeed.

Marching into the parking lot, she looked at the back of her new company commander. Her success, and in turn, the success of the evaluation, rested heavily upon that man, Captain Stanley Wittworth. He could make or break her in a dozen different ways. From the tasks he assigned her, to the personnel he placed in her platoon, Captain Wittworth held the key to her future. Though Kozak tried to convince herself that the same was true for any second lieutenant, the consequences of her failure would be more than a simple statistic.

Preoccupied with these thoughts, Kozak almost missed Wittworth's order to halt. Catching herself in time, she came to a halt, and, on command, faced to the left. Clutching her fists and wincing, she uttered a silent curse, reminding herself that she had to keep her head out of her ass and pay attention. First and foremost, she had to keep her eyes and ears open and her mouth shut.

After dismissing the company, Wittworth wandered back to his office. He was in no hurry. All that waited for him there was paperwork and a line of soldiers waiting to see him about some damned thing or another. He didn't feel much like dealing with trivia at that moment. Instead, he needed to get his own head together. The nice, organized, and controlled world he had created for himself as a company commander had hit a speed bump named Nancy Kozak.

Although he had known that having a female second lieutenant in his company was going to bring a certain amount of problems and difficulties with it, he hadn't reckoned on some of his problems coming from his own commander. Wittworth had been hoping for guidance and support, or at least some empathy. Instead, he got nothing. What little was said appeared, to Wittworth, to be interference bordering on micromanagement.

The parade rehearsal that morning, the first official duty in which Lieutenant Kozak had participated, had served as a warning to Wittworth. Offering what appeared to be a simple recommendation, the battalion commander had suggested that Lieutenant Kozak be placed so that she was in the right-hand file of the company for the retreat parade. Wittworth had no way of knowing that the reason the battalion commander wanted Kozak to be on the right was so that she would be visible for everyone on the reviewing stand to see when the battalion marched by. It was the battalion commander's way of proving that he had taken Big Al's "suggestion" and become a team player, and that Lieutenant Kozak was fully integrated in the battalion, like she was supposed to be.

The message that the battalion commander's recommendation drove home to Wittworth was that she would receive more interest from the battalion commander than the average run of the mill second lieutenant. The battalion commander, and probably the entire battalion staff, would be watching her. This, in turn, meant that he would be watching Wittworth, or at least what Wittworth's company was doing. What exactly all this meant was not entirely clear to Wittworth. About the only thing that was clear was that somehow his career was now tied to the fate of a brand-new second lieutenant, a female lieutenant at that. If that was true, then it behooved Wittworth to find out, as quickly as possible, what results the battalion commander expected. In a nutshell, he had to know whether Second Lieutenant Kozak was to be a success or a failure. Once he had that figured out, he could act accordingly.

ALONG THE RIO SALADO, NORTH OF MONTERREY, MEXICO
1035 HOURS, 3 JULY

Around one end of the dirt runway stood three buildings, all in varying degrees of collapse. The main building was a one-story cinder-block structure with a tin roof that had once served as a terminal and office. To the right was a hangar, in which two helicopters were hidden behind doors that hung from rusting hinges. To the left, in a lean-to shed that had more wooden planks missing than present, were a jeep and two well-used pickup trucks hidden under canvas tarpaulins. Built on the flood plain of the Salado river by a mining company, the airfield had been officially abandoned for over twenty years. A quick glance, from the ground or air, would have convinced the casual observer that it still was. Childress and his small crew of mercenaries had spent hours making sure the airfield appeared unoccupied. Only the occasional reflection of light from the lookout's binoculars betrayed their presence.

While Childress and the others could jokingly call the abandoned airfield the next best thing to home, the thought of having lost his precious Chinampas and having to hide like a common criminal amongst a group of cutthroat mercenaries made Alamán physically sick. In private, he would look up at the sky and ask, Why, my Lord, have you forsaken me? Not that he expected an answer. Though his mother had endeavored to raise him in the ways of the church, the reality of life in the slums of Mexico had made Alamán a realist and a survivor. Already, in his mind,

an idea for extracting revenge and restoring himself to power was forming
in his mind.

While Alamán sat alone in his room in the abandoned airfield's terminal, dreaming of the future, Childress and the handful of mercenaries that
had escaped from Chinampas dealt with the present. A shout from the
lookout on the roof alerted them that someone was coming. Scrambling
up a rickety ladder, Childress went to where the lookout was posted.
Even without binoculars, he could see the clouds of dust rising like
rooster tails, indicating that two vehicles were approaching, long before
he heard the roar of the vehicles' engines.

As he handed the binoculars to Childress, the lookout asked, "Delapos?"

Putting the binoculars up to his eyes, Childress did not respond at first,
not until he had confirmed that there were two vehicles. "No, not likely.
Delapos and Luis had only one vehicle. I can't think of a good reason
why they should have taken a chance and stolen another. They were only
on a simple supply run."

"Alert the rest?"

Childress put the binoculars down. "Yes, alert the rest. But no shooting unless we have to. Clear?"

With a nod, the lookout backed away toward the ladder. "Clear."

As the vehicles approached the ford site to cross the river, they both
stopped. In the lead vehicle, an open jeep, a tall lean man got out. Putting
binoculars to his eyes, he scanned the airfield. Childress did likewise.

In an instant, Childress knew who it was. The maroon beret of the
Foreign Legion parachute regiment and the motley camouflage jacket
could only belong to Lefleur. Letting the binoculars down, Childress
thought, well, you little bastard, you did show up. Though he too was a
mercenary, Childress felt that Lefleur could not be trusted. As long as he
had known him, Lefleur had shown no trace of humanity, conscience, or
integrity. He was, Childress thought, a man who would stab his own
mother in the back.

Still, they were, at least for now, on the same side and working for the
same man. Standing up, he waved his right hand, shouting to his men
below to stand down, that friendlies were coming in. From across the
river, Lefleur saw Childress and returned the wave before getting back
into the jeep. With Lefleur's men, they would have a total of twelve men,
not counting the two pilots and Alamán. It wasn't much, but it was a
start. Childress paused. A start for what? What exactly would they be
able to do? And why? Up to this point, he, and everyone else, had been
taking things one step at a time. It was time now for some serious
discussions about the future.

HEADQUARTERS, MINISTRY OF DEFENSE, MEXICO CITY, MEXICO
1045 HOURS, 3 JULY

Without a word, Guajardo, his hat pulled low over his eyes, his head
fixed straight ahead, entered the outer office. Mechanically, he walked
past his secretary and adjutant and headed straight for his own office,
where he entered without a word, quietly closing the door behind him.
For a moment, the secretary and the adjutant looked at each other. Then,
without uttering a single word, they busied themselves with whatever it
was they had been doing. Both knew that Guajardo, having just returned
from reporting to Colonel Molina on the raid at Chinampas, needed to
be alone.

With his hands clasped together at the small of his back, Guajardo stood
at the window, rocking back and forth on his heels as he looked out at the
street below. That his meeting with Molina could have been worse was the
only bright thought that lightened his dark mood. Knowing that Guajardo
openly despised his adjutant, Major Puerto, Molina had arranged that
Puerto be on an errand while Guajardo was in the office. For himself,
Molina could not have been more understanding, without being condescending.
    Guajardo, after having ignored the advice of almost everyone on the
council concerning the plan for the elimination of Alamán and Chinampas, had come prepared to hand over his resignation. Molina, anticipating
his friend, was ready for such a move. He spoke to Guajardo as a brother,
neither condemning him nor ignoring the issue. He freely admitted that
the loss of Alamán was a disappointment in an otherwise flawless seizure
of power. That, however, Molina pointed out, did not justify losing one
of the council's most capable members, and that this was no time for
heroic gestures. They had all faced the prospect of failure, he continued,
and still did. Now was not the time to start tearing apart the system they
had built so carefully, simply because perfection had not been achieved
on the first day. Though he would consider accepting his resignation,
Molina asked Guajardo, as a personal favor to him, to reconsider his
position and stay with the council. When the two men parted, they were
choked with emotion, embracing each other as brothers.
    During his return to the Ministry of Defense, Guajardo had realized he
would not resign. As terrible a burden as his failure would be, to abandon
the people's struggle simply because of a matter of honor would be
foolish. Molina knew this, and so did Guajardo. Perhaps, Guajardo
thought, this was a good thing. A man, regardless of who he is, needs to

be humbled, in order to be reminded that he is only human. Yes, I must learn from this.

Guajardo did not hear the first soft knock at the door. The second, a little louder, caught his attention. Without moving, Guajardo called out, "Yes?"

The door opened wide enough for the adjutant to slip partway into the room. "Sir, Lieutenant Blasio is here as ordered. Shall I have him wait?"

Looking at his watch, Guajardo noted that Blasio was ten minutes early. "No, send him in."

The adjutant disappeared, closing the door. A moment later another knock. Again, without moving from his position at the window, Guajardo called out, "Enter."

Guajardo heard the door open, then close, followed by four short steps ending with the clicking of two heels brought together. "Sir, Lieutenant Blasio reporting as ordered."

Guajardo did nothing. Up to that moment, he hadn't thought much of what he would do with the man who had compromised the attack on Chinampas. He had read the reports from both Blasio and the lieutenant who had commanded the platoon Blasio had been transporting. Both men were good men who had done what they had thought appropriate. So what was he to do with Blasio, the man who, through an error of commission, had allowed Alamán to escape?

Turning, Guajardo laid eyes on the lieutenant for the first time. He was still standing at attention, his hat tucked under his arm, his eyes fixed on Guajardo. What, Guajardo thought, am I to do with you, my friend?

Walking around to the front of the desk, Guajardo paused, then leaned back against it, half sitting, half standing. Folding his arms, he continued to stare at Blasio. Was there, Guajardo thought, any difference in my failure in judgment in using so complex a plan for Chinampas, and this lieutenant's for landing his aircraft due to a relatively minor mechanical problem? And, Guajardo asked himself, were they in fact failures, or simply a series of bad decisions made independently of each other, that, together, had created a failure? Guajardo, after all, knew that he had come so close, so very close to pulling off the raid as he planned. Only Blasio's forced landing changed that. And why, he thought, place all the blame on Blasio? The infantry lieutenant commanding Group N could have continued immediately with the second aircraft instead of waiting for Blasio to finish. Did that mean the infantry lieutenant was responsible for the failure?

Looking down at his shoes for a minute, Guajardo decided that it would be wrong to punish this officer for doing what his training had dictated. As senior aviator on board the helicopter, he was responsible for the lives of his crew, his passengers, and his aircraft, all of which were valuable commodities in the understaffed and underequipped Mexican Army. Had this been a peacetime exercise, Guajardo knew that Blasio's decision to land at the first sign of trouble would have been the correct one, just as Guajardo's plan of attack would have been considered an acceptable option.

Looking back up at Blasio's face, Guajardo studied the lieutenant for a moment longer before he decided what to do. "Do you know why you are here, Lieutenant?"

Turning his head to look at the colonel, Blasio responded promptly. "Yes, sir. To explain my actions during the raid of Chinampas and receive whatever punishment you deem fit, sir."

For a moment, Guajardo hesitated. Blasio, as Guajardo had been, was ready to atone for his error. But we cannot afford such sentiment. Molina was right about that. There is too much to do and there are too few good men. In an instant, Guajardo decided.

"Lieutenant, I do not need you to explain your actions. Your report, and that of the infantry officer commanding the assault force, were quite satisfactory." Guajardo paused, allowing Blasio to sweat a little longer. "As for your punishment, you will be relieved from your current posting and be assigned to my staff as my personal pilot."

Not quite understanding what he had heard, Blasio turned toward Guajardo. "Excuse me, sir. Am I to understand that I am to be your pilot?"

With an expression that betrayed no emotion, Guajardo responded, "Yes, that is correct. Now, you will report to my adjutant for further instructions. Once you have found quarters, you will find yourself a good watch. I demand punctuality. Understood?"

Blasio, struggling to maintain his decorum, simply responded, "Understood," leaving Guajardo's office as quickly as possible, as if he feared the colonel would change his mind.

ALONG THE RIO SALADO, NORTH OF MONTERREY, MEXICO
2135 HOURS, 3 JULY

Finishing their meals, the three men picked at bread or sipped coffee as they talked amongst themselves. Freely switching from French to Spanish, then to English and back in an effort to impress each other, the three men discussed their future plans. Delapos, for all his bluster, would, with little doubt, stay with Alamán. "Things will, eventually, settle down, and when they do, there will be the need for a man like Alamán."

Besides, Delapos said, they were both Mexicans. Despite the hard times, he had confidence things couldn't get worse. Childress toyed with the idea of going back north. It had been, he claimed, too long since he had seen real snow. It was time to head back to Vermont and enjoy some of his pay. Lefleur, a Frenchman through and through, talked only of Paris, then perhaps a job in Africa, where he had served with the Legion. It was idle chat, no different than that of any other soldiers who had, in reality, no clear idea of what the future held for them.

From out of the shadows of the doorway of the terminal office where the three men sat, Alamán emerged. He had been listening to their idle chatter for several minutes in an effort to gauge their dedication and attitude. When he was satisfied that he had a feel for where each man stood, he came forward.

The sudden appearance of Alamán caught the three mercenaries off guard. Turning to face the apparition, Delapos began to stand. Alamán indicated to Delapos to keep his seat with a motion of his right hand. Striding over to the one side of the table where no one was seated, Alamán stood there for a moment before speaking. Then, almost shyly, he asked if he could have a moment of their time.

Since their arrival, this was the first time that Alamán had come forward and addressed them, either separately or together. Now, standing there before them was the man who had once considered his power in Mexico equal to that of the country's president. Though his clothes showed spots of dirt and were stained with sweat marks, they were neatly arranged, like his hair. With an air of confidence that made him appear larger than he was, Alamán looked at each man without speaking. Each of the mercenaries, realizing that he had a proposal, said nothing when he looked at them in turn. When Alamán began to speak, they were all ears.

"If we are to believe the news on the radio," Alamán stated, "there is no possible way for me to reestablish my operations under the current regime in Mexico City. The military appears to have a solid base of power and no viable opposition. In addition, the Council of 13 has gained great popular support from both the middle and lower classes. The council's program of taking immediate and direct action against corrupt officials and government employees, while encouraging the people to help them track down and identify those officials, seems to have captured the imagination of the people. The people are finally being allowed an opportunity to vent their frustrations against a government that has long abused and ignored them and provided us with a 'comfortable' environment to work in."

As Alamán spoke, he began to circle the table. Delapos, always captivated by his fellow countryman's fairy-tale success story, watched every move Alamán made and took in every word. Childress and Lefleur, on the other hand, began to wonder where Alamán was going with this lecture. Both men shot furtive glances at each other before turning back to watch Alamán.

"Under these circumstances," Alamán continued, "there is little that we, the four of us and the handful of guards who survived the raid, can do on our own to remove the new government or alter its policies from within. The climate," he stated as he paused, lifting his right hand up to his side and holding the index finger of that hand in the air for dramatic effect, "is not suitable for us at this time. But that does not mean that all is lost." As a conclusion to his meandering introduction, Alamán stated, "If *someone* were to remove the new regime, then things could once more return to normal. It is up to us, the four of us, to precipitate that change."

As Alamán spoke, Delapos nodded every so often in agreement. As a Mexican, he understood. Childress, poker-faced, sat and listened in silence, knowing that the other shoe was about to drop. Lefleur, though he was just as curious about what Alamán had to say as Childress was, feigned a lack of interest. When Alamán paused again, the three men looked at each other, then back at Alamán. As their leader, and the one most loyal to Alamán, Delapos asked the question that was on all their minds. "How, Señor Alamán, do you propose we do that?"

With a smile that lit his entire face, Alamán whispered, as if he were saying a prayer in the Catedral Metropolitana, "The Americans, my friends, the Americans. They will be our salvation."

Alamán's comment caught Childress and Lefleur off guard. They had been expecting something more dramatic, such as assassination or bribery. Only Delapos understood. In a flash, he jumped to his feet and embraced Alamán. "Brilliant, señor! Brilliant!"

8

The first law of war is to preserve ourselves and destroy the enemy.

—Mao Tse-tung

CAPITOL, WASHINGTON, D.C.
1030 HOURS, 3 AUGUST

There was little enthusiasm that morning for much of anything. Even the ceiling fans gave the impression that they had no great drive as they spun lackadaisically at half speed around, and around, and around.

Below them, the monotone drone of the current witness reading his prepared statement reminded Ed Lewis of a faulty fluorescent light, a low, annoying buzz that quickly got on your nerves. The witness, a third-echelon flunky from the office of the CIA director, was as exciting as a white plaster wall, but not nearly as interesting. He was dressed in a dark blue, three-piece suit, a white shirt, and a thin red tie that was decorated with those funny little multicolored shapes that looked like pears and didn't have a name. The thin, narrow face, accented by advanced balding at the temples and round horn-rimmed glasses, was indistinguishable from the faces of four out of five bureaucrats who wandered the streets of the capital. Lewis had no trouble seeing that the witness would be just as comfortable conducting audits for the IRS, handling a divorce trial, or prosecuting a malpractice suit. For a moment, Lewis wished the CIA had had the common decency to send over an attractive female spokesperson to deliver the prepared statement like some of the more astute agencies did. At least a well-attired and -groomed woman provided a pleasing distraction from the dull, arduous task of patiently listening to drivel while one waited one's turn to verbally rip the witness to pieces. But, Lewis lamented, no such luck today, as he watched the geek from the CIA drone on, and on, and on.

Like most prepared statements, this one was being delivered with a zeal that matched the ceiling fans' slow and tedious rotations. It was cluttered with redundancies, stuffed with embellishments, and liberally sprinkled with caveats. The prepared statement, in short, was ninety percent grade A, government-inspected horseshit. Still, Ed Lewis listened intently, for he knew that there was no such thing as pure horseshit. Somewhere hidden in the horde of words the witness was issuing was an idea, a grain of truth, a real and cognitive thought. It was the task of Ed Lewis, and the other members of the House Committee on Intelligence, to capture those few precious thoughts and truths as they whizzed by and beat them to death during the questioning that would follow.

The likelihood of that happening this day, however, was quite remote, and the witness knew that. At least his bosses did, which is why only a relatively low-ranking administrative assistant had been sent to deal with the congressional committee. With the summer recess about to begin, Lewis, by pushing for hearings on the crisis in Mexico, was fighting the annual drive to finish up or postpone all business that might force the congressmen and their staffs to prolong their stays in D.C. Opposition from every quarter, including an occasional plaintive whimper from his own staff, had threatened to postpone the hearings until the Congress met again in October. It was only through threats and a few well-chosen comments to the press that Lewis had been able to convince his fellow congressmen on the committee to hold preliminary hearings on the failure of the nation's intelligence community to predict and accurately track recent events in Mexico. In an election year, when the race was close, the last thing an incumbent could do was appear to be negligent in his duties, especially when they were connected to the crisis du jour.

Lulled into inattention by the lackluster delivery of the prepared statement, the assembled congressmen took a few seconds to realize that the CIA man had finished. There was a momentary shifting in seats and reshuffling of papers as people throughout the chamber stirred themselves back into a state of mental awareness. When the chairman of the committee finally roused himself to speak, his voice and comments betrayed his lack of interest and focus. Even his questions were rather perfunctory.

The witness, sitting across from the committee members, stared at them through his large, round, horn-rimmed glasses. With his hands folded on the table, he responded to each of the chairman's questions with stock answers that were as uninformative and evasive as they were predictable. In some cases, Lewis had great difficulty relating what was given as a response to the question that had been asked. Still, no one seemed to mind. A function was being performed. Like cogs, and wheels, and gears of a great machine, the congressional hearing was grinding on as scheduled.

When the floor was turned over to Lewis to ask his questions, he paused before proceeding. Looking over at his colleagues, and then at the witness, he considered his approach for a moment. On one hand, he could follow suit, asking mundane questions that avoided controversy, thereby ensuring that the hearing would end on time and in a nice, neat, tidy manner. Or he could, as his instincts told him to, go for the throat. By choosing the latter, he would be assured some media coverage, incur the wrath of his fellow committee members who wanted to end this session, and, possibly, just maybe, put some people in the intelligence community on notice that their poor performance in Mexico to date would not escape punishment.

Had Lewis chosen the easy out, he would have surprised both friends and foes. A former officer in the National Guard, he had participated as a battalion executive officer in the Persian Gulf war and had experienced, firsthand, the price of poor intelligence. The people who had paid the price for those failures had been his friends and the soldiers who had entrusted their lives into his care. To allow the intelligence community to do whatever it wanted, without regard to consequences, would be, to Lewis, a betrayal of those he had left behind.

He could not, therefore, do otherwise. Of all his congressional duties, Lewis considered the time spent working as a member of the House Intelligence Committee as being the most important and, potentially, as having the greatest impact. He could not, and would not, fluff off the witness simply for the sake of convening on time. Like a samurai warrior about to do battle with an opponent, Lewis held the papers in front of him in both hands like a weapon, leaned forward, and stared the witness in the eyes.

Stressing the word *Mister* as a way of reminding everyone present that the witness was without a title, an important distinction in Washington, Lewis began his questioning. "I've read the report submitted by your agency, *Mister* Napier, with great interest. Are you familiar with its contents?"

The CIA rep leaned forward to the microphone. "Yes, Congressman Lewis, I wrote it."

There was a hint of pride in Napier's response, which bothered Lewis. Everyone knew Napier had written the report. Napier's comment, as far as Lewis was concerned, was nothing more than a stab at publicly receiving credit for simply doing the mundane job he was being paid to do. After glancing at the report, then at Napier for a few seconds, creating a pause for effect, Lewis grunted, "Uh-huh." Looking back down at the report for a few more seconds, Lewis gave the impression he was considering his next question, even though he already knew what it and the following questions would be. "This report is quite informative, Mr. Napier. In it, you describe CIA operations in Mexico, providing dates, details, facts, and figures galore. Were someone to read this in isolation, he, or she, could not help but get the impression that we had the means in place to monitor trends and developments in Mexico that could pose a threat to the United States. And yet, the events of June 28 through June 30 of this year do not bear this out. Comparatively speaking, the people at Pearl Harbor on December 7, 1941, were wide awake and alert. How, sir, do you explain the discrepancy between the means available, as delineated in your report, and the poor results, as demonstrated by recent events?"

Napier was prepared for the question. A smirk lit his face as he leaned back in his seat before answering, unaware that he was being set up. "Well, Congressman Lewis, as a member of the House Committee on Intelligence, you are well aware of the many requirements placed on the intelligence community of the United States. You are also aware, I am sure, of the budget with which we are expected to execute the multitude of tasks necessary to fulfill those requirements. There is, and again, I am sure you are aware, a discrepancy between many requirements and too few funds. We, therefore, have to make hard choices, prioritizing our efforts based on what we perceive to be the greatest need at any given time."

"Who, Mr. Napier, makes those choices?"

Napier responded with a tone that emphasized his confidence, and a wave of his hand. "The director, of course, based on recommendations from subject-matter experts and area specialists."

Lewis cut in. "Such as yourself?"

Cocking his head back, Napier responded, with pride, "Yes sir, like me."

"Do you, Mr. Napier, provide much input to the director concerning affairs in Mexico?"

"Yes, Congressman, of course. Central America, and Mexico in particular, is my responsibility. Just about everything concerning Mexico comes across my desk for my review, screening, and reworking before going to the director, or higher."

Like a skilled hunter, Lewis continued to close, preparing to snare Napier as his prey, while turning Napier's own arrogance against him. "Then, I assume, Mr. Napier, that you also advise the director on what requirements should be pursued and how best to allocate funds and re-sources to meet those requirements?''

"Yes, Congressman, of course. The director, responsible for many areas, normally goes along with our recommendations.''

For a moment, Lewis had to suppress the urge to lash out at the pompous bureaucrat seated before him. Instead, in a rather nonchalant manner, Lewis struck. "Then, Mr. Napier, you accept responsibility for the CIA's failure to understand the threat to the Mexican govern-ment and the Agency's inability to predict the military coup that brought it down at the end of June.''

Lewis's statement struck Napier like a bullet. Sitting upright, his face flushed, Napier stared blankly at Lewis before answering. His response was quick and reactive. "I said nothing of the sort. There was no failure on our part. As my report states, the events of this past June were totally unprecedented, unexpected. The spontaneous action on the part of a handful of military officers could not possibly be predicted.''

It was now Lewis's turn to settle back in his chair and snicker. "You would have us believe that this entire crisis was a bolt out of the blue, that these thirteen colonels woke up one day and suddenly decided to over-throw their government?''

Napier was angry. Lewis was trying to make him look like a fool and he didn't like it. He was, however, too rattled to respond rationally, and it showed. "Of course not, *Mister* Congressman. You just don't pull off an operation like they did without detailed planning and preparation. Such things take time, as well as motivation.''

"And your agency detected none of this detailed planning and prepa-ration? And, *Mister* Napier, you just stated that the coup was spontane-ous. Which is it? Deliberate and premeditated or spontaneous?''

Caught between a rock and a hard place of his own creation, Napier slowed down this time before answering. His next response was more controlled. "As I have already pointed out, Congressman Lewis, our efforts were oriented toward gathering information on drug-trafficking operations. I didn't believe . . . the Agency didn't see any need to ques-tion the stability of the Mexican government or the loyalty of the Army.''

Shooting forward in his seat, Lewis looked Napier in the eyes. "Then, sir, you failed. You failed to do what the CIA is supposed to do. In the twinkling of an eye, the entire government of a nation that shares a fifteen-hundred-mile border with the United States was eliminated and replaced by a group of men whom we know absolutely nothing about. If that, sir, is not a failure, then what is?''

Napier, at a loss for words, fumbled about in an effort to find a suitable response. Lewis, however, did not give him the chance. He had the floor, Napier was on the ropes, and it was time to go for the kill. Lewis was not interested in hacking up a minor flunky. He was going for bigger things, the entire intelligence community. Napier was just a foot soldier who had been placed in the line of fire and had been shot.

Turning in his seat and facing the chairman of the subcommittee, Lewis addressed him specifically, and the entire chamber in general. "As in the past, the United States finds itself caught off guard and reacting to an international crisis. Instead of being forewarned and prepared, the leadership of this country has no better understanding of events in Mexico today, five weeks after the event, than the average man and woman on the street." Holding Napier's report up in one hand and crumpling it like a piece of scrap paper, Lewis drove on. "I find it totally reprehensible that Jan Fields, a simple reporter for a news network, who just happened to be in Mexico City at the time of the coup, is providing better information, and greater insight into this crisis, than an agency that we annually sink billions of dollars into. Now, I really do not expect anyone to justify this, for in my mind, there is no reasonable justification. What we should be interested in, Mr. Chairman, is what Mr. Napier, and his agency, are going to do to correct this glaring deficiency. That, sir, is what we need to work on. We owe it to the American public and ourselves. To do anything less would be criminal."

Though most of his fellow committee members were not at all pleased with the line of attack that Lewis had taken, no one dared challenge him. His approach had been sound and his speech was real mom-and-apple-pie stuff, the kind that made good press in an election year. After a moment of reflection, the chairman, realizing that these proceedings were out of his control and were not going to be wrapped up before the summer session ended, called a recess. Lewis had skillfully put them on the offensive and now, in order to save face, and perhaps enhance his re-election efforts, the chairman had to figure out where to go with the attack on the intelligence community.

MEXICO CITY, MEXICO
1155 HOURS, 3 AUGUST

Anyone who knew Jan Fields and followed her work would have been surprised by Ed Lewis's description of Jan as a simple reporter. Were it not for what some called an illogical love affair with a lieutenant colonel in the U.S. Army, Jan would have been able to name her price in any national network news slot she chose. Even after she had spent three years in self-imposed exile as a simple correspondent, the current situation in Mexico, and her coverage, had once again catapulted her to the front of the pack. It was a feat that pleased her no end and earned her both the respect and envy of a horde of reporters currently flooding Mexico City in search of a story.

It didn't take the correspondents coming into Mexico City long to figure out that, regardless of how good they were, no one could catch Jan Fields. From day one of the crisis, she had dominated the field as if it were an exclusive. While everyone else reported the coup in traditional terms of sinister assassinations and rising military dictatorship, Jan presented to the American public the story behind the story. Opening with a hard-hitting ten-minute WNN special report that laid out in clear and striking terms the story behind the coup, Jan had captured the attention of the American public and never let go. While other reporters found it a struggle to make even a simple phone call, let alone arrange an interview with a government spokesman, Jan floated through the corridors of power like a summer breeze. To her credit was a series of thirteen interviews, one with each member of the ruling council, a visit to each of Mexico's thirty-one states, and numerous tours and trips to every nook and cranny of Mexico City, from the barrios to the presidential palace. Throughout, there was no doubt that Jan was in her element, in charge, and determined to stay there.

Doing so, however, was not as easy as some would think. For every flashy and intriguing interview Jan did, there were three she would rather have ignored. The story she was covering at that moment, the public execution of criminals for crimes against the state, was a prime example.

Most Americans, including Jan, accepted that there had been a need for change in Mexico. The Council of 13 had proven quite astute at mustering support for their cause in the United States through the use of the media and the large Hispanic-American community. Even the most ardent opponent of the new regime in Mexico had to concede that the Council of 13 was justified in seeking a change. It was some of the methods used by the council that caused a major split in the United States between those who pushed for acceptance and support of the new regime and those who advocated action to restore the old government. No issue caused more debate and concern than the use of summary trials, conducted by military tribunals.

From the beginning, the Council of 13 understood that the success or failure of their efforts rested upon their ability to win popular support. The revolution had to be a revolution of the people, not just of a select group of individuals, if it were to have meaning and a chance to succeed. As far as the council was concerned, they were doing nothing more than continuing the Revolution of 1917, bringing it back on course and to the people of Mexico, where it belonged. Molina, Guajardo, Zavala, and the others understood this and believed in it. They had to, in order to justify themselves individually and collectively to the striking down of the government that they had sworn to defend. Convincing the people of Mexico, grown cynical after living under a corrupt and ineffective government for decades, was a different, and more difficult matter. The members of the council, trained in the art of war, naturally sought measures that would be swift, positive, effective, and would touch every citizen. The specter of the failed Soviet coup in August 1991 guided their planning as they worked to ensure that they did not repeat the errors of the Soviet conspirators.

The council approached the problem in a cold and analytical manner. Conditions in Mexico were bad, and they knew those conditions would grow worse, considerably worse, before the council would be able to show a real and widespread improvement for the nation and its people. The council, as the PRI had done many times before, was going to have to ask an impoverished people to make new sacrifices in order to save their future. What the council had to demonstrate to the people, in a way that would be of immediate and direct benefit to them, was that it not only was sincere about saving Mexico, but that it had the ability to actually effect sweeping changes that would reach all citizens. Unable to provide food, money, or jobs to the people, the Council of 13 attacked two of the major things that had contributed to the people's disillusionment with their own government: corruption and unrestrained crime.

The elimination of corruption at all levels throughout the country using swift and uncompromising justice would have many benefits. By administering it at the local level in every state and town, it would be highly visible and provide every citizen in Mexico the feeling that the revolution was a national undertaking, not simply confined to the capital. The use of public executions would also serve as a warning to anyone who entertained the notion of resisting the will of the council. One could turn off the radio or the television or throw away a newspaper. Executions, on the other hand, were an entirely different matter. Most people in Mexico found it difficult to ignore the crack of rifles and the smell of fresh blood on hot summer days as the council sought to stamp out corruption and consolidate power.

Corruption was a way of life in Mexico. Everyone, or so it seemed to the poor, from the highest official to the policeman on the street, had a price. To Americans, a country that took its civil servants for granted, the idea of having to pay a policeman a bribe in order to get him to investigate a theft was alien. But in Mexico, it was necessary. If you wanted a telephone, you paid for the installation plus a little extra to the clerk before he processed your request, and then to the man who actually installed the phone. Not to pay simply meant not getting the service you desired. Requests for phones could easily be lost in mountains of paperwork. Just as easily as the man installing the phone could discover that he was missing a part that could take months to order or was back at the office and he didn't know when he could possibly come back your way. Jan was familiar with the system. That is why she, and all the foreign correspondents, required a "fixer," a Mexican who knew everyone and everything, including the going rates for bribes. The fixer made the necessary arrangements and was paid a set fee to ensure that matters were expedited. Not to have a fixer was akin to wandering through Wonderland without a map.

It was on the elimination of this corruption that the Council of 13 staked its success or failure. Besides, the restoration of law, order, and discipline through direct and immediate action held a natural attraction to military men that could not be resisted.

The system used to execute this policy was a simple one. Any government official suspected of crime or corruption, regardless of rank or position, could be turned in to a representative of the ruling council by any citizen. The representative was normally an Army or Air Force officer, a captain or major who was familiar with the district or town, and was responsible for supervising the operation of government at the local level. Once a citizen had made a complaint, the officer was duty-bound to investigate.

The investigation, by any measure, was quick. An effort was made to corroborate the accuser's statements by questioning other residents or possible victims of the corrupt official. Once the officer was reasonably sure the charges against the accused official had merit, the officer had the official arrested, and convened a summary trial, usually the following day. Evidence from both parties was heard and considered by the officer before he made his judgment and announced his sentence. Execution of the sentence was swift. By far the most popular was death by firing squad, a technique that ensured there would be few appeals, kept the prison population down, provided the victim with a clear and decisive resolution to his accusation, and served as a warning to other real and potential offenders.

To some Americans, educated that rights of the accused took precedence over justice, surrounded by lawyers who used the letter of the law to drag out litigations, and unable to come to grips with capital punishment, the use of military tribunals and public executions seemed barbaric. Even the most ardent supporter of the new regime in Mexico felt the need to publicly condemn the use of what was being called drumhead justice. This issue, more than any other single action by the Council of 13, kept the government of the United States from accepting the council as the legitimate representative of the people of Mexico. This was, after all, an election year in the United States and law and order, a perennial issue, was viewed as the key to success or failure for most officials running for office. Most American politicians found it impossible to run on a platform of law and order while supporting a government that was in the process of meting out drumhead justice. So they opted for the easy solution, public condemnation of the Council of 13. After all, there were few votes to be gained in Mexico.

Although the council had expected the government of the United States to protest the policy of summary trials and executions, the members of the council had hoped that the overall good of the long-term benefits would be seen to justify the means. When it became obvious that they had miscalculated, several members had urged the others to abandon the program as a sop to the government of the United States.

Molina, however, supported by Guajardo, saw no other alternative. The support of the people was critical. On one hand, the program to eliminate corruption had captured the imagination of the people of Mexico and was doing what it had been intended to do, win their support and prepare them for the long struggle to reform Mexico. On the other hand, the same program was preventing the establishment of an accord between the government of the United States and their fledgling government. U.S. acceptance of a legal representative of Mexico, which would be followed by economic assistance and business opportunities, was just as important to their success as the support of the Mexican people. But it was argued that to publicly buckle under pressure from the United States could kill their cause in the eyes of the Mexican people and other Central and South American governments. As Molina had stated in a public address on the subject, ''It is better to be poor, hungry, and master of our own house than to be slaves to the whims of a foreign government.''

While such a statement appealed to the machismo pride of the Mexican people, it did not solve the problem of winning recognition by the government of the United States. To do this, Colonel Molina turned to the media, as he had done before, to place their case directly before the American public. Some members of the council urged Molina to reconsider. Allowing the American press to report on the trials and executions was an unnecessary risk which, if not properly handled, could backfire on them. When challenged to come up with a practical alternative, however, none did, and with great reluctance, they accepted Molina's solution. Molina assigned to Guajardo the task of seeing that the matter be given the priority and emphasis that it deserved.

Guajardo, while stating that he was not the best choice for the job, nevertheless went about doing as he had been directed. It was no surprise to Molina and the other members of the council when Guajardo recommended that Jan Fields be given free rein to study the program and report on it as she saw fit.

At first, Jan Fields had been reluctant to tackle the assignment. There was in the United States, despite the popularity of gratuitous and graphic violence on television, a great reluctance to broadcast real executions. She recognized, however, that this story was not only important, but also would be a challenge to shoot and have broadcast. Besides, the opportunity to have the freedom to do what she wanted was too hard to resist. In the end, the very fact that it was such a great challenge was what had driven her to accept the invitation.

The only real hang-up Jan had concerning the story was the need to work with Colonel Guajardo. Within the crew, Ted referred to Guajardo as Darth Vader, while Joe Bob preferred Attila the Spick. Their new fixer called him "the Dark One." Jan found all those names apt and useful. Despite the fact that he had been instrumental in putting her and her team in the enviable position of being able to go anywhere and talk to anyone, Jan didn't like working with the man. He had even arranged for the new fixer who now traveled with them, a young and very likable man with an excellent command of English. Everyone suspected the fixer was with Mexican Army counterintelligence. His actions, especially in the presence of senior Army officers, reinforced this suspicion. Still, he, like the association with Guajardo, was useful and, in Mexico, very necessary, especially since "the Purification" had begun.

Stories of members of the former government being arrested, tried, and shot the same day were legion. The program, unofficially dubbed "the Purification," was rumored to be widespread and to touch every level of society. There were no news releases that spoke of the Purification and no statistics available that delineated its scope and effectiveness. It was just there, like a shadow, following everyone. And yet Jan and her crew had noted in the streets and markets as they traveled about the country that the people radiated a degree of happiness and energy she had never seen before in Mexico. When the average Mexican discussed the Purification, he did so enthusiastically and with a smile on his face. Only those who had been connected with the former government or who might have been involved in some form of corruption betrayed a sense of apprehension that bordered on fear. On the surface, it appeared as if the Purification was both popular and effective, a theory Jan intended to prove or disprove.

The problems she faced in putting together her report on the Purification were monumental. In a nutshell, Jan Fields had to create a piece that covered an emotional and controversial subject in a very detached and objective manner. Even her own crew was split over the issue. Ted, her shooter, was adamantly against what he called the nationalization of vigilante justice. Joe Bob, on the other hand, thought it was great, recommending that they take copious notes in the hope that they might convince the president of the United States to adopt a similar program. Jan, for her part, kept her own counsel. She had her opinion, but worked to keep it to herself and off camera.

The approach she had taken was typical of Jan Fields. Told she had a free hand to do as she pleased, she took Guajardo at his word. Searching for what appeared to be a typical case, Jan had sat in a district courthouse she had selected from a list of all courts in the Federal District of Mexico and waited for a complaint to be filed against a corrupt official or criminal. She didn't have long to wait.

Within an hour, an old lady dressed in black hobbled into the courthouse and asked to see the captain of the guard. When Jan and her crew followed her into the captain's office, the old lady almost left before filing her complaint. The captain, a friendly man, slightly overweight and with a broad mustache, convinced her to stay. Hesitantly, she told her story.

It seemed a shopkeeper in the market was routinely overcharging his customers. The old lady, tired of this, complained to a policeman. The policeman, feigning concern, followed her to the shop. There, in her presence, he asked the shopkeeper some questions. For his part, the shopkeeper made a great to-do about the high cost of transportation and produce, showing the policeman a ledger that was supposed to be a record of receipts. The policeman, appearing satisfied with the answer, according to the old woman, turned to her and told the woman that all was in order. Not convinced, the old woman left the shop but did not go home. Instead, she crossed the street and watched through the window. What she saw confirmed her suspicions and angered her. The policeman, convinced she was gone, was sharing a drink with the shopkeeper, laughing and talking. The old woman, sure they were laughing at her, waited until they parted, shaking hands, before coming down to the district court.

The captain, taking notes and nodding on occasion, listened to the old woman while he tried to ignore Jan and the camera. When she was finished, the captain thanked the old woman and, aware of the importance this case had assumed because of Jan's presence, immediately began his investigation.

Much of the work was done by the captain himself. In this way, there were fewer hands involved, a safeguard against new opportunities for compromise and corruption. After a few phone calls, the captain was able to find out the name of the officer who had been on duty in the area where the shop was, which station he worked out of, and when he would be available. He also called several markets and stores, asking each of them what it cost them to purchase selected items and what they, in turn, charged their customers for the same items. He checked the prices with an officer in the Ministries of Commerce and Agriculture. Finished with these preliminaries, the captain, followed by Jan and her crew, left the courthouse for the shop where the old woman had been.

En route, the captain explained that much of their success in finding true offenders was the speed and surprise that they achieved. Jan at first took this as a warning that she and her crew were to be as circumspect as possible. The captain, however, went on, stating that often the sudden and unexpected appearance of an Army or Air Force officer asking questions resulted in immediate and profuse cooperation. "The longer an investigation lasts," he pointed out, "the more time the accused has to fabricate a story. If you come in quickly, without warning, and armed with a few facts, often the accused will crumple under the initial impact and confess in the hope of clemency."

From her seat in the van, Jan leaned forward with a mike extended to catch the captain's response. "Do they often get clemency for such cooperation, Captain?"

The captain turned and looked out the front window, considering his answer. Then he turned back to Jan. "In truth, Señorita Fields, even if I knew the statistics which you are interested in, I could not tell you. The number of people involved in these cases, the total number of cases that have been handled, the results of the investigations, and the number and types of sentences carried out are all considered to be state secrets. You see, that is part of the shock value of the Purification. When I walk up to a person under investigation and begin to ask questions, that person has no idea what lies in store for him. He has no way of knowing what his odds are. The number of investigations that have failed to turn anything up is not known or publicized. Only those that result in a conviction are. Therefore, in the accused's mind, the first image that comes to his head is the worst possible result, a firing squad."

Jan looked at the captain. She must have had a perplexed look on her face, for he smiled and continued. "You see, señorita, a man in shock does not think straight. It is difficult to fabricate a credible cover story while the image of a firing squad is dancing before his eyes. Truthful responses are therefore more likely."

She was still pondering the validity of that position when they arrived at the shop. Stepping from the van, the captain adjusted his uniform, took a deep breath, puffed out his chest, stepped off with a purpose, and entered the shop. With the grace of a circus parade, Jan and her crew followed him in, filming as they went.

The shopkeeper was, as the captain predicted, quite befuddled by his sudden appearance. Though Jan was sure he had noticed her and her crew, the shopkeeper's eyes were riveted on the captain. For his part, the captain ignored the shopkeeper. Instead, he went to the shelves, took from his breast pocket a small notebook in which he had a list of selected items and their prices at other shops, and began to search for those items. When he found one, he would compare the price, write down the price on the item in the shop, and continue his search for the next item.

The shopkeeper became quite concerned. Within minutes, and without a word being exchanged, he understood what the captain was doing. His nervousness betrayed itself when he offered to help the captain in any way he could. For his part, the captain ignored the shopkeeper except for an occasional cold, unfeeling glance. By the time the captain had completed his search, the shopkeeper was shaking. Still, the captain did not address him directly, brushing him aside as he went to the counter, thumped his notebook down on the wooden surface, and demanded that someone bring him the shop's ledger and receipts for merchandise. In short order, these were produced by a young girl with dark skin and round eyes that betrayed her apprehension.

Using a soft and friendly tone with the girl, the captain asked her to find the entry that listed the cost to the shopkeeper for each item on his list. As she found each item, she would show him. The captain, in turn, would look at the entry, written in the shopkeeper's own hand, and make a mark next to it in the ledger. When he was satisfied he had seen enough, the captain turned to the shopkeeper and addressed him directly for the first time. "Señor, you will come with me now." With that, a soldier who had been standing just inside the shop door came forward, grabbed the shopkeeper's arm, and escorted him to the waiting van.

The subsequent questioning at the courthouse was quick and enlightening. The shopkeeper, Jan discovered, was not the person the captain was after. He was only a source of information and evidence. This included the names of other shops in that neighborhood involved in jacking up prices above what the government permitted, and the names of policemen who, for a share of the profit, turned a blind eye to the practice. Finished with the shopkeeper, the captain instructed that he be held until further notice. Leaving the courthouse, the captain, Jan, and her crew next went to the police station where the policeman under investigation was stationed.

Like the shopkeeper, when confronted with the sudden appearance of the captain and the information he had, including the shopkeeper's statement, the policeman broke, providing the names of all his fellow officers who took bribes. Included in his list was the name of his superior, a police lieutenant. Finished with the first officer, the captain asked to see another policeman whose name appeared on the new list of offenders.

The second officer, brought into the interrogation room, was as nervous and skittish as the shopkeeper and the first officer had been. Glancing at Jan and her crew, he didn't know what to expect. The captain, on sure ground now, switched tactics. When the officer was seated at a table opposite the Army captain, the captain leaned over the table and, in a very low voice, informed the police officer that he was under investigation for corruption, namely accepting bribes from local shopkeepers. The officer, wide-eyed, began to protest. The captain, however, cut him short by slapping down his notebook and screaming that if he did not cooperate, things would not go well for him.

During the questioning of the second officer, many things became clear to Jan. The Army captain's statement about the effect of surprise and the image of a firing squad before the accused's eyes made sense. She could tell that the policeman was shaken and unable to think clearly. When the captain began his questioning again, the policeman shot out the first answer that came to his mind without pausing to consider what had been asked before or what might be coming up next. In this way, the captain was able to ask several questions about the police lieutenant's involvement without the policeman realizing it.

It wasn't until the captain had finished asking his questions that Jan realized who was the true target of the investigation. The shopkeeper, the two policemen, and a third who would be brought in later were of no interest to the Army captain. He did not want to bother with what he considered the crust of the problem. He wanted a target that was both worthy of his efforts and would serve as an example to more than a single shopkeeper. In due course, the lieutenant was arrested, presented with the evidence, and confessed his guilt.

The trial, held at the courthouse the next morning, with the captain serving as the judge, was quick. The shopkeeper involved, present as a witness, was fined and released. The police officers on the list, also present as witnesses, were demoted one step in grade, fined, and released. The police lieutenant was duly found guilty of encouraging his subordinates to accept bribes, which he shared in, from shopkeepers who were overcharging their customers. He was sentenced to death by firing squad, to be carried out the following day before noon. Without further ado, the court was adjourned and the Army captain prepared to work on his next task.

Before she left, the Army captain asked Jan what she thought of the whole affair. Jan didn't quite know how to respond. She, like the accused, found that the speed of the whole affair had left her little time to organize her thoughts. Her first response, that she thought shooting the police lieutenant was rather severe and cruel, resulted in a perplexed look on the captain's face. "Señorita Fields, to have shot all the policemen and shopkeepers involved would have been cruel. Besides, we do not have enough bullets in all of Mexico to shoot everyone who, under the old regime, was corrupt. No, instead, we slapped the underlings and shot the biggest fish we could catch, the more influential and visible, the better. Now all the shopkeepers and policemen in that precinct, and no doubt the neighboring precincts, know what can happen if they attempt to take advantage of their position. No, señorita, a simple and hard-hitting example of what can happen is best.''

Where the investigation and trial had proceeded with a speed that was staggering, the events leading up to the execution of the sentence had been painfully ponderous. Taken from the courthouse, the police lieutenant was held overnight at a prison within the city. That night, with Jan and her crew watching, he was permitted a visit by his wife and children. In a scene that brought tears even to Joe Bob's eyes, the police lieutenant's wife cried with abandon while his children clung to him, as if this could prevent him from being taken. For his part, the lieutenant stood in stunned silence, overwhelmed by the events of the past two days. Overwhelmed herself with sympathy for the poor wife, Jan chose not to wait for their departure. Instead, she cut the taping and left. The next day, she knew, would be difficult.

She was right. When Jan arrived the next morning, she found the police lieutenant awake. A breakfast served earlier sat next to his bed untouched. Though she suspected that the lieutenant had not slept, he seemed to be fully alert and at peace. In a short interview, he spoke freely, confessing his sins in the same manner that he would to a priest in an effort to absolve himself of his guilt, admitting that it had been wrong for him to encourage his subordinates to neglect their duties and accept bribes. To ignore shopkeepers and tradesmen who exploited the poor, he said, was evil and should be stopped. Alas, he lamented, he was but a weak mortal who, raised in a corrupt system, had done what everyone else was doing. When Jan asked if he thought that the sentence he had received was too harsh, he looked at her for a moment before answering. "This is, señorita, a revolution, or more correctly, a continuation of that great revolution fought by our grandfathers that has made Mexico the great country that it is today. I am guilty of betraying that revolution and I am prepared to pay the price, like a man, for my sins against the people."

Though Jan suspected that the lieutenant had been coached before she had arrived, there was no denying that he meant what he said when he told her that he would face his death like a man. In the courtyard there were four groups of people. In the center stood a firing squad. Because the accused was a police officer, the firing squad was made up of ten policemen, all from different precincts. The officer in charge was also a policeman, a lieutenant, just like the accused. The significance of all this did not escape Joe Bob, who suspected that Colonel Guajardo had arranged it. The second group was a cluster of police officers of assorted ranks. They were there to witness the execution and learn. The third group was private citizens, including the old woman who had brought the original charges against the shopkeeper, and the shopkeeper himself, to watch justice dispensed. The final group was Jan and her crew. Though Ted preferred to shoot with the camera on his shoulder, he had it mounted on a tripod that morning. Though it would limit his ability to move around, he knew the extra support was necessary, since he didn't like guns and had a tendency to jump every time he heard one fired.

When all was set, the police lieutenant to be executed, accompanied by a priest, was led to a spot in front of a wall opposite the firing squad. Jan watched the preliminaries without comment as Joe Bob adjusted his equipment so that the tape would pick up every word. There was, after all, nothing to be said at this point. Everything was self-explanatory, readily evident.

As in any B movie, the priest said a final prayer, the officer in charge read the charges out loud, and the accused manfully refused a blindfold. Only this wasn't a B movie. Jan kept telling herself that. This, she knew, was real. The man standing less than fifty feet from her was about to die and there was nothing that she could do to stop it. All she could do was watch, like everyone else in the courtyard. That was, after all, her job, to watch and report what she saw. She didn't make news, she didn't change it. She only watched events in the making. This, she repeated to herself, over and over, was just another event. No different than a tornado, or a fire, or any other story. It was just a story.

Still, as the officer in charge of the firing squad began to issue his orders, Jan felt light-headed. In response to the officer's crisp, clear, and exaggerated orders, the firing squad brought their rifles to bear and took aim. At the last moment, before the crack of the rifles announced that the sentence had been carried out, Jan turned away and hung her head. This was not just a story. And she knew it.

From a small room overlooking the courtyard, Colonel Guajardo watched the execution below. He observed Jan Fields intently as he listened to the commands. When she turned just before the command to fire was given, Guajardo smiled. Before the first trigger was pulled, Guajardo knew that the firing squad had hit its mark. Once again, through a happy combination of luck and subtle manipulation, he had managed to turn a potentially bad situation into a favorable result. Though he didn't know what she would say, Guajardo counted on Jan's story to do what the Council of 13 couldn't do on its own.

Looking up at the clear blue sky, he ignored the report of the rifles. Without turning to his adjutant, he mused, "It is going to be a beautiful day today. Far too beautiful to spend in the city."

Understanding his colonel's meaning, the adjutant asked, "What shall it be, sir, flying or riding?"

"Riding, I think." Slapping his right hand on his chest, Guajardo looked over to his adjutant. With a smile on his face, he grabbed the adjutant's arm and began to guide him down the corridor. "Come, we will make short work of the paper monsters that threaten to consume us and then we will each find a fine horse that demands to be ridden hard."

WEBB COUNTY, TEXAS
1230 HOURS, 3 AUGUST

In his fifteen years as a member of the border patrol, Ken Tinsworthy had never known a man who could get lost more than his best friend, Jay Stevenson, could. Stevenson, himself a veteran of fourteen years with the border patrol, never had mastered the fine art of map reading. For this reason, the duty roster was always arranged so that Stevenson was paired with someone who could read a map or who knew the area.

The current problems in Mexico, however, had screwed up the duty roster, along with everything else for the men working out of the Laredo office. Though the news reports continued to tell of the popularity of the new Mexican government, the increased flow of Mexicans north, into the United States, told Tinsworthy and his fellow border patrolmen that not everyone in Mexico agreed with that assessment. The big difference with many of the Mexicans coming north was that they were coming from a better class of people than in the past. Former government officials, policemen, merchants, lawyers, and even an occasional priest made up the bulk of the new wave headed north. Increased movement of illegal immigrants north meant increased patrols, which, in turn, meant longer hours and the need to put new and partially trained men into the field as soon as possible. Everyone with over ten years service was paired off with a new man. In this way, the system of putting Stevenson with a proficient map reader got screwed up. Too proud to complain, Stevenson had gone out the night before with the new man, named Mikelsen, driving while Stevenson tried to find the easiest and most obvious route to their checkpoints.

When Tinsworthy and the rest of the day shift had been greeted at 7:30 that morning with the news that Stevenson and the new man had still not checked in, no one was surprised. Someone recommended that before anyone got excited, they check with the Louisiana, Arkansas, and Oklahoma highway patrols. They were even betting money on why Stevenson wasn't answering the radio. Half felt he was too embarrassed. The rest claimed that he was too far out of range. Still, when nothing was heard from Stevenson and his partner by nine o'clock in the morning, their supervisor had ordered all patrols to begin to converge on the area where Stevenson and Mikelsen should have been.

Tinsworthy was in the process of checking the high ground overlooking the Rio Grande when his partner spotted a light green and white Border Patrol four-by-four sitting on a knoll in the distance. Since they were the only ones in that area, they knew it had to be Stevenson's. Turning off the trail, Tinsworthy headed straight for the stationary vehicle while the new man tried unsuccessfully to raise Stevenson on the radio.

At a distance of one hundred meters, Tinsworthy suddenly slowed down. The new man looked at Tinsworthy, then at Stevenson's vehicle, then at Tinsworthy again. Tinsworthy, both hands on the wheel, was staring intently at the other vehicle. The new man, not understanding why they had stopped, tried to figure out what Tinsworthy was staring at. "What's the matter?"

"Somethin's not right here." Stopping his vehicle fifty meters short of the stationary four-by-four, Tinsworthy took his hands off the wheel, unsnapped the strap of his holster with his right hand. He opened the door with his left and began to get out, all the while watching the vehicle on the knoll. "You stay here and cover me."

The new man, spooked, looked back at the vehicle and the knoll, then to Tinsworthy. "Cover you? Cover you from what?"

Tinsworthy had no time to explain. How could you explain a feeling to a new man? How could you tell him that the cold chill down your back told you something was terribly wrong? Instead, he just repeated his instructions, never once taking his eyes off of the knoll. "You just do as I tell you. Cover me and be ready to call in for help." Without waiting for a response, Tinsworthy began to inch his way up the knoll.

Despite the heat, Tinsworthy felt as if a cold hand had been placed on his back. With his right hand on the butt of his pistol, he slowly moved forward. Though he continued to face the stationary vehicle on the knoll, his eyes scanned to the left and right, watching for movement. Halfway up the knoll, he noticed that there was someone in the driver's seat, his head bare and resting on the steering wheel as if he were asleep. Pausing, Tinsworthy took a long look at the vehicle's driver, then looked about, turning until he could see his own vehicle and partner behind him. The new man, standing behind the passenger door of their vehicle, had the window down and the shotgun resting on the door. Tightening his grasp on his own pistol, Tinsworthy continued to advance.

At a distance of ten meters, he stopped when he saw a jagged line of bullet holes in the door. Drawing his revolver, he closed on the vehicle, holding his pistol with both hands pointed up and over his right shoulder. He heard the sound of the flies before he saw them buzzing about and landing on the head of the man in the driver's seat. When he reached the vehicle, he took a quick glance inside, then around the entire area. Seeing nothing that looked suspicious, Tinsworthy moved closer to examine the body draped over the steering wheel. It was Mikelsen. Tinsworthy reached into the cab, feeling Mikelsen's neck for a pulse with his left hand while still keeping his pistol at the ready. Though the stench of blood exposed to the summer heat for hours and of human waste released when the bowel muscles lost tension told Tinsworthy that Mikelsen was dead, he still felt for a pulse. As he did so, he wondered why there appeared to be no blood, though he could smell it. It wasn't until he finished trying to find a pulse and walked around to the passenger side that he saw it.

The passenger's door was open. Seeing that the radio was on, Tinsworthy reached in to grab the hand mike. As he did so, he examined

Mikelsen's body from that side. At his feet, down on the floor, Mikelsen's cowboy boots were awash in his own blood. The seals of the door and the hump where the transmission was had caught Mikelsen's blood as he had bled to death.

Drawing in a deep breath, Tinsworthy took the hand mike and called the base station, requesting backup and an ambulance. The dispatcher, taken aback by Tinsworthy's request, paused before putting their supervisor on. In a solemn voice, the supervisor asked what Tinsworthy had.

"Not good, boss. Mikelsen's dead. Looks like they were hit with automatic fire while they were sitting on a knoll watching the river. I haven't found Stevenson yet. The passenger door was open and there's no bloodstains on his side of their vehicle. I'm going to go find him."

"Negative, not until you get some backup. Stay with your partner. We have the chopper en route now."

"Can't do that, boss. Jay might need my help."

"Ken, I repeat, stay where you are. Do you hear me?"

Tinsworthy didn't answer. Dropping the hand mike on the seat, he turned and began to search for his friend. When he found him after what seemed like an eternity, he wished he had listened to his supervisor.

In a gully, down by the riverbank, Ken Tinsworthy found Jay Stevenson's body. The first thing he heard was the snarling of two wild dogs fighting. Drawn to the commotion, he saw the two dogs alternating between chewing on Jay's body and snarling at each other. Without thinking, Stevenson lowered his gun and fired twice, dropping one of the dogs, scaring off the second, and causing his partner, who had lost sight of him, to panic and report on the radio that they were under fire.

Moving down into the gully, Tinsworthy looked down at his friend's corpse. He didn't need to read the name plate to recognize that the body at his feet belonged to his best friend. The sight of Jay Stevenson, his feet and hands bound and his head blown off at point-blank range, was too much for Tinsworthy. Dropping to his knees, Ken Tinsworthy looked up at the clear blue sky and began to cry for his friend. As he cried, he first asked God why he had let such a terrible thing happen. Then he began swearing to revenge his friend's death, crying out loud through his tears, "God help the fucking spick that killed Jay. God help him."

9

The instruments of battle are valuable only if one knows how to use them.

—Ardant du Picq

FORT HOOD, TEXAS
0545 HOURS, 8 AUGUST

Watching Second Lieutenant Kozak as she conducted her final precombat inspection of the 2nd Squad, Sergeant First Class Rivera wondered what it was with infantry second lieutenants. Perhaps, he thought, Fort Benning makes them that way. It had to be. After being a platoon sergeant with the same platoon for twenty-six months, he was in the process of breaking in his third brand-new, fresh-from-Fort Benning platoon leader. And each and every one came into the platoon full of piss and vinegar, ready to set the world on fire, and hell-bent for leather to lead a bayonet charge.

Even his new lieutenant, a woman for Christ's sakes, was just as gung ho, and as intolerant of anyone who wasn't, as his first two lieutenants had been. It wasn't until they became captains, or so it seemed, that they discovered that just maybe sergeants weren't so dumb after all. Rivera wondered if his counterparts in the field artillery and tank corps had the same problems. Probably did, he thought. A lieutenant, after all, was a lieutenant, was a lieutenant, was a lieutenant. Maybe the first sergeant was right. He always told his platoon sergeants to save their breath when dealing with new officers. Instead, he told them, they should just take their new lieutenants out into the boonies and beat them senseless with a two-by-four for a half hour before starting their training. That was the only way, the first sergeant contended, that you could, A, get rid of some of the foolish stuff they filled their heads with at Benning, and, B, be reasonably sure you had their attention.

That day's operation was a prime example. The platoon's mission was to establish an outpost forward of the company's battle position. The task, as it was explained by the company commander, was rather simple. One squad was to move forward where it could observe the main avenue of approach into the company's engagement zone. All Wittworth wanted was a few minutes warning so that he could coordinate the direct fires of the company with the indirect fires of the artillery.

Lieutenant Kozak, however, felt that it would be better if an antiarmor ambush was established in addition to the outpost. Rivera pointed out that the purpose of the outpost was to provide security and early warning to the company, nothing more. The lieutenant, however, believed that they could do that just as easily by establishing an ambush. An ambush, she pointed out, would begin the process of attrition and perhaps confuse the enemy as to where the company's main positions actually were. Rivera made an effort to point out that they stood just as good a chance of becoming confused as the enemy. It didn't take long, however, before he realized that he was fighting a losing battle. Watching her eyes and listening to her tone of voice as she explained her reasoning in great detail, Rivera decided that perhaps it was best to let the lieutenant have her way. Sometimes, he knew, it was better to leave lieutenants to discover the grim facts of life themselves. Perhaps she just might pull it off, though he doubted it. She was, after all, here to learn, and Rivera knew that sometimes the best lessons in life came from the biggest screwups.

If Rivera's goal was to let her learn the hard way, Kozak did everything she could to help him. The plan she had come up with the previous night placed one squad, armed with a single Dragon antitank guided missile, half a dozen antitank mines, and four light antitank rocket launchers, on the forward slope of a hill. The squad's M-2 Bradley was concealed in a hide position on the reverse side of the hill. Not only did it not have any field of fire, it was over a kilometer away from where the dismounted members of the squad would be waiting in ambush. As tactfully as possible, Rivera pointed out that the dismounts would never be able to make it back up the hill to their Bradley. The enemy force, he pointed out, would overrun the dismounts, pound them with artillery, or simply deploy and gun them down when the dismounts tried to move.

Again, Kozak explained that dismounted infantry, taking advantage of the confusion caused by the ambush, would never be seen by the enemy. With a bland expression, achieved through years of practice, Rivera gave a dry "Yes, ma'am" and went about organizing the platoon's battle position while the lieutenant prepared her operations order. As he did so, he wondered where he could find a two-by-four at that hour of the night.

What never occurred to Rivera as he ambled away was that, for the first time, he hadn't thought of Kozak as a woman first. Instead, he had subconsciously lumped her into the same category as every other infantry second lieutenant he had ever known, and had treated her accordingly. Though not a red-banner day for women's rights, it was, nevertheless, a necessary step if the platoon was to become an effective unit, and not just a showpiece.

From the front seat of Scott Dixon's Humvee, Captain Cerro watched Second Lieutenant Kozak prepare her antiarmor ambush. While the squad setting up the antiarmor ambush might have been able to get away with occupying its positions after dawn, the movement of their platoon leader from one place to another in an effort to check weapons and fields of fire compromised the entire ambush site. Even without binoculars, at two hundred meters Cerro could see people moving and bushes shaking. He had no doubt that the enemy scout track two hundred meters further up the road, hidden in a shallow arroyo and covered with camouflage nets, saw everything.

As Cerro waited for the inevitable, Specialist Eddie Jefferson, nick-named Fast Eddie, sat next to Cerro, intently studying Cerro's map and the notes written on the margin of the map case that detailed Kozak's plan. Bored, Cerro turned to Fast Eddie. "What's so interesting?"

Eddie furrowed his brow in confusion, answering Cerro without look-ing away from the map. "This here plan, sir. It don't make any sense at all." Draping the map across the Humvee's steering wheel, Eddie pointed to the blue symbol on the map that indicated where Kozak had placed the antiarmor ambush. "Look. That dumb bitch puts her squad here, on the wrong side of the hill," running his finger from the squad symbol to a blue symbol for a Bradley, "and the Bradley all the way over here, on the other side of the hill. No way they'll make it back."

Wincing, Cerro reminded Fast Eddie that he was talking about a lieu-tenant and "bitch" was not quite appropriate terminology. Eddie looked over to Cerro. "Oh, sorry, Cap'n." Then, turning his attention back to the map, he continued. "And on top of that, that dumb lieutenant puts the Bradley in a hole where it can't use its sights or shoot."

Shaking his head, Cerro gave up. Eddie Jefferson appeared to be a good troop, intelligent and motivated. There was no need to hassle him. After all, Kozak was being a bit dumb and it showed. Christ, Cerro thought, maybe he should have sent Eddie out there to set up the outpost. He couldn't have done any worse than Kozak was doing.

As they continued to watch, it occurred to Cerro that if Eddie, sitting here with a map, could figure out the lousy spot the squad was in, the men in the squad had to know it. If no one else, at least the platoon sergeant and squad leader must have realized that the plan wouldn't work the way Kozak had briefed it. If that were true, Cerro wondered if the NCOs in the platoon had pointed it out to their lieutenant and been overridden by an eager beaver LT with a better idea, or if they had kept their own counsel and were letting Kozak make a fool out of herself. Either way, he was not happy with what he saw, although he could understand it if Kozak had overridden the NCOs. As a young, hard-charging airborne infantry lieutenant, Cerro had once thought that he could conquer the world single-handed. It took a few years and a war to convince him that he was outnumbered and needed, on occasion, a little help. His battalion commander had referred to that process as becoming a mature leader. His first sergeant had called it pounding some sense into Cerro's thick head.

With nothing better to do, Cerro asked Eddie how he would have set up the outpost. They were in the middle of this discussion when another Humvee, flying the orange flag of a fire marker team, rolled up to where Kozak's dismounted squad was located. The driver, leaving the road, slowly began to drive along the tree line where the antiarmor ambush was set up. The passenger in the fire marker Humvee, holding a box of artillery simulators in his lap, took one simulator at a time, held it at arm's length, pulled the white cap and string that activated the simulator with a quick jerk, and threw it into the tree line as they went by. After dropping half a dozen simulators that were meant to represent three volleys fired by a 155mm artillery battery, the Humvee drove away, leaving Kozak's squad in the process of putting on their gas masks.

The squad had just finished that task and were settling back down when a line of four enemy Bradley fighting vehicles, with 25mm cannon and 7.62mm machine guns firing blanks, burst out of the tree line across the narrow valley from Kozak's squad and began to advance against the squad's position. Though the fire was inaccurate, the speed and violence, not to mention the surprise, unnerved Kozak, who stood up and ordered her squad to withdraw.

There was, however, little chance of the squad making it. A healthy infantryman, with equipment, can run one kilometer in five minutes, or at best four and a half. A Bradley, moving at twenty miles an hour, can cover the same distance in less than two. It was, as Eddie had predicted, no contest. Nor was the confrontation between the four attacking Bradleys and the squad's lone vehicle. Because the squad's Bradley was on the other side of the hill, the first indication that the crew had that they were under attack was the flashing of their kill light. Listening to both A Company's radio net and that of Kozak's platoon as he watched from the G3's Humvee, Cerro heard no one report the engagement. As far as Captain Wittworth, Kozak's company commander, was concerned, at that moment, everything was in order. Because of Kozak's failure and the swift, well-coordinated attack by the enemy on her squad, Wittworth wouldn't get the two-minute warning he had been counting on.

"How long that take, Cap'n?"

Cerro looked at his watch, then at Kozak's squad as they moved out of their positions, into the open, and fumbled about. "Three minutes, four if you count the artillery."

Eddie let out a sigh. "Geez, ain't that some shit. Four minutes to fill ten body bags. Hope she learned somethin'."

"Oh, I'm sure she did. But, just to make sure, Eddie, let's mosey on over there and have a talk with the young lieutenant while her company gets overrun."

Grinning, Eddie fired up the Humvee and drove over where Kozak's squad was rallying. As he did so, Eddie took great care to watch for the rest of the attacking enemy company as it rolled south down the road in an effort to catch up with its four lead Bradleys that had overrun Kozak's squad. The squad was still getting out of their masks, looking for a green key to turn off the buzzer on the MILES belts that had been activated when lasers simulating enemy gunfire had hit them, and accounting for weapons and gear, when Cerro arrived.

Already angered and upset by the total failure of her squad's ambush, Lieutenant Kozak became depressed when she saw that the bumper number of the approaching Humvee identified it as the division G3's vehicle. The appearance of a captain, and not the G3 himself, did nothing to improve her state of mind. The captain, no doubt, would tell the G3, who in turn would tell the division commander, who in turn would tell the corps commander, etc., etc., etc. Still, there was nowhere to hide and no escaping the inevitable. It had been her plan and now she would take the beating.

Going up to the Humvee after it stopped, Kozak saluted and reported to the captain in the passenger seat even before he had a chance to get out. The captain, returning her salute with a casual wave of his hand, reached over to retrieve his map from his driver and climbed out without a word. Moving around to the front of the Humvee, he laid his map out on the hood, looked at it for a moment, then turned to Kozak. As he did so, she recognized him as the same captain that she had bumped into on her first day at Fort Hood. Remembering the small kindness he had shown her when she had lost a clip off of one of her badges, she was about to say something about that, but then decided not to. That had been, she realized, another time and place. Right now, under the circumstances, it didn't seem like a good idea to start with idle chatter.

When the captain was ready, Kozak realized her assessment of the situation, this time, had been on the mark. Captain Cerro, his eyes shaded by the brim of his helmet, stared down at her. "Lieutenant Kozak, what was your mission?"

Assuming a relaxed position of parade rest, she looked up at Cerro's hidden eyes. "To establish an outpost with one squad, sir."

"What, Lieutenant, was the purpose of that outpost?"

"To provide early warning to the company of the enemy attack."

"And did you accomplish that mission, Lieutenant?"

Kozak hesitated before answering. Maybe she did. Perhaps the Bradley had reported in. Or maybe the company had heard the engagement. She didn't know and told Cerro that she wasn't sure, attempting to explain that maybe the squad's Bradley had escaped and reported, or had reported before it had been destroyed.

Cerro, however, didn't let her finish. "Why don't you know, Lieutenant?"

"Well, I am temporarily out of contact with my platoon."

Placing his hands on his hips, Cerro leaned over toward Kozak, the brim of his helmet almost touching hers. His voice, when he answered, was harsh and cold. "Temporary my ass, Lieutenant. You're permanently out of contact with your platoon. Your ability to move, shoot, and communicate was degraded one hundred percent for eternity. That's because you're dead, remember? Dead, D-E-A-D, dead. And do you know why you're dead, Lieutenant?"

Taken aback by Cerro's aggressive stance, Kozak was about to take a step back, but changed her mind. Instead, she held her ground, allowing the brim of her helmet to make contact with the brim of Cerro's. "Yes sir. We screwed up."

"Correction, Lieutenant, you screwed up. Again, what was your mission?"

As Kozak pondered Cerro's last repetitive question, she fought back the urge to move back and away from him. She could feel his breath on her face and the unrelenting pressure of his helmet touching hers. His stance was, she felt, quite intimidating. No doubt, she thought, it was meant to be. For a moment, she allowed her eyes to drop down and look at the narrow space of ground that separated the toes of her size-five-and-a-half narrow combat boots from his eleven wide jungle boots. She hadn't been treated like this since she was a plebe at West Point.

Then, suddenly, it dawned upon her what Cerro was driving at. Looking Cerro in the eye, Kozak regained her composure. "Our mission was to provide the company with an early warning so they would be ready when the enemy came. By concentrating on the antiarmor ambush, and not putting the Bradley where it could use its sights to see the enemy and its radio to report, I set us up for failure."

After a pause, Kozak noticed a slight softening in Cerro's expression. Though she wouldn't call it a smile, it was close enough. Standing upright, and folding his arms across his chest, Cerro, and Kozak in turn, relaxed. "Bingo, Lieutenant. You win your first brass ring. Your commander, no doubt, expects you to take the initiative. And, if he's anything like me, doesn't explain everything, including his reasons for giving certain orders, to his people every time. What that means, is that you are going to have to learn when you can use your initiative, and when you need to follow his orders to the letter. I'm here to tell you, learning that isn't easy. Some people never do. Hopefully, you will. Understand?"

Kozak nodded. "Yes sir, understood."

"And another thing, Lieutenant, you need to use your NCOs." Turning to where Kozak's squad was assembling, Cerro waved his hand. "Your platoon sergeant never should have let this happen. If he warned you and you ignored him, that's an ah shit on you. If he didn't, then he isn't doing his job and you need to talk to him. Bottom line, Lieutenant, is that while you are getting paid to think, you don't have a monopoly on it and, more important, you don't have the experience yet. Your NCOs do. Use 'em. Clear?"

Again, Kozak nodded. "Yes, sir, clear. It's just that, well, this was my first time out and, well, I wanted to make an impression. You understand, don't you?"

For the first time, Cerro laughed. "Yeah, I understand. And you succeeded. You've made one hell of an impression on this squad, the rest of your platoon, and no doubt, your company commander. You better hope he has a short memory or a forgiving streak a mile wide."

Kozak winced. She was not looking forward to explaining herself to Captain Wittworth. Cerro, seeing her squirm, put his hand on her shoulder. "Listen, I know exactly what you did and why you did it. Every new second lieutenant that's worth a damn comes out of Benning hell-bent for leather, ready to make his mark on the world. If he's a natural, and very lucky, he pulls it off. If he's like the rest of us, he makes a lot of mistakes and gets beat up often before he learns his trade." Turning his head toward the squad, Cerro pointed. "Don't ever forget, Lieutenant, that the lives of those soldiers depend on you and your decisions. So don't let your ego, pride, and ambitions override your common sense and training." He looked back at her, and their eyes met. "Do what's right, and what you're told, and you'll do all right. Got it?"

For the first time, Kozak smiled. Stepping back, she saluted Cerro. "Yes, sir. Got it. Thank you, sir, I appreciate it."

Again, with a casual wave of his hand, Cerro returned her salute. "No problem, LT. That's what I get paid for. Carry on."

GRAND CAYMAN ISLAND IN THE CARIBBEAN
0740 HOURS (CENTRAL TIME), 8 AUGUST

Slowly walking along the beach, with his right hand resting on the smooth and narrow hips of his latest lover, Alamán found it difficult to believe his good fortune. Everything, even the reactions of the American public and their government to the first small raids along the border, was playing into his hands.

Leaving the chore of creating a viable force from the remnants of his personal bodyguard that had survived the Mexican Army raid at Chinampas to Delapos, Alamán had left Mexico, seeking a secure base from which he could mobilize his vast resources, talents, and network to achieve his goal of returning to Mexico. Though his reputation was tarnished as a result of his failure to foresee the military coup, there were many who still needed Alamán's talents and connections. Some even shared his dream of a new Mexico where their opportunities to conduct their illegal trades would be greater, not less, than before the military coup of June 29. It was, therefore, not difficult to find a place that suited his needs and tastes. At the home of an associate on Grand Cayman Island in the Caribbean, Alamán had found an ideal site where he could work from.

Building upon the contacts he had had in the United States before the revolution, Alamán quickly found new contacts, including people within the United States Border Patrol, who could provide the information that Delapos and his team leaders needed. With information on everything, ranging from schedules and patrol routes to weapons used and personalities involved, Alamán's tiny army hoped to create an effect all out of proportion to its size. With that in hand, and anticipating future needs, Alamán was currently working on establishing contacts in the Texas

National Guard, a feat that was proving more difficult than he had anticipated. Still, all in all, Alamán was more than happy with how things were progressing.

Delapos, assisted by Childress and Lefleur, had recruited, armed, and organized six teams as a start at the abandoned airfield along the Rio Salado. By using the collective knowledge and experience of those mercenaries, coupled with Alamán's money, connections, and unique organizational talents, they would translate Alamán's strategy for the reestablishment of his business in Mexico into action.

That strategy was as simple in concept as it was complex to execute. The key elements were the fear among the leaders of Mexico of America intervening in Mexico's internal affairs, and the American habit of doing so. The fear was both natural and historical. Historically, it was the end result of a collision in 1836 between a growing United States, eager to fulfill its manifest destiny, and newly independent Mexico. It had become an article of faith for years that the Anglo-Saxon population had achieved moral ascendancy over their poor, misguided southern brothers with the defeat of the Mexican Army by Sam Houston and the Army of the Republic of Texas on the banks of the San Jacinto River on April 21, 1836. Since that war, Americans had seldom hesitated to intervene in Mexico whenever they felt that it was to their advantage. In addition to a divergence of national goals and prosperity, underpinning this unhappy history was an assumption of racial superiority on the part of most *norteamericanos* in their dealings with Latinos.

From the first hours of the coup by the Council of 13, the resurrection of these fears and feelings had been fueled by both the Mexican and American media. Although the council tried to be sensitive to American concerns, it had many hard choices to make and few good solutions. Inevitably, it had to take actions that were not understood, or were frowned upon, by the United States. The American media naturally picked up on this friction, which was exacerbated by the fact that in the United States it was an election year with few issues of importance to separate the candidates. Politicians in the United States, regardless of their party affiliation or position, were being hammered from both the left and right. Conservatives pushed liberal politicians to ensure that American business interests in Mexico and the territorial integrity of the United States were protected. The vision of revolution spreading north through the huge Hispanic-American population of the Southwest sent shivers down the back of every self-proclaimed patriot. From the left, demands that the conservative politicians take action to halt civil rights violations resulted in daily demonstrations in both Washington and in state capitals throughout the Southwest. What exactly needed to be done to protect the United States and the poor oppressed people of Mexico laboring under a military regime was a matter of great and heated debate. Plans ranged from recognition of the current regime to direct and immediate intervention. It was, as Alamán pointed out, as if a boat were sinking and no one could decide what to do to stop it. As the parties argued, Alamán planned to use his tiny army to set the boat on fire.

With the warm waves of the ocean washing over their feet as they slowly walked along the shoreline, Alamán explained to his lover, called Anna, how he would make the military buffoons in Mexico City pay for what they had done to him. "At this minute, my love, I have forty men spread out along the border of Mexico and the United States, men with no other purpose in life than to kill Americans and spread terror along the border. Most of these mercenaries, some of whom are former leftist guerrillas, are all experts in antiterrorist operations or have been terrorists themselves. None of them, to a man, has a single moral fiber in his body. They are mine, and will soon create the havoc that will sweep me back to my beloved Mexico."

For her part, Anna merely listened as he spoke of his plans and the actions of his tiny mercenary army. She was content to allow Alamán to pamper her in ways she had never been pampered before while she indulged both his sexual appetite and his need to brag, both of which seemed insatiable. With only a slight nod of her head, Anna listened as they walked and Alamán droned on. "Assigned a sector along either the Texas or New Mexico border, each team, with six to eight men, is allowed to develop its own techniques, schedule, and operations. The only restrictions I have placed on them is their choice of weaponry, the vehicles they use, and almost total segregation between the teams. Weapons, of all caliber and type, are limited to what is currently issued to the Mexican Army. Likewise, the vehicles used by the teams must be either the same type as used by the Mexican Army or equipped with tires used on Mexican Army vehicles. Communication, either by radio or telephone, is forbidden. Even in extreme emergencies, the teams are not permitted to contact Delapos, whom I hold responsible for supervising the actual operations. Instead, Delapos comes to me for my orders and, in turn, travels from one team to the next, reviewing their past actions and approving the team leaders' plans and issuing new instructions, when necessary. In this way, only I and Delapos know where everyone is and what is actually happening along the border."

Pausing, Alamán looked out at the rising sun. "This, my love, is beautiful. But not as beautiful as in Mexico. You will see."

Taking her cue, Anna bent down, kissing him softly on his lips, then along the side of his neck. Running her hands along his naked side, Anna lowered herself to her knees, lightly kissing his chest. When her hands reached his waist, Anna inserted her fingers between the waistband of Alamán's swim trunks and his body. Catching the waistband with her thumbs, she lowered the trunks to Alamán's knees. All the while, Alamán continued to stare out over the ocean as he took Anna's head and gently guided her to him. "You will see, my love. I promise you."

MAVERICK COUNTY, TEXAS
0745 HOURS, 8 AUGUST

Peeking out through the narrow gap between the edge of the camouflage net and the ground, Childress made a quick scan of the horizon. Seeing no motion, he turned his attention to the road that ran at an angle to their position, some one hundred meters away. Starting at the small culvert that concealed a forty-pound cratering charge, Childress ran his eyes along the length of dirt road until it disappeared over the horizon, some five kilometers in the distance. Nothing would be able to come and go along the road without his men being able to see it.

It had taken Childress over two days to find this spot, a spot which, for his purposes, was ideal. The gully where he and two other men, manning a .30-caliber M-1919 machine gun, lay hidden, provided both cover and concealment from the road. It also offered them an excellent covered route of retreat back to their vehicles, hidden farther down the gully. A branch of the same gully, off to their right, provided the same features to the other three men of Childress's team. In this way, if something went wrong with the ambush, both sections of his team would be able to make it back to their vehicles secure in the knowledge that their opponent would be unable to see them, let alone put effective fire on them as they did so. This last item was all-important to the six men protected from the searing morning sun by the tan and brown nets. They were, after all, doing this for the money. Neither glory, nor honor, nor decorations motivated them. A medal presented to a next of kin posthumously had no meaning. The only bottom line that mattered was a healthy bank account and an equally healthy body with which to enjoy it. Escape routes, both primary and alternate, were therefore a critical element of every plan for Childress and the other team leaders of Señor Alamán's private army.

To achieve the effect Alamán desired, every raid had to be as bloody and terrible as it was precise and swift. Lefleur, who had the honor of striking first, had set the tone. To create the desired effect, nothing had been left to chance. Binding one of the border patrol officers and shooting him execution-style had been intended both to infuriate and to horrify those who found him, and the media that reported the incident. The wheel tracks, going into and out of the point where Lefleur had forded the Rio Grande, had been found and plaster casts dutifully made. Also found and identified by the highly trained FBI forensic experts had been a pile of .30-caliber ammunition, an unusual caliber used by few modern machine guns. So as not to make the setup too obvious, Lefleur left no other traces. As it was, the 5.56mm slugs found in the skull of the executed border patrolman and the .30-caliber slugs found in his partner were enough to get the FBI onto the trail Alamán was baiting.

Childress, for his part, preferred to do things in a big way. Having worked with explosives, he liked the effect a little well-placed C-4 could achieve in short order. Besides, he felt Lefleur's approach was far too subtle. While anyone could obtain 5.56mm and .30-caliber ammunition, few people could legally buy a standard military cratering charge. The significance of this would alert even the dullest investigator.

In case, however, this failed to put those coming behind them on the right trail, Childress had added a twist that was unpopular. The idea of making a hit in broad daylight had at first been greeted with horror by his men. The idea of tromping about in the open desert in broad daylight seemed, on the surface, suicidal. Childress had explained, however, that Americans found it difficult to maintain a high state of vigilance around the clock. There was, he noted, a tendency to be on guard at night, and then, when the sun came up, to relax. "The enemy," he had pointed out, "always attacks at dawn in the movies." Besides, he had continued, smugglers, pushing both drugs and illegal aliens across the border, normally operated at night, avoided contact, and fought only when cornered. They didn't lie in ambush and blow up roads in the middle of the day. Only well-trained soldiers did that.

A slap on the shoulder and a finger pointed to the west alerted Childress to the approach of the border patrol. As predicted, there were two jeeps headed their way. Both had their canvas tops off, but their windshields up. Childress thought this was a mistake. Had he been in charge of that patrol, he would have ordered the windshields down to provide a better view and to prevent flying glass in the event of a hit.

The two vehicles, traveling fifty meters apart, each contained two border patrolmen. Even from this distance, Childress could see that the passenger of each vehicle held a shotgun across his lap. Another bad call, he thought. Shotguns were great for coyotes and close-in work. Against automatic weapons at long range, they were useless. Childress faced the man to his side. "These people aren't taking this seriously yet."

Tightening his grip on the machine gun's handle as he tracked the second vehicle, the man shrugged. "That, my friend, is fine by me."

Further conversation was cut off by the detonation of the cratering charge. As the front tire of the lead jeep reached the culvert, one of Childress's men in the other gully twisted the red handle of the blasting machine. The result achieved bordered on perfection. The lead jeep was lifted off the road and flipped end over end amid a growing pillar of black smoke and brown dirt. The driver of the second jeep panicked, hitting his brakes and cutting the steering wheel. The sudden locking of the brakes and the turn, coupled with the jeep's own forward momentum, caused the second jeep to turn over as the machine gunner next to Childress opened up with a long burst that racked the jeep as it rolled over and over down the road toward the growing pillar of dirt and smoke. The machine gunner continued to fire until the jeep made one final flip and disappeared into the gaping crater where the road had once been.

Even before the first jeep finished its wild tumbling and crashed with a great thud, Childress knew they had succeeded. There was, he knew, no way that anyone in the second jeep could have made a radio call. There just hadn't been that kind of time. Five seconds, maybe ten, was all it had taken. Two days of planning and recon, six hours of waiting, and ten seconds of killing. That, he thought, was the way it should be.

Standing up, he grabbed the camouflage net and began to pull it down, yelling for the others with him to get the gun and move out. They had done what they had set out to do. Now it was up to others to harvest the crop that they had so carefully sown.

10

How can any man say what he should do himself if he is ignorant what his adversary is about?

—Henri de Jomini

GEORGETOWN, TEXAS
0505 HOURS, 11 AUGUST

Carefully rolling over onto his left side, Scott Dixon eased himself into position. Though it was still dark, he didn't need any artificial illumination for this particular maneuver. His movements were well rehearsed and the terrain before him was familiar. With great care, he brought his right hand up, easing it onto Jan Fields's bare thigh. Slowly, gently, he began to run his hand up her thigh, around to the front of her stomach, and then up until he was able to cup her right breast in his hand. The quiet darkness of their room, the warmth of her naked body against his, and the smoothness of her skin under his hand were, to Dixon, the most erotic sensations he could imagine. Tenderly kneading the breast in his hand, Dixon could feel himself becoming aroused, causing him to gradually apply more pressure and slowly intensify his manipulation of Jan's breast.

The effect on Jan was predictable. At first, she let out a low, barely audible sigh as she thrust her bottom out toward Dixon. This action accelerated Dixon's mounting desire and his manipulation of Jan's breast. Sensing that she was ready to execute phase two, he lifted his head from his pillow, twisting his head and upper body around until he could reach the side of Jan's exposed neck with his lips. Ever so lightly, he began planting a string of kisses starting on her neck and leading up to her ear. By the time he finished, she was beginning to wake.

Rolling over to face Dixon, Jan opened her eyes and looked into

Dixon's. As she stretched, she broke Dixon's grasp on her breast and caused him to move his head away a few inches. There was a mischievous smile on her face. "And what do you want, Colonel?" Jan's voice was low and provocative.

With Jan on her back, Dixon brought himself around so that he had himself propped up with one hand on either side of her, stuck between her arm and chest. Leaning forward until his nose touched hers, he grinned. "Well, my dear, I'm going to do what every soldier dreams of, I'm going to fuck with the media."

"You know you could get in serious trouble for screwing with the press. Let me remind you, Colonel, that I'm protected by the First Amendment of the Constitution, and you're pledged to uphold that."

Bringing his right leg around so that he now straddled Jan, and shifting his weight to his knees, Dixon moved his hands to either side of Jan's rib cage. "Oh, yeah! Is that what you think? Well, I'll show you what I'm committed to uphold right now." With that, he began to tickle her under the arms and along the base of her breasts, sending her into a spasm of laughter and beginning what, for them, was serious play.

Wearing only gray Army running shorts and a gray VMI T-shirt, Dixon wandered into the kitchen. Even the cool tile floor on his bare feet failed to rouse him out of his early morning stupor. Jan often commented that it was amazing how, in a matter of minutes, Dixon could go from being Tarzan, King of the Apes to a cast member from *Night of the Living Dead*. Food, mixed with numerous cups of coffee, seemed to be the only thing that could get Dixon going and keep him going.

To this end, Dixon negotiated the perils of the cold tile floor in his pursuit of nourishment and stimulants. With the grace and determination of a wire-guided antitank guided missile, Dixon moved toward the refrigerator. Opening the door, he stood there for a minute while his eyes and brain attempted to make contact with each other. Not that there was much thinking that Dixon needed to do. Inevitably, he would remove the same items from the refrigerator that he removed every morning. The only problem he faced was locating those items. As in all homes populated by children, items stored in Dixon's refrigerator had a tendency to migrate from one spot to another in an unpredictable and random manner. Simply because Dixon had put something on a shelf that he had designated as its proper place was no guarantee that he would find it there the next day. Whenever Dixon complained about this phenomenon, Jan would chide him, claiming that he needed to be a little more flexible, exclaiming, "You need a little challenge every now and then, Scotty."

A new challenge was the last thing Dixon needed when it came to Jan. Both of them had, from the beginning, realized that if their love affair was going to work, it would require both of them to work at it. While Jan had been more than willing to leave behind her globe-trotting as a hot-shot correspondent for WNN for Dixon, it was too much to expect her to leave her career completely. Not even in his wildest fantasies could Dixon imagine Jan playing the role of the good little Army wife. The image of Jan Fields spending her days making cookies for community bake sales and patiently waiting at home for him with a warm meal and a sympathetic ear whenever the Army decided it was finished with Dixon for the day, simply did not register. Of course, no one else shared that image either, especially since Jan Fields and Scott Dixon were not married.

Like their lovemaking, Jan and Scott's approach to life was, some would say, rather unconventional and very unpredictable. A widower, Dixon had no interest in a new wife. He had had one of those already and really didn't see the need for another. He had loved his first wife, and was sure that she had loved him. But he knew that it would be impossible to find another woman who could fill her place. Wives, he once told a sergeant, after all, were not like replacement parts. You couldn't, he said, simply wear one out, and then expect to be able to requisition a new one that would be able to fit in where the old one had been. So he had never tried. He didn't need to, for Jan was there when he needed a friend and lover who could accept him for what he was.

Slowly, Dixon began to find what he was searching for. As he found each item, he took it out with his right hand and passed it to his left in a ritual that he repeated every morning. When he finally had a tub of margarine, a jar of grape jam, and a pitcher of orange juice cradled in his left arm, Dixon closed the refrigerator and turned toward the kitchen table. For a moment, he considered going over to the counter where the bread was kept to pick up his English muffins. That, however, did not seem like a good idea, especially since there was no assurance that there would be any left. As he continued toward the table, the sound of the television being clicked on behind him told Dixon that Jan had joined him and was beginning her breakfast ritual.

Dressed in an oversize pink T-shirt that sported Minnie Mouse, Jan made sure that the kitchen television was set to the proper channel before moving to the coffeemaker. With an occasional sweep of her left hand to push her hair from her face, she went about making their first pot of coffee as she listened to the morning news.

Jan, like Dixon, wasn't in the market for a spouse. She needed something more than a husband could provide. That is why she valued Scott as a friend, a lover, and a confidant. But a husband, no. Jan, when she described the perfect husband, found herself describing her father. Her father was a sweet and kind man, and she loved him very much, but he, or someone like him, was the last person in the world she wanted to spend her life with. In her heart, she knew she could never surrender her individuality and freedom as her mother had. Jan's mother loved her father, and she had no complaints about her life. But she had never been a happy woman. Often, as she grew into adulthood, Jan could see a sadness in her mother's eyes. It was a sadness born from dreams and ambitions that her mother had never been able to fulfill. For most of her life, she had let her dreams, like hundreds of meals, grow cold while she tended the needs of husband, home, and children. Though she admired her mother, Jan knew she could never be like her. So, she had never tried.

It had taken her years, however, to find that she couldn't have it both ways, either. The image of a cosmopolitan woman, doing whatever she pleased and passing from one affair to another as she saw fit, was hollow. She found that she could not be a free-floating electron for her entire life. In Scott she had found a person she could both respect and enjoy, a person so different from what she was used to, and yet so comfortable, that the thought of being without him was painful. Scott never sought to dominate or change her. Instead, he challenged her, reveled in the diversity and unpredictability that she brought into his life. She, in turn, enjoyed the idea of being a consort rather than a spouse. When asked why they didn't marry, Jan's response, only half in jest, was that her love for Scott and his friendship was far too valuable to her to screw up with marriage.

The weatherman's announcement that it would be another bright and sunny day, with temperatures reaching one hundred and five degrees throughout most of central Texas, failed to get a reaction from either Jan or Dixon. The statement by the bright-eyed and well-dressed female co-anchor that they would have more on the previous night's attacks along the border after a commercial break, did.

Finished depositing his first load on the table, Dixon turned and headed for the counter where the muffins were kept. ''Another bad night for the home team?''

Jan, with another sweep of her hand, shrugged as she continued to prepare the coffeemaker. "Seems so. I suppose you don't know anything that you'd care to share with me?"

"Yeah, it's going to be sunny and hot today throughout central Texas. How's that for a beginning?"

Jan was about to make a comment when the news show continued. With well-practiced tones appropriate for the seriousness of the story, the perky young female co-anchor started with a recap of the morning's top story. As she had done each morning, with the help of a map in the background, the newswoman enumerated in detail the location, nature, and losses from each of the three incidents that had occurred overnight. As the newswoman spoke, both Jan and Scott continued to move about in silence, glancing at the television screen every now and then as they continued to prepare their own breakfast. Only when the next commercial cut in did either speak.

"I just don't understand, Scott, why the CIA or the FBI haven't been able to find something. My God, it's like a plot from a cheap horror movie, bodies cropping up everywhere without a trace or clue."

Dixon grunted. "Well, my dear, don't feel like the Lone Ranger. There's a whole bunch of people in Washington, including our dear friend Ed Lewis, who are asking the same question. I just hope those people keep asking questions and looking for the answers before someone does something unsmart and buckles under to the demands for action."

"Is there really the prospect of some kind of military action in the offing, Scotty?"

Pretending not to hear Jan's question, Dixon pulled his English muffins from the toaster and prepared to spread margarine and jam on them. Jan looked up at him and saw that he was ignoring her, a sure sign that she had hit close to home. Knowing that he would continue to ignore her if she continued to persist in her questions, Jan decided to pull her horns in. "Busy day ahead of you?"

Relieved that Jan had changed the subject, Dixon turned his attention away from the newswoman's monotone account of the raids. In another hour he would get a detailed briefing by the division duty officer and on-call intelligence officer on all of that. Moving to the table, Dixon sat down, poured himself a tall glass of orange juice, and began to munch on his muffins, talking to Jan between mouthfuls. "Oh, nothing exciting. Just the usual stuff. We have a couple of briefings to finish and rehearse, training inspections, and a meeting with some members of Congress and their staff. Seems we lost some facts and they feel the need to come down here and personally find them."

Though Scott tried to shrug off the congressional visit, Jan knew exactly what it was for, based on the members of Congress who had come. Congressman Harriman, chairman of the House Armed Services Committee, along with Congressman Ed Lewis from the House Intelligence Committee, had been dealing with only one subject for the past week; how would the Army secure the nation's southern border? Harriman's inquiries into plans to use the military had, to date, been stonewalled by both the White House and the Pentagon. Only Lewis's investigation into the failure of the CIA to predict the coup in Mexico, now broadened to include its inability to find an explanation for the border raids, was yielding any measurable action. The continuation of the raids, however, without producing any worthwhile clues or information, made those efforts appear to be weak and feeble. Jan knew that Scotty was working on some kind of contingency plans, and that eventually both the White House and the Pentagon would have to give in to pressure to do something. Only a show-stopping revelation would stop that.

Still, Jan knew that, when it was time, she would find out from official sources, just like every other newsperson. She loved Scott Dixon too much to jeopardize her relationship for a fleeting news story. Deciding to avoid the subject, she asked if the reception for the congressmen was still being held that night.

Spitting out tiny chunks of muffin as he spoke, Dixon cynically remarked that such affairs were where congressmen usually looked for the facts they were after. Then, as an afterthought, he asked Jan if she was still going to delay her trip to Brownsville and attend the reception.

With a sweet smile, Jan cocked her head to one side and held her coffee cup out. "Now, Scotty dear, what do you think?"

"Just checking, just checking. You remember how to get to the officers' club, Jan?"

"Yes, dear, I do. And Scotty, please do me the favor and wash your hands before meeting me there tonight. The last time I went to one of these after-duty things it took me a trip to the cleaners to get the smell of tank out of my clothes and two days to get it off my skin."

Dixon smiled. "Why, Jan, are you objecting? If you remember, we had some of the best sex we ever had during those two days. You know how excited tankers get when they smell gunpowder and diesel."

"Scotty, if that's what it takes to get you up, then I think we need to take a serious look at our relationship."

Finished, Dixon stood up and walked around the table until he stood behind Jan. Reaching down, Dixon ran his right hand along Jan's neck and into the wide opening of the oversize T-shirt she wore. With a light, gentle touch, Dixon began to play with Jan's nipple as he bent over and kissed her on the right side of her neck. "Okay, we'll talk, but later."

MEXICO CITY, MEXICO
0815 HOURS, 11 AUGUST

While Colonel Salvado Zavala discussed the need to end bread rationing in the southern states with the minister of agriculture, Guajardo looked about the table and considered his fellow council members. How well Molina had chosen them for the positions in which they were now serving. Colonel Emanuel Barreda, responsible for foreign affairs, was an excellent example.

Since the twenty-ninth of June, Barreda had been in almost constant motion, visiting every capital throughout Latin America as well as Japan, the People's Republic of China, and many nations in Europe. Publicly, his meetings were aimed at recognition of the new regime and laying the groundwork for economic cooperation. As an aside, Barreda was to sound out fellow Latin American leaders and find out what, if any, cooperation Mexico could expect if the United States attempted to intervene in Mexican affairs militarily. With this last item in mind, Barreda timed his visits so that each one followed, within a matter of days, sometimes by hours, a similar visit by the secretary of state from the United States. So close were their visits that in Buenos Aires, Argentina, the honor guard that had seen the American secretary of state off had to double-time over to the spot where they were to greet Barreda. In this manner, Barreda was able to gain a feel for what the United States was trying to do about the revolution while he was promoting it.

Many of the responses Barreda received were surprising. From the president of Venezuela, who had come to the airport personally to greet Barreda, came the suggestion that if the United States attempted intervention, Mexico should appeal to the Organization of American States for support. The president of Venezuela gave his personal pledge that if Mexico did so, he would support them. In Nicaragua, the minister of state, a former Sandinista general, offered to loan Mexico any weapons the Nicaraguan Army had in its vast inventory if there ever was need to defend themselves from the imperialists. Even those nations in Central and South America that publicly condemned the Council of 13 stated privately that, in a confrontation with the United States, they would support Mexico. It was, as the president of Brazil told Barreda, ''time that the United States began to treat Latin American republics as equals and learn that the new American world order is not the only solution.''

These pledges of support, as important as they were, could not, in themselves, protect the revolution or the Council of 13. Mexico needed to present a viable deterrent. That was what Guajardo had to provide.

Again, Molina had shown great wisdom when he had appointed Colonel Guajardo as the minister of defense. Guajardo's attendance at many United States Army schools had given him a familiarity with and insight into the American way of war that few of his brother officers could equal. The list of schools was long and diverse, including Ranger and Airborne training at Fort Benning, Georgia, the Armor Officers Advanced Course at Fort Knox, Kentucky, the Command and General Staff College at Fort Leavenworth, Kansas, and the School of the Americas back at Fort Benning. All of this had been no accident. Under the old regime, Guajardo had been being groomed to be the attaché in Washington, D.C., and the foreign-area expert on the United States for the Ministry of Defense. Even Guajardo's assignment to the critical State of Tamaulipas had been part of that plan. Any move into Mexico would include an effort to seize the natural gas areas located in the northern regions of that state and the oil fields in the south. Tamaulipas's location on the Gulf Coastal Plain also made it the most vulnerable to American forces, both land and seaborne. Such vulnerability would be too tempting to an invader looking for a quick knockout.

So Guajardo was doing what he was trained to do and what he did best, as he prepared Mexico for an invasion from the north. Like Barreda, Guajardo spent much of his time traveling. Using a pair of Bell Huey helicopters, Guajardo and his small staff crisscrossed northern Mexico, inspecting training and overseeing the arming and reorganization of local militia units. As he did so, Guajardo visited area and garrison commanders, briefing them on the part they were to play in the defense of Mexico. The plan for this, based on an older version, had been revised by Guajardo before the twenty-ninth of June. He had personally written the threat assessment, providing both the Council of 13 and his subordinate commanders with a realistic view of what the United States was capable of doing, what it would probably do, and how best Mexico could defeat American intentions. Based on this assessment, a plan that included the needs of the Army and militia, down to the smallest detail, had been ready for execution once the council was in power.

Unfortunately, no one, not even Molina, could have predicted the strange border attacks that the United States was complaining of. Though no one doubted that something was happening along the border between the United States and Mexico, everyone was at a loss to explain who was behind it and why they were attempting to provoke the United States. Each member of the council had his own pet theory, based on his personal and political beliefs. Zavala was convinced that the provocateurs were leftists, attempting to egg the United States into doing what they themselves could not do, eliminate the Council of 13. Colonel Angel Ruiz, minister of justice, agreed with the motivation but thought that the drug lords were involved in the raids, providing financial support if not manpower.

Molina, ever the great mediator, refused to publicly support any theory. Instead, he took a very practical approach. It didn't matter, he pointed out, who was behind the raids against the Americans. What was important was the fact that they were occurring and, more importantly, that they were preventing the recognition of the council by the United States and driving American politicians toward extreme measures for solving the problem. To succeed, the council needed time to establish itself and its authority, reorganize state and political apparatuses, and, equally important, revive Mexico's economy. A war, regardless of how short, would cripple these efforts. With this in mind, Molina, with the backing of the entire council, gave Guajardo a free hand to deal with the problem as he saw fit. The only restriction placed upon him was the need to do so quickly and without causing the Americans any further alarm.

Guajardo, as he half listened to his fellow councilmen, wondered how he could achieve the last. Any efforts to reinforce or increase military activity in the northern states were bound to increase American suspicions and fears. How, he had asked, can a man go about arming himself without worrying his neighbor? Eventually, he pointed out, that neighbor will feel the need to do likewise in order to protect himself. Not to do so, he said, would be, in the eyes of his family, criminal. Molina, speaking for the rest of the council, simply replied, "Do your best, my friend. That is all we can ask of you."

HEADQUARTERS, 16TH ARMORED DIVISION, FORT HOOD, TEXAS
0915 HOURS, 11 AUGUST

Finished with his morning run and fresh from a shower, Scott Dixon was ready to begin some serious work. Walking through the admin section of the G3 shop in search of his first cup of coffee, he told his deputy to have someone from the G3 plans section bring all of the GREEN plans and the briefing slides for them to his office and that no one, under pain of death, was to disturb him.

While Dixon sat at his desk, sorting through the heap of papers and memos stacked in his in-box, a clerk from the plans section came into his office and set a thick green loose-leaf binder, a large covered map board, and a stack of framed transparencies on the end of the conference table that sat perpendicular to his desk. As the clerk left, he asked her to close the door behind her. For a moment, Dixon looked at the loose-leaf binder, then at the muddle of notes and papers he still had left in his in-box. He thought about leaving the in-box until later, but decided against that. Maybe, just maybe, he thought, there might be something of importance hidden deep in there. Against his better judgment, he finished sorting through his in-box. No doubt his deputy, whose task it was to ensure that all paperwork was straight, accounted for, and on time, would be relieved.

His routine complete, Dixon took his coffee cup and the stack of papers he had reviewed and written comments on and walked out to his deputy's desk. Dropping the papers in the center of the deputy's otherwise neat desk, Dixon wandered over to the coffeepot, refilled his cup, and then returned to his office to review the GREEN plans.

The name of the division's contingency plans for intervention in Mexico had a story all its own. Before World War II, the army had a comprehensive series of war plans, referred to as the RAINBOW plans, to deal with the threats that faced the United States in 1940. These plans were based on individual single-color war plans developed by the War Department, as the Department of the Army was then known, between 1920 and 1940 to deal with each nation that was considered a threat to the United States. Under that system, any plan dealing with Mexico was referred to as a GREEN plan. The GREEN plan, the most highly developed of all the War Department's plans, was in turn a derivative of the General Mexican War Plan that was first drafted in 1919.

The 1919 plan called for sealing the borders of the United States, seizing the Mexican oil fields in Tampico as well as the coal fields just south of Texas, blockading the principal Mexican seaports, and cutting Mexico off from other Central American countries. Since many of the goals of the current XIX Corps war plans were the same as the old GREEN plans, Dixon, with a degree in history from VMI, had decided to name the 16th Armored Division's draft war plans for Mexico the GREEN plans. Big Al, the division commander, who liked to keep things simple, had kept the name.

There were actually six different and distinct contingency plans within the GREEN plans. GREEN ONE was purely defensive, dealing only with the sealing of the border of the United States and the repelling of attacks up to the Mexican–United States border but nothing beyond. The sealing of the border, the primary operation in GREEN ONE, was only an initial phase in all other GREEN plans. GREEN TWO included the sealing of the border but assumed the active assistance of the Mexican military, which allowed combined Mexican-American operations south of the border. GREEN THREE called for destruction of hostile forces south of the border, but assumed that the Mexican military would neither cooperate with nor interfere with those operations. GREEN FOUR assumed that the Mexican military would defend its territorial integrity if the United States attempted to follow and destroy hostile forces south of the border. GREEN FIVE called for occupation of selected areas in northern Mexico as a buffer against incursions against the United States. GREEN SIX, the thickest of the plans, called for an all-out invasion with the goal of toppling the military regime and reestablishment of a freely elected democratic government. There was a GREEN SEVEN plan, but since it included the employment of nuclear weapons, it was classified top secret, special compartmented information, and not available to the 16th Armored Division.

Each of these contingency plans, in turn, had at least three variations. For example, GREEN ONE-1 included only the two active-duty brigades of the 16th Armored Division. GREEN ONE-2 required three brigades, with the third brigade being the 173rd Infantry Brigade from Fort Benning, Georgia. GREEN ONE-3, also calling for three brigades, required the mobilization and deployment of the 16th Armored Division's National Guard round-out brigade from Mississippi.

While it was the responsibility of the G3 plans section to draft all the plans and their various permutations, based on the division commander's general concept of operations and Dixon's specific instructions, Dixon had to ensure that the plans were complete, made sense, and had been coordinated with the other staff sections. This was not easy, especially when Dixon often found the intelligence estimates upon which the plans were based wanting. Unable to gather their own information, the G2 intelligence section of the division depended on the intelligence estimates provided by the XIX Corps G2 section. These estimates, in turn, were based upon those produced by national-level agencies, namely the CIA and the DIA, whose products Dixon had good reason to suspect. Using those estimates for the creation of operational war plans was, as Dixon pointed out on numerous occasions, like building a house on a dung heap. Still, until those estimates changed, they were all he had to work with.

Dixon, scheduled to brief the concept of GREEN plans to a group of visiting congressmen and their staffers that afternoon, needed to refresh his knowledge and make notes for the briefing. Under normal circumstances, he would have spent little if any time preparing for a congressional delegation. Ordinarily, few, if any, of the members of the delegation would have had any real conception of what was being discussed. Today, however, Congressman Ed Lewis of Tennessee would be present. Lewis, a veteran and a member of the House Intelligence Committee, knew his stuff. Dixon wouldn't be able to hip-shoot with him in the audience.

With his feet up on the table, his coffee cup in one hand, the green loose-leaf binder in his lap, the map board showing the operational graphics before him, and the slides to one side, Dixon prepared himself for the briefing.

OFFICERS AND CIVILIANS' OPEN MESS, FORT HOOD, TEXAS
1845 HOURS, 11 AUGUST

Jan had so seldom come onto post that she had needed to stop for directions three times before she found the officers club. Embarrassed at being late, she decided to say nothing about why she was late. Instead, she entered the room where the staff of the 16th Armored Division was gathered, careful not to attract attention while looking for Scott. When she spotted him talking to the division intelligence officer, she maneuvered herself until she was able to approach him from behind. Coming up to his side, she slipped her hand around his arm and gave it a gentle squeeze. "There you are! I've been looking all over for you, Scotty dear."

Looking over at her, Dixon grinned. He was about to ask if she had gotten lost again when Big Al came up.

With a loud and sincere welcome, Big Al greeted her. "Well, I see Scott has unshackled you from the stove long enough to come out and join us."

Towering half a head over Big Al, Jan looked at the general, then turned to Dixon. "Scott dear, do we have a stove?"

This caused the general to laugh and Dixon to roll his eyes. Grabbing Jan by the arm, Big Al began to escort her away. "You, my dear, will probably dehydrate if you wait for that tombstone of a boyfriend to get you a drink. Come with me and let a dirty old man buy you one."

"That, sir, would be a pleasure. No doubt Scott has told you I specialize in dirty old men, which is what keeps me going with him."

Again, the general let out an unabashed laugh. "Scott, this is too much woman to be wasted on a tanker. She deserves an aviator, like me."

Dixon threw his hands out in mock surrender. "As always, sir, you know best."

With a smile the general pointed at Dixon. "Damn straight, that's why

I'm the general. Now, if you'll excuse us, Colonel, I would like to introduce Jan to some people.''

With Jan gone, Dixon headed for the cash bar. En route, he ran across Captain Cerro, who was carrying two bottles of beer. Dixon stopped and looked at the young officer and the beer in his hands, and raised his eyebrows. ''A real two-fisted drinker.''

Cerro looked at the beers, then at Dixon. ''Well, no, not actually. One of them is for someone else, but I can't find him right now.'' Then as an afterthought, he offered one to Dixon. ''Here, sir, might as well before it gets warm. I hope you don't mind Corona. I hear tell that's the official drink of the 16th.''

''Actually, I'm a Coors Light man myself, but since division policy states that field grade officers cannot refuse free beer, I couldn't possibly refuse.'' He took a sip, then held the bottle out at arm's length. ''Well, it ain't Coors, but what the hell.'' Turning back to Cerro, he asked how he was getting on in his new job.

As Cerro began to talk, recounting an incident of several days ago with one of the female infantry lieutenants, he realized that he had been with the G3 section for over a month, and yet this was only the second time he had had the opportunity to talk to the G3 one on one. It wasn't like Dixon had been hiding. Dixon was always there. In fact, sometimes, it appeared that he was everywhere. Even when he was out inspecting training or at a briefing, his presence still seemed to permeate the offices of the G3 section. His majors, and he seemed to have a lot of them, referred to him as El Jefe, Spanish for ''the leader.'' He, in turn, referred to them as his Middle-Aged Mutant Ninja Majors.

The entire section, and how it operated, threatened to cause Cerro to redefine how he viewed staff officers and, in particular, Lieutenant Colonel Scott Dixon. The casual and seemingly relaxed atmosphere that had struck him in the beginning as the sign of a slack organization was, in truth, the outward indication of a well-working machine. It was a machine cast in the image of its creator, Lieutenant Colonel Dixon. Like him, the G3 section always seemed to be in motion, moving forward, in many directions, in a very deliberate and purposeful way. What was most amazing to Cerro was the efficiency of the whole operation. There was little wasted motion. In the month that he had been there, he had heard of only one meeting between the G3 and his majors, and that had lasted less than half an hour. And yet, Dixon seemed to be on top of everything. Cerro had watched one day as a parade of officers, both G3 officers and officers from other staff sections, went into and out of Dixon's office. Each officer, with a different subject or problem, had filed into Dixon's office, summarized what he needed from the G3, and, in turn, received guidance or new instructions from Dixon. Without skipping a beat, Dixon had listened, considered, decided what needed to be done, and issued his instructions in terms that even a finance officer could understand.

Cerro had also noticed that Dixon had no patience with people who could not think on their own, were indecisive, or could not keep up with Dixon's physical or intellectual pace. The people in the G3 shop were what someone referred to as high-speed, low-drag majors. Anyone who couldn't hack it, Cerro was told, soon found his way to the door. Though most everyone complained at times about the work load, long hours, and Dixon's treatment of them, they knew they were learning from a master and, when their time came, that they would be rewarded with a choice assignment in a troop unit somewhere in the division.

As he talked with Cerro, Dixon noticed a tall man in a light tan three-piece looking over at them. For a moment, he ignored the man's presence and his efforts to attract Dixon's attention. Instead, Dixon continued to listen to Cerro with only an occasional circumspect glance to the tall man in the light tan suit.

Cerro, seeing Dixon's attention distracted by someone behind him, glanced over his shoulder, then at Dixon, who was making no effort at all to acknowledge the presence of the tall man. Instead, with his face locked in an impassive stare, Dixon continued to pay attention to Cerro. Suddenly, Cerro realized that Dixon was intentionally ignoring the man behind them. He was, in his own way, fucking with the guy, making the stranger choose between being rude and breaking in or giving up and walking away. Since Cerro had no idea who the man was, he took his cues from Dixon and continued. Dixon, slowly taking a sip of his beer, watched Cerro's eyes and continued to ignore the stranger. The stranger, for his part, was becoming agitated. Cerro, finally, threw the game by turning to the stranger and ending his conversation with Dixon.

Unable to pretend any longer, Dixon turned to face the stranger. Changing expressions from blank to surprised with well-practiced ease, Dixon acknowledged the man. "Well, Congressman Lewis, how pleasant to see you again. Been here long?"

Lewis shrugged, pretending to ignore Dixon's attempt to rebuff him. "Not long, Colonel."

Pointing to Cerro, Dixon introduced him. "I'd like you to meet my new acquisition, Captain Harold Cerro, VMI graduate, airborne ranger infantry, and holder of the Distinguished Service Cross, Silver Star, and the Purple Heart.''

Knowing that Dixon was also VMI, Lewis saw a chance to pay back Dixon's rebuff. ''How'd you earn your Purple Heart, Captain, from one of the female cadets at VMI?''

For a second, Cerro imagined himself as a helpless infantryman pinned down between the crossfire of two opponents. Unable to figure out how best to respond, he was rescued by Dixon. ''Ah, hell, no, Congressman. Captain Cerro is a member of the old corps, when men were men and girls were dates.''

A smirk lit Lewis's face. ''I see. Now I understand why you have Captain Cerro in charge of the program designed to evaluate the effectiveness of female combat officers.''

Lewis's comment smacked Dixon like a two-by-four. Well, Dixon thought, I should have known better than try to mess with this guy. Begrudgingly, he acknowledged that Lewis was too sharp to play games with. Mustering a smile, he took a sip of his beer and asked Lewis what he could do for him.

''I was hoping to have a word in private with you.''

''Of course.'' Dismissing Cerro, Dixon escorted Lewis to the patio. ''What can I do for you, Congressman?''

Lewis leaned against a table, half sitting on it. ''Today, in the briefings, I detected a certain amount of dissatisfaction with both the intelligence summaries coming from the DIA and the war plans you briefed. In fact, you went out of your way to accentuate every negative aspect of the plan. I was, to say the least, quite taken aback by the fact that an officer with your reputation would get your commander to buy into such a gloomy and pessimistic briefing.''

Dixon looked down at his beer, swirled the bottle, and took a sip before answering. For a moment, he tried to come up with an evasive answer, but decided to pass on that idea. It was, after all, hard to bullshit a bullshitter and Lewis, he realized, knew bullshit when he saw it. ''Big Al never buys into anything he doesn't want to.'' Dixon let that comment hang in the air for a moment while he took another sip from his beer. Ready, he looked Lewis in the eye. ''You're right, I am not at all thrilled with what we have to work with, intelligencewise, that is. Nor am I thrilled with our strategic goals, and when I say strategic, I'm talking about political goals and objectives. I especially don't like the idea that there are people who seriously believe in using the American military to salvage a bankrupt foreign policy.''

Taken aback by Dixon's comments, Lewis paused for a moment before continuing. Though Lewis had used the same arguments, and had, in a different way, said the same thing, Dixon's accusations hit him like a slap in the face. As a member of Congress, and a prominent figure in Washington, he was guilty, through association, of both the good and the bad calls that came from that city.

Though he wanted to, Dixon fought the urge to smirk. He saw that Lewis was both surprised by his response and somewhat embarrassed. The jerk, he thought, had asked for it. Still, he had to remember that Lewis was, after all, a congressman, while Dixon was a mere lowly lieutenant colonel. Lewis was the maker and giver of policy, Dixon a simple swordbearer for the realm. He therefore decided to ease off and defuse the tension between them. "Congressman, have you ever studied the Little Big Horn campaign?"

Relieved that Dixon was changing the subject, Lewis went along. "I've read about it, but never really studied it. Why?"

"In 1875 we had elements in our country who viewed the American Indians as an 'inconvenience' to their plans. Land, and the resources those lands contained, were, in their opinion, wasted on the Indians. In order for the nation to grow, and, oh by the way, to amass a fortune for themselves, these well-meaning advocates of manifest destiny did their best to remove that inconvenience. The motivation they relied on to precipitate action was the unthinking hatred that white America had for the red savages. The tool they used was the U.S. Army."

Lewis put his hand up. "Okay, Colonel, hold it. Are you saying that today's version of the robber barons are out to start a war and that we are unjustified in defending ourselves?"

Without skipping a beat, Dixon continued. "No, I am not. I have no reason to believe that anyone in the United States is involved in precipitating this crisis. What I am trying to point out is that there are people, well-meaning people in this case, who are using their influence to apply political pressure on our national leaders to take a course of action that is both ill-advised and could result in embarrassment and disaster."

"If that is true, Colonel, why are you the first soldier I've heard come out so strongly against such an operation?"

Dixon looked at his bottle, and gave it a swirl. "There are any number of reasons for not doing so, just as there were many reasons why the U.S. Army did what it did in 1876. First, there is the philosophy that we are soldiers and our job is simply to obey. The president and Congress decide national policy, we only execute. You know, the old 'Roger, out, can do' attitude."

"You think that's wrong?"

"It's not my place to decide right or wrong. It is my duty to point out what is possible and what is not. You see, I happen to believe in the American system. But, having said that, we cannot ignore the dark side of some of the people in the American military." Dixon lifted his beer bottle and used the index finger of the hand holding the bottle to point at Lewis. "You see, Congressman, every time the Army is ordered out, we can justify our existence. Whenever you give us a mission, we salute with one hand and reach out with the other for more funds, since every time the United States is without an enemy or a viable threat, the Army shrivels up into an unimportant and expensive inconvenience. A small Army with no mission means slow promotions and little opportunity for fame and glory."

"I thought you guys prided yourself in your selfless service and professionalism?"

Dixon laughed. "If you still believe that, I would appreciate it if you went back and looked at recordings of the news broadcasts shot during Just Cause and Desert Storm. More than a few senior commanders and officers took great pains to make themselves available to the television cameras so as to 'help' the American public understand the war. And, when it was over, they sacrificed their military careers, retiring so that they could travel the speaking circuit, for a fee of course. No, Congressman, egos and self-interest do not disappear when you put on a uniform. Though Mexico ain't the evil empire Russia used to be, it happens to be the only game in town, for the moment."

"What's your alternative? Do nothing? Let the raids continue? Surely even you can appreciate that there isn't a single congressman or senator from the southwest who is willing to sit and do nothing in Washington while their constituents are being shot in their own backyards? The demand for direct and effective action is becoming too compelling to ignore. That, Colonel, is a political reality."

Nodding his head, Dixon agreed. "I understand that. Just as Terry did when he left Fort Abraham Lincoln in 1876 to catch the Sioux, and Pershing went to Texas to punish Pancho Villa. We'll go where we are sent and do what we are told. That, however, doesn't mean that it's the right or proper thing to do."

Lewis grunted. "I see you believe in the Pancho Villa theory."

"Not necessarily. Though that line of thinking is, in my opinion, the most logical, no one can confirm it. And that, Mr. Congressman, is exactly my point. No one is able to confirm or deny any of the theories concerning the raids along the border. Yet, in spite of this lack of solid evidence, everyone is chomping at the bit, demanding that we commit the Army. What's going to happen, to us and the future of our two countries, if we find out, after all the shooting is over, that we shot the wrong guy? My God, sir! Even the most brutal murderer in the United States must have overwhelming and irrefutable evidence brought against him before he is punished. Shouldn't the Mexican people be given the same courtesy?''

"We are not dealing with criminal law here, Colonel Dixon. This is not a nice, clean courtroom in some city far away. We are talking about the real world. Again, let's do a reality check here. We are dealing with politics and national passions. Both of these can be very irrational and uncompromising. When you add fear and coat that fear with liberal quantities of American blood, like the people who are conducting these raids on our borders are doing, logic goes out the window.''

Dixon was about to answer when Jan came up from behind and grabbed his arm. Leaning over and planting a kiss on his cheek, she turned to Lewis and smiled. "Scotty sees nothing wrong with our strategy, so long as it includes dinner, soon. Right, dear?''

Dixon looked at Jan. The look in her eyes and her speech told him she was feeling no pain. Taking her hand from his shoulder, he lifted it to his lips, lightly kissed it, and lowered it halfway. "You, my dear, are drunk.''

Pulling her hand away, Jan protested. "Drunk? I am not drunk, sir. Your general's drunk. I'm just hungry, nay, starved. And I demand food, now.''

Amused, Lewis watched for a moment before he cut in. "I had no idea you two were married.''

Seeing a chance to get away from Lewis, Dixon turned to him. "Us, married? No way, Congressman. We just sleep together.''

Putting her hands on her hips, her eyes aflame in mock rage, Jan scolded Dixon. *"Scott B. Dixon, how dare you imply I'm a kept woman?''* She turned to Lewis. "Do you know what the *B* in his name stands for, Congressman? It stands for 'Bad.' And if he doesn't take me to dinner right now in an effort to make up, it's going to stand for 'bye,' as in bye-bye, gone, adiós, adieu, farewell.''

Dixon turned to Lewis and shrugged. "I'm terribly sorry, Congressman, but duty calls. Perhaps we can continue this later.''

Lewis raised his glass. "Yes, maybe later.''

After Jan and Dixon had reentered the building and were on their way to the dining room, arm in arm, Jan leaned over to Dixon and whispered in his ear. "I saw you cornered and figured you needed to be rescued.''

Slowing down, Dixon turned and lightly kissed her cheek. "And that, my dear, is why I love you."

PRESIDIO, TEXAS
2355 HOURS, 11 AUGUST

The evening shift wasn't half over and already it promised to be a slow and boring night. Tom Jerricks, sitting at the dispatcher's desk, put down the well-worn magazine he had been leafing through, then looked about the office for something new to read. He glanced at the lieutenant, sitting with his feet up on his desk watching television, then over to the shelf where the coffeepot and a stack of magazines sat.

At that moment, they were the only ones there; everyone else was on patrol. Since the beginning of August, everyone had been working twelve-hour days, six days a week. Already, that and the tension were beginning to wear on everyone in the office. No one, it seemed, was getting any smarter and none of the banditos, as the unknown raiders were being called, had been hit, let alone killed, as far as anyone knew. It was as if they were fighting shadows. Those shadows, Jerricks knew, had teeth. On the blackboard, where the patrols were briefed, was a message, updated nightly, that reminded everyone of that gruesome fact. Across the top was written, "Banditos 14, Border Patrol 0. Don't Become 15."

Standing up, Jerricks walked over to the coffeepot, poured himself a cup, and began to sort through the stack of magazines in search of something to read. His back was to the radio when the shrill voice of a patrolman, with the sound of breaking glass and gunfire in the background, broke the silence.

"We're under fire. We're under fire. Presidio Base, Presidio Base, this is . . ."

Dropping his coffee as he spun around and dashed for the radio, Jerricks grabbed the microphone, hit the transmit button, and responded. "Last station, this is Presidio Base. Identify yourself and give us your location, over."

As he prepared to call again, the lieutenant came up behind Jerricks, placing his hand on Jerricks's shoulder as he leaned over to listen to the speaker. Jerricks repeated his call. "Last station, this is Presidio Base. Identify yourself and give us your location, over."

There was nothing. Silence. Both men looked at the radio speaker and waited for a response, just as every border patrolman on that net sat listening, waiting. When there was no further broadcast, the lieutenant ordered Jerricks to have all patrols report in, give their location, and report anything that they might know about the reported shooting.

It took what seemed to Jerricks an eternity for all of their patrols to report in. After each report, there was a pause before the next patrol checked in, just in case the patrol under attack was able to make another report. But there was no further report of an attack. Only the patrols reporting their locations and that they had negative contact came in. After three minutes, all but Ed Kimel and Hernando Juarez were accounted for. As Jerricks called them by name, an effort that yielded no response, the lieutenant went to the map and traced their assigned patrol route. When he had a fix on the approximate location where they should have been at the time of the reported contact, the lieutenant directed the patrols on either side of them to converge on that spot. Although he knew he didn't need to, the lieutenant instructed the converging patrols to exercise extreme caution.

NORTH OF INDIO, TEXAS
MIDNIGHT, 11 AUGUST

From a distance of two miles, Delapos could see the border patrol jeep come screaming down Highway 170 in an effort to find the missing patrol. Delapos, of course, already knew where the missing patrolmen were. He and four of his men had killed them over an hour ago. After dragging the bodies of the border patrolmen off the road, removing the radio from their jeep, and disposing of the jeep, they had moved farther north and set themselves up in a new ambush site. When his men were ready, Delapos had turned the radio on his jeep to the same frequency that had been set on the border patrol jeep, sent out a frantic distress call, and waited for a reaction.

As the border patrol jeep approached and his men prepared to fire the two Claymore mines set on the road, Delapos smiled. The reactions of the border patrol had been both timely and, as he had anticipated, predictable. Two patrols, in two different locations, attacked by the same team, would be a first. Sooner or later, Delapos knew, the border patrol would need to admit that the situation was out of hand. If the double ambush, and the fact that the second patrol was lured in by a false radio call, didn't convince them of that, then nothing would.

11

Guns are left to do what words might have done earlier, rightly used.

—John Walker

ABILENE, TEXAS
1845 HOURS, 12 AUGUST

With a few sharp turns of the steering wheel and a casualness that frightened some, Jimmy Sullivan backed his eighteen-wheeler up to the loading dock. Sullivan loved driving the big rigs, and looked forward to the day when he would be able to own a rig himself. Glancing from the left side mirror to the right side mirror, Sullivan eased the truck back until he felt a slight thump, telling him the rear of the truck had made contact with the thick rubber bumper on the loading dock.

Shutting down his rig, Sullivan shoved his portable cassette player into his gym bag, grabbed his clipboard with the manifest on it, and began to climb down. As he did so, his supervisor, Tom Henry, yelled to him from the dock. "Hey, Jimmy, your old lady wants you to call her right away."

On the ground, Sullivan yelled back. "Did she say what she wanted?"

Without looking up from the clipboard, Henry yelled back, "Yeah, she said some guy at the armory has been tryin' to get you all day."

Slamming the cab door, Sullivan threw the clipboard down on the ground. "Ah shiiit. Not again."

Looking up, Henry watched Sullivan standing next to the truck, with his hands on his hips and his head hanging down, cursing and kicking imaginary rocks with the tip of his cowboy boots. "Hey, Jimmy."

"What!"

Henry smiled. "Your wife's pissed too."

"Thanks, boss, I needed that. I really fuckin' needed that." Sullivan

picked up his clipboard, straightened out the papers on it, and headed for
the phone in the locker room. He knew what the call from the armory was
about. Ever since the raids along the Mexican border had begun, rumors
concerning the use of the National Guard to seal the border between
Mexico and Texas had been running wild. Some of the old-timers in the
unit Sullivan belonged to said it was just a matter of time. The new men,
defined as people who had joined after the war in the Persian Gulf, were
excited. Sullivan, who had been mobilized for that war, did not share
their enthusiasm.

The Guard, for Sullivan, had started as a fun thing to do. He had enjoyed
his three years in the Army and saw the Guard as a means of making extra
income while having the opportunity to enjoy the friendships and excitement he had experienced while on active duty, without having to put up
with the chickenshit that the regular Army seemed to thrive on. Soon, the
Guard took on a greater importance to Sullivan. With a wife, a son, and
another child on the way, his regular income was quickly eaten up by the
day-to-day cost of living. His dream of buying his own truck was quickly
dying. Only by staying with the Guard, and saving every penny he made
during weekend drills, could he keep that dream alive. Combined with a
Veterans Administration small business loan, which he would soon qual-
ify for, Jimmy figured he could make it.

Sullivan's plans, however, were not without their problems. His wife,
a good woman by any measure, had no problems with his driving all over
the Southwest for the trucking company. That, after all, was what put
food on the table. Even the thirty-nine days a year he spent with the
Guard were tolerable, since that would make their dream of owning their
own truck a reality. For years she had accepted Sullivan's time with the
Guard as a necessary evil. That attitude, however, had changed when
Sullivan was mobilized and shipped to the Persian Gulf just before Christ-
mas 1990.

With less than two days' notice, Sullivan had left his pregnant wife in
Abilene as he went to war. Suddenly, because of the actions of a single
man, their entire future had been threatened. It was more than putting
their dreams on hold. They had done that before. When Sullivan had
broken his leg and couldn't drive for two months, everything they had
planned had had to be postponed. The war in the gulf, however, was
different. The broken leg could be dealt with. The doctor could tell them
when the cast could come off. He could prescribe what therapy was
needed for full recovery and how long that recovery would take. And

Sullivan and his wife could plan accordingly. The war, however, had been like a huge gaping abyss, undefined, seemingly endless, and very, very black. Sullivan's call to the colors to serve in the gulf did more than put their future on hold. It had challenged the very roots of their relationship and tested his wife's character as nothing had ever done before. The war had found both their relationship and her character lacking. As a result, their marriage had never been the same since. Sullivan's only hope, his only logical plan, to salvage his marriage and start all over again, was to buy a truck and become his own boss. Like a drowning man grabbing for something, he saw that dream as the stick that would save him. And that stick, until he got his loan, was owned by the National Guard.

Once in the locker room, Sullivan grabbed the phone, then paused, trying to decide who to call first. While there were pros and cons for calling his wife first, he decided that it would be wiser to call the armory first. Perhaps the unit wasn't being mobilized. Perhaps there was a change on the upcoming weekend drill or an admin problem with his pay voucher. Maybe this whole problem wasn't a problem at all. At least by calling the armory, he would be able to find out exactly what he had to deal with.

Mike Lodden, the unit's full-time training NCO, answered. "Sullivan, where you been, boy? We've been tryin' to get hold of you since eight o'clock this mornin'."

Sullivan wasn't in the mood for idle chatter or beating around the bush. "I've been out earnin' an honest living. Now what's all so hell-fire important that you need me for?"

Lodden skipped the pleasantries and got down to business. "The governor's callin' out the Guard. Border patrol was hit last night and hit hard. This mornin' at six o'clock the head of the region covering Brownsville to El Paso informed his boss in Washington that the situation was out of hand and his boys were refusing to go out on patrol. Till we get there, the border's wide open. Even the customs boys are pullin' back."

Sullivan let out a moan even Lodden could hear. "What about the Army? Why in the hell aren't they goin' down there?"

"Jimmy, don't you lis'n to the radio?"

"No, Mike, I don't. I'm ignorant, okay? Now tell me, if it ain't too much trouble, what in the hell are the regular pucks doin'?"

"Well, accordin' to the news and what the colonel told us, the president and the National Security Council is meetin' this morning to discuss the matter and review their options. In the meantime, accordin' to the news, the president doesn't want to do anything that would upset the Mexicans or might provoke 'em."

"Provoke 'em! Provoke 'em!" Sullivan's screams caused Lodden to pull the phone away from his ear. "What in the hell does that fool think the goddamned Mexicans have been doin' down here? Is he for real?"

Though Lodden wanted to end the conversation, he couldn't help but throw his two cents in. "Well, that's what we get for electin' a bleedin'-heart liberal from New England. Anyway, you need to get your butt down here yesterday. The battalion XO is leaving with the advance party tonight."

Sullivan paused. "You know, Mike, Martha's gonna be pissed."

Lodden chuckled. "I don't mean to make fun of ya, old boy, but she already is. Damned near blew my eardrum out when I called her for the second time."

For a second, Sullivan got excited. "Did you tell her already?"

"No, no, of course not. But be realistic, Jimmy. I didn't have to. Women kinda know these things. It's like radar. They can pick up bad news a mile away."

"Yeah, tell me about it. Okay, I'll be in as soon as I can. When we supposed to move out?"

"Don't know, Jimmy. But when you come in, don't plan on goin' home again. The adjutant general and the governor are in a low hover. They say every state legislator and big-city mayor from the border area is on the phone every five minutes demandin' to know where the troops are. Like I said, they wanted us yesterday."

With nothing more to say, Sullivan hung up the phone and prepared to call home, then paused. As distasteful as it was, he decided that this was the kind of news he had best tell his wife in person. Turning away from the phone, he shuffled down to John Henry's office to tell him he wouldn't be in for work for a while.

La Sauceda, Mexico
2045 hours, 12 August

No one paid any attention to the tall blond gringo sitting in the back corner with two Mexicans. In this cantina, it was not healthy to stare at anyone for too long, let alone ask questions. No one seemed to notice that the gringo had entered through the back door and everyone pretended that the pistol sticking out of his boot didn't really exist, although the gringo had taken great pains to make sure everyone could see it.

Of the two men sitting across from Childress, only one was really a Mexican. The other was a former colonel in the Nicaraguan Army whose sole claim to Mexican citizenship was the forged Mexican passport and identification papers he carried. A lifelong Sandinista, the Nicaraguan had found that he not only had a knack for waging guerrilla war, he actually enjoyed it. Peace, and the shift toward democracy in his home country, had left him little opportunity to use his one God-given gift.

Originally sent to Mexico as part of a delegation to assist in the transfer of surface-to-air missiles and antitank guided missiles to the new Mexican government, the Nicaraguan had been recruited by Alamán through a third party to provide a similar service to Delapos's growing army. It was because of this man that Delapos felt some confidence in his group's ability to continue its campaign of terrorism against the Texas National Guard with some hope of success. Deciding on the exact mechanics of dealing with that new threat, and what to do while the Guard was still in the process of deploying and the border was uncovered, was the purpose of this meeting.

The Nicaraguan colonel, though he spoke with great authority and confidence and took the lead in the discussions, was anxious. He wanted to become involved in anything that would embarrass the United States. Only the presence of the tall blond American across from him kept the Nicaraguan from saying so. Childress, for his part, said little, though he sensed the Nicaraguan's contempt for him. Instead, Childress merely leaned back in his chair, his right hand listlessly dangling down and within easy reach of the pistol sticking out of his right boot. With his left hand, he slowly turned the bottle of beer on the table, looking at the Nicaraguan with cold, steady, unemotional eyes. Though he knew that what the Nicaraguan was saying made sense, Childress didn't know whether he agreed or not. Until he could sort out his own emotions, Childress hid them as best he could behind a mask of stone.

For his part, Delapos, the third man at the table, also had concerns and reservations about some of the Nicaraguan's suggestions. The idea of hitting purely civilian targets, though logical, bothered Delapos. He was a mercenary, yes, but not a murderer. Though many of his own men would argue that such a fine distinction was purely academic, Delapos had for years maintained standards of conduct that had allowed him to keep his sanity and justify his work. A self-imposed prohibition against killing innocent civilians had been one of those standards. Now, it seemed, he would have to violate that prohibition, for logic told him that regardless of what he personally thought, such actions, in order to achieve what they desired, were necessary. After all, it was the attack on civilians by some of Pancho Villa's men in 1916 that had brought the American Army south of the border. When Delapos and Alamán had made their pact at the beginning of July, exactly that reaction was what they had hoped for. Now, when such a possibility was there for the taking, Delapos could not hesitate. He had, after all, pledged his personal loyalty to Alamán and his quest. To back off now would be both dishonorable and, for him as a professional mercenary, disreputable. Besides, the project would go on with or without him. Others, men with no moral scruples, would gladly take up where Delapos left off.

Without looking up from the beer bottle that he continued to turn slowly, Childress summarized the major points of their discussions. "As I see it, the colonel has some very valid points. Even with the improved weaponry that he will be providing, and the inside information Alamán is able to provide concerning American operations, the National Guard will be able to achieve superiority over our people every now and then. The National Guard can afford to lose both men and matériel. We cannot." Childress paused, lifted his beer bottle, took a sip, then pointed it at Delapos to drive home his point. "You might be able to explain away the loss of a single team to bad luck. After all, accidents will happen and everyone understands that. But if we start taking casualties, you're going to have some real problems. We are, after all, businessmen, not patriots. There is no profit in becoming a dead hero."

Delapos, looking down at the drink he was holding with both hands, shrugged. "I cannot argue with such logic. We must stay one step ahead of the Americans. We must maintain an edge." Delapos looked up at Childress, then the Nicaraguan. "Like you, my friends, I see that we have no choice." Lifting his drink, Delapos proposed a toast to seal their agreement. "It is time to end this discussion. There is much to do, and the sooner we start, the better."

Both the Nicaraguan and Childress brought their own drinks up, tapped Delapos's drink, and took a long sip. As they sipped, each man watched the other out of the corner of his eye, for each man knew that they were, at best, reluctant partners, temporarily joined by necessity. All three understood that each of the others, and Alamán, had his own agenda, one that was self-serving and had limits. In a pinch, each man would betray the next. They were, after all, businessmen.

AUSTIN, TEXAS
1030 HOURS, 13 AUGUST

The hostility that permeated the conference room poisoned every conversation, every comment. Even when no one was speaking, Dixon felt as if his body were being shredded by a deluge of invisible daggers from the governor and his staff seated across from them. It was for him, and all of the Army briefers from Fort Hood, a most difficult experience. Combat, Dixon thought, was preferable to the verbal and mental abuse they were being subjected to. In combat, at least you could do something. Here, in the presence of the governor of Texas, his adjutant general, and all their staffs, the only thing the Fort Hood people could do was preach the party line, take their lumps, and keep smiling.

The briefings being presented addressed how the regular Army planned to deal with the problems on the Mexican border. They were to have taken place at Fort Hood in another five days as part of a conference, a real dog-and-pony show meant to reassure the governors of the Southwestern states that the federal government was not ignoring them and had a plan to deal with the Mexican problem. Unilateral withdrawal of the U.S. Border Patrol and the deployment of the Texas National Guard to seal the border, however, had shot that plan all to hell. Instead of controlling the situation and providing a solution that would allow some flexibility for diplomacy, the federal government now found itself reacting to the initiatives of the governor of Texas. Part of that reaction was sending the corps commander and selected officers from his corps, to brief the governor of Texas on the Army's contingency plans for dealing with Mexico. Big Al, along with Dixon and the division intelligence officer, were among them.

The move by Governor Wise was a gamble. In a televised speech, Wise had stated, "Action, only action could protect the citizens of Texas and their property. Direct and unhesitating action, therefore, would be the order of the day in Texas. I am therefore ordering the Texas National Guard to do what the federal government seems incapable of doing, consequences be damned."

While his speech was stirring and his motives understandable, the Texas National Guard, despite its size, simply wasn't up to the task of sealing the border with Mexico. At best, the Guard would be able to establish outposts at critical crossing points along the border and patrol the rest. Even that would be difficult, for the bulk of the state's units were not structured for such operations. The largest unit, the 36th Mechanized Infantry Division, was designed to fight a high-tech foe on a modern battlefield using tanks, heavy artillery, and attack helicopters in swift, sweeping maneuvers. Its force structure, equipment, and training were ill-suited for the task of patrolling and securing the border. And even if the 36th Division, along with other Guard units, could do so, the cost of operating the equipment and paying its troops would soon bankrupt the state. Personnel and operating costs alone would cost the state of Texas several million dollars a day. Without federal manpower and funds, Texas alone could not accomplish what the governor publicly had set out to do.

That was where Governor Wise's gamble came in. Politically, he could ill afford inaction. Although he knew the state could not afford full-scale deployment of the National Guard without federal aid, he also knew that the president, and most of the Congress, could not, politically, afford to do nothing while Americans were being killed and the nation's southern border violated with impunity. What he needed to do was precipitate action. With Texas committed, he hoped to force the president to make a decision, one way or the other. Sending the National Guard to the border was a challenge that the president could not ignore.

Nor was it a challenge that the Mexican government could afford to ignore. Within an hour of the announcement of the deployment of the National Guard along the Texas border, the Mexican representative to the United Nations, supported by every Central American government and most South American governments, called for an emergency session of the UN. Within two hours a representative of the Mexican government was at the State Department demanding an explanation as to why the United States was militarizing the border between their nations. When the secretary of state commented that the action had been a unilateral one on the part of the governor of Texas, and that the president of the United States had not sanctioned such a move, the Mexican ambassador threw back a comment, word for word, that the secretary of state had used on the Mexican ambassador several times in recent weeks. "If, sir, your government is unable to control what is happening along its own borders, then my government will have no choice but to take action to control matters on our side of the border." In addition to the diplomatic moves, the CIA reported that the Mexican Army was finally beginning to stir itself.

For his part, the president had wanted to wait, allowing the Mexican government a period to establish itself and stabilize its own border. Like many in Washington, he and his closest advisors were puzzled by the raids. Privately, he favored the theory that forces opposed to the new regime were attempting to precipitate a crisis between the United States and Mexico. While that was a popular concept, called the Pancho Villa theory, the fact that the Mexican government could not control its borders and prevent such raids from taking place could not be ignored. More and more, the president was bombarded by calls to do what the new Mexican government could not do: to take action to secure the border. With the national presidential convention of his party less than a week away and that of the other party opening the next day, decisions had to be made.

Governor Wise's move, therefore, could not have come at a worse time, or in a worse form. In one fell swoop, the governor of Texas, and the reaction by Mexico, had all but eliminated diplomacy as an option. It was, as one presidential advisor mused, a shotgun wedding, with Governor Wise's finger on the trigger.

The commander of the Tenth Corps nodded to Big Al Malin. He, in turn, leaned over and whispered to Dixon the old gladiator's refrain, "We who are about to die salute you."

Dixon turned and looked Big Al in the eye. "Right behind you, boss."

While Big Al and Dixon stood and moved to the front of the room, the corps commander explained that the 16th Armored Division, with three active brigades and no units out of place due to training exercises, and because of its proximity to the border, was the best-prepared division to move to the border and would probably be the first to do so. The governor of Texas cut the corps commander off, dryly reminding him that the 36th, the division that had spearheaded the first bloody attempt to cross the Rapido River in Italy during World War II, was already headed there and that the 16th would be the second.

What the corps commander did not tell Governor Wise was that the 16th was the only division that had taken this particular contingency seriously and therefore was the only division with complete and updated plans for such an operation. Besides, Big Al and Scott Dixon made an unbeatable pair when it came to conducting a briefing. If they couldn't satisfy the Texans, no one could.

While Dixon managed a blizzard of slides, charts, and maps with overlays, Big Al did his thing. He started by stating that the United States Army, once deployed, had to consider the entire border with Mexico, not just the portion adjoining Texas. That, he explained, represented a grand total of 1,933 miles, or 3,111 kilometers, which included mountains, desert, and urban terrain. With that as a given, Dixon showed a slide that listed the amount of front a typical platoon, company, and battalion could defend, or cover, according to current doctrine, and handed out paper copies of the same slide to the governor and his adjutant general.

Taking great care, Big Al explained the problems that the Army would face if it were sent to the border. "As you can see, Governor, a mechanized infantry battalion, ordered to defend a piece of terrain, can effectively hold ten kilometers of front. To spread that battalion out further would mean leaving holes, or gaps, in the line. Even with this density, however, you are looking at one combat soldier every thirty-three meters. Were we faced by a mechanized foe, armed with tanks, armored personnel carriers, and such, that density, with the weapons available to the soldiers of a mechanized infantry battalion, would be able to stop the foe. Unfortunately, we are facing a light infantry threat, a guerrilla force not unlike the Viet Cong. Even with extensive barriers such as barbed wire, land mines, antivehicle ditches, active and passive sensors, and aggressive patrolling, the best infantry unit cannot prevent a determined foe from infiltrating through our defenses. We ourselves train to do just that, and the enemy, whoever he is, has demonstrated that he is both a skilled and clever opponent. Complicating this is the fact that in a typical mechanized infantry division, such as your 36th, only six battalions are infantry. The other four are tank battalions. In my division, I have the opposite mix, six battalions of tanks and four of infantry. While tank battalions are the cornerstone of offensive operations, they do poorly, almost without exception, in a static defense. The opponent we face would have little difficulty finding weak points and infiltrating at will.''

Shifting in his seat, Governor Wise grumbled. ''Opponent, my ass, they're goddamned murderers. And it's my people they're murdering.''

Big Al paused, allowing the governor to vent his spleen before carrying on. When Governor Wise had settled back into his seat and appeared ready to listen again, Big Al continued. ''The orders we received from the Tenth Corps state that my division is to be prepared to seal the border between the United States and Mexico from Laredo to Rio Grande City. We assumed that 'sealing' means preventing the movement of any hostile force north of the border.''

Governor Wise again cut in. ''Brilliant damned assumption, General. Did you come up with this on your own, or did you need some help from Washington?''

Ignoring the governor's attempt to provoke him, Big Al carried on as if the governor hadn't said a word. ''Given that interpretation, we could not accomplish our mission given the forces at my disposal and the length of the border assigned.''

The last comment, delivered in such a cool and unemotional manner, almost went over Governor Wise's head. It took him a moment to understand what Big Al had just said. When he did, Governor Wise shook his head and blurted out, ''You mean to say that you cannot do what your own commander told you to do? And that the United States Army cannot defend its own borders?''

In the same controlled and unemotional manner, Big Al responded without hesitation. ''Yes, sir, that is correct. Let me explain. In order to seal the border, we would be obliged to deploy in the manner shown on this slide, using the deployments and densities we have just gone over. Now, not every battalion can be on the front. We also assume that this will be a long-term mission, requiring the Army to be deployed for months, perhaps years. You cannot keep a unit on the front line forever. Therefore, some system of rotating units from the front to the rear would be necessary. One way of doing this would be to have each brigade, with an average of three battalions, hold one battalion in reserve. This reserve battalion, freed from frontline duty and the associated stress of that duty, would be able to rest, train, receive replacements for soldiers whose enlistments have expired, send some of its personnel on leave, and be ready to respond to any penetration of the frontline battalions. This reserve battalion would give us tactical depth, a deeper sector that any enemy force would be required to traverse if it penetrated the front line, and a force available to deal with such penetrations. Assuming each brigade was organized with three battalions, the division, in turn, would retain one battalion, the tenth battalion, as a division reserve for much the same purpose. Using that system, a division would have six battalions forward deployed, allowing each division to cover sixty kilometers of front.''

Understanding where Big Al was going, Governor Wise cut in again. In a briefing presented by his own military people a week earlier, he had been told much the same thing. ''Okay, so what you're trying to say is that the United States Army cannot accomplish its most fundamental mission, securing its own borders.''

Drawing in a deep breath, Big Al looked at the corps commander, then back at Governor Wise. ''In a nutshell, yes. We simply do not have enough troops and units, even with the National Guard and Army reserve federalized, to totally close down the border between the United States and Mexico.'' Anticipating what was coming, Dixon threw up a slide that showed the total number of divisions and personnel the Army would require to secure the border. ''As you can see on this slide, to establish a defensive system like the one I just briefed, which I repeat is by no means solid, would require fifty-two divisions, or an army of approximately two point six million soldiers. That figure is roughly five times the current standing Army authorized today. And that figure does not leave any units left to deal with other national and international contingencies. Two divisions in Europe, one in Korea, one in the Middle East, and a rapid-deployment force of three divisions would bump the number of divisions up to fifty-nine and the total strength of the Army to just under three million.''

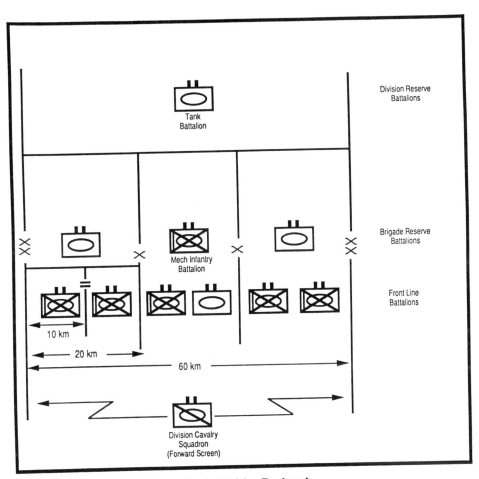

Briefing Slide Showing an Example of a Division Deployed

Before the shock of those figures wore off, Dixon threw up another slide labeled "Barrier Material." Big Al looked at the new slide, then at Governor Wise. "Now, we all know that we cannot simply put troops out into defensive positions without some sort of barrier to protect their positions and cover the gaps between those positions. Normally, a barrier combining triple strand concertina wire—that is, barbed wire—and antipersonnel mines is used when the threat is primarily dismounted personnel. This slide shows the amount of material needed to construct a simple, continuous barrier, from the Gulf of Mexico to the Pacific."

BARRIER MATERIAL

Standard Barbed Steel-Taped Concertina	611,830	rolls
Man-hours to Install Concertina	312,000	hours
Antipersonnel Mines at a 0-2-0 Density	14,508,000	mines
Man-hours to Lay Above Mines	1,810,000	hours
Truckloads Required to Haul Above Material	28,000	loads

"Please bear in mind, Governor, that these figures are approximations only and probably on the low side. Various areas, such as the mountainous area around Big Bend National Park, would require more material and time than a flat open stretch of border." The mention of Big Bend National Park caused the governor to wince, as Big Al had expected. After all, the vision of laying mines and stringing barbed wire through a national park was, to most Americans, a very disturbing thought. If anyone had missed the significance of Big Al's definition of "sealing the border" before, the last series of slides left no doubt as to the magnitude of what that task would entail and, as a follow-on, what it would cost, both financially and, more important to some, politically.

Pausing to allow these figures to sink in, Big Al waited until Governor Wise was ready. "Both you and I know, General, that the American people, and Congress, are not going to give you an army of three million men. On the other hand, the same American people and Congress will not, cannot, tolerate a do-nothing attitude. Surely you must realize that?"

Folding his arms in front of his chest, and looking down at the floor, Big Al nodded in agreement. "Yes, sir, you're right. The Army will be required to do something if our diplomats and the Mexicans don't solve the problem." Big Al then looked up and stared into Governor Wise's eyes. "We know that and we understand political reality. But you, sir, and the people in Washington, must understand military reality. If we are not given an army of sufficient size to defend the United States along its established borders, then we must either move those borders south, establishing a very wide security zone that can be patrolled with the small mobile forces we have, or we must remove the current government of Mexico and replace it with one that can control its own borders. Any way you look at it, the only practical military solutions available to us all start with an invasion of Mexico.''

For the first time during the briefing, Governor Wise remained silent as Big Al let the meaning of his last statement seep in and take root. During this lull, the corps commander caught Big Al's eye. With a faint smile and a slight nod of his head, he congratulated Big Al for wrestling the initiative away from Governor Wise and putting him into a receptive mood. The corps commander knew that the rest of the briefing could now proceed without trouble.

NUEVO LAREDO, MEXICO
1230 HOURS, 14 AUGUST

From the doorway of the commander's office, Colonel Guajardo watched soldiers of the local garrison company issue members of the Rural Defense Corps new weapons. In the upcoming confrontation, the Rural Defense Corps, a force of over 120,000 men, would play an important role in the defense of Mexico. These men, peasants from the surrounding countryside, would form the core of a stay-behind force that would provide information on the activities of the invading force and harass the rear areas of that force. It would be a difficult task and, no doubt, a costly one. After all, these men, who ranged in age from eighteen to fifty, were farmers and part-time volunteers, not trained soldiers.

Organized into eleven-man units called *pelotones*, they were used under normal circumstances by the governing body of the *ejido*, or local land-holding commune, to protect the peasants. With training that was limited, equipment which was almost nonexistent, and leadership that understood only the most rudimentary tactics, there was little that would make them an effective guerrilla force. In open combat, against a modern, well-trained, high-tech army, they would be brushed aside like so many flies. Even with their newly issued German-made H-53 rifles and Mexican-produced RM-2 machine guns, man for man, they could not hope to stand up to American mechanized infantry. Guajardo, however, had no intention of pitting them against American infantry.

There was little that Guajardo could give these men, other than the new rifles and one machine gun with 2,000 rounds per *pelotón*, to improve their odds. But that was enough. What they lacked in weapons and skills, they more than made up for in spirit and will. Even without the new weapons, the men of the Rural Defense Corps would have fought. They, and not the politicians in Mexico City, were the true grandchildren and great-grandchildren of Juárez and the Revolution. From early childhood, they had been raised to revere the deeds and struggles of their forefathers, to have faith in the Virgin of Guadalupe, and to jealously protect their land and rights from all quarters. Almost all had, at one time or another, been shown a picture of a relative who had fought in the Revolution. The image of that relative, standing tall in a wide sombrero, bandoliers criss-crossed over a proud chest thrown out, and holding a rifle at the ready, was burned into their memories. Some even had the ancient Mauser rifles that their grandfathers had carried when the picture was taken. Properly used, these men could tie down enemy forces many times their size. And with the prospect of an American invasion becoming more and more likely, the question of how and when to use them, and every other military and paramilitary unit in Mexico, was a question that Guajardo had to answer.

The deployment of the Texas National Guard to the border had come as no surprise. Every member of the Council of 13 knew that the United States would, eventually, do something. The only surprise was that the move had been a unilateral one made by the governor of Texas.

There was no question among the members of the council that some type of reaction to the provocative American move was required. The only questions were what kind and how much were necessary at this time. The session of August 12, convened late in the afternoon to discuss the issue, had degenerated into a long, heated debate that created the first rift in the council since the June 29 coup.

Colonel Barreda, minister for foreign affairs, had opened the session with a review of the responses he had received through diplomatic channels at the UN and in Washington, D.C. That the movement of American troops would act as an impediment to his ability to deal with the American government could not be denied. "How can they expect us," he said, "to take them seriously when they offer one hand in friendship and talk of peace while they hold a gun in the other hand behind their backs?"

Barreda ended his review with an impassioned speech that was also supposed to be a warning. "Once a sword is drawn," he said, "for whatever reason, it is hard to return it to its sheath without showing some kind of victory. And that victory can only come at our expense." Walking about the table, his arms waving, and caught up in the passion of the moment, Barreda continued. "The governor of Texas, no doubt with the sanction of their president and in an effort to test our resolve, has declared, in his own words, a 'holy war' against us, referring to us as evil and murderers." Barreda ended by warning that if they did nothing, if they allowed the United States to dictate policy to them, they, the Council of 13, would lose face and fall. Caught up in the heat of the moment, however, Barreda forgot about his call for moderation and, instead of warning against precipitous actions, swung toward a call to arms. "As our forefathers did in 1846, so must we send our Army to the Rio Grande. To do less would be criminal and cowardly. And so, as Major General Mariano Arista did in 1846, Colonel Guajardo must be ordered north to the Rio Grande with the Mexican Army to face an American Army sent by their government to threaten us."

Barreda's rhetoric began to sway some of the moderates on the council. As Guajardo watched the foreign minister deliver his inflammatory oration, more and more members of the council began to nod their heads in agreement. To counter this groundswell of support for military action, Guajardo believed that he had to be the cold, practical realist. He therefore commenced his review of Mexico's military situation by reminding them what had happened when General Arista went north to respond to President Polk's stationing of Zachary Taylor's army in Texas. Arista, with a larger force, had been defeated by Taylor at the battles of Palo Alto and Resaca de la Palma, leaving his army routed and Mexico open to invasion. Guajardo's task, as minister of defense, was to protect the council from all major threats, both internal, which he emphasized as he looked at Barreda, and international.

The move by the governor of Texas, Guajardo warned, could be a small-scale test to see how they, the Council of 13 and the people of Mexico, would react to an overt military threat. If that were true, then they, the Council of 13, had to do something soon, but something that matched the threat and did not result in an escalation of the crisis. Instead, Guajardo stated, "We must, in this case, play the innocent victim. Our efforts to defend ourselves must be measured, but not provocative. Otherwise, we stand to lose any sympathy that we might gain from other nations, not to mention providing the Americans with more justification for these moves and more dangerous ones in the future. No, we must stay the course and continue as planned."

Referred to as the Dark One, Guajardo relied on few for counsel and provided little indication of what he was thinking or planning as he carried out his duties. With the exception of Colonel Molina, few could penetrate the mask of stone that Guajardo wore to hide his thoughts, his feelings, and his fears. Often, his subordinates were told only what they needed to know in order to execute their next mission. In part, this was a holdover from the days before the twenty-ninth of June, when secrecy had been of the greatest importance. But that was not the whole reason. Guajardo, despite the fact that he had been raised in a society where men used boasts and rhetoric to intimidate their adversaries and promote themselves, disliked boastful men. Instead, he prized men of action, men who did, rather than bragged, men who saw things that needed to be done and did them with little fuss and no need for praise or physical reward. Action and results were what mattered to Guajardo. Everything else was, to him, a waste of time.

The plan that he spoke of staying with was one designed to fill the gaps left by the purges of the federal police and intelligence agencies. The Rural Defense Corps was a critical part of that plan, a plan that had already been accelerated as a result of the mysterious raids just north of the Rio Grande. Though the plan did call for an increase in both readiness and training of regular Army units, it intentionally avoided any increased military presence along the United States–Mexican border. Guajardo ended by stating that any movement of the Army north would only increase the tension that already was building. "I realize that it may be true that the Americans have a gun behind their back. That, however, does not mean that we must put bullets into it for them."

Spurred on by Barreda's stirring speech, Colonel Zavala led the faction calling for full mobilization. Guajardo's actions to secure the northern borders and his call for moderation were, in Zavala's words, timid, insufficient, and dangerous. "To do as our brother suggests," Zavala stated, "is tantamount to leaving our northern border undefended. How can we expect to command the respect of our own people, let alone the Americans, if we do nothing in our own defense? This is no time for half measures." Zavala's conclusion of his appeal to his brothers on the council was an emotional one, one that was meant to embarrass Guajardo as much as to rally support for Zavala's position. "Our honor as Mexicans and the Revolution demand that every inch of Mexican soil be defended. It is the only manly thing we can do at times like this."

Throughout the night, Guajardo continued to appeal to reason and sanity. "We can no more stop the Americans from coming, if they choose, than they can occupy all of Mexico. Sending the entire Army to the border to defend our masculinity is absurd and wasteful. No, we must restrain ourselves from overreacting. We must move slowly and cautiously, or we stand to lose everything that we have gained since the twenty-ninth.'' Although Molina favored Guajardo's position, as the president of the council, he kept out of the debate, allowing Guajardo to present his position. If the matter came to a tie vote, Molina would throw his behind Guajardo.

That, however, was not necessary. When the final vote was taken just before midnight on the 12th, seven members of the council voted to declare full mobilization and meet the challenge from the north as best they could. So, when President Molina announced from Mexico City that morning that it was with a heavy heart that he was ordering the full mobilization of the Army and militia in preparation to go north to the border, he meant it.

The rearming of the Rural Defense Corps, planned before the current crisis, fell into place with the defensive plan that Guajardo was now developing as a result of the council's call for full mobilization. Even before the current crisis, Guajardo had felt that there was a need for the rearming, and so he had issued the appropriate orders. At that time, he himself could not have explained to his own satisfaction why he felt that doing so was necessary. Events had proved him right, though not for reasons he could have foreseen at the time.

The Rural Defense Corps, on horseback and foot, and supplemented by mechanized cavalry units of the Mexican Army, would patrol the border, providing both a visible presence and information. The last point, the gathering of information, was both critical and, for the Council of 13, a sore point. The Purification had, when it came to purging Mexico's intelligence apparatus and both the national and state police forces, gone too far too fast. While few members of the intelligence community and the police had been arrested, the number of those under suspension had been quite large, accounting for over one-third of all members of those agencies. In addition, many of those who were not affected by these actions deserted, either fleeing north to the United States or back to their home villages. This accounted for another third of the force. Within the ranks of those that remained, morale was almost nonexistent and reliability even lower. After all, as Colonel Zavala pointed out, to the intelligence community and police forces of Mexico, the interests of Mexico and of the PRI had been one and the same. "How can we trust men," Zavala had stated before June 29, "who owe everything they have to men whom we are about to kill?"

Perhaps he had been right, Guajardo mused as he watched a *pelotón* of Rural Defense Corps reassemble after receiving their new weapons. The men, smiles on their faces, were busy chatting amongst themselves while they worked the actions on the rifles and machine gun and inspected the sights by aiming at distant objects around the courtyard. These men, who had also been part of the PRI's power structure, would now have to do the bulk of what trained and organized professionals had once done. And their task would be complicated by the need to look both ways, for it was Guajardo's intent to use this force to not only keep track of activities north of the border, but also on their own side. Perhaps, he thought, they, people from the local communities along the border, could discover who it was that was working so hard to start a war between Mexico and the United States. Any information, any clue, any tiny break could make a difference, a difference that could end the current crisis and buy the council the time to work the miracle so desperately needed to save Mexico.

But as far as Guajardo was concerned, time and hope were running out. Each day brought the possibility of open conflict between the two nations closer. And as that gap closed, the possibility diminished that the United States would believe any evidence offered by the Council of 13 that it was not responsible for the border raids.

12

The country must have a large and efficient army, one capable of meeting the enemy abroad, or they must expect to meet him at home.

—Sir Arthur Wellesley, Duke of
Wellington

ON U.S. HIGHWAY 83, 10 KILOMETERS NORTH OF SAN YGNACIO,
TEXAS
1745 HOURS, 29 AUGUST

Moving far too fast to observe anything along the route, the lead Humvee of Sergeant Jimmy Sullivan's scout section raced along the deserted highway to their assigned observation post. Two hundred meters behind, the second Humvee of the section, an armored Humvee armed with an M-60 machine gun, was pushing it to keep up with Sullivan. Were it not for an occasional reminder from Private Tod Alison, who normally drove Sullivan, Sullivan would have gone faster and lost the heavier and slower vehicle. Losing the second vehicle, however, was the least of his concerns. With both hands gripping the steering wheel, Sullivan ignored the speedometer and leaned on the accelerator in an effort to make up the time they had lost getting ready back at the battalion's base camp. In the backseat, Andy Morrezzo, a scout observer, held onto his map with one hand and the radio mike with his other, keeping track of their progress and calling off checkpoints as they went whizzing by. While he was doing so, Morrezzo hoped that no one back at the battalion was noticing that they were hitting the checkpoints rather fast.

There were any number of excuses Sullivan could use, if necessary, to explain why they had started late. After all, this was only their third day on the border, using equipment that was relatively new to them, and working as a section for the first time. Even under the best of circumstances, it took the men of the 1st Battalion, 141st Infantry, most of the first week of annual summer camp to get into the groove of tactical operations. After all, you simply cannot jerk eight hundred men from their homes scattered all over central Texas one day and expect them to be up to speed, working as a battalion, the next.

To say that the conditions they were working under were far from the best would be an understatement. To start with, instead of going to Fort Hood, where their equipment was located, the battalion had assembled at Camp Mabry in Austin, Texas. There, they were reorganized and issued a mix of Humvees and ancient M-151 jeeps instead of their armored vehicles. The wheeled vehicles, which were cheaper to operate and more suitable for patrolling the vast stretch of border which they were responsible for, were nonetheless new to the men and required some retraining as well as rethinking on how to employ them. In the case of Sullivan's section, this meant reorganization as well as training. At Camp Mabry, Sullivan found that his scout section, authorized at five men and one M-3 Bradley fighting vehicle but consisting of four men and one M-113 armored personnel carrier since it was short personnel and modern equipment, now consisted of six men and two Humvees. One of the Humvees he was issued was a stripped model with nothing but a radio. It could carry four men and their equipment. The second Humvee, borrowed from an MP unit, was an armored version with a roof mount for the M-60 machine gun. The FM radios in both vehicles, VRC-64s, were built in the 1960s and had a planning range of twenty-five kilometers, or sixteen miles, which would be woefully inadequate for what they would have to do. Sullivan still wasn't sure how best to use this combination of equipment when they were moved to their sector on the border.

Sullivan's personnel status was just as bad. Of the three men assigned to his scout section before the call-up, one announced on the day everyone reported to the armory that he was nondeployable due to his job with the state police. This cut Sullivan's section down to three, including himself. To make good this deficiency, three new men were assigned to his section after they had arrived at Camp Mabry. One man, the best of the lot, had just left active duty. Although he had been an artilleryman while in the Army, he at least was trained. Of the other two, one had not yet had a chance to attend basic training while the other, Jack Lyttle, Sullivan suspected, was a dud transferred from one of the infantry companies. Jack was a nice enough guy, anxious to please, but seemingly incapable of doing anything without close supervision. Sullivan thought that Jack's nickname, Gomer Pyle, gave him too much credit, since, as Sullivan put it, at least Gomer knew how to wear his uniform properly.

With this mix of new equipment, men, and mission, with almost no time to organize and train properly, Sullivan didn't have to fabricate a reason for not making their start time. In the words of his first sergeant, the scout platoon was an accident waiting to happen.

While Sullivan knew he could get away with such excuses, he didn't want to if he didn't need to. To do so at this early stage would be unwise. The good ole boy system had no place in the 1st of the 141st. Instead, both the company commander and the battalion commander judged their people on their performance, not who they were or who they knew. Those who performed were rewarded, those who didn't got extra training or the boot. The day would come, Sullivan knew, when he would need a favor, such as a couple of days off to go home and see his family. When that time came, the last thing he wanted to have was some officer pull out his notebook, flip to a page, and inform Sullivan that on 29 August he and his patrol had been thirty minutes late getting into place. And Captain Terry Wilkes, his company commander, was just the kind of guy to do that. So Sullivan told his normal driver to hop in the passenger seat, took the wheel, and made a beeline for the site where they would set up their first observation post that night. Along the way, he decided to reduce the number of stops to check crossing points from six to three and make a visual inspection of the other three as they went by. It was a gamble that Sullivan thought was worth taking.

The truth was, it didn't make any difference. Even had Sullivan stopped at each of the six crossing points in his sector, neither he nor his section would have found any traces of Lefleur and his team. They, like all the other teams, were already north of the border, preparing to operate from new locations in the United States, not Mexico.

In a stroke of real genius, Delapos had ordered his teams to go north and find base camps on the U.S. side of the Rio Grande before the Texas National Guard was able to close on the border and replace the U.S. Border Patrol. The advantages of doing so were numerous. By operating in the United States, Delapos's men could avoid the need to sneak through the increasing Mexican patrols, crossing a border that was coming under intense scrutiny by human and electronic surveillance on both sides, and then, when finished, come back after everyone was alerted. Their earlier operations, against the border patrol, had more than established the idea in everyone's mind that the raids were coming across the border. There was, therefore, no need to reinforce this. What was necessary was to maintain a high success rate without compromise or loss. Actions by both the Mexican government and the state of Texas were making this harder. Capitalizing on the fact that the Americans were becoming both frustrated and mesmerized by the ability of the raiders to move across the border without detection, both Delapos and Childress suspected that each success would cause the Americans to panic, redoubling their intelligence efforts at or south of the border, not north of it. If this in fact happened, Delapos figured that their operations would become easier as more troops and efforts were piled up on the border and drawn away from the interior.

Besides being able to avoid crossing the border, Delapos would be able to supply, pay, reinforce, and communicate with his people with greater ease. In the days after June 29, it had not been a problem to move men, weapons, and money about in Mexico while the Purification was decimating Mexico's police and intelligence agencies and causing panic among those that remained. Deployment of the Rural Defense Corps, movement of regular Army units to the border, and acceptance of the Council of 13 by the people, however, had made operations south of the border hazardous.

Coupled with an increase in the odds of being discovered while operating on the border itself, was the fact that the Council of 13 was beginning to gain a firm grasp of Mexico's institutions and systems. Banks, now under control, were limiting the amount of funds that could be transferred in and out of the country. The purge of customs officials, as well as of the police at seaports and airports, was over. Those who remained took the lessons of the Purification to heart and were, at least for the time being, incorruptible. To ensure that they remained so, the customs officials and police were being rotated to other assignments randomly and at irregular intervals, making it difficult to bribe them and allow arms and military supplies to be smuggled in. Against such moves, there was little Alamán or Delapos could do. Even communications and movement were becoming more difficult. The comings and goings of strangers were being tracked and reported. The telephone system was susceptible to being tapped. And roving roadblocks, set up without notice and at random intervals, were making movements of equipment difficult to plan.

The situation in the United States, however, was different. If anything, the shifting of operations north simplified matters. Despite the fact that the raids had created a panic in Texas and the National Guard had been called out, no one, not even the governor of Texas, was prepared to suspend civil liberties by declaring martial law or restricting movement of civilians. It was therefore possible for Delapos's men, especially those who were North American or European, to travel near the border in pickup trucks and scout out their next ambush sites and watch the National Guard as it deployed and maneuvered. Some, like Childress, actually went up to the National Guard observation posts. Striking up a conversation with the guardsmen, Childress would share beer he just happened to have in a cooler in the back of his pickup, telling them how glad he was to see them on the job, and swap war stories. And while the guardsmen drank his beer, Childress carefully noted how they were equipped, asking seemingly innocent questions about their unit and mission, and listened to their reporting procedures. That they were being set up was the last thing on their minds. After all, he spoke the language, looked like them, and had been in the Army himself. The enemy, according to the commanders, were sneaky little Mexicans. As far as the soldiers were concerned, Childress was just another good ole boy who really knew how to support the troops.

Not that Childress really had to do this. To ensure that the border was properly covered, and that military operations did not interfere with civilian operations, all American patrol plans, roadblocks, and OP locations had to be determined well in advance, coordinated with state and local authorities, and approved. If an OP was to be located on private property, the owner of the land had to be notified. In this way, a great deal of detailed information was available and passing through many hands on a daily basis. It was therefore not difficult for Alamán to energize his own intelligence network. The fact was, some of the state and local officials who were handling the military information were already on Alamán's payroll, holdovers from when Alamán's efforts had been simply to facilitate the movement of drugs and illegal aliens.

Movement of new personnel, funds, and even military hardware, was no problem. In fact, using Alamán's connections, it was surprisingly easy. Secondhand weapons no longer needed by the Nicaraguan and Cuban governments were purchased by Alamán's agents and shipped to Colombia. There they were combined with regular drug traffic organized and run by Alamán's associates in that country and sent on flights being made into the United States. Once in the United States, the new personnel, funds, weapons, and equipment were moved by road using a trucking company owned by another of Alamán's associates. In this way, Delapos was able to provide antitank guided missiles and portable surface-to-air guided missiles to his teams within a matter of weeks.

Though outdated, the new heavy and precision-guided weapons gave Delapos's teams an edge that the National Guard was unaware of. When they did find out about it, and American intelligence began to look into the matter, they would find little useful or conclusive information, be-

cause the Nicaraguans were providing the same weapons to the regular
Mexican Army. Even this effort was planned in such a way as to reinforce
the confusion within the American intelligence community about whether
the Mexican government, through intent or ineptitude, was implicated.

By using the same Nicaraguan colonel who was handling the movement of weapons to the Mexican Army, Alamán could avoid duplicate
systems. Both he and the Mexican Army were drawing from the same
stock of weapons. The Nicaraguan colonel, for his part, ensured that
weapons and ammunition provided to either the Mexican Army or Alamán
did not have consecutive serial numbers, but were mixed. For example,
a shipment of surface-to-air missiles was arranged so that the Mexican
Army received weapons with serial numbers one through three, while
Alamán received the missile with serial number four, the Mexican Army
numbers five and six, Alamán seven and eight, and so forth. In this way,
if the Americans were able to obtain the original manufacturer's serial
numbers, and track them through Nicaragua, there was the possibility that
some would be found to be in the hands of the Mexican Army while
others, with consecutive serial numbers, were found conveniently discarded at ambush sites in the United States.

There was little, therefore, from Delapos's standpoint, to fear from the
National Guard. With the Guard in place and settled into a discernible
routine, and his own teams rearmed and set north of the border, Delapos
was more than ready to open the next phase of Alamán's reign of terror.

From the seat of the division commander's command and control helicopter, Scott Dixon watched the two Humvees below for a moment
before returning his attention to the border to the south. This was his third
trip to the border in ten days and, with pressure increasing for the federal
government to take an active role in securing the border, he knew it
wouldn't be his last.

The recons, by Dixon and other key members of the division, were
meant to prepare them for what some called the inevitable deployment of
the division south. Rather than increase his knowledge of the area and
better prepare him, however, each successive recon only served to
heighten Dixon's sense of foreboding and apprehension. Even Jan, during their brief reunions, noted that Dixon was treating the entire subject
of the use of American military forces on the border with great trepida-
tion. In one halting discussion over dinner, he kept pointing out that
unless someone came up with what he called a "war-winning strategy,"
they were not only wasting time and manpower, but were leaving them-

selves open to a situation that had no definable goal and little direction other than the perceived need to "teach the Mexicans a lesson." In his heart, Dixon knew that if the Army deployed to the border, someone, for some reason, would find an excuse for using it in Mexico. And once that happened, there would be no peace for years, on either side of the border. With a heavy Hispanic population throughout the southwestern United States and a strong anti-American sentiment in Mexico and Central America, the resulting mess would make the Israeli-Palestinian problem in the Middle East look like child's play.

Turning his thoughts away from the politics of the problem, which were not his concern anyway, and back to the immediate military situation, Dixon looked out the open door. The terrain below, the area where the 16th would be operating, was a real horror story. Looking down at his map, Dixon tried to figure out where they were. In the process of trying to solve the problems of the world, he had lost track of his location. When he couldn't relate the terrain he was looking at to the symbols on the map, he flipped the map over and refolded it to uncover the next sheet, taking great care to hang on to it as he did so lest the wind rip it from his hands and out of the helicopter. To lose one's map was the nightmare of every officer, the supreme moment of embarrassment. As a young company commander, leading his tank company on his first major tactical exercise in Germany, Dixon had lost his map doing just what he was doing now. The image of his wayward map, lazily floating away down the long column of tanks after being ripped from his hands, was burned into his mind as one of the three most embarrassing moments in his life. Though he didn't take the precaution of tying his map to him with a string, like they taught at the infantry school, he was always extremely careful and very mindful of what he was doing whenever he handled his map while on or in a moving vehicle.

It therefore came as a surprise when, after refolding his map, he looked up and saw a UH-1 helicopter flying parallel to them south of the border. Running his hand along the intercom cable until he found the intercom button, Dixon pressed the button and blurted, "Who's that?"

The pilot, a young warrant officer, responded without thinking. "It's a helicopter, sir."

Taken aback by the comment, Dixon tried to decide if the aviator was trying to be a smartass or didn't understand what Dixon wanted. Either way, he decided that he should have gotten a better answer. He therefore decided to give the young warrant a verbal shot in the head. "No shit, Sherlock. You figure that out on your own or did the co-pilot help?"

There was a pause while the pilot figured out that Dixon was not pleased with his first response. In a more respectful and less flippant tone, he corrected himself. "Sorry, sir. It looks like a Mexican Air Force Bell 212. It came up from the south, from our seven o'clock position a few seconds ago and began to parallel us. He's still on his side of the border, traveling at approximately one hundred knots."

Dixon only grunted in response as he looked across the open space between the two aircraft in an effort to find any distinguishing marks or equipment that would help him identify it later. The Mexican Air Force helicopter, like his, had its doors wide open. He could clearly see its pilot and co-pilot, the crew chief, and the door gunners. On the right side of the cargo bay, a lone passenger sat. He, like Dixon, held a map on his lap and was watching Dixon watch him. No doubt, Dixon thought, the lone passenger was an officer, like him, making his recon in order to prepare himself for the deployment of his forces to the border. The irony of the situation did not escape him. Keying the intercom again, Dixon instructed the pilot to slowly increase their air speed. Dixon wanted to see how badly the Mexican, whoever he was, wanted to play chicken.

Colonel Guajardo had no doubt that the American UH-60 helicopter his helicopter was paralleling was a command and control aircraft. The symbol of the 16th Armored Division, painted in bold colors, was all over it. That, and the lone passenger seated before a huge radio set in the cargo bay, left little doubt that the anonymous American was doing the same thing that he was. And the presence of door gunners, on the American aircraft as well as his own, told Guajardo how seriously both sides took the current situation.

As he watched the American door gunner that faced him, Guajardo noted that he held the spade grips of his M-60 machine gun with his right hand angled down and away from Guajardo. Guajardo knew, however, what the American gunner was thinking. Even with the American's sun visor down, Guajardo could almost feel the eyes drilling a hole through him as the gunner mentally noted range and computed the angle of deflection he would need to apply in order to hit Guajardo's helicopter. Such thoughts, Guajardo knew, were expected. In fact, only a poor soldier would have been thinking of other things. And the odds were nonexistent that a poor soldier would be part of the crew on a command and control helicopter.

The thought of flying in such close proximity to a group of men who were prepared to kill him without hesitation, on order, was sobering. How easy, Guajardo thought, it would be for the American door gunner to pull his weapon over into firing position and engage his aircraft. A simple pulling in of the right arm until the spade grips were in front of the door gunner's chest, a lifting of his left hand to the spade grips, a pause to sight the gun, and a downward motion with his two thumbs were all that was necessary for the gunner to engage Guajardo's helicopter and start a war. So simple, so easy. Yet the American would not do it, at least not yet. There were still a few hands left to be played out by the politicians and the diplomats. Until these hands were played, it was the task of Guajardo, and no doubt of the unknown American officer in the other helicopter, to keep stupid mistakes from starting something that would cost both sides more than either could possibly imagine.

An increase in the vibration of his own helicopter rattled Guajardo back to the present. He looked to the American helicopter and noted that it seemed to move forward slightly. Then there was an increase in the vibration of his own helicopter as the pilot pushed the old Bell 212 to keep up. Looking toward his own pilot, he noted that First Lieutenant Blasio's head was turned toward the American helicopter, watching its every move and matching it. Guajardo, realizing that the American was intentionally increasing his speed, knew that Blasio could not possibly match the speed and performance of the American. The American was only playing with him, egging Blasio on until he couldn't keep up. The American would then kick in whatever power he had left and leave Blasio behind. In order to spare Blasio such an undeserved humiliation, Guajardo ordered him to stand by to execute the sharpest left turn he could, telling Blasio that he wanted to show the American the backside of a Mexican Air Force helicopter.

This order was greeted by Blasio with great pleasure, for he also realized that he must soon fall behind the American. This way, at least he could show the American some of his skills as an aviator. When he was ready, he informed Guajardo, warning everyone to hang on. "Very well then, Lieutenant. On the count of three. One . . . two . . . three . . ."

As he finished three, Blasio jerked up on his lateral, twisted his collective to get whatever power he had left, and threw the stick to the left as hard as he could. The American helicopter, and Guajardo's view of the ground, disappeared in a flash as the helicopter practically stood on its side in a violent power turn. Guajardo could feel himself being forced back into the seat, as if by a giant hand, throughout the turn, by the increase in speed and climb. By the time the helicopter was back in level flight, the American helicopter was nowhere in sight.

Satisfied that Blasio's pride had been saved, Guajardo instructed him to come around and back onto their heading for Nuevo Laredo. Guajardo was anxious to arrive at the garrison headquarters there and talk to the officers of the cavalry units before they moved out for their nightly patrols. As with the other units along the border, Guajardo wanted to impress upon his officers and men the gravity of the situation. Common sense, tempered by healthy discretion, were the order of the day. Although every man was expected to do his duty, investigating anything and everything of note during their patrols, they were to do their utmost to avoid provoking the Americans. In order to rally world support and opinion in the event of a confrontation, Mexico had to be the offended party.

NUEVO LAREDO, MEXICO
1925 HOURS, 29 AUGUST

Standing alone, Lieutenant Augustín Martí watched the colonel's helicopter lift itself through the cloud of dust created by its own rotors and jet engines. Even after the helicopter was aloft and on its way to its next stop, Martí continued to stand there, almost as if he expected Colonel Guajardo to turn around and come back. But Martí knew that would not happen. There was much that the colonel needed to do and so little time. Such an important man could not afford to explain everything in detail to every lieutenant in the Mexican Army. It was not up to the colonel to explain everything, for if that were the case, there would be no need for lieutenants. No, Martí thought, it was his task to understand what the colonel had said and act accordingly.

Still, as Martí turned and headed back to his platoon, he wished that he were clever enough to grasp exactly what it was that the colonel expected of him and his men. That the situation along the border was serious was well understood. One only had to listen to the news, both from Mexican sources and Spanish-speaking radio and TV stations in America, to know that there was a great deal of mistrust and tension between the two nations. Even the dullest peasant in his platoon felt a sense of foreboding as they approached their duties. All of this was known. All of this was understood.

Why, then, Martí kept asking as he slowly shuffled through the dust, did the colonel, a member of the Council of 13, feel it was so important that he take time from his busy schedule to come all the way from Mexico City and personally deliver a message such as the one he had just given? Did he doubt the ability of the Army to act in an appropriate manner? Or was there some hidden meaning in what he had told them? Perhaps that was it. Perhaps, Martí thought, the colonel wanted them to do their duty, but not too well. Or was it that he wanted them to do their duty only so long as it did not interfere with the Americans? And what was he to do if the Americans did do something that violated Mexican territory? Martí understood the need to avoid provoking the Americans. That was simple. But did that mean avoidance to the point of surrender? What was he to do if the Americans provoked him? And what, he thought, constituted provocation?

Stopping just short of his platoon, Martí turned and looked back in the direction that Guajardo's helicopter had disappeared. Why hadn't he asked Guajardo his questions when he had the chance? Why had he stood there, like a lump, and nodded dumbly, acting as if he understood when he didn't? Martí wondered if his pride was so important that he was willing to sacrifice himself and his platoon rather than ask questions that should have been asked, regardless of how elementary they were. Was that it? A simple question of pride?

Shaking his head, he turned and looked at his platoon. His sergeants were already gathering their men in preparation for his return and final instructions. Well, Martí thought as he shook his head, the colonel is gone. It is now up to me to do what is necessary. After whispering a short prayer to the Virgin of Guadalupe to watch over him and his platoon, he stepped off with a confident pace in an effort to mask the doubts he felt, and prepared to execute his duties as he saw fit. After all, what else could he do? It was him, and only him, that was left. In the end, Martí thought, that must have been the way it always was. The pride and security of a nation entrusted to the hands and judgment of a junior officer and his men.

OFFICERS AND CIVILIANS' OPEN MESS, FORT HOOD, TEXAS
1925 HOURS, 29 AUGUST

Coming to the officers club had been a big mistake. Nancy Kozak knew that now. Not that it would have made any difference where she went. Her feelings of loneliness, self-doubt, and inadequacy would have followed her wherever she went. She just thought that perhaps, at the officers club, she could escape them or, at least, submerge them for a while.

She couldn't do that in her small one-bedroom apartment, a place that she had yet to be able to call home. It was a place to sleep, a place to store her things, a place to shower and change her clothes. But it was not a home, a place where she could go and leave the world behind, where she could let herself go, where she could relax. Instead of being a nice little cozy niche, a safe haven, it seemed, at times, to be a vise, its walls closing in on her and accentuating her loneliness rather than offering an escape from it. So, instead of being a refuge, her apartment became another place that she needed to escape from.

Escape, what a thought. As Kozak stared mindlessly down at her plate, poking her chicken with a fork, she wondered what she was trying to escape from. Loneliness, yes, she wanted to do that. Everyone wanted that. But escape did not solve the problem. It only delayed resolution. That's what she wanted. That's what she needed. A solution. But in order to have a solution, you need to have a definable problem to deal with. And that, Kozak knew, was the crux of the matter. After being at Fort Hood for two months, she had never taken the time to sort herself out, to stop and absorb what she had learned and come up with an effective means of dealing with her new world.

The Army, she had found, was far different from what she had experienced at West Point. Although everyone had known that the real Army would be different, few of her classmates had really understood how different it would be. Though 2nd Battalion, 13th Infantry, was a disciplined unit, its discipline was different from West Point's. At times, rather than acting as a single, coherent entity operating under a hierarchical system of command, her platoon appeared to be a loose association of sergeants and soldiers who functioned as crewmen, squads, and platoon through cooperation and mutual consent. In some cases, the junior soldiers seemed to be more influential and capable than their sergeants. This should not have been a surprise to Kozak—but understanding such things and dealing with them were two different matters. This, in itself, was a challenge that she had still to master.

Then there were the people themselves. No amount of reading, no role-playing in leadership classes, could possibly prepare a person for dealing with real people with real problems. From the sergeant who had bouts with alcoholism and wife-beating to the married soldier who went to pieces every time the platoon rolled out to the field, Kozak found herself facing things she had never dealt with before. And each situation, each member of her platoon, and each of their problems, demanded a solution that was correct and appropriate to the individual.

On top of all this came the warning order to be prepared for immediate deployment to the Mexican border. How, Kozak thought, could she possibly deal with her own problems and those of the world at the same time.

Looking up for a moment, Kozak scanned the room. There were officers, some in uniform, some not, scattered about in groups or with their
spouses. Their age, their deportment, and the company they were in made
it easy to identify their rank. There were young company-grade officers,
lieutenants and captains, who sat together in groups. Their laughter and
conversation was free and unrestrained. Their faces and manner betrayed
a certain arrogance and cockiness born of innocence and youth, an innocence Kozak herself could identify with. At the other extreme were the
lieutenant colonels and colonels. They sat quietly with their wives, and
their manner, just as much as their looks, spoke of maturity and wisdom
gained through experience and endurance. Their wives, graceful orna-
ments, complemented them, as good Army wives should. A third group,
senior captains and majors, were liberally scattered about the room, filling the spaces between the colonels and the lieutenants and providing a
buffer, both real and psychological, between the two groups. These officers were in transition. No longer young and innocent like the lieutenants, this last group had not yet achieved the qualities, loosely referred to
as maturity and experience, that allowed them to face the world with the
cool, calm demeanor that the colonels displayed. The senior captains and
majors were in training, eager to please and do whatever was necessary
to prove themselves ready to join the colonels. For they knew, even in
this setting, that they were on display, being watched by both superiors
and subordinates. If, in their hearts, they might still feel the urge to join
the laughter and light conversation of the younger officers, the majors
knew they had to demonstrate to the colonels that they were like them in
every way, mature, socially competent, and cool.

While all of this was very interesting to speculate on, it did little to
relieve Kozak of her own feelings of loneliness and inadequacy. Had the
colonels, she wondered, felt the same things at one time that she was
feeling now? Had they been overwhelmed by dealing with the hail of
pressing problems of leading while learning? Was the reason they sat
there, quiet and subdued, because the attrition of years of dealing with
such problems had worn away their youth and drive? Kozak wondered if
someday she too would be sitting there quietly, looking at the world with
an unemotional, almost placid face.

As she finished scanning the room before returning to a dinner turned
cold, Kozak noticed Captain Cerro enter the room with a woman she
assumed was his wife. His appearance caused Kozak to take heart. Of all
the officers she had dealt with to date, Captain Cerro was the only one
who had come across as professional, honest, and sincere in his dealings
with her. Only he seemed able to break through the glass barrier that kept

other infantry officers from dealing with her in the manner she thought was appropriate for an infantry second lieutenant. Though a couple of their run-ins had been less than pleasant, they had been open and, in retrospect, appropriate for the situation. Not even her own company commander, Captain Wittworth, could overcome what Kozak perceived as hang-ups in his dealings with her. Too bad, she thought, there weren't more officers like Captain Cerro. Maybe some of the problems that she lugged about wouldn't be problems.

But he wasn't her commander. That was not reality. Whatever solutions she developed, whatever methods she devised to deal with her problems, had to be based on reality, not wishes and dreams. Time for that was over. Her dream of becoming an infantry officer had been fulfilled. Now it was time to make it work.

In an instant, she realized that she had hit upon something. She had to make it work. She would be, and in fact always had been, the one who had to make it work. That's what Captain Cerro had tried so hard to tell her, in his own way, every time they had crossed each other's path. She was alone, and perhaps she was supposed to be alone, somewhat aloof and above the nitty-gritty. Was that why the colonels sat alone? Was it that they, in order to deal with their world, distanced themselves from part of it? The idea was intriguing and worth considering, Kozak thought. Definitely worth considering.

As she watched Cerro and his wife move to their table, Kozak considered catching his attention and saying hello. She paused, however. Not knowing the protocol for such an occasion, and unsure who the woman was, Kozak decided not to. If the woman was a date, Kozak's attention might not be appreciated. No doubt Captain Cerro's wife, or girlfriend, felt safe in the knowledge that he, as an infantry officer, worked in an exclusively male world. Such a thought, Kozak knew, was a comfort to some wives who feared the danger of their husbands becoming involved with a woman while away from home in the field. Kozak's appearance, in the flesh, might shatter that illusion, which, surprisingly, continued to exist, despite the presence of Kozak and her sisters in other combat units.

So Kozak let the moment pass, turning her attention back to her meal. Better, she thought, to settle her own problems before creating problems for other people, especially people who were sympathetic to her efforts to become the best infantry officer that had ever pinned on the crossed rifles.

While seating his wife, Cerro noticed Lieutenant Kozak sitting alone at a table in the corner of the dining room. For a moment, he considered going over and saying hello, perhaps even introducing her to his wife, Ann. But he didn't. Not knowing how Ann would react to a female infantry officer, he decided against it. Had it been the wife of another officer that he knew, sitting there and eating alone, Cerro wouldn't have hesitated to bound across the room and invite her to join them. This situation, however, was different. There would be many problems, even if he had simply introduced Kozak to Ann. Having been associated with the Army for years, and well indoctrinated in the protocol and military etiquette, Ann knew how to deal with other wives and other officers. Each, she had been taught, required a different touch, appropriate to the rank of the officer or the officer's wife. Dealing with female officers, however, was still difficult, at best. It was doubly so for an officer and his wife who had spent their entire career, up to that point, in the comfortable company of airborne or air assault units. Though there were many women even in those elite combat units, they had always belonged to someone else, another unit, another commander. So Harold and Ann Cerro had never had to confront the issue and develop an appropriate set of rules.

This, Cerro decided, was not the time or place to start doing either. When he finished seating his wife, Cerro moved around to his own chair and seated himself. As he did so, Ann leaned over toward him. "Something wrong, dear?"

Cerro looked at her, thought for a moment, then shook his head. "No, nothing, why?"

Ann leaned back and gave him a sideward glance. "Don't give me that, Harold Cerro. I can tell when your mind has left the here and now. Are you going to share your deep dark thoughts with me or not?"

While still looking into her eyes, Cerro picked up the menu and opened it. He smiled. "Dear, I'm sorry. It's all highly classified and hush-hush. If I told you, I'd have to kill you and that, my dear, would spoil my appetite." Without another word, he looked down at the menu.

Slouching down in her chair, Ann reached out with her leg under the table and kicked him in the shin. "I'll give you something that'll spoil your appetite."

Doing his best to ignore the kick, Cerro looked up. "Did you say something, dear?"

Leaning over in order to get close, Ann squinted her eyes, wrinkled her nose, and whispered, "Harold Cerro, sometimes you can be a real asshole."

Smiling, Cerro pinched Ann's cheek. "I try, dear, I really try."

The border crossing in Brownsville, Texas
2025 hours, 29 August

Despite the fact that the sun was well on its way down, it was still hotter than hell. Jan Fields, standing in the shade of the American customs building, was still sweating. Her bright yellow short-sleeved cotton blouse was streaked with dark spots from the perspiration that ran down her back. Even her tan walking shorts were soaked at the waistline. God, she thought, how she hated to sweat. Deciding to toss out all thoughts of feminine poise and charm, Jan reached up behind her head and untied the yellow cotton bandana that was holding her hair back. Carefully folding the bandana on her right hand, she began to mop the beads of perspiration on her forehead and cheeks, finishing with wide sweeps along the sides of her neck. Turning to Ted and Joe Bob, she called out to see if they were finished. Ted, who had his back to her, merely lifted his right hand and waved. Joe Bob, who was facing Ted, looked over Ted's shoulder at Jan and yelled, "Hey, Jan, Ted wants to know if there's something really important you need to do or if it's just one of those woman things."

Putting her hands on her hips, with her chin stuck out, Jan shot back, "Okay, you guys. How 'bout moving your male bonding back to the hotel pool. I hear water spots is all the rage now with the guys."

Joe Bob just smiled a big toothy grin as he continued to hold a white panel Ted was using for judging light conditions. "God, Jan, you're really sweet when you're angry."

Ted, who had had his head bent over reading a light meter, looked up into Joe Bob's eyes. "Cute, really fucking cute. Now how about holding the bloody panel still so we can all get out of here."

Looking from Jan to Ted, Joe Bob's expression changed to mock surprise. "Oh, what do we have here? Sympathetic PMS syndrome?"

Without looking up at Joe Bob, Ted continued to fiddle with his light meter. "Joe Bob, if you don't hold that panel still and shut up, I'll stick this meter up your backside and see just how true it is that the sun never shines there."

Sighing, Joe Bob lamented to himself, but loud enough so Ted could hear, "Jeez, I really hate it when this time of month comes around."

Unable to hear what Ted and Joe Bob were saying, Jan turned her attention to the story that they were to shoot tomorrow. It was already decided that the opening shot would be here, on the bridge that separated Mexico from the United States. Preliminary surveys showed that this was the best

place in Brownsville for getting, in a single shot, a picture of Texas
National Guardsmen and Mexican Army soldiers, each on their own side
of the border, facing off.

She would start the piece by referring to the speech President Ronald
Reagan had given in the early eighties in which he warned the people of
America that unless they did something to stop the spread of communism
in Central America, Brownsville, Texas, would become the front line.
Jan had learned from Scott to use historic quotes that appeared to be
applicable. It gave people, he said, the impression that you had done
some research and, therefore, knew what you were talking about. His
comment was only half in jest. Though Jan loved to spend as much time
as possible on research, there just wasn't time to learn everything about
a story that was really necessary. Time, and the pressing demands of the
network, simply did not permit a correspondent the luxury of becoming
an expert on every subject she covered. So Jan, like most of the people
in her field, did the best she could with the time and resources available,
and winged the rest.

Pulling out a small pad and pen from her pocket, Jan jotted down a few
quick notes. On the bridge, they would talk to the soldiers on duty and get
their impressions and comments. From there, they would go to the headquarters of the 1st Brigade, 36th Infantry Division, and interview the
brigade commander. After that, downtown to city hall for an interview
with the mayor, then out onto the street in the shopping district for some
opinions from the people of Brownsville. Jan was hoping to get comments from both the Hispanic citizens and the Anglos, or what Joe Bob
referred to as "real Americans."

Scanning the shooting schedule before putting it back in her pocket,
Jan noticed that the sweat running down her arm and hand had left a damp
thumbprint on the page of the pad, smearing the ink. Looking up at Joe
Bob and Ted, she called out, "Will you two stop playing grab-ass in
public and get a move on."

Joe Bob smiled and waved, whispering to Ted as he did so, "Better
hurry there, friend. Her highness is overheating. Whatever it is you need,
buddy, you can get tomorrow. There'll be plenty of time."

13

10 KILOMETERS NORTHEAST OF SAN YGNACIO, TEXAS
0115 HOURS, 30 AUGUST

Unable to focus his eyes any longer on the Louis L'Amour novel he was reading, First Lieutenant Ken Stolte, the executive officer of a 155mm howitzer battery, swung his feet off the table and onto the ground and put the book down on the table. As he stood, his calves pushed back the old folding chair he had been sitting on. As it moved, the chair, painted several times too often, folded and collapsed, creating a clattering that surprised the nodding duty NCO seated at the TAC fire set in the M-577 armored command post carrier. Noting the puzzled look on his sergeant's face as he held his hands over his head, leaned back and stretched, Stolte smiled. "What's the matter, Buck, losing it?"

Sergeant Buck Wecas saw the lieutenant stretching and the chair folded behind him on the ground. Putting two and two together, he relaxed and smiled. "No, no. Nothin' like that. I just thought we had gooks in the wire."

"Gooks in the wire? Where'd you hear that, in a war movie?"

Standing up, Wecas came out of the command post carrier, stepped down off the carrier's rear ramp, and headed over for the coffeepot. "Ya

228

know, Ken, not everyone was born yesterday. There's still a few old farts
from Nam around.''

Closing his eyes and rotating his neck as he continued to stretch, Stolte
sighed. ''Yeah, you're right on both counts.'' Dropping his arms, he
turned toward Wecas, who was pouring himself a cup of coffee. ''You're
old and a fart.''

Wecas was about to remind Stolte that his silver bars protected him
only up to a point, when the radio blared:

''Mike one Victor three two, Mike one Victor three two, this is Charlie
four Charlie eight eight Bravo, over.''

Stolte looked at Wecas. ''Who the hell is Charlie four Charlie eight
eight?''

Shrugging, Wecas took a sip of coffee and walked over to the carrier,
reaching in and pulling out a small chart that listed all the radio call signs
and frequencies in use that day. ''According to this, Charlie four Charlie
eight eight is the scout platoon of 1st of the 141st. Bravo must be one of
the scout sections.''

As Stolte and Wecas considered that for a moment, the voice on the
radio repeated the call. ''Mike one Victor three two, Mike one Victor
three two, this is Charlie four Charlie eight eight Bravo, over.''

''Find out what he wants, otherwise he'll keep callin' and callin.' ''

Putting the board down, Wecas climbed into the track, mumbling so
that Stolte could hear, ''Yeah, we'd hate to have someone call and disturb
your reading with business.''

Picking up the hand mike, Wecas keyed the radio. ''Charlie four
Charlie eight eight Bravo, this is Mike one Victor three two, do you have
traffic for this station, over?''

''Yeah, roger, Victor three two. I am unable to contact my higher,
Tango seven Kilo six nine, and submit my sitreps. Can you relay for me,
over?''

Looking over to his chart, Wecas saw that Tango seven Kilo six nine
was the call sign for the command post of 1st Battalion, 141st Infantry.
''Charlie eight eight Bravo, this is Victor three two. I'll try. If I do
contact them, is there something you need to report, over?''

''Yeah, roger, Victor three two. Tell them I can't reach them from
here. I've been tryin' for the last fifteen minutes. Tell 'em I'm still at
checkpoint Quebec five two and have a negative sitrep. Also, I would
appreciate it if they would try to contact me, over.''

Considering the request for a moment, Wecas decided to honor it. It
was not unusual for units to use other stations to relay radio traffic when
direct contact had been lost. Even more common was the habit of using

artillery units, such as Wecas's, for relay. For some reason, Wecas noticed, artillery units always seemed to have better comms than line units. Maybe, Wecas thought, it was because without comms, his firing battery would be worthless. Or perhaps, he thought, it was because the artillery attracted and kept people like him, old-timers who knew how to keep their ancient radio equipment running. Whatever the reason, Wecas knew he had to help this poor jerk out and had no earthly reason for doing otherwise. Informing Charlie eight eight that he would call his higher, Wecas ended the conversation, then looked on his chart for the frequency of 1st of the 141st. Flipping the knobs to change the frequency, Wecas set the proper frequency for the 1st of the 141st command radio net and passed Charlie four Charlie eight eight Bravo's message to a radio telephone operator at 1st of the 141st who sounded as if he was half asleep.

5 KILOMETERS NORTH OF SAN YGNACIO, TEXAS
0121 HOURS, 30 AUGUST

After hanging the hand mike of the radio back on a hook made from a coat hanger and attached to the roll bar of the Humvee, Andy Morrezzo leaned back in the backseat and stretched. He had been twenty minutes late checking in with the battalion command post through the artillery unit. It would be another forty minutes before his next scheduled report. That one, he knew, had to be on time. It was okay to be late on one, every now and then. But to miss two in a row was unforgivable, even if comms were bad. Scouts, according to their battalion commander, were supposed to be resourceful and tenacious, whatever that meant. Looking at his watch, Morrezzo decided that at one thirty in the morning it was hard to be resourceful. Hell, he thought, it was hard just staying awake.

Opening the door of the Humvee, Morrezzo decided to get out and walk around for a few minutes. Maybe he'd go over to the armored Humvee and see if the new kid was awake.

Carefully, Morrezzo reached over, resting his left hand on the tube of an AT-4 light antitank rocket launcher in order to reach the AN-PVS 5 night-vision goggles sitting on top of the radio located in the front of the Humvee. Taking care not to wake Sullivan and Alison, both of whom were asleep in the front seats, Morrezzo grabbed the goggles carrying case, slowly lifted it, and eased himself back and out of the Humvee. He didn't need to worry about waking his companions. Both sleeping soundly, neither man noticed him leave. Morrezzo didn't bother to take his helmet, resting on top of the AT-4 antitank rockets. Nor did he, in his concern over waking his companions, notice that he had failed to turn the radio back to the battalion command frequency, leaving it instead on the frequency of the artillery unit he had just contacted.

Once outside the Humvee, Morrezzo paused, taking in a deep breath and stretching. The cool night air felt good. Though eighty degrees was still warm by any measure, eighty degrees without the sun was a damned sight better than one hundred and five with the sun and no shade. Looking about, Morrezzo allowed his eyes to adjust to the darkness. In the pale gray light of a quarter moon setting in the western sky, he could clearly make out the form of the armored Humvee parked one hundred meters to the right of Sullivan's. Between Morrezzo and the other Humvee was a concrete and stone picnic pavilion sheltering concrete and stone picnic tables. Checkpoint Quebec five two, selected by the battalion intell officer because of its view of the road and border, had been chosen many years before by some state park official as a great place for a roadside park and picnic site for the same reasons.

Walking over to the picnic tables, Morrezzo boosted himself up on the top of one of them. Setting his feet on the bench and resting his elbows on his knees, he opened the hard plastic case containing the night-vision goggles and took them out. Still not fully awake, it took Morrezzo forever and a great deal of fumbling to find the switch to turn the goggles on. Finally finding it, he flicked the switch to the on position and looked down at the goggles until he saw the soft green glow that emanated from the eyepieces inside the headpiece. Ready, he lifted the goggles to his eyes and began to scan the Mexican side of the border for banditos and other such bad guys.

The image of two armored vehicles on the other side of the Rio Grande, their gun tubes pointed right at him, was, to say the least, quite unexpected. Startled, Morrezzo jerked upright as if an electric shock had been applied to the base of his spine. Pressing the night-vision goggles tightly against his face, Morrezzo locked onto what appeared to be the nearest of the two armored vehicles and studied it for a moment. Although he couldn't identify the French-built Panard ERC-90 Lynx for what it was, Morrezzo knew it wasn't American and, more importantly, it was on the other side of the river. Hence, it was the enemy.

After studying the boxlike armored vehicle with the big long gun for another moment, Morrezzo threw his legs over the side of the picnic table, hopped down, and stood up, all the time holding the night-vision goggles to his face as if they were glued to it. Only after he was satisfied that the enemy vehicles were not moving and had apparently not seen him, did he turn and head back to Sullivan's Humvee to inform him of the sighting.

                        *   *   *

The sudden shifting of his target, followed by a quick turn and movement away from him, did not bother Lefleur. He merely continued to smoothly track the target and slightly, ever so slightly, elevate the barrel of the 7.62mm sniper rifle to compensate for the increased range. When he felt good about his sight picture, Lefleur squeezed the trigger, firing a single hollow-point bullet.

Morrezzo never heard the report from Lefleur's rifle. Nor did he feel the impact of the hollow-point round as it struck the base of his skull. And even if he did feel the impact, it was only for the briefest time, for the bullet struck true, doing what it was designed to do. Penetrating the skull bone at a slightly upward angle, the soft lead of the bullet pushed a chunk of shattered bone in front of it. As the bullet and the chunk of bone continued forward, the bullet began to slow down, spreading out into a wad the size of a quarter. In a single, continuous motion, this wad, with the bone chunk in front of it, began ripping through the soft brain tissue that stood in its path, compacting the tissue that wasn't pushed to either side of the moving mass against the bone plate that formed the forehead. When the pressure of the ever expanding mass of bullet, bone, and brain tissue became too great, the front plates of Morrezzo's skull, from his hairline down to the base of his nose, blew out, freeing the wadded bullet from the mass of bone and brain tissue that had obstructed its flight path. The wadded bullet momentarily accelerated as the obstructions fell away and traveled a little further before finally falling to the ground. Morrezzo, however, was dead before that happened.

Lefleur's single shot initiated a fusillade which, in the best traditions of the French Foreign Legion, achieved its objective quickly, violently, and completely. First to fire after Lefleur was the RPG team. They engaged the armored Humvee first, firing at a range of less than one hundred meters. Their first round hit the engine compartment head-on. The jet stream created by the shaped-charge explosion sliced through the upper part of the engine, through the fire wall, and into the passenger compartment. Though it missed the two men asleep in the front seats of the Humvee, the white-hot pencil-thin shaft of flame cut through the fiberglass tube containing one of the stored AT-4 antitank rockets, igniting the rocket propellent. This explosion, in turn, detonated the high-explosive antitank warhead of a second AT-4 rocket launcher stored next to the one that had been hit. From where the team sat, it seemed as if the armored Humvee blew itself apart, with doors flying open and a sheet of flame shooting up and out of the open hatch in the roof, engulfing the machine gunner who was standing watch in the hatch. For the machine gunner, as well as the two men inside the armored Humvee, the heavy duty construction and special Kevlar armor of the vehicle worked against them by containing and magnifying the effects of the explosions better than a simple canvas-covered Humvee would have. All three men were dead in a matter of seconds.

Even before they died, a hail of machine-gun and automatic-rifle fire raked the left side of Sullivan's Humvee. Sullivan, still sitting in the driver's seat with his head resting on the steering wheel while he slept, caught the full weight of the initial machine-gun burst. Tod Alison, in the passenger seat, was shielded, for the most part, by Sullivan's body. Even so, Alison took one round in the left shoulder and one in his right knee as well as numerous fragments from flying glass, fiberglass, and metal. The sting of his wounds, as well as the shock of suddenly being under fire, momentarily paralyzed Alison. His first reaction was an instinctive pulling away from the source of the pain.

Reaching around with his right hand to grab the door handle while he watched in horror as Sullivan's body jerked as more bullets hit it, Alison threw open the Humvee's frail door just as secondary explosions rocked the armored Humvee, lighting up the night. Turning to watch the death of the armored Humvee, Alison realized that there was no escape in that direction either. The first conscious thought that flashed through his mind as he watched the machine gunner of the armored Humvee, his body engulfed in fire and writhing in pain, was that he too was about to die. His next thought was to report the attack before that happened. Twisting about in his seat, his body responding spasmodically as a result of multiple wounds, shock, and panic, Alison grabbed for the radio hand mike. Someone had to be told. Someone had to help them.

The sudden flash, followed by one of the American Humvees blowing up, startled Lieutenant Martí. His first thought was that the Lynx that was overwatching him had fired. Standing upright in the open hatch of his own Lynx, Martí twisted about and looked at the other Lynx. He could see no indication, however, that it had fired. He was still puzzled when the sound of small-arms fire drifted across the river to his position. Looking back to the American position, he could see muzzle flashes spewing out streams of tracers at the American recon vehicles.

Reaching down, Martí grabbed the radio hand mike and lifted it to his mouth. He was about to key the radio and submit an initial report, but he hesitated. What exactly was he going to report? What was it he was looking at? Unable to answer those questions and knowing that they were the first ones that his troop commander would ask, Martí put the radio hand mike down and, instead, ordered his driver to start the engine. They needed to get closer and investigate a little more before they reported. Better, Martí thought, that he submit a complete report that clarified the situation than a partial one that confused or caused undue panic at head-quarters.

As the engine of the Lynx choked to life, the gunfire on the American side of the river died down. Ordering his second Lynx to cover his move, Martí switched back to the intercom and then instructed his driver to move forward. As they began to roll out of the shallow gully they had been in, Martí watched the far side of the river intently. Whatever had happened, Martí thought, was over. Perhaps that would make it easier to sort the situation out.

"Any station this net, any station this net! This is Charlie eight eight Bravo. We are under attack! Repeat, we are under attack! We need medevac and backup, over!"

For several seconds, Sergeant Wecas, back in front of the TAC fire unit, turned only his head and looked at the radio. Lieutenant Stolte, having resumed his position at the table with feet propped up and leaning back in the folding chair as he read, lowered his book and looked at Wecas in the command post carrier. Stolte was about to ask what the last call was all about when the radio blared again.

"Any station this net! This is Charlie eight eight Bravo. We are under attack! We need help, ASAP! Answer me. Someone, please answer me!"

Sitting up as if he had been shocked, Wecas grabbed the radio hand mike and keyed the radio. "Charlie four Charlie eight eight Bravo, this is Mike one Victor three two. Give me your location and your status, over."

There was a pause. While he waited, Wecas was motionless, staring at the radio in front of him. Stolte, realizing by now that something was going on, put his book on the table, swung his feet to the ground, and was in the process of entering the command post carrier when the voice on the radio came back. "We're under attack, damn it. The sergeant's dead. I'm hit. The other Humvee blew up. I need help. Please God. I need help."

Though Wecas didn't understand exactly what was happening, he understood that whoever was calling was hurt, frightened, and in need of help. In Vietnam he had heard many calls like this one. Young soldiers, often alone and in combat for the first time, trying to find someone, anyone, to help them and their buddies. Although the voice calling itself Charlie eight eight Bravo wasn't the same one that had called before when they couldn't reach their own battalion CP, it didn't matter to Wecas. The first caller might already be dead, or wounded. Wecas didn't know. Nor did that matter. What did matter was that the fear, the excitement, the anger that came out of the radio speaker in the command post carrier was real. Someone, another American soldier like him, was in trouble out there. Wecas was not about to let him die alone.

"Charlie four Charlie eight eight Bravo, this is Mike one Victor three two. Can you give me your location and a target reference point? I can have a fire mission for you in a minute, but I need your location and a target reference point, over."

The shooting had stopped. For a moment, there was an eerie silence, punctuated only by a low roar of flames consuming the armored Humvee and an occasional *pop-pop* as small-arms ammo in the armored Humvee cooked off. Thankful that someone had answered his call, Alison calmed down and considered what he should do next. He had no idea who had fired upon them and only a vague idea where the fire had come from. Though he thought that the attackers were close and somewhere to the front, he couldn't be sure. Whoever had fired on them was, no doubt, still out there. They might even be closing in. If that was the case, he needed to get out of the Humvee and hide, or at least get into a position where he could defend himself. Dropping the radio hand mike in his lap, Alison reached behind for his M-16 rifle. As he did so, a series of sharp pains wracked his body. Laying the rifle across his lap, he realized that escape would not be possible. Though he didn't know how bad he had been hit, he intuitively understood that he would not be able to get out of the Humvee and evade his attackers.

"Charlie four Charlie eight eight Bravo, this is Mike one Victor three two. I say again, give me your location and a target reference point. I need your location and a target reference point, over."

Looking at the radio, Alison realized that his only salvation was to give whoever Mike one Victor was what he asked for. Letting go of his rifle, he seized the radio hand mike with his right hand and the map, which was wedged under the radio, with his left hand. As he put the map in his lap, he keyed the radio. "Last station, this is Charlie eight eight, give me a minute, over."

Calmer now that he had someone out there ready to help, Alison pulled the flashlight off of the clip that held it to the front windshield frame, flicked it on, and began to search the map for a mark that showed where they were. When he found the point on the map, Alison held the index finger of his left hand on the spot while he keyed the radio mike with his right hand.

He was about to speak when the door of the Humvee flew open. Jerking about to see what was happening, he looked up. In the darkness, he could see no facial features, no details, only the black outline of shoulders and a head. He didn't even see the automatic pistol as the apparition shoved it into his face. All Private Tod Alison felt was the sudden shock of the cold metal barrel slam into his jaw before the apparition pulled the trigger.

Wecas watched the orange radio call light come on, signaling the beginning of a transmission. Prepared to copy the information he had requested from Charlie eight eight and punch the data into the TAC fire computer, the sudden blast that came out of the radio speaker, followed by the call light going off, caught Wecas off guard. For a second, he didn't move, waiting for the radio to come to life again. Stolte, now standing behind Wecas, looked at the radio, then at Wecas. "What was that all about?"

Though Wecas knew, he didn't answer. Instead, he keyed the radio mike. "Charlie four Charlie eight eight Bravo, this is Mike one Victor three two. I say again, give me your location and a target reference point. I need your location and a target reference point, over."

Finished, Wecas picked up the hand mike for the radio set on the firing battery net and gave the fire direction center an order to be prepared to receive and fire a real mission.

Lefleur was in the process of putting his automatic pistol back into its holster when the orange call light of the Humvee's radio came on and he heard a voice, asking for a location and target reference point. Looking at the radio, then down at the body in front of him, he noticed a map. Picking up the flashlight and shining it down, Lefleur studied the map. As he did so, one of his men came up behind him.

"Everyone in the other vehicle is dead. Poof, all gone. And one of the Mexican recon vehicles is moving down to the river to get a closer look."

The voice, belonging to a Mexican-American mercenary, gave Lefleur an idea. Turning to his man, Lefleur surprised him. "Amigo, do you remember how to direct artillery fire?"

Straightening up and puffing out his chest, the Mexican-American responded with pride, "I was in force recon for three years. Every marine in force recon knows how to call for and direct artillery fire. Child's play, mere child's play."

Reaching into the Humvee, Lefleur pried the radio hand mike from the dead guardsman's hand. Turning around, he handed the mike to the Mexican-American. "Then this should be fun. Here, call Mike one Victor three two and tell them you are at . . ." Lefleur paused as he leaned over to shine the flashlight on the map and find the information he needed. "Ah, here we are. Tell them you are located at checkpoint Quebec five two and the target, two Mexican armored cars, is located near target reference point . . . Yes, target reference point Bravo Tango zero one five. Got that?"

The Mexican-American shrugged his shoulders. "No problem." Keying the hand mike, he began the call.

Before he spoke, Lefleur put his hand over the mike. "When you talk, sound excited, frightened, amigo. Sound like you are under attack. And ask for DPICM. No adjusting rounds. Let's do this right."

Again the Mexican-American responded with a simple, matter of fact "No problem, boss."

Stolte, still standing behind Wecas, suddenly realized what was going on. With an appreciation of the situation came a sudden feeling of disbelief. For a moment, he stood riveted to the floor of the command post carrier, watching and listening while Wecas yelled at the chief of the gun section to get his men out of the sack and ready to fire. The gun section chief, like Stolte, was having difficulty believing that they were about to execute a real fire mission. Stolte was about to interfere, asking Wecas if it was a good idea to process the fire mission without permission from battalion first, when Charlie eight eight Bravo came back on the air. Rather than interfere, Stolte watched Wecas take down the data coming in. As he did so, Stolte noticed that the voice was different. It was lower, calmer, more collected. That, however, changed when the sound of a three-round burst of rifle fire screamed over the radio, followed by a loud "Jesus," then silence. The attack, apparently, was still in progress.

The sudden burst of rifle fire behind his back caused the Mexican-American literally to jump. In the process, he dropped the radio hand mike. Turning around, his eyes as big as saucers, the Mexican-American saw Lefleur, a broad smile on his face, standing behind him holding a smoking M-16, taken from the dead guardsman, pointed in the air. *"What the fuck did you do that for, you stupid bastard?"*

Lefleur chuckled. "My friend, you were not excited enough. You were not convincing. I thought you could use a little help."

Reaching down to retrieve the hand mike, keeping an eye on Lefleur as he did so, the Mexican-American warned him that if he pulled a stunt like that again, he would shove the M-16 up his ass.

When the voice of Charlie eight eight Bravo came back on the air, it seemed more animated and a little shaken. Wecas confirmed the target location and signed off. As he began to punch the data into the TAC fire computer, Stolte, for the first time, intervened. "Buck, shouldn't we call someone first and get permission before we shoot?"

Without looking up or stopping what he was doing, Wecas brushed Stolte off by merely mumbling that there was no time. Stolte, however, persisted. "I don't like this, Buck. We need to tell someone what's going on before we do this. That target is across the border."

Spinning about in his seat, his face contorted with anger, Wecas screamed at Stolte. "People are dying out there, Lieutenant. Our people. And we're the only ones who can help. I'll be goddamned if I'm going to sit here and let that happen." Without waiting for a response, Wecas returned to the TAC fire computer and finished inputting the data. When he was finished, he stood up, taking the mike to the radio that the gun section was on in one hand and the hand mike to the radio that Charlie eight eight Bravo was on in the other. When the gun section chief reported that the first round was on the way, Wecas relayed that information to Charlie eight eight Bravo while Stolte stood behind him, watching in silence.

The small submunitions of the first dual-purpose, improved conventional munitions round, or DPICM, impacted less than fifty meters in front of Martí's Lynx. The surprise and shock of the chain of exploding submunitions and the sudden blinding flashes directly in front of him caused Martí's driver to jerk the steering wheel to the right. This unexpected violent maneuver threw Martí off balance just as he was dropping into the safety of the Lynx's turret. It took Martí a second to regain his balance, and the driver a little longer to get the Lynx under control again. In that time, three more rounds from the 155mm howitzer platoon that had responded to Wecas's fire mission detonated over Martí's Lynx, raining a shower of armor-piercing submunitions down on it.

From their location at Sullivan's Humvee, Lefleur and the Mexican-American mercenary observed the strike of the first volley of artillery fire. When three rounds engulfed the Lynx that had been moving down to the river, the Mexican-American mercenary turned to Lefleur, a broad grin illuminating his face. "See, boss, I told you the United States Marine Corps did everything right first time, every time."

Lefleur grunted. "So you did. So you did. In the Legion, however, we never used four rounds when one was all that was needed." Holding up a pair of night-vision goggles that he had recovered from the body of the national guardsman he had shot, Lefleur looked to the west, across the river. "On top of that, amigo, your job is only half done. There is another recon vehicle out there, three hundred meters west of where you just hit the moving vehicle. Let us see how well you can adjust fire."

Proud of his handiwork, despite Lefleur's comment about wasting rounds, the Mexican-American mercenary prepared to call in the adjustment. "Three hundred meters, you say. Are you sure?"

Without taking the night-vision goggles down, Lefleur responded. "Yes, three hundred meters, due west."

The Mexican-American mercenary had just finished calling in the adjustments for the next volley when a flash, followed by the streak of a tracer, announced that the second Mexican Lynx was returning fire at them. Lowering the night-vision goggles, Lefleur announced to his companion, "I think it is time that we leave."

As the first round from the Lynx impacted to the left and short of Sullivan's Humvee, the Mexican-American dropped to the ground. When he looked up and saw Lefleur still standing there watching to the west, the Mexican-American mercenary shook his head. "Okay, you proved you got balls. Now let's go before you lose both yours and mine."

The second fire mission was faster and easier. The ice had been broken. They were committed. Though he was still uncomfortable with what was happening, Stolte did nothing as he watched Wecas process the request for adjustment and a repeat of the fire mission. Standing there, Stolte began to wonder how he had lost control of the situation. Not that he had ever been in control. Through his lack of action, he had surrendered all initiative to his sergeant, who, instinctively, had done what he had done as a young soldier in Vietnam and during numerous training exercises and drills since: receive and process calls for fire. How terrible, Stolte thought, how terrible and tragic it would be if this was all a mistake, all one big tragic and terrible mistake. Who, he wondered, would be guilty? Who? That thought was still lingering in Stolte's mind when the gun platoon leader announced that the next volley was on the way.

Noticing that their first round had missed the American vehicle that was not yet burning, the commander of the second Lynx cut short his report to this troop commander and prepared to adjust his gunner's fire. Though he could hear his troop commander's yells in the earphones of his helmet, the Lynx commander ignored them, calmly giving his gunner directions. There would be plenty of time to report once the enemy vehicles were destroyed.

When he was ready, the gunner announced he was firing, providing the rest of the crew time to brace for the shock of firing and gun recoil. As he squeezed the trigger, he closed his eyes and pressed his forehead against the brow pad of his sight. When he felt the gun fire and the Lynx rock back, then settle forward, he opened his eyes and watched the tracer of his second round arch up, then slowly begin its downward descent, holding his breath as it did so. Only after he saw his round impact on the enemy vehicle, obliterating it in a blinding explosion and great clouds of smoke and dust, did he relax and breathe again. He had no way of knowing that everyone in the Humvee had already been killed. Nor did he realize that the breath he was taking was his last, for Lefleur's estimation of the range had been very accurate, and the 155mm howitzer fire direction center and gun crews had done a magnificent job of computing and firing the mission.

From the rim of the gully where their pickup trucks were hidden, Lefleur looked to the west. When the second Mexican Army recon vehicle began to burn, he turned to the Mexican-American mercenary. "See, three hundred meters. Just as I said."

14

There can be no fifty-fifty Americanism in this country. There is room only for one hundred percent Americanism.

—Theodore Roosevelt

BROWNSVILLE, TEXAS
1015 HOURS, 3 SEPTEMBER

The people of Brownsville were used to traffic jams in the summer, especially during holiday weekends as throngs of tourists poured into and out of South Padre Island to escape the Texas heat, or across the border to Matamoros in search of bargains. Labor Day weekend, the end of the summer, was traditionally the busiest weekend of the year. So it wasn't the volume of traffic or the delays caused by it that was different this year. It was the nature of the traffic that caused people to pause, stare, and become concerned. Few Americans were prepared for the sight of a twenty-five-ton combat-loaded Bradley fighting vehicle sitting on their front lawn. Nor were they quite ready to share Main Street with a column of M-1A1 tanks whose 120mm main guns had brought the Iraqi Republican Guard to bay.

Even the sight of the soldiers, American soldiers, armed to the teeth, was unnerving. Most vestiges of their humanity were hidden under thirty-five pounds of helmet, special protective sunglasses, flak vest, load-bearing equipment, desert camouflage uniform, and heavy boots. Rather than friendly protectors, the soldiers of the 52nd Mechanized Infantry Division appeared like alien invaders. Thus the descent of the United States Army upon Brownsville on Labor Day weekend did little to calm the people of south Texas. Instead of the military's deployment bringing an end to the panic and terror that had gripped the border communities,

241

the chain of disasters that had befallen the Texas National Guard and the sudden appearance of the regular Army only served to heighten the fears and apprehensions of the Texans.

It should not have come as a surprise, therefore, that people long used to peace and able to take a stable border for granted took refuge in flight rather than face the prospect of living in a free-fire zone. Nor should it have been a surprise to local, state, and federal officials when their pleas to the people of the border areas to stay in place fell on deaf ears. The inability of the National Guard, after a barrage of media hype, to solve the problems along the border doomed claims by the federal government. And the image of a battery of 155mm howitzers setting up in a public park, broadcast across the nation by the media, with high-explosive shells piled in the lee of a child's swing, did nothing to calm the public. So, as military convoys moved south, following in the footsteps of Zachary Taylor and John J. Pershing, caravans of refugees moved north.

In the middle of this muddle, a term Joe Bob used to describe Browns-ville, was Jan Fields. Her "right place at the right time" theory handed Jan and her crew an opportunity that almost matched the coup they had pulled off in Mexico City in late June. For they were there, in Browns-ville, to record the reaction of the people when the president of the United States announced that he was federalizing the National Guard of Texas, New Mexico, Arizona, and California, as well as deploying four Army and one Marine divisions to the border. Ted's camera captured the image of the members of the 52nd Division's advance party as they rolled into Brownsville in the predawn light the day before Labor Day. Joe Bob's recorder picked up the stiff and stilted conversations between officers of the regular Army and those of the National Guard as the former relieved the latter and issued them their first orders under federal control. And the ubiquitous Jan Fields, ever searching for the shot that, in a single glance, spoke louder than a tirade of commentary, was seen and heard that night and every night across the nation. In one shot, she was standing next to Mexican Army officers on the southern side of the bridge over the Rio Grande, listening to their comments as they watched American soldiers erect wire entanglements, barriers, and sandbag emplacements complete with machine guns, on the north side of the bridge. In another shot, made less than two hours later, she was seen talking to the commander of the 1st Brigade, 52nd Division, about his mission. Even Joe Bob, a man who was not easily impressed, was becoming awed by Jan's unerring ability to move through the chaos of the day and sift through the myriad opportunities, capturing in a few brief minutes those images and words that brought everything together in a clear, concise, and hard-hitting package. No amount of technical training, no course of study, could produce a correspondent with the skills that Jan possessed. When asked by a cameraman from another crew to describe her, all Joe Bob could do was look at the cameraman and say, in reverent tones, "That girl's good. She's damned good."

Of course, what made her good, as she always was the first to admit, was luck and hard work. Having been in Brownsville for a week, Jan and her crew knew the city and surrounding area, not to mention where the best shots could be obtained as well as who to stroke and who could do what for them. While other news teams were pouring into the airport at Harlingen as fast as the airlines could get them there, Jan, Ted, and Joe Bob were taping. One New York news team, in an effort to make up for lost time and gain an edge, tried following Jan's van. When Joe Bob, who was driving, noticed he was being tailed by the New Yorkers, he decided to ditch them. Stopping in the middle of the street, Joe Bob stuck his head out of the window and yelled, "Eat my dust, you Yankee queers." With that challenge, he took off, driving down alleys and up one-way streets the wrong way as fast as their van could carry them. After ten minutes of fast driving and running two red lights, three stop signs, and one railroad guard that was about to close, Joe Bob managed to lose the New York news team in the worst possible part of town and still get Jan to her next appointment with time to spare. So while everyone else was trying to figure out what stories were valid and what was useless, Jan Fields was coming across with solid, well-orchestrated pieces.

What didn't come across on Ted's camera or on Joe Bob's microphone was Jan's growing sense of concern and apprehension. Part of Jan's success was her ability to see and understand the broad context of the story she was covering, and an ability to personalize that story so that it could be seen and understood by her primary audience, the American public. In most stories, Jan was able to remain aloof, emotionally and intellectually detached from the issues at hand. In this case, however, it was becoming more and more difficult.

The internal changes in Mexico, Jan now understood, were necessary, as was the deployment of some forces, by both the United States and Mexico, to the border. For the United States, it was a matter of defending against the mysterious raids, while the Mexicans were responding to the American buildup. While that was all logical, it was also logical that the military buildup, as well as the shooting incident of four days before, would create situations in which more incidents would be likely.

As frightening as a conflict between her country and Mexico was in itself, the question of where her loyalty went was even more frightening. After all, how could she, an American, continue to produce objective stories about the Council of 13 when she knew that they were, at that moment, planning how best to kill her own countrymen? Especially Colonel Guajardo. To Jan, he had come to personify the new revolution. He was a man, she was convinced, who was capable of using anyone for whatever he wanted and, if it suited his purposes, of having them disposed of quickly, completely. Though she knew him to be educated, articulate, a family man, and in his own way quite charming, Jan also knew there was a dark side to him, a dark side that was as black and as bottomless as a tar pit.

Adding to her difficulties in reporting the story was the fact that the man she loved, Scott Dixon, was now an active player. As Guajardo represented the Council of 13 in her mind's eye, Scott was coming to represent the American soldier on the front line. Since the introduction of the National Guard, but even more so in the last two days, Jan found herself surrounded by sights and sounds that only served to heighten her feelings of concern and uneasiness. The American soldiers manning the border crossing in Brownsville were no longer simple props and objects to be used for a news story. They were real people, soldiers, soldiers just like Scott. When she interviewed commanders and senior staff officers, she found herself thinking about Scott, for they looked, spoke, acted, and even smelled like him. The dry, subtle humor and the cocky, "can do" attitude the officers displayed when interviewed could just as easily have come from Scott's mouth, for she had heard it from him many times before. Slowly, unavoidably, this story was taking on a personal twist that was becoming unsettling to Jan. Though it was only a feeling, an uneasiness, she couldn't avoid it. Soon, she knew, she would have to confront it and deal with it.

So on this Labor Day weekend, as Texas prepared itself for a journey into the unknown, Jan wondered how much longer she would be able to deliver the same cool, objective view of the crisis that everyone had grown to expect from her. She wondered how she could go back to Mexico City and treat the members of the Council of 13 in a professional, civil manner. For it was more than the memories of the criticism that Americans who had stayed in Baghdad during the Persian Gulf War had taken from their fellow Americans that concerned her. Jan had taken heat before and, in her own way, enjoyed a little controversy. It wasn't that. It was the idea of sitting down with a man who, regardless of how justified his cause, no matter how righteous his principles, could be the instrument of death to a man Jan so loved. That, above all else, upset her, leaving her to wonder if she could do it.

That such a decision was not hers to make hadn't dawned upon her yet. But that was not unusual in these days, for people far wiser than she still imagined that they were in control of the situation. Men in both Mexico City and Washington, D.C., continued to act as if they directed the situation. The only difference between them and Jan was that they were not yet ready to acknowledge their own dark foreboding. Instead, they pushed aside such feelings as frivolous and continued to seek a "correct" and "logical" solution that was at the same time politically acceptable— where no such solution existed.

MEXICO CITY, MEXICO
1315 HOURS, 3 SEPTEMBER

With a flurry, Colonel Guajardo stood up from the small desk he had set up in the operations center and walked across the room to look at the situation map posted on the opposite wall. He remained there for several minutes, his hands behind his back, studying intently the designation and location of symbols that represented new U.S. units deployed along the border. When he got bored with this, he walked over to where the assistant intelligence officer on duty sat, reviewing incoming reports and scribbling notes for himself and his subordinates. The assistant intelligence officer, used to the colonel by now, ignored Guajardo and continued to jot down notes as he pored over the messages coming in faster than he could review them.

When Guajardo tired of being ignored, he walked over to where the assistant operations officer sat. He, like the assistant intelligence officer, was reviewing incoming reports as he prepared to write his summary of the Mexican armed forces activities for the past twelve hours. Like the assistant intelligence officer, he also ignored Guajardo. It was not that either of the officers, both majors, was disrespectful. It was just that they knew that if they stopped and talked to Colonel Guajardo every time he came by and looked over their shoulders, they would never be able to get anything done. Both understood that Guajardo, with nothing of value to do, was nervous, and anxious to do something, anything, to work that nervousness off. Wandering around the operations center, looking here and there, was just his way of doing that. For those who had to work there, it was at times unnerving, but since the colonel was the minister of defense, and this was his operations center, anything he did was right and, as a result, had to be tolerated.

When he finished his aimless rounds of the operations center, Guajardo walked over to the door leading into the main corridor and stopped. He turned and looked back into the room before leaving. Everyone, he thought, was busy, doing something. Everyone but him. There had to be something worthwhile that needed tending to that only he could do. But what? At that moment, he could think of nothing. Until the Americans finished their latest deployments and made their intentions clear, there was no need to act. All units of the Mexican Army were deployed or completing deployment according to their war plans. Every one of his subordinate commanders knew what to do and was doing it. In effect, Guajardo thought, he had planned so well that he had, for the moment, put himself out of a job. If that was so, then why did he feel so uneasy about what was happening?

Turning away, he headed down the corridor to the latrine. Although there was a private facility that he could have used next to a private office reserved for him just off of the operations center, Guajardo preferred to use the common latrine. An American friend of his, an infantry officer, had once told him that as a method of checking on what the troops were thinking, he would go into the latrines used by his troops and read the graffiti they left behind. In a few minutes, he told Guajardo, he knew what officers in his unit were unpopular, and what the soldiers were unhappy about. As an aside, he also noted that he sometimes got some real hot telephone numbers. Guajardo, always one to try new things, had adopted the practice after returning to Mexico and found that it was, indeed, quite useful, as well as entertaining.

As he relieved himself, Guajardo thought it was good for his soldiers to see that he, their leader, was no different than them. There was a certain leveling that took place when men understood that their leaders were men, men who put their pants on one leg at a time just as they did, and who had human needs just as they did. Besides, Guajardo thought as he finished stuffing himself back into his trousers, he had nothing at all to be ashamed of. If anything, he could be quite proud of his manhood.

From behind, Guajardo heard the door of the latrine open slightly. The voice of the assistant operations officer hesitantly called through the partial opening, "Colonel Guajardo. Sorry to disturb you but Colonel Molina is on the phone. He would like to speak to you."

"Did you tell *el presidente* that I had my hands full, Major?"

There was a pause. "Ah, well, no, sir. I told him you had a pressing matter that needed your personal attention."

Turning around and heading for the sinks, Guajardo groaned. "Good lord, man! Now Colonel Molina will think I've been screwing a secretary on that beautiful mahogany desk in my private office. Go back and tell him I am on my way.''

With a crisp ''Yes, sir,'' the major disappeared and left Guajardo laughing to himself.

Deciding to take Molina's call in his private office so that he could speak freely, Guajardo seated himself at the large mahogany desk, its shiny surface clear of everything but one black telephone. Picking up the receiver, Guajardo informed Molina's adjutant that he was ready to speak to the president. When Molina came on and began to speak, Guajardo cut him off. ''My friend, before you say anything, I was taking a piss.''

Guajardo could hear Molina laughing on the other end of the line. When he finally spoke, Molina asked Guajardo if he had a guilty conscience, to which Guajardo responded, no, just a full bladder. Again, there was laughter that lasted several seconds before Molina was finally able to regain his composure.

''Well, I am glad that you have things down there well in hand, Colonel Guajardo.'' Now it was Guajardo's turn to laugh.

When he was ready, Guajardo continued. ''I am sure, Hernando, that you did not call me because you needed a break in the dull routine of running this country. How can I serve my president?''

''Actually, you've already done wonders for me, Alfredo. I haven't had anything to laugh at all day.''

Guajardo, knowing that the conversation would soon turn serious, could not resist playing with his friend a little longer. ''Oh? And when you need a little levity in your life, you call the Army?''

When Molina spoke again, Guajardo noted that his voice had grown serious. ''Well, if I was looking for humor, I definitely would not call Barreda at Foreign Affairs.''

In an instant, Guajardo understood. ''Is Salvado climbing the walls again?''

''No, Alfredo, he is well past that. Our foreign minister has gone through the ceiling. It seems that the American ambassador had no sooner left his office after explaining that the deployment of the American Army was only defensive when a special report on American television announced that a group of American congressmen had drafted a resolution that would authorize the president of the United States to invade Mexico.''

Guajardo shot upright in his seat. ''Are you serious? The American Congress throwing away their ability to control their president's use of the military? Did he say which congressmen made the statement?''

When Molina read the list of senators and congressmen who had already stated that they would support such a resolution, Guajardo could not speak. He had hoped, as had Barreda, that the American Congress would act as a brake on what they considered precipitous action on the part of the American president. Instead, if what Molina had told him was true—and Guajardo had no reason to doubt it—then the American Congress was in fact expediting, not hindering, the possible use of force.

For a moment, there was silence as both men, alone in their own offices, pondered the real purpose of this latest American action. Was it meant to intimidate them? Or was it a warning? Guajardo, as well as Molina, knew that a similar resolution had been passed by the American Congress just before the Americans commenced military operations against Iraq in 1991. Perhaps, in their own way, the American Congress was telling them that it was the eleventh hour. But for what? Finally, Guajardo spoke. "What, *el presidente,* do you need from me?"

Understanding that Guajardo had intentionally addressed him with his formal title to signal him that it was Colonel Guajardo, the minister of defense, asking the question, Molina responded as the president. "As much as you dislike the idea, it is time for you to personally contact the military chiefs in Guatemala, Honduras, El Salvador, Nicaragua, Costa Rica, Panama, Colombia, Venezuela, and Cuba in order to establish command and control procedures for the incorporation of their forces into our defensive plans. Colonel Barreda is in the process of sending an official request to those governments for the assistance they promised."

"What about the UN and the Organization of American States? Has he called for an emergency session of those organizations?"

"Yes, Alfredo, he has done so. What happens with them is not your concern. Defense of the republic is your only concern now, my friend."

Molina's last comment was an order. For the time being, Guajardo was to remain out of international politics. Still, he could not resist the urge to add a warning. "You realize, my friend, that such assistance will not come cheaply. Each of our new allies will have a price that they will expect us to honor. Especially the Cubans, and you know I cannot trust the Cubans."

"Nor I, Alfredo, nor I. But what else can we do? Pray for a miracle? Hope that the Americans will see the error of their ways and reason with us an equal? No, it is not their way. So long as they view us as something less than equal, as naughty children who must be taught a lesson every now and then, they will not listen to reason, from us or anyone else. As much as I hate it, I see no other course than to offer armed resistance against any and all violations of our borders."

There was another pause before Guajardo asked the question that had to be asked. He spoke slowly, clearly, and concisely. "I assume then, *el presidente,* you are ordering the Army to repel any and all incursions by the Americans, with the use of force if necessary."

"Yes, Alfredo, those are my orders. Do you have any further questions?"

Guajardo didn't. There was nothing more to say. It had all been discussed, it had all been debated. In order to stay in power and succeed in rebuilding their beloved country, the Council of 13 had to prove it could defend the Republic of Mexico and its people. To back down and freely allow the Americans to occupy even a single square meter of Mexico would be viewed as weakness, and the council would lose face with its people. After telling Molina that he had no further questions, Guajardo hung up the phone, leaned back in his seat, and stared at the blank walls for a moment.

Then he surprised himself by doing something he had not done since he was a little boy. In the silence of his cold, barren office, he found himself praying to the Virgin for guidance and solace.

WASHINGTON, D.C.
1715 HOURS, 3 SEPTEMBER

The sudden impact of Senator Jimmy Herbert's fist on the picnic table sent a spoon flying, knocked down two paper cups full of iced tea, and brought a stunned silence to people seated at the picnic tables flanking Herbert's. Herbert, however, didn't notice any of this, for his entire attention was riveted on the only other person seated at his table, Representative Ed Lewis of Tennessee.

Lewis, used to evoking such a response from his colleagues, calmly sat across from Herbert, righting one of the spilt cups with one hand and carefully sopping up the tea with a napkin in the other. "Why, Senator Herbert, all I said was that your resolution was the dumbest piece of legislation since the Gulf of Tonkin Resolution. The only difference is that the men who drafted the Tonkin Resolution, in comparison, knew what they were getting into."

Thrusting his head closer to Lewis, his face still red and contorted with the effort to control himself, Herbert growled at Lewis, "Damn you to hell, Mr. Congressman Ed Lewis. I heard what you said the first time. And damn you for even suggesting that what happened in Southeast Asia had any similarities with what is happening down in Mexico. The Vietnam War is over. It's history. Or haven't you heard?"

Lewis was still calmly cleaning up the mess created by Herbert. "Ah, yes, I remember the former president mentioning that." Then, pausing in his cleanup, Lewis looked up at Herbert. "But I don't think he meant that we were supposed to forget about it, and the lessons it taught us about the limitations of military intervention."

Herbert leaned back, throwing his hands up in the air. "What military intervention? We have no intention of intervening in the internal affairs of the Mexican government and my resolution does not authorize such actions."

It was now Lewis's turn to become angry. Lewis threw the sopping napkin he had been using to clean up the iced tea on the ground. "Oh, come off it, Mr. Senator! Who are you trying to bullshit? The problem with all you goddamned lawyers in Congress is that you start believing that the fancy words you use to hide the meaning of your actions fools people. Listen, do you and all your supporters really believe that your resolution authorizing the president to, and I quote, 'use whatever means necessary along, and beyond, the borders of the United States in order to protect the people of the United States and guarantee the territorial integrity of the United States,' will frighten the Mexicans into backing down and do what we want them to?" Lewis pointed his finger at Herbert to make his point. "Now, you can call the action you have authorized anything you want. But I'll tell you what the Mexicans will call it. They'll call it an invasion."

Seeing that he had Lewis riled up, Herbert regrouped, relaxed, and, with the ease of a professional politician, let a smile light his face. "Okay, so it's an invasion. So what? What are the Mexicans going to do? Bombard us with taco shells?"

While Lewis's last outburst had been staged, the one he unleashed now was from the heart. "I don't believe you! You don't understand what you're doing, do you? I hope you realize that the gulf we're talking about is the Gulf of Mexico, not the Persian Gulf. Those aren't Arabs down there. They're Mexicans. Fellow North Americans. People related to almost five percent of our own population. They're not going to simply sit on their hands and watch American combat troops tromp about their country. They'll do what they always have done whenever we've gone south, they'll fight." Lewis paused, turning away from Herbert. Then, as an afterthought, he added, "Besides, we don't even know if the current regime in Mexico is responsible for the border raids. For all we know, someone could be staging those raids, trying to embarrass the Council of 13 in order to get us to invade, just like Pancho Villa did in 1916."

"What difference, Ed, does it make who is responsible for the raids? None. None at all. What matters, my dear distinguished colleague from the state of Tennessee, is that Americans are dying, right here, in their own country, defending their own borders. When it comes to defending your home and family, it doesn't matter who, in reality, is responsible for the danger." Standing up, Herbert prepared to leave, but paused long enough to finish his speech to Lewis. "Even your high-minded ideals don't matter. What matters, dear boy, is the fact that someone is threatening the United States and we, the leaders of the nation, must do something to end that danger."

Lewis, still turned at an angle, mockingly clapped his hands. "A wonderful campaign speech by any measure, Senator. The only thing you forgot was to mention Mom, apple pie, and the girl next door. The voters back home always love that."

Infuriated, Herbert was about to tell Lewis to fuck off, but held back. Instead, he clenched his fists, turned, and went storming off, leaving Lewis alone and, for the moment, at a loss as to what to do to forestall what he saw as a disaster in the making.

5 KILOMETERS SOUTH OF LAREDO, TEXAS
1945 HOURS, 3 SEPTEMBER

While the problem that Second Lieutenant Nancy Kozak faced that evening was, in comparison, trivial to people like Jan Fields, Colonel Guajardo, and Ed Lewis, it was, nonetheless, a very real and pressing matter to Kozak. In the excitement and haste of the 16th Division's load-out and deployment, Kozak had forgotten what time of month it was. It was only that morning, shortly after breakfast, when the first menstrual cramp struck, that Kozak realized she had forgotten to throw a box of sanitary napkins in her rucksack.

Knowing full well that sanitary napkins were the last thing the company supply sergeant and battalion S-4 would think of, Kozak decided to use a field expedient napkin to hold her over until she could find some. In the privacy of the mesquite bushes one hundred meters from her platoon's perimeter, Kozak dropped her trousers and squatted. Ripping open her personal first aid package, she took out the large compression bandage meant to be used for large wounds, and used it in lieu of a proper sanitary napkin. While it more than did the job for the balance of the day, by late afternoon Kozak could feel the compression bandage begin to get soggy. While she could, with effort, hide her discomfort, there was nothing she could do to mask the odor, especially in the close confines of the turret of a Bradley fighting vehicle on a hot summer Texas day.

Sooner or later, she was going to have to change the bandage. The question was with what? She could always use another compression bandage. The Bradley's larger first aid kit had several of them. But her crew might not appreciate that. That first aid kit was there for a reason. It and its contents could mean the difference between life and death if they were hit. No one, even the most sympathetic member of the crew, would look kindly upon Kozak's use of medical supplies in such a manner. While she understood that it didn't matter to them what she did with her own compression bandage, the first aid kit belonged to the crew.

As they rolled down the two-lane road, merrily ignoring the occasional cars and pickup trucks that swerved to give the twenty-five-ton tracked vehicle a wide berth, Kozak continued to work on a solution. She thought about using toilet paper, but quickly discarded that idea. A friend of hers at West Point had tried that one night during a field exercise. The only thing the toilet paper produced was a bloody, soggy mess. The bag of cloth rags they carried for cleaning their weapons and checking the Bradley's oil levels was a possibility, but not a good one. Most of them were already filthy.

When the Bradley came whipping around a curve in the road, Kozak saw the answer to her prayers. There, on the side of the road, less than one hundred meters away, was a gas station with a convenience market. Excited, Kozak keyed the intercom and yelled to the driver to pull into the gas station and stop.

Surprised by Kozak's order and startled by her high-pitched screech, Specialist Louie Freedman jerked the steering wheel to the right and pulled into the parking area of the gas station, barely missing a pickup sitting at the gas pumps. When the track came to a stop, Kozak dropped down inside of the turret, took off her armored crewman's helmet, grabbed her web gear and Kevlar helmet, and prepared to dismount.

Her gunner, Sergeant Terry Tyson, looked at her. "What's the matter, Lieutenant? Where are you going?"

Looking at Tyson for a moment, she considered giving him a line about needing to check something out, but decided not to. Looking him in the eye, she told him the truth. "Well, if you must know, I need to go into that store to buy some sanitary napkins."

For several seconds, they stared at each other while Kozak's announcement registered. When it did, he blinked. "Oh, okay, Lieutenant. I just need to know in case the CO called."

Kozak's eyes grew large. "If the CO calls, don't you dare tell him why we stopped."

"What should I tell him, Lieutenant?"

"I don't care. Tell him I'm reconning another platoon position or something. Tell him I'm going to the bathroom. Tell him anything but . . ."

"Okay, no problem, Lieutenant. I'll cover you."

Smiling, Kozak thanked Tyson and hoisted herself up and out of the open hatch. After she had climbed down the front slope of the Bradley and gone into the store, Freedman called Tyson over the intercom. "Where's the lieutenant going?"

"The LT's on the rag and she needs to buy some Kotex."

Freedman was unable to tell if the tone in Tyson's voice was disgust or impatience. Keying his mike, he decided to harass his sergeant. "Oh, is that what that smell was."

"Jesus, Freedman, haven't you ever smelled a bitch in heat?"

"Yeah, Sarge, lots of times. But never in a Bradley."

With a distinct note of sarcasm in his voice, Tyson replied, "Well, welcome to the new Army. You'd best get used to it."

"Hey, it ain't so bad. After putting up with your greasy farts for all these months, I can deal with this, provided she buries them herself."

Watching his lieutenant walk out of the store, a bag under her arm and a smile on her face, Tyson didn't respond to Freedman's last comment. Instead, he just watched his lieutenant and wondered if he would ever get used to her. Maybe, he thought, it would be easier if she was ugly. At least then, he wouldn't have to worry about hiding the occasional erection he got when they sat together in the close confines of the Bradley's small two-man turret.

After she climbed on the Bradley, Kozak put her paper sack down, reached in, and pulled out two cold cans of soda, handing one to Freedman and one to Tyson. As Tyson took his can, she smiled. "Thanks, Sergeant. I appreciate your covering for me."

Tyson, opening the can, smiled back. "No problem, LT. We're a crew. Ain't that right, Freedman?"

After taking a sip of his soda, Freedman looked up at Kozak, then at Tyson. There they were, him a black kid from Cleveland, Tyson, a redneck from Georgia, and the lieutenant, a twenty-two-year-old female from some nice middle-class suburb, sitting on the border of Texas, drinking soda. Yeah, he thought, they were a crew, a real far-out crew. "Sure thing, Sarge. Whatever you say."

15

There is no approved solution to any tactical situation.

—George S. Patton

LAREDO, TEXAS
0905 HOURS, 7 SEPTEMBER

Neither Alverez Calles nor his brother Julio had any intention of starting a war. All they were interested in that morning was robbing a bank, a task that seemed rather easy to do in America. After all, there were banks all over south Texas, each one lightly protected and most near major roads and highways. It would be nothing, they told their two friends, to walk into any of the branches in the suburbs, threaten the bank staff with automatic weapons, and collect more money in five minutes than they could possibly earn in a year delivering pizzas.

Alverez, the older of the two brothers, had no problem winning his brother over to his scheme. And their two friends, tired of living in the slums of south Texas, needed little convincing. Living in America for two years had taught them all several hard truths. First, despite the fact that they, as Colombians, were ethnically Caucasians, just like the Anglos, in America they would never be considered white. The second truth, however, served to balance the first. Money, according to conventional wisdom, was the great leveler. With enough money, money that seemed readily available to those bold enough to take it, even they could live as well as the whites.

The presence of armed American troops didn't bother the Calles brothers and their partners. After all, armed troops were a permanent fixture in Colombia. Since the Calleses knew that soldiers were the same everywhere, they saw no difference between them and the city police officers who frequented doughnut shops and drove about in big, underpowered American patrol cars. Besides, with two assault rifles, a shotgun, and three automatic pistols, Alverez Calles knew they could discourage the local police from following too closely. Few people, he knew, were willing to lay down their lives to defend the wealth of others.

While the Calles brothers were in the process of psyching themselves up for their great leap into fame and fortune, Captain Stan Wittworth was in the process of making his morning rounds, or at least trying to. Parked across from a doughnut shop, Wittworth and his driver were waiting in his Humvee for Deputy Sheriff Glenn Briscoe to come out. Looking at his watch, then across to the shop, then back at his watch, Wittworth became impatient. There were places he needed to go and things he needed to do. Briscoe, liaison from the sheriff's office to Wittworth, following a routine he had followed for the past fifteen years, was keeping Wittworth performing duties he was neither trained for nor comfortable with.

Despite the fact that Briscoe wore a uniform, Wittworth still considered Briscoe a civilian. The deputy was quite knowledgeable in his duties, but that was not the problem. In the past week, he had been very helpful in showing Wittworth and his officers the area, explaining the lay of the land as well as providing them a feel for local politics and people. Wittworth was even impressed by the way Briscoe handled himself when dealing with other civilians who had run afoul of the law. Still, Wittworth found Briscoe far too casual in both his dress and conduct when not performing his duties. Even his conversations, when Wittworth allowed himself to be drawn in, were about things that had nothing to do with their mission. In no time at all, Wittworth became convinced that to Briscoe his position as a deputy sheriff was nothing more than a job, a means of earning a living. He lacked, in Wittworth's mind, the singular dedication to duty that separated a professional from a civilian. So Wittworth tolerated Briscoe and used him as necessary, but decided that, if push came to shove, he would use his own judgment and people, people who were dedicated, well-trained, and disciplined.

Seeing that Briscoe was deep in conversation with two of the other patrons of the doughnut shop and in no hurry to leave, Wittworth studied the map board in his lap. On one side of the board was a street map showing a section of southeastern Laredo, where his 1st and 2nd platoons were deployed. On the other side was a topographical map showing the countryside to the south and east of Laredo, where his 3rd Platoon con-

ducted mounted patrols and manned a roadblock. Both maps were covered in clear acetate on which were marked black triangles with letters in
them that represented observation posts, numbers in boxes representing
checkpoints, and dotted lines connecting them defining patrol routes used
by his company. While necessary, the military symbols, written with
wide markers, obscured some of the street names and map symbols under
the acetate. Still, enough showed so that even without Briscoe, Wittworth
could now find his way about Laredo.

Looking back at the doughnut shop, Wittworth saw Briscoe, one foot
up on a chair, still talking to his two friends. Looking at his watch,
Wittworth decided to give Briscoe five more minutes before he would
leave without him. There was, after all, a limit to how far this civilian-
military cooperation could be pushed.

Pulling up in front of the bank they had selected, Julio Calles stopped.
From the side door of the white van, decorated with the logo of the pizza
shop where they worked, Alverez Calles emerged, holding a large, square
pizza warming pouch in his left hand. Leaving the door of the van open,
he looked to his left and right before entering the bank. Seeing his two
friends, each approaching from opposite directions, Alverez nodded, then
proceeded to enter the bank.

Once inside, he looked about for a moment, then turned and headed for
the office where the manager of this branch was seated. The guard, a man
of about fifty, looked at Alverez quizzically for a moment, then turned to
ask one of the tellers standing near him how anyone could stand to eat
pizza that early in the morning. In the process of doing so, the guard
failed to notice the entrance of either of Alverez's accomplices. One of
them, a tall, lanky man with jet black hair and carrying a white plastic
shopping bag, stayed at the door. The other, a short stocky man with eyes
that darted from side to side, crossed the floor to the far side, turning
around once he got there so that he could see Alverez, the guard, and the
tall man at the door.

Entering the bank manager's office without pausing, Alverez said nothing when the manager, a man of about forty, looked up. At first, he
merely stared, wondering why a pizza deliveryman was standing in front
of him. He was about to ask, when Alverez, in one easy motion, reached
into the warming pouch and pulled out a black automatic pistol with an
oversize magazine protruding from its handle.

*   *   *

Wittworth was looking at his map again when his driver grunted. "Looks like trouble in the doughnut shop, sir."

Not understanding, Wittworth looked up at his driver, who was pointing across the parking lot. Wittworth turned and saw Briscoe, without a hat, come flying out of the shop. There was an anxious look on Briscoe's face as he ran for the Humvee, holding his small handheld radio to his ear all the while. As he watched, the first thought that came to Wittworth was that this was the fastest he had seen Briscoe move all week. In a single bound, Briscoe was up and in the back seat of the topless Humvee, shouting to the driver to get moving and to take a left once they were out of the parking lot.

Obediently, the driver cranked up the Humvee and prepared to move. Wittworth, however, signaled him to hold it for a moment by holding up his left hand. Wittworth turned to face Briscoe. "Where we going, Deputy?"

Thrusting his head forward between Wittworth and the driver, Briscoe, sweat beading up on his forehead, turned to Wittworth. "Some Mexicans are hitting a bank two blocks from here. Shots have been fired and an officer's down."

For a moment, Wittworth considered his situation. A bank robbery was definitely a civilian matter. Even if Briscoe, a civilian law enforcement officer, felt obliged to respond, Wittworth, an Army officer, wasn't sure he was required to transport Briscoe to the scene. On the other hand, however, the fact that Mexicans were involved changed the nature of the situation. Why the Mexicans would hit a bank didn't bother him. Wittworth knew that, in the closing days of the Civil War, the Confederacy had staged raids from Canada into Vermont, robbing banks in order to finance their war effort. What worried Wittworth was the fact that they were doing this in broad daylight, in the presence of regular Army units. That, to him, didn't make sense. It was almost as if they had a death wish.

Watching Wittworth sit like a bump on a log, pondering the situation, was infuriating to Briscoe. "What the hell are you waiting for, Captain? A goddamned invitation from the governor? Americans are being killed by Mexicans. You gonna sit here and do nothin' about that?"

Briscoe was right. Regardless of the motivation or the question of jurisdiction and authority, the fact was Americans were being killed and he and his company had been sent down to prevent that. The raid by the Mexicans, regardless of why they were doing it, suddenly became a personal affront to him, his company, and the United States Army, an affront that could not go unpunished.

Without further thought, Wittworth ordered his driver to move out and follow Briscoe's directions. Once they were on the street and rolling, Wittworth took the radio hand mike and began to issue orders to his platoons, translating Briscoe's civilian terms into military terms that his platoon leaders could understand.

Sitting on the side of the road near the roadblock established by her platoon on U.S. 83 south of Laredo, Lieutenant Kozak was finishing her breakfast. Carefully picking at an unidentified edible object that the company first sergeant had plopped down in the center of her breakfast plate, she was debating if she should eat it or toss it when Sergeant Tyson, sitting on top of their Bradley, called her. "Hey, Lieutenant, hot flash from the CO. He wants the company to stand to."

Looking up at Tyson, Kozak was about to become upset when she realized that he had not been guilty of making a sexist remark, only of poor terminology. Letting that pass, she turned to the matter at hand. "Stand to? Why?"

"The CO didn't say much, just that the Laredo police were engaging some Mexicans in a firefight in town."

Kozak looked at Tyson for a moment. Didn't say much? There's a firefight in progress and Tyson thinks the CO didn't say much? Tyson's comments and reactions didn't match. Setting her plate down, Kozak decided she had better contact the CO herself and find out what was going on. Her breakfast could wait. After all, she thought, whatever it was that the first sergeant had served her that morning had been dead for a very long time and could only improve with age.

As his Humvee took a right turn off of Guadalupe Street onto Cedar Avenue a little too fast, Wittworth had to hang on as the centrifugal force threw him over to the left. They were halfway through the turn, veering over into the left-hand lane, when a white van with a plastic pizza attached to its roof came tearing around the same corner, headed in the opposite direction. The speed of the van and the sharpness of its turn, like that of Wittworth's Humvee, was causing the pizza van to veer over into the center of the street. With a flick of his wrists, Wittworth's driver cut the steering wheel as far to the right as it could go, missing the van by inches and, in the process, running the Humvee up onto the sidewalk, and running over two newspaper machines before coming to a jarring stop. In the process, Wittworth watched the van go zinging by. In the open side door, he saw two dark-skinned men holding weapons.

In an instant, the van had disappeared down the street they had just come up. Realizing that the van had to be the one they were pursuing, Wittworth turned to his driver and ordered him to move out and follow the van. The driver, however, did not immediately respond. With his hands frozen to the steering wheel in a death grip, his eyes wide open and his mouth gaping, he was hyperventilating, trying hard to catch his breath and calm down. Wittworth's first attempt to get his attention by yelling elicited no response. The man was shaken. Reaching over, Wittworth grabbed the man's arm and yelled again. The driver, his mouth still gaping, slowly turned his head toward Wittworth and stared at his commander with wide, unblinking eyes. Wittworth shook him and repeated his order. There was a moment's hesitation before a weak, high-pitched "Okay" issued from the driver's throat.

By the time Kozak had mounted her Bradley and put on her armored crewman's helmet, Wittworth was back on the radio, issuing orders as he tried desperately to find his location on the street map and hang on at the same time. Briscoe, unable to do anything but hang on, watched the white pizza truck zigzag in and out of traffic. Briscoe thought about putting on his seat belt, but decided against it. To do so would keep him from sticking his head between Wittworth and the driver. But even with his head next to Wittworth's, the only thing he could get through to Wittworth above the noise was that they were on U.S. 83 headed south out of town.

The Humvee driver, having regained his nerve, used the superior mobility of his vehicle to close the distance, running up over sidewalks and across lawns, and scattering pedestrians that stood in their way as they continued their pursuit. He was in the process of negotiating a street-corner while Wittworth was looking down at his map when the rear doors of the van flew open. The only warning Wittworth and his driver got was Briscoe's yelling, above the roar of the engine, *"Jesus Christ! Duck!"*

Looking up from his map, Wittworth was just in time to see the muzzle flash from an assault rifle aimed right at him. The driver saw the same thing and, as before, reacted by jerking the wheel to the side, running the Humvee into an aluminum street lamppost. For an instant, the Humvee pitched up, as if it were about to climb the post, before its weight brought the lamppost crashing down, impaling the Humvee on the stump of the post and pitching Briscoe forward over the windshield and onto the hood. The same jarring stop launched Wittworth forward just as he was ducking to avoid the gunfire. The forward movement and stop drove Wittworth's Kevlar helmet into the glass windshield like a battering ram.

When everything finally settled, the driver jumped out of the Humvee and turned to Wittworth, who was in the process of freeing his helmet from the glass windshield and slowly sitting up. "That's *it,* Captain. That's it. Twice in one day is enough for me. Damned sure not gonna try for strike three."

Shaken by a near collision, being fired at, and piling up on a streetlamp post, and dazed by the impact of his head into the windshield, Wittworth looked to his right at the ground, noticing the front wheels of the Humvee were off of it. Without admitting it, he too realized that he had had enough for one day. But he wasn't ready to give up. As he sat upright and shook himself out, Wittworth's shock was quickly replaced by embarrassment, then, in quick order, by a fit of rage. Grabbing the radio hand mike, he keyed the radio net and ordered all his platoon leaders to pursue and stop a white pizza van with Mexicans in it at all costs. Those bastards, he thought, were not going to embarrass the United States Army and get away with it.

At 3rd Platoon's roadblock, Kozak and her people waited. The 3rd Squad, who had been on duty at the roadblock when the call came in, continued to man it. Their Bradley, with the engine running, the gunner and track commander up and alert, the main gun pointed north toward Laredo, sat blocking the right side of the road. Kozak's Bradley sat on the opposite side of the road, also with its engine running and main gun pointed toward Laredo. The other two squads, with SFC Rivera, were mounted and ready to move out, their Bradleys sitting just off the road fifty meters south of Kozak's and the 3rd Squad's Bradley.

As they waited, watching for any sign of the enemy pizza van, Kozak tried to contact Wittworth, who, for some reason, was not responding. She was unsure of her instructions. His last orders, "to pursue and stop" the pizza van, were, at best, ambiguous. Kozak didn't know if she was required to challenge the people in the pizza van, offering them an opportunity to submit to a search or surrender before she opened fire. If they showed any signs of resistance or flight, was she authorized to use deadly force? What, she wondered, constituted resistance, and how much deadly force was too much? What did Wittworth have in mind, Kozak wondered, when he ordered them to stop the pizza van? A simple physical roadblock? Warning shots from small arms? Or did he expect her to use 25mm high-explosive rounds and simply blow the van away?

All these questions, and more, were racing through Kozak's mind when Tyson yelled into the intercom, "Here they come! There's a white van heading for us. And he's in a hurry."

Hoisting her binoculars up to her face, Kozak searched the road to the north. The white van Tyson had spotted was, indeed, headed south toward them as fast as it could go. On top of the van's roof, a red plastic pizza identified the van as the one they were after. This was it. There wasn't any time for questions, no time for clarification. She was on her own. Self-doubt and the uneasy feeling that comes with it were gone. In its place, a nervous rush of anticipation and a tingle of excitement. This was it.

Letting the binoculars fall until the strap around her neck stopped them, Kozak stood up on her seat, bending over until she could see Staff Sergeant John Strange, squad leader of the 3rd Squad. Leaning against the side of his Bradley, Strange was talking to one of his soldiers when he heard Kozak yelling for him to come over closer to her Bradley. Picking up his rifle, Strange began to trot over toward Kozak.

Kozak didn't wait for Strange to reach her before she began to issue her orders. "Sergeant Strange. The white van coming down the road, stop it. But do not, repeat, do not shoot unless fired on. Is that clear?"

Stopping short, with his M-16 in his left hand, Strange waved his right hand and nodded. Without further ado, he turned in place and, in a booming voice, called his squad to action. "Okay, 3rd Squad. This is it. Show time. I wanna see everybody up and ready. And no shootin' unless I or the LT say so." He looked around as his people put on helmets, crouched behind the concrete road barrier, and prepared themselves. Just to be sure, he repeated the last part of his order. "No shootin' until you hear the order from me or the lieutenant."

Satisfied that all was ready where she was, Kozak keyed the radio tuned to the platoon frequency. Turning around in the open hatch and looking south toward the other two Bradleys of her platoon, Kozak alerted Rivera that she thought the van they were watching for was coming at them. She instructed Rivera to stand by with the 1st and 2nd squads and be ready to move. Rivera acknowledged her orders with a short, functional "Wilco, out," and dropped off the air. With the platoon ready, Kozak next dropped down into the turret and prepared to switch the radio frequency to the company command net when Tyson's voice came over the intercom. "They've seen us and stopped, LT."

Forgetting about the company net, Kozak put her head up to the eyepiece of the primary sight. Tyson already had the van in the sight, crosshairs laid on the center mass of the vehicle, which was sitting some five hundred meters north of them on the road. "Are you sure they saw us, Sergeant Tyson?"

Taking his eyes off his sight, Tyson looked at Kozak, seated to his right, for a second. At a range of five hundred meters, he thought, even if he missed the red and white fifty-five-gallon drums, concrete Jersey barriers, barbed wire, and stop signs of the roadblock, even a blind man would see the two twenty-five-ton, nine-foot-nine-inch-high Bradleys, standing right behind the roadblock. Holding his tongue, he gave a simple, short response. "Yeah, LT, they saw us."

"They're backing up."

Swinging back around to his sight, Tyson caught the image of the van just before it completed a wild U-turn in the middle of the road. Even before the van finished the turn, Kozak was up out of the hatch and yelling orders to Sergeant Strange. "Sergeant Strange, you stay here with the 3rd Squad. I'm taking the rest of the platoon and going after the van."

As she dropped down and ordered Rivera to bring the rest of the platoon up, Strange had his people open a gap in the barrier. Hearing Kozak's order to Strange, Freedman, her driver, anticipated her next order. He let the park brake off, put the Bradley's transmission into gear, and prepared to roll. Without waiting for the rest of the platoon, Kozak told Freedman to move out.

Scurrying out of the way just in time, the men of 3rd Squad watched as Kozak's Bradley whipped around the barrels and wire, knocking one of the barrels over in the process. Its engine whining to a high pitch, then dropping as the next higher gear caught, the Bradley cleared the barrier and took off down the road. Seconds later, the other two Bradleys, with Rivera perched high in the commander's hatch of the first, came tearing through. They were already close to reaching top speed and less able to negotiate the twists and turns of the roadblock. It came as no surprise to anyone in the 3rd Squad, now standing on either side of the road at a respectful distance, when Rivera's Bradley ran over and crushed flat the fifty-five-gallon drum Kozak's Bradley had knocked over. The 3rd Platoon was in hot pursuit of a dangerous pizza van and nothing was going to stop them.

As they closed to where the van had disappeared, Kozak watched as three police cars in pursuit of the van went careening around the corner, down the side road where the van had disappeared. Looking down at her map, then at the street sign as they closed on and turned the corner, Kozak noted that they were now on Masterson Road, which ran due west and ended just short of the Rio Grande. Between ducking low branches from trees along the road and working out in her mind exactly what they would do with the van if and when they caught it, Kozak wasn't paying attention when her Bradley came to the end of the road and almost rammed a Laredo police car sitting sideways in the middle of the road.

The driver's door, facing the oncoming Bradley, was open, with a Laredo policeman standing next to it, radio hand mike in one hand, looking west, across the river, when Kozak's Bradley appeared out of nowhere. Both Kozak and the policeman saw each other at the same instant, their eyes flying open in surprise. Freedman, too, saw the danger. Honking the steering wheel over to the left, he felt the Bradley slide forward on the dirt road a few meters before it began a hard left turn. Missing the front of the police car by inches, the Bradley crashed through the brush on the side of the road and down the embankment toward the river where other policemen and sheriff's deputies were standing.

Although Freedman had control and was already in the process of stopping the Bradley, the policemen and deputies didn't know that, and didn't give a hoot about their pride. Like chickens scurrying to get out of the way of the fox in the hen house, the policemen and deputies turned and fled when they saw Kozak's Bradley come crashing down the embankment, throwing dirt, dust, and rocks everywhere.

After Freedman finally did manage to bring the Bradley to a stop, everyone stopped in place and looked at it. Kozak, stunned by the near collision, stood up in her hatch and looked behind her to make sure they hadn't run over anything or anyone of importance, then turned to the nearest policeman. *"Where'd the white van go?"*

The policeman, still recovering from his close encounter with Kozak's Bradley, just looked up at her for a second. The fact that the commander of the huge combat vehicle was a woman was as much a shock to him as his close brush with sudden death. What in the hell, he thought, was she doing up there? Kozak looked at him for a moment before repeating her question. "Where'd the white van go?"

Realizing that she must be for real, the policeman pointed toward the river. "They tried to ford the river. Van got stuck and they took off, on foot into Mexico."

Looking over into the river, Kozak could see the white van, all its doors wide open, awash in the center of the Rio Grande. Taking a deep breath, she realized that the enemy had evaded them. With nothing else to do, she dropped down and switched the radio frequency over to the company command net. The CO had to be told the bad news.

Pacing back and forth to work off his anger and nervous energy, Wittworth heard Kozak's call just as the aidmen were about to pull Briscoe's body off of his Humvee's hood. Ignoring them, Wittworth ran over to the Humvee and reached for the radio hand mike. Keying the mike, he responded to Kozak's call using his standard company call sign, Alpha 6.

"Alpha thirty-six, this is Alpha six. Send your traffic, over."

"Alpha six, this is thirty-six. We were in pursuit of the white van. They have abandoned the van and fled on foot. We have broken off the pursuit and are . . ."

Kozak's comment that they had given up the pursuit simply because the Mexicans had taken off on foot pissed him off. Even before Kozak finished her report, Wittworth squeezed the talk button with all his might and began to yell into the mike. "Damn you, thirty-six. Get out of your tracks and follow them, over."

Letting up on the talk lever on her CVC helmet, Kozak was surprised to hear Wittworth's voice come booming over the radio. Since she was transmitting and his radio couldn't override her transmission, all she caught of Wittworth's transmission was the last part, the part that instructed her to follow the Mexicans. Obviously, she thought, he didn't understand that the Mexicans had fled over the river into Mexico. Keying the radio again, she tried to inform Wittworth of the real situation.

"Alpha six, this is Alpha thirty-six. I don't think you understand the situation, over." Kozak's response caused Wittworth to lose whatever self-control he had left. Mashing the hand mike as if he were trying to crush it, he yelled back at Kozak, "This is Alpha six. You get your ass off your tracks and get those bastards or don't come back. Out." With that, Wittworth threw the hand mike into the Humvee, turned and went storming off, looking for some way to vent his anger.

Kozak was still trying to raise Wittworth on the radio when Rivera's Bradley pulled up next to hers. Taking off her CVC, she yelled to Rivera, "Have you been listening to the company command net?"

Rivera nodded his head. "Yeah, I heard. What do we do, Lieutenant?"

"I don't think he understands that the Mexicans are across the river."

Rivera looked down, thought about that, then looked back at Kozak. "He must. All these police have been following them. He's got a sheriff's deputy with him. He's got to know. Why else would he order us to pursue? Besides, don't the rules of engagement say something about hot pursuit in life-and-death situations?"

He was right, Kozak thought. The rules of engagement did say something about hot pursuit. While she didn't remember exactly what they said, surely Wittworth did. Otherwise, he wouldn't have ordered them to pursue. As she pondered this, neither she nor Rivera thought to ask the deputies, now wandering about in an effort to recover from their close call, if any of them had contact with the deputy who was Wittworth's liaison. Instead, Kozak accepted Rivera's logic. Looking over at the river and the far bank, she decided to do as she had been told.

"Sergeant Rivera, have the dismount teams from 1st and 2nd squads dismount and form up at the riverbank. We're going after them on foot." Dropping down, Kozak recovered her web gear, rifle, and Kevlar helmet. As she did so, she told Tyson to stay with the track and on the radio, even though he already knew this without her telling him. Tyson, a senior sergeant E-5, was familiar with his duties. At times, he resented having Kozak remind him of them, like now. It was, to him, almost as if she didn't trust him and she felt it was necessary to constantly remind him. Though he knew most new lieutenants were like that, it didn't make him feel any better about it.

Once outside the track, she trotted down to the riverbank, where Rivera was already forming the two squads. Quickly scanning the length of the river, with the stalled van in the center, Kozak decided it wouldn't be a very formidable barrier. A dry summer had dropped the water level, leaving several exposed sand bars that would make their crossing easier. For a second, she thought about leaving Rivera with the tracks. She should. It was the normal practice in mech infantry platoons to leave the platoon sergeant with the carrier teams while the platoon leader led the dismounts. In this situation, however, Kozak felt it would be better to have him with her. The tracks weren't in danger, and the men, she knew, would feel better going into battle if Rivera was with them.

Suddenly, Kozak's heart skipped a beat. It had just occurred to her that they were, in fact, about to go into battle. They were crossing an international boundary, locked and loaded, in pursuit of an armed foe. This was no exercise. No drill. When they pulled the trigger, real bullets, not laser beams, would be launched. When she reached the river, she looked at the two squads of soldiers, the 1st Squad on her right, the 2nd on her left. All eyes were on her. She returned the stares. Since most of her men were taller than she was, she had to look up. That, however, didn't seem to matter, for they were all waiting for her orders. Even Rivera, understanding the gravity of the situation, said nothing. He could have, but to do so would have undermined Kozak. This, she suddenly understood, was it. This, as the books say, was the moment of truth.

Without further thought, Kozak ordered the 1st Squad to deploy in line and follow her. Turning to Rivera, she ordered him to follow with the 2nd Squad, providing overwatch to the 1st. When Staff Sergeant Roger Maupin had his 1st Squad deployed, Kozak plunged into the knee-high water of the river and began to head into Mexico.

16

War means fighting, and fighting means killing.

—Nathan Bedford Forest

Through the shallow river and up the steep embankment on the Mexican side, Kozak led the 1st Squad. At the top of the embankment stood a row of brush and bushes that Kozak, without thinking, crashed through. As soon as she did, she realized her mistake. Once clear of the bushes, she found herself alone and in an open field, just her and her M-16 rifle, held at the ready. From the line of bushes to her rear, there was no cover or concealment until a row of houses, which stood over one hundred meters distant to her front and right. For several long seconds, she hesitated, wondering whether she should turn around and go back into the bushes or continue forward. In the bushes, she could wait until the two squads closed up, leaving 2nd Squad to cover the move of the 1st Squad across the open area to the buildings. Tactically, that would be the wise choice, the safe bet. Her other option was to continue forward once 1st Squad reached her, a move that would temporarily separate the two squads. That would be faster, allowing them to make up some of the time they had lost, but it entailed risks. If, while the 2nd Squad was still scaling the embankment, the 1st Squad, in the open, took fire, SFC Rivera and the 2nd Squad would not be able to cover or support the 1st.

Kozak was about to back up, opting for the safe bet, when the entire 1st Squad, in line, came crashing out of the brush. Coming up next to Kozak, the squad leader whispered into Kozak's ear, "Sorry, LT. The embankment was a little slippery. Took me a few seconds to rally the squad."

Seeing that it would screw things up to stop the squad, turn them around, and go back into the brush, Kozak changed her mind. "No problem. Let's go." With that, she stepped off and headed for the houses.

As they moved forward, they came across a road that ran perpendicular to their line of advance. The road led, to their right, into the row of houses, and, to the left and at a greater distance, toward buildings that looked like a school complex. Kozak had not noticed these buildings before. She hesitated for a moment and reconsidered their situation. She could see that they were entering, in all probability, the outskirts of Nuevo Laredo. Given a choice, she had no doubt that the Mexicans they were pursuing had gone right, since the houses were closer and would offer the Mexicans a better chance to hide or blend in with the populace. Using her right arm to signal the squad, she indicated they were to turn and follow the road toward the houses.

When the squad had finished wheeling to the right, Kozak turned around and began walking backward. In the line of brush along the embankment, she could see that Rivera had deployed the 2nd Squad. Without having to be told, Rivera had held the 2nd Squad there in order to cover the move of the 1st into the built-up area. That's why, she thought, she had brought Sergeant Rivera, to cover the mistakes she was making. The danger had passed, for now at least. "Okay, 1st Squad, let's pick up the pace." With that, she spun about and began to quicken her own pace.

With one problem addressed and her mind freed from worrying about it, another concern immediately popped into Kozak's head. As she turned her attention to the buildings they were fast approaching, the reality of the situation hit her like a head-on collision. She, Second Lieutenant Nancy B. Kozak, was leading American combat troops in a foreign country against a hostile force of unknown composition. And there was nothing between them and her except fifty meters of open space and her M-16 rifle. Yet there was no great paralyzing fear, no panic. Her concerns and thoughts, up to now, had been about practical matters, technical and tactical concerns. Only now, when they were deep in the execution of their pursuit, when all appeared to be going well, and all necessary deployments and decisions had been made, were concerns over personal safety beginning to emerge.

As she continued the approach, alert for any sign of movement, Kozak wondered if her conduct and the disregard for personal safety that had, up to then, come to her so effortlessly meant that she was brave. Or was it that her mind, so crowded with other concerns and thoughts, simply had not gotten around to alerting her to the fact that she was headed into real danger? What, she wondered, was courage and heroism? Was there any difference between them and stupidity and foolishness? After all, had it been smart for her to turn her back to the buildings, buildings that might be occupied by enemy soldiers, as they advanced, while she looked to see if Rivera and the 2nd Squad had come up? At the moment she had done it, it had been the right thing to do. Now, in retrospect, such a thing seemed dumb. Was that it? she thought. Were courage and heroism simply a question of doing what appeared to be right at a moment of danger and surviving? Strange thoughts. Strange questions. Thoughts and questions that had no place in her mind at that moment. For in an instant, they were at the first row of buildings and new problems demanded Kozak's attention. Lofty thoughts of courage and personal conduct, for the moment, were replaced by the immediate tactical situation, which demanded Kozak's full attention.

Without having to be told, Sergeant Maupin deployed his five men. He, and three of his people, took to the right side of the street, flattening themselves against the buildings along the narrow street while the other two men of 1st Squad went to the left side of the street where Kozak and her radio man were. In two single files, they slowly moved down the street, the lead man in each file looking to the front, and those following automatically staking out a sector of responsibility across the street from them, searching for any signs of trouble. After moving down the street some fifty meters, Kozak signaled for 1st Squad to halt. Immediately, Maupin relayed the signal. His men stopped and squatted in place, their backs against the wall or in the doorways of the building they were in front of. With their rifles held at the ready, thumbs lightly brushing the mode selector switches, only their heads moved as they slowly scanned their sector of responsibility.

When she saw that all was calm and that they were in no immediate danger, Kozak decided it was time for her to report their progress to Wittworth and wait for Rivera to bring up 2nd Squad. While she scanned the street and buildings to her front, wondering why, in the middle of the day, there were no people or signs of activity, Kozak ran her hand down her right leg to grab the map she kept in the large pocket on the thigh. Only after the fingers of her right hand had climbed over the flap and into an empty pocket did she realize that she had left her map on her Bradley. For the briefest of moments, the image of the map, wedged under the open sight of the Bradley where she used it when mounted, flashed across her brain. In her excitement, she had forgotten it.

Pulling her right hand out of the empty pocket, she balled it up into a fist and pounded her thigh with it. Stupid, she thought. Stupid! All she seemed to be doing was bumbling from one dumb mistake to the next. Thank God, she thought, there had been no contact. Even that thought triggered a new alarm. Since they began this wild goose chase, there had been no contact with the people they were supposed to be pursuing. By now, for all she knew, they could be halfway to Mexico City. And who, she wondered, were they pursuing? For the first time, she realized she had no idea how many people they were after, what they looked like, how they were armed, or even if they were all men or men and women. All she knew for sure was that she, and fourteen soldiers, were sitting on the outskirts of a Mexican city, with over two hundred meters, a river, and a row of bushes separating her from the rest of the United States Army.

With no idea of where, for sure, she was, who they were after, and what they faced, the absurdity of their situation suddenly became crystal clear. Though the thought of returning empty-handed, a failure in her first real-world test, was distasteful, she saw that to continue would be stupid. Kozak could, after all, justify her decision to withdraw. Even Wittworth would understand. Other than her own ego, and orders that had been suspect from the beginning, there was no reason for going on. Without further thought, she decided it would be pointless to go any further. From her position, she ordered Sergeant Maupin to send two men down the street a little ways to provide security and early warning. They would need that while she issued the necessary orders and regrouped for their withdrawal back to the American side of the Rio Grande.

Kozak watched Specialist Ron Cody and Private John Gunti move out down opposite sides of the street. They had just disappeared around a slight bend to the right when Rivera came up behind her, bumping her slightly before stopping to watch the 2nd Squad closing up on the 1st. Kozak, not expecting the contact, lost her balance from the bump, and almost toppled over onto her face. Steadying herself, she twisted about and faced Rivera, noticing that, despite the exertion and excitement, he wasn't breathing heavily. In fact, as she looked at him, she saw that he was hardly sweating. As Rivera continued to scan the area, Kozak looked down at his right leg to the pocket where she knew he kept his map. With great relief, she noticed the top of a folded map sheet sticking out of the large pocket on his thigh. Now all she had to do was figure out how she could get him to pull his map out without alerting him to the fact that she didn't have hers. Innocently, almost nonchalantly, she asked, "Sergeant Rivera, where do you put us?"

Without looking at her, he pulled out the map and looked down at it for a moment. When he found the right spot, he pointed to it and shoved it in front of Kozak. "Here, I think. We're right here, just inside of this village."

Taking the map, Kozak looked at the spot, running her finger over the route they had taken from the river to where they were. As she did so, Rivera got closer to her and whispered in her ear. "Hey, Lieutenant. We gotta talk. I don't think this is a good idea anymore."

As she looked up from the map, a smile lit Kozak's face. "Ah, gotcha there, Sergeant Rivera. Already ahead of you on that. You're right. In fact, it's half past time to go back."

Rivera returned the smile as he backed away a couple of feet. "Well, there's hope for you after all. Okay, should I pull 2nd Squad back to the row of bushes now while 1st covers from here?"

Rivera's comment was more than a question. It was, Kozak understood, a very tactful way of making a recommendation. She was about to reverse the order, wanting instead to lead off with the 1st Squad, but changed her mind when she saw Rivera's logic. First Squad was already in place, with a two-man security team out to cover the withdrawal. To pull 1st Squad out first would entail unnecessary confusion. "Good. I'll remain with 1st here. When you're ready, move out with 2nd. We'll follow as soon as you're set."

Rivera, relieved that their insane little foray into Mexico was about to end, gave Kozak a "Wilco, no problem." He was in the process of ordering Sergeant Russel Poer, squad leader of 2nd Squad, to take the squad back to the river embankment, when the sound of gunshots cut him off. For a second, there was dead silence as everyone in the 1st and 2nd squads froze in place. Kozak and Rivera looked at each other, realizing that the rifle or rifles that had fired the two rounds were not M-16s. Kozak turned for a moment, looked down the street in the direction the shots had come from, then turned back to Rivera to tell him something just as a hail of gunfire shattered the silence. This time, the distinctive *pop-pop* of the M-16 could be heard mixed in with the crack of a high-power, larger-bore rifle. Cody and Gunti were in contact.

When the firing stopped, and without waiting to consult with Rivera, Kozak began to issue her orders. "First Squad, inside the buildings. Second Squad, pull back to river embankment and be prepared to cover the withdrawal of the 1st Squad."

Without having to be told twice, Maupin was up and yelling to his squad. "Rupp, Salas, into that house with the LT. Everyone else, in here with me. *Move!*"

Poer, likewise, was on his feet, rifle at the ready and crouching low as he ran down the street in the direction of the river. "Okay, people! You heard the lieutenant. Let's look alive and get a move on, *now!*"

For several seconds, Rivera stood behind Kozak, watching her, the squad leader, and the response of their people to the orders. Only when he was satisfied that everyone was responding as they should and Kozak had a handle on the situation, did he grab Kozak's arm. "I'll stay here with 1st Squad, Lieutenant, and cover the move of 2nd. I'll give you two minutes to get set at the river embankment before I pull out of here."

Turning her entire body around to face Rivera, Kozak reached out with her left hand and put it on Rivera's right shoulder. "No. I'll stay here with 1st Squad. You go back with 2nd."

Rivera was about to protest, but Kozak cut him off. "It's my job, Sergeant Rivera. First in, last out and all that other horseshit. You know that. Now get moving."

Looking in her eyes, he gave up. This was no time to argue. Besides, she was right. Had she been a man, he would never have made the suggestion. His offer, he knew, had been a knee-jerk reaction. For a second he had thought of her as a woman first, not as an infantry officer. He would have to watch that in the future. Silently he turned and began to follow 2nd Squad, pausing for a second and yelling back to Kozak, "Don't fuck around and get sucked into a firefight, Lieutenant. Two minutes, no more." With that, he was gone.

Turning her attention back to the direction the gunfire had come from, Kozak wondered where Cody and Gunti were. She was just beginning to become concerned, wondering if she should go up to the corner in order to check on them, when she heard the thumping of boots on the pavement coming toward her. Watching where the street bent around to the right, she could see chips of concrete and plaster fly off the walls from the impact of bullets an instant before she heard the report of the rifles that had fired those bullets. Since there was no return fire from an M-16, and the pounding of boots was growing louder, Kozak assumed that Cody and Gunti were coming back, under fire.

Straightening up, she lowered her rifle to waist level, flicked the mode selector switch with her thumb from safe to three-round-burst mode, and prepared to go forward to cover Cody and Gunti. She had taken no more than two steps when Specialist Cody, followed by Private Gunti, came tearing around the bend in the street, followed by another volley of rifle fire. Flattening herself against the building she was next to and raising the muzzle of her rifle, Kozak watched as Gunti spun around, lowered his rifle, and fired a three-round burst at an assailant Kozak could not see. This stopped the rifle fire only long enough for Gunti to turn about and continue running toward Kozak.

As Cody came up to her, she yelled and pointed to an open door behind her. "In here." Without pausing, Cody was past Kozak and through the open doorway. With Cody back and safe, Kozak turned her entire attention to Gunti, watching his every move with no thoughts of anyone or anything else. Gunti, still at the corner, had paused for a second to face his attackers before continuing on toward Kozak. As if the whole scene were in slow motion, Kozak watched Gunti as he began to turn toward her and safety. Suddenly, when he was midway through the turn, his eyes flew wide open, as if in surprise. At the same time, his body began to move sideways instead of forward. Pivoting on the one foot still on the ground, Gunti slowly turned away from Kozak and faced back toward the direction he had just come from, his arms flying out as he did so as if he were trying to balance himself. He couldn't regain his balance, though. Instead, he began to fall over backward, arms over his head, his rifle flying through the air, and his one foot on the ground coming up and out from under him. To Kozak, Gunti's actions reminded her of a man who had lost his footing on ice. But there was no ice. Gunti had been hit and was going down.

There was no conscious thought as Kozak leaped forward, away from the relative safety of the wall, and began running to where Gunti was still in the process of falling. Not even after she was in the middle of the street, bounding toward Gunti as fast as her legs could carry her, did Kozak begin to think. Her only conscious thought, if indeed it was a thought, was to reach Gunti. What she was going to do when she reached him hadn't occurred to her yet. She was running purely on adrenaline and driven by reactions.

As she neared Gunti, she held her rifle by the front guard in her left hand, and reached down with her right hand for Gunti. Grabbing the shoulder strap of his web gear harness without stopping, Kozak began to turn and head for an open door to her left. Gunti, however, didn't budge. The inertia of his six-foot two-inch, 195-pound frame resisted Kozak's efforts to move it while her own forward momentum tore her grip from Gunti's harness. The sudden turn, combined with the resistance, threw Kozak off balance, leaving her falling backward. Though she didn't know it, this was fortunate for her, because her wild and unpredictable gyrations ruined the aim of the Mexican soldiers who had just unleashed a volley of fire at her. She hit the hard pavement butt-first, and the impact knocked the wind out of her and sent her sprawling. Only by sheer determination and luck did she hang on to her rifle.

For what seemed to be an eternity, Kozak lay on her back, looking up at the sky as she tried to catch her breath. For the first time since leaving the safety of the buildings, she thought about what she had done and of her current predicament. Every thought that popped into her dazed mind told her that she was not in a good spot. She was in the middle of the street, with the body of one of her soldiers a few feet away from her, under fire, and unable to move the other soldier or herself. In her excitement to rush to Gunti's aid, she had failed to give Maupin any orders or even ask someone to cover her. She and Gunti, at that moment, were on their own. And as if that weren't bad enough, she could hear voices speaking in Spanish growing closer. No, she thought, this is not good. Not by a long shot.

Drawing in a deep breath, Kozak rolled over onto her side. Sliding her left arm and head through the sling of her rifle, she maneuvered it over her head and onto her back. Grabbing a handful of Gunti's uniform with both hands, she swung her legs around so that she could dig her heels into the pavement as she pulled. When she had one leg on either side of Gunti, and a firm grasp on him, Kozak half sat up and began to tug at him. Her first efforts, while they managed to move him, were disappointing. After dragging him a foot, she had to stop, scooting herself back a foot, before trying again. Kozak's second try yielded the same result. She managed to move him another foot. As she repositioned herself for her next tug, she looked behind her to see how far they had to go. The ten feet between them and the open door, to Kozak, seemed like ten miles. But she had no choice. Determined to finish what she had started, she turned around and prepared to give the next tug.

A shadow blocking Kozak's view of the sky and buildings across from her was the first hint that he was there. Like an apparition that had popped out of the ground, the largest Mexican that Kozak had ever seen was standing in front of her, looking down at her and Gunti. From Kozak's reclining position, the Mexican, holding an assault rifle at the ready, looked like he was over ten feet tall and weighed half a ton.

For the briefest of moments, they looked at each other. Kozak, wide-eyed and mouth hanging open, sat with one leg on either side of Gunti's body, hanging onto him ready for the next pull. She was shocked to see a Mexican soldier so close. The Mexican soldier, rifle clutched across his chest, his legs straddling Gunti's body, looked down at Kozak, almost as surprised to see an American woman soldier in the middle of a firefight as Kozak was to see him. It was as if both of them, carried forward by the excitement of the battle, had suddenly come across a situation that neither was prepared for. Kozak, with her rifle slung across her back and Gunti's body half on top of her, could do little to defend either herself or Gunti.

The Mexican, fired up with passion and hate, had been ready to rush forward and slit the throats of the invading gringos. The situation he found himself in, however, left him at a loss. He didn't quite know how he was expected to deal with the wounded man and woman at his feet.

These, he thought, were not the ten-foot-tall *norteamericanos* who threatened his home and family. They were, he thought, just people, one an injured man and one a helpless woman trying to rescue him. How could he, he wondered, be expected to kill them in cold blood. Without a second thought, he slung his rifle over his shoulder. Bending down, he took Gunti's hands, pulled Gunti up over his shoulder and onto his back. Without looking back at Kozak, the Mexican soldier began running toward the open door Kozak had been headed for.

Kozak, still trying to get over her close encounter with the Mexican soldier, watched in amazement as he lifted Gunti and carried him away. As soon as she could recover her composure, she was up and headed for the open doorway where the Mexican and Gunti had disappeared. Rather than hassle with her rifle, she unholstered her 9mm pistol, charged the slide to chamber a round, and went into the building after the Mexican, ready to save Gunti from capture.

Running into the dark room after having been in the bright sunlight, Kozak found herself momentarily blinded. She was therefore unable to see Gunti's body, left just inside the doorway, when she came charging in. Tripping over his legs, Kozak went down on her face, bashing her nose and chin on the tile floor. Pushing herself up with her hands, she shook her head, then looked around. Between the stars that floated before her eyes from the collision with the floor, and the adjusting of her eyes to the dark room, she almost missed the Mexican soldier. He paused long enough, however, for her to see him looking down at her. Still at a loss as to what to do, the Mexican, with his rifle in his left hand, raised his right hand, waved at Kozak, whispered *"Vaya con Dios,"* and then disappeared down a dark hall toward the back of the house.

Kozak was still on the floor, looking down the dark hall where the Mexican had disappeared, when someone else came charging through the front door. Like Kozak, the new arrival failed to see Gunti's body just inside the doorway. And, like Kozak, the new arrival tripped and went sprawling, head-first, into the house. Fortunately for the new arrival, Kozak's body cushioned his fall, which shoved her face back down onto the tile floor. Cursing, Kozak tried to push herself up, but found that it was impossible while the new arrival was still on her.

"Jesus, Lieutenant! I'm sorry. I didn't see you." Turning her head, she saw that the new arrival was Sergeant Maupin.

"Apology accepted. *Now get the hell off of me!*"

In a flash, Maupin was on his feet and helping Kozak, all the while looking about the room. "Where's the Mexican? Did you get the Mexican that carried Gunti in here?"

With her right hand, which still held her pistol, she pointed to the hall while she carefully felt her nose with her left hand. "He went that way."

Maupin, running over to where she had pointed, looked down the hall. When he didn't see anyone, he looked at Kozak, then at Gunti. "You mean he just brought him in here, then left? Did you get a shot at him?"

It was broken. Kozak realized her nose was broken. Letting it go, she tilted her head back and crossed her eyes in an effort to see how badly her nose was broken. She couldn't. But she could feel the pain, pain that spread across her face like a blanket. And, even worse, she could feel the blood running down her nostrils and around her upper lip. With her nose broken and clogged with blood, she sounded like a person who had a severely stuffed-up nose. "No, I didn't shoot him. What the hell is going on outside?"

"Nothing, right now. I left 1st Squad in place to cover us."

Moving to the side of the doorway, Kozak carefully peeked around the corner and looked down the street in the direction that the Mexicans would be coming in. "Any sign of the bad guys?"

Maupin, coming up to the other side of the doorway, also peeked out, then faced Kozak. "No. Only one we saw was the one who grabbed Gunti. But there's got to be more out there. No doubt, they're closing in."

Kozak was still looking down the street while she held her nose with her left hand. "Yeah, no doubt. We need to get outta here." Seeing nothing moving, she turned to Maupin. "Can you move Gunti back to where your squad is or do you need help?"

Looking at Gunti's body, Maupin thought about it for a moment, then nodded. "I can do it. No problem." Looking back at Gunti where they had left him sprawled in the middle of the floor, Maupin asked Kozak how bad Gunti was hit.

Like a shot in the head, it struck Kozak that in all her excitement she hadn't even looked to see where Gunti had been shot and how bad it was. She didn't even know if he was alive. Glancing back over her shoulder, she stared at Gunti's body. For the first time she noticed the pool of blood on the floor under Gunti. Oh my God, she thought, he's probably bleeding to death and I never looked or did anything for him. "I don't know. See what you can do for him before you move out. But hurry."

Without a word, Maupin moved over to where Gunti was, leaving Kozak to silently curse herself as she watched for any sign of the Mexicans.

After several seconds, Maupin grunted. "Geez, LT, this guy's a mess. I can't do shit for him here. We gotta get him back to the aidman, fast."

Kozak, still at the door, looked back over at Maupin, down at the floor at Gunti, then back to Maupin. While she put her pistol back into its holster and took the rifle off her back, she considered her next move. "All right, Sergeant Maupin. When you're ready, take Gunti out of here. I'll cover you from here and follow once you're clear. If we don't draw fire by the time you reach where the rest of your squad is, keep going. I'll gather them and bring 'em along. Got any questions?"

"No, no questions, LT. Just give me a minute." Maupin slung his rifle over his back and bent down. Grabbing Gunti's hand, he pulled Gunti up and over one shoulder into a fireman's carry. After bouncing up and down a couple of times in an effort to shift Gunti's body into a comfortable and balanced position, Maupin informed Kozak that he was ready.

Hoisting her rifle into the ready-to-fire position and bracing it against the doorway to steady it, she told Maupin to go. As the sergeant ducked and ran under the muzzle of her rifle, Kozak wondered if she should fire some random shots, in the hope of making the Mexicans seek cover, or if she should just hold her fire and return aimed fire after the Mexicans opened fire and revealed their positions. Maupin, with Gunti on his back, however, was gone before she had made a decision.

Counting slowly to ten, Kozak held her position, slowly scanning the street to her front for any sign of a reaction to Maupin's appearance. When she saw and heard nothing after reaching ten, she went out the door and headed down the street where 1st Squad waited.

Alerted by Maupin as he went by, the rest of 1st Squad was ready to move when Kozak came running by. "First Squad, out and back to the river, now!"

As the members of 1st Squad came out of the buildings they had been in, Kozak, standing in the middle of the street, turned and looked back, holding her rifle at the ready and searching for pursuers. Their roles, she thought, were reversed. Her platoon had come into Mexico pursuing the Mexicans, and now they were being chased out of Mexico. Looking over her shoulder, she yelled to her people to get a move on. Only after the beating of boots on the pavement began to fade did she turn around and follow them at a run, breathing through her mouth and trying hard to keep the blood and snot running down from her broken nose from going into her mouth.

With far more fanfare than it had begun with, the latest incursion by the United States Army came to an end as Second Lieutenant Nancy Kozak, her nose bent to one side and bleeding, came sliding down the embankment, into the Rio Grande, across the river, and into the ubiquitous eye of Ted's camera.

On television sets across the nation, people barely heard Jan Fields's running commentary. Instead, the image of the lone infantry lieutenant, with blood dripping down her chin, wading back across the river after a brief pursuit of Mexican raiders, stirred viewers' emotions as no words could. Blood had been drawn. American blood. They had watched the body of one of her soldiers carried across the river. They had seen the medics working frantically to save the soldier. Then, when hope was gone, the television viewers had watched as the medics, in disgust, turned away when they realized they had failed. And finally, the young female officer who had led her men in an effort to punish the enemy came back, wounded but undefeated. Such images stirred the passions of a nation and washed away any vestiges of logic or reason that might have remained. While the National Guard incident could have been a mistake, few could find any defense or justification for this latest spilling of American blood. In the minds of millions of Americans, the war with Mexico was a reality.

17

The first casualty when war comes is truth.

—Senator Hiram Johnson

CITY HALL, LAREDO, TEXAS
1905 HOURS, 7 SEPTEMBER

Working her way through or around barriers was as much a part of Jan Fields's job as shooting a story. A fighter by nature, who enjoyed the fight just as much as the fruits, Jan never took no as an absolute answer. Rather, it was a signal that the approach she was using wasn't working, and that a different appeal to "be reasonable" or for cooperation was required. Military police were no different. If anything, they were easier to deal with. Well trained to perform specific combat-related tasks, the young soldiers who made up the military police corps often lacked the depth of experience veteran civilian police had when it came to dealing with civilian media. So Jan was able to use her entire repertoire of tricks and pleas to get what she wanted. The only time she ran into serious problems was when the senior MP on site was female.

This evening, this was not the case. The young staff sergeant whose squad was augmenting the sheriff's deputies and the Laredo City police at city hall was an easy mark. The conversation started with Jan insisting that she had an appointment with Lieutenant Colonel Dixon, the G3 of the 16th Armored Division. When the MP sergeant responded that he didn't know who Dixon was and doubted he was there, Jan happily pointed to Dixon's Humvee parked ten feet away from them. Embarrassed at being caught off guard and beginning to wonder if the female reporter badgering him did, in fact, have an appointment, the sergeant sent one of his people into the courthouse to check. Jan, with the confident smile of a cat who was about to pounce on the cornered mouse, waited with the MP sergeant.

Her smile disappeared, however, when the MP sent to summon Dixon returned. Reporting to his sergeant, he stated that Colonel Dixon not only had negative knowledge of an appointment with a female reporter, but couldn't even seem to place the name Jan Fields. Jan blew a gasket. Scott was playing with her and she was in no mood to be messed with. With her eyes reduced to angry, narrow slits, and her forehead furrowed with rage, Jan turned to the MP who was patiently waiting and pointed her index finger at him. "Look, soldier, you march right back where you came from and tell that pompous ass that if he doesn't haul his butt out here in two minutes, it will be a cold day in hell before he beds this broad again. Got that?"

The MP, taken aback by Jan's response, looked at her with wide eyes for a few seconds, then turned to his sergeant for guidance. The sergeant, not sure what to make of the angry woman with the violent temper, was unsure what to do. If he sent his MP back to the G3 with the message Jan had just relayed, and the G3 really didn't know who this reporter was, he might find himself relieved or something even worse. On the other hand, if he didn't send the MP back with the new message, he would have to deal with the crazy woman standing less than two feet in front of him. Between the look on her face and her proximity to him, Jan appeared to be the greater of the two threats at that particular moment. Deciding that the old saying that discretion was the better part of valor applied, the sergeant turned to his MP and told him to inform the G3 that the young female correspondent was quite insistent and was threatening him with grave domestic consequences if he did not respond to her request. The MP, trying hard to suppress a grin, shook his head, turned, and disappeared into the courthouse.

By the time Dixon came out onto the steps where Jan had been waiting, she had, for the most part, calmed down. Dixon's appearance, in desert camouflage uniform, along with his web gear arranged for field duty, holster and pistol, protective mask, and helmet, took her aback for a moment. They were serious, she thought. The appearance of Dixon in downtown Laredo, ready for battle, finally convinced her that the government of the United States was really serious about fighting. Without having to be told, and not needing to do any complicated analysis in which she weighed all available evidence, Jan knew that there would be war. In her heart, she knew it.

Still, she had a little fire left from the joke Dixon had played at her expense. When he reached her, Dixon fanned that fire into a raging flame by greeting her with hands held out and a broad smile as if he had done nothing. "Jan, what a lovely surprise."

With her hands on her hips, her upper torso angled forward, and her feet spread shoulder width apart, Jan greeted Scott with a growl. "Scott Dixon, you can be a real jerk sometimes. And don't give me that 'What did I do now?' look either."

Stopping a few feet from her, he paused for a few seconds to admire Jan, who remained standing on the steps below him in her defiant pose. Her long, dark brown hair was pulled back, probably done up in a French braid. Her oval face, though masked with an angry expression, was tanned from hours of tromping about shooting stories in south Texas. If she was wearing makeup, it was applied with such skill that it blended nicely. The white cotton blouse she wore, no longer crisp and neat after a day in the late summer heat of Texas, had the top three buttons undone. The khaki walking shorts she wore ended just above her knees. Although Dixon found the knees one of the more unimpressive parts of the female body, he admired the calves and thighs that they connected. He was therefore willing to overlook the imperfections that naked kneecaps abounded in. All in all, though few people would call Jan Fields a natural beauty, the image before him, and the person that it represented, had come to mean more to Dixon than anything else. Raising his hands in mock surrender, Dixon called out, "Okay, cease fire, I give up," as he shuffled down the last few steps that separated him from Jan.

Still angry at the fun Dixon had had at her expense and wanting to play out her show of rage and indignation a bit longer, Jan folded her arms across her chest as Dixon approached, and turned away from him. Dixon, stopping on the step above the one Jan was on, looked down over her shoulder, staring at the exposed cleavage that Jan's folded arms raised and accentuated. For a moment he stood there, both to admire the view and to evaluate her mood, though he already knew that she wasn't really mad at him. If she were, she would have turned on him like a cat on a strange dog. No, Dixon decided, it was her turn to have some fun with him. He had embarrassed her in front of the MPs, who were still watching at a respectful distance, though they both tried to pretend that they weren't. Without a word, he knew that before they could continue, she would have to have her pound of flesh, or at least an apology appropriate to the offense.

Walking around her and down two steps so that he now faced her on a slightly lower level, Dixon took off his helmet, tucked it under his left arm, extended his arms, palms up, and looked up at her. "Dear Jan, I do humbly apologize for making you look like a fool. It's just that doing so is so easy. And besides, I can't help myself."

Jan looked at him, thinking about what he had just said. He was still mocking her, but she really didn't want to continue to press the point. He was obviously in a playful mood that she didn't feel up to matching. His hair, receding at the temples and graying on the sides, was cut ludicrously short. The sides, clipped in what Dixon referred to as whitewalls, looked more like beard stubble than hair. Jan ran her fingers through the scant hair left on top. She enjoyed running her hands through Dixon's hair, when he had enough, and was always saddened when he had it chopped away. Taking a deep breath and letting it out, she looked into his eyes. "See you got yourself a haircut."

Dixon, using the palm of his right hand, wiped away the sweat that had beaded up on the right side of his scalp above his ear. "Well, until someone figures out a way to improve the ventilation in the Kevlar helmets, short hair is the way to go."

When he dropped his hand to his side, Jan raised her two hands to his head, running them along his temples and stopping when they came to rest on his cheeks. With a gentle squeeze, Jan held his face in her hands, tilting it up toward hers. "We have nearly an hour until the president comes on TV and enlightens us with his latest pearls of wisdom. All will be forgiven, provided you buy me something cold and wet. I'm dying of thirst."

Dixon smiled. "Your wish, my dear, is my command. I happen to know this great little convenience mart a few blocks from here that sells the greatest thirty-two-ounce drinks this side of the Rio Bravo."

As they walked to the convenience mart, Dixon, for the most part, was silent as Jan talked about the shooting she had done during the past few days as well as what she was planning to do next. Much of her activity had included a healthy dose of the history of Texas, which she was using as background for her stories, and which she now related to Dixon. In one piece, shot outside Meir, Texas, Jan recounted how a small group of Texans, bent on invading Mexico in 1842, had been captured by the Mexican Army. She used this as a lead-in to a story that recounted the problems the Republic of Texas and the Republic of the Rio Grande had had with Mexico after the War for Texas Independence. These incidents, Jan explained, coupled with vigorous lobbying from Texans and expansionists in the United States, had led to what she now referred to as the first Mexican War. That war, Jan told Dixon, had resulted in strained relations between Mexico and United States that had never healed and often resulted in misunderstandings and, at times, incidents like the one that had just occurred in Laredo. In another piece Jan had done, she told of some of these minor border incidents between the American Army and Mexican forces at the beginning of the first Mexican War. Not far from McAllen, Texas, Jan and her crew visited the site where a patrol of sixty-three U.S. dragoons, led by Captain Seth Thornton, was intercepted and ambushed by Mexican General Anastasio Torrejón on April 23, 1845. When they shot that piece, Jan had intended to use it for another story. Instead, she explained how she'd use it as a lead-in during her report on the incursion into Mexico by U.S. forces that morning.

After buying their drinks, and as they returned to city hall, Jan told Dixon all was not going well, though. She and her crew had planned to cross over into Mexico to visit several historic sites over the next few days as well as to interview local Mexican officials. That, she pointed out, was highly unlikely after the incident of that morning.

While she spoke, Dixon marveled at Jan's ability to travel about with her little crew and do what she did. Conventional wisdom viewed Dixon's duties, those of an American soldier, as dangerous and difficult. Dixon, however, didn't feel that way. While being a soldier entailed danger and the requirement to place life and limb in harm's way, on command, what Jan did was often times as dangerous, and infinitely more difficult. Dixon, especially as a general staff officer, operated within a very large and complex organization known as the United States Army. The Army delineated his exact duties and responsibilities, provided training until he mastered those duties, and for the most part then told him what to do, when to do it, and where to do it. To perform his assigned duties, Dixon had a large number of soldiers to assist him. Like Dixon, these soldiers had well-defined duties and the training required to perform those duties, as well as the necessary equipment. In addition, the Army provided for the physical well-being of Dixon and his soldiers by creating and following them with a support system that provided them with their meals, clothing and personal equipment, supplies used to perform their duties, health and comfort items, and medical support. There were even special units, called Greggs, short for "grave registrations," that would tag, bag, and bury Dixon or any of his men should they die in the line of duty. In the United States Army, and all of its sister services, it was an article of faith that the soldiers who had volunteered to go forth and do battle for their country would receive all the support and help that the nation and its government could provide those soldiers.

In Jan's field, by contrast, she was on her own. Everything, from learning the techniques of her craft, to learning how to hustle a news story, was up to her. The only thing she and her crew got from WNN, whom she was now working for, was the equipment needed to shoot and transmit their stories. Everything else, from clothing to lodging, was up to them to obtain. While they did receive a nice per diem rate that was meant to cover all their personal needs, it was far different from having someone hand them to you, like the Army did for Dixon.

Even more significant was the fact that, legally and practically, the rights and protection afforded to Jan and her crew were no different than those of any ordinary citizen. When Jan and her crew were out chasing a story, whether it was in Austin, Texas, or in the mountains of Mexico, they were on their own. They had to protect themselves, and if one of them became injured, they had to fend for themselves. By comparison, even though Dixon was the soldier, he was relatively safe, protected by distance from the forward edge of the battle area, and by units such as the MP platoon assigned to guard the division command post and commanding general. Drawn to where the action was by the need to get her story, Jan had no one and nothing to protect her. Dixon thought on that for a moment, reflecting how strange it was that he, pledged to defend and uphold the Constitution, could, in reality, do nothing to protect his lover from the danger she so readily put herself in. Not that there was anything he would do to change such things. Both he and Jan were adults, two people who had their own aspirations and callings, and at the same time, they loved each other so much that neither wished to change the other.

When they got back to the steps of city hall, Jan and Dixon sat as far away from the main entrance as they could. For a moment, there was a pause as each tried to find something to talk about. Dixon, with full knowledge of the current situation on both sides of the Rio Grande, as well as what the president was going to announce in less than thirty minutes, had to be careful what he said, or even implied. Jan, a reporter by profession and nature, had to suppress her natural desire to probe for the information she knew Dixon had. It was not the nature of the trite conversation that mattered, however; it was the proximity of the person that each loved, the sound of their voices, and the tone of the conversation they fell onto. The time they spent that evening on the steps of the Laredo city hall was, for both, a period of rest and renewal as they drew upon each other's strength in preparation for the ordeal each knew was coming.

Dixon heard the tromp of combat boots approaching on the steps behind him before Jan did. The steps were hurried, which meant the owner of the boots wasn't coming over for a social call. For a moment, he tried to ignore the approaching boots, hoping they were headed somewhere else—but he wasn't that lucky. When the sound of the boots was only a few feet away, the voice of the general's aide called him. "Colonel Dixon, the CG needs to see you ASAP."

Twisting his head around, Dixon watched as the division commander's aide came down and around until he was facing Dixon and Jan. "Sorry to disturb you, sir, Ms. Fields. But we just got this in." With that, he thrust out a sheet of yellow paper, folded in half, that Dixon recognized as a spot report form.

Dixon unfolded the spot report and read it. Jan, anxious to see what was on it, nevertheless restrained herself, concentrating on taking a long, slow sip from the soda she held. Folding the paper in half again and handing it back to the aide, Dixon told him he would be along in a minute. The aide saluted, then went scurrying back up the steps. When he was gone, Dixon reached out with his left hand and put it on Jan's legs. "Well, my dear, duty calls."

Leaning over so that her right arm was against his left, Jan looked at Dixon, who was staring off into the distance. "Hot date with Big Al?"

Patting her leg, he turned and looked Jan in the eye. "Well, I guess you'll find out soon enough. Seems our friends south of the border aren't going to buy the president's plan."

Jan was intrigued. "What plan?"

Looking away from her, back to the distant object that he had been staring at, Dixon slowly, carefully, explained to Jan. "The president of the United States is going to announce to the American public in twenty minutes his proposal to solve our little border problem, a solution that the American ambassador presented to the Council of 13 in Mexico City a little over four hours ago." Dixon paused, took a drink, and then continued. "In a nutshell, the president is going to announce that the armed forces of the United States are going to establish a security zone south of the Rio Grande, to be patrolled by us, with or without the cooperation of the Mexican government."

Jan sat there for several seconds, absorbing what she had just been told. "How do you know that the Council of 13 is going to reject it? Have they made an announcement?"

Dixon, his face showing no signs of concern, played with his drinking straw as he answered. "No, not that I know of. But there are subtle ways soldiers have of broadcasting their intentions. Take that spot report, for example. It was from the division cav squadron watching International Bridge Number One five blocks from here. Right now, as we speak, the Mexicans are preparing their side of the bridge for demolitions." He turned and looked at Jan. "Call me paranoid, but it seems to me that our friends south of the border are trying to tell us something, and it ain't 'Welcome.' "

MERCY HOSPITAL, LAREDO, TEXAS
2025 HOURS, 7 SEPTEMBER

With nothing to do while he waited for the doctor to finish working on Lieutenant Kozak, Harold Cerro reread her report concerning her platoon's foray into Mexico that morning. It didn't get any better with the third reading. Grammatically and structurally, it was quite good, unusual for a junior Army officer. Its tone and content, however, were self-demeaning and apologetic in the extreme. Were the investigation into the cause of the border incident to be based solely upon Kozak's statement, an uninformed person would walk away with the impression that Kozak had planned and been responsible for everything that had occurred from the loss of the Alamo in 1836 to the overthrowing of the old Mexican government in June. It was no wonder that Colonel Dixon had sent him to talk to her, both to assess her mental state and to get her to reconsider her first report and rewrite it.

Though Cerro didn't relish his role as a "special projects" officer—which, translated to English, came out as "shitty little jobs" officer—it was better than sitting in the current operations van at the main command post, answering telephones and watching majors thrash about and ping off the walls. It seemed even the most mundane things sent everyone at the CP into orbit on days like this one, especially when no one knew for sure what was going to happen. Staff officers from subordinate brigades, especially the operations officers, were on the phone every hour, asking for current updates on pending orders or changes to the rules of engagement. Staff officers from the corps command post called more frequently, asking for additional information on the border-crossing incident. It seemed, at times, that the people at corps wanted to know everything about the platoon, down to the names of each individual who had crossed, their ranks, race, the amount of time they had spent in the unit, etc., etc., etc. About the only thing that the corps staff hadn't asked for by the time Cerro left was what color eyes Kozak's people had, though there were bets that someone would get to that question sooner or later. Such questions, in and of themselves, were bad enough. What made it worse was that the staff at corps never appeared to share any information with each other. In one incident, two corps staff officers, who Cerro knew sat next to each other, called within a single ten-minute period to ask the same question. Therefore, when Colonel Dixon had come up to him and handed him the file containing the reports of the incident, notes of the commanding general's initial impression, and instructions to find Kozak, talk to her, and see if she wanted to change her statement, Cerro jumped at the chance.

"Captain Cerro, you can come with me now. The doctor is just about finished with your friend."

Looking up from the report on his lap, Cerro saw the emergency room nurse he had talked to earlier. Far from being an angel of mercy, the nurse that stood before Cerro looked more like a sitcom character. The short, round Hispanic woman, in her late thirties, had a figure that had all the definition of a bowling ball. She wore her hair pulled back from her round face in a bun. The whites she wore, which no doubt had been fresh and clean hours ago, were soaked with sweat and stained with drops and smears of blood. Were it not for those bloodstains, as well as the haggard look and eyes that showed signs of emotional exhaustion, the nurse would have been an object of humor. But she wasn't. While the chaos and pace of her activities differed from Cerro's as night does from day, her look told Cerro that she, like him, had been dealing with the real world too long that day.

In silence, she led him to an examining room, where she entered after looking in at the small square window in the door. Opening the door for Cerro, she let him enter and left without a word, headed for her next task. Lieutenant Kozak, lying on the examination table, had her legs dangling off the edge, her hands behind her head, elbows out, and eyes closed. Before he said anything, Cerro studied her. Her boots, as well as the pants of her uniform, were covered with dried mud, which, Cerro thought, was from the crossing of the Rio Grande. From the waist up, she wore only a brown, regulation T-shirt stained with wavy white lines of salt from her perspiration, which made the shirt appear to be tie-dyed. With her hands held behind her, her breasts, straining against the brown T-shirt, stood like two firm mounds, perfect and round. Since her eyes were closed and the nurse had left, Cerro stood for a moment and gauged, from a distance, their approximate size. He had always pegged her as having a B cup. Now, without the bulky class-A greens or the baggy camouflaged battle dress uniform to obscure them, he could clearly see that young Lieutenant Kozak was a healthy C cup.

Cerro was assessing Kozak's dominant features when the door behind him burst open and a doctor came into the examination room, talking without looking up from a chart he carried. "Well, you're in great shape there, Lieutenant. No concussion, no signs of fractures, nothing broken, except your nose."

The doctor's sudden appearance caused Kozak to take her hands out from behind her head and, grasping the sides of the examination table, push herself up into a sitting position. As she did, she noticed Cerro standing next to the door, blushing slightly, as if he had just been caught doing something wrong. It never occurred to her that he had been standing there eyeing her while she rested.

*   *   *

Looking first at the doctor, Cerro didn't notice that Kozak had sat up. When he had recovered from the sudden appearance of the doctor, as well as his personal embarrassment, he looked back at the lieutenant. It was only then that he realized he had been so busy staring at her breasts that he had not seen her face. What he saw bore no resemblance to the clean, soft face that he had come to associate with the young lieutenant. Her gentle features were obscured by a swollen nose covered with a piece of wide medical tape. Only the tip, swollen, scraped, and red from soreness, showed below the tape. Protruding from her nostrils were the ends of white cotton packing. As bad as her nose looked, however, the blue-black circles that began at her nose and surrounded her eyes made Kozak look like a boxer who had been knocked out. Without thinking, Cerro shook his head and mumbled, "Jesus, you look like hell."

Unable to turn away from the doctor, who had tilted her head back and was looking at her nose, Kozak was about to give Cerro a cynical "Thanks" for the less-than-cheerful comment, but thought better of it. She had no idea why he was here. Even though she was convinced that, at that moment, she didn't have a friend in the world, she didn't want to take any chances and alienate a possible friend. So she held her tongue, letting the doctor complete his examination and allowing Cerro's comment to pass unanswered. She would let Cerro initiate the conversation and set the tone when he was ready.

Assuming that Cerro was there to pick Kozak up, the doctor, finished with his examination, turned away from her and said to Cerro as he prepared to leave, "Well, Captain, she's all yours. You should keep the packing in the nose for twenty-four hours." Pausing at the door, the doctor looked back at Kozak. "Next time something like this happens, don't wait ten hours before coming in. It would have been a lot less painful had we been able to work on your nose immediately after your accident." Without another word, the doctor left. Kozak stared at Cerro, waiting for him to say something.

Feeling awkward, and not knowing how to start, Cerro stalled, moving over to a chair. Taking his Kevlar helmet from under his right arm, he dropped it on the floor from waist level, making a loud clunk that reverberated in the small examining room. Sitting down on the edge of the seat, facing Kozak, Cerro tucked his feet up under the chair but allowed his knees to spread apart. He held the folder containing the reports on the foray into Mexico against his stomach with both hands, and looked at Kozak for a moment, considering how he was going to do this.

From the examining table, Kozak watched Cerro as a bird watches a cat circling the tree it's in. He kept staring at her face, which no doubt looked like hell. At least, she thought it did. If it looked half as bad as it felt, it was terrible. During the initial exam, one of the nurses had looked at Kozak's face with a pained expression. With a sigh, the nurse had grasped her hand, telling her not to worry, that the black and blue would go away as soon as the swelling went down. Instead of serving to calm Kozak, it had only worried her, creating an uncontrollable urge to find a mirror and see what it was that caused everyone to stare. With Cerro sitting there, holding folders that no doubt contained statements and reports concerning the crossing of the Rio Grande, it would be a few more minutes before she got to look at her own face.

Seeing that Lieutenant Kozak wasn't going to make his task any easier by initiating the conversation, Cerro decided that he might as well just launch into it. After all, diplomacy, subtlety, and regard for someone's feelings never seemed to blend well with the spirit of the bayonet. Praised by raters throughout his career for his direct, frank, and uncompromising approach to all matters, Cerro now found himself wishing he had a few more skills in dealing with people. Sidetracked for a moment by that thought, he wondered if he was concerned about his approach because Kozak was a woman. No, he was sure that wasn't it. On the day he had observed Kozak's squad get overrun, he hadn't even considered the gender issue when he "counseled" her. No, that wasn't the reason he was uncomfortable. Was it because she was hurt? That could be. After all, he felt the same way whenever he had seen any of his own men wounded or injured. But that wasn't it completely, for in the past Cerro had always been able to say something to the wounded. Even when faced with a man from his own unit who had lost a limb, Cerro had been able to work through his natural revulsion of injured people and say something appropriate. Yet here he was stymied by a lieutenant with a simple broken nose and two black eyes.

That was it. Suddenly, like a bolt of lightning, the reason for the unaccustomed empathy that was hamstringing his efforts to carry on, struck Cerro. Instead of looking at Second Lieutenant N. Kozak, infantry platoon leader, Cerro had been looking at himself. Without realizing it, he had projected himself into Kozak's position as he read the reports and weighed her actions. The feelings that he was experiencing were not those of a male seeking to protect the female of the species. Nor were they of one human experiencing sympathy for an injured fellow being. Instead, Cerro found himself having trouble dealing with Kozak because he had true insight into the emotional upheaval that she was going through, the same upheaval he, as a second lieutenant, had experienced after his introduction to combat. For the briefest of moments, he was able to see Kozak in a light that transcended all differences. He saw her not as a person of a different rank, or sex, or age, or anything. She was, at that moment, the newest recruit to what W. E. B. Griffin referred to as the brotherhood of war.

With his own emotions in check and a clear idea of how to approach Kozak, Cerro started. "The G3 has sent me to talk to you, one on one, after reviewing all the statements and reports concerning this morning's crossing of the border by your platoon."

Once Cerro finally began to speak, Kozak breathed a sigh of relief. He had, while he had sat there staring at her, made her feel uncomfortable and very vulnerable. It had been as if she were a specimen under a microscope, open to examination and unable to do anything. Now that he had started talking, at least she could respond to his initiatives and comments. Grasping the edge of the examining table, Kozak nodded, responded with a "Yes, sir" that was barely audible even to herself, and waited for Cerro to play out his initial hand.

Deciding to cut to the heart of the matter, Cerro moved his feet out from under the chair and planted them firmly on the floor, leaning forward, resting his elbows on his knees. When he was settled in his new position, he looked into Kozak's swollen black eyes. "The G3 believes that you need to rewrite your statement. It is his opinion that you are being far too critical of your actions. Were this report to go forward as is, there is the chance that you might open yourself to undeserved criticism and possible disciplinary action that would be unwarranted."

After a short pause, during which she looked down at the floor, then back into his eyes, Kozak asked Cerro what he thought. Although he knew that she was asking specifically about the proposition that he had presented to her—the rewriting of her report—Cerro understood that what she was really asking for was his opinion of her actions as a platoon leader, as an infantryman, and as a soldier. Deciding that this was no time for great philosophical discussions or subtle mental jousting,

Cerro decided to talk to Kozak in a manner that he wished someone had used with him after his first battle. He dropped the folder with the reports to the floor and linked his hands. "Lieutenant Kozak, you done good."

Though Kozak had been hoping to get around to Cerro's assessment of her performance, he had surprised her by doing so right off, and it showed. As before, she sat on the table, in silence, and let Cerro go on.

"What you're going through, right now, is no different than what just about every second lieutenant goes through the first time they survive a firefight. Oh, I suppose there is the odd character who charges into his first battle and walks away from it without a second thought. But those creatures are rare and, if they exist, dangerous. You see, West Point and the Army have filled your head with a lot of ideas and theories about war and leadership that you, under peacetime conditions, cannot possibly understand and sort out. While it's true that we can teach you the technical skills needed to employ the weapons and people under your command, and provide you with an idea of what it's going to be like through realistic training, there is no way in hell that West Point, sitting in splendid isolation high above the Hudson, or the Army, or anyone, can adequately prepare you for the experience of being shot at and watching people, your people, die. There's just no way."

Since Kozak had expected, at best, an inquisition, Cerro's comments were a welcome relief, at first. Slowly, however, she began to wonder if they were simply fluff, a standard "You're okay, kid, now drive on" speech given to every lieutenant after their first action. Abandoning her position of leaving the initiative to Cerro, Kozak asked him how he'd felt after his first firefight.

Sliding back into his seat, Cerro crossed his legs, allowing his hands, linked together, to come to rest on his stomach. He looked down and a slight smile lit across his face as he let out a small chuckle. "You know, Colonel Dixon, the G3, and I were talking about that just before I came over here. My first action." Cerro looked up at Kozak, and his smile widened. "I was lucky it happened in the middle of a war and not, like yours, alone and on national television, 'cause it was a fucking disaster." Cerro paused. "Even today, years later, I still can't think about it without wondering how I survived without killing myself and every man in my platoon." Suddenly, as if someone had hit a switch, Cerro's smile disappeared. When his eyes locked onto Kozak's, she could almost see a cold emptiness in them. When he spoke, he did so with an even tone that lacked all feeling, all emotions. "It was a night jump to seize an airfield. We went out at five hundred feet. Though I was in the air less than two minutes, with all the tracers flying this way and that, it seemed to take forever. I hit the concrete runway like a ton of bricks, knocking myself silly. I wasn't even able to unhook myself from my harness for several minutes. Imagine, lying there in the middle of a firefight. Explosions going on all around you, people screaming, officers and NOCs shouting orders, your platoon out there, somewhere in the middle of the darkness and chaos, running about and fighting. And there I was, lying flat on my back after screwing up the simplest of all airborne skills, the parachute landing fall, unable to do squat.''

Cerro paused, looking up at the ceiling as he took in several deep breaths. ''In those few seconds, I was convinced that I was the dumbest, most incompetent, most worthless piece of shit God had ever placed on the face of the earth.'' Slowly, his head moved from side to side. ''God, I can't imagine anything before or since that compared to what I felt that moment.'' When he looked down at Kozak again, she could see his eyes were moist, almost as if he were on the brink of tearing. Not that it mattered, for she realized that he was no longer with her. Though he was looking right at her, she knew he didn't see her. Instead, images she could only vaguely picture were dancing before his eyes, images that were burned onto his brain by the fear and horror that his words could never do justice to.

Slowly, methodically, Cerro continued. As he did so, he picked his words with great care, more out of the desire to do justice to the memory of that moment than for impact. ''We lost the CO that night. He had a malfunction and creamed into the runway. Didn't find his body till next morning. I lost my first man too. Young black kid from Jersey. He joined the Army to get away from the slums and gangs. Specialist Ellis J. Johnston wasn't the smartest person in the world. Nor was he the best soldier. In fact, he was, at times, a downright pain in the ass. But he was mine. And I lost him. He was blown away by a twenty-three-millimeter antiaircraft gun while I was lying out on the runway thrashing about and trying to recover from my own stupidity.''

Leaning forward, with his elbows resting on his knees and the index finger of his right hand pointed at Kozak, Cerro drove his next point home as if he were drilling her with a machine gun. ''Now I know, today, in retrospect, that there was nothing I could have done to prevent Johnston's getting killed. He landed three hundred meters from where I did and was drilled by the antiaircraft gun before he got his harness off. Had I been there with him, I would have been killed too. It was just one of those things. But such logic, that kind of clear, uncompromising logic, didn't mean shit to me the next day, when it was all over, as I watched his squad leader dropping the pieces of Specialist Ellis J. Johnston into the body bag. It took me over three years to finally see that what happened to him wasn't my fault.''

Suddenly, Cerro scooped up the folder from the floor and stood up. ''Johnston was a soldier. He knew what that meant. And what happened to him was no different than what happened to lots of other guys in that war and every war before and since. I knew that, too. VMI, Fort Benning, and every officer and NCO that had trained me had taught me that. I knew men died. I knew that I could die. I knew that. But at that moment, when I looked down on the shattered remains of a man who had placed his faith in my abilities to lead him and pull him through, I damned near folded up. All the lectures on leadership, all the great examples of famous 'heroes' who had faced combat and come through, all the training in the world didn't mean shit to me or Specialist Ellis J. Johnston. He was dead and I wasn't.''

There was a sudden, embarrassing pause as Cerro suddenly realized that he was no longer looking at Johnston, that he was standing there, lecturing to Kozak. Her face, turned up toward his, was masked with an impassive stare that belied the pathos she was trying hard to suppress. He hadn't come to lecture her. He hadn't come to tell stories. Cerro's only task had been to get her to consider rewriting her report. Now, he wondered if he had succeeded or failed. That, however, was no longer the issue. He had tripped out, crashed, and burned on memories he had thought he had buried. Unable to continue, and not really caring, Cerro plopped the folder containing Kozak's statement on the chair he had been sitting on. For a moment, he looked at it, then turned to her. ''You did extremely well, Lieutenant Kozak, given the situation you were in. You have nothing to be ashamed of and nothing to regret. I would advise you to do as the G3 recommends and rewrite your statement, taking all the whining, sniveling, self-flagellating bullshit out and sticking with the facts.''

Cerro moved to the door, opened it, and started to leave, then stopped. He spun about and faced Kozak. ''If you're half the infantry officer I think you are, you'll rewrite it.'' Without further comment, Cerro walked out, leaving Kozak sitting on the examining table, tears streaking down her cheeks and soaking the cotton packing that protruded from her nostrils.

INTERNATIONAL BRIDGE NUMBER 1, LAREDO, TEXAS
2210 HOURS, 7 SEPTEMBER

From the south bank of the river, Guajardo watched his combat engineers, hanging precariously above him from ropes, preparing the bridge for demolition. From dangling pouches they wore, or from pallets held up by ropes of their own, the engineers took blocks of military explosives, securing them to cross members and stringers that supported the roadway above. When enough explosives had been packed up against the cross member or stringer, an engineer carefully took blasting caps from a separate pouch and placed them into the mass of explosives. When the blasting caps were set, a companion followed, wiring them together. This was no easy task. From the main firing line, branch firing lines to the individual blasting caps set in the explosives needed to be cut the same length so that the explosives on a span of the bridge went off simultaneously. Since several spans were being dropped, the wiring had to be arranged so that the bridge span farthest from the blasting machine, used to initiate the demolition sequence, went off first, followed by explosives on the next span closer in. If the closest span were dropped first, the explosion and the falling debris could sever the wires leading out to the farther span and stop the sequence of destruction.

In addition to the exactness required for the placement of explosives, size of the charges at each location, and wiring sequence, backup systems and booby traps to hinder sabotage were necessary. Less than an hour after the engineers had started working, a group of American Army officers had gathered on the north bank, watching every move. One of them, a lieutenant colonel, Guajardo saw, wore a green beret. To Guajardo, the appearance of the American lieutenant colonel in his green beret was an arrogant challenge. Though Guajardo knew that the Americans would use special operations people to try to prevent the destruction of the bridge, he at least expected those people to be a little more discreet. This lieutenant colonel, however, made no secret of his presence. By standing there with his green beret on, it was if he were shouting to Guajardo, "Here I am. I'm going to stop you from blowing your bridge and there's nothing you can do."

If that were the lieutenant colonel's intent, Guajardo and his engineers were not about to let his challenge go unanswered. To complicate any efforts to prevent destruction of the bridge by cutting the firing wires, a dual firing system, with one electric and one nonelectric primer, was being emplaced. In addition, the engineers were installing a series of booby traps, some hooked in series, some independent, as discreetly as was possible, as they went along, in such a manner that it appeared to be part of the main demolition effort. Though Guajardo knew that the American special forces were good, and that the odds were better than even that they would be able to prevent the destruction of the bridge, he knew they wouldn't be able to do so without paying a price.

And that, Guajardo knew, was the purpose of this entire exercise: to make the Americans pay the price. In fact, that was what their entire war-winning strategy was based on. No one on the Council of 13 had any illusions about the initial outcome of a confrontation between the United States and Mexico. In the beginning, the American Army, Air Force, and Navy would be able to go wherever they wanted and do whatever they wanted. Guajardo's forces simply would not be able to match the American weapons or technology. Even when the full weight of Nicaraguan and Cuban assistance came to bear, weapon for weapon, they would be outclassed.

But if it were true that the Americans would be able to go wherever they wanted, it was equally true that they would not be able to stay. While Colonel Barreda, the foreign minister, traveled through the councils of the world, screaming righteous indignation and demanding that the Americans be forced to leave Mexico, Colonel Zavala, the minister for domestic affairs, would be mobilizing the people for the great patriotic struggle against the invading Americans. With the forces he already had, those that Barreda could arrange for from the Latin American nations, and those that Zavala could mobilize within Mexico, Guajardo would wage a protracted campaign whose sole goal was to fill body bags with American dead. Eventually, he knew, the American public would tire of burying its young. Though many of his own people would also die, at least they knew what they were fighting for. Some Americans, on the other hand, were already questioning their goals and the methods of their leaders. Guajardo would give them something more to consider. Debate, he knew, would redouble when the flag-draped coffins began to appear in every little town and city across the United States.

Though Colonel Ruiz, minister of justice, cautioned that Saddam Hussein had hoped to do the same in Kuwait and had failed, Guajardo reminded him that they were not Arabs. Instead of drawing lines in the sand and hurling empty challenges, Guajardo told his brothers on the Council of 13, they should fight as the Vietcong and their grandfathers had. "Our war will be a righteous war, a war fought to defend our homes and our honor against the colossus from the north. So long as we do not admit defeat, we cannot be beaten. Remember, our people, like us, have nothing to lose except our pride. And even the most sophisticated missile or the biggest, most modern tank cannot strip that from us. Only we can throw that away. And I, for one, will die leading our people into battle before I let that happen."

Although he had not intended to make such a melodramatic speech to the council, Guajardo didn't regret it. He had meant every word. They were, after all, a passionate people, used to giving way to their passions when appropriate. At least his brothers knew where he stood. Soon, the Americans would too. If the Americans wanted to come, they would. In the beginning, they would find nothing, just poor villages, old men and women, and destruction. In the beginning, their sweep into northern Mexico would, no doubt, be compared to the almost bloodless American victory in Iraq by their own media and the pseudomilitary ''experts'' they employed. Guajardo had taken great pains to arrange his forces so that it would appear so. But he would watch, and wait. As the great cats of Africa track a herd, his forces would watch the Americans. When the Americans were comfortable and elation over their ''success'' was at its height, his forces would come, seeking the strays that wandered too far from the herd.

In time, Guajardo knew, they would prevail. They always had. The Americans had come before and, when they had tired of Mexico, they had left. This time would be no different. It never was. And when they left, Mexico and her people would still be there. They always were.

18

Hurrah, boys, we've got them!

—George Armstrong Custer before the
Battle of the Little Big Horn, as quoted by
Giovanni Martini

ARLINGTON, VIRGINIA
0035 HOURS, 9 SEPTEMBER

Reaching over with her right arm, Amanda Lewis spent several minutes of fruitless searching before she realized that the only thing her hand could find on Ed's side of the bed was crumpled sheets and a vacant pillow. With her mind clouded with sleep, she was not quite up to the challenge of solving the mystery of the missing husband. Satisfied that she had done all she could, she rolled over and began slowly drifting back to sleep, until the muffled voice from downstairs began to bring her back. Opening her eyes, as if that would help her hear better, Amanda listened for a moment. From the direction and the tone, she could tell that Ed was still on the phone, yelling at someone. Squinting in order to read the digital numbers on the clock, Amanda debated whether she should stay in bed and let Ed vent his spleen or go down and lend him some moral support. After listening for another minute and noticing no change in Ed's pitch or tone, she opted to go down. At least, she thought, she could try to calm him, though she doubted it. Once Ed Lewis started chasing windmills, only a punch in the nose or a bout of high blood pressure could stop him. Though she couldn't fend off the former, at least she could try to do something about the blood pressure.

Throwing on a robe, Amanda quietly went down the stairs to the kitchen to brew a pot of decaffeinated coffee. She didn't even pause as she passed the door of Ed's home office. Even through the closed door,

Ed's words could be heard clearly down the hall and in the kitchen. Tuning out his outburst, punctuated with an occasional pause while the other party talked, Amanda busied herself preparing a tray for their coffee. When all was ready, she took the tray and headed for Ed's office, reaching the door just as Ed slammed the receiver down. Leaning over to listen at the door, Amanda didn't hear a sound. Deciding that he was finished with whoever he had been talking to, she balanced the coffee tray in one hand while opening the door with the other.

Walking in as if nothing were out of the ordinary, Amanda began searching for any flat surface free of stacks of books, folders, papers, and magazines. She moved to a small table that appeared to offer a reasonably level spot on top of a small stack of books. Even on her way to the table she had to be wary, taking care to step over a briefcase, assorted books, and one of Ed's shoes. As she crossed the room, she watched her husband from the corner of her eye.

Seated at his desk, his chair turned sideways to face the corner of the desk where the phone was, Lewis had yet to acknowledge her presence. Instead, he merely sat there, reclining in his chair, hands folded on his stomach, staring at the phone. Even when Amanda finished preparing his mug of coffee, leaning over his desk to hand it to him, Lewis didn't look at her. Mechanically, he reached out, took the mug in one hand, and slowly brought it to his lips, holding it there for a moment with both hands, all the while watching the phone.

It wasn't that Ed was ungrateful or rude. When it came to a loving husband and an understanding father, there wasn't any better and Amanda knew it. After twenty-two years of marriage, the only regret that she had was that she had given in to his desire to run for Congress. Even his tour of combat duty in the Persian Gulf as a battalion executive officer had not been as hard on her as his five years in Congress. In those years, she had watched the man she loved begin to turn solemn and cynical. Though he denied there were any differences in him, Amanda knew better. These changes, along with a growing threat of hypertension accentuated by a poor diet due to long hours of work, threatened to destroy the only man that Amanda had ever loved, the man to whom she had devoted her entire life. Quietly taking her mug of coffee, Amanda moved over to a chair across the room from him, bending down to remove several file folders from the seat cushion. Sitting down, Amanda Lewis began to sip her coffee as she watched Congressman Ed Lewis and waited patiently for him to finish his thoughts.

When the phone rang, Amanda jumped. Lewis leaped forward, grabbing for the phone with his right hand. Without looking, he swung his left

arm, holding the coffee mug, toward the desk, and set the mug precariously on top of a jumbled stack of papers. Amanda was about to say
something when Lewis responded to the party on the other end of the line.
"Yes, I'll hold."

Settling back in her seat, Amanda watched Lewis, while casting an
occasional glance at the coffee mug that threatened to topple over from its
awkward perch. Only when he began speaking did Amanda understand
his lack of concern.

"Yes, Mr. President, this is Ed. I am sorry for waking you at this hour,
but I wanted to ask you one more time to reconsider your decision."

Amanda's eyes narrowed. Bullshit, she thought. Ed wasn't sorry for
waking the president. Nor was she sorry that he had.

"Yes, sir. I understand your position. And I understand the need to do
something about the raids across the border. Hell, Mr. President, I'd
rather be down there, on the front line, than stay here in Washington any
day of the week."

With her eyes narrowing even more, Amanda felt like shouting "Good,
let's go, tonight, and get the hell out of this rat race," but restrained
herself.

Lewis continued. "No sir, I have not changed my view. It is, and will
remain, a mistake to take direct military action against the Mexican
government. I am convinced that they are as anxious to stop those raids
as we are."

As she lowered her mug to her lap, Amanda shook her head. You'll
never give up, she thought. You'll never give up chasing those windmills, you old fool.

"No sir, I do not believe what the CIA, the DIA, the NSA, or the FBI
are saying. They're full of shit and you know it."

Looking over to the clock behind Lewis's desk, Amanda knew the
conversation would be ending soon. Presidents, after all, don't have to
listen to congressmen curse like that at one o'clock in the morning. She
was sure the president got enough of that during the day.

"In the first place, they have a piss-poor record, starting from when
Fidel took Havana all the way up until now and every point in between.
Second, and most importantly, the Mexicans will fight. Both you and I
know we will never be able to bring the Council of 13 down. Hell, even
with the whole world behind us and his armed forces shattered, we
couldn't get rid of Saddam. What makes you think this is going to go any
better?"

Odds, Amanda thought. After all, any Vegas gambler knew that if you
threw the dice enough, you would eventually come up with a winning

number. After Korea, Cuba, Vietnam, and Iraq, some president had to get lucky. Suddenly, she realized that she was beginning to sound as cynical as Ed. With a shake of her head, she stood up and moved over to the tray to pour herself another cup of coffee.

"You, Mr. President, may be committed. But I am not obliged to follow. This is a dumb move, a move that neither you nor I, in the end, will pay for. I just pray that next week, when the body bags start coming back, you can find a way to explain to Johnny Jones's mother that her son died for political necessity." After listening for another minute, Lewis heaved a sigh. "Yes, Mr. President. It will be a long day. But not near as long for us as it will be for our people moving into Mexico."

Without any further response, Lewis hung the phone up. Turning away from the tray, Amanda saw him sitting there, still holding the receiver with his right hand while bending over, staring at the floor in silence.

He had lost, again. Heaving a great sigh, Amanda felt the urge to go over and take him in her arms. But she knew that this wasn't the time for that. Instead, she lifted the pot of coffee and quietly went over to his desk.

As he heard more coffee being poured into his mug, which still sat teetering on the papers he had put it on, Lewis sat up and turned to his wife. For the first time, he took note of her smiling face framed by her long, ruffled hair. When she was finished and began to return to her seat, leaving the pot on the tray as she did so, he reached over for his mug, taking a sip before saying anything. When he did speak, it was in a low, almost plaintive tone. "This, my dear, isn't a good night to be an American."

Resuming her seat and picking up her own cup, Amanda gave him a sympathetic smile. "I heard, dear. How about telling me all about it."

EAST OF LAS JOSEFINES, ON THE TEXAS SIDE OF THE RIO GRANDE
0405 HOURS, 9 SEPTEMBER

For the briefest of moments, the sky above Laredo lit up. Though she couldn't hear the muffled explosion over the whine of her Bradley, Kozak knew someone had blown something up somewhere. She had no way of realizing that she had just witnessed the explosion that claimed the first American dead of the day. The war of attrition, a war the Mexicans felt that they couldn't possibly lose, had begun.

Turning her attention back in the direction in which they were moving, Kozak squinted slightly, searching through the dust thrown up by the lead vehicles for the chem lights marking the Bradley to her immediate front.

It took her a few seconds to identify the faint glow of the three red chem lights hanging vertically from the back of the turret of the 1st Squad's Bradley, the lead track in her platoon. Each company in 2nd of the 13th Infantry used different colors to identify their vehicles. Her company, A Company, used red stripes painted on the base of the 25mm cannon for visual recognition during the day and red chem lights or red-filtered flashlights at night. B Company used white, C Company blue, D Company yellow, and all headquarters vehicles green. Within the company, platoons were identified by the number of stripes or lights used. First Platoon had one stripe or light, 2nd Platoon two, 3rd Platoon, her platoon, three, and the company commander's Bradley used four. By using such a system, commanders, at a glance, could tell who they were looking at in the heat of battle when a friendly vehicle appeared on their left or right.

Satisfied that her driver was keeping the proper interval, Kozak twisted about, looking behind for the 2nd Squad's Bradley, which was supposed to be following hers. The 3rd Squad, with Sergeant Rivera, was taking up the rear of the platoon and the company. As she looked, it occurred to Kozak that she had fallen into the habit of assigning missions and establishing the order of march for her platoon in such a manner that it was always 1st Squad in the lead, 2nd Squad next, and 3rd Squad in the rear. Although Staff Sergeant Maupin was the most experienced and competent of her squad leaders, it wasn't fair that he should always lead. Kozak had been taught that such a practice had a tendency to make the other squad leaders lazy, dependent on the map-reading skills of Maupin and secure in the knowledge that Maupin's Bradley, and not theirs, would catch the first land mine or antitank round in a firefight. The same considerations put continuous pressure and stress on the men of the 1st Squad. That such feelings were real struck home when Kozak noticed that two riflemen from Maupin's squad had scribbled ''First to Fall'' on the camouflage bands of their helmets. The use of such graffiti, thinly disguised as humor, was a subtle method used by soldiers to communicate dissatisfaction with leadership or unit policies or practices. That Maupin, who had to have seen the slogan, allowed the two riflemen to continue to display it, told Kozak that he agreed with its sentiment.

Not that she could blame her own people for feeling that way. With Captain Wittworth's habit of placing her platoon at the rear of the company column during every road march, or in reserve during most operations, she was beginning to sympathize with the feeling of the men in 1st Squad. At first Kozak had accepted Wittworth's practice of putting her platoon in the rear without much thought. When she began to notice that he continued to do so, she had passed it off as common sense. Wittworth, she told herself, was simply giving her a chance to learn her trade without the added pressure of being in the lead. That rationale, however, began to wear thin when Wittworth rotated 1st and 2nd Platoons, while keeping Kozak's in the rear or sending her on every mission that required a platoon to be detached from the company. Though she tried hard not to become paranoid, Kozak began to wonder if Wittworth was trying to discourage her or keep her at arm's length. Regardless of the reason, it was becoming apparent to her, and to her platoon, that Wittworth was, in his own way, telling the 3rd Platoon that it wasn't good enough yet to be part of the company.

Besides the psychological cold shoulder, there were practical concerns. Being the trail platoon meant that the 3rd Platoon had the honor of eating the entire company's dust on long road marches. When traveling on dirt trails, especially on the tank trails at Fort Hood, where the dust had been ground into fine powder by the passage of thousands of tracked vehicles since 1940, the dust clouds could reach great heights and linger forever. It was not unusual to end a road march covered with a thick layer of dust that clogged every pore, violated every crack, crevice, and opening on your body, and turned dark green camouflage uniforms almost white. For Kozak, whose nose was still stuffed with cotton wadding and who was still breathing through her mouth, this was particularly annoying. In fact, she had even considered scribbling a motto of her own on her helmet, such as ''The Dust Devils'' or ''The Last of the Least.'' But Nancy Kozak was an officer, a new and junior officer, who was being watched and evaluated by everyone who outranked her, which, to a second lieutenant, seemed like everyone in the Army. So she bit her tongue and did as she was told. Her day, she knew, would come. Until then, all she could do was follow and, for the time being, eat more dust, a commodity that 2nd Platoon was currently supplying lots of as they headed south into Mexico.

SHERATON HOTEL, SOUTH PADRE ISLAND, TEXAS
0815 HOURS, 9 SEPTEMBER

Each page of the thick document sitting on the breakfast table served only to discourage Childress, though he didn't show it. There was a reason, he knew, for his being shown this particular report. When he asked Delapos, who sat across from him, sipping coffee and eyeing the waitresses, how he had managed to obtain it, Delapos smiled. ''The Council of 13, my friend, no longer thinks as one.'' If, in fact, the document he was reading was authentic, then Delapos's words were true, and Alamán, the manager, had succeeded in penetrating the belts of security that had surrounded the council.

The summons to meet Delapos at South Padre, along with the announcement that U.S. forces had crossed into Mexico that morning, had cheered Childress like nothing else in a long time. While waiting for Delapos to meet him in the restaurant, Childress had wondered why he had felt that way, for he had quickly realized that his sudden euphoria was more than the satisfaction one gets when a difficult and well-paying job is coming to an end. He had finished many other jobs, a few even more difficult than this one, and had never felt like he had that morning. Nor was the elation due to his anticipated return to his beloved Vermont mountains, though the prospect of being there for foliage season was, in its own way, exciting. It wasn't until he had met Delapos and found out that Alamán had decided that their campaign of provocation and agitation, rather than ending, needed to enter a new and more deadly phase, that Childress finally understood the reason he had been overwhelmed with joy when he thought his role in provoking the war was over. Despite denials to himself, Delapos, and other Americans employed by Alamán, Childress had never been able truly to reconcile himself to the fact that his actions were resulting in the deaths of fellow countrymen. The idea that his actions were treasonous was never far from his mind. The document he read, and the new instructions from Alamán, only served to reinforce that idea.

The document Delapos had handed Childress was a white paper, dated three days after Lefleur's incident with the National Guard, which summarized what Colonel Guajardo called the Council of 13's war-winning strategy. Written by both Guajardo, the minister of defense, and Colonel Barreda, the foreign minister, it laid out their strategy, not only for defending Mexico, but for achieving clear and unchallenged power as well as legitimacy for the council as the sole and rightful governing body of Mexico.

As a preamble, the paper stated in clear and uncompromising terms that, barring an unforeseen act of God, Mexico had no hope of achieving any type of military victory over American forces. In the next breath, however, the report stated that, so long as the Council of 13 and the Mexican people acted with prudence and restraint, the final political victory, the one that mattered, would be theirs. Guajardo, carefully citing American experience in Vietnam, pointed out that despite the fact that the American military had never lost a major engagement to either the Viet

Cong or the People's Army of Vietnam, politically they had lost every-thing in Southeast Asia. The report discounted the apparent evidence of recent American military prowess demonstrated in Grenada, Panama, and the Persian Gulf, pointing out that in all three cases, the opposing gov-ernments had underestimated the American willingness to use force and its effectiveness, and had overestimated their own military position. Even more importantly, however, Guajardo pointed out that the opposing gov-ernments had lacked the type of popular support, and the willingness of their people to endure the kind of sacrifice, necessary for the conduct of a protracted war of attrition. In Guajardo's words, "The Americans won in the Persian Gulf, not by breaking machines, but by breaking the will of the soldiers and the people it fought. In Mexico, the Americans will find, as they did in Vietnam, that we have few machines to break, and a people that cannot be broken. A people who will not admit defeat cannot be defeated."

The heart of the report was an astute blend of military and political maneuvering that never left the realm of reality. In all, it was an effort that would have brought tears of happiness to the eyes of Machiavelli, the fifteenth-century Florentine theorist who had elevated modern political-military thinking to an art. Knowing full well that the American president would never be able to muster the support needed from either the Amer-ican Congress or the people for a full declaration of war, and citing past American incursions into Mexico, Barreda anticipated that the issue the American president would use to justify their invasion was that of secu-rity. Guajardo, in turn, pointed out that, like Winfield Scott in 1848, and John J. Pershing in 1916, the American military lacked the forces nec-essary to occupy all of Mexico. Therefore, Guajardo went on, the Amer-ican Army would instead seize whatever terrain it determined was necessary to meet the stated objective of ensuring the security of its people, property, and land.

Three key considerations would dictate the amount of territory seized by the Americans and its location. The first was the size of force available to the Americans to seize it and hold it. Initially, this task would fall to the regular Army, consisting of twelve divisions, and the Marine Corps with two. Of these, only seven Army and one Marine division could be deployed, since two Army divisions were still in Europe, one was in Korea, and the sole American airborne and air-assault divisions could not be committed by the United States without emasculating its ability to respond to unexpected contingencies outside of Europe, Korea, or Mex-ico. The use of reserve and National Guard units, Guajardo pointed out, would be limited by law as well as readiness.

Once committed, the American ability to keep its forces in Mexico would limit their effort. Supply lines, called lines of communications or LOCs for short, from the United States, through occupied territories, to the most advanced American unit, would have to be established and kept open. In 1848, Winfield Scott had gambled when he intentionally severed his lines of communications with the sea at Veracruz and marched overland into Mexico City in order to end the war. Unlike that of his modern counterparts, his army consisted only of men, mules, and horses, allowing him to live off the land as he went. That option, given the size and sophistication of the modern American Army, was out of the question. A single M-1A1 tank could consume over 500 gallons of diesel fuel in a day. In comparison, the case of rations consumed by its crew was negligible. A division, with over 300 such vehicles, would require 150,000 gallons a day for its tanks alone. Added to the fuel needed to run the tanks, infantry fighting vehicles, self-propelled howitzers, helicopters, and supply vehicles were specialized lubricants, spare parts, medical supplies, engineer material, ammunition, water, food, mail, and a host of other items that a modern American army found indispensable. In the end, the needs of the American Army would place a requirement for moving anywhere from 100 to 200 pounds of supplies per soldier in Mexico each and every day he was there.

The final limiting factor, one few outside the military profession ever considered, was the difficulty the Americans would encounter in controlling, feeding, and administering any local inhabitants that remained in the territory occupied by American forces. Once a territory was occupied, it fell to the occupying force to administer, feed, and care for the people in that territory. Modern conventions and law, as well as moral and ethical codes, demanded that. As all civil-military units in the United States were reserve units, and they were few, the number of populated areas that could be effectively governed and administered by those units, not to mention supplied, was limited. Matamoros alone had close to 400,000 inhabitants, and Monterrey nearly four million. These populations would need to be supported by the conquering Americans.

Given an analysis of American capabilities, and assuming that American goals would be limited to the establishment of a security zone, Guajardo estimated that the American limit of advance into Mexico would be north of a line defined by Tampico, Ciudad Victoria, Monterrey, Chihuahua, Hermosillo, and Kimo Bay. Whether or not the cities mentioned would be included in the security zone depended on the American ability to support the population of those cities versus the value of controlling the road and rail networks that converged in them. Though the occupation of Veracruz could not be ruled out, such an action would be inconsistent with the announced limited objectives.

It was at this point that Barreda took the lead again. Mexico, he pointed out, should allow the United States to define the parameters of the conflict. Once the Americans announced their goals, they would be hard pressed to change them unless the Council of 13 did something to justify an escalation or change in goals. The occupation of Veracruz, located on the eastern coast of Mexico well south of the Rio Bravo, would be inconsistent with the stated goal of establishing a security zone to protect the American border. Such inconsistencies, Barreda pointed out, if they occurred, would be useful in driving a wedge between the American president and his supporters. If the council could fuel the political and moral debate that already existed within the United States, support for the war would erode faster and demands for a negotiated settlement would only be a matter of time.

On the international level, not only would the UN and the Organization of American States be used to apply pressure, but the establishment of a coalition of Central American countries would add to the pressure on the United States. Already, a combined military command, under Mexican control, including forces from Guatemala, El Salvador, Nicaragua, Honduras, Panama, Colombia, and Venezuela, had been formed. Though the contribution of some of the countries was insignificant, the mere formation of such a coalition, Barreda pointed out, could not be ignored by either the United States or the world community. Mexico, by using the rallying cry of oppression by a superpower, would be able to bring pressure to bear from those nations who wished to embarrass the United States or repay real or perceived past transgressions.

A benefit of this whole process, Barreda emphasized, was that the Council of 13 would, out of necessity, receive recognition as the legal government of Mexico, almost by default. Barreda ended his section by stating, ''By casting ourselves in the role of the oppressed, and ensuring our military operations are conducted in accordance with all international accords and protocols governing warfare, the same international system that the United States has so successfully manipulated in the past to achieve her national goals will give us our ultimate victory.''

Childress paused when he read this, noting that the section, ''ensuring our military operations are conducted in accordance with all international accords and protocols governing warfare'' was underlined, twice. Without any need for explanation, he knew what Alamán had in mind. Sliding the document back into a plain manila envelope, Childress looked up at Delapos. ''How sure are you that this is real?''

Taking a sip of coffee, Delapos glanced about the room before answering Childress. "As I said, the Council of 13 is no longer of one mind. There are those who feel the manipulation of internal American politics is a game that is far too dangerous to become involved in. It is, as one of the members of the council said, like twisting the tail of the bull. These same men are also ashamed of what they call a strategy of cowards. Rather than surrender Mexican territory, they demand that every effort be made to defend every inch or perish in the effort. Yes, my friend, this document is real."

Although Childress had, by now, pretty well figured out what Alamán was now demanding of Delapos, Childress wanted Delapos to tell him. Perhaps, Childress hoped, the actual plan was not as outrageous, or as gruesome, as what he was then picturing in his mind. Eager to tell Childress, Delapos explained how he and Alamán saw things happening. "The Americans will, or I mean, have invaded, moving south to secure a line similar to the one defined by Guajardo. The Mexican Army will offer only token resistance to that advance, just enough to appease Mexican machismo and provide the people with new heroes and martyrs that could be used to rally the nation behind the Council of 13. Once the Americans reach the limit of their advance, a stalemate will settle in, during which the Americans will try to clean out any groups of bandits or criminals within the security zone it occupies, while the Council of 13 applies diplomatic pressure, as well as manipulating antiwar sentiment within the United States, in an effort to force the Americans out. Eventually, Señor Alamán sees negotiations that will end with the United States claiming its goals have been met and withdrawing. The Council of 13, for their part, will be able to claim victory, pointing out that they had prevented the total defeat and occupation of Mexico. In the end, a status quo ante bellum will be reestablished and relations between the two nations will resume, with the Council of 13 formally recognized, by both the people of Mexico and the world, as the sole and legal government of Mexico."

Pausing, Delapos looked at Childress for a reaction. When he saw that he would not get one from the poker-faced American, he continued. "To prevent this from happening, Señor Alamán intends to move our teams south again, once the American forces reach the limit of their advance. Operating from base camps behind Mexican lines, we will conduct raids against isolated outposts and along the extended supply lines that the Americans will have to use. Though we expect the Mexican Army to do the same, those conducted by our forces will be brutal, committing the most vicious and heinous atrocities possible. By doing this, we will cause the Americans to overreact and either retaliate in kind or, even better, modify their limited war aims to include the overthrow of the Council of 13.''

Childress, for his part, remained calm. Delapos, however, was animated by his own dialogue. His face lit by glowing eyes and a smile, he continued, talking faster and faster and waving his right hand as he proceeded. ''That such sentiment can be mustered in the United States is possible. Many Americans, after the war in the Persian Gulf, felt that it was a mistake to leave Saddam Hussein in power. The atrocities committed against the Kurdish rebels in the north and Iraqi refugees in the south by a man left in power were a stain that marred an otherwise brilliant feat of American arms. If we can make the Council of 13 appear to be as evil as that Iraqi dictator, the Americans may demand that steps be taken to prevent a repeat of their failure in the Persian Gulf, especially since the victims, this time, would be Americans.''

Finished, Delapos again waited for Childress to respond. In Delapos's eyes, Childress could see both excitement and joy. After having listened in silence, struggling to avoid any emotional response, Childress finally had to say something. Several thoughts ran through his mind. First and foremost was the realization that he was, despite years of self-denial, still an American. The idea of being a man without a country, which had been appealing to him in his youth, was wearing thin as he began to look for a life that held more than just danger, excitement, and adventure. At thirty-five, Childress wanted to make peace, with himself and with a country he had so long ignored.

Hand in hand with this realization was the impression that, just as he was too much an American, Delapos was too much a Mexican. The same forces of heritage, birth, and experience that made Childress undeniably American made it impossible for Delapos to be anything but a Mexican. In his enthusiasm to follow Alamán, a man Delapos had begun referring to as a great Mexican patriot, Delapos was ignoring the stupidity of using mercenaries in an area contested by two standing armies. Cold hard logic told Childress that, regardless of how vast the area of operation and how dispersed the opposing forces were, of how good and secretive the mercenaries were, and of how inept the Mexican Army was, the mercenaries would eventually run out of luck—or, worse, their usefulness to Alamán would end. How easy, Childress knew, it would be for Alamán to arrange for information regarding the location of his mercenary base camps to fall into the hands of the American CIA or Mexican intelligence. Once this was done, every asset from high-performance bombers to special-operations forces would be used to eradicate the mercenary teams, relieving Alamán of the necessity of paying them.

Despite the reservations he harbored, however, Childress found himself seriously considering going along. Such a risky venture, he knew, would require that Alamán pay top dollar to his mercenaries. It would take little effort to convince him, through Delapos, that all payment had to be in advance. Childress, therefore, saw an opportunity for one last hurrah, one more job that would, if he survived it, let him leave his chosen profession and retire to his beloved Green Mountains. Though the idea of building his future on the bodies of his fellow countrymen was never far from his mind, Childress was able to keep those thoughts in check. He was, he told himself, just like the American politicians in Washington, D.C., who were enhancing their political careers by sending Americans to fight another war that was, by any measure, wrong, immoral, and unwinnable.

35 KILOMETERS SOUTH OF NUEVO LAREDO, MEXICO
1310 HOURS, 9 SEPTEMBER

With the passing of the scout helicopters, quiet returned to the arroyo. That they had once again escaped detection by the Americans both surprised and worried Guajardo. For he knew that, as good as the sensors and optics of the American recon aircraft were, the camouflage and positions of his men were bad. Not that the men, or their leaders, were slack or undisciplined. On the contrary. The morale and spirits of both leaders and led were high, almost euphoric. Though much of the euphoria was nothing more than a thin veil to hide their nervousness, Guajardo could tell there was a true desire to do well in the soldiers he had selected to fight the rearguard actions. No, Guajardo knew, it wasn't really their fault that things were not perfect. It was just that they were not as well trained as they should have been, and lacked the experience that served to both motivate and focus one's efforts in combat.

To some extent, he blamed himself, for the mechanized cavalry platoon waiting in ambush was from the military zone he had been responsible for before the June 29 revolution. During his tenure as their senior commander, part of his responsibility had been to train and prepare them for this day. That he felt uneasy now, when his soldiers were about to engage in their first battle, was natural. That he also saw only the negatives, and imagined the worst possible outcome, was also natural. His admonishments to subordinates during peacetime training exercises, telling them that perfection in war was an illusion, did not, at that moment, help relieve the anxiety he felt, for he knew that errors cost men their lives and lost battles.

*   *   *

Yet, despite his reservations, there was nothing, in reality, that he could do. Technically, by all measures, Guajardo had done everything expected of a senior commander. He had formulated his strategy, had it approved by the council, issued the necessary orders to implement it, and done everything that was prudent and within his power to ensure that his subordinates carried it out. Now, all he had to do was have the courage of his convictions and see those plans through. The most difficult part of command, Guajardo was beginning to realize, was letting go, trusting in subordinate commanders and allowing them the freedom to do their jobs.

Still, there had to be something he could do, some way that he could influence the battle. This very question had, in the past, often nagged Guajardo. Over the years, he had studied how various commanders, both Mexican and foreign, had sought to exercise command and control, to influence their subordinates by thought, word, and deed. At an early age, Guajardo had rejected the manners and techniques used by his fellow Mexican officers. They were, he felt, too self-serving. While some of the battlefield exploits of his ancestors provided stirring accounts and inspiration, they offered little in the way of practical war-winning advice. While the story of the young cadet who plunged to his death wrapped in the flag of Mexico at the Battle of Chapultepec on September 13, 1847, made a great and inspiring legend, it scarcely provided a commander with a solution to command and control problems on the modern battlefield.

At first, Guajardo thought American leadership techniques could provide an answer. Quickly, however, he found that American commanders depended far too much on sophisticated equipment, equipment that Guajardo knew the Mexican Army would never have. In addition, and to his surprise, he found that the practices of many American officers, too, were quite self-serving. In their own way, the "professional" military officers in the United States made just as many decisions based on domestic and international political considerations as did officers in Mexico, although no one would ever admit to such a thing. Finally, the American character, both national and individual, greatly influenced their system. American professional journals and doctrine preached a policy of centralized planning and decentralized execution, in which the subordinates supposedly had great latitude in deciding how to perform assigned tasks. In practice, however, sophisticated communications systems provided very senior commanders, commanders who were conscious of the fact that their careers depended upon the success or failure of their subordinates or who were lacking confidence in those subordinates, the ability to actively intervene in operations in which they had no business. Rather than having freedom to fight their own battles as they saw fit, American commanders, Guajardo found, were hamstrung by demands to submit frequent and detailed reports and were often victimized by recommendations and advice from commanders too far removed from the reality of battle.

Rejecting the American way of war, Guajardo briefly considered the Soviet technique. In many ways, it was attractive. Its reliance on standardized battle drills and clear, concise doctrine took much of the guesswork out of the decisions of junior commanders. But this, too, was rejected by Guajardo as being too inflexible. The conformity demanded by Soviet techniques was unsuited to the Mexican temperament. It was too mechanical, too cold, too precise. His men, he knew, were men of flesh and blood, men of passions. Such men, Guajardo knew, could never be made into the machines the Soviet techniques required. While one could not build a system using only the example of the Niños Perdidos of Chapultepec, the occasional display of passion, courage, and sacrifice, which Mexicans abounded in, and which the Soviet system discounted, was needed to stir a fighting man's blood.

It was only after many years that Guajardo had realized that he would never find, in a foreign army, an ideal technique that could be grafted onto his army. Instead, he opted for a mix, a hybrid system combining the strengths of his army with suitable techniques and practices from other armies. Of all the armies he studied, the system he followed most closely was the German. Though it was the system that the Americans pretended to follow, Guajardo knew they had lost focus when they diluted it with particular American practices and idiosyncrasies. Guajardo, on the other hand, chose only two features of the German system that he knew he could implement and influence. The first was a small, well-trained staff that created plans, coordinated them, and then provided necessary synchronization when the plans were implemented. The second feature, which Guajardo himself endorsed, was leadership from the front. It was only from the front, Guajardo knew, that officers could see and understand what was happening. A man sitting in a safe, comfortable bunker, miles from danger, could not possibly feel or understand a battle in progress. Only a leader standing shoulder to shoulder with his men could gauge what was possible and what wasn't. Besides, Mexican character responded to such leadership. It, in fact, demanded it. So Guajardo found little difficulty in justifying why he, the senior military commander in Mexico, was standing in a hastily dug position on the forward edge of the battlefield. After all, how could he demand that his subordinates lead from the front if he himself didn't. And it was only by using such excuses that he was able to escape the chaos of the capital and go where he could be with men he understood and do what he was trained to do.

A young captain of cavalry, who commanded the mechanized cavalry units in this area, lightly tapped Guajardo on the shoulder to get his attention, then pointed to the north, toward the road. Taking his time, and making a great show of a calmness that he really didn't feel, Guajardo hoisted his binoculars to his eyes and began to search in the direction indicated by the captain.

At first, Guajardo didn't see what the captain was pointing at. Then, as if it simply had popped out of nowhere, he saw a dark green vehicle moving down the road. With his binoculars, he studied the vehicle. It was a Bradley, probably the scout version. If that was so, there had to be another, somewhere near. Following the road back to the north, Guajardo searched for another vehicle. He saw none. Perhaps it was halted, covering the lead vehicle from a concealed position. Without stopping his search, Guajardo asked the cavalry captain if he saw any other vehicles. The captain responded with a curt no, he did not.

Guajardo grunted. Perhaps, he told the captain, the scout vehicle was being overwatched by attack helicopters. Still searching, the captain responded that he had thought of that, but saw no dust or shaking vegetation that normally betrayed the presence of a hovering helicopter. Again, Guajardo responded with a grunt. "Perhaps," he said, "we have a careless scout."

The captain of cavalry lowered his binoculars, scanning the horizon with his naked eyes before responding. "Perhaps, Colonel, that is true. The only way to be sure of that, sir, is to fire."

Guajardo, his binoculars still riveted to the enemy scout vehicle, didn't react at first. Then, understanding that the captain was seeking permission, he turned his head, calling over his shoulder while still holding his binoculars up. "Then, Captain, perhaps you should do so."

Unfamiliar with the proper etiquette for starting a war, the captain snapped to attention, saluted, and responded to Guajardo's comment with a resounding "Sí, Colonel."

As the captain of cavalry issued the order to open fire, Guajardo chuckled. In time, he knew, after they had been brutalized by combat, such giddiness would be gone. Only then, when the enthusiasm of the first battle had been washed away by blood, would he know if his soldiers could do what was expected of them.

Though he knew where the Panard recon vehicles were hidden, Guajardo could not see them as they pulled out of hidden positions and into their firing positions. Even after they fired, throwing up plumes of white smoke and dust from the muzzle blast, Guajardo still could not see the two vehicles.

Neither, he noted, could the American. Both Panards had fired within a second of each other. And both missed. The round of one Panard impacted on the road just in front of the American Bradley while the round of the second hit the shoulder of the road to the left of the Bradley. Even before the dirt thrown up by the near misses began to fall back to earth, the Bradley jerked to the left. For a second, Guajardo caught a glimpse of the Bradley's commander as he dropped out of sight and pulled his hatch shut. It was obvious that the driver, seeing the explosion to his immediate front and not the one to the left, had reacted instinctively and without guidance from his vehicle commander, for his maneuver was taking the Bradley right into the guns of the Mexican Panards. Of course, Guajardo thought, maybe the Bradley driver did know what he was doing. After all, standard drill in an ambush was to turn into the ambush.

That possibility, however, was quickly dismissed when the Bradley began belching smoke from its on-board smoke generator. Rather than hide the Bradley, which the white billowing smoke would have done if the Panards were behind it, the smoke now silhouetted the Bradley, making it an ideal target. Not that the smoke was necessary. The first round that had impacted to the front of the Bradley had landed short because the commander of the Panard that had fired it had made an error in estimating the range. By turning toward the Panard's position, the Bradley had closed the range, eliminating the ranging error. The commander of the Panard, unable to see the strike of his first round because of the muzzle blast and the dust kicked up by it in front of his vehicle, fired a second round without making any corrections. Thus, the actions of the Bradley's driver, and the failure of the Panard's commander to make any corrections, established a perfect ballistic solution for the Panard's second round.

Striking just below the driver's hatch on the Bradley, the Panard's 90mm high-explosive antitank, or HEAT, round detonated. A HEAT round has a shaped-charge warhead which, when detonated, forms a superheated, pencil-thin jet stream of molten metal molecules. These molecules, which come from the metal cone in the warhead that forms the jet stream, can exert over 125,000 foot-pounds of pressure against a single point. In the case of the Bradley, this force easily defeated the vehicle's aluminum armor. In a span of time that lasted less than a second, the superheated molecules in the jet stream from the Panard's round literally pushed the molecules of the Bradley's armor out of the way. Once inside the Bradley, the superheated molecules of the HEAT round, now joined by molecules from the Bradley's own armor, cut through anything that stood in their way, including the chest of the driver. As it ripped through the crew compartment of the Bradley, the jet stream cut through anything it made contact with, igniting fires as it went. When the stream hit one of the TOW antitank guided missiles stored in the Bradley, itself a HEAT round, and penetrated the thin aluminum skin of its warhead, a chain reaction was initiated.

From where Guajardo stood, the impact of the 90mm round on the front slope of the Bradley, followed by secondary explosions, was spectacular. One second the Bradley was there, blindly charging for all it was worth toward the Panards. In an instant, a sudden flash and a great puff of thick black smoke obscured the Bradley. Then, before the puff of smoke disappeared, the Bradley shuddered and threw off a coat of dust, like a dirty metal toy that had been hit by a hammer. Almost instantaneously after that, the hatches on the turret and in the rear of the Bradley blew open, venting great sheets of flame that leaped up for a split second, then disappeared. Still, the Bradley rolled forward, trailing thick, dirty white and black smoke from numerous openings. A second series of internal explosions, caused by the detonation of more warheads stored on board, caused the Bradley to shudder again. This time, as the sheets of flame, which were caused by the burning of the TOW missiles' rocket fuel, appeared, the Bradley slowed, veered to the left, then rolled to a stop. The lone scout was dead.

The scene elated the captain of cavalry. "We have done it, Colonel Guajardo. We have killed the Bradley. And with only three rounds!"

Watching the burning Bradley, Guajardo's response was cold. "Four rounds, Captain. Your Panards fired four rounds. The second round of the other Panard flew over the Bradley. The commander of that vehicle either overcompensated, adding too much of a correction, or did not take into account the fact that the American, headed toward him, was reducing the gun-to-target range." Turning away from the burning Bradley, Guajardo looked into the eyes of the surprised captain of cavalry. "Either way, you need to talk to both of those commanders. They were in ambush. They should have known the exact range to the road before the American came. Such errors in the future will cost us dearly if we do not make corrections now. Is that understood?"

Snapping to attention, his face showing confusion because of what he took to be a rebuke, the captain of cavalry responded with a crisp "Sí, Colonel."

After an awkward moment, Guajardo placed his right hand on the captain's shoulder. "It was a good kill, Captain. I do not begrudge you that. But it was only one kill. The American 16th Armored Division alone has 316 Bradleys. If we hope to make an impression upon them, we must make every shot and every life count. You understand, don't you?"

The captain of cavalry looked down at his feet, then up to Guajardo's eyes. "Yes, Colonel, I do. Forgive me for being so foolish. This is, you see, my first battle."

Grasping the back of the captain's head, Guajardo shook it. "You do not need to apologize. This is new to all of us. Now, quickly, move your people before those other 315 Bradleys come thundering down on us."

20 KILOMETERS SOUTH OF NUEVO LAREDO, MEXICO
1315 HOURS, 9 SEPTEMBER

"Colonel Dixon, the 9th Cavalry is in contact!"

The sudden announcement, blurted over the helicopter's intercom, caught Dixon dozing off. Up since 0200 hours that morning after less than two hours sleep, Dixon had been on the move since then. He had been on hand in Laredo when the Mexicans had blown up two of the three bridges on the Rio Grande in the faces of the Special Forces teams that had tried to seize them at H-Hour, 0400 hours. After that, he had driven south of Laredo to watch the river crossing of the 2nd of the 13th Infantry, lead unit of the 2nd Brigade. When he saw that all was going well there, he had flown over to Roma, where the 1st Brigade had its forward command post, to see how their initial operations were going. Only after Dixon had been satisfied that all was in order did he return to the division tactical command post, or TAC CP, located outside of Laredo, to monitor the battle and confer with the corps G3 over a secure land line.

Arriving at the TAC CP shortly after 1000 hours, Dixon had been off again by 1200 after receiving an update from the division assistant intelligence officer, his own current operations officer, and conferring with Big Al, the commanding general, whom Dixon had met coming in as he was going out.

It was not surprising, then, that the steady beating of the helicopter's blades and the rhythmic vibration of the engine were all that was needed to put Dixon to sleep. Blinking his eyes, Dixon looked about for a moment in order to get himself oriented. Once his head was as clear as it was going to get, he hit his intercom button. "Say again that last report, Chief."

His pilot, Chief Warrant Officer 3 Bomaster, realized, from Dixon's voice, that he had been asleep. "We just heard a spot report over the division command net that 1st of the 9th Cav had made contact. No grids or specifics were given, sir."

Taking a deep breath, Dixon pulled the map case that had partially fallen off of his lap up to where he could see it. In one corner of the map case was a small card that had the call signs and frequencies of selected division units on it. Finding the frequency for the 1st of the 9th Cavalry Squadron's command net, he reached over to the command and control console of the helicopter, and set that frequency on one of its FM radios.

As soon as he did, the silence of the headset he wore was shattered by a string of excited conversations. The use of illegal call signs, and familiarity with the voices, made it easy for Dixon to identify who was talking on the radio. The squadron commander, using his nickname Scout 6, was grilling his A Troop commander, who responded to the call sign Alpha 6. Every now and then, the squadron operations officer, with the handle Scout 3, would cut into the conversation with a question. The operations officer, however, was for the most part ignored, as squadron commander talked to troop commander.

"Alpha six, say again the location of the ambush, over."

"This is Alpha six. I do not have a six-digit grid on it. We have only an initial contact report, over."

"This is Scout six. As I recall, an initial contact report includes location and nature of contact. If you have that information, then pass it on. If not, tell me, so I can get division off my back, over."

There was a pause. From the squadron commander's tone of voice and questions, Dixon could tell that he was about to lose his temper. Not that he blamed him. It was obvious, from the short conversation that Dixon had already heard, that the troop commander was waffling, that one of his lead elements had screwed up and been caught, and that the troop commander was in the process of trying to cover either his own stupidity or that of one of his subordinates. Dixon could almost picture the A Troop commander, sitting in his command post, trying to come up with at least some kind of useful information to mollify his enraged squadron commander. The urge to protect his troopers, not to mention his own pride and career, Dixon knew, was strong. While such sentiment was laudable and acceptable by many in peacetime, in combat, when timely and accurate reporting meant the difference between success and failure, there was no room for such sentiments. Failure equaled lives lost for nothing and that, to Dixon, was intolerable. Unable to restrain himself, Dixon was about to key the radio and turn the screws another notch. The squadron commander, however, beat him to the punch.

"Alpha six, this is Scout six. Okay, lad, answer me, yes or no. Do you know where the contact took place, over."

"This is Alpha six. Negative."

"Do you have contact with the element in contact or anyone who can observe them, over."

"This is Alpha six. Negative."

"Do you have any idea of the size, location, or nature of the enemy force that was engaged, over."

"This is Alpha six. Negative."

There was a pause. When the squadron commander came back, he did not bother to hide his anger. "Alpha six, do you fucking know anything? Over!"

Again, there was a pause before the troop commander replied. When he did, his voice was low, almost sheepish. "This is Alpha six. Roger. A scout track from the Alpha two one element moving south on the main red ball called in that he was under fire. Alpha two one has been unable to contact him after that report. Over."

The squadron commander articulated the anger that Dixon felt. "You mean to tell me that you had one Bradley, all by itself, running down the main road? That you may have pissed away the lives of five men just to find out there's Mexicans out there who are willing to fight?"

After a moment, a moment that Dixon knew had to be the most difficult one in the life of the young A Troop commander, he came back and answered his squadron commander. "This is Alpha six. Affirmative. Over."

Having heard enough, Dixon turned the radio off. For a moment, he merely stared out the window of the helicopter, watching the sparse vegetation of northern Mexico go by. Why, he thought, did every war have to start the same way? Why did young soldiers always have to pay with their lives so that their leaders could learn their trade? As much as Dixon felt sorry for the troop commander, he knew that he had to go. Not only had he sinned by sending out a single vehicle on recon, he had tried to cover up his mistake. Officers, especially cavalry officers, who thought that it was permissible to submit false or inaccurate reports in combat could not be tolerated. Too many lives rode on the decisions that were made based on what the cavalry reported. Besides, after the verbal beating and public humiliation the troop commander had received on the open-air radio net, Dixon knew the troop commander's confidence would be broken beyond repair. So, to the five scouts who everyone was now assuming were out there somewhere killed or wounded, Dixon added a sixth casualty, the troop commander, who would become a psychological casualty, probably for life.

In the current operations van, located in the division main command post, Cerro turned the FM radio frequency from the cavalry squadron command net back to the alternate division command net. Like Dixon, he had been listening to the squadron commander, eavesdropping as they called it. Like Dixon, he was depressed after listening to the conversation, but not for the same reasons. The A Troop commander, Cerro felt, had been incredibly stupid. Relief, Cerro felt, would be too good. For what the commander had done, anything less than public castration would be too light a punishment. The thought of sending a lone scout out into hostile territory was, doctrinally as well as in terms of common sense, nothing less than criminal.

No, it was not the fate of the scouts or their troop commander that concerned Cerro. It was the death of innocence that depressed him. Right up to H-Hour, just before the Mexicans dropped the bridges into the Rio Grande, there had been division staff officers who had believed that the Mexicans, knowing full well that it would be futile to resist any American military initiative, would do nothing. After all, as the division G2 pointed out, in 1916, when Pershing chased Pancho Villa into Mexico with three U.S. Army brigades, the Mexican Army had done nothing other than put on a show of force. This attitude, with reports from J-Stars and long-range ground recon teams, which had reported that major Mexican units had already withdrawn south, had encouraged the feeling that this exercise would be a piece of cake. The G3 plans officer, a major of great intellect, had thought that the division would push south to Monterrey unopposed, occupying and patrolling its assigned sector while the two governments negotiated. When all the media hype had died down, which he estimated would take no more than six weeks, and both sides could reach agreement without losing face, he had predicted, U.S. forces would declare the operation a success, disengage, and withdraw north.

The shedding of blood, on both sides, however, made such a scenario unlikely. As the sinking of the HMS *Sheffield* and the Argentine cruiser *General Belgrano* during the Falklands War had demonstrated, once blood has been shed and the resulting national passions unleashed, talk of logic and common sense is drowned out by the cries for revenge and victory to justify the sacrifice. Blood, once spilled in the name of God and country, could only be satisfied with more blood. That the Mexicans would have allowed the Americans to enter their country unopposed had, in Cerro's mind, been a foolish notion to begin with. All that remained to be seen, at this point, was how much Mexican pride was worth, how much the American government was willing to sacrifice to support an ill-chosen policy, and how much of a sacrifice the American public would tolerate once it found out that there could never be a clean, decisive victory.

Standing up, Cerro looked about the van. Such thoughts were, at times, mind-boggling, especially for a not-so-young-anymore infantry captain. Turning to the operations NCO, he asked what was for lunch. Reaching down into a box of MREs under his desk, the sergeant grabbed a brown plastic sack, pulled it out, and read the label.

"Gee, sir. You're in luck." Tossing the plastic sack to Cerro, he waited until Cerro had caught it before he announced, with a great flourish, "And the captain gets, ta-da, pork patties."

Making a face, Cerro looked at the black lettering on the pouch to confirm the sergeant's verdict. Then he turned to the other people in the van and said, "Well, it's a dirty job, but someone's got to eat 'em." With that, he pivoted and left the van in search of a quiet, shady spot where he could choke down his lunch unmolested by the thoughts and noise of war.

19

The true chief is one who knows how to ally firmness with wisdom, professional knowledge with resolution in action, the art of the organizer with that of the executioner. It is thus that he wins confidence.

—Marshal Philippe Pétain

MEXICO CITY, MEXICO
0900 HOURS, 11 SEPTEMBER

Little had surprised Jan Fields as much as Colonel Guajardo's request to see her, without the rest of the camera crew, before she departed Mexico City. Though she could think of a dozen excuses for not going, as well as a dozen good reasons to accept the invitation, it was the manner in which the colonel had made the request that convinced her to go. Less than an hour after she had informed the Ministry of Information that she and her crew would be departing Mexico, an Army major had appeared at Jan's hotel room. Handing her a small envelope, he informed her that he had been instructed personally by the minister of defense to wait for an answer regardless of how long that took.

The envelope contained a simple piece of yellow paper, the kind used to take phone messages. Written in beautiful, flowing handwriting, the message was simple and to the point:

Señorita Fields,

I request the honor of your presence at breakfast at eight thirty A.M. tomorrow. It would mean a great deal to me to be afforded an opportunity to bid you farewell, in private.

Your respectful servant,
Guajardo

When to her own surprise, and later to the surprise of the crew, she had told the major she would go, the major had informed her that he would come by the following morning to pick her up and escort her to the Ministry of Defense. When Joe Bob found out what she had done, he did his damnedest to talk her out of it. "Jesus Christ, Jan. What possible good could seeing Darth Vader alone do? In case you haven't heard, our countries are at war and he, by the way and as a matter of fact, just happens to be the numero uno head military spick. Jesus, I don't know what gets into you sometimes."

Jan, however, didn't pay Joe Bob any attention. She had committed herself and she intended to go. If nothing else, she was a gambler and an opportunist, and this, in Jan's book, was an opportunity, handed to her on a silver platter.

The breakfast was a light affair in Guajardo's formal office. Rolls, fruit, coffee, and juice. As they ate, making small talk between bites, Jan noted that Guajardo seemed both well rested and at ease, not at all what she had expected of a man whose country was under attack by the United States. There were no signs of loss of sleep or nervousness. He seemed, as he always seemed to her, in control of himself, calm and confident. In a way, that worried her. If he, as Joe Bob put it, "the numero uno head military spick," showed no signs of concern despite the fact that an American army was barreling down on top of him, then perhaps all the talk by Pentagon officials that this would be a quick and easy operation might be ill-founded. As she talked to him, she watched his eyes, eyes which—like those of her lover, Scott Dixon—she knew looked out upon the world from the mind of a professional killer, betraying no secrets or emotions.

When the food trays had been cleared away, Jan and the colonel moved to two large overstuffed chairs where they finished their coffee. Guajardo began by explaining that he could not allow Jan to leave Mexico City without expressing his personal gratitude, and that of the president of Mexico, for the fair and objective manner in which she had treated the June 29 revolution and the Council of 13. Since he had to be in Mexico City for an important meeting of the council the previous day, Guajardo explained, he had decided to do so in person. "Few of your fellow correspondents," he explained, "have taken the time to look beyond the sanguine events of the day and gain an appreciation for the issues that made those events necessary. In your own way, Señorita Fields, you have shown that it is possible to bridge the cultural gaps that separate our great nations and see our side of the story."

More accustomed to critics, Jan was, for a moment, speechless. The sincerity of the compliment, given at such a time, by a man who had much to do, struck a chord in her heart. Here, she thought, was a man of great passions and thought. A man who, despite his heavy duties, felt the need to take the time to personally thank her for something she would have done anyway. For the longest time, she struggled in an effort to come up with a response that was appropriate. In the end, she could not. The best that she managed was a simple thank you, whispered in tones that told Guajardo her words were heavy with emotion.

For a moment, there was an awkward silence, the kind of silence that fills a room when great passions are alive and where there are a man and a woman, alone. Clearing his throat, Guajardo offered Jan another cup of coffee. Though she didn't want one, she accepted his offer. Freed from the silence by action, Guajardo leaped from his seat and walked to where the coffeepot sat, and back to Jan's chair. As he poured for her, he turned to the next matter at hand.

"You realize, Señorita Fields, that you are the only American who has availed herself of the opportunity to talk to each and every member of the council since the twenty-ninth of June?"

Jan hadn't thought of that. In a way, the idea appealed to her. She could use that angle. Then, in the next instant, what he had just told her hit her like a slap in the face. Her country, her beloved America, which at that moment was in the process of invading his country, had not taken the time to sit down and talk to the people who were its declared enemies. How could that be? Looking up as Guajardo resumed his seat across from her, she pointed out that she knew that the American secretary of state had met with Foreign Minister Barreda on three different occasions and that a special White House envoy had been to see Colonel Molina, the president of the council, twice.

Guajardo chuckled, leaning back into his seat. "You did not listen to what I said, señorita. I said, talk to us. Your representatives did not talk to us. They lectured us, they threatened us, they even tried to dictate to us. But talk, as you and I have, never. Not in July. Not in August. Not ever. A meaningful dialogue cannot be established between men when one enters the room with an arrogance nurtured by an assumed superiority that his culture and position encourages. Though each of your nation's representatives was an educated man, each thought—correction, knew—he was right and we were wrong. Every representative that your president sent could never overcome the idea that the person he was talking to, my brothers, were poor, misguided soldiers, untutored in the skills of politics and diplomacy. In the same way that Lyndon Johnson viewed Ho Chi Minh as a peasant and terrorist and based his policies accordingly, your representatives see us as petty dictators and buffoons.''

Guajardo paused. He realized that his tone had turned bitter and harsh. He could see it in Jan's face. Grasping the arms of his chair, he looked up at the ceiling, taking deep breaths in an effort to compose himself before he continued. Ready, he looked back at Jan, who sat wide-eyed and waiting.

"Forgive me, Señorita Fields. But these are very trying times. I did not mean to frighten you or take my frustrations out on you. I am afraid that your pleasant visit has been ruined by my lack of self-control.''

Jan shook her head and shrugged, telling him that it was no problem, that she understood.

"Señorita Fields, I would like you to do one more thing for me, a personal favor, if you would?''

Jan told him she would, anything.

"Your CIA, no doubt, knows you are here this morning. I made no effort to keep it a secret. They, the CIA, will, no doubt, contact you. When they do, tell them you have a message from the president of Mexico, a personal message that is for the ears of the American president only.''

Jan blinked. God, she thought to herself. Joe Bob was right. She should have stayed away. Now she was becoming involved in secret messages, the CIA, and God knew what else. Still, she simply nodded and said she would do her best. What else could she do? To start with, she was, she realized, at that moment the original captive audience. The image of Princess Leia telling Darth Vader to piss off popped in and out of her mind in a flash.

As real as that thought was, accompanied by an uncomfortable feeling of vulnerability, it was not the deciding factor that made her accept Guajardo's "request.'' The idea of being offered an opportunity to do something real, something tangible to end this war, was very compelling to Jan. It was more than a sense of duty to God and country, though that was present. Instead, she was being offered the chance to do something that would take Scott out of harm's way, to do something to protect the man she loved from the dangers he so willingly thrust himself into. That alone was justification to deliver Guajardo's message.

"Tell your president about us. Tell him what you think of us. Use your words to create in his mind an image of each of us, as people, not as members of the enemy government. Then tell him what you saw, and what you think of us, of Mexico, and what we are doing. If you have gotten this far, and he is still listening, then give him this message. We do not want trouble with the United States. Our futures, like our histories, are interwoven. One cannot exist without the other. We are, in many ways, the same. We are both, in our own eyes, great people, with a pride in our heritage and dreams for a better future. All we ask for is an opportunity to work for that future, in peace, as we see fit. We are asking for nothing that we do not already have, except peace and respect. And tell him, Señorita Fields, if he cannot see fit to grant us peace, then tell him we have no choice but to fight for that respect on the field of battle, a field of his choosing.''

5 KILOMETERS WEST OF SABINAS HIDALGO, MEXICO
1830 HOURS, 11 SEPTEMBER

Arriving late in the afternoon by helicopter, Guajardo prepared himself for the first major confrontation between his forces and the Americans. Noting the time on a wall clock, he knew it would be dark soon, time for his soldiers, like the predators of the desert, to begin to stir.

From a command/observation post hidden near an old mining operation, Guajardo could observe American units moving into positions. Though he was interested in what units they were and where they were, he also knew that, like his own, they would reshuffle themselves under the cover of darkness. Much of what the Americans were allowing him to see was for his benefit, a deception. Like a poker player, the American commander was holding his good cards close to his chest until it was time to play them.

Not that it would make any difference. What the American commander in this sector did in the next few hours, and during the upcoming battle, would not cause Guajardo to change his own plans for the defense of Monterrey. After having exercised great caution, with a few exceptions, in their advance south, the American 16th Armored Division had paused, closing up its combat power north and northeast of Monterrey. With one brigade concentrated north of Monterrey around Lampazos, another south of Vallecillo, and the third, to the south of Agualeguas, the 16th Armored Division was positioned for a move on Monterrey.

The distance between American brigades told Guajardo that the commander of the 16th Armored Division was not concerned about a counterattack by Mexican forces. Had he been, he would have kept his brigades closer together, deployed so that they could provide mutual support. Superior communications, as well as numerous aviation units capable of patrolling the gaps between the brigades, provided the Americans the ability to disperse their combat power and threaten Monterrey from three directions. Any offensive action against one of the dispersed American brigades by a mechanized unit larger than a company would be easily detected and parried by ground attack aircraft and attack helicopters well before the Mexican force could close with American ground units.

Guajardo, however, had no intention of throwing his valuable mechanized units away in a futile counterattack, at least not yet. He, like the American commander, used deception. Like a poker player with few blue chips, he did not want to throw them away early in the game. So, from the beginning, Guajardo was prepared to cede this hand, the battle of Monterrey, to the Americans. It was, after all, theirs for the taking.

But while he had no intention of playing any blue chips in the defense of Monterrey, neither was he ready to give the hand away cheaply. Though he could not beat the Americans here, he could bleed them a little, perhaps make them a little cautious. In the course of the play, if Guajardo was attentive enough, he might even be given an opportunity to cause real damage to the Americans. Such opportunities, Guajardo knew, had to be made. So Guajardo prepared his units to play the opening game for Monterrey.

With that thought in mind, he deployed his forces. Two battalions of infantry, both militia units, were deployed to the north in and around the city of Villaldamo. There, they would be able to delay an attack coming down the valley from the north by the American brigade located at Lampazos. In the Mamulique Pass, two infantry battalions, one militia and one regular army, reinforced with an antitank company, covered the direct route from Laredo, to the northeast, into Monterrey. To the northeast of Monterrey lay the Sierra Picachos, with the Mamulique Pass in the west and open flatlands to the east and southeast. In that area, centered on a town named Nuevo Repueblo, a small regular army brigade with one infantry battalion, one mechanized infantry battalion, one militia battalion, two batteries of artillery, and a mechanized cavalry troop were deployed to defend against a sweep south of the Sierra Picachos. It was here, in the east, that Guajardo expected the American 16th Division to make its main effort. A move from Lampazos would force the Americans to advance down a long, narrow valley, dotted with many villages and towns. An attack through the Mamulique Pass would force the Americans to fight on ground favorable to the defender. Only in the south, around

Nuevo Repueblo, was the ground favorable for wide, sweeping maneuvers by mechanized forces. The American commander had, to date, used every advantage he had to avoid direct assaults on positions that could easily be defended. Guajardo did not expect him to change.

For that reason, he stationed the only powerful force he intended to sacrifice in the defense of Monterrey, a battalion of Nicaraguan T-72 tanks, south of the city in the town of Marin. From there, the Nicaraguan tanks could move to the north to hit an American force coming south out of Mamulique Pass, or east to hit an American force moving through Nuevo Repueblo. These tanks had been moved from Nicaragua under great secrecy. Every trick had been used. The thirty tanks that composed the battalion had been moved at night, along the most roundabout routes, individually. It had been a great effort, too great an effort in the opinion of some, especially since even Guajardo expected American attack helicopters to make short work of this force. Still, it was not their added combat power that Guajardo counted on. It was the mere appearance of Nicaraguan tanks, especially T-72s, this close to the United States and so early in the campaign, and the resulting shock that such an appearance would generate, that Guajardo aimed to achieve.

Not everyone agreed with the use of the Nicaraguans this early in the fight. Guajardo's decision to deploy them was opposed by some of the Council of 13, a body of men that was becoming more and more divided. A few felt that by using the Nicaraguans, they would be forcing the Americans to broaden the conflict. The threat of an invasion of southern Mexico, or a bombing campaign throughout Mexico, to isolate the country from the rest of Latin America frightened some of the council. It would not be wise, they warned, to anger the Americans in this way. Others insisted that the initial part of the conflict should be an all-Mexican affair, keeping other national forces out of the fighting. It would not do, they insisted, to give their rivals to the south the impression that Mexico could not fight its own battles.

Both Guajardo and Barreda, however, agreed that it would be a good thing to let the Nicaraguans bleed a little. While it was true that such an action would broaden the conflict, the same action would also serve as a warning to the Americans, showing that the war could be broadened beyond their control. The Americans had, after all, come to Mexico in search of security, not to start an intrahemisphere conflict. Furthermore, if the council involved its allies early, and let some of their blood be shed, those allies would be more committed. So long as the other Latin American countries were left out of the actual shooting, it would be easy for them to change their minds and withdraw their forces and support. Once

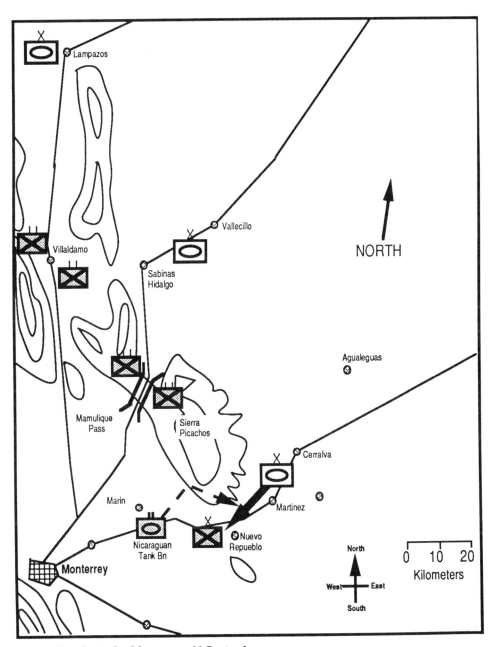

Map 8: The Battle for Monterrey, 11 September

bloodied, however, they could not do so without losing face in the eyes of their own countrymen and the other Latin American nations. Blood, Barreda pointed out, would bind them together.

In private, Guajardo confessed to one more reason for committing the Nicaraguans. He knew that he could not win the battle of Monterrey. He knew that the fight would be quick and bloody. A defeat involving only Mexican forces would be an embarrassment and would leave the ability of the Mexican Army open to question. By involving the vaunted Nicaraguan Army, and allowing them to share the defeat, Guajardo could humble some of the Sandinista officers who were trying to tell him how to do things, and show them, and the other allies, that American technology and combat power were not to be taken lightly.

With his plans set and dispositions completed, Guajardo's role in the upcoming battle would be simple. He had only two decisions to make, and two orders to issue. The first involved where and when to commit the Nicaraguan tanks into battle. Once he knew where the main American effort was, he would make that decision and issue the appropriate code word to launch that counterattack. The second decision would be when to break off the battle. That decision would be made when, in Guajardo's opinion, his forces had done all they could do and further sacrifice would be pointless. When that point was reached, he would have the code word transmitted that would allow his subordinate commanders to break contact with the Americans. Withdrawing to new positions south and west of Monterrey, they would regroup and wait as the initiative moved back into the hands of the politicians and diplomats.

12 KILOMETERS SOUTHWEST OF VALLECILLO, MEXICO
1840 HOURS, 11 SEPTEMBER

With nothing to do before the lead units of the division crossed their lines of departure, and too keyed up to sleep, Big Al and Dixon sat in the G3 Plans van in the division main CP and rehashed how they saw the battle developing the next morning. Of the three options available to the division, Dixon still favored punching through the Mamulique Pass with the main effort. It had, he pointed out, the advantage of being the least likely choice while being the most direct into Monterrey. Eventually, since the hills on both sides of the pass needed to be cleared anyway, an assault on the pass would be necessary. The division, Dixon claimed, had more than enough direct and indirect firepower to suppress the defenders in the pass while dismounted infantry were airlifted to the flanks and rear of the defenders to isolate them. Once in control of the high ground, the dismounted infantry would be free to rout out those defenders still wanting to resist.

It was not that Dixon lacked imagination or was, by nature, bloody-minded. It was important, he pointed out to Big Al, and anyone who would listen, to demonstrate early in this war the effectiveness of American firepower, the damage it could inflict, and the American resolve to use it. In a set-piece battle, such as Dixon was advocating, all the weight of the division could be brought to bear on a single point. The slaughter of the defenders, which would be great, could not be ignored. Besides, by taking the best-defended and most difficult position, the division would be making it clear to the leadership of the Mexican Army, in a less than subtle manner, that no position, regardless of how well defended, could be held. The technique of attacking into the teeth of apparent strength was often used by the Opposing Force Brigade at the National Training Center at Fort Irwin in order to shake the confidence of units training there. Dixon, having been on the receiving end of one of those attacks, understood the psychological value of such an action.

Big Al, however, was a maneuver man, a soldier who preferred to use the tracks of his tanks rather than their guns to achieve victory. The end run south of the Sierra Picachos, where the ground was more open and therefore more conducive to maneuver by mechanized forces, appealed to him. The Mexican defenders, notoriously weak in mechanized forces and totally lacking modern antiarmor weapons, would be quickly overwhelmed by a mounted attack. Besides, Big Al's preference just happened to coincide with the general order from the Department of the Army that major confrontations that would result in high casualties and protracted combat be avoided, when possible. That order, coupled with a restriction on both Air Force and Army aviation that limited it to no more than fifty kilometers from the forward edge of friendly forces, bothered Dixon. It was as if, Dixon quipped, they were being ordered to kill the Mexicans only a little. Though Big Al agreed that it was ludicrous to establish such limitations now that they were engaged in a shooting war, he, as the commander, had no choice but to comply.

With the time for debating and decision-making over, and the success or failure of the next day's operations in the hands of the captains and lieutenants, Big Al and Dixon compared Zachary Taylor's campaign of 1846 with their own. Their one lament was the amount of control people outside the theater of operations exerted on their current operations. Had Taylor been burdened with the communications that the current president had at his disposal, Dixon pointed out, the 16th Armored Division would be preparing to seize Kansas City, not Monterrey.

5 KILOMETERS NORTHEAST OF MARTÍNEZ, MEXICO
0050 HOURS, 12 SEPTEMBER

The promise of action in ten minutes, after a sudden and unexpected road march, no longer thrilled Second Lieutenant Nancy Kozak. In part, this was due to the road march that had taken the 2nd of the 13th Infantry from the division reserve at Vallecillo to their current location behind the 3rd Brigade. Moving all night, the 2nd of the 13th had arrived in its new assembly areas just as the sun crested the horizon to the east. Rather than being thrown into the growing battle around Nuevo Repueblo, as the battalion commander had expected, the 2nd of the 13th had been placed in reserve again. The situation that had existed when the 2nd of the 13th began its move had completely changed. Instead of achieving a break-through, as the 3rd Brigade commander had expected to do when 2nd of the 13th was released to his command, he had encountered unexpected resistance on the part of the Mexicans which had changed the entire picture by the time 2nd of the 13th arrived in the 3rd Brigade's area.

At an update held by Captain Wittworth after he returned from the battalion CP, Nancy Kozak found out that, rather than giving ground without a fight, the Mexicans facing the 3rd Brigade's sweep south of the Sierra Picachos mountains had merely moved to other positions under cover of darkness. The lead elements of the 3rd Brigade's attack, finding that those Mexican positions that had been occupied earlier were vacant, had assumed the Mexicans had withdrawn. Ordered to switch from con-ducting a deliberate attack to a headlong pursuit in an effort to catch the fleeing enemy, the two lead battalions of the 3rd Brigade had been in the process of changing formations, on the move, when they made contact with the actual Mexican fighting positions. The resulting combination of surprise, stiff enemy resistance, and the change of formations during a night battle resulted in confusion that stalled, then halted, the 3rd Bri-gade's advance. Rather than continue thrashing about in the dark, and risk fratricide, the commander of the 3rd Brigade had ordered all units to break contact and assume hasty defensive positions. The attack, Witt-worth told his platoon leaders, would begin again, after dawn, using only those elements that were currently in contact. Until such times as the situation was fully developed, the 2nd of the 13th would remain, as it had been since the beginning of the invasion of Mexico, in reserve.

For Kozak, this was not all bad. The reason she accepted the role of being in reserve, again, was a feeling that things in her platoon were not right. Despite the fact that she could not quite put her finger on exactly what those things were, she did not feel comfortable with the way her people had been acting the past few days. Though she was mentally ready for combat, she wasn't sure that her platoon in general, and her platoon sergeant, Sergeant First Class Rivera, were ready. Since entering Mexico, the attitudes of both had changed, and she wasn't sure if the two changes were related.

When she had mentioned her observation to Staff Sergeant Maupin the day before, he had admitted, in an unusually candid conversation, that he hoped that they would be allowed to do something worthwhile, which, to Maupin, translated to being committed to combat. He went on to explain that the prospect of getting mauled or killed didn't thrill him or anyone in his squad. While everyone in his squad wanted to go back north, meaning back to the United States, they wanted to do it under their own power. It was just that the idea of going through the entire operation with all the discomforts, fears, and stress that go with an active campaign in the field, not to mention family separation, without having an opportunity to shoot someone, was, in his words, ''shitty.''

That her men felt that way was a revelation to young Lieutenant Kozak. That she felt the same way was a shock. She kept telling herself that this was not, after all, a video game. That the next time she put the sights of her Bradley onto a target, it would be a live target, manned by real people. Still, the idea of going into battle, and the thought that she was finally going to be given an opportunity to prove to herself and everyone else that she had ''the right stuff,'' fascinated her like nothing else ever had. That real people would have to die in order to satisfy this urge seemed unimportant, a remote consideration at best.

As difficult as this was to deal with, Rivera's strange conduct was more difficult. Though Captain Wittworth had discussed the possibility that some of the soldiers of Hispanic origin might be reluctant to engage in combat, Kozak had never imagined that her platoon sergeant, the cornerstone of the platoon, would have second thoughts. That he did was becoming more apparent every day. Instead of the dynamic, hard-driving NCO he had been back at Fort Hood, Rivera had, since the border incident on September 7, kept to himself. Though he performed his assigned duties, he did so in an impersonal and mechanical manner, almost by rote. Even the soldiers, used to being jumped on by Rivera for the smallest infraction, began to mumble, loud enough that Kozak could hear, that Rivera had gone off the deep end.

Though something needed to be done, and done soon, Kozak didn't quite know how to approach the matter. On the single occasion when she tried mentioning that she had noticed a change in his attitude, he had all but snapped at her, asking her to enumerate exactly what he was doing wrong. When she responded that he wasn't doing anything really wrong, Rivera had surprised her by telling her that if she wasn't happy with him, then she should relieve him and find someone who suited her. Frustrated by the direct approach, Kozak had mentioned the conversation and her concerns to the company first sergeant. He hadn't proved to be much help. With a simple shrug, the first sergeant told Kozak not to worry. Everyone, he said, got a little funny in a war. The first sergeant assured her that, when the shooting started, the old Sergeant Rivera would pop out, as if by magic, and everything would be back on track. Though the first sergeant's words did little to allay her concerns, she dropped the subject. Maybe, she thought, he was right. He was, after all, a first sergeant and a combat veteran. Surely he, if anyone, knew what he was talking about.

Looking at her watch, then at those vehicles that she could see, Kozak decided there was little more to be done. All was, as far as she could tell, ready. Bringing her hands up to her face, she carefully rubbed the sides of her nose with her index fingers. Damn, she thought, as a flash of pain ran through her body. When will this damned nose stop hurting?

While Second Lieutenant Nancy Kozak made every effort to sort out the problems within her platoon, her peers in the two lead battalions of the 3rd Brigade had more immediate concerns to deal with. After shifting through all information available concerning the location of Mexican positions, including reports based on a hasty recon by division air cavalry scouts, the commander of the 3rd Brigade ordered the lead battalions to conduct a movement to contact commencing at 0600 hours. It was his intent, stated in a verbal order issued to his battalion commanders at 0400 hours, to find and fix the enemy. Once the brigade and battalion commanders had a firm grasp of where the enemy main positions were, they would pile on with everything he could get his hands on. Without realizing it, the commander of the 3rd Brigade had lost sight of the division commander's concept, moving away from an operation based on maneuver and gravitating toward one based on the direct approach and use of overwhelming firepower. It was an approach to war that was more familiar to American soldiers and resembled Dixon's original approach.

Though all this was, to the brigade and battalion commanders, important, it didn't matter what approach they used if the young captains and lieutenants in command of tank and mechanized platoons couldn't get their people motivated and moving. Even a professional soldier gets tired. No amount of battle drill, no amount of physical training, no amount of benefits, real or imagined, could change the fact that a human body and mind can only go so long without sleep, real sleep, before it up and quits. The soldiers of the 3rd Brigade were fast approaching that point.

On the previous day, in order to deceive the Mexicans, the brigade had been shifted to an assembly area twenty kilometers east of Nuevo Repueblo. Only after darkness on the night of 11 September had the brigade been moved to its actual attack positions. That movement had been orchestrated in such a manner that, just as the last unit was closing on the attack position, the lead elements of the brigade were crossing the line of departure and going into the attack. Timed to commence at 2200 hours, or ten P.M., the attack had appeared to go well at first. Initial contact, made at 2215 hours, had been light and along the line where the brigade had expected to find the enemy. When, by 2235 hours, contact had been broken and initial reports were stating that the lead units were overrunning many abandoned positions, the brigade commander had ordered the lead units to shift from a deliberate attack into a pursuit.

It was at this point, while the lead battalions were changing from being dispersed for an attack into the tighter formations used in a pursuit, that contact with the main Mexican positions, positions that had not been identified by earlier reconnaissance, had been made. As these were initially believed to be delaying positions, used to cover the withdrawal of the main body of troops, preparation for the pursuit had continued. It was not until sometime after 2300 hours, probably 2320, that the truth had become known. By then, companies lined up in columns of platoons, with artillery units limbered up and closed up on top of them, had been decisively engaged in close combat.

In several places, company commanders reacted by redeploying their units and conducting hasty attacks on the fly. Some of these attacks succeeded, allowing the company commander to press on to the southwest toward his distant objective. Other attacks failed, with the company thrown back onto itself. A few company commanders, unable to assess what was going on, simply stopped where they were, coiled their units up into a tight defensive posture, and waited for orders. Within minutes, effective command and control at battalion level and above ceased to exist.

Confusion was not limited to the battalion and brigade commanders alone. Command and control also ceased to exist within some companies. A failed night attack, at its best, bears a striking resemblance to a nightmare. Burning tracks, both tanks and Bradleys, cast an eerie illumination over the area where the attack had taken place, an area still dominated by fire from enemy positions and artillery that the attack had failed to destroy. Into this area medics and recover teams, under the control of the company first sergeant, must move to save the wounded and retrieve damaged vehicles. Sometimes these people, in the process, also become casualties.

While all this is going on, the company commander, if he has survived, is trying to rally the survivors of the attack, count noses to find out who he still has, figure out what happened so that he can submit a timely and accurate report to his battalion commander, and reorganize his unit. This entire effort usually is complicated by the fact that sometimes leaders, including the company commander, are among the casualties that the first sergeant is trying to recover. When that happens, platoon sergeants—or if they are also gone, squad leaders—must step forward and assume the duties of platoon leader, doing things they have never trained for, under the worst possible circumstances.

A failed attack almost always appears worse than it actually is. It takes time, however, to sort that out. And even when a unit is finally reorganized and recovered, the psychological impact of the failure, coupled with the exhaustion from the physical exertion, stress of combat, and trauma of a confused night battle, is usually enough to make the unit combat-ineffective for hours. It is at this time, in the midst of a seemingly impossible situation, that the young officers who lead the companies and platoons earn their pay. For inevitably, from out of the darkness, through the use of the magic we call radio, the voice of some unseen staff officer comes to the young captain or lieutenant, giving him new orders, orders that will require his unit to expose itself again to the horrors it has just survived.

It is at this moment, in the brief span of time that separates the commander's acceptance of his new orders and the issuance of his own orders to his own unit, that many young combat leaders experience a loneliness and despair that knows no bounds. Exhausted himself, the company commander must find, from the depth of his own soul, not only the courage and fortitude to propel himself forward again into combat, but enough to motivate almost one hundred men to follow him as he does so. Some call this courage. Others, simply a commander's duty. Regardless of what it is called, it is hard, and some people simply cannot do it.

By midnight, the entire 3rd Brigade was in disarray. Some companies were pressing on, unchecked, toward Monterrey. Other companies that had initiated hasty attacks and failed were scattered about and in the process of recovering. As the chances of units becoming isolated, or firing on other friendly units in the confusion of the night, became more and more likely, the brigade commander had to face the fact that his brigade was falling apart. Once he accepted this reality, and being unwilling to expose his units to unnecessary risks, it was easy for the brigade commander to issue the order shortly after midnight to break contact, assume hasty defensive positions, and be prepared to conduct a movement to contact at 0600 hours.

In those six hours, there was no time for battalion commanders, their staffs, company commanders, and platoon leaders to rest. Instead, they scurried about the battlefield, assessing the status of their units and their personnel, arranging for and supervising the rearming and refueling process, and receiving and issuing new orders for the next operation. All of this, done under the cover of darkness, after a failed attack, took its toll on what little mental and physical strength those leaders had. The commander of the 3rd Brigade, himself feeling the effects of the long, hard night, knew that his unit had only a few good hours left before it could go no further. Hence, the need for the division reserve battalion. In a three-way conversation with the division commander and the division G3, the 3rd Brigade commander explained that he intended to punch through whatever Mexican positions he encountered with his own battalions. Once he was sure they had cleared the main defensive belt, he intended to commit the division reserve, pushing the 2nd of the 13th Infantry through the gap created by his lead battalions and toward Monterrey.

Though Big Al did not like the idea of plowing head-on into the Mexican defenses, he was under the mistaken impression that the 3rd Brigade was too heavily committed to break contact and maneuver, an impression created by the reports submitted by the 3rd Brigade staff. Dixon, seeing the situation in the same light as the 3rd Brigade commander, had come up with the same solution. Dixon therefore endorsed the option selected by the 3rd Brigade commander. Trusting in the judgment of the commander on the scene, and himself suffering from lack of sleep and nervous tension, Big Al approved the plan that would throw Second Lieutenant Kozak's platoon, ready or not, into the heat of battle.

20

Our hatred knows no bounds, and the war shall be to the death.

—Simon Bolívar

The movement of Kozak's platoon through the gap created by the 3rd Brigade was a sobering experience. The first vehicles they encountered were ambulances, both tracked and wheeled, rushing past them with the wounded. Next came the battlefield itself. The axis of attack that the 3rd Brigade had followed was dotted with shattered and burning vehicles. Here and there, neatly laid out beside the abandoned combat vehicles, were body bags, filled with the remains of crewmen who had died in their vehicles.

The column that Kozak's platoon was in was slowed by combat engineers, who directed the lead elements of 2nd of the 13th toward marked lanes through minefields. Slowed almost to a crawl, Kozak had more time to inspect the point where elements of the 3rd Brigade had made contact with the Mexican forces. As they neared the Mexican positions, the number of American vehicles destroyed and damaged increased, belying the reports by the battalion intelligence officer that the Mexicans had few antitank weapons. Some of the vehicles burned furiously, throwing off great billowing clouds of black smoke. Others, their guns aimed into the vastness of space, just sat there, abandoned and forlorn. The only motion on these vehicles came from the flapping of green, yellow, and red flags, left on the stricken vehicles by surviving crewmen to help harried recover teams determine the nature of their problem and know whether or not wounded were on board.

Kozak, watching a recovery vehicle hook up to a damaged Bradley, didn't notice the Mexican defensive works until her own Bradley hit a sudden bump. Looking down to see what they had run over, her eyes fell on a length of trench, its floor covered with bodies. Before she could react, the forward motion of the Bradley took that image away, replacing it with that of an American aid vehicle parked just beyond the trench. The aid vehicle was surrounded by wounded soldiers, American and Mexican, some lying on stretchers or ponchos, most on the bare ground. On one side of the vehicle, she could see teams of medics working on several of the wounded in a frantic effort to save lives while other wounded men, with lighter injuries, watched and waited their turns. On the other side of the aid vehicle, a lone chaplain, the purple vestment about his neck in stark contrast to the brown and tan camouflage uniform, knelt before a motionless figure, administering last rites. This figure belonged to another group, one in which those too badly wounded to help were put to wait until those who could be helped were, or until they died.

To actually see triage, the separation of the wounded into three groups, in practice, hit Kozak hard. Unable to watch, she turned away, scanning the horizon. This brought her no relief, though, for the horizon was dotted with more burning vehicles, more aid stations, and more trenches littered with dead. This was the face of battle, a face that had, until then, been to her only an imagined notion. Now, and for the rest of her life, it would be very real.

After her Bradley was clear of the marked lane, a soldier Kozak recognized as Wittworth's driver flagged her down. Ordering her driver, Specialist Freedman, to stop, Kozak took her crewman's helmet off and leaned over to hear what Wittworth's driver wanted. Pointing to a cluster of three Bradleys to the right, he shouted above the rumbling of the Bradley's engine that the CO was over there, about to issue a frag, or abbreviated order. Giving Wittworth's driver a thumbs-up to indicate that she understood, Kozak put her crewman's helmet on and radioed Sergeant Rivera that she was going over to the CO's track to receive a frag order, and that he was in charge until she got back. In her haste, she took her helmet off before Rivera could ask where she wanted him to park the platoon. When he received no response from Kozak, he looked toward her track. By then, Kozak was on the ground, trotting over to the CO's track with that distinctive and female walk that Rivera now associated with his platoon leader. Mumbling a curse to himself, Rivera looked for a vacant spot to take the platoon that was as far as he could get from the stench of death and from the 3rd Brigade units still eliminating pockets of resistance.

                    *   *   *

As soon as Kozak joined the circle of lieutenants gathered about Wittworth, he looked at them and asked, "Is that everyone?"

The lieutenants, in turn, looked at each other. It was obvious that he
knew they were all there, he had just looked at them. Why, Kozak
thought, had he asked that? Strange, she thought. Captains can sometimes be really strange.

After his XO responded that they were all present, Wittworth turned
toward the front slope of his Bradley, where his map was laid out. With
a marking pen, he pointed to the symbols and locations he mentioned as
he briefed his lieutenants. "We are currently located here, on the northern edge of Objective Amanda. The rest of the battalion is spread out
south of here. The attack this morning by 3rd Brigade succeeded in
penetrating the enemy's main defensive belt and routing the enemy."

Kozak, taking a quick glance at the devastation, wondered who had
been routed.

"The battalion," Wittworth continued, "after having completed a passage of lines through the 3rd Brigade, will conduct a movement to contact
toward Objective Beth, located just south of this town, named Marin, and
then to Objective Carrie. Deployed in a diamond formation, with Team
Charlie in the lead, Company B on the right . . ."

The sudden *thump-thump-thump* of a Bradley's 25mm cannon firing
less than one hundred meters to their rear caused Kozak to jump. Twirling
around, she saw the Bradley, sitting at one end of a trench, firing its
cannon into the trench. For a moment, Kozak and the other lieutenants,
also caught off guard by the sudden firing, watched as members of the 3rd
Brigade carried out the grisly task of "mopping up" enemy positions that
had been bypassed. The Bradley was firing in support of an M-1A1 tank.
The tank, with a dozer blade attached to its front slope, was in the process
of pushing dirt into the trench, starting at the end farthest from the
Bradley. Taking its time, the M-1 tank would drop its blade and move
forward, pushing a pile of dirt over to the trench where the dirt would
disappear from view as it fell. Backing up, the tank would shift over a
little, closer to the Bradley, and repeat the process. Every now and then,
as the M-1 was in the process of backing up, the Bradley would pump a
few more rounds into that part of the trench that was not yet covered.

Curious as to why someone would waste time and ammunition doing
something like that, Kozak turned to Wittworth and asked. Wittworth
took a deep breath. "Well, I guess the Mexicans in the trench don't want
to surrender."

Kozak's eyes betrayed her shock. She took a quick glance at the trench, just in time to see the tank push another scoop of dirt over the edge. Looking back at Wittworth, she asked if anyone had tried to talk the Mexicans into surrendering. Wittworth chuckled. "I doubt, Lieutenant Kozak, if anyone in the 3rd Brigade was in the mood to try. It's a general rule of thumb that the longer you defend, the less likely it is that the attacker will be in a mood to accept your surrender. Besides, they're only Mexicans."

After one more long look at the trench, Kozak turned her back to the scene. But she couldn't turn her mind away from it. The laboring of the tank's engine as it pushed more dirt into the trench, and the occasional *thump-thump-thump* of the Bradley's cannon reminded her of what was going on. What do you call men who would rather be buried alive than surrender, she wondered. Were they heroes? Or fools? Was it courage and pride that made them do such a thing? Or was it insanity? In her wildest dreams, she could never imagine anyone in her platoon, even the most gung-ho soldier, sitting in a trench, calmly waiting to be shot or buried. Taking one more fugitive glance over her shoulder at the scene, Kozak decided that, as for herself, she would rather take a 25mm shell in the chest than allow herself to be buried like that.

With her mind awash with images and thoughts of the trench, Kozak missed most of Wittworth's order. Not that it made much difference. Company B was on the right, its normal location with the battalion deployed in a diamond formation. Her platoon, the 2nd, would be the right flank guard, deployed 1,500 meters to the right of the rest of the formation. Though Wittworth warned her that since her platoon would be cutting across a series of dry streambeds, or arroyos, forcing the platoon to go slower than the battalion's main body moving on flatter ground, she didn't appreciate what he was telling her. Instead, Kozak's mind was in the process of grappling with the cold, uncompromising inhumanity of war, an inhumanity that enveloped her like sackcloth.

10 KILOMETERS NORTHWEST OF NUEVO REPUEBLO, MEXICO
0955 HOURS, 12 SEPTEMBER

As more and more American tanks and infantry fighting vehicles came pouring over the trenches of the brigade defending around Nuevo Repueblo, Guajardo knew the end was in sight. So did the colonel who commanded the brigade being overrun by those vehicles. Unable to watch any longer or listen to the cries for help from his subordinates, cries that he could do nothing about, the brigade commander turned away from the observation slit of the bunker and faced Guajardo. With tears running freely down his cheeks and his great chest heaving, the brigade commander struggled to look Guajardo in the eye. Finally, with the greatest of efforts, he blurted out his apology. "Forgive me, Alfredo Guajardo, for I have failed you and the people of Mexico."

Overwhelmed by the passions of the moment, Guajardo stepped forward, embracing the brigade commander with a bear hug. Then, stepping back but still grasping the commander by the shoulders, Guajardo told his fellow officer that there was no shame. He and his men had done magnificently against terrible odds. His men, Guajardo told him, had shown the Americans, and the world, that Mexico would never bow its head for any man or nation. Theirs, he said, was a victory of the spirit and of the heart.

When he had managed to compose the brigade commander, Guajardo ordered him to break off contact and pull back as many of his units as he could. Their task, he told him, was over for now. It was important that those who could do so rally and prepare for the next battle. With renewed confidence and sense of purpose, the brigade commander saluted Guajardo, then turned to his staff and began issuing his own orders.

Guajardo watched for a moment. It had been, he knew, a long and hard fight. All of them, including him, were nearing the limits of their own endurance. While what he and the brigade commander had been exposed to, physically, bore no resemblance to what the common infantryman in the most forward trench had to face, the stress and strain of command coupled with a lack of sleep quickly took its toll, especially on older men. It was time, he knew, to bring the battle to a close. It had been a good fight, far exceeding his wildest expectations. They had repulsed one night attack, fought another nearly to a standstill, and, more important, stood their ground. No, he thought, the Mexican people had been well served. There remained only one more hand to play out in this game.

Satisfied that all was in order again, he turned to his aide. "Contact the Nicaraguan commander. Tell him he may begin his attack toward Nuevo Repueblo. And, Juan, tell him I recommend that he use the northern route, through the arroyos. It is slower, but offers more concealment."

15 KILOMETERS EAST OF MARIN, MEXICO
1110 HOURS, 12 SEPTEMBER

The heat of the sun beating on the Bradley was, for Kozak, almost unbearable. How the soldiers in the rear of the vehicle stood it was beyond her. As a vehicle commander, and the platoon leader to boot, she got to stand up in the open hatch of the Bradley's two-man turret and take advantage of the cooling breeze generated by the Bradley's forward motion. That she was recklessly exposing herself, from the waist up, to enemy fire or bodily injury as she stood in the open hatch, her crewman's helmet cocked back on her head, didn't occur to her at that moment. Even the constant climbing out of and back down into the numerous arroyos they had to cross didn't bother Kozak. All that mattered, at that moment, was that there was a cooling breeze, no matter how slight, and she was able to take advantage of it.

Kozak's enjoyment of the breeze was interrupted by a spot report from Sergeant Maupin, whose Bradley was on the far right side of the platoon wedge formation, that there was a large cloud of dust to the platoon's front right. Looking over in that direction, Kozak saw the dust cloud. For a moment, she wondered what could be making such a large cloud. It was, she knew, definitely dust. But whose? Looking down at her map, she confirmed that no one was supposed to be to the right or front of her platoon. According to Wittworth's order and the graphics he had given her, her platoon was on the right side. Glancing up from her map, she counted her own tracks. All four were there. Next, she looked to her left, down into the flatter lands below. At a distance of fifteen hundred meters, more or less, she could see the other vehicles of Company A. Although they were a little ahead of her, due to the rougher upland terrain her platoon had to fight, everything seemed to be in order there. Turning back to her right, she studied the dust cloud for a moment before making a decision.

Satisfied that the dust wasn't being created by friendly forces, Kozak studied her map again. She decided that whatever was kicking up the dust was in the next arroyo, which was roughly parallel to the one her platoon was in. According to the map, it was a relatively wide one that meandered and twisted as it ran downhill. Narrow at the top, it widened as it reached the open country below. Deciding that it would probably be unwise to take the entire platoon out of the arroyo they were in and expose them to whatever was creating the dust cloud, Kozak ordered the platoon to halt just before it began its assent out of the arroyo. Contacting Rivera, she told him to remain there, with the tracks, while she dismounted, with a radioman, in order to go forward on foot to take a look-see.

Without waiting to receive an acknowledgment from Rivera, Kozak took her crewman's helmet off. Sticking her head down and to the left, she opened the turret compartment door that separated the turret crew compartment from the rest of the Bradley and shouted down into the rear for the radioman to dismount. After she was sure he had heard her, Kozak took her rifle, Kelvar helmet, and web gear, tossing them out of the hatch and onto the top of the turret. Climbing out, she stood up, put her gear on, arranged it, then carefully began to climb down.

In the past, she had jumped from the side of the vehicle onto the ground. Since breaking her nose, she had been more careful, especially since even a slight jarring was enough to send a spasm of pain shooting from her nose, across her face, and throughout her head. Every time that happened, she cursed herself. Of all the stupid, childish injuries she could have gotten. Though she wasn't thrilled about the injury, and how she had gotten it, it did, she thought, have its advantage. Through roundabout means Kozak had found out that, in a matter of days, her nickname in the platoon had been changed from Lieutenant Lips to "the Nose." Though being referred to as "the Nose" didn't do much for her self-image and ego, at least her new nickname was nonsexist.

On the ground, Kozak was greeted by Specialist Billy Bell, her radio telephone operator, or RTO. His uniform was soaked with sweat. Still, there was a smile on Billy Bell's face. "What's up, LT?"

Even the fact that everyone called her LT, short for lieutenant, didn't bother Kozak anymore. In the beginning, the soldiers in the platoon, used to working in an all-male world, had responded with "sir" when talking to her. This had, on several occasions, resulted in blushing and embarrassment, followed by apologies that sometimes were sincere. Though the proper response was "ma'am," the soldiers of 2nd Platoon, somehow, couldn't bring themselves to utter that word. So an unspoken compromise had been reached. The soldiers, from Rivera on down, used LT, and Kozak said nothing. Everyone, she knew, had to make compromises.

Sticking her folded map into the large pocket on her right thigh, she looked at the dust cloud, which appeared to be getting closer, then at Bell. She pointed with her rifle. "We're going to trot on over to the hill and see who's making that dust."

Bell sighed. "Do we have to trot, LT? It's hotter than hell."

Ignoring Bell's glib comment, Kozak turned and began to climb the wall of the arroyo, taking great strides as she did so, and calling back, "Come on, Bell. You could use the exercise."

Looking down at his stomach, then at Kozak, he shook his head. Damn, he thought, as he began to scale the wall of the arroyo behind her. Was she ever going to get off his case about his beer gut? It was only a little one.

Once out of the arroyo, Kozak got her bearings and they began to head for the dust cloud. As they did, neither of them took any great care, standing upright as they jogged toward the crest of the mound that separated the arroyo her platoon was in from the one that the dust appeared to be coming from. Once they reached the crest, Kozak stopped, kneeling as she caught her breath, and surveyed the ground before her. For the first time, she listened. To her front, from the direction of the dust cloud, Kozak could hear the squeaking and popping of tracks being pulled through drive sprockets, mixed in with the low rumble of laboring diesel engines.

Tanks! There were tanks to their front. But whose? The throaty rumble of the engines didn't sound like the whine of an M-1A1's turbine. Though there was the possibility that the terrain, heat, and distance could be distorting the sound, Kozak didn't think they were friendly. Coming up behind her, Bell shouted, "I'm here, LT. Late but . . ."

Turning, she put her right index finger up to her lips, indicating that she wanted him to shut up. Pausing, Bell looked at her, then over toward the dust cloud, listening to the sound of the tank engines. Without any need for more cues from Kozak, he understood what was going on. Crouching next to her, Bell held his rifle at the ready as he watched his platoon leader and waited for her next move.

Kozak knelt there for another second, watching, thinking. She could feel her stomach muscles begin to tighten as her heart rate slowly began to climb. With sweat running down her spine in tiny rivulets, Kozak's body prepared itself for fight or flight while her mind pondered their next move. When she was ready in body and mind, Kozak slowly rose and began to advance, her unblinking eyes glued to the edge of the next arroyo. Bell, without a word, followed, his eyes darting from Kozak's back to the edge of the arroyo and the cloud of dust that was being thrown up from it by the unseen tanks.

When they were within two meters of the edge, Kozak paused, then slowly lowered her body to the ground, crawling on her stomach up to the edge. When Bell saw she was at the edge, he did likewise, coming up on her right. When he reached the edge he looked down just in time to see what looked like the biggest tank in the world pass less than six feet below them. Forgetting their predicament, Bell gasped. "Jesus Christ! What in the fuck are those?"

Kozak, struggling to control herself as she watched the tank pass below them, didn't answer right away. When she was finally able to talk, all she could get out was, "It's a tank." Then, as an afterthought, "A T-72."

Their attention was suddenly drawn away from the tank trundling on down the arroyo below them as another tank materialized out of the cloud of dust created by the tank that had just passed below them. As if from nowhere, it appeared at the lip of the arroyo across from them and a little to their right, at a range of one hundred meters. The new tank, on reaching the edge, slowed almost to a stop as the driver lost sight of the ground to his front. With the tank commander leaning out of his hatch and directing him, the driver inched forward until he could feel the tank teetering on the edge. When he felt that, the driver nudged the accelerator of the tank ever so lightly, giving the tank enough of a kick to push it over the edge and into the bottom of the arroyo. As the tank came over the lip, Kozak noted that, from where she and Bell were, the entire top of the turret and the back deck were exposed for two or three seconds. Once in the arroyo, the tank turned to the right and passed below them, following the first one that was now beginning to disappear in its own dust further down the arroyo.

Although Kozak had no idea who was manning the tanks, or where they came from, she knew that they were not friendly, and worse, that they were headed downhill and straight into the right flank of 2nd of the 13th. Pushing away from the edge of the arroyo, Kozak and Bell moved to where they could sit up. Pulling out her map with one hand, and grabbing the radio mike with the other, Kozak reported her sighting to Rivera in as calm a voice as the situation and her excited state permitted. Knowing that it was only a matter of minutes before the enemy tanks made contact with the rest of the company, and not wanting to waste time while Rivera reported to the CO and they waited for him to issue orders, Kozak began to issue her own. She was, after all, the flank guard, charged with protecting the battalion from an attack from that area. She was expected, according to doctrine, to take action. And she didn't need anyone to tell her to do it.

The arroyo, according to the map, opened up just south of where they were. It was there, Kozak thought, that the tanks would deploy before hitting 2nd of the 13th. Since the 25mm guns and TOW missiles of the Bradleys would be of no use at close range, Kozak decided to send the Bradleys, under Rivera, to the open ground to the south, where they could engage the tanks at long range. And rather than send the infantry dismounts with the Bradleys, where they would be of no use in a long-range antitank fight, Kozak ordered Rivera to send all the dismounts with man-portable antitank weapons to where she was. In that way, she could break the column in half while Rivera dealt with those tanks that had already gone past Kozak's position by hitting them in their flank and rear as they massed before attacking the battalion. She could only pray that artillery, which Kozak told Rivera to request when reporting to Wittworth, and attack helicopters, which she hoped Wittworth would request, would be enough to deal with the unknown number of tanks that were still to come.

Finished with her orders, she gave the hand mike back to Bell. Noticing that he was staring at her, Kozak forced a smile. "Looks like we're about to get into some really deep shit."

Bell nodded. "Yeah, big time."

"You ready, Bell?"

For a moment, he looked her in the eyes. If there was fear there, she wasn't showing it. Slowly, he smiled. "Fuckin' A, LT. Fuckin' A."

With Sergeant Maupin in the lead, Kozak deployed her three dismounted squads. To the right, she placed Maupin and his 1st Squad. She recommended that he use the Dragon antitank guided missile, and told him that if he waited to fire until after the tank entering the arroyo began to go over the edge, the thin armor of the tank's top would be exposed. At the range they would be engaging at, the missile would have just enough time to arm. The missile's flight time, which would be less than three seconds, wouldn't give the enemy tank commander much time to react. The way Kozak figured, the forward momentum of the tank, and the resulting lack of control as the tank dropped into the arroyo, would prevent the crew from avoiding the guided missile even if they saw it. Because of the need to time the shot, 1st Squad would fire first and initiate the ambush. When Maupin nodded that he understood, Kozak sent him and his squad on their way as she moved to the next squad leader.

In the center, she placed Staff Sergeant Strange and his 3rd Squad. Because they were too close to use their Dragon, she told him they would have to use the AT-4 light antitank rockets. She told Strange that, by crawling up to the edge of the arroyo, where she and Bell had been, he and his squad could fire right down on top of any enemy tank passing below them. Kozak cautioned him, however, to let the tank go a little farther down the arroyo before his squad fired, lest fragments from the explosion of their own antitank rockets on the enemy tank fly back into the gunner's face.

When Sergeant Zeigler and his 2nd Squad came up, she ordered them to the left. Their mission was to engage any tanks that had gotten past Maupin's or Strange's squads. Because the dust might cause problems with the Dragon, she told Zeigler to use his best judgment in deciding which weapon to use. When Zeigler and his squad were gone, Kozak looked about, watching as the three squad leaders quickly positioned their men.

The thought of failure, and its consequences, never crossed her mind. Nor had she considered what they would do once the ambush had been initiated and the first three tanks were taken out. Kozak, in the rush of events, was taking the problems on one at a time, as they presented themselves to her. Right then, at that particular moment, Kozak's only concern was that the squads would be set, in place, before the last enemy tank rolled past their position. With the squad leaders doing their jobs, and nothing more for her to do, Kozak placed herself in the center, with the 3rd Squad.

Back at the edge of the arroyo, Kozak crawled up next to Strange, who was peering over the edge. When he saw her, Strange leaned over and whispered, "Any time you're ready, LT."

Scooting herself back a few feet, Kozak got up on her knees and looked to her right. Maupin, who had been watching, waved his hand. He was ready. Looking to her left, she caught the attention of Zeigler, who also waved. Turning back to Maupin, she pointed at him. With an exaggerated salute, Maupin acknowledged the order to fire. Turning away from Kozak, Maupin leaned over to look into the arroyo, placing his left hand on his Dragon gunner's back as he did so. She watched as the two men, squad leader and Dragon gunner, waited for their opportunity. When she saw Maupin's hand rise, then slap the gunner's back, she knew it had begun.

Bracing himself for the shock of firing, Maupin's Dragon gunner leaned into his sight, took one more deep breath, then squeezed the trigger. The whoosh of the missile rocket engine, and the *pop, pop, pop* of the tiny guidance rockets firing on the sides of the missile, caused everyone in 2nd Platoon to jump a little. Across the arroyo, only the commander of the tank being engaged saw the incoming missile. As Kozak had predicted, there was nothing he could do. Holding onto the edge of the open hatch to his front, he could only watch, eyes and mouth wide open in disbelief, as Maupin's missile closed on his tank.

The Dragon impacted on the flat turret roof just in front of the tank commander. While the hatch protected his body, his face and head had no protection whatever when the shaped-charge warhead of the Dragon missile detonated. If the injuries to the tank commander's head and face from the detonation of the Dragon's warhead were not fatal, the secondary explosion of on-board ammunition was. To protect the main gun ammunition on a T-72, all rounds were stored under the turret floor, in a circular carousel. The angle of attack Maupin's Dragon gunner used, however, defeated that system. The jet stream from the Dragon's shaped-charge warhead was driven straight down into the stored ammunition.

Maupin and the rest of his squad watched as a sheet of flame leaped up, engulfing the tank commander. Then, to their utter amazement, the tank shook, then exploded, ripping the turret off the chassis and into the air. Oblivious to the danger of flying scraps and shrapnel thrown up as the enemy tank tore itself apart, Maupin's men turned their faces skyward, mouths gaping, as they watched the tank's turret twirl. It was the first time any of them had seen a tank die.

Though they could clearly hear the destruction of the tank Maupin's squad had engaged, the rest of 2nd Platoon was too busy to watch. Both Strange's and Zeigler's squads were using AT-4 antitank rockets to deal with their target. Because 1st Squad initiated the ambush, and the 3rd Squad could not fire while its intended target was right below it, a strange standoff existed for several seconds between the 3rd Squad and the tank commander on the vehicle below them. Looking back to see what had happened to the tank to his rear, the commander of the vehicle below Strange's squad looked about, and then up, right at the men of the 3rd Squad.

Had it not been war, the scene would have been comical, with the tank commander, mouth open and eyes wide, looking up at the faces of Strange's men as they trained two AT-4 antitank rockets on the tank less than six feet below them. The panicked screams of the tank commander were as clear to Strange's men as they were to his own crew. Only when the commander reached for his machine gun did someone finally do something. Without a second thought, Strange raised his M-16, flipped the safety off with his thumb, and squeezed off a three-round burst. Hit in the back and shoulder, the tank commander dropped down the open hatch of the turret, out of sight, as the tank continued to move down the arroyo and away from Strange's men. When he thought that there was a comfortable distance between his men and the tank, Strange gave his gunners the order to fire.

Both antitank rockets impacted, striking the top of the engine compartment. Though their effort yielded a less spectacular result than that of the 1st Squad's, the resulting damage and fires caused by the antitank rockets were enough to stop the tank. For the longest time, Strange and his squad watched and waited, their rifles and automatic weapons ready, prepared to gun down the crew of the burning tank as they abandoned it. But no men came out. Only the screams of the crewmen burning to death, screams that seemed more animal than human, came out of the stricken tank. That the tank crew chose to die as they did was almost a disappointment to Strange's squad. It was a feeling akin to what a hunter experiences when denied the pleasure of a kill he feels he deserves.

Kozak had no time for such feelings. Looking to the left, she noted that Zeigler's squad had already engaged their tank. She watched as, for whatever reason, a second volley of AT-4 antitank rockets was launched into the tank being engaged by Zeigler's gunners. Beyond Zeigler's squad, Kozak could just make out pillars of black smoke farther down the arroyo. That had to be Rivera and the Bradleys. They were engaged.

Waving to Bell to come over, Kozak looked around while she waited, her eyes falling upon the far side of the arroyo, the side the enemy tanks had come from. The fear of not being able to deploy her platoon in time to catch some of the enemy tanks was now replaced with an uneasiness that, in all probability, there were more tanks over there, tanks that could, at that very moment, be massing for an attack. The artillery mission she had requested should have come in by now but hadn't. When Bell handed her the hand mike, Kozak keyed the radio and called for Rivera.

Instead of Rivera, however, Sergeant Kaszynski, the assistant squad leader for the 1st Squad, replied. Kozak was puzzled. "Alpha two one Alpha, this is Alpha two six. Do you have contact with Alpha two four, over."

There was a pause before Kaszynski answered. "Two six, this is two one Alpha. Alpha two four's track has been hit. Over."

It took Kozak a second to realize the significance of Kaszynski's statement, given in such a matter-of-fact manner. Her platoon sergeant's Bradley had been hit. How, she asked herself, could that be? "Alpha two one Alpha. How bad is the damage to two four? Is two four still operational? Over."

As she waited, Kozak looked around. Still no artillery on the far side of the arroyo. On this side, all her men were, like Kozak, watching the far side for more tanks. "Two six, this is two one Alpha. We're kinda busy here right now. Two four's track is still moving. There's a red flag on it. Can't talk now. We're engaging a tank. Out."

A red flag, that meant wounded on board. For a moment, Kozak looked about her and took stock of her platoon's situation. Deciding that it was pointless to try to talk to Kaszynski while he was engaging, Kozak dropped the matter. By doing so, Kozak realized, she was abdicating control of half her platoon. Not that she could have done much from where she sat, since the Bradleys were somewhere off to her left and out of sight, commanded by assistant squad leaders in combat for the first time, fighting an unknown number of enemy tanks. That left the rest of her people with her, and with no way of getting around except by foot, facing an imminent attack by God knew what from across the arroyo. On top of that, she had no way of knowing for sure if Rivera had ever managed to get a report in to the company commander. Reaching the conclusion that she had screwed things up about as bad as she could on her own, Kozak decided it was time to report directly to Wittworth.

Ordering Bell to turn around so she could change the radio frequency to the company net, Kozak decided that it was time to find out. Using a small plastic-covered card she kept around her neck on her dog-tag chain, she looked up the company frequency and set it on the radio. When it was set, she took the hand mike, keyed the radio, and tried to contact Wittworth.

"Alpha six, this is Alpha two six. Over."

Wittworth's response startled Kozak. "Alpha two six, this is Alpha six. Where in the hell have you been? What in the hell are you doing? Over."

With Rivera possibly out of action, she wondered how much Wittworth knew. Deciding that she should start by giving him a full report, Kozak tried but was cut off by Wittworth. "Two six, this is six. I say again, what in the hell is going on? Over."

"Alpha six, this is Alpha two one. Dismounts are located one point three klicks north of checkpoint Charlie three three. We have engaged and destroyed three enemy T-72s at that location. Break. Alpha two four and the tracks are engaging more T-72s vicinity of checkpoint three three. Alpha two four has been hit. Over."

"Alpha two six, this is Alpha six. Request you confirm that you are engaging T-72s. The Mexicans don't have T-72s. Over."

Wittworth's last comment struck Kozak, causing her to hold the hand mike out at arm's length and look at it with a strange expression on her face. Sergeant Strange, who had been watching and listening to what she was saying, asked her what was wrong. Kozak let the hand mike fall to her lap and looked at Strange. "The CO says the Mexicans don't have T-72s. He wants us to confirm that we're engaging T-72s."

Leaning over, Strange looked into the arroyo at the burning T-72 less than ten meters from his location, then back to Kozak. "Well, LT, they got 'em now."

Kozak chuckled as she picked up the hand mike. "Alpha six, this is Alpha two six. Affirmative. We are engaging T-72s. Over."

Without a pause, Wittworth shot back, "This is Alpha six. That's not possible. Over."

Before she realized what she was doing, Kozak keyed the hand mike. "Six, this is two six. Well they got them now. If you wait a minute, I'll let you talk to one of their tank commanders. Over."

Strange, as well as those members of his squad who could hear, began howling over Kozak's statement. As she waited for Wittworth's response, she looked up at Strange and his soldiers. Unable to restrain herself, she also began to laugh. What an idiot, she thought. He's nowhere near the fighting and he's telling me what I see. What an idiot!

The next voice that came over the radio surprised both Wittworth and Kozak. Blue 6, the battalion commander, had been listening on the company radio net.

"Alpha two six, this is Blue six. I've monitored your report and have your Bradleys and the T-72s in sight. You're doin' a great job, two six. I have some fast movers and snakes coming your way. Do you have smoke to mark your position? Over."

Though she had no idea what snakes were, Kozak asked Strange if he had any colored smoke. Pulling a canister from his web belt, he showed it to Kozak. "Is violet okay, LT?"

Giving Strange the thumbs-up, Kozak informed the battalion commander that she had colored smoke.

"Okay, Alpha two six. The forward air controller is asking to pop that smoke now. The fast movers will be coming in from the southeast. Over."

Hesitating, Kozak wondered if it was such a good idea to mark her own position. If friendly forces could see the smoke, the enemy forces could also. Still, the battalion commander had told her to pop smoke. Without another thought, Kozak told Strange to pop the smoke and toss it to the rear of their position so they could mark it for an air strike. She waited until the dark violet smoke cloud was well developed before she reported back.

"Roger, Alpha two six. We have your smoke. Fast movers inbound now. When they finish, I want you to collect some prisoners, pronto. We need to find out who's driving those tanks. Over."

"Blue six, this is Alpha two six. Wilco on the prisoners. Will advise you when we have them in hand. Over."

When neither the battalion commander nor Wittworth responded to her last transmission, she figured that they were done with her for now. Turning to the southeast, Kozak watched, shouting to her squad leaders to spread the word that an air strike was coming in. Bell, who was also watching, saw them first. "There they are, LT."

Following his finger, Kozak finally saw two black dots coming toward them fast. Within seconds, the black dots became black blobs. Then the black blobs appeared to sprout wings. Finally, just before they passed overhead, the two blobs with wings began to take on the distinctive form of F-16s. When they released their loads before they passed her platoon's position, she thought, Christ, they're going to hit us! Controlling her panic, she held her breath as she watched the bombs fall away from the jets. Only when the cluster bombs, already split open and spewing hundreds of small bomblets, had cleared the platoon and began to impact on the far side of the arroyo, did Kozak begin to breathe again. Though she could not see the impact, a series of secondary explosions told her the F-16s had found the mark. A second pass, and the appearance of a company of Apache attack helicopters, was anticlimactic.

She had pulled it off. Second Platoon, Alpha Company, the "Dust Devils," had pulled it off. Now, all that remained for her to do was to find out how much their small victory had cost them.

10 KILOMETERS SOUTHEAST OF VALLECILLO, MEXICO
2245 HOURS, 12 SEPTEMBER

From his position, Captain Nino Garza watched the trucks of the 16th Armored Division's main command post move like a great snake crawling along the road leading southeast out of Vallecillo. The information he had been given, six hours before, that the division command post was preparing to move, had been right. Even more gratifying was the fact that his guess as to the road it would use had also been right. If that guess had been wrong, he would have been guilty of unnecessarily exposing the one hundred and fifty members of the Rural Defense Force he now had deployed along that road, waiting to ambush the American command post. Taking one last look, Garza struggled to suppress the giddiness he felt at the prospect of impending battle.

Finally ready, Garza eased himself down off the rock he had been watching the road from and joined his subordinate commanders, who were gathered to receive his final instructions. "Remember, no one is to fire until the mortars fire. I will have them alternate the high-explosive rounds with illumination rounds so that we can keep the column illuminated. And, remind your men, a green flare means they are to rush the column. I will do that only if conditions are ideal. Do not rush the column on your own, no matter how good conditions appear to be to your front."

Garza paused, looking at each of his subordinate commanders as they nodded that they understood. Though he was far from being the patronizing type, Garza knew that the men entrusted to his command were simple farmers and shopkeepers. He not only had to keep everything simple, he also had to remember that each of these men had a family that depended upon him. Though the men were patriots, and each and every one was willing to die in the defense of his home and Mexico, as their grandfathers had been, Garza never forgot Colonel Guajardo's admonishment to him and other guerrilla leaders like him: "While we need patriots to fight this war, never forget that only live Mexicans can build our future." So Garza was careful to ensure that, if nothing else, everyone in his command understood the dispersal plan and the signal to initiate it. "Regardless of what happens or what you are doing," he stressed to his subordinates, "when I or my deputy fires a red flare, the company will disperse. Do not wait for me, or anyone else. Take your people back to their rally points, have them clean their weapons before they bury them, and send them home. I will contact you when I can. Is that understood?"

With a final nod, each of Garza's subordinate leaders moved off into the darkness, back to his unit where he would wait with his men for Garza to initiate the ambush.

Stuck in the rear seat of Major Nihart's vehicle, amidst a tumble of personal gear and boxes, Captain Harold Cerro was asleep. To him, *convoy* and *sleep* were synonyms. Since his earliest days in the Army, he had found that the slow, serpentine pace of a convoy, coupled with the steady hum of an engine running at the same speed hour after hour after hour, was the best sleep aid ever invented. Cerro could last for ten, fifteen minutes tops, in a convoy before going to sleep. While sleep was always a commodity soldiers sought, it was not acceptable for the senior occupant of an Army vehicle to be seen sleeping while the vehicle was moving. Though Cerro understood the reasoning behind that rule, he also understood that no one could regulate biology and human nature. Cerro had therefore developed a system for accommodating both. After being reprimanded on several occasions for sleeping, he now took the precaution of training his drivers to be on constant lookout for officers of the rank of major and above when he was asleep. When the driver saw the senior officer, it was the driver's duty, Cerro would explain, to wake him.

That night, it would take more than a nudge by the driver to wake Cerro. It had been a difficult and trying day for him, far more demanding than he had ever thought possible. Though the threat of danger had been absent, along with the stress of being a leader in battle, the strain on the body and mind he had experienced that day was no less debilitating. Division staffs are dominated by lieutenant colonels, who are the principal staff officers, and majors who are punching their tickets while they wait to become lieutenant colonels. Captains serving on division staffs don't make any real decisions and don't really get the chance to do much of anything. Their days, split into twelve-hour shifts, consist of numerous little tasks, such as answering the phone; filling out, receiving, and submitting reports; asking questions of staff officers on subordinate unit staffs or answering questions asked by staff officers from higher headquarters staff; updating maps or redoing map graphics; searching to find the answer to a question posed by a senior officer; and dozens of other relatively simple and mundane things. Each of these actions, in and of itself, is simple, ludicrously simple. Doing all of them at once, however, in an area the size of a small hotel room crammed with tables, chairs, radios, telephones, map boards, computers, and a dozen other members of the staff is not only hard, it is physically and mentally demanding.

As in the experiment in which rats are made to live in overcrowded conditions, it is not long before the stress and strain of operating in an overcrowded van causes the members of a staff to turn on each other. Though Cerro and the other members of Major Nihart's current-operations shop got along with each other under normal circumstances, the demands of the last twenty-four hours would have turned a saint into a chain-saw murderer. Even Colonel Dixon, normally a rock, had broken that day. During a heated conversation with the corps G3, Dixon had reached his breaking point. When he terminated the conversation by throwing the telephone across the current-operations van, barely missing Cerro, everyone in the van froze. Looking about at everyone in the van—all of whom were, in turn, looking at him—Dixon, a little embarrassed, mumbled, "Stupidity knows no bounds," before he turned and left. Though no one had any idea what he meant, as soon as Dixon was gone, everyone went back to work without giving the incident a second thought. Such scenes were becoming more and more common.

Unable to vent the stress and frustrations of the day through physical means, as he had been able to do when he had commanded an airborne infantry company, Cerro sought escape through sleep. A sleep that nothing could disturb. Or so he thought.

Cerro hadn't counted on Captain Garza and the members of the Rural Defense Force. No one, in fact, had. And that was about to become apparent.

*   *   *

When the convoy reached the point where Garza wanted to initiate the ambush, he fired a white flare, the signal for the mortars to commence firing. Five hundred meters to his rear, a man old enough to be Garza's father, a cobbler by trade, watched the white star cluster climb into the sky and burst before he gave the three mortar crews under his command the order to fire. The mortar on the left, manned by a farmer and his two sons, had the honor of being the first to fire.

Cerro's eyes popped open when the first 6omm mortar round, the one fired by the farmer and his sons, detonated less than one hundred meters in front of them. The odds against a mortar round, especially the first one, impacting on a moving truck were, even when the range was known, astronomical, under the best of circumstances. But it was also true, in the game of probability, that eventually someone had to be that "one" in a situation that measures the million-to-one odds.

As the G2 current-intelligence van, hit dead on, flopped over into the ditch on the side of the road, small-arms fire began to rake the column. In the darkness, to his right, Cerro could see the flashes of rifles and machine guns. As he struggled to find his own rifle, hidden amongst the tumble of gear and equipment, Cerro heard a *thump-thump-thump* on the side of the vehicle, followed by a scream from Major Nihart. "Jesus. I'm hit. I'm fucking hit!"

Thrusting his head between Nihart and the driver, Cerro could see Nihart bent over, grasping his right thigh with both hands. Though he couldn't see the blood, the grimace on Nihart's face told him he had been hit bad. Cerro turned to the driver. "Left. Go left and get off this road. Now."

For a moment the driver looked at Cerro, then at Nihart. Thrusting his head forward so that it blocked the driver's view of Nihart, Cerro repeated his order. "Get this piece of shit off the road to the left now, before we all die."

When, out of the corner of his eye, the driver saw another truck further down the road blow up, he snapped out of his shock. He cut the wheel to the left with all his might, stepping on the accelerator as he did so. The vehicle almost jumped. The ditch to the left, though it wasn't very wide or very deep, was wide enough and deep enough to bring the vehicle's sudden burst of energy to a bone-crushing halt. Cerro was thrown head-first into the dashboard. Nihart, still clutching his leg, let out a piercing scream.

Panicked, the driver pushed the accelerator to the floor to no avail. "We're stuck! We're stuck!"

Pulling himself back, Cerro shook his head. Now, he thought to himself, he finally understood why everyone insisted that soldiers wear their helmets when in a vehicle. Though he knew his neck would be stiff, his Kevlar helmet had saved him from a cracked skull. After shaking his head again, Cerro turned to the driver. In a rather calm tone of voice, he told the driver to let up on the accelerator and engage the four-wheel drive before trying again. Though the rear window of their vehicle was shattered by another volley of rifle fire, the driver complied. This time, they cleared the ditch, crawling up into the open field on the left side of the road and away from the ambush.

Sergeant Major Aiken, Dixon's senior NCO and operations sergeant, was in the cab of the truck immediately behind Major Nihart's vehicle. He was in the process of swinging the ring-mounted .50-caliber machine gun that was attached to the cab of his truck toward the ambushers when he saw Major Nihart's vehicle clear the ditch and move into the field to the left. Deciding that it might be smarter to follow the major, Aiken leaned over and yelled to the truck driver to follow Nihart into the open field. Though he knew that there might be mines or more enemy troops lying in wait on the left side of the road, Aiken also knew that the odds would be better moving around in an open field instead of sitting on the road.

Though he hadn't intended it to, Cerro's action created a chain reaction. Behind Nihart's vehicle and Aiken's truck, every truck that could make the left-hand turn began to follow them. Though the drive across the open field was almost unbearable for Major Nihart, as each bump sent a spasm of pain through his body, it quickly became clear to Cerro that they were moving out of the kill zone of the ambush and mortar fire. It was only after he looked back to confirm this that he noticed that he was being followed. After traveling several hundred meters away from the road, a trip that seemed to take forever, Cerro told the driver to stop. Climbing out over him, Cerro ordered the driver to tend to the major, then set out to set up a defensive perimeter.

Once on the ground, he headed for the first truck he came to. Aiken, seeing Cerro, who he thought was Major Nihart, on the ground, ordered his driver to stop. Dismounting even before the truck stopped rolling, he began to head for Cerro. "If you start forming the perimeter, Major, I'll direct the other vehicles over to you."

Cerro ignored the fact that Aiken thought he was the major. "Sounds good to me, Sergeant Major."

Confused, Aiken walked up to Cerro, confirmed who he was, then apologized. "Sorry, thought you were Major Nihart, sir."

"The major's been hit. He's out of it for now."

"Anything we can do?"

Cerro looked around as he answered. "No, the major will be all right, I think. His driver's with him now, taking care of him. Besides, you and I got a lot to do out here. If you will go on over there, Sergeant Major, and direct the incoming trucks to me, I'll start circling the wagons."

Aiken was about to respond when a red star cluster popped over the portion of the column that was still on the road. "What do you suppose that means, Captain?"

Cerro looked at the star cluster, noting that the ambushers were increasing their rate of fire. "I don't know, Sergeant Major. But I have a sneaking suspicion we're gonna find out. Until then, let's get a move on and form this here perimeter."

Aiken, looking at the road one last time before setting out, sighed, "Big Al's going to be pissed."

"Pardon my apparent disrespect, Sergeant Major, but screw Big Al. Right now, I'm more concerned about the yahoo that's directing the ambush and what he's thinking."

Almost a kilometer away, on the other side of the road, Captain Garza, the yahoo that Cerro was referring to, decided to break off the attack. The sudden separation of the rear of the column had come as a surprise to him. From where he sat, it looked as if the Americans had been less surprised than he had hoped, and were responding better than he'd expected. There was no telling what they were about to do and how they were going to respond. Rather than press his luck, Garza decided to break off the attack.

Firing the red star cluster, he paused for a moment and watched the response of his men. As instructed, some of the men increased the rate of fire while others, under the direction of their leaders, began to move back to their rally points. The mortars also increased their fire, switching to firing all high-explosive rounds instead of a mix of illumination rounds and high explosives. The mortars would be the last to stop, as they covered the withdrawal of the rest of the force. Garza's planned route of escape took him right past their position. He personally would give them permission to leave.

Satisfied that all was in order, he turned to the militiaman who was serving as his radio operator. "We have done well tonight. Tomorrow, there will be many gringo families mourning."

In the fading light of the last illumination rounds, Garza could see the militiaman's face. The young farmer, a boy of sixteen, was smiling. "And we, *el capitán,* will have much to celebrate."

21

The morality of killing is not something with which the professional soldier is usually thought to trouble himself.

—John Keegan, *The Face of Battle*

WASHINGTON, D.C.
1045 HOURS, 15 SEPTEMBER

The shock wave generated by the battle of Monterrey, what some were calling America's second Tet, was just as great in Washington as it had been to the troops who had fought it. Instead of the simple, controlled occupation of a security zone, an image that the president and his advisors had worked hard to cultivate, the American public found itself involved in a full-scale war. Though the battle was technically a victory, since the Mexicans had been forced to break contact and withdraw and all U.S. forces had more or less reached the southern limit of advance that defined the security zone, few people in America saw it in those terms. In that single attack, and the operations immediately after it, the United States Army had suffered more casualties than it had during the entire Persian Gulf War.

The impact of the battle had been magnified by the news stories, uncensored by the military. In contrast to its policy in the Gulf War, where it held a tight rein on what correspondents could see and what they could release for public broadcast, the military had felt that, due to the nature of the operations in Mexico, no censorship would be necessary. Both the administration and the Pentagon, however, had soon regretted that decision. To counter statements made during briefings by Pentagon spokesmen, who continued to assure the public that the fight around Monterrey had been a tactical victory, newscasters freely used film footage fresh from the battlefield, showing the devastation. One network newsroom ran a two-minute segment during which the soundtrack of a Pentagon briefing was dubbed over footage showing burning American vehicles, rows of filled body bags being tossed into trucks, overcrowded aid stations, and soldiers, dazed from combat, stumbling back to the rear. Such techniques, coupled with interviews with soldiers fresh from battle and still reeling from the impact of losing a friend, made the statements by military officials in Washington seem trite and out of touch with the reality of the situation in Mexico.

For those in Congress who had been opposed to the establishment of a security zone in Mexico, warning that such a move was not only dangerous but unnecessary, the news from Mexico was vindication. Congressmen like Ed Lewis, who had been vocal in their opposition, redoubled their efforts, taking every opportunity to drive home the point that the longer U.S. forces stayed in Mexico, the more both nations would suffer. The entire affair, Lewis pointed out, had been ill-conceived and based on too many false assumptions. On the day after the battle of Monterrey, after emerging from a special briefing at the White House for selected senators and congressmen, Lewis summed up the administration's problem. When reporters asked him what he and the other members of Congress had been told, Lewis smiled. "The president," he told the reporters, "has assured us that we have that tar baby just where we want it and, any day now, we're going to teach it a thing or two."

Into this growing controversy came Jan Fields, bearing her message for the president from the Council of 13. When she was told that it was not possible for her to deliver the message in person, as Colonel Guajardo had requested, by a condescending third-echelon White House staffer, who informed her that the president could not possibly see her, Jan decided not to get mad. Instead, she delivered the text of the message in a special fifteen-minute segment aired by the World News Network. With a summary of the events that had led up to the current crisis, along with her own observations based on interviews with participants on both sides as a lead-in, Jan delivered Colonel Molina's message. The result exceeded anything Jan could have imagined. The effect was akin to the dumping of gasoline onto a smoldering fire. Within hours, Congress, with Ed Lewis in the vanguard, opened a formal investigation into the administration's handling of Mexico since the beginning of the June 29 revolution.

That he had been called to the White House along with two dozen other congressmen and senators for a special briefing the day before had come as no surprise to Ed Lewis. That he had been invited back, alone, did.

Perhaps, he thought, the president, stung by his tar baby comment, was going to give him a piece of his mind. That caused Lewis to chuckle. God, he thought, the last thing this president needed to do was to give anyone a piece of his mind. He already had too little to work with as it was.

Lewis was still in the midst of his private joke when the president's national security advisor came out of the Oval Office and started to walk over to him. A college professor before joining the White House staff, William Hastert gave new meaning to the word *wimp*. With men like this to advise the president, Lewis mused, how can he possibly go right? When Hastert reached Lewis and greeted him, there wasn't a hint of warmth in his handshake or smile. Instead, Hastert only mumbled that both he and the president were glad that Lewis had been able to make time in his busy schedule and come over on such short notice. That Hastert placed himself before the president did not escape Lewis's attention.

Wanting to understand a little about what was going to be discussed before he walked into the Oval Office, Lewis held onto Hastert's hand when they finished their perfunctory handshake, much to Hastert's discomfort. "Who will be joining us, Mr. Hastert?"

Pulling his hand free, Hastert looked at it, then back at Lewis. "No one else, Congressman Lewis. The president wanted to talk to you in private. The president is ready to see you."

Unable to discern the subject of the meeting, and taking Hastert's less than subtle hint, Lewis decided to trust his luck and skill in dealing with this impromptu meeting. "Well then, Mr. Hastert, we mustn't keep the president waiting. After you."

Trailing Hastert, Lewis weaved his way around the desks of the outer office and past two security men standing outside the Oval Office. Once inside, Lewis saw that the president stood motionless at the french doors behind his desk, staring vacantly out into the Rose Garden. That man, Lewis thought, is not a happy one. With his arms folded tightly across his chest, his shoulders rolled forward, and his head down, the president appeared to Lewis to be a man under considerable stress. After Hastert announced that Lewis was there, the president hesitated before turning to face the two men. When he did, he kept his arms folded and his head down, looking up instead at Lewis with eyes that were puffy and surrounded by dark circles. "Thank you for coming over so fast, Ed." Even when he dropped his arms, motioning as he walked over to an arm-chair for Lewis to take a seat, the president's head still drooped down, his chin almost coming to rest on his chest. "Please, take a seat. Would you like some coffee?"

Lewis was about to say no, then reconsidered. Ever since his wife, Amanda, got on her decaffeinated kick, he never passed up the chance to get a real cup of coffee when he thought he could get away with it. Amanda had even managed to infiltrate his own office in the congressional building, instructing his staff to serve only decaf to him. Though it was a foolish gesture, out of habit Lewis looked about furtively to see if there was anyone in the room who would tell on him before he accepted the president's offer.

When everyone was seated and Lewis had been afforded the opportunity to savor his coffee, the president started. "As you so eloquently put it yesterday, Ed, we, I've got both hands full with a tar baby."

Lewis sighed. He was almost sorry that he had made that comment. After all, it had been a cheap shot that not even this guy deserved. Still, there was nothing he could do about that now. Though he thought of apologizing, he didn't. While it might have been a cheap shot, Lewis decided, in the end it had been all too true.

"Ed, I'm in a very bad spot, and you know it."

Looking up from his coffee cup, Lewis smiled. "You're sort of like the guy who has his private parts caught in his fly. Even though he knows he needs to do something, and soon, he also knows that, no matter what he does, including nothing, it's going to hurt like hell."

While Hastert frowned, the president laughed. "That's what I love about you, Ed. You have a unique way of putting things." Then, in a flash, the laughter was gone. "You're right, of course. We are in a bad spot and need to do something, even though it's going to hurt like hell."

For a moment, Lewis looked at the president. He agreed with neither the man's politics nor his policies. He didn't even like the president as a man. Still, he was the president, and a person. For a moment, in the president's eyes, Lewis saw a human being who was in trouble and needed help. Rather than let the president thrash about, trying to save whatever pride he could, Lewis decided to let him off the hook. Besides, it would be wrong to use the president's current predicament for political or personal ends. Whatever personal satisfaction he might derive from such an effort would be washed away by Lewis's conscience, something that he still had despite his five years in Congress. "What, Mr. President, can I do to help?"

Relieved of the need for further groveling, the president launched into his proposal. "I need someone to go to Mexico, someone with military experience, and yet not connected with the military, who can give me a clear, unbiased, and objective view of what the commanders in the field are thinking and how they view the situation, from a military standpoint."

Lewis gave the president a sideways glance. "Are you telling me that you don't trust what your own Joint Chiefs are telling you?"

"Ed, it's not that I don't trust them. It's just that I do not believe that they can be objective about this anymore. They, like the CIA, got caught short by the fight around Monterrey and active participation by the Nicaraguans. Between trying to explain away their failures by justifying their initial positions and scrambling to make the current battle plan work, everyone in Washington has lost sight of the long-term goal, national security. I need solutions, real solutions, not fixes. And before I can come up with those solutions, I need some solid, unvarnished information." Leaning forward toward Lewis, the president looked into his eyes while he rested his elbows on his knees and brought his hands together, almost as if he were begging. "Ed, will you go?"

For a moment, Lewis considered the president's offer. What a great way, he thought, of getting an opponent out of the way. Was the president, he thought, using the old adage that it was better to make friends rather than multiply enemies? Was he buying time, in the hope that by sending Lewis to Mexico he could appease his critics and hope that the Mexican government would buckle under? Or was the president sincere? Was he really seeking a real solution? "Who, Mr. President, are you sending with me, whom do I answer to, and what restrictions are there on my comings and goings down in Mexico?"

The president opened his hands. "You may take whomever you like, you report back to me when you are ready, and you will have a free hand to go wherever you want and speak to whomever you feel you need to talk to. You have a free hand."

That, Lewis thought, was inviting. Turning the idea over in his mind as he took a long sip of coffee, he decided to press for more. After all, if he was going to become involved, he wanted to be part of the solution, to do something meaningful, and not just become a storefront dummy. He looked down at his cup. "If that reporter, Jan Fields, is to be believed, we have not done all we could to reach an understanding and appreciation of the situation that the Council of 13 is dealing with." With a glance over to Hastert, Lewis continued. "It says a lot when a foreign government is forced to use a TV correspondent as a means of passing messages to us." As Hastert struggled to contain his anger at the slap Lewis had given him, Lewis turned to the president. "Any solution will need to involve the Mexicans. Unilateral action, as we have seen, is a noncontender. Therefore, if I go to Mexico, I want to have the ability to travel to Mexico City, with this Jan Fields, and open a dialogue with the Council of 13 on your behalf."

As if he had already considered that request, the president responded without even bothering to look over to Hastert. "That, Ed, is more than what I had in mind, but you're right." The president eased himself back into his seat. Though he didn't like the idea of Lewis, trailed by a high-speed correspondent like Fields, running around in Mexico City, the president decided that he had little choice. He had, in fact, decided before Lewis had arrived to accept just about whatever Lewis asked, since, as he had put it so eloquently, there would be pain involved no matter what the president did. "You are right. We were, in fact, discussing just how best to respond to the council's message when you arrived. You, if you would be so kind, can carry my personal message back to the Mexican government. When can you leave?"

"Will tonight be soon enough?"

"Tonight will be just fine. Besides making the necessary arrangements and coordination, is there anything else I can do to help you?"

Lewis was about to say no, but changed his mind. "Yes, Mr. President, there is. Could I have another cup of coffee?"

HEADQUARTERS, 16TH ARMORED DIVISION, SABINAS HIDALGO, MEXICO
1705 HOURS, 15 SEPTEMBER

Officially referred to as an operational pause, the order to halt all offensive operations and avoid contact with Mexican forces came as no surprise to Big Al and Scott Dixon. It was, Big Al dryly commented, about time that someone in Washington took note of the fact that maybe the Mexicans had different ideas about the presence of U.S. forces in Mexico. Still, the cost of the battle of Monterrey, and the sudden reversal of government policy immediately after, put Big Al, and all American commanders in the field, in a difficult position.

Too much hype about their own capabilities and too little regard for that of the Mexicans hadn't prepared the American soldiers going into Mexico for the kind of war that they now faced. They were willing, one soldier told a reporter, to do their jobs. All they asked for, he went on, "was for someone to tell us the truth, for a change." Unfortunately, with "the truth" changing almost by the hour, there was little that Big Al and other commanders like him could do. Every new directive, every new change in policy, evoked the same response from him: "It's Vietnam all over again." He did what he could, and asked the soldiers in his command to bear with him.

One thing that he could do was protect his force, deploying it in such a manner that it could protect itself without leaving any elements exposed to unnecessary risk. With the 16th Armored Division spread out like it was, this would be no simple task. As the ambush on the division's own CP, and numerous other attacks throughout the division's rear areas, showed that, while the Mexicans might have given ground, they had conceded nothing.

As part of the reshuffling of forces into a defensive posture, the 3rd Brigade was ordered to release the 2nd of the 13th Infantry, which, in turn, reverted back to division control as a reserve. Because the threat from small, lightly armed raiding parties in the rear areas was greater than that of a major attack by Mexican forces, it was decided to disperse elements of 2nd of the 13th to various rear-area facilities in an effort to discourage raids.

Though many would like to believe otherwise, the influence that egos and politics have in the decision-making process is, at times, just as important in troop units as it is in Washington. The manner in which 2nd Platoon, A Company, 2nd of the 13th, found its way to the division CP to provide security is an example. When Major Tod McQuirer, the operations officer of 2nd of the 13th, was informed that they were going to be tasked to provide a platoon to the division CP for security, he saw an opportunity to help out his friend and drinking buddy, the commander of A Company. Calling Wittworth to the battalion CP, McQuirer discussed the matter with him.

"Stan, we just got a tasking from brigade to detach one platoon to go back to the division CP in order to provide security for them." With a knowing smile, he looked Wittworth in the eyes. "Do you think you could help?"

Seeing an opportunity to rid himself of the 2nd Platoon and its platoon leader, Second Lieutenant N. Kozak, Wittworth said, "Sure. Though it will be hard, I think I can spare 2nd Platoon."

Though McQuirer knew that Wittworth was full of shit, he played along for the benefit of the officers and NCOs in the CP who just might overhear the conversation. Ever since Kozak had changed her statement about the September 7 incident, Wittworth had been looking for a way to get rid of her. The second statement had not only put Wittworth on the spot, her change of mind had shown that she didn't have the slightest thought of loyalty for him, her commander. McQuirer had agreed, especially after

Wittworth showed him the part that stated her orders "were not clear and did not appear to consider the situation at our location." That had been enough. Unfortunately for Wittworth, she went on to state, "Despite repeated efforts to advise my commander of the nature of the situation, he simply repeated his initial order." The second statement resulted in Kozak's being exonerated and earned him a written reprimand. McQuirer hadn't helped Wittworth's state of mind by telling him that, if Kozak had been an ordinary infantry officer—i.e., a male—the second statement would never have been accepted.

As bad as that incident had been, it didn't even compare to what had happened outside of Monterrey on the twelfth of September. Her disrespectful manner to him on an open radio net that was being monitored not only by every leader in Company A, but also by the battalion commander, had been bad enough. That the battalion commander not only had ignored Kozak's snide comment, but had congratulated her, then and a second time after the battle, made it worse. When, on the thirteenth of September, Wittworth went to see the battalion commander to protest, he was again reprimanded for his conduct and, this time, for his pettiness. Kozak, Wittworth knew, had to go.

With a wink, McQuirer discounted Wittworth's feigned concern. "Well, I'm really sorry to hit you up like this, but I'm afraid you'll just have to make due with two platoons." So that it appeared to be a choice based on sound logic, rather than hurt egos, McQuirer explained his "official" reasoning. "Since your 2nd Platoon is short a platoon sergeant, and the Bradley that the platoon sergeant had been on has lost its fire-control system, they are the least combat-ready platoon. Back at the division CP, the platoon sergeant and damaged Bradley won't be missed."

Making a show of it, Wittworth sighed. "Well, sir, you're right. I guess I have no choice. When do they leave?"

For Kozak, the assignment was welcome. Getting used to Staff Sergeant Maupin as the platoon sergeant and Sergeant Kaszynski as the 1st Squad leader was no big problem. In fact, the only problem she saw that needed to be tended to was with herself. In a span of less than a week, her entire world had been turned upside down.

Up until the seventh of September, the day they had gone into Mexico after the bank robbers, Kozak had thought nothing could be worse than her first six months at West Point. The physical and mental stress and strain of that six months, however, now seemed trivial when compared to the demands of command in combat. After the firefight in Nuevo Laredo, Kozak had almost lost it when Rivera pulled the zipper up on Private Gunti's body bag. She still found it impossible to pull up the zipper on her own sleeping bag without panicking. And then there was the sight of Sergeant Rivera himself after the fight with the tanks, laid out on a stretcher, his face as white as a sheet from shock and the loss of blood. The seemingly cold, matter-of-fact comment by his gunner, who had been sitting next to Rivera when their Bradley was hit, still echoed in her mind. When Kozak and the dismounts rejoined the Bradleys after their fight at the arroyo, and she asked how Rivera was, the gunner had looked up at her. "Oh, he'll be okay, I guess. Sarge is lucky. He only lost an arm."

It was in the calm after the battle that Kozak had been able to consider what had happened and, even worse, what could have happened. Like a person who walks away from an auto accident, it was only after the danger had passed that Kozak began to shake as the images of what might have been became clear to her. The thought that an entire enemy tank battalion might come crashing down on her and the handful of dismounts she had deployed never occurred to her before she initiated the antitank ambush. Her failure to contact Wittworth herself and push for the support they needed would have been fatal had the battalion commander not been in a position where he could see what was going on and quickly put two and two together. It was, Kozak realized, the same situation she had faced at Fort Hood, only bigger this time. It was as if she hadn't learned a thing from Captain Cerro that day. And if that were true, would she, could she, ever?

So when the order came down to 2nd Platoon, Company A, to report to the division's headquarters commandant, Kozak was hard-pressed to hide her relief. Back at the division CP, tucked safely in the division rear areas, she would have time to sort herself out. She needed time to absorb the horrors of combat. Like her nose, the wounds of her spirit and mind needed time to heal.

20 KILOMETERS WEST OF SABINAS HIDALGO, MEXICO
1935 HOURS, 15 SEPTEMBER

Like clouds on the distant horizon that foreshadow a coming storm, forces were in motion that would deny Kozak what she needed most, time.

The operational pause that was meant to provide the people in Washington with time to reassess their policy toward Mexico was a godsend to Señor Alamán. It provided him and his mercenaries with conditions that couldn't be more perfect for what they intended to do. With U.S. forces deep in Mexico, spread very thin and operating in the midst of a hostile population that provided cover for an active guerrilla force, it would be easy for Delapos's teams to move about and attack isolated American outposts and columns. That the Mexicans would be blamed for both the attacks and the atrocities Delapos's people would commit was without doubt. And for the American soldiers who would witness the results of the atrocities and have to live in fear of them, the desire to exact revenge from the nearest Mexican would, Alamán knew, soon become overpowering. With atrocity repaying atrocity, it would not be long before the bloody cries for revenge drowned out the calls for diplomacy and reason. It was now simply a matter of timing. As with the raids along the Texas border, Alamán warned Delapos to take his time and set the stage properly before acting. "It would be a shame," Alamán repeated at every chance, "to come this far and lose everything because we were in too much of a hurry. Time now is a friend that we can use freely. So long as we are willing to be a little patient, the opportunities that will bring us success will come our way."

All of this, to Jean Lefleur, that evening, was purely academic. He seldom bothered himself with the details of his bosses' ambitions or goals. His needs were few. In fact, his only needs were money and job satisfaction. So long as someone was willing to provide both, he was happy. As he sat in the passenger side of his newly acquired four-by-four, feet up on the dash and headed toward Sabinas Hidalgo, there was a smile on his face as he hummed old marching songs from the French Foreign Legion.

At that moment, it seemed like he had it all. Alamán's call for the mercenaries to continue their agitation in Mexico, at triple the pay they had been receiving, paid in advance, was an offer only a fool would turn down. That in itself would have been more than enough to satisfy Lefleur. What really capped the offer was a change in his status within Delapos's small army. The American, Childress, who had served as Delapos's unofficial deputy and advisor, had fallen out of favor. Lefleur couldn't tell for sure what had caused the problem between Childress and Delapos. Part of it, he knew, was the fact that Childress was lukewarm to the idea of committing what Childress called murder. Though the atrocities they intended to carry out exceeded what they had done in the past, however, that in itself was not enough to explain Childress's mood.

No, Lefleur thought. That was not at the heart of the problem. The real problem, Lefleur suspected, was the obvious one, one that neither man was willing to admit. Childress, despite all his training and years as a mercenary, was and would always be an American, just as Delapos could never be anything but a Mexican. The impressions and beliefs left by the cultures that had spawned them and raised them left a mark upon the two men that no amount of money could ever wash away. Childress did little to hide the agitation he felt when Delapos bragged about the manner in which the Mexican Army had beaten the arrogant gringos. Nor could Delapos ignore Childress's use of the words *dago, greaser,* and such when referring to Mexicans. As the war between their homelands expanded, so too, Lefleur knew, did the gap between the two men. And it was into that gap that Lefleur intended to insert himself.

No longer able to trust Childress, Delapos began to turn to Lefleur for the advice that Childress used to provide. For Delapos, so anxious to please Alamán, had great difficulty making major decisions on his own, a fact that both Childress and Lefleur had used to their own advantage so many times before. Needing someone he could trust to help him talk his way through to a decision, and unable fully to trust Childress any longer, Delapos accepted Lefleur's counsel more and more. Even the grueling task of reconnaissance, long hours of driving about coupled with the need to dodge or bluff through both Mexican and American outposts and lines, provided another chance for Lefleur to increase his value to Delapos, not to mention his salary. While Childress was left to organize and defend the base camp, Lefleur went out on reconnaissance, familiarizing himself with the ground and seeking routes that could be used for infiltration and vulnerable spots that were susceptible to attack. With intimate knowledge of the terrain and unit dispositions, Lefleur, not Childress, would be able to influence Delapos and future operations.

Armed with a false passport and other ID that identified him as Paul Perrault, a real correspondent for the French National News Network, Lefleur had no trouble moving about the American sector. Since the other men who traveled with Lefleur carried IDs that supported Lefleur's, and enough camera and sound equipment to support their claims, few Americans at roadblocks and checkpoints bothered to search them or their vehicle. Even if the Americans had found the MP-5 submachine gun under Lefleur's seat, or the weapons each of his men kept concealed within arm's reach, Lefleur felt that he could easily talk his way out of any difficulty. There were, after all, banditos about, and he as well as his crew had the right to defend themselves.

*   *   *

So when Lefleur and his men came up to a checkpoint manned by half a dozen MPs at the entrance to the gap between mountains that led to Sabinas Hidalgo, where the CP for the American 16th Armored Division was, Lefleur didn't give it a second thought. Still, he instinctively evaluated the situation and assessed his chances should it become necessary to fight his way out.

After they stopped a respectful distance from the wire entanglement the MPs used to block the road, a lone MP, armed with an M-16 rifle, approached them on Lefleur's side. From the rank on his helmet and collar, Lefleur guessed that he was their leader. Behind him, at the wire entanglement, stood two more MPs. One was armed with an M-16 slung over her shoulder, while the other had an M-203, which is an M-16 with a 40mm grenade launcher attached to the front hand guard. The two vehicles belonging to the MP squad were sitting on either side of the wire entanglement. Lefleur identified them as armored Humvees. Though the vehicles could easily protect the American MPs from the automatic weapons he and his team had hidden but ready, none of the MPs were, at that moment, availing themselves of that protection. Even the MPs manning the weapons mounted on top of the Humvees, an M-60 machine gun on the left and an M-19 40mm grenade launcher on the right, were fully exposed as they sat on top of the Humvee in order to escape the heat of the vehicles' interior. A sixth MP, a female, sat in the shade of the Humvee on the right. With her helmet off and her M-16 leaning against the side of the Humvee, she was busy eating from a brown plastic sack, paying Lefleur and his people no attention. Even before the MP sergeant reached him, Lefleur already had decided that, if push came to shove, they could easily take the Americans.

"Howdy. What brings you folks out this way?"

The casual approach to war and soldiering that Americans reveled in never ceased to amaze Lefleur. In the Foreign Legion, had he run a checkpoint the way this sergeant did and challenged an unidentified vehicle with such a greeting, he would have been flogged. That the Americans won so often in war proved, to Lefleur, that there was no justice.

When the MP sergeant stopped next to Lefleur, Lefleur pulled out a card that identified him as a correspondent. "My name is Paul Perrault. I am a correspondent for the French National News Network." Then he pointed to the others in his vehicle, one at a time. "And he is my cameraman, my sound technician, and my driver and interpreter." Each man in Lefleur's vehicle smiled and waved with his left hand as Lefleur pointed to him, while they kept their right arms close to their side.

Lefleur's response caused the MP sergeant's smile to broaden. "Oh, then you must be with Congressman Lewis's party."

Lewis's name rang a bell in Lefleur's head. He was one of the American congressmen who was opposed to intervention in Mexico. Not having any idea what the MP sergeant was talking about, but seeing an opportunity to expedite their passage through the checkpoint, Lefleur responded that they were, but that they had become separated from the congressman.

The MP sergeant smiled again. "Well, partner, you're in luck. The congressman and his party passed through here not five minutes ago, headed east. If you hurry, you can catch up to them before they get into town."

Although he still didn't quite know what the MP was talking about, Lefleur saw an opportunity. Looking away from the MP, down the road to the east, Lefleur considered the information the sergeant had so freely given him. As Lefleur pondered, for a moment, what he could do with it, the MP sergeant looked puzzled as to why Lefleur was waiting. "You know, you don't have much time. It'll be dark soon and you'll lose 'em."

If Lefleur had learned one thing in his years with the Legion, it was to trust one's instincts. Those instincts, at that moment, told him that somewhere, up on the road ahead, there was a prize waiting for him, a prize for the taking. What he would do with that prize, once he had it, he didn't know. But he knew it could not be ignored. And, Lefleur reasoned, if they were going to start a campaign of terror, this was as good a time and place as any to start.

Lefleur, turning back to the MP sergeant, smiled as he looked into the sergeant's eyes. "Yes, it is true that I do not have much time. But I have more than you."

Unable to figure out what Lefleur meant, the MP sergeant continued to stare into Lefleur's eyes, never noticing that he was reaching under his seat with his right hand.

The sudden burst of fire surprised everyone. The MPs at the wire entanglement froze as they watched the body of their squad leader fly backward, away from the vehicle he had been next to. It took them several seconds to realize that he had been shot by the vehicle's passenger, seconds that the vehicle driver put to good use. Rising from his seat, pulling out his own submachine gun as he did so, the driver popped up over the windshield and fired a short burst at the two MPs at the wire entanglement. The first burst hit the MP with the M-203 just as he was leveling it at Lefleur's vehicle. The other MP, struggling to take her M-16 off her shoulder, paused to watch her partner as he fell over backward. Looking back at the man who had just shot him, the second MP renewed her efforts to bring her rifle into play. It was, however, no contest. The driver, satisfied that the first MP was finished, shifted his MP-5 to the right a little, took aim, and fired at the second MP at the wire entanglement. As with the first, his aim was true and the impact of his burst threw the second MP back and out of the fight even before she could get into it.

Lefleur's two men in the backseat didn't need any special instructions from him. Both, like the driver, drew their weapons out and rose up, firing at the MPs manning the heavy weapons on the Humvees as they did so. Only the MP on the M-60 was able to bring her weapon into play before she was hit. Fortunately for Lefleur, her first burst was high and wild. The mercenary taking her vehicle under fire never allowed her the chance to adjust her aim. Her counterpart, across the road on the M-19 grenade launcher, went down before he even managed to get the safety off his weapon.

That left only the female MP who had been eating. Lefleur, satisfied that the most immediate threats had been dealt with, turned his attention to the last MP. When he looked where she had been, however, only a discarded brown plastic sack and her helmet marked the spot. For the first time, Lefleur was worried. Knowing she couldn't have gone far, he began to scan the area around the Humvee she had been leaning against.

A three-round burst, and a scream of pain from the man standing behind Lefleur, announced the last MP's presence. Though he knew that the noise behind him was the sound of the body of one of his men hitting the pavement, he paid no attention. After catching a glimpse of the offending M-16's muzzle disappearing behind the front left tire of the Humvee, Lefleur leaped out and ran toward the right side of the Humvee. Covering the distance in four or five easy bounds, he didn't pause, but continued around to the rear of the vehicle. As he did so, he ran into the last MP as she was slowly backing around to the rear of the Humvee from her side. Without a second thought, Lefleur leveled his submachine gun at his side and squeezed off a burst into the back of the last MP, who was now less than a meter from him. The kick of the submachine gun caused the strike of the rounds to climb up the MP's back, with the first round hitting her at the base of the spine and the last one in her right shoulder. Several more rounds flew over her shoulder, but that didn't matter. As her body collapsed, Lefleur knew she was finished.

For a moment, he stood and looked at her. What a waste, Lefleur thought, of a good woman. The idea of raping her entered his mind, but he quickly dismissed it. While such an action would have been in line with their program of atrocities, Lefleur had bigger game in mind. Lowering his submachine gun, he fired into the MP's body until the thirty-round magazine was empty. That would have to do for now, he thought, as he ran back to his vehicle.

His driver, with the engine running, was ready to leave. Behind the vehicle were the other two members of his team. One man, a Colombian, was lying on the ground in a pool of blood. The other man, a Canadian by birth, was kneeling over him. Lefleur walked over, looked at the Colombian, and asked how he was. The Canadian looked up and shook his head. "What the hell did you start shooting for? We could have gotten through and they would have been none the wiser."

Lefleur was not used to explaining his orders to anyone. Besides, the Canadian knew just as well as any other man in the group that the last thing they could afford to do was to leave witnesses behind. The MP sergeant had seen his face and would, no doubt, be able to put two and two together when the congressman showed up missing. Besides, Lefleur thought, what a great way to start a terror campaign. Ignoring the Canadian's question, he asked how the Colombian was.

"He's bleeding like a stuck pig. He won't make it if we can't stop the bleeding and get some serious medical attention quickly."

Lefleur looked at the Colombian, then to the east. "All right then, take his ID and weapon. We need to get moving."

The Canadian hesitated. "We're going to leave him?"

Lefleur looked down into the Canadian's eyes. "You yourself said he would die if we didn't get him help right away. We have no way of doing that. Besides, he looks like a Mexican. When the Americans find his body here, they'll think that he is a Mexican, and blame them. It will help our efforts. Now, get moving. We have to catch up to the congressman before it gets dark."

The Canadian looked at his wounded comrade, unconscious and breathing irregularly, then back at Lefleur. Realizing that Lefleur was right, and that they had all signed on for what they knew was going to be a difficult job, the Canadian emptied the Colombian's pockets and hopped into the vehicle. Lefleur looked down at the Colombian one last time before he followed suit. He had considered finishing off the Colombian, but decided against that. To do so in front of the other two would be a bad business practice. You do not, Lefleur knew, inspire confidence and loyalty by shooting your own wounded. Besides, the American high command had placed a mandatory restriction on unnecessary movement at night. With no prospect of anyone coming by that checkpoint before daybreak the next morning, the Colombian would die anyhow, on his own. Without another thought, Lefleur walked around, got into his seat, and ordered his driver to move out to the east as fast as he could.

5 KILOMETERS WEST OF SABINAS HIDALGO, MEXICO
1945 HOURS, 15 SEPTEMBER

When the driver of the Humvee Ed Lewis was in saw the flashing headlights of a vehicle coming up behind him, he slowed down.

Noticing the reduction in speed, Lewis leaned over and asked what the problem was. The driver, twisting his head around and looking out his window to see if the van with Jan Fields and her camera crew was also slowing, didn't answer at first. Lewis repeated his question. The driver, looking back to the front, eased his Humvee over onto the shoulder of the road and stopped it before answering. "Sorry, sir, but there's someone coming up fast behind us that either wants to pass or wants us to stop."

The young lieutenant, a public-affairs officer who was serving as Lewis's escort, had been asleep. It wasn't until the Humvee hit the gravel on the shoulder of the road that he realized they were stopping. "What are we stopping for, Jackson?"

Specialist Jackson, the driver, repeated his explanation to the lieutenant. Opening his door, the lieutenant saw the four-by-four coming up, horn honking and lights flashing. Since they were already stopped, the lieutenant saw no harm in finding out what the people in the vehicle wanted. As a courtesy, he asked Lewis, though he had no idea what he would do if Lewis told them to keep going. "If it's all right with you, Congressman, I'll find out what the problem is with these people."

Lewis, having been in the National Guard, understood these things and simply nodded his approval. Besides, he needed to get out, stretch his legs, and take a leak.

Behind the Humvee, in the van, Jan asked the same question. Joe Bob, who had been driving, just shook his head. "Don't know, boss lady. They stopped and I thought it would be a good idea to stop too."

Though Jan didn't like Joe Bob referring to her as "boss lady," she said nothing. Instead, she opened her door and began to get out, just as the four-by-four that had been racing up the road to catch them went screaming by. Jumping back into the van and closing the door behind her, Jan looked out the window to see if there was another vehicle coming before she tried to get out again.

"Guess now you know why we stopped, hey, boss lady?"

Jan shot Joe Bob, who was laughing, a dirty look. "I'll get you, smartass."

From the backseat, Ted woke up and asked Joe Bob what was going on. "Piss break, my friend."

Jan ignored Joe Bob's comment. "Let's get out and see what's so hell-fire important."

The strangers in the four-by-four, parked on the other side of the road, didn't get out right away. Instead, they waited until the public-affairs officer crossed over to them. While the lieutenant was doing so, Lewis, along with Jackson, the driver, had moved around to the far side of their Humvee where each man took up position before one of the Humvee's tires and began to relieve himself. Joe Bob and Ted got out and did likewise behind their van.

As he sat there, watching the American officer approach him, Lefleur considered his options. Logic told him that the quickest and most efficient means of dealing with this was just to kill everyone there outright and leave. That would conform nicely to their strategy and tactics. But Lefleur also knew that this group of Americans was no ordinary group. Had they been simple soldiers, like the MPs at the roadblock, he wouldn't have given the matter a second thought. But a congressman, along with a news correspondent to boot, now this was something entirely different. The fact that one of their own was missing might spur the rest of the American congressmen to drop their differences and press for further, more severe measures, an effort the American media would, no doubt, give great coverage to, since one of their own was also involved. Besides, Lefleur thought, he could always have them killed later if things didn't work out and deposited somewhere that would be embarrassing to the Mexican government.

Jan, ignoring the joy that Lewis and the rest got from peeing on tires, began to walk across the road to see who the strangers were. The man seated in the passenger seat, as well as the one in the rear, had already gotten out, but remained on the far side of their vehicle. They too, Jan thought, were getting ready to pee. Just as she was beginning to wonder if she was the only one who could control her bladder, she heard the front passenger in the four-by-four identify himself as Paul Perrault. Jan froze. Looking at the man in the growing darkness, she knew that whoever he was, he wasn't Paul Perrault. Jan and Paul had been lovers when Jan had worked in Paris years before. When Jan heard him continue, stating that he was a correspondent for the French National News Network, she knew they were in trouble. While there was a possibility of there being two Paul Perraults, the odds of both of them being correspondents and working for the same agency were just too great. Without waiting to hear more, Jan turned and began to walk back to the van as quickly as she could without raising any suspicions.

The Canadian, however, who had been watching her, noted her strange behavior, and alerted Lefleur that they had been read. After a quick glance to assess the situation, Lefleur raised the submachine gun he had been concealing and shot the lieutenant standing on the other side of the four-by-four.

The sudden rip of machine-gun fire caught everyone in Lewis's party off guard. Even Jan, her back to the four-by-four, jumped before she dove for the open cargo door of the van. The Canadian, who had been watching Jan's van as well as her, lifted his submachine gun and raked the van, from front to rear, with a long burst. He missed Jan by inches and didn't hit Joe Bob or Ted, who were standing on the other side. Still, the burst had the desired effect, causing all the men who had been on the other side of the Humvee and van to flatten on the ground, seeking cover behind the tires they had just urinated on.

Before anyone could recover from their shock and react, the Canadian and Lefleur's driver were across the road, training their weapons on Lewis and his party. With a crisp, clear shout, Lefleur ordered everyone up and into the middle of the road. Slowly, Lewis and Jackson, as well as Joe Bob and Ted, responded. The emotion and fear displayed by each man differed. Jackson, Lewis's driver, was shaking as he looked at Lefleur's driver, then back to his Humvee where his rifle was still sitting in the rack. Lewis tried hard to suppress his fear, eyeing Lefleur's driver as he rose from the ground.

Behind the Humvee, at Jan's van, the Canadian gathered Joe Bob and Ted. Joe Bob, more embarrassed than shocked, eyed the Canadian, assessing what his chances were of rushing and overpowering the mercenary. Ted, totally shaken by the incident, was slow to get up. When he did, he trembled like a leaf.

As Jan lay stretched across the front seat of the van, half in and half out, she saw the handle of Joe Bob's pistol sticking out from under the driver's seat. For an instant, she considered reaching over and pulling it out. The voice of the mercenary, the one who claimed to be Paul Perrault, stopped her. "Mademoiselle, if you would be so good as to join us?"

He was standing right behind her. Jan took one last look at the pistol, then gave up the idea. Lightning reactions had never been her strong suit. Slowly, she eased herself out of the van.

Once Lefleur, escorting Jan, reached the others, who were already gathered in the center of the road, Lewis tried to assert himself. "Who's in charge here?"

Lefleur, without so much as a word, walked around Jan, over to where Jackson and Lewis were standing side by side. Lefleur jammed the muzzle of his submachine gun under Jackson's chin and fired a burst, showering Lewis with blood, bone fragments, and brain tissue before he could react.

Jan lost it. She was hardly conscious of the urine running down her leg as she screamed.

Ignoring Jan's screams, Lefleur smiled at Lewis. "Does that, my friend, answer your question?"

Lewis, eyes wild, also lost his self-control. "What in the hell did you do that for? Are you mad?"

Lefleur shrugged. "Why, Congressman, did you not ask who was in charge?"

"You didn't need to kill a man to prove that to me, did you?"

Lefleur looked down at Jackson's body, then at Lewis. "True, but he had to go anyway. Excess baggage. Now, talking about going, if you would all please move over to the van, we can leave."

Jan, finally able to control her voice, asked what the rest of them were thinking. "What are you going to do to us?"

Lefleur, turning away from Lewis, walked over to Jan. For a moment, he looked her up and down, a grin on his face. Joe Bob, unable to restrain himself, stepped forward, muttering as he did so, "Don't even think of it, you fucking shit."

With a simple flick of his wrist, Lefleur turned his submachine gun on Joe Bob. Jan screamed again. "No! Joe Bob! The bastard will kill you!"

Pausing, Joe Bob looked down the barrel of Lefleur's gun before backing off.

Looking back at Jan, Lefleur noticed her pants were wet. "I must apologize to the lady. It seems my melodramatics have caused you to, how can I say, lose control of yourself." Jan's face turned red from anger. He was baiting them, just playing with them and goading them to react so that he could shoot someone else.

When he saw that no one else was going to respond, Lefleur looked at the setting sun. "We are wasting time. There is a long and, for you, mademoiselle, uncomfortable journey ahead." With that, he signaled the

Canadian and his driver to begin moving them to the van. Lewis, Jan, Ted, and Joe Bob were bound, gagged, and thrown into the back. Leaving the bodies of the public-affairs lieutenant and his driver, as well as their Humvee, Lefleur headed back to the base camp with his trophies. If this didn't get a rise out of the Americans, nothing would.

22

The good fighting man who honestly believes himself to be a pure mercenary in arms, doing it all for the money, may have to guard his convictions as vigilantly as any atheist.

—General Sir John Hackett

4 KILOMETERS SOUTHEAST OF EJIDO DE DOLORES, MEXICO
0615 HOURS, 16 SEPTEMBER

Childress stormed into the one-story cinder-block building that had housed the offices of the abandoned mining camp, pushing an Irish mercenary against the wall as he did so. Regaining his balance, the stunned Irishman was about to lunge at Childress, but missed his chance as Childress threw open the door of Delapos's office and flew into the room, slamming the door behind him.

Stunned by Childress's sudden and violent appearance just as much as the Irishman, both Delapos and Lefleur ceased their discussion and turned to stare at the tall American standing before them, his nostrils flaring and face contorted in anger. Paying no attention to Lefleur, Childress rushed at Delapos. "What in God's name do you think you're doing? Hostages were never part of the plan. And why in the hell wasn't I notified when they were brought in?"

Delapos's surprise turned to anger. "What do you mean, coming into my office like that and speaking to me like I was some kind of peon?"

Too enraged to be brushed off with such a comment, Childress raised his right hand, his index finger uncurling from a tight fist. "I asked you a question, Delapos. What in the hell are we doing with those hostages? Have you lost your mind?"

If it was to be a challenge, then Delapos was ready to meet it. Kicking the chair that he had been sitting on out of his way as he stood, Delapos

378

turned toward Childress and assumed a fighting stance. "I am not going to stand here, in my own office, and be threatened by you, or anyone else, in this manner. When the time comes, I will tell you what I choose to tell you. Until then, your only concern is defense of the two base camps and, while they are here, the guarding of the prisoners."

Still uncowed by the angry Mexican standing across from him, Childress continued to yell as he began to move closer to Delapos. "Have you lost your fucking mind? This is stupid, fucking stupid. When did you . . ."

Instinctively responding to the threat that Childress presented, Delapos reached down with his right hand and pulled a commando knife from his boot. In a single, smooth motion, he brought it up to waist level, threw his left arm out for balance, and hunched down as he prepared to meet the American.

Without thinking, Childress stopped and prepared to defend himself, reaching down to grab for his pistol. There was, however, no pistol to be found. In his haste, Childress had forgotten to strap his ankle holster on. This sudden discovery flashed across his face, causing him to pause, then step back away from the menace Delapos now presented.

Delapos, alert and ready, had seen Childress's move and knew what he was doing. He was about to lunge forward in order to strike before the American was able to bring his pistol into play, but stopped when he saw the expression on Childress's face change. When he glanced down and saw Childress's right hand was empty, Delapos relaxed slightly and checked his attack.

"Did you forget something this morning, *mon ami?*"

In his anger, Childress had ignored Lefleur. While keeping an eye on Delapos, Childress slowly cut his eyes to his right. Lefleur, in his indomitable fashion, was seated next to a table, lounging back in a chair with his left elbow resting on the table and his legs crossed while he slowly sipped from a beer. Finished, he held his bottle of beer out in front of him, smacking his lips and belching before turning to Childress. "It seems, my friend, you have come up empty-handed. Would you like to borrow my knife?"

Defenseless and caught off guard by Lefleur, Childress took another step back. Though he dropped his menacing stance and stood upright, he kept his guard up while turning slightly to his right so that he could watch both Delapos and Lefleur. "Was this your idea, you ignorant son of a bitch?"

Lefleur refused to allow Childress to provoke him. Instead, he just played with his beer bottle while he spoke to Childress without looking at him. "When I started, I really didn't know what I was going to do with the Americans. I suppose we could have killed them where we found them. But that seemed such a waste. Congressmen and star reporters are a rarity in these parts, you know."

As intolerable as Lefleur's arrogant mocking was, Childress managed to keep his anger in check. "So why didn't you kill them? That's what we're supposed to do. What in the hell are you going to do with them now?"

Placing the bottle on the table, Lefleur uncrossed his legs, planting both feet on the floor. Taking a deep breath and letting it out, he placed his hands on his knees with an audible slap and looked straight at Childress. "Oh, I suppose, eventually, we will kill them. In fact, Señor Delapos and I were discussing that when you, ah, decided to join us. The only question seems to be how we can do so while achieving the greatest shock value from the act. Since neither of us is as well schooled in the fine arts of terror as Señor Alamán, we decided to send a message to him and ask for his advice in this rather delicate matter."

"Lefleur, you're nuts."

Lefleur laughed. "Yes, that may be true. But at least, *mon ami,* I am armed."

"Get out of here," Delapos snarled. "Get back to your duties and don't ever try this again. Do you understand?"

Turning his attention back to Delapos, Childress saw that his boss and former friend hadn't budged an inch or changed expression. He still stood ready, knife in hand, to strike. Without a word, and keeping his eyes on Delapos, Childress reached behind him and felt for the doorknob. When he opened the door, the Irishman he had shoved was in the hall and waiting for him. The Irishman, however, moved away and allowed Childress to back out of the room when he saw Delapos, standing there with a look of hatred in his eyes and his commando knife in hand. Whatever had transpired didn't concern him and he had no desire to become involved in a dispute between his boss and one of his lieutenants. The pay was too good.

When Childress was gone and Delapos relaxed, Lefleur stood up. "It seems that our American friend is not happy with our decision."

"He has lost his edge. He cannot be trusted."

Trying hard to conceal his gloating, Lefleur sighed. "Perhaps, amigo, our American friend has lost his taste for American blood."

Replacing his knife, Delapos grunted. "Perhaps. Whatever the reason, he cannot be trusted."

Allowing Delapos's comment to hang in the air for a moment, Lefleur began to smile. "Well, it is getting late. I must be going. I have not finished my reconnaissance and there is little time. Perhaps, by the time I get back, you will have a response from Señor Alamán. Either way, please do me the favor of saving the Americans for me?"

Taking deep breaths to calm himself as he thought about Childress's insult and challenge to his authority, Delapos considered Lefleur's request. "Yes, I will do that, under one condition."

"Why, yes, of course. Whatever you say, *mon ami.*"

"Before you dispose of the congressman and his party, you get rid of Childress. He cannot be trusted anymore."

"Ah, I see," Lefleur mocked. "A little pleasure before business. How nice."

The heat in the small metal-covered shed where Jan had been thrown the night before was stifling even though the rays of sunlight pouring through the gaps in the walls told her it was still early in the morning. As she lay there, bound and gagged on the dirt floor, looking around, Jan began to regret that she had not gone for Joe Bob's gun. At least, she thought, had she done so, her problems would be over. It would have been quick, clean, and final. This, she thought, as she looked about the shed that was no bigger than a closet, was hell.

Since their arrival at this base camp, as the Frenchman had called it, no one had come by, no one had spoken to her, no one had bothered to untie her. She had not been given anything to eat, nothing to drink, and she had been unable to relieve herself. They had simply opened the door of the shed, thrown her in, and closed the door, leaving her in the dirt to sweat and lie in her own filth. She doubted that the door of the shed was even locked. Not that it mattered. She was gagged, and bound like a calf at a rodeo, hands and feet together. Though there were cracks and gaps around the door and here and there in the walls through which light entered the small room, they were not big enough to allow a breeze in. The only things that did come into the shed through those cracks were bugs and flies, which were having a field day as they crawled all over her, and dust that settled on her body and turned to a thin layer of mud as it mixed with her sweat. As much as all that bothered her, she knew that it wouldn't be long before she was past caring. Already she could feel herself alternating between periods of faintness and nausea from lack of water. Eventually, she would either go mad or die. At that moment, she didn't care which came first.

When the door of the shed flew open, the bright light hit her face and blinded her, causing her to roll over and away from it. With her back to the door, she felt someone grab the gag and pull it away from her head, stretching the corners of her dry mouth further. For a second, there was the sensation of cold metal next to her ear, then the ripping of cloth as the gag was cut. When the gag finally fell away from her mouth, Jan let out a series of coughs.

She was still hacking away, trying to catch her breath and clear her dry throat, when the man who had cut her gag reached over her, grabbed her hands and feet, and cut the rope that had bound them together. When the knife cut through the ropes, Jan found she had no control over her arms and legs. Instead, they sprang apart like a rag doll's. For the longest time, all she could manage to do was lie spreadeagled on the floor, staring at the ceiling as she let the muscle spasms and pain in her arms, wrists, legs, and ankles subside. She was oblivious to whoever had freed her. She was even oblivious, for the first time, to the bugs, insects, and flies that were still scurrying across her body. The only thing that mattered was that she was no longer bound and gagged. Thoughts of escape were the farthest thing from her mind. All she wanted at that moment was for the pain to stop and a drink of water.

After a minute or so, a hand reached around the back of her neck and lifted. Before she knew what was happening, the stranger put a cup to her lips and began to pour water into her mouth. Although Jan wanted to drink the water, her first reaction was to cough and spit it back out. When she did so, the stranger paused for a second, allowing her to catch her breath again, before pouring more water. This time, she was able to swallow it. When the stranger went to pull the cup away again, she panicked, trying to reach up and grab the cup so she could keep drinking. Her arms, however, would not respond. Instead, all she managed to do was shake and wiggle, causing the stranger to spill water down her face and neck.

"Whoa, lady, take it easy. Relax. There's more."

The voice was that of an American. The Army! Delta Force! They were here to save her! Jan opened her eyes. Still blinded by the bright light coming through the doorway, she couldn't see the face or clothes. What she could see was the outline of the man's head. His hair, she realized, was too long for an American soldier. No, she hadn't been saved. It wasn't Scott and the 7th Cavalry. But he had water. And for now, that was all that mattered.

After waiting a minute, the stranger pulled Jan up into a sitting position and offered her the cup of water. Finally able to control her wobbly arms, she took it and gulped it down. Only after she had finished it and sat there in silence, savoring her freedom and the taste of the water, did she begin to look around and wonder who her savior was, and, more importantly, what was going to happen next.

Anticipating her questions, Childress decided to tell her what he thought was safe before she began with a thousand questions. "There's not much I can tell you. In fact, the less you know, the better off you are. First, your friends are, for the moment, all right. Someone is taking care of them as we speak. Second, I can't tell you who we are, where we are, or what we are doing. Like I said, it's to your advantage that you don't know. Finally, I have no idea what's going to happen to you. Until my boss hears from his boss, I can't tell you what is going to happen."

The woman on the floor played with the cup she held in both hands for a moment before looking at him. "You mean, you don't know how you're going to murder us."

Had the woman slapped him in the face, Childress could not have been more hurt. She was right. He knew that, in the end, Delapos would have no choice but to murder her, the congressman, and the camera crew. There was simply no way that they could be allowed to live after having seen Lefleur and his people. Such loose ends could not be permitted. Besides, logic told Childress that the abduction of a congressman, followed by his brutal murder, fit perfectly into Alamán's strategy to enrage the American military and public. The rape and mutilation of a TV reporter, especially one who had so recently come out in support of the Mexicans as Jan Fields had, was a bonus that simply could not be passed up. He knew that she was right.

Childress sat there and looked at the woman, her words and his thoughts tearing at the lining of his stomach like a wild cat in a sack. What a loathsome creature he had become. A snake that slithered about on its belly could take greater pride in what it did than Childress could. The snake, after all, killed its victims quickly and only to feed itself or in self-defense. Lefleur, Delapos, and the others, including him, killed for money and to prove that they were real men.

It wasn't that Childress was having an attack of conscience. He had been a mercenary too long for that. In fact, in many respects, he was like Lefleur, eager to prove to himself and to his peers that he was a skilled practitioner of the fine arts of war. Unlike Lefleur, however, Childress preferred to work at long range, claiming that it took greater skill to take down a man a mile away with a single bullet. While that was true, and many of his peers agreed with him, Childress knew the real reason for his preference. At a range of sixteen hundred meters, it was impossible to see your victim's eyes. Even with a high-powered scope, the entire process was remote, impersonal, unreal. You couldn't hear the scream. It was not necessary to watch the shocked expression as the victim's life drained away. Even the smell of fear, mixed with the sweet scent of warm blood, was missing. It was, Childress thought, more like shooting targets.

This was different. Looking down into Jan's eyes, he could see the fear and hatred she held for him. When it came time, and he knew that that time would come, there would be no skill involved in killing this woman. It would be murder, simple and outright murder.

Unable to look at Jan any longer, knowing that he was as responsible for her death as the man who would eventually pull the trigger, Childress stood up and turned away from her. It was incredible, he thought, how far from God and his beloved Vermont he had come. No matter how much he was paid, no matter how anyone dressed it up, what was about to happen would leave Childress no pride, no satisfaction, and worse, no peace.

Without saying a word, Childress dropped the canteen of water he held onto the floor, walked out of the shed, and nodded to the man posted outside to lock it.

ARLINGTON, VIRGINIA
1615 HOURS, 16 SEPTEMBER

Although Megan Lewis knew that her efforts would be futile, she asked the caller if he would hold for a moment while she checked to see if her mother was available. Carefully laying the phone's receiver on the countertop, Megan left the kitchen, tiptoeing as she approached the door of the den that her father had used as an office. Pausing before she knocked, Megan listened at the door for her mother. When she heard nothing, Megan gently tapped on the door. "Mother, it's the White House again. The president's secretary says that the president would like to talk to you. He wants to offer you his condolences."

Megan's efforts were greeted with silence. "Mother, please say something. This is the third time he's called. It won't hurt to at least listen to what he has to say." Her pleading, however, elicited no response. After waiting a few more seconds, Megan sighed. "I'll tell them that you're not available, to call back tomorrow. Will that be okay, Mom?"

When even that failed to elicit a response, Megan turned and slowly walked back to the kitchen. Her mother, she knew, could be just as impossible as her father when she wanted to be.

Inside the den, Amanda Lewis sat in the chair she always sat in across from Ed's desk. She knew that her daughter, despite three years of college and grades that assured her acceptance to any medical school in the country, wouldn't understand. How could she. She was young and just beginning to learn about the real world. Megan had yet to love as she had. Megan had yet to discover that pompous titles and age did little to make some men any wiser or more compassionate. Even Ed, for all his strength, was just a human trying to make sense out of a world that, on occasion, found it necessary to turn and devour its own children in a fit of mindless passion.

When the flashing red light on Ed's phone went out, telling Amanda that her daughter had hung up, Amanda continued to stare at the phone. Had it been like that, she thought, for Ed? One minute, there was the flickering of life, a steady glow of life, and the next, nothing? And was that all that Ed's life had been, a brief and insignificant flickering of light? Looking about at the stacks of papers and files and books, Amanda wondered if all his efforts, all his dreams, all his hopes that lay hidden in the stacks of files and papers would, like the flashing light, disappear in an instant.

No, she thought. No, Ed deserved better than that. There was a real purpose behind what Ed had devoted his life to. What he had been doing was no illusion, no dream. His efforts to bring peace and sanity may have cost him his life, but that didn't mean that they, like him, should die. Although she didn't quite know what she could do, Amanda decided that the dreams and goals, no matter how unrealistic they appeared at times, would not die. As he had said so many times before, a person must do more than protest an injustice, he must do something to make it right. Amanda's refusal to allow the president to ease his conscience by consoling her was a protest, but one that would have no meaning if she didn't follow it up with action.

Moving around Ed's desk, Amanda sat in his seat, absentmindedly opening the first file that her hand fell upon. Reading the handwritten notes, Amanda began to look for a way to keep her husband's dreams alive and keep other wives and mothers from going through what she was experiencing. Perhaps she could make someone pay attention to what Ed had been trying to say. Perhaps she could make a difference. She didn't know if she could, but she could try, if for no other reason than to give the loss of her husband some meaning, some value.

SANTA GENOVEVA, MEXICO
1845 HOURS, 16 SEPTEMBER

With two men set at the roadblock, Fernando Naranjo returned to the side of the road where the other two men in his small detachment worked at starting a fire for the coffee that they hoped would keep them alert throughout the coming night. Not that anyone expected all five men to stay awake all night. After all, they were farmers and ranchers. While the duty they performed for the defense of Mexico was important, the necessity of making a living and providing for their families was critical. Like thousands of other militiamen and members of the Rural Defense Force, Naranjo and his four men were only part-time soldiers, doing what they could when they could. That night, their task and instructions were simple: set up a roadblock just behind Mexican lines and prevent anyone, other than Mexican Army soldiers, from passing through.

Though Naranjo would have preferred to be doing something a little more active, he knew he didn't belong out there, behind American lines, with his son and oldest grandson. He was too old, too slow. Though he could have insisted on going, doing so would have been foolish vanity. Besides, someone needed to remain behind to take care of the ranch and the women. His two youngest grandsons could not have done it on their own. So he stayed, doing what he could with the Rural Defense Force when his aging body and work at the ranch allowed him.

With great care, and using his 1898 Mauser rifle to steady himself, Naranjo began to lower himself down onto a blanket across from the two men preparing the coffee when he heard the sound of a vehicle coming up the road. Pausing, Naranjo leaned on the rifle and looked down the road in the direction of the sound, then over to the roadblock. His two men on the road, also aware of the sound, were turned facing down the road, their rifles at the ready. Deciding that perhaps he should wait before relaxing, Naranjo told the two men with him to wait on the coffee. Though he didn't expect any trouble, he wanted them to stay where they were and be ready to help the men at the roadblock if necessary.

With a push, Naranjo stood upright and headed down to the roadblock just as the lone vehicle came around a bend in the road and into sight.

Asleep, Lefleur didn't see the roadblock until his driver slowed, then stopped just short of it. Stirring himself, Lefleur, noting that they were not at the base camp, asked why they had stopped. The Canadian mercenary, riding in the backseat, laughed. "It is nothing. Just some old men manning a roadblock."

Sitting up, Lefleur studied the barrier to his front and the two men, rifles at the ready, standing behind it. When he saw that they were armed with 1898 Mauser bolt-action rifles, he joined the Canadian as they both tried to make a joke of the whole affair. "Which do you suppose," he quipped, "are older? The rifles or the men?"

When the old man who appeared to be in charge began to approach the vehicle, followed by the two men who had come out from behind the barrier, the Canadian chuckled. "The men. Definitely the men. How much will you bet they are out of breath before they reach here?"

As he approached, Naranjo saw that the gringos were laughing. This angered him, for he took his duty seriously. Becoming incensed, he decided to make the strangers pay for their laughter. Pointing his rifle at Lefleur, he demanded that everyone in the vehicle show proper identification.

The sudden belligerence of the old man and the muzzle of the rifle waving two feet in front of his face wiped the smile off of Lefleur's face. The old fool, he thought, was dangerous. Raising his right hand, palm out, Lefleur gestured to the old man, while he dug in his pocket with his left hand for his false French ID and passport. Deciding that there was no need to antagonize the old simpleton, Lefleur turned over his papers.

The ID, of course, meant nothing to Naranjo, who could not read French. Determined to show that he had authority, and to teach the arrogant foreigners a lesson, Naranjo informed Lefleur that he would need to come back to the village and have the army officer in charge of his militia company check out his papers.

Suddenly, the situation was no longer a laughing matter. Lefleur and the Canadian went silent as they prepared to go for their weapons. Naranjo and his companions, however, noticed the change in attitude of the strangers. They were ready when Lefleur's driver reached under the seat for his weapon. Without warning, the man who had been covering the driver fired. Whether he did so because he was nervous or because he saw the driver's weapon will never be known. But he did. When hit, the driver jerked upright, causing his hand to pull his submachine gun out and into the open where Naranjo, who was still covering Lefleur, saw it. As Naranjo shoved his rifle into Lefleur's stomach, the third militiaman, who had been at the rear of the vehicle, put the muzzle of his rifle next to the Canadian's ear.

For their efforts, Naranjo and the militiamen who had helped apprehend Lefleur were given the submachine guns that they found on their captives. Not only would the modern weapon be useful when Naranjo led his men on future occasions, but it would provide proof of his feat to his son and grandchildren. The submachine gun, Naranjo knew, would become a family heirloom that was worthy to pass on to his son, just as the 1898 Mauser he carried had been passed on to him from his grandfather.

As important as this was, the gift Naranjo and his men presented Guajardo with was one beyond measure. With Lefleur, Guajardo had a key that, if used properly, would give him what he wanted most: Alamán.

23

MEXICO CITY, MEXICO
1935 HOURS, 17 SEPTEMBER

Sitting alone, at the end of a long table, Lefleur stared at the two Mexican soldiers at the door. Though the accommodations in the Mexican jail were far better than he had imagined, such thoughts did nothing to dispel his anger or embarrassment at having been caught by peasants. It had been such a stupid affair. A stupid and unnerving affair.

When there was a knock at the door, one of the soldiers turned and opened a small viewing window in the center of it to identify who was on the other side. Closing the viewing door, the soldier unbolted the door and opened it to allow the visitor in. As soon as the door began to open, the soldier returned to his position, but came to attention, shouting an order for the other guard to do likewise. Not having seen such a reaction from his guards before, Lefleur figured that he was about to meet someone important.

The Mexican Army colonel who entered, followed by a lieutenant, was tall and lean. Lefleur gave him the once-over. There were few ribbons on his chest, which meant that the colonel had done nothing to earn his rank, or else he was a modest man, something Lefleur doubted. It was not possible, he knew, to be a colonel and be modest. The colonel wore his hat with its brim pulled down so that his eyes were not visible. He was here, Lefleur decided, to intimidate him. He thought about that for a moment, then laughed to himself. What could a Mexican colonel possibly do to him that a good sergeant in the Legion, and half a dozen trained professionals after that, hadn't already tried?

As he was studying the colonel, Lefleur did not notice that the lieutenant who accompanied the colonel had dismissed the guards, closing and bolting the door after they left. Taking up his station at the door, he nodded to the colonel that he was ready.

Taking off his hat, Guajardo placed it on the table, then slowly walked past Lefleur so that he was now behind him. Guajardo stood there for a moment before starting, as if he were pondering his first question. When he finally spoke, it was in English. "I already know what brings you to Mexico, Señor Lefleur, so we can dispense with many of the preliminaries."

Lefleur, without looking at Guajardo, decided to play with the colonel. Folding his arms in front of his chest, Lefleur protested. "My name, *señor colonel,* is Perrault, Paul Perrault. I am a correspondent for the French National News Network. I have no idea why I am here and demand that I be allowed to see a member of the French embassy staff."

Lefleur could hear the colonel heave a great sigh before he spoke again. "Do not, Señor Lefleur, play the fool with me. Your friend the Canadian was most talkative."

Unable to help himself, Lefleur quipped, "Well, if the Canadian was talkative, then you do not need me."

There was a pause. Unable to see the colonel's face, Lefleur did not know how his comment had gone over. The lieutenant at the door, still wearing his hat, betrayed no reaction. So Lefleur sat there, waiting.

"Ah, well, Señor Lefleur, as I said, your friend was most talkative. But no more. Alas, he was not as hardy as we had thought. His physique was very deceptive. You see, your friend died an hour ago."

For the first time, Lefleur felt a twinge of fear. Though he tried not to, he stiffened slightly at the news of the Canadian's death. For a minute, Lefleur tried to convince himself that the Mexican colonel was bluffing. They would not beat or torture a man to death. They were professional soldiers. Yet, in the back of his mind, he knew it was true. He had no idea who this colonel was or what he wanted. But he did know that Mexico was a country in the middle of a revolution and at war with the United States. Given those circumstances, and if what the colonel said was true, Lefleur realized that anything was possible. It was time to start cooperating, a little. "What is it, Colonel, that you want?"

Without hesitation, the colonel responded. "I want Alamán."

Lefleur hesitated. The Canadian had talked a lot. Still not ready to roll over, Lefleur shrugged and threw his hands out to his side. "I am sorry, Colonel. I cannot help you. I do not know a person by the name of Alamán."

Though he had expected the Frenchman to play games with him, Guajardo was still angered by the man's manner and arrogance. Looking over to his side, Guajardo snapped, "Juan, your pistol."

Marching from his post at the door, past Lefleur, Juan came up to Guajardo, unholstered his pistol, and handed it to Guajardo. The sound of the pistol's slide being pulled back and released, an action that chambered a round, caused Lefleur to flinch. Lefleur could hear the lieutenant pivot and begin to head back to the door, where he resumed his post. Lefleur noticed that there was a slight smile on his face. It was a wicked smile, a smile that increased Lefleur's apprehension. Whatever was going on, Lefleur realized, had been planned and rehearsed.

"Señor Lefleur, if you would be so kind as to place both hands on the table, palms down and fingers apart, we can continue our conversation."

Having no idea what was going on, Lefleur complied. He could feel the sweat begin to bead up on his forehead as he placed his hands on the table.

Without a word, without a warning, the pistol flashed past the right side of Lefleur's head. Before he could react, Guajardo placed the muzzle of the pistol on the lower knuckle of the right-hand pinkie and pulled the trigger.

Expecting a violent reaction, Guajardo pulled away and to one side as Lefleur pushed himself away from the table, howling like an injured animal. Guajardo, seeing the chair begin to slide back, stuck his foot behind its rear leg, stopping it from sliding any farther, and causing it to tip over. The chair tilted back, then toppled, sending Lefleur sprawling on the floor, blood squirting out of the nub on his right hand where a finger had once been.

Once he was able to recover from the shock and surprise of being shot, Lefleur grabbed his right wrist with his left hand and looked at the nub. As he was studying the damage, he began panting, almost unable to breathe. Guajardo, who had taken a step back, looked down at Lefleur and smiled. "Señor Lefleur, you may, if you choose, continue to be stubborn. But I must warn you, I will surely outlast you. You see, I have fourteen bullets left. You, only nine fingers."

Lefleur had had enough. He was, after all, only a mercenary. There was no honor in dying for Alamán. There was nothing worth throwing his life away for. It was not in his own interest to continue with this insanity. As soon as he had composed himself, he blurted that he didn't know where Alamán was. He was, he explained, only one of many mercenaries.

Guajardo walked over and looked down at Lefleur. "Yes, that may be true. But you are going to take me to the man who does know where Alamán is. You will, my friend, lead me to Señor Delapos and deliver him to me. For if you do not, I will personally see that your death is a slow and painful one, the kind where the victim's voice gives out from incessant screaming days before the body dies. Do we understand each other, señor?"

HEADQUARTERS, 16TH ARMORED DIVISION, SABINAS HIDALGO, MEXICO
0635 HOURS, 18 SEPTEMBER

The calm that Dixon tried to feign fooled no one. Though he was far from being a basket case, Big Al considered putting him on furlough for a week, maybe two. Big Al, however, appreciated that such a move would only serve to magnify Dixon's sense of loss. So long as he continued to function and perform his duties, the division commander would leave Dixon be. In his own time, in his own way, Big Al knew that Dixon would finally come to grips with the loss of Jan Fields.

It was not that anyone had given up. On the contrary, the president, under pressure from Congress and the media, and fueled by Amanda Lewis's agitation, was making every effort to find out what had happened to Congressman Ed Lewis, Jan, and her crew. From the branch of the Red Cross that dealt with prisoners of war, to the United Nations, representatives of the United States were demanding that the Mexican government stop denying any knowledge of the incident and surrender the hostages immediately. The Mexican government, for their part, denied that it had any part in or any knowledge of the incident. The CIA, working inside Mexico, could not find any evidence that they were lying. On the contrary, their agents reported that several Mexican intelligence and police agencies were also involved in trying to find Congressman Lewis and party. Though some believed that the efforts by the Mexican intelligence agencies were a sham, created to back the Mexican government's claim that it had no knowledge of the incident, it could not be ignored.

Within the 16th Division's sector, ground and air patrols, starting at the site of the abduction and spreading out in ever-widening circles, continued to search for the raiders and for Lewis and party, or for any clue as to where they might have disappeared to. That Lewis and the members of his party might be dead was not discounted by anyone. Included in the instructions of all patrols involved was to keep an eye open for anything that resembled freshly dug graves.

Though Big Al favored these actions, he was concerned that his soldiers, incensed over what the media were calling the brutal murder of the MPs and Lewis's military escort, might seek revenge on innocent Mexicans. Already there had been two incidents in which nervous guards, already on edge due to the sporadic guerrilla attacks that were becoming more and more numerous, had fired on civilians. If this were allowed to continue, Big Al could face a situation that would compel him to quit the area that his division had paid so much to take.

Cerro walked into the current-operations van, ready to relieve his counterpart from the night shift, Captain Mark Grumpf. Cerro was about to slap Grumpf on the back when he noticed Dixon, sitting at a field table in the corner. Alone, his head propped up with his right hand, Dixon was poring through the duty log, reading every entry and report. Cerro leaned over and whispered in Grumpf's ear, "How long has he been here?"

Grumpf looked over at Dixon, then to Cerro. "He left at oh-two hundred this morning and was back in at oh-five thirty."

Cerro stood up and looked at Dixon for a moment. He felt sorry for the man. A few years before, Dixon had lost his wife in a bombing while he was assigned to the Middle East. Though Cerro had been told that they were estranged, the loss had to have been hard on him. Now, in the middle of a war, he had lost his . . .

Cerro paused. He didn't quite know what to call Jan Fields. What was Jan Fields to Dixon anyway? A lover? A friend? A roommate? It was a strange relationship, at least for the military, which prided itself as being the last great bastion of conservative values and such. No one talked about Jan and Dixon's relationship, but it was one that meant a great deal to Dixon, and one that he never tried to hide or apologize for. To be sure, Jan was good-looking, for an older woman. And she had a great personality. In many ways, she matched Dixon perfectly. Still, Cerro couldn't figure out what to call the relationship between them. Perhaps there wasn't a name for it. Perhaps, Cerro thought, the relationship they had was like Dixon's military career, one of those things that simply defied definition and refused to be classified.

Shaking his head, Cerro was about to join Grumpf, who had moved to the map in preparation for giving Cerro a quick update, when the division G2 came rushing into the van. "Scotty, we've got 'em."

Startled, Dixon looked up at the G2 with blurry eyes. "Got who?"

"Remember me telling you that I thought it was strange that there were no weapons missing from the MP or Lewis ambush sites?"

Not really remembering, Dixon nevertheless nodded his head in order to get the G2 to make his point a little faster.

Continuing, the G2 pointed a finger toward Dixon to emphasize his points. "In every other ambush, those that we know were made by units of the Mexican Army or guerrilla units led by Mexican Army officers, every piece of equipment and weapon that looked like it would be of value was missing. Even when they didn't overrun the unit under attack, the Mexican guerrillas were reported to take what commanders in the field considered extraordinary risks to collect whatever they could before withdrawing. You see, the Mexican Army, especially guerrilla units, are still quite poor when it comes to weapons and equipment, and they refuse to miss an opportunity to make up that deficiency." The G2 was talking too fast for Dixon to follow, but Dixon didn't stop him. He was too tired and only wanted the G2 to finish. "In addition, in the two cases where prisoners have been taken by the Mexicans, the International Red Cross had the full name, rank, and Social Security number of the prisoners within twenty-four hours."

In his own roundabout way, the G2 was preparing to make a point, a point that Dixon wished he would get to. "Okay, so this ambush isn't like the others. What's it mean?"

A smile lit across the G2's face. "The Mexican Army didn't ambush the MPs or Lewis. Their story that they don't know anything about the ambushes, and the one being put out by the government, is true. They didn't do it."

Dixon shook his head. "Okay, you've lost me. Seems like the info about the weapons being left behind is all very nice, but doesn't mean much by itself. Anyone can make a mistake. Hell, I got two weeks' worth of duty log that will prove that."

The G2 held out a small folder with yellow TOP SECRET cover sheets. "That Mexican we found at the MP checkpoint that was hit came to last night long enough for our people to interrogate him."

Dixon, wide awake now, sat up. "And?"

"Well, what he said, by itself, didn't make a whole lot of sense. Most of what he gave us was gibberish. He's in really bad shape, you see. Doctors say he should have died. But that's not important right now. What is important is that the little info he gave us, combined with other bits and pieces, like the fact that no weapons were taken from either site, adds up."

Dixon was becoming impatient. The G2 was beginning to ramble. "Adds up to what?"

Not to be rushed, the G2 used his fingers as he enumerated his points. "First off, he's not a Mexican. In fact, he's not even working for the Mexican government. That we know. As it turns out, he's a Colombian mercenary. The CIA confirmed that a few hours ago. Seems he's working for some drug lord he kept calling El Dueño, that's Spanish for 'manager.' We're not sure why he's called that, but right now, that's unimportant."

Dixon threw his hands up. "Look, I'm beat. Could you please tell me what *is* important?"

The G2 looked around to see who was in the room. Then he pushed the folder a little closer to Dixon. "I can't tell you. Not in here. It's classified, special compartmented information. You can either read this or come over to my shop and I'll brief you on what we think this Dueño dude's been managing." After Dixon took the folder, the G2, unable to restrain himself, added, "If half the shit that's in there turns out to be true, our fearless leader in the White House and half the CIA's staff better find themselves new jobs."

PALACIO NACIONAL, MEXICO CITY, MEXICO
0915 HOURS, 18 SEPTEMBER

With their meeting coming to an end, Molina turned to Barreda. "Then we are agreed, Felipe. Your actions must be timed so as to ensure that Colonel Guajardo will have achieved everything that he can. Do you see a problem with that?"

Barreda shook his head. "No, there is no problem from our side. The problem all hinges on what the commander of the American 16th Armored Division decides to do. I will be prepared to go either way. If the American does not agree to the meeting that Alfredo is trying to set up, or if they run to their government after the meeting and drop the matter into their State Department's hands, then I will contact the American chargé d'affaires and give him everything we have. If, on the other hand, the American division commander agrees to cooperate with Alfredo, then I wait to meet with the chargé d'affaires until seven AM on the twentieth."

Closing his eyes, Molina nodded. "Things will go better for you, Felipe, and for us, if we are able to point to a success."

"As Alfredo and I have pointed out, Carlos, that depends upon the Americans themselves."

Opening his eyes, Molina turned to Guajardo. "Is there no way to go in and destroy the mercenaries' base and free the American hostages ourselves? Must we depend on the Americans?"

Guajardo answered without looking up from the folder in front of him. "Yes, we could try. And I can give you my assurance that none of the mercenaries would escape. But I cannot guarantee the safety of the Americans, especially since we know that there are traitors amongst us, even on the council."

Guajardo's comment about traitors on the council made Molina flinch. He, and he alone, had invited each and every man on the council to join. The idea that his judgment had been flawed, and could result in the total failure of their efforts, struck him hard. "What makes you think that the American soldiers will be able to do any better than your men?"

Looking up at Barreda, then over to Molina, Guajardo answered slowly and deliberately. "Nothing, absolutely nothing. They, like us, will be going in blind. The big difference is that they will be in control. It will be, essentially, their operation and, God forbid, their failure if the hostages die in the process."

Molina stood up from his seat at the desk, looked down at the papers that Guajardo had handed him, glanced over to his minister of defense and friend, and sighed. Lifting his face toward the ceiling before looking down at Guajardo again, Molina took a deep breath, then sighed again. Turning away from his desk, Molina walked over to the window. With his hands behind his back, he looked blankly out into the square below. After a minute or two, he turned his head slightly toward Guajardo. "Had you come to me with a story that the man in the moon was waiting to see me outside my office, I could not have been more shocked."

Looking back out the window, Molina folded his arms across his chest and shook his head. "Are we being too clever, my friend? Are we trying to be too clever for ourselves? I still feel the better, safer course would be simply to announce publicly what we know, or turn over the information we have on the mercenaries to the Americans. This military operation of yours, Alfredo, and Felipe's diplomatic brinksmanship, is risky." Pivoting, he looked at Guajardo. "No, I believe we should simply tell the Americans what we know and be done with this."

From his seat, Guajardo looked down at his hands, held loosely in his lap. "We must be realists, who deal with the truth as it is, not as we would like it. We all know that as soon as we pass any information through formal channels, no matter how hard we try to safeguard it, Alamán will know. My God, we cannot even trust our own brothers on the council." Guajardo looked up and fixed his eyes on Molina's. "Yes, this entails great risk. But if we hope to end this, we must accept the risks. And part of those risks include using the American military to free their own people."

"Do you agree, Felipe?"

"We must not ignore the fact," Colonel Felipe Barreda pointed out, "that a success in this operation will provide both of our nations with an opening for an honorable resolution to this conflict. I fully agree with Alfredo. There is too much at stake to gamble on our ability to pull this off. Even an American failure will give me a basis for opening a dialogue with them."

Turning about, Molina walked to his desk, gathered up Guajardo and Barreda's report, and waved it at Guajardo. "You two realize that if the Americans refuse to believe us, then we may not have a future. The future of Mexico that we have brought our people will be one of disgrace and conquest. A future dominated by the gringos and drug lords. Is that what our efforts will bring us?" Letting the papers fall from his hand, Molina walked away from his desk again.

Guajardo's retort was given in a calm, determined voice. "I intend to ensure personally that everything happens as we have planned."

Walking around to where Guajardo sat, Molina stopped and looked down at him. "I am sorry, my friend, I cannot allow you to do what you are proposing."

Guajardo slowly rose. Looking his friend in the eye, he smiled. "Carlos, my friend, I am not asking for your permission. I seek only your blessing."

Blinking, Molina realized that Guajardo was serious. "It is bad enough, Alfredo, that we are going to do this without consulting the other members of the council. When they find out, I will need you here, at my side while Felipe deals with the American diplomats."

The smile left Guajardo's face. "Where I go, as the minister of defense, is purely an operational matter. Since this operation concerns national security and, as such, falls completely within my authority as the minister of defense, it is my responsibility to ensure that it is carried out as planned."

There was a pause for several seconds as both men looked at each other. Finally, Molina grasped Guajardo's arms. "You are a fool, Alfredo, an old and stubborn fool." Then, slowly, a smile crept across Molina's face. "You do not know how much I wish I could come with you. When do you leave, my friend?"

"As soon as I notify my adjutant to deliver the letter to the Americans, I will depart for Saltillo."

As his eyes began to moisten, Molina squeezed Guajardo's arms. *"Vaya con Dios*, my brother. *Vaya con Dios."*

"Hey, Sarge! We got someone coming up the road and he's in a hurry."

Though most of the men at the roadblock didn't understand the warning specialist Terry Alison blurted out, his high-pitched squeal was all that was needed to tell them that something was coming down.

Scrambling for their weapons and gear, the men of Staff Sergeant Darrel Jefferson's squad raced for their positions while Jefferson, with flak vest open and web gear flopping about, ran to join Alison. Like a runner stealing a base, Jefferson slid into the narrow opening of the forward bunker, almost hitting Alison in the rear with his boot as he came to a stop.

Alison heard Jefferson but did not move. Leaning forward, he was steadying his M-16 on the sandbags as he tracked the approaching vehicle. Even when Jefferson came up next to him and spoke, Alison kept his rifle trained on the approaching target.

"Okay, hot shot, whatta we got?"

"A jeep of some kind. He's tooling up the middle of the road like nobody's business."

Picking up a pair of binoculars from a case next to the bunker's forward aperture, Jefferson rested his elbows on the sandbags and brought the binoculars up to his eyes. Jefferson studied the approaching jeep. "Do you see a white flag?"

"I see two, Sarge, one on each side of the bumper."

Lowering the binoculars, Jefferson grunted. "Yeah, I see 'em too. Do you suppose they want to talk?"

As if on cue, the jeep slowed, then stopped about one hundred meters short of the bunker where Jefferson and Alison sat. Both men could clearly see the two Mexican soldiers sitting in the open jeep staring in the direction of the bunker, waiting for some sort of acknowledgment from the Americans.

"Well, either that or these people have a real death wish." After a second, Alison turned and looked at Jefferson. "Well, Sarge, what do we do?"

"You stay here. I'm going to see what they want."

Leaving the bunker, Jefferson ordered the other members of his squad to hold their fire. Then, after calling for one of the men nearest him to follow, Jefferson turned and began to approach the passenger side of the stationary jeep while he directed his companion with his right hand to stay behind him and to his right.

When he reached the jeep, Jefferson placed the butt of his M-16 on his right hip, muzzle pointed to the sky. The passenger, an officer wearing a clean uniform, had no weapons showing. Assuming that he spoke English, Jefferson decided to skip the formalities since this officer was, after all, the enemy. Besides, Jefferson had no idea of what the officer's rank was. For all he knew, this could be nothing more than a second lieutenant. "What do you want?"

"I am Major Antonio Caso. I am here on behalf of Colonel Alfredo Guajardo, the minister of defense for the United States of Mexico. I have a personal message from Colonel Guajardo for the commanding general of the 16th Armored Division."

Jefferson looked at the Mexican officer for a moment. The first thought that popped into Jefferson's head was one of dread: Shit, why in the hell does this kind of stuff always happen to me? Manning an outpost was one thing. He knew how to deal with that. Talking to the enemy and receiving personal messages for the division commander was something that was a little bit more than he could deal with. Still, he had to do something. After all, this Mexican was obviously serious. "Let me see the letter."

Without flinching, Caso shook his head. "I am sorry, Sergeant. I cannot let you have the letter. My orders are to personally deliver it to your division commander."

Seeing that the major's eyes betrayed no fear, no hesitation, Jefferson knew that he was serious. Without another thought, he decided it was time to pass this off to someone who got paid to deal with this kind of crap. "Okay, Major, you and your driver stay right here. I'm going to get my CO out here. He'll know what to do." Suddenly, Jefferson laughed as he thought about his young company commander. Like hell he'll know, Jefferson thought. Like hell.

63 KILOMETERS NORTH OF MONTERREY, MEXICO
2230 HOURS, 18 SEPTEMBER

As they waited for the Mexican Army colonel to be shown in, Big Al sat in a chair turned sideways at an old wooden table, staring at the floor with a vacant look on his face while Dixon nervously paced. The only sound was the hiss of the kerosene lantern that sat on the table and provided the only light in the room.

That he was allowing himself to be sucked into this was as much a surprise to Malin as it was to his staff. Big Al had no doubt that what he was about to do far exceeded his authority. Both he and Dixon knew that, when this incident was reviewed by people back in Washington, D.C., sitting in air-conditioned offices after having had a good night's sleep in a clean bed followed by a hearty breakfast, no amount of reasoning or logic would be able to save them. After all, the entire affair sounded more like a script from a mystery movie than a military operation.

From the beginning, everything, from the appearance of the Mexican Army major to their covert meeting in an old ranch house just behind the front line trace, was so unreal, so new. Even the means of contacting the Mexican minister of defense had been strange, almost comical. When Dixon had asked Major Caso how they were to give Colonel Guajardo their response, Caso had informed them that the postmaster in Sabinas Hidalgo had a secret phone line that the leader of the local guerrilla unit had been using for receiving his orders and reporting American troop movements. "We are," Caso told the Americans with a smile, "keeping that line open so that, when you are ready, it will ring in Colonel Guajardo's forward command post in Saltillo."

Still, Big Al had decided that it was a chance worth taking. Therefore, without so much as a word to the corps commander, Big Al and Dixon had gone to the ranch that served as a battalion CP to meet with Colonel Guajardo, minister of defense and member of the Council of 13, in order to find out what he knew about Congressman Lewis and Jan.

When the door opened, an infantryman, his M-16 held at the ready, entered the room, then stepped aside to make way for the tall Mexican officer who was following him. In the shimmering light, both Big Al and Dixon recognized Colonel Guajardo. Stepping up to the edge of the table, opposite where Big Al was seated, Guajardo stopped and saluted. "Colonel Alfredo Guajardo, at your service, General Malin."

Big Al, caught off guard, stood, returned the salute, and then, without thinking, reached over the table and offered Guajardo his right hand. Mechanically, Guajardo took the general's hand and shook it. For a brief moment, while they still held each other's hand, the two opposing commanders stared into each other's eyes. It was as if they were gauging each other's strength and honesty.

Big Al took his seat while Guajardo pulled a chair out on his side of the table and sat down. Dixon, standing in the corner, caught the attention of the infantryman who had escorted Guajardo into the room. "That will be all, soldier. Close the door when you leave."

Without hesitation, the soldier saluted Big Al with his rifle and left the room, executing sharp, quick turns as he did so. When the door shut, Big Al waved over at Dixon. "This, Colonel Guajardo, is Lieutenant Colonel Dixon, my operations officer."

Guajardo and Dixon looked at each other and nodded. How peculiar, Guajardo thought, that he should finally have the opportunity to meet Jan Fields's lover under such circumstances. Still, Guajardo knew, these were strange times. At times like this, nothing, not even this improbable meeting, a meeting between men who were supposed to be trying to kill each other, was odd.

Not understanding why Guajardo was staring at Dixon, Big Al hastened to explain his operations officer's presence. "I brought him along as a sort of note taker, nothing more. You see, Colonel, my memory isn't what it used to be." Then Big Al turned and shot Dixon a glance that could only mean "Keep your mouth shut and ears open."

Guajardo nodded. "I understand. It is no problem." Then, leaning forward, he placed two folders before Big Al. "I am in your debt for honoring my request for a parley. Under the circumstances, had you refused, I would have understood."

Big Al grunted. "Hell, Colonel. After the thumping your people gave me outside of Monterrey the other day, my career is in the shitter anyway."

The attempt by Big Al to put him at ease, and the compliment, whether intentional or not, pleased Guajardo. Perhaps, he thought, this would not be as hard as he had expected. "The folders in front of you, General, each contain a copy of a report I submitted after interrogating a mercenary being employed by a man named Alamán."

At the mention of Alamán, Big Al snapped his head around and looked at Dixon. Guajardo saw the reaction and the surprised look on their faces. They already know, he thought, something about this. But how? Was their CIA that good? When Big Al looked back at him, Guajardo continued. "Rather than my trying to explain, it might help if you both read through these. The translation of the report is far better than my English."

Big Al handed one of the folders to Dixon before he began to read his copy. As the two men read, Guajardo watched them, looking for a reaction. When neither man showed any, Guajardo knew that the Americans already knew something about Alamán and his mercenaries. For a fleeting moment, Guajardo panicked. Were the Americans, he wondered, in league with Alamán? Had they, in order to provoke a war with Mexico and occupy its northern states, used Alamán to instigate a war? Were the Americans capable of such a thing?

Guajardo's mind was still racing with such thoughts when Dixon, and then Big Al finished reading the report and closed the folders. Tossing his copy onto the table, Dixon turned to Big Al. "It agrees with what the G2's people got out of the Colombian."

Big Al nodded. Then, seeing that Guajardo was looking at them with quizzical eyes, he explained. "We found a wounded Colombian mercenary at a checkpoint that Alamán's men hit ten kilometers from where we found Congressman Lewis's vehicle and the dead escort officer and driver." Big Al thumped the report with his finger. "Although he didn't provide as much detail as this Lefleur character, everything that he told us agrees with what Lefleur said." Big Al paused, sucking in a deep breath before he continued. "We, our nations, have been had. The question is, Colonel Guajardo, what do you expect us to do? Why did your government not take this through diplomatic channels to my government? Why go through us?"

"That will be done, at the proper time. But first, there are things that need to be done before Alamán and his people find out how much we know about them. To do these things, I need your help, General Malin. And you, mine. You see, my government has already been corrupted by Alamán. There are members of the Council of 13 who no longer support our efforts and have been providing information to this bastard. Although I could, eventually, pull together a force of loyal soldiers, it would take too long. My best and most capable leaders are scattered all over Mexico, many of them operating behind your lines as leaders of guerrilla units. By the time I pulled them back, your congressman and Miss Fields would be dead."

The mention of Jan's name caused Dixon to straighten up. "You know where she is?"

Guajardo nodded. "Lefleur has agreed to lead us to their base camp."

Big Al looked at Dixon, then Guajardo. "This man has already betrayed his boss and comrades. Can he be trusted?"

Guajardo's response was dry and cold. "Lefleur is a mercenary. Trust has nothing to do with this. His only concern is money and survival. He must survive in order to enjoy the fruits of his labor. Lefleur has no loyalty to Alamán. He would receive no bonus that he could enjoy by dying for him. There is no honor or principle attached to what Lefleur has done. He is a businessman, a man who provided Alamán a service and received money for that service. Right now, Lefleur is no longer in a position to provide that service or to be paid. At the present time, it is in his own best interests to cooperate." Then, as a fleeting smile crept across his face, Guajardo added, "Besides, Lefleur and I have an understanding."

After thinking about Guajardo's response, Big Al looked at Dixon, then back to Guajardo. "You obviously have something in mind, Colonel."

"Yes, I do. Based on what Lefleur has told me, the congressman and Miss Fields are, probably, still alive. But that will not last for long. Once the mercenaries figure out that Lefleur is not coming back, they will assume the worst and move their base camp. When they do this, we will have nothing. Therefore, it is critical that we act soon if you are to save your people and I am to find a way to Alamán. Therefore, I am offering you the services of Lefleur as a guide, and safe passage through our front lines and into our rear for a raiding party."

Dixon came over to the table and leaned over toward Guajardo. "If you know where this base camp is, and you have Lefleur as a guide, why do you need us?"

In tones that were dispassionate and cold, Guajardo explained. "The mercenaries are holding an important member of your Congress and a noted television reporter hostage. Even if you believe this report, how would your government and your people react if, during a raid by my people, your congressman and reporter were killed?"

Dixon stood up. Jan had told him, on several occasions, that Colonel Guajardo was a cold, calculating bastard. While what he proposed made sense, it didn't make it any more palatable. If the Mexican Army tried to save Lewis and Jan but failed, they would get the blame. By letting the Americans go in, the Mexicans got rid of the mercenaries and, as a bonus, washed their hands of all responsibility for whatever happened to Lewis and Jan. It was, for Guajardo, a true win-win situation.

Big Al, coming to the same conclusion as Dixon had, thought about Guajardo's offer. "What, Colonel, do you expect in return?"

"First, I will accompany the assault. I will bring Lefleur with me. He should prove useful in helping us find our way about. Second, I will use my own helicopter. Although I realize that my Bell 212 will be slower than your Blackhawks, it is important that I go into battle in one of our own aircraft, not an American aircraft."

Dixon shot a glance at Big Al. Big Al could tell by Dixon's expression that he didn't like the idea of including a Mexican helicopter in any operation they would be running. But Big Al, who had worked with other military forces, understood exactly what Guajardo was doing. As the minister of defense, the leader of the Mexican armed forces, and a member of the Council of 13, Guajardo was an important man in Mexico. As such, he had an image which he had to maintain. Even though the operation would be an all-American effort, it would be politically suicidal for Guajardo to be carried into battle in an American helicopter. For him to do so would make it look as if he didn't trust his own pilots and equipment and, more importantly, that he had to depend on the Americans for everything. That would never do in a nation where appearances were often more important than fact. Although it was pure tokenism, Big Al knew the Mexican helicopter had to go and, more importantly, it had to make it.

"Finally," Guajardo continued, "I must be given the one named Delapos, who is the leader of these mercenaries, alive, at the end of the raid."

For a moment, Big Al waited for more demands. But there were none. "Is that all? What about after the raid?"

Guajardo smiled. "We, General, are soldiers. What happens after the raid is best handled by the politicians and diplomats. It would be foolish for us to become involved with anything other than the immediate problem."

Both Big Al and Dixon agreed. By keeping it at that level, they would be able to justify their action. Although the rules of engagement that they currently were operating under forbade U.S. forces from crossing over the front line held by Mexican forces, they did allow commanders to take whatever actions they deemed necessary to protect American lives. As Big Al saw it, he had the authority and the responsibility to do what Guajardo proposed. Without any further thought, Big Al decided to do it. When he stood up, Guajardo did likewise.

"When, Colonel Guajardo, do we go?"

"Tomorrow."

HEADQUARTERS, 16TH ARMORED DIVISION, SABINAS HIDALGO, MEXICO
0105 HOURS, 19 SEPTEMBER

Big Al and Dixon started planning while they were en route back to the division main command post. Poring over data concerning the area of operations and disposition of Mexican forces as well as information provided by Lefleur that Guajardo's aide had given them, they developed several options and discussed them. By the time the general's command and control helicopter landed at the CP, they had already come up with a basic concept and some rules of engagement that would govern the operation. One thing that both men agreed on was that the fewer people that knew and were involved, the better.

Once they were on the ground, they called in the division G2. Together, in a van that served as the commanding general's office, Dixon and the intelligence officer drafted a plan that Big Al approved. Next came the question as to what forces would be used and who would command them. Dixon recommended that Captain Cerro, an officer who had conducted numerous air-assault operations, be designated as the ground force commander. Big Al concurred and sent his aide to roust Cerro out of bed.

Next, the question of troops came up. It was decided that only a single infantry platoon, supported by attack helicopters, would be necessary. Fewer people on the ground and fewer aircraft in the air meant less confusion. With so little time to prepare, it was mandatory that everything be done to keep the plan simple. Besides, the division had to stay within its limited resources. The division did not have a lot of UH-60 Blackhawks available for troop transport. So one platoon, possibly reinforced, was the limit. The division aviation officer concurred. Since he would plan and coordinate the air movement, he had been added to the growing conference. There would be no time, he pointed out, for the air crews making the raid to do a rehearsal before the actual event. If for no other reason than that, it was critical that the number of aircraft involved be as few as possible.

When Cerro arrived, Dixon quickly briefed him on the mission, his role, and what had been discussed up to that point. When he was asked if he had any recommendations as to where the platoon should come from, Cerro didn't hesitate. He told Dixon that the 2nd Platoon, Company A, 2nd of the 13th Infantry should go. They were, after all, right there at the division CP, they had been tested in combat and had done well, and they were rested. When Big Al asked who the platoon leader was and Cerro informed him, there was silence in the van.

In the silence that followed Cerro's recommendation, he watched Dixon look at Big Al, and Big Al, in turn, look back at Dixon. Cerro knew what the problem was, a problem no one, apparently, was going to be the first to mention. Looking at Big Al, Cerro stated, without any flourishes, without undue emotion, that Nancy Kozak was as good as they came and if he was going to go in, he wanted her and her platoon to go with him. Big Al smiled as he looked about the room. "Well, that's good enough for me. Scotty, would you have my aide go get Lieutenant Kozak?"

*   *   *

Shaken out of a sound sleep, Kozak took a minute to understand that the man who was shaking her was the general's aide. It took her even longer to understand what he wanted. Crawling out of her sleeping bag, she rummaged about for her gear for several minutes, slowly pulling herself together as the aide waited impatiently. Finally ready, Kozak followed the aide to the general's van.

Though she had seen the vans that made up the division main command post, she had never been in them. It was, to her, like entering another world. The radios, telephones, computers, and other electrical equipment that did things she had no idea about made her platoon's radios look puny. As they went through vans, along ramps, past staff officers, and around desks piled high with stacks of paper, Kozak didn't notice a single officer below the rank of captain. She was, she realized, walking through the rarefied air of a higher headquarters. She hardly noticed the stares of both staff officers and NCOs who wondered, just as she did, what she was doing there.

Finally, they arrived at the commanding general's van. The aide knocked, then opened the door without waiting for a response. He, however, did not go in. Instead, he motioned for her to enter. As she walked into the van, her helmet on and rifle slung over her right shoulder, she felt like a Christian entering the arena. The stare of the faces that turned toward the door as she entered only served to reinforce that feeling.

Once inside the door, Kozak stopped. Reaching across, she grabbed the sling of her rifle with her left hand and saluted with her right. "Sir, Lieutenant Kozak reporting."

For a moment, Big Al looked at her. Her uniform was dirty and torn. Her gear was hanging about her loosely. Her face still showed the results of her broken nose, and of her having been awakened in the middle of the night: patches of black and blue under drawn, baggy eyes. Turning to Cerro, Big Al dryly commented, "I thought you said they were rested."

Cerro shrugged. "Sir, that's what a well-rested infantryman looks like."

As Dixon, the G2, and the aviation officer laughed, Kozak looked at Cerro, then at the general. When she spoke, she surprised everyone but Cerro. Though her comment made no sense, its meaning and the enthusiasm with which it was delivered were understood by all. "Sir, 2nd Platoon is ready and can do."

The laughing stopped. Big Al looked at Cerro and nodded his approval. "If the rest of the platoon is like her, they'll do."

Then, after looking at Cerro and then the general, Kozak asked, a little less enthusiastically, "Excuse me, but what is it exactly, sir, we're supposed to do?"

24

The Spartans do not ask how many the enemy number, but where they are.

—Agis of Sparta

7 KILOMETERS NORTHWEST OF SAN LAZARO, MEXICO
0600 HOURS, 19 SEPTEMBER

Carefully picking his way through the loose rocks of the gully, Childress paused as he left its cover. To his front, the ground finally began to flatten out. Though the sparse chaparral that seemed to spread out before Childress without end appeared desolate and uninviting, it was far more hospitable than the barren hills behind him. He would be glad, he thought, to leave, for this land, like his profession, no longer suited him.

From the east a sudden breeze swirled around him, sending a chill down his spine. Looking to the left, he could see the sun peeking over the tops of the Sierra de la Garia. It was not, however, an inviting sun. Instead of the usual pale yellow ball of fire that he had come to associate with this part of the world, Childress watched as a strange reddish-orange orb struggled to climb above the distant mountain peaks. The glow that it cast across the plain before him bathed everything, even the colorless rocks at his feet, in an eerie, almost blood-red hue. While Childress viewed this strange sight, an old sailor's ditty about the sky came to his tired and troubled mind. The lines ran through his head as if someone were behind him, whispering them in his ear: ''Red sky at night, sailor's delight. Red sky in the morning, sailor take warning.''

Glancing over his right shoulder, Childress looked back at the twin peaks of the hills he had passed through for any activity or signs that he had been followed. There were none. Not that Childress had expected any. He had been careful to avoid the sentinels posted around Delapos's base camps. Since it had been his task to set up security for the base camps, and he had personally walked the hills, he knew where every outpost and sentinel was posted.

The greatest threat, when he and Delapos had been setting up the camps, had appeared to be from the hills to the north and east that dominated the mines and mining camps that they were using. If a raiding force was able to secure that high ground while blocking the trails leading from the east and west into the camps, escape would be difficult, at best. Since seizing the high ground and attacking downhill was a technique favored by both the Americans and Mexicans, Delapos had put most of his efforts into guarding against such an attack from those hills. Since the approach from the village of Ejido de Dolores provided an attacker with a quick and direct route into the base camps, it also had received a great deal of attention. By the time they got around to the south and east, there had been few assets left to guard against attack from those quarters. Not that either man considered an attack from those directions very likely. Both expected that any attacker, if one came, would be drawn to the natural benefits of the northern and western approaches.

It was for those reasons that Childress chose to leave by the southern route now that he had decided it was time to terminate his association with Delapos, Alamán, and their schemes. He had, Childress decided, overstayed his welcome in Mexico. Though he was a mercenary, and felt no need or desire to apologize to any man for that, he was not a terrorist. He would leave such things to men like Lefleur, who saw no difference between the profession of arms and murder.

To his front, the red stain of the morning sun was beginning to fade. The sun, a little higher in the sky, was beginning to wash out. Adjusting the straps of his rucksack, Childress prepared to continue his journey to San Lazaro, then south to Saltillo. Eventually, all of this—Delapos, Lefleur, the desolate landscape, and the war—would be behind him. With luck, he would be back in his beloved Vermont in time to see the foliage change and watch the first snow fall.

HEADQUARTERS, 16TH ARMORED DIVISION, SABINAS HIDALGO, MEXICO
0715 HOURS, 19 SEPTEMBER

Even though Kozak hadn't told the members of her platoon the nature of the mission, they could tell. Instinctively, in a way that only a long-serving soldier knew, every man could sense that something was going

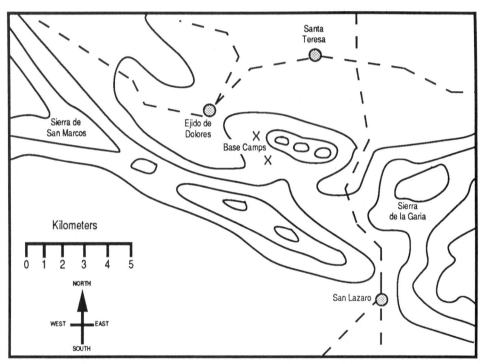

Map 9: Mercenary Base Camps

down. As she followed Captain Cerro down the ranks of her platoon during his first precombat inspection, Kozak could see the emotion each man felt in his face. Most showed a confidence that bordered on arrogance. The faces of other soldiers, despite their best efforts to hide them, betrayed small, unmistakable signs of fear. A few were even impatient. Though they didn't know where they were going, when they were going, what they would do when they got there, or why, all they wanted to do was to get on with the mission, whatever it was.

Passing from one soldier to the next with little to do but look each man in the eye as Cerro inspected him, Kozak wished that somehow some of the confidence she saw in some of their faces could, like magic, flow from them to her. But she knew that such things did not happen. The confidence she needed that morning had to come from within. No one, not the general with all of his rank and authority, not Colonel Dixon with his plans and reputation as a fighter, not even Cerro with the air of professionalism and confidence that he wore like a cloak, could give Kozak what she needed most. Only trial by fire would tell if she was what she had so long pretended to be, a soldier.

As much as she would have liked to believe in herself, the two fights which she had already participated in hadn't given her the assurance that she was what she wanted to be. Though the two fights, the one in Nuevo Laredo and the one north of Monterrey, had been very different, they had been similar in one important point. In each case, Kozak had simply reacted. Neither situation, even the battle against the tanks, had given her an opportunity to think more than one or two minutes in advance. Everything had been quick, unexpected, and unpredictable. They had been more like car wrecks than battles. Though she had done well, or so she was told, Kozak still lacked the confidence that came from knowing, in her heart as well as her mind, that she had what it took to be a leader.

So she both looked forward to and feared the upcoming raid. No wargame or drill, no reading or lecture, no badge or ribbon, no peacetime test or physical exam, could tell her, or any infantryman preparing to go into battle, if she was a true combat leader. Not until it came time to go over the top, to face, as they used to say, the push and pull of the bayonet, would she know for sure if she was a combat leader.

Nearing the end of the last rank, Kozak wondered how many good men had been lost in battle because, at the last minute, their leader suddenly discovered that he didn't have the right stuff. How many graves were filled with the corpses of trusting soldiers who were betrayed by a system that allowed untried and unfit leaders to take them to war. Pausing, she looked back along the rank she had just passed, praying to herself that her vanity and ego, her single-minded drive to be the first woman infantry officer, wouldn't cost these men their lives.

From the shade of one of the CP's vans, Dixon watched Cerro and Kozak complete their inspection. They would, he thought, make a good pair. Cerro had more than enough confidence for both of them, and Kozak had a quiet, businesslike manner that made shoestring operations like this one possible.

From the east, the beating of helicopter blades through the quiet morning air announced the approach of the Blackhawks. Squinting, Dixon searched the sky until he saw the five helicopters. Though the operation needed only four, three in a pinch, Dixon had decided to add a fifth as an added margin of safety. They had only one chance to get this thing right and he didn't want what happened to the Teheran raid to happen tonight. He had, after all, a personal stake in the success, or failure, of this operation.

The choppers were no sooner on the ground than Cerro gave the order to commence loading. Besides Kozak's platoon, two medics and an extra radioman for Cerro would go. The radioman, at Cerro's request, was Dixon's own driver, Fast Eddie. Though Eddie, like Kozak's platoon, didn't know where he was going, he was glad to get out of the division main for a while, even if it meant carrying a radio.

Besides the rations and water they would need for the next twenty-four hours, and their basic load of ammunition, Cerro was taking nine AT-4 antitank rocket launchers to be divided between the three squads, and two M-60 machine guns with 600 rounds per gun. Though the banditos, as everyone now referred to the mercenaries, didn't have anything bigger than a pickup truck, rocket launchers and M-60s would be useful in taking out machine-gun positions or banditos holed up in a building that 40mm grenades and the 5.56mm squad automatic weapons could not reach. Cerro had even tried to get a 60mm mortar, but couldn't find one in time. The consummate American warrior, Cerro was in love with firepower; the more, the better.

Once the helicopters were loaded, they would take Cerro's force to an isolated spot where he could brief the ground force, conduct some re-hearsals, link up with Colonel Guajardo and his helicopter, and rest his troops. By noon, he would have everything except the Apache attack helicopters in hand, briefed on the mission, and at least one short re-hearsal completed. If necessary, he would then have the balance of the afternoon to refine his plan, conduct another rehearsal, or rest his troops. Either way, Cerro showed no worry about being able to make their scheduled 2100 hours liftoff time.

*   *   *

"I thought I would find you here, Scotty."

Turning, Dixon didn't even salute Big Al as he came up to stand next to him and watch the ground force prepare for departure. Instead, he stood there for a moment without looking at the general, then spoke. "Have you reconsidered my request, sir?"

Without turning toward Dixon, and not wanting to rehash the conversation, Big Al simply told him no in a manner that could leave no doubt in Dixon's mind that all discussion was at an end. After a couple of minutes' silence, however, during which Big Al began to feel like a heel, he turned to Dixon. "Look, Scotty, you're too goddamned old to be crawling around in the dark, on your belly, like a twenty-two-year-old ranger candidate. And it won't do you any good to remind me that the Mexican colonel is at least five years older than you. I'm not responsible for him." Big Al paused, softening his tone before he continued. "Besides, the last thing we need is a person emotionally involved, like you, dicking around out there tonight. Given your current state of mind, not to mention lack of sleep, you'd be of no use to the mission or Jan, not to mention yourself. As much as I would love to let you go, Scotty, I am ordering you to stay."

Dixon had expected Big Al's answer. He knew Big Al was right. He knew that it would be pointless for him to go out there. That wasn't his kind of war. That wasn't what he was trained for. He would be, as Big Al pointed out, a threat, not an asset. Dixon had done everything he could to plan and prepare the mission. All of that was, he knew, logical and correct. Still, the thought of staying behind, doing nothing while others prepared to go out and save the only person in the world that really mattered to him, cut him to the bone. The idea that he had done his best, and that that might not be good enough to save Jan, broke down whatever restraint and reserve of calm Dixon had left. As he watched Cerro walk from helicopter to helicopter, making sure everyone was in place and all was ready for liftoff, tears began to streak down Dixon's cheeks. Big Al pretended not to notice. Instead, he just stood next to his G3, watching the helicopters as, one by one, they lifted off and disappeared to the south.

4 KILOMETERS EAST OF EJIDO DE DOLORES, MEXICO
1200 HOURS, 19 SEPTEMBER

Delapos turned away from the window and again began pacing the small room that served as his office. He did so for several minutes before he stopped by the window, looked out in the direction of Ejido de Dolores for a minute, and went back to his pacing. The thought that he could lose both Childress and Lefleur did not seem possible. It did not seem fair, either, especially since Lefleur had dumped the American congressman and his companions and left, leaving him the responsibility of deciding what to do with them. It would have been better, Delapos kept thinking, if the fool had simply killed the Americans and been done with them. As it was, if neither Lefleur nor Childress showed up, and he received no suggestions from Alamán, he would have to decide how and when to dispose of the matter himself.

While he was pacing, the idea that the two of them, Childress and Lefleur, were in league, and had deserted together or betrayed him, crossed Delapos's mind briefly. He quickly dismissed that thought, however. The only thing those two had in common was the naked hatred each had for the other, a hatred that Delapos had used, on occasion, to his advantage. No, he thought, those two could never work together on their own.

Though there was always the chance that one or both of them had been captured, Delapos was sure that he would have heard, by now, of such a thing or, worse, have had a visit from the Mexican Army. There was nothing, however, that indicated any danger. Still, as a precaution, he had ordered the number of outposts and lookouts on the hills to the north and west doubled. He had even sent extra people into the villages to listen for news of any increased patrols or activities by the Mexican Army. If there was trouble coming, Delapos felt comfortable that he would hear of it in time to flee.

That, however, did nothing to relieve his concern and apprehensions concerning the whereabouts of his two best men. Stopping at the window again, he looked vacantly toward the west, trying to clear his mind. He would give them until that evening to show up before he notified Alamán and began preparations to move his base of operation. He was too committed to Alamán's program of terror to let the mistakes of a few of his people, no matter who they were, stop him from succeeding. If, in the end, they could do what Alamán said they could, and Alamán regained the power and status he'd had before the June 29 revolution, Delapos could end his wanderings and retire a rich and powerful man in his own right.

Yes, he would do that. In the morning, if Childress or Lefleur still hadn't shown, he would begin sending his people and equipment out to the alternate location before they commenced their operations on the twenty-first. As for the Americans, they would be disposed of as part of the move. He would send the Americans out with the first team. They could be killed somewhere along the way.

Turning away from the window, Delapos resumed his pacing but abruptly stopped when he was struck by a sudden inspiration. What if, he thought, he sent that first team out before dawn with the dead Americans to Saltillo, where his men could leave their fresh bodies at the doorstep of the military garrison wrapped in the morning paper. Such an act would be a worthy beginning to their war of terror. Besides, it would pass on to the Mexican government a problem that not even the cleverest member of the Council of 13 could explain to the Americans. Yes, he would do that.

10 KILOMETERS SOUTH OF SABINAS HIDALGO, MEXICO
1758 HOURS, 19 SEPTEMBER

Sucking in his breath, Lieutenant Blasio looked at the gathering of American pilots, then marched over to join them. It would be difficult, he thought, to work with these men. After all, only a few hours ago they had been the enemy and would be, perhaps, again tomorrow. Still, if his colonel felt comfortable with the Americans and could work with them, so could he. The men he would work with were, after all, aviators, no different from himself.

When he was within a few feet of the American pilots, their conversation began to die out as one of them noticed him and then, attempting to be discreet, warned the others that "he" was coming. By the time Blasio joined the circle of aviators waiting for their final briefing, the silence was total. The American Army colonel, the aviation officer for the 16th Armored Division, who would be giving the briefing, glanced at his watch before he looked about, first at his people, then at Blasio. Satisfied that everyone who needed to be there was present, he began.

"Okay, since everyone is here and eager to start, we'll begin early. By now, you've all had an opportunity to look over the route and the order. The key to this operation, as if you haven't heard it enough today, is simplicity and synchronization. Although there are only, relatively speaking, a few aircraft involved, and we're going to be playing follow the leader, everyone needs to be on his, or her, toes and ready to take the lead at any time. Should you find yourself in the lead, remember the lowest common denominator."

When the American colonel mentioned lowest common denominator, he was looking at Blasio. Though he could feel the anger in him welling up, Blasio did not show it. Instead, he returned the colonel's stare without so much as a blink. Why, Blasio thought, did the Americans think themselves so superior simply because they had better machines? Without having to ask, he knew that he had more flying hours, under worse conditions, than most of the American pilots sitting there. It was only natural, since Mexico had so few helicopters and so many demands. With, perhaps, the exception of the colonel doing the briefing and one or two of the older aviation warrant officers, Blasio knew in his heart that he would have little difficulty matching or besting the skills of any pilot there, given a machine of equal ability. And yet the gringos assumed, just because they had newer, faster, more complex, and more expensive aircraft, that they were somehow better than he. While he would never be able to change their minds, he was determined to give the gringos a reason for doubting their groundless preeminence. Blasio knew that he not only had to defend his own pride—he was, that night, representing the honor of all Mexican military pilots. He would not let them down.

As the American colonel continued, Blasio had to push those thoughts from his head. The briefing was being given in English. Though he spoke and understood English, he had to give all of his attention to that effort. "Right, from the top, one more time. At 2100 hours, three hours from now, the lead Blackhawk, the CG's command and control bird, will lift off carrying Captain Cerro, his RTO, and two two-man pathfinder teams. Colonel Guajardo of the Mexican Army and a guide will follow the CG's bird in his own helicopter."

Good, Blasio thought. At least they had stopped referring to them as "the Mexican bird" as if it were a strange and foreign creature.

"Cruising at one hundred knots, and flying at an altitude of one hundred feet above ground level, they'll go in using contour flying. That will put them on the LZ, here, west of San Lazaro, at 2210 hours. Once the captain, one pathfinder team, and the colonel are on the ground, those aircraft will move to the rally point, here, and wait."

Using a map behind him, the colonel traced the routes he was discussing as he went, tapping the map at the proper location with a small collapsible silver pointer when he mentioned a point of interest. "The captain, with an RTO, and Colonel Guajardo with a guide, will move along the dismounted approach to recon the route and the bandito base in advance of the main body. The pathfinder team that they dropped off will mark the LZ and provide security, while the second pathfinder team will mark the rally point when they get there. At 2200 hours, the main body, under Lieutenant Kozak, will depart in the three vanilla Blackhawks, followed by the air ambulance. Using the same route, speed, and altitude, they will hit the LZ at 2310. Any questions or problems so far?"

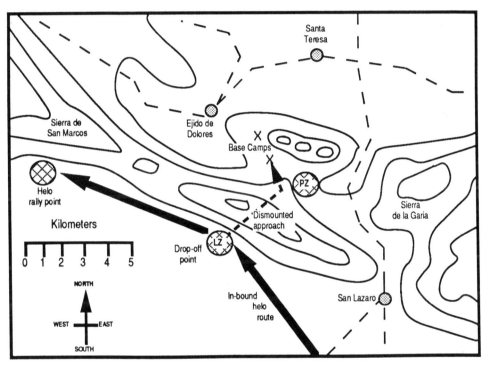

Map 10: Deployments for the Raid

A warrant officer, seated in the front, raised his hand. "Excuse me, sir. But why, may I ask, are we dumping the grunts that far away from the camps, and in the south? It seems to me that it would make sense to either just go zooming in there and drop everyone in the middle of the camp, or, if they wanted to go in quietly, drop them off north of the camps, using the hills there to cover our approach."

"You're right. Both of those solutions are the most direct and the most obvious. That's why we're doing what we are. It appears, if the information that the Mexicans gave us is correct, that the banditos have already considered both of your approaches and are prepared to meet them." Referring to a small green notebook and pointing to the map, the colonel located known enemy positions for the assembled pilots. "There are three .50-caliber machine guns, here, here, and here. There are at least two surface-to-air missiles at each of those locations. From these positions, the banditos can fire down on any helicopter making a direct approach into either camp. Observation posts, here and here, would give them ample warning of our approach from the north. From those OPs, they can see everything as far north as Santa Teresa. Odds of our being able to sneak up on them, even in the dark, are nil. And since we suspect the hostages are in Bandito Base East, it is pointless to go around the hills to the west and through Bandito Base West first or directly over the hills and through the OPs and machine-gun positions. Both options would require fighting and give the banditos an opportunity to dispose of the hostages. While the approach march will take longer, it gives us the best chance of surprise."

The colonel waited for any more questions, scanning the gathering of pilots as he did so. Though Blasio understood the tactics, he had no idea what the difference between a vanilla Blackhawk and a regular Blackhawk was. This, however, was not the time for such a trivial question. Perhaps, he thought, he could find out after the briefing without making his ignorance too obvious.

"Captain Cerro is leaving five hours for the five-kilometer march over the hill, through the saddle, and down into the valley where the bandito bases are. Though they may not need that much time, the going may prove rough, especially since we will have less than twenty-percent illumination tonight. The actual raid, which should take less than thirty minutes, start to finish, will commence sometime after 0400 hours, just before dawn. Therefore we need to be ready to pull pitch, at a moment's notice, from 0400 on. Right now, the plan is to pick everyone up at the PZ, here. The situation on the ground, and the condition of the hostages, however, may dictate that we go right into the bandito bases in order to extract them. If we do—I say again, if we do—make sure your flares are armed and ready. The banditos have both SA-7 and Redeye surface-to-air missiles here, on the hill to the north overlooking their base.''

Blasio took in a deep breath. His helicopter had no flare dispensers with which to spoof the heat-seeking missiles. If he was engaged by one, he would have only speed, radical maneuvers, and luck to protect him.

Nervously, the colonel tapped his small silver pointer against his leg as he added another word of caution. ''The only jokers in the deck will be the Apaches. They will be working independently, coming into the area of operation just before 0400 and taking up positions near the LZ. From there, they will respond to requests for fire support from the ground force commander. This may include the supression of enemy ground fire when we go in for the ground force. That means they can be anywhere. So keep your eyes and ears open. You need to pay attention to where the Apaches are and what they are doing because once they start engaging, they won't have time to look out for us.''

Finished, the American colonel collapsed his pointer by pushing the point into the palm of his left hand. ''If all goes well, we'll be back in time for breakfast. Gentlemen, and ladies, what are your questions?''

For a few seconds, everyone looked at their notes, their maps, and each other. When he saw that no one was going to ask a question, the colonel wished them luck and dismissed the group. As everyone stood and prepared to leave, Blasio looked around to where the Blackhawks were parked. Determined to find out what a vanilla Blackhawk was, he turned to a young aviator next to him. ''Excuse me. But would it be possible to see one of your magnificent machines? I have heard so much about them but have never had the opportunity to see one up close.''

The young warrant officer looked at Blasio, and then the colonel who had conducted the briefing. The colonel looked at Blasio, then back to the warrant. ''Sure, Tim, go ahead.''

Like a child freed to show off his toy, the young warrant smiled. ''If you would come this way, Lieutenant, I'll give you the nickel tour.''

25

The onset of bayonets in the hands of the valiant is irresistible.

—Major General John Burgoyne

4 KILOMETERS SOUTHEAST OF EJIDO DE DOLORES, MEXICO
0415 HOURS, 20 SEPTEMBER

Their approach march up the hill from the LZ, through the saddle between the two peaks, down the hill, and finally to the easternmost mercenary base camp had been more difficult than Cerro had expected. The time he had allotted for that movement, five hours, had seemed more than sufficient when he had looked at the map back at the division main command post. Now, as Cerro looked at his watch, he realized he wouldn't be able to meet his original schedule. He would be hard pressed to conduct his recon to find out where the hostages were, get back to where Kozak was holding her platoon, and lead the platoon into the base camp before dawn.

Not that it mattered, he thought. He had no pressing engagements back at the division CP. Besides, an attack just after dawn was, given the circumstances, not a bad idea. The idea of attack helicopters zipping all over the place, trying to provide fire support, at night, bothered Cerro. Though he knew the pilots and gunners were good, and the Apaches had dynamite thermal sights, Cerro also knew that people, in the weird green and black image created by a thermal sight, all look the same. In the daylight the Apache gunners would be able to use their daylight sights and look before they shot. At least, he hoped they would. There was, Cerro knew, no way of predicting what the rotorheads would do.

Ready to leave the cover of the gully they had been crawling in for the past thirty minutes, Cerro looked back at Colonel Guajardo and nodded. It was time for Guajardo and his ''guide'' to take the lead.

Pulling the tape from Lefleur's mouth, Guajardo looked at him and whispered his warning again, just in case Lefleur had forgotten. "Cooperate, and you will see the sun. Cross me, and you are a dead man. Do we understand each other?"

Lefleur, wiping his mouth, nodded.

Removing his pistol from its holster, Guajardo pointed toward the base camp. "After you, my friend."

With Lefleur in the lead, followed by Guajardo, then Cerro, and finally, Fast Eddie, the four men rose up out of the gully and began to move toward the rear of the building that Lefleur had identified as a cantina. Located on the eastern side of what everyone called Bandito Base East, the cantina was used as a mess hall for the mercenaries. On the south side of the camp, a large storage shed and machine shop served as billets for most of the mercenaries. An administrative building, on the western side of camp, was used by their leader, Delapos, as a headquarters as well as for additional billeting space.

While Guajardo was interested in the administrative building, where Delapos would be asleep, Cerro's attention was riveted on the tool shed and garage on the northern side of the base camp. It was in these buildings, according to Lefleur, that the American hostages had been put. Cerro's task, during the recon, was to confirm that. If he could, it would make life so much easier when Kozak and her platoon came tearing into the camp. Perhaps, Cerro thought, with a little luck, some of Kozak's people could even secure the hostages before the shooting began. In that case, it would be a simple matter of putting Kozak's platoon in a line abreast and marching them into the bandito base, shooting everyone in front of them as they went.

Upon reaching the rear of the cantina, the four men flattened themselves against the wall and crouched to catch their breath and listen for the movement of any guards. After waiting a minute, Guajardo turned to Cerro. "Well, my young companion, this is where we must part."

Even in the dark shadow of the cantina, Guajardo could see the shocked expression on Cerro's face. It was only with the greatest effort that Cerro kept his voice down. "'What do you mean?"

"I am, my young friend, after their leader. I cannot take the chance that we will be able to find him and keep him alive once your lovely lieutenant and her men begin shooting. So, I am taking our guide and leaving to find and secure Señor Delapos, for safekeeping. You understand, of course."

Cerro couldn't believe it. The colonel, he realized, had been planning this the entire time. The bastard. The fucking bastard. Well, Cerro

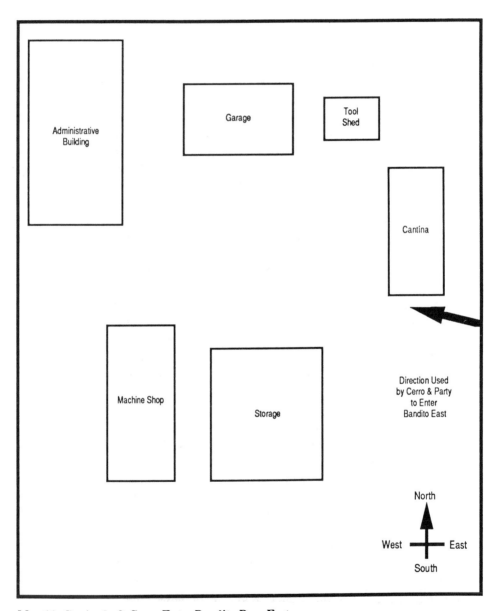

Map 11: Guajardo & Cerro Enter Bandito Base East

thought, two can play hardball. "No, I do not. That was not the plan. You, Colonel, must understand that if you go jerking around in the dark, on your own, I cannot be responsible for your safety. When the shooting starts, I cannot guarantee that you, your guide, and your hostage won't be hit by friendly fire."

Guajardo nodded. "I understand. But I am sure you will do your best. *Vaya con Dios.*"

Without another word, Guajardo grabbed Lefleur by the collar and pushed him ahead of him out into the open and toward the rear of the storage building. Fast Eddie, who hadn't heard the conversation between Cerro and Guajardo, leaned forward and whispered in Cerro's ear, "Where they goin', sir?"

Disgusted, tired, and momentarily flustered, Cerro mumbled a curse Fast Eddie didn't hear, then over his shoulder, he whispered, "They're off playing cowboys."

When Cerro turned his attention back to his front, Fast Eddie thought about Cerro's response. He had no idea what the captain meant. He didn't remember anyone mentioning anything about the Mexican doing his own recon. Not that it mattered. Fast Eddie reminded himself that he was, after all, only a grunt. Nobody ever told him anything. All he was expected to do was carry the radio and follow the captain.

2 KILOMETERS SOUTHEAST OF BANDITO BASE EAST, MEXICO
0420 HOURS, 20 SEPTEMBER

They were late. As Kozak looked at her watch, she realized that they still had two kilometers to go. If everything had gone well with Captain Cerro's recon, and she had no reason to suspect that it hadn't, he would be waiting for her and her platoon, at that moment, at the designated jumpoff point just east of the enemy base camp. Unless they did something soon, there was no way that they could make it to the jumpoff point, get Cerro's briefing on the layout of the camp, and attack before dawn. A decision had to be made. Another one of those one-time-only, guess-wrong-and-die decisions.

Throwing her right hand up over her shoulder, palm out, she signaled her platoon to halt. Like a ripple, starting with the man behind her, every man repeated the motion, then squatted, watching to either the left or right as he waited for further instructions. Only Staff Sergeant Maupin, the platoon sergeant, kept going. Turning to the man following him and telling him to stay, Maupin worked his way up the file of men to where

Kozak, at the head of the column, stood looking to the north and west. When he reached her, he looked around in the same directions, then leaned over and whispered, "What's up, LT?"

Looking toward the base camp, its buildings barely visible in the distance, she sighed. "We're late."

Maupin looked at his watch. "Took longer than the captain thought. He's probably late too."

Kozak shook her head. "Can't count on that. If we don't get moving fast, we'll never be in place and ready to attack before dawn."

Maupin was about to ask what she intended to do, but he realized that she was already considering her options. So he stood next to her and waited. He thought about offering her his advice, but decided not to. Ever since their deployment from Fort Hood south to the Mexican border, she had called everything right. Even Rivera had been surprised how well she had done, commenting to Maupin after the incident in Nuevo Laredo that second lieutenants just didn't come any better. So Maupin simply watched her and waited.

Seeing no signs of anything that looked like an outpost between them and the base camp, and remembering the French mercenary's comment that most of their attention was oriented to the north and west, Kozak decided to take a chance, a big one. She turned to Maupin. "Okay, Sergeant Maupin. We're getting out of this ditch and double-time down to the jump-off point. Wedge formation once we're in the open. First Squad in the center, 2nd Squad on the left, 3rd to the right. Place one machine gun each with both 2nd and 3rd squads. I'll lead, you take up drag. Pass the word."

Without hesitation, Maupin turned and prepared to move back down the column to relay Kozak's order to the squad leaders, when Kozak reached out and grabbed his shoulder. "And Sergeant Maupin, pass the word. Fix bayonets."

BANDITO BASE EAST, MEXICO
0422 HOURS, 20 SEPTEMBER

When they finally reached the rear of the administrative building, both Guajardo and Lefleur paused to catch their breath. After he had done so, Lefleur, twisting his head around, whispered over his shoulder to Guajardo, "This is the rear door. Inside, a corridor runs through the building to the front. Two rooms on each side of the corridor. Delapos uses the second one to the right as an office. He also sleeps in there." Lefleur turned his head back and waited. He had, he knew, fulfilled his end of their bargain. He had led Guajardo to where Delapos was. Now, he waited for the Mexican to let him go, as he had said he would.

What he would do, once freed and a safe distance from the Mexican, was a good question, one that Lefleur had been pondering all night. The Mexican, with an HK-53 submachine gun, which he carried slung across his back, as well as the 9mm pistol he had held at Lefleur's back as they moved to the admin building, was too well armed to take on. At least, right away. No, Lefleur thought, it would be pointless to risk his life right there, in such an uneven fight. He would wait. And, he thought, if a chance to take out the Mexican didn't come, it was no loss. He had, after all, been paid in advance.

The gleam of a blade flashing in front of his face caught Lefleur's attention just as Guajardo's left hand came around and clamped down on his mouth. In a single, smooth motion, Guajardo jerked Lefleur's head back and onto his left shoulder as he brought the bayonet in his right hand across in front of Lefleur's face. Pressing the bayonet against the skin just under Lefleur's left ear, Guajardo jerked to the right, using all of his strength to rip Lefleur's throat open, just above the wind pipe, from ear to ear. The only sound Lefleur made was a gurgling sound as blood from his severed artery mixed with the air escaping his lungs through the slit in his neck. For an instant, Lefleur's body jerked, then stiffened in shock and surprise. When he finally went limp, Guajardo removed his hand from Lefleur's mouth, allowing the body to fall in a heap at his feet.

After looking around to see if his action had attracted any unwanted attention, Guajardo bent over Lefleur's body. Pulling Lefleur's shirttail out of his pants, Guajardo first used it to wipe the blood from his bayonet before returning the bayonet to its scabbard. Then he wiped Lefleur's blood off his hands as best he could. He looked around again as he unslung his submachine gun and pulled the bolt of his weapon back. Ready, he stepped over Lefleur's body and entered the administrative building.

Once inside, Guajardo paused, flattening himself against the wall to his left while he allowed his eyes to adjust to the darkness of the building's interior. Within seconds, he could make out the four doors Lefleur had spoken of. At the end of the corridor, under the door of the room that Lefleur had indicated Delapos used for his office, there was light coming out. Guajardo could see something blocking the light under the door every now and then. Someone was up and moving around in the room.

Keeping his back against the wall and his submachine gun trained on Delapos's door, Guajardo began to move down the corridor. As he passed a door behind him, he glanced back for a split second, then returned his attention to the door where the light was coming from. When he was finally standing across from it, he steadied his submachine gun in his right hand while he slowly reached across the corridor for the doorknob with his left. Once he had a firm grip on it, he slowly began to turn the doorknob, listening for any sound and watching the light under the door. When it would turn no more, he froze and listened a little longer. Taking several deep breaths, he prepared to go in.

Delapos was bent over, reaching down to pull up his trousers, when the door to his room flew open. Looking up, he was startled to see a tall soldier, dressed in tiger-striped camouflage fatigues and training a submachine gun on him, standing in the doorway. Like a statue, Delapos froze, watching the man with the submachine gun as he took a quick step into the room, then a step to the right, closing the door with his left hand and holding the submachine gun in his right. Easing himself back so that he was leaning against the wall, the man with the submachine gun brought his left hand up to the front hand guard of the weapon before he motioned for Delapos to stand up by wiggling the barrel of the gun up and down.

Standing upright, and recovered from his initial shock, Delapos studied the man's face for several seconds before he realized that he was looking at Colonel Alfredo Guajardo, minister of defense, member of the Council of 13, ''the Dark One.'' The revelation only served to heighten Delapos's sense of shock and panic. If he, the Dark One, was standing there, in his own office, Delapos thought, then it was all over. Everything was lost. Everything, including his life, was finished.

BEHIND THE CANTINA, BANDITO BASE EAST, MEXICO
0424 HOURS, 20 SEPTEMBER

After circling the outside of the buildings, and seeing what he thought to be the hostages where the French mercenary had said they should be, Cerro and Fast Eddie prepared to head back to the jumpoff point. For a moment, Cerro glanced back at the tool shed as he reconsidered his decision to leave without freeing the hostages. It wouldn't, he thought, take that long. Five minutes tops. With the hostages out of the way, the rest of the operation would be a piece of cake, a real breeze. But going in like that, with only Fast Eddie as backup, was a big risk, a risk that he wasn't ready to take. At this stage of the game, there was no need to take any more chances. He'd do just like he'd briefed, go back, brief Kozak's platoon, lead them forward, position them, and then, when everything was ready, start the attack. Doing all that would take time. But in the end, Cerro knew, it was the smart thing to do.

Just as Cerro and Fast Eddie stood up and prepared to leave the shelter of the cantina, the door of the storage building facing into the center of the compound opened. Dropping down, Cerro and Fast Eddie froze in place as they watched three mercenaries leave the building and head for a pickup truck parked in front of the storage building. All three carried weapons, but they had them in one hand while hauling bundles of gear in the other. Cerro heaved a sigh of relief, realizing that he and Eddie had not been spotted.

His relief didn't last long. After dropping their gear into the open bed of the pickup truck, one man, the shortest of the three, opened the door on the driver's side while the other two shuffled across to the garage where Cerro believed some of the hostages were. When they entered the garage, the mercenary wearing a green camouflage shirt turned on the garage's outside and inside lights, just as the short one in the pickup truck flipped on the headlights. The whole open area in the center of the compound was now illuminated by the light coming from the garage and the pickup. The odds of anyone being asleep in the mining compound were now less than remote and getting worse by the minute.

Pulling back into the dark shadows of the cantina, Cerro watched as the mercenary in the green camouflage shirt came out of the garage. With his rifle slung over his shoulder, he was pushing one of the male hostages in front of him as he dragged another behind him. Both hostages, their hands bound in front of them, came out reluctantly. The mercenaries were, Cerro thought, about to move the hostages.

Turning to Fast Eddie, Cerro took a grenade off a loop of his web belt. "Can you manage to get a grenade into the back of the pickup in one try?"

Eddie leaned over and looked past Cerro at the pickup. "Sure thing. Why?"

The mercenary in the camouflage shirt, instead of taking his charges over to the pickup, put them up against the front wall of the garage.

Walking away from them, he was joined in the center of the open area by the short mercenary, who had turned on the lights of the pickup. As they stood there together, the mercenary in the camouflage shirt took his rifle off his shoulder and pulled the bolt back, looking at the two hostages. Cerro looked at Fast Eddie, the mercenaries in the open area, then at Fast Eddie again, tossing him the grenade. " 'Cause I said so. When I say go, chuck the grenade in the truck. After it goes off, you head for the garage. Get the hostages back inside and stay in there. I'm going after the woman in the tool shed. Got that?''

While he was in the process of slipping the radio off his back and studying the pickup, Fast Eddie nodded. "Sure. But wouldn't it be a good idea to wait for everyone else?''

The short mercenary was also preparing his weapon, looking at the two hostages standing against the garage wall, when Cerro looked back. They weren't moving the hostages, they were going to shoot them."No time. Besides, once she hears the shooting, I'm sure Lieutenant Kozak will come.'' At least, Cerro thought, that's what he hoped. That she might still be climbing down the mountain and be too far off to get there in time didn't really matter. What mattered was that he and Fast Eddie had to stop the mercenaries from shooting the hostages.

The sudden blaze of lights from the center of the compound startled Kozak. Without a thought, holding her rifle by the hand guard in her left hand, Kozak threw out her right hand with the palm open toward the platoon. Without a word, everyone, including Kozak, dropped down on one knee as they waited to see what was going on. Though they were less than fifty meters from the jumpoff point, Kozak knew that things were in the process of changing. The lights meant that some of the mercenaries were up and moving about. That, in turn, meant that the platoon's ability to meet Cerro, get briefed on what he had seen, and use that information to conduct a slow, quiet approach, was out.

Looking back over her shoulder, Kozak studied her platoon for a moment. The men, kneeling or squatting where they had been when she had signaled them to halt, grasped their weapons as they waited. Though it was dark, and their eyes were hidden by the deep shadows of their helmets' brims, Kozak could feel every man's eyes riveted to her, waiting for her to make a decision that would throw them into battle again. There would be no need for dramatics, no long or stirring speech. Once she had made her decision, a few words, one quick command, was all that would be needed. She knew that they were ready to follow, but more important, Kozak knew she was ready to lead.

Taking a deep breath, she took one more look at her people before turning back to watch and listen. At least, she thought, they were in an assault formation that would lend itself to just about anything.

Lifting his rifle, Cerro flipped the safety off with his thumb and took aim at the mercenary in the green shirt. He ignored the appearance of the third mercenary in the door of the garage, pushing the last of the male hostages in front of him. "Okay, Eddie, throw it." To his rear, Cerro could hear the grenade's spoon and safety level flip up and the striker hit the primer. He even heard Fast Eddie count to three before the crunching of dirt and a grunt from Eddie told him the grenade was on the way. Without waiting for the detonation, Cerro squeezed off two quick rounds.

The report of Cerro's rifle, and the collapse of the mercenary in the green camouflage shirt next to him, surprised the short mercenary. He looked down at his friend as he fell at his feet just as the grenade went off. Jumping and turning at the same time, he was in the process of looking for his friend's assailant when Cerro fired on him. Hit once in the chest and once in the left shoulder, the second mercenary went down, falling backward and over the body of his partner.

Jumping up, Cerro ran a few feet into the open, yelling as he brought his rifle up to his shoulder, "Go, Eddie, go."

The mercenary in the door of the garage, seeing Cerro, pushed the third hostage out of the way and began to bring his rifle up to his shoulder. Cerro, however, was ready before the mercenary. Taking the best aim possible, he began firing away, one round at a time. Even after he hit the mercenary and saw him go down, Cerro continued to fire into him until Fast Eddie came around in front of him and blocked his view. Only then did he let the muzzle of his rifle down as he spun about to see what reaction their sudden attack had caused.

The two hostages who had been against the wall were still on the ground. Cerro couldn't tell if they were hit until Fast Eddie, coming up to them, started yelling for them to get up and back into the garage. Looking to his right, he saw the third hostage struggling to get up from where the mercenary had pushed him. Leaving Eddie to deal with them, Cerro took off for the tool shed, reaching the door in four or five quick bounds.

When she heard Cerro's rifle fire, followed by the detonation of Eddie's grenade, Kozak was up in a flash. That was it. Whatever was happening was happening now and happening fast. Without any further thought,

Kozak leveled her rifle and took off at a run, yelling over her shoulder as she did so, *"At the double, 2nd Platoon. Keep your eyes open and follow me!"*

At the door, Cerro saw a bolt and lock securing it. He put the muzzle of his rifle under the lock and prepared to shoot it off, but decided against that. There was no way of telling where all the shit from the shattered bolt and bullet would fly once he fired. Stepping back slightly, he lifted his right foot and kicked in the door near the bolt with the sole of his boot. The dry wood gave way, letting the door fly open and throwing Cerro off balance. Once he had both feet on the ground, Cerro stepped forward into the doorway and looked inside.

"Miss Fields, we're Americans. You in here?" From the corner of the room, Cerro saw something move. Turning, he trained his rifle on it.

Seeing the black figure in the door, outlined by the light of the burning truck, and hearing the words "We're Americans" overwhelmed Jan. It took her a second before her dry throat could choke out, "Yes, yes. I'm okay. I'm okay." She was just beginning to cry for joy when the soldier in the door suddenly jerked, as if hit from behind, fell to his knees, and then flopped onto his face, his rifle landing on the ground just in front of Jan.

The shock of being shot took a moment to sink in. At first, as he had stood in the doorway, exposed, all Cerro had felt was a burning sensation in his calves of his legs and back. It was as if someone was jabbing hot needles into him. Only when he began to go down did it dawn upon him that he had been shot.

When he came to, everything seemed to have changed. There was a woman screaming in his ear. His face, in the dirt, was lying in something wet and sticky. His body felt weird, numb, sort of, and his mind seemed to be floating. Pulling his hands to his sides, he tried to push himself up. This effort, however, was greeted with a spasm of pain that caused him to scream, falling back into the dirt after only lifting himself a few inches.

Cerro's second attempt to do something was more modest. He merely rolled himself over onto his back. As he lay there, he could hear gunfire out in the compound. The burning pickup lit the inside of the tool shed with a strange, flickering light. Moving his head about, he saw Jan for the first time. "You okay, Miss Fields?"

*   *   *

The captain's question caught Jan off guard. Jesus, she thought, what kind of a question was that? After all, here was this man, lying in his own blood, shot God knew where, and the first thing that came to his mind was her safety. It was the kind of thing that she expected from Scott. He would say something like that. He was always doing that to her, trying to play the he-man and overprotective male. When he did, it angered her. It was as if he considered her incapable of taking care of herself, treating her like a child.

But instead of anger, instead of being insulted that Cerro was acting like a typical male, Jan was touched. Gently taking his head in her hands, she bent over and kissed his forehead. "I'm okay."

He had no idea why she had kissed him. Everything was so weird. Cerro could hear shooting, but he couldn't decide what to do. People were shouting, too, but he couldn't understand what they were saying. He knew he had to do something, but he wasn't sure what to do first. At least, he thought, he wasn't in pain anymore. The sharp, burning pain was gone. Instead, he felt warm. Not hot. Just warm. It was a nice, comfortable feeling, like you get when you're wrapped in a comfortable blanket. Whatever it was that he needed to do could wait.

From the building next to the shed she was in, Jan could hear a nervous, anxious voice calling out, "Captain Cerro. Hey! Captain Cerro. You okay?"

Jan looked down at Cerro. He was out of it. "Captain Cerro's been wounded."

There was a pause, followed by a volley of rifle fire, before the voice outside came back. "You okay, lady?"

"Yes, I'm fine. But your captain needs help. Right away."

There was another pause. "Sorry, lady, but I'm hit too. They got my arm. Can you get over here, into the garage?"

Jan looked at Cerro. Though he was breathing and awake, he wasn't with it. She knew she couldn't lift him. And she knew she wasn't going to leave him. "No. I can't."

The next voice she heard was Joe Bob's. "Jan, stay where you are. I'm on my way."

*   *   *

After handing Ed Lewis the assault rifle he had taken from the dead mercenary in the doorway, Joe Bob looked over from the window at the soldier. "When you hear me yell, open up and see if you can keep those bastards busy. Got it?"

Fast Eddie thought the big cowboy was crazy, but he didn't say anything to stop him. Instead, he just nodded. "Yeah, I'll do what I can." Turning away from the crazy cowboy, Eddie eased himself into the most comfortable firing position he could. When he was set, he peered out across the compound toward the storage building where most of the enemy fire seemed to be coming from. Ready, he lifted his rifle, took aim as best he could, and began to squeeze off three-round bursts.

Without another word, Joe Bob looked out the window over to the tool shed where Jan was, then hoisted himself up and out of it as soon as Fast Eddie began to open fire. As soon as he hit the ground, Joe Bob flattened himself out against the wall of the garage, looking about to see if he had attracted any attention. When he was sure he had not been observed, he got to his feet and prepared to cover the few feet between the garage and the door of the tool shed. That part, he knew, was going to be tricky. When he was ready, he moved out.

With the mercenaries' attention centered on Fast Eddie and Lewis, Joe Bob jumped out of the shadows, taking great strides as he made for the door of the shed. Though he drew fire, it was wild and late, but not by too much. Joe Bob had barely cleared the door and thrown himself on the floor next to Jan and Cerro when a hail of gunfire from the storage building sent splinters and chips of metal flying about the tiny tool shed. When there was a pause in the firing, Joe Bob pushed himself up off the floor and looked around the room, before he turned to Jan. Seeing that she was safe, he smiled. "Thought you could use a little company."

With Guajardo hovering over him like the angel of death, Delapos watched the firefight unfold. From where he sat, on the side of a small mound just south of the eastern camp, Delapos could see his men scurrying about as they came out of the rear of the storage building and ran to take up positions in the machine shop and to reinforce the people in the admin building. A few, running over to the cantina, he knew, would not make it. For out of the darkness, coming from the east, he could see the forms of more soldiers emerging from the darkness. It would be over as soon as those soldiers hit the camp.

What happened there, however, no longer mattered to him. That Guajardo wanted something from him was obvious. Otherwise, Delapos knew, he would have been dead already. Though he suspected he knew the reason he was being kept alive, he wanted to confirm it. He didn't take his eyes off of the unfolding battle three hundred meters away when he began to question Guajardo. "What do you intend to do with me?"

Standing behind Delapos, his feet spread at shoulder width and his submachine gun at the ready, Guajardo heard Delapos's question but did not answer him immediately. He, too, was watching Kozak's platoon, rifles held at the ready, bayonets fixed, as it rushed to join the fight already in progress. Although he had no idea why the young American captain had started the firefight on his own, Guajardo didn't care. He had been right to leave the American cowboys to their games and take what he had come for. Even if every one of the American hostages died in the next few minutes, Guajardo knew they had achieved a great victory.

Looking down at Delapos, Guajardo smiled. "Whether you live or die, my friend, makes no difference to me. Your life, in the scheme of things, is not important. What you can do for me, in exchange for that life, is. The choice will be yours. I trust that when the time comes, you will choose wisely." Looking back at the compound, Guajardo watched Kozak's platoon join the fight. Though he couldn't tell which of the running figures was Kozak, he could hear the female's high-pitched voice over the rifle fire as she issued her final orders. "Until then, my friend, sit back and enjoy the show."

While they were still approaching the compound, Kozak turned and issued her orders, trotting backward as she did so. "Sergeant Strange, take your squad to the right and secure the tool shed and garage. Watch for the hostages. Sergeant Kaszynski, you clear the cantina. Sergeant Zeigler, set your machine gun up to sweep the open area in the compound while your squad clears the storage building. Sergeant Maupin, go with 3rd Squad, I'll stay with 1st."

For a few seconds, Kozak watched as the 2nd and 3rd squads split off and headed for the buildings she had indicated to them. Satisfied, she turned around. "Okay, Kaszynski, let's go." Picking up the pace, Kozak closed the last few meters of open ground.

Just as she was passing between the cantina and the storage building, a figure jumped out from the front of the cantina and began running toward the storage building. Though he was silhouetted against the burning pickup, Kozak couldn't tell, at first, if he was friend or enemy. Only after the figure heard the tromping of Kozak's people coming up behind him did he turn away from the firefight in the compound and toward her. When he did, Kozak saw that his weapon and clothing weren't American.

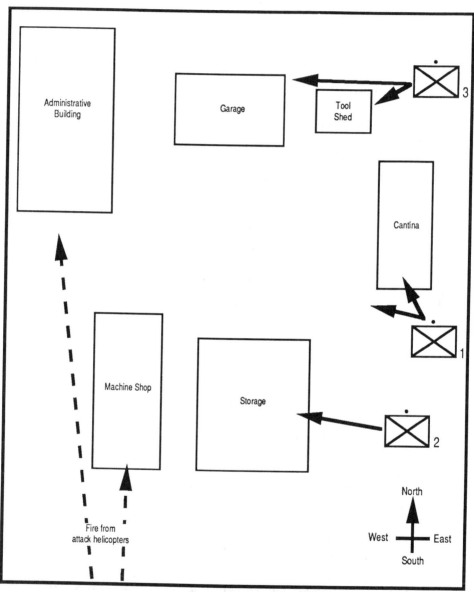

Map 12: Kozak's Attack

Bringing her rifle down, Kozak attempted to fire from the hip, but got no response. Desperately she tried a second time, but the trigger wouldn't budge. There was no time to find out what was wrong. In another second she would either be on top of the figure or he would recognize the threat she presented and fire on her. Leveling her rifle, she thrust it out in front of her, locked her elbows and arms stiff, aimed for the figure's midsection, and charged.

Surprised by the sudden appearance of armed soldiers out of the darkness, the mercenary stopped and threw down his rifle as he prepared to surrender. Kozak's forward momentum, however, carried her through. As soon as she felt her bayonet enter the mercenary just above his groin, she began to pull the front of her rifle up with all of her might while pushing the mercenary over to her left. Screaming, the mercenary grabbed for Kozak's rifle as he toppled over.

From behind, Maupin saw that his platoon leader was in trouble. Picking up his pace, he rushed forward, yelling, first to the right, then to the left, so that everyone could hear: "Mark your targets and fire at will. Mark your targets and fire at will." Although it was terminology better suited for a rifle range, the soldiers of 2nd Platoon understood what he meant and began to go to work.

Reaching the corner of the cantina, Sergeant Strange and 3rd Squad were greeted by a large-caliber machine gun firing down into the compound from a position on the hill to their right. Going to ground, it took them several seconds to figure out that whoever was manning the machine gun had not observed them yet. Instead, the machine gun's fire was wild and unaimed. Directing the crew of his M-60 to set up in the lee of the cantina, Strange ordered them to engage the enemy machine gun with a plunging fire. Though he doubted that his gun crew would actually be able to put the machine gun on the hill out of action, at least his crew would be able to suppress it while the rest of 3rd Squad cleared the tool shed and garage.

Happy to have the chance finally to use the large machine gun and boxes of ammo that they had been hauling around all night, Strange's gun crew was ready to fire in a matter of seconds. When they were set, they waited a few more seconds, watching for the enemy gun's muzzle flash. When they were sure they had it pinpointed, they began to fire bursts of fifteen to twenty rounds, adjusting their aim by walking their gun's tracer rounds into the enemy position. Once the gunner was satisfied, he began to fire longer bursts.

Satisfied with the effectiveness of his own gun's fire on the enemy position, Strange pushed himself off the ground, yelling to his squad to follow as he headed for the tool shed.

Though they knew that someone was close when the machine guns began to exchange fire, the sudden banging on the east side of the tool shed, followed by a booming voice, still caused Jan to jump and Joe Bob to turn the M-16 he had picked up off the floor at the source of the noise. *"Captain Cerro, Eddie, you in there? It's Sergeant Strange!"*

Recovered from her shock, Jan answered first. "Captain Cerro's in here, but he's hit bad."

The voice on the other side responded, "Okay, lady, hang on, we're comin' through."

Looking at each other, Jan asked Joe Bob what they meant. "Are they going to use explosives to blow a hole in the wall?"

Joe Bob shrugged, looking about the small confines of the tool shed. "Shit, I hope not."

Instead of C-4, however, Strange had two of his men take the bayonets off their rifles and pry a loose sheet of metal off the shed. When it was off, Strange sent a rifleman, followed by a medic, through the hole. Before Strange left, he yelled to Jan through the hole, "Stay put, lady. I'm goin' over to the garage."

When Strange was gone, and while Jan held a flashlight for the medic working on Cerro, Joe Bob looked over at the rifleman who had joined him at the door facing into the compound. "Exactly where in the hell does your sergeant think me and the little lady are going to go, especially at this time of night?"

Rolling into a tight turn, Blasio aimed the nose of his helicopter due west at the eastern mercenary camp. Once the camp was in sight, Blasio straightened out his aircraft, bringing it down as low as he comfortably could while increasing his speed. Though he had no idea what had gone wrong with the plan, he knew that his colonel, as well as the prisoner he was after, were down there somewhere, in the middle of the firefight, waiting to be picked up. When his co-pilot asked how he knew that, Blasio, in a rather offhand manner, responded that Colonel Guajardo wouldn't have it any other way. Though the co-pilot really didn't understand, he did as Blasio instructed.

To the right, from the hills, Blasio could see tracers streaking down into the compound from the .50-caliber machine-gun positions that the

American colonel had mentioned in his briefing. Though his speed and altitude would give those guns little opportunity to hit his aircraft with more than one or two aimed bursts of fire, Blasio didn't want to take the chance. After all, he was on the right side and it took only one .50-caliber round to kill a man, aimed or not. Easing his joystick over to the left and down slightly, Blasio decided to fly to the south of the camp, using the buildings to shield his helicopter from the enemy guns to the north.

They had no sooner made that correction than the commander of the American Apaches came on the air, announcing that his four gunships were in position south of Bandito Base East and ready to engage. If that was true, and they began engaging, Blasio's present course, while protecting him from the mercenaries to the north, would place him, his crew, and his aircraft right in the American gunships' line of fire.

Realizing the danger, the co-pilot began to yell over to Blasio that they had to break off and go around, looking for another approach. Blasio, however, did not respond to his co-pilot's warning. Instead, he took a deep breath, twisted the throttle on the collective a little more to increase their speed, and fixed his attention straight ahead. "Keep your eyes open for the colonel. He will be waiting for us."

From across the open area of the compound, Kozak heard Strange call. "Lieutenant Kozak. We got the hostages. The garage and tool shed are secured."

Sticking her head around the corner of the cantina, near the ground, she replied to Strange's report. "Okay. Hold there, Sergeant Strange."

Pulling her head back, she looked over to the storage building. From where she sat, leaning against the south wall of the cantina, Kozak could hear gunfire and the explosion of grenades inside the storage building. As she was staring at that building, a head came thrusting out of the window of the cantina behind her. This caused Billy Bell, Kozak's radioman, to pull back a few feet and aim his rifle at the head protruding from the window. Sergeant Kaszynski ignored Bell, however, when he saw Kozak. "Hey, LT. The cantina's secured."

Without looking back, she ordered Kaszynski to stand fast with his squad in the cantina. While the machine gun next to her was firing, raking the administrative building with a long burst, Kozak reached out with her left hand and yelled, *"Bell!"*

From behind, Bell handed her the radio mike. "Sky King, this is Alpha two six. Over."

The warbling voice of the Apache attack helicopter company commander came back over Kozak's radio. "Alpha two six, this is Sky King. What's going on down there? Do you have contact with Grunt six? Over."

"Sky King, this is two six. Grunt six is down. Break. We have secured the garage, the tool shed, the cantina and are clearing the storage building. Break. Bad guys in machine shop, admin building, and hills to the north. Request you hit them and anyone in Bandito Base West. Over."

There was a pause before the Apache company commander replied. "Understand we are cleared to attack machine shop, admin building, and Bandito Base West from the south. Over."

"This is two six. Affirmative. Start your attack when ready. Over."

"Two six. This is Sky King. Wilco, out."

Reaching back, Kozak returned the hand mike to Bell. She was about to get up and go over to the storage building when Sergeant Maupin came up behind her and told her that 2nd Squad had cleared the storage building. After telling him to pass the word that the attack helicopters were coming in, Maupin saluted, responded with a "Yes, ma'am," and headed out to spread the word.

Maupin had no sooner disappeared into the darkness than a huge apparition, screaming in from the east, went streaking past Kozak's eyes like a runaway locomotive. The high-pitched whine of engines, along with a sudden blast of wind and sand that lashed at both Kozak and Bell, caused Bell to flatten out on the ground and scream, *"Jesus Christ, what the fuck was that?"*

Looking over to the storage building, behind which the blur had disappeared, Kozak brushed the dirt off her uniform as if this were an everyday occurrence, and grunted, "Oh, I'd say it was a UH-1 helicopter."

Bell, still shaken, picked up his weapons. "Well, what in the hell was he doing?"

Kozak laughed. "Oh, I'd say about one hundred miles an hour at an altitude of one foot."

The same high-pitched whine of engines that shook Bell caused Guajardo's ears to perk up. Orienting on the approaching sound, Guajardo took a red-filtered flashlight from his pocket and flicked it on. Though he knew there was the remote possibility that doing so would draw fire, he also realized that if he didn't do so, Blasio would never find him. As an American friend had once told him, half jokingly, everything you do in combat, including doing nothing, draws fire.

*   *   *

"Over there, Lieutenant. To the left, a red flashlight."

Blasio hadn't even waited for his co-pilot to finish that simple statement before he had begun to reduce speed and carefully turned slightly to
the left. Once he had the flashlight in sight, Blasio eased the helicopter
over, ignoring the firing to his right and rear. He didn't even pay attention
to the instruments to his front. Instead, with his eyes fixed on the red
light, he felt his way forward until he was satisfied that he was where he
needed to be. When he was ready, it took only a slight lowering of the
collective and a twist of the throttle to bring the helicopter to rest on the
ground.

Noting that only two men boarded the helicopter, Blasio felt a moment
of panic. Had the colonel lost the man he was after?

Guajardo's greeting, however, told him that he had not been disappointed. "You are, Lieutenant Blasio, right on time. My new friend here
was getting quite bored watching the Americans."

Picking up on the colonel's good mood, and relieved that all was well,
Blasio shot back, "Well, sir, is there somewhere I can take you that will
be more to his liking?"

Guajardo turned to watch as the crew chief secured Delapos across
from him. "Well, perhaps he might not enjoy it, but, yes, indeed, there
is one more trip we need to make. But not tonight." Then, turning to
Blasio: "Whenever you are ready, Lieutenant."

Easing back in the nylon seat, Guajardo allowed himself to relax.
There was nothing more to do. The crew chief and the soldiers he had
brought along would watch Delapos. By the time Blasio had cleared the
compound and reached an altitude of two hundred feet, Guajardo was
sound asleep.

With nothing better to do, Kozak sat and watched the machine gun next
to her continue to hammer away at the administrative building even
though there was no longer any return fire coming from it. Bell, crawling
up next to her, watched for a minute, then looked at his platoon leader.
"Now what do we do, LT?"

Watching the machine-gun crew at work, Kozak said nothing at first.
Then she sighed. "That," she said, "is a good question." With the 3rd
Squad in control of the garage and hostages, 1st Squad secure in the
cantina, and 2nd Squad mopping up the storage building, there really
wasn't much to do. As she rested against the wall of the cantina, the only

thing that came to Kozak's mind was the fact that she was thirsty. Reaching around, she unsnapped her canteen cover and pulled her two-quart canteen out. After taking a long swallow of water, she looked back at the machine gun.

Watching the machine-gun crew do their thing, and listening to the shouts of her NCOs going about their tasks, Kozak finally understood what Cerro had been driving at back at Fort Hood. Though she could have gone over to any of the squads and watched them, it would have served no purpose other than to occupy her time and give her the false impression that she was really doing something, when in fact she would only be hindering progress. No, Kozak knew that Cerro had been right. The NCOs knew what they were doing and they were doing it well.

Although things had not gone as planned or as she had expected, she felt good about what her platoon had done, and about her conduct. Even the little incident with the mercenary she had encountered when entering the compound, when she had forgotten to take the safety off before trying to fire her rifle, didn't bother her. She had reacted well and in an appropriate manner. Though she couldn't put her finger on what the difference was between this night's operations and her previous experiences, she felt good about herself.

Looking at her watch, then over to Bell, she offered him a drink from her canteen. "It's about time for us to go home, Bell. All we need to do now is wait for the fat lady to sing."

As if on cue, a volley of 2.75-inch high-explosive rockets, fired by the Apaches hovering off to the south somewhere, slammed into the machine shop and the administrative building. The glare of the rocket motors, and their detonation against the sides of the targeted buildings, lit up the predawn darkness, bringing the battle for Bandito Base East to a close.

Epilogue

Veni, vidi, vici. (I came, I saw, I conquered.)

—Julius Caesar

PALACIO NACIONAL, MEXICO CITY, MEXICO
1105 HOURS, 1 OCTOBER

The pace at which Molina led the American delegation through the corridors of the presidential palace was slow and deliberate. He hoped to allow them an opportunity to think about what he had just said, and also to view some of the murals that adorned the walls. Perhaps, Molina thought, the Americans will begin to appreciate that we are a proud people with a proud past.

Though Ed Lewis did not understand Molina's intent, he nevertheless was struck by the beauty of the murals. While the secretary of state and his assistants moved briskly behind Molina, holding hushed conversations amongst themselves, Lewis followed at a leisurely pace, looking at the colorful and vibrant murals as he passed them. As beautiful as they were, Lewis thought, they were trying to tell him a story, a story that he didn't know. When he came across a mural showing a number of men, Lewis finally recognized one of the faces. It was Pancho Villa. Pausing, he looked at the face for a moment, then at the others around it. He noticed that Villa's face, the only one he knew, was only one of many and, more importantly, did not occupy a central or important position. How terrible, Lewis thought, the only famous Mexican whose face I recognize is one we consider a bandit.

It was several moments before Lewis, lost in his thoughts, noticed that he was no longer alone. Turning his head to the left, he was not at all surprised to see that President Molina had come up from behind and was

standing next to him looking at the same mural. Without looking over at
Lewis, Molina began to speak, using hushed, almost reverent tones.
"These murals were painted by Diego Rivera between 1929 and 1935.
They trace the history of our country from the Aztecs up to the end of the
Revolution. This one depicts the fathers of our Revolution, the men who
gave us modern Mexico."

Lewis was about to ask who each of the figures was, but decided that,
at the moment, it would be inappropriate. There was, after all, still much
that needed to be worked out between the two governments. The disen-
gagement of forces, the joint manhunt for Alamán and his network of
informers, and a joint border patrol agreed on over the past week were
only Band-Aids. To solve the problems that had plagued their two nations, Lewis knew, would take years. With a sigh, he turned to Molina.
"There is much, Mr. President, about your nation that we must learn. I
only hope that we can find the time and a common voice."

Molina looked at Lewis and smiled. Taking his arm, he began to lead
him down the corridor. "We, Congressman Lewis, must make that time.
We are, after all, men, not victims. If we do not make the effort to learn
how to live with each other, then it is our fault"—he pointed back to the
murals—"not theirs."

GRAND CAYMAN ISLAND
1420 HOURS, 1 OCTOBER

Although he was surprised to see Delapos, Alamán was genuinely glad.
There was, he told Delapos, much to do now that the Americans were
preparing to withdraw from Mexico. After a warm embrace, the two
men, accompanied by two associates Delapos had brought, walked along
the beach. Though Delapos's two companions looked vaguely familiar,
especially the blond American, Alamán paid them no attention. With few
exceptions, he never bothered learning the names or faces of the hired
help.

Although Alamán listened attentively to Delapos as he explained
what had happened in the end, Alamán was not interested in the past.
Though he was disappointed in their failure, especially since they had
come so close, he was a businessman who could accept his losses and
move on to new business without much trouble. When Delapos was
finished, Alamán began to outline his new strategy for returning to Mexico. By the time he had finished, they had reached a secluded part of the
beach. Pausing, Delapos asked Alamán why, when he could live in a

place such as Grand Cayman, he insisted on returning to Mexico. "Despite the many attractions that a place such as this has," Alamán said as he spread his arms out, "my first love has always been Mexico."

Delapos nodded in agreement. "Yes, Mexico. She is a lovely and demanding mistress."

"Come," Alamán told Delapos, "enough of this longing for Mexico. We shall see her soon enough. Let us return to the house and celebrate your return from the dead properly." Turning, Alamán began to walk back up the beach toward the house.

Delapos, however, did not follow. By the time Alamán stopped to find out why he was not coming, Delapos's two companions had stepped forward. After taking one more look at his former employer, Delapos turned his back and walked a little farther down the beach, leaving Alamán staring at the two men for the longest time. Finally, the taller of the two stepped forward, removing his sunglasses and reaching behind his back with his right hand. When his right hand came back to his side, it held a pistol with a silencer attached.

Rather than fear, anger welled up in Alamán's face. "What treason, Delapos, is this? Do you now conspire to murder me? For what purpose do you do this?"

Delapos did not answer. Instead, the tall man with the pistol replied to Alamán's challenge. "How dare you speak of treason and murder? How dare you speak of Mexico with such loving words after what you have done to her?"

Turning to the tall one, Alamán demanded to know who he imagined he was, to speak to him in such a manner.

Alamán's words did not bother the tall man. In fact, they seemed to have no impact on him. Not even a hint of a smile showed on the tall man's face as he responded to Alamán's insults. "If I have committed murder, it has been, truly, for the people of Mexico. Unlike you, I seek nothing for myself. It is for our children, the children of Mexico, that I have done what I have done."

Alamán was becoming more angry. "Who are you, you bastard?"

"I, Señor Alamán, am Colonel Alfredo Guajardo."

Alamán's angry expression dropped, replaced with a stunned look. How, he thought, could that be? The chief of the Mexican Army? Here? Regaining his composure, Alamán pointed to the blond American next to Guajardo. "And he?"

The American, in broken Spanish, responded that he was CIA, here to bring Alamán to justice.

Looking back at Guajardo, Alamán regained his composure. "Ah, I see. The Americans. You have surrendered the pride and glory of Mexico to be a hired gun for the Americans.''

Guajardo, tiring of the conversation, looked at the American, then at Alamán. Knowing the American's command of Spanish was limited and confined to Castilian Spanish, Guajardo began speaking to Alamán using the Mexican twist of the old language. ''Señor Alamán, in the name of the Republic of Mexico, and its people, I charge you with high treason and murder. As a member of the Council of 13, I find you guilty and sentence you to death.''

Unable to keep up with what Guajardo was saying, the CIA man was shocked when Guajardo lifted the pistol in his hand and fired three hollow-point 9mm bullets into Alamán's stomach. As Alamán fell to his knees, his face turned up to Guajardo and his eyes betraying his surprise, the CIA man yelled at Guajardo, ''You said we were bringing him in! You said that you were going to turn him over to us!''

After he watched Alamán keel over face first into the white sand, Guajardo turned to the American. ''I lied.''

INTERNATIONAL BRIDGE NUMBER 2, LAREDO, TEXAS
1725 HOURS, 2 OCTOBER

Leaning back and turning in the hatch of her Bradley, Lieutenant Nancy Kozak took one long last look at Mexico. How much, she thought, had changed in the last month. At least, the way she looked at the world, and herself, had changed.

It was wrong, she knew, to say that she had grown up. By any measure, she had been an adult before she had gone to Mexico, before she had gone to war. Perhaps, she thought, the veterans of the Civil War put it best. She had, as they would say after participating in battle for the first time, ''seen the elephant.'' And, like them, her life would never be the same again.

While it would be a while before she understood the full effect of the war on her, she realized a few things now. The desire to be the first female infantry officer, to prove that women could do anything, didn't matter to her any longer. In truth, she really didn't know the answers to those questions and others like them. Others, she knew, whether they truly understood the nature of the problem or not, would decide those issues. What did matter to Kozak that day, as she led her platoon back north into the United States, was that she belonged where she was. She had not only earned the right to be called a combat leader, she *was* one, in body and spirit.

Leaving the bridge, the column Kozak's platoon was in turned to move onto the interstate and continue north, out of town, to assembly areas. At the turn, Kozak noticed a Humvee parked under the shade of a tree. A woman and an officer, whom she recognized as Lieutenant Colonel Dixon, were sitting on the hood of the Humvee, their feet resting on the I-beam front bumper. Both of them were sipping sodas from oversize cups and watching the column go by. Coming to a rigid position of attention, Kozak rendered Dixon a sharp hand salute, holding it until she had gone well past his Humvee.

After returning Kozak's salute, Dixon picked up his forty-four-ounce drink and took a long sip. He watched a few more Bradleys go by before he said anything to Jan, who was busy with her own drink. "So, you were saying that our young hero is raising hell with the nurses."

Finishing her sip, Jan let a tank go by before she tried to answer. "What I said, dear, was that Captain Cerro had been raising hell with the nurses until his wife got to town today. The head nurse said his wife has gotten him straightened out."

Dixon raised an eyebrow. "You mean he's healthy enough for that already?"

Jan looked at Dixon. "Healthy enough for what?"

"Sex."

"Scott Dixon, I said nothing about sex."

"Yes, you did. You said his wife got him straight today."

Making a face, Jan didn't reply. Instead, she turned her attention to taking another sip and watching more tanks go by. After a few minutes, Dixon sighed. "Talking about getting things straight. Do you think, Jan, that a high-speed news correspondent could ever find true happiness married to a broke dick tanker?"

Jan took a sip of her diet Coke before answering. "Maybe. Why, do you know a broke dick tanker who has the hots for a reporter?"

Dixon, after taking a sip from his drink, looked at her. "Maybe."

For several minutes, neither of them said anything as they continued to watch the column as the tanks finished passing and another unit of Bradleys began to go by. To the west, the sun was beginning to dip low on the horizon, casting its reddish-orange rays on everything it touched. Dixon looked at the sun, then at Jan. "Well?"

"Well, what?"

"Well, do you think a news correspondent could be happy married to a broken-down tanker like me?"

Jan looked Dixon in the eyes. "Is this a proposal?"

"Maybe."

Pulling the straw from her drink, Jan played with the ice in her cup. "Ever notice how much ice they give you in these things? It's almost criminal."

Dixon, serious about his proposal, was tiring of the game they were playing. Taking Jan's hand and pulling her to him, he decided it was time to get a straight answer. "Damn it, Jan, yes or no."

Knowing that he was on the verge of losing his patience, Jan decided to play out Scott's own little game a little longer. With a feigned look of confusion on her face, she cocked her head to one side. "I'm sorry, what was the question again?"

"Jan, will you marry me?"

With a mischievous smile and a sparkle in her eyes, Jan took another sip of her Coke before she looked at Dixon. "Maybe."